Norman Mailer

THE EXECUTIONER'S SONG

A R

An Arena Book
Published by Arrow Books Limited
62–65 Chandos Place, London WC2N 4NW

An imprint of Century Hutchinson Limited

London Melbourne Sydney Auckland
Johannesburg and agencies throughout the world

First published in Great Britain by
Hutchinson 1979

Arrow edition 1980
Reprinted 1983 and 1984
Arena edition 1989

Printed and bound in Great Britain by
Cox & Wyman Ltd, Reading

ISBN 0 09 968860 3

To Norris, to John Buffalo, and to Scott Meredith

Contents

Deep in my dungeon
  I welcome you here
Deep in my dungeon
  I worship your fear
Deep in my dungeon
  I dwell.
I do not know
  if I wish you well.

  — old prison rhyme

CHAPTER I

The First Day

1

Brenda was six when she fell out of the apple tree. She climbed to the top and the limb with the good apples broke off. Gary caught her as the branch came scraping down. They were scared. The apple trees were their grandmother's best crop and it was forbidden to climb in the orchard. She helped him drag away the tree limb and they hoped no one would notice. That was Brenda's earliest recollection of Gary.

She was six and he was seven and she thought he was swell. He might be rough with the other kids but never with her. When the family used to come out to Grandpa Brown's farm on Decoration Day or Thanksgiving, Brenda would only play with the boys. Later, she remembered those parties as peaceful and warm. There were no raised voices, no cussing, just a good family get-together. She remembered liking Gary so well she would not bother to see who else was there — Hi, Grandma, can I have a cookie? — come on, Gary, let's go.

Right outside the door was a lot of open space. Beyond the backyard were orchards and fields and then the mountains. A dirt road went past the house and up the slope of the valley into the canyon.

Gary was kind of quiet. There was one reason they got along. Brenda was always gabbing and he was a good listener. They had a lot of fun. Even at that age he was real polite. If you got into trouble, he'd come back and help you out.

Then he moved away. Gary and his brother Frank Jr., who was a year older, and his mother, Bessie, went to join Frank Sr., in Seattle. Brenda didn't see any more of him for a long time. Her next memory of Gary was not until she was thirteen. Then her mother, Ida, told her that Aunt Bessie had called from Portland, and was in a very blue mood. Gary had been put in Reform School. So Brenda wrote him a letter, and Gary sent an answer all the way back from Oregon, and said he felt bad putting his family through what he did.

On the other hand, he sure didn't like it in Reform School. His dream when he came out, he wrote, was to be a mobster and push people around. He also said Gary Cooper was his favorite movie star.

Now Gary was the kind of boy who would not send a second letter until he received your reply. Years could go by but he wasn't going to write if you hadn't answered his last. Since Brenda, before long, was married — she was sixteen and thought she couldn't live without a certain guy — her correspondence lapsed. She might mail a letter from time to time, but Gary didn't really get back into Brenda's life until a couple of years ago when Aunt Bessie called again. She was still upset about Gary. He had been sent from Oregon State Penitentiary to Marion, Illinois, and that, Bessie informed Ida, was the place they built to replace Alcatraz. She was not accustomed to thinking of her son as a dangerous criminal who could be kept only in a Maximum Security prison.

It made Brenda begin to think of Bessie. In the Brown family with its seven sisters and two brothers, Bessie must have been the one who was talked about the most. Bessie had green eyes and black hair and was one of the prettiest girls around. She had an artistic temperament and hated to work in the field because she didn't want the sun to make her tough and tanned and leathery. Her skin was very white. She wanted to keep that look. Even if they were Mormons farming in the desert, she liked pretty clothes and finery, and would wear white dresses with wide Chinese sleeves and white gloves she'd made herself. She and a girl friend would get all dressed up and hitchhike to Salt Lake City. Now she was old and arthritic.

Brenda started writing to Gary once more. Before long, they were into quite a correspondence. Gary's intelligence was really coming through. He hadn't reached high school before they put him in the Reformatory, so he must have done a lot of reading in prison to get this much education together. He certainly knew how to use big words. Brenda couldn't pronounce a few of the longer ones, let alone be sure of their meaning.

Sometimes, Gary would delight her by adding little drawings in the margin; they were damn good. She spoke of trying to do some artwork herself, and mailed a sample of her stuff. He corrected her drawing in order to show the mistakes she was making. Good enough to tutor at long distance.

Once in a while Gary would remark that having been in prison so long he felt more like the victim than the man who did the deed. Of course, he did not deny having committed a crime or two. He was always letting Brenda know he was not Charley Good Guy.

Yet after they had been sending letters for a year or more, Brenda noticed a change. Gary no longer seemed to feel he would never get out of jail. His correspondence became more hopeful. Brenda said to her husband, Johnny, one day, Well, I really think Gary's ready.

She had gotten into the habit of reading his letters to Johnny, and to her mother and father and sister. Sometimes after discussing those letters, her parents, Vern and Ida, would discuss what Brenda ought to answer, and they would feel full of concern for Gary. Her sister, Toni, often spoke of how much his drawings impressed her. There was so much sorrow in those pictures. Children with great big sad eyes.

Once Brenda asked: "How does it feel to live in your country club out there? Just what kind of world do you live in?"
He had written back:

I don't think there's any way to adequately describe this sort of life to anyone that's never experienced it. I mean, it would be totally alien to you and your way of thinking, Brenda. It's like another planet.

— which words, in her living room, offered visions of the moon.

Being here is like walking up to the edge and looking over 24 hours a day for more days then you care to recall.

He finished by writing:

Above all, it's a matter of staying strong no matter what happens.

Sitting around the Christmas tree, they thought of Gary and wondered if he might be with them next year. Talked about his chances for parole. He had already asked Brenda to sponsor him, and she had replied, "If you screw up, I'll be the first against you."

Still, the family was more in favor than not. Toni, who had never written him a line, offered to be a co-sponsor. While some of Gary's notes were terribly depressed, and the one where he asked if Brenda would sponsor him had no more good feeling than a business memo, there were a few that really got to you.

Dear Brenda,
Received your letter tonight and it made me feel nice. Your attitude helps restore my old soul. . . . A place to stay and a job guarantee me an awful lot, but the fact that somebody cares, means more to the parole board. I've always been more or less alone before.

Only after the Christmas party did it come over Brenda that she was going to sponsor a man whom she hadn't seen in close to thirty years. It made her think of Toni's remark that Gary had a different face in every photograph.

Now, Johnny began to get concerned about it. He had been all for Brenda writing to Gary, but when it came down to bringing him into their family, Johnny began to have a few apprehensions. It wasn't that he was embarrassed to harbor a criminal, Johnny simply wasn't that sort of person, he just felt like there's going to be problems.

For one thing, Gary wasn't coming into an average community. He would be entering a Mormon stronghold. Things were tough enough for a man just out of prison without having to deal with people who thought drinking coffee and tea was sinful.

Nonsense, said Brenda. None of their friends were that observing. She and Johnny hardly qualified as a typical straitlaced Utah County couple.

Yes, said Johnny, but think of the atmosphere. All those super-clean BYU kids getting ready to go out as missionaries. Walking on the street could make you feel you were at a church supper. There had, said Johnny, to be tension.

Brenda hadn't been married to Johnny for eleven years without coming to know that her husband was the type for peace at any price. No waves in his life if he could help it. Brenda wouldn't say she looked for trouble, but a few waves kept life interesting. So Brenda suggested that Gary might only stay weekends with them, but live with Vern and Ida. That satisfied John.

Well, he told her with a grin, if I don't go along, you're going to do it anyway. He was right. She could feel awfully sympathetic to anybody who was boxed in. "He's paid his dues," she told Johnny, "and I want to bring him home."

Those were the words she used when she talked to Gary's future parole officer. When asked, Why do you want this man here? Brenda answered, "He's been in jail thirteen years. I think it's time Gary came home."

Brenda knew her power in conversations like this. She might be that much nearer to thirty-five than thirty, but she hadn't gone into marriage four times without knowing she was pretty attractive on the hoof, and the parole officer, Mont Court, was blond and tall with a husky build. Just an average good-looking American guy, very much on the Mr. Clean side, but all the same, Brenda thought, pretty likable. He was sympathetic to the idea of a second chance, and would flex with you if there was a good reason. If not, he would come down pretty hard. That was how she read him. He seemed just the kind of man for Gary.

He had worked, Mont Court told her, with a lot of people who had just come out of prison, and he warned Brenda that there would be a recycling period. Maybe a little trouble here or there, a drunken brawl. She thought he was broad-minded for a Mormon. A man couldn't, he explained, walk out of prison and go right into straight normal living. It was like coming out of the Service, especially if you'd been held a prisoner of war. You didn't become a civilian immediately. He said if Gary had problems, she should try to encourage him to come in and talk about it.

Then Mont Court and another probation officer paid a visit to Vern at his shoe shop and looked into her father's ability as a shoe repair man. They must have been impressed because nobody in these parts was going to know more about shoes than Vern Damico, and he would, after all, not only give Gary a place to live, but a job in his shop.

A letter arrived from Gary to announce that he was going to be released in a couple of weeks. Then, early in April, he called Brenda from the prison and told her he would get out in a few days. He planned, said Gary, to take the bus that went through Marion to St. Louis, and from there connect with other buses to Denver and Salt Lake. Over the phone, he had a nice voice, soft spoken, twangy, held back. A lot of feeling in the center of it.

With all the excitement, Brenda was hardly taking into account that it was practically the same route their Mormon great-grandfather took when he jumped off from Missouri with a handcart near to a hundred years ago, and pushed west with all he owned over the prairies, and the passes of the Rockies, to come to rest at Provo in the Mormon Kingdom of Deseret just fifty miles below Salt Lake.

2

Gary couldn't have traveled more than forty or fifty miles from Marion, however, before he phoned in from a rest stop to tell Brenda that the bus ride so far had been the most kidney-jogging experience he ever felt and he'd decided to cash in his ticket at St. Louis and come the rest of the way by plane. Brenda agreed. If Gary wanted to travel deluxe, well, he had a little coming.

He called her again that evening. He was definitely on the last flight and would phone once more when he arrived.

"Gary, it takes us forty-five minutes to get to the airport."

"I don't mind."

Brenda thought this was a novel approach, but then he hadn't been taking a lot of airplanes. Probably he wanted time to unwind.

Even the children were excited, and Brenda certainly couldn't sleep. After midnight, she and Johnny just waited. Brenda had threatened to kill anybody who called her late — she wanted that line to be open.

"I'm here," said his voice. It was 2 A.M.

"Okay, we're coming to get you."

"Right on," said Gary and hung up. This was one guy who wouldn't talk your ear off for a dime.

On the ride, Brenda kept telling John to hurry up. It was the middle of the night, and nobody was on the road. John, however, wasn't about to get a ticket. They were traveling the Interstate, after all. So he kept at 60. Brenda gave up fighting. She was altogether too excited to fight.

"Oh, my God," said Brenda, "I wonder how tall he is."

"What?" said Johnny.

She had begun to think he might be short. That would be awful. Brenda was only five feet five, but it was a height she knew well. From the time she was ten years old, she had been 130 pounds, five-five, and wholly equipped with the same size bra as now — C cup.

"What do you mean, is he tall?" asked Johnny.

"I don't know, I hope he is."

In junior high, if she put on heels, the only person big enough to dance with her was the gym teacher. She used to hate like hell to kiss a boy on the forehead and tell him good night. In fact, she got so paranoid about being tall it could have stunted her growth.

It certainly made her like boys taller than herself. They let her feel feminine. She just had this nightmare that when they got to the airport, Gary would only come up to her armpit. Why, she would abandon the whole thing right there. Shift for yourself, she would tell him.

They pulled up to the island that ran parallel to the main entrance of the terminal building. So soon as she got out of the car, there was Johnny over on the driver's side, trying to tuck his shirttail in. That annoyed Brenda no end.

She could see Gary leaning against the building. "There he is," Brenda cried, but Johnny said, "Wait, I have to zip my pants."

"Who gives a shit about your shirttail?" said Brenda. "I'm going."

As she crossed the street between the parking island and the main door, Gary saw her and picked up his satchel. Pretty soon they were running toward each other. As they met, Gary dropped his bag, looked at her, then encircled her so hard she could have been hugged by a bear. Even Johnny had never gripped Brenda that hard.

When Gary put her down on the ground again, she stood back and looked at him. She had to take him all in. She said, "My God, you're tall."

He started to laugh. "What did you expect, a midget?"

"I don't know what I expected," she said, "but, thank God, you're tall."

Johnny was just standing there with his big good face going, um, um, um.

"Hey, coz," said Gary, "it's fine to see you." He shook hands with Johnny.

"By the way, Gary," said Brenda demurely, "this is my husband."

Gary said, "I assumed that's who it was."

Johnny said, "Have you got everything with you?"

Gary picked up his flight bag — it was pathetically small, thought Brenda — and said, "This is it. This is all I have." He said it without humor and without self-pity. Material things were obviously no big transaction to him.

Now she noticed his clothes. He had a black trench coat slung on his arm and was wearing a maroon blazer over — could you believe it? — a yellow and green striped shirt. Then a pair of beige polyester trousers that were badly hemmed. Plus a pair of black plastic shoes. She paid attention to people's footwear because of her father's trade and she thought, Wow, that's really cheap. They didn't even give him a pair of leather shoes to go home in.

"Come on," said Gary, "let's get the hell out of here."

She could see then he'd had something to drink. He wasn't plastered, but he sure was tipped. Made a point of putting his arm around her when they walked to the car.

When they got in, Brenda sat in the middle and Johnny drove. Gary said, "Hey, this is kind of a cute car. What is it?"

"A yellow Maverick," she told him. "My little lemon."

They drove. The first silence came in.

"Are you tired?" asked Brenda.

"A little tired, but then I'm a little drunk too." Gary grinned. "I took advantage of the champagne flight. I don't know if it was the altitude, or not having good liquor for a long time, but, boy, I got tore up on that plane. I was happier than hell."

Brenda laughed. "I guess you're entitled to be snockered."

The prison sure cut his hair short. It would, Brenda judged, be heavy handsome brown hair when it grew out, but for now it stuck up hick style in the back. He kept pushing it down.

No matter, she liked his looks. In the half-light that came into the car as they drove through Salt Lake on the Interstate, the city sleeping on both sides of them, she decided that Gary was everything she expected in that department. A long, fine nose, good chin, thin well-shaped lips. He had character about his face.

"Want to go for a cup of coffee?" Johnny asked.

Brenda felt Gary tighten. It was as if even the thought of walking into a strange place got him edgy. "Come on," Brenda said, "we'll give the ten-cent tour."

They picked Jean's Cafe. It was the only place south of Salt Lake open at 3 A.M., but it was Friday night and people were sporting their finery. Once installed in their booth, Gary said, "I guess I got to get some clothes."

Johnny encouraged him to eat, but he wasn't hungry. Obviously too excited. Brenda felt as if she could pick up the quiver in each bright color that Gary was studying on the jukebox. He looked close to being dazzled by the revolving red, blue, and gold light show on the electronic screen of the cigarette console. He was so involved it drew her into his mood. When a couple of cute girls walked in, and Gary mumbled, "Not bad," Brenda laughed. There was something so real about the way he said it.

Couples kept coming from parties and leaving, and the sound of cars parking and taking off didn't stop. Still, Brenda was not looking at the door. Her best friend could have walked in, but she would have been all alone with Gary. She couldn't remember when somebody had absorbed her attention this much. She didn't mean to be rude to Johnny, but she did kind of forget he was there.

Gary, however, looked across the table and said, "Hey man, thanks. I appreciate how you went along with Brenda to get me out." They shook hands again. This time Gary did it thumbs up.

Over the coffee, he asked Brenda about her folks, her sis, her kids, and Johnny's job.

Johnny did maintenance at the Pacific State Cast Iron and Pipe. While he was blacksmithing now, he used to make iron pipe, fire it, cast it, sometimes do the mold work.

The conversation died. Gary had no clue what to ask Johnny next. He knows nothing about us, Brenda thought, and I know so little about his life.

Gary spoke of a couple of prison friends and what good men they were. Then he said apologetically, Well, you don't want to hear about prison, it's not very pleasant.

Johnny said they were only tiptoeing around because they didn't want to offend him. "We're curious," said Johnny, "but, you know, we don't want to ask: what's it like in there? What do they do to you?"

Gary smiled. They were silent again.

Brenda knew she was making Gary nervous as hell. She kept staring at him constantly, but she couldn't get enough of his face. There were so many corners in it.

"God," she kept saying, "it's good to have you here."

"It's good to get back."

"Wait till you get to know this country," she said. She was dying to tell him about the kind of fun they could have on Utah Lake, and the camper trips they would take in the canyons. The desert was just as gray and brown and grim as desert anywhere, but the mountains went up to twelve thousand feet, and the canyons were green with beautiful forests and super drinking parties with friends. They could teach him how to hunt with bow and arrow, she was about ready to tell him, when all of a sudden she got a good look at Gary in the light. Speak of all the staring she had done, it was as if she hadn't studied him at all yet. Now she felt a strong sense of woe. He was marked up much more than she had expected.

She reached out to touch his cheek at the place where he had a very bad scar, and Gary said, "Nice looking, isn't it?"

Brenda said, "I'm sorry, Gary, I didn't mean to embarrass you."

This set up such a pause that Johnny finally asked, "How'd it happen?"

"A guard hit me," said Gary. He smiled. "They had me tied down for a shot of Prolixin — and I managed to spit in the doctor's face. Then I got clobbered."

"How," asked Brenda, "would you like to take that guard who hit you, and get ahold of him?"

"Don't pick my brain," said Gary.

"Okay," said Brenda, "but do you hate him?"

"God, yeah," said Gary, "wouldn't you?"

"Yeah, I would," said Brenda. "Just checking."

Half an hour later, driving home, they went by Point of the Mountain. Off to the left of the Interstate a long hill came out of the mountains and its ridge was like the limb of a beast whose paw just reached the highway. On the other side, in the desert to the right, was Utah State Prison. There were only a few lights in its buildings now. They made jokes about Utah State Prison.

3

Back in her living room, drinking beer, Gary began to unwind. He liked beer, he confessed. In prison, they knew how to make a watery brew out of bread. Called it Pruno. In fact, both Brenda and Johnny were observing that Gary could put brew away as fast as anyone they knew.

Johnny soon got tired and went to sleep. Now Gary and Brenda really began to talk. A few prison stories came out of him. To Brenda, each seemed wilder than the one before. Probably they were half true, half full of beer. He had to be reciting out of his hind end.

It was only when she looked out the window and saw the night was over that she realized how long they had been talking. They stepped through the door to look at the sun coming up over the back of her ranch house and all her neighbors' ranch houses, and standing there, on her plot of lawn, in a heap of strewn-about toys, wet with cold spring dew, Gary looked at the sky and took a deep breath.

"I feel like jogging," he said.

"You've got to be nuts, tired as you are," she said.

He just stretched and breathed deep, and a big smile came over his face. "Hey, man," he said, "I'm really out."

In the mountains, the snow was iron gray and purple in the hollows, and glowed like gold on every slope that faced the sun. The clouds over the mountains were lifting with the light. Brenda took a good look into his eyes and felt full of sadness again. His eyes had the expression of rabbits she had flushed, scared-rabbit was the common expression, but she had looked into those eyes of scared rabbits and they were calm and tender and kind of curious. They did not know what would happen next.

CHAPTER 2

The First Week

1

Brenda put Gary on the foldout couch in the TV room. When she began to make the bed, he stood there smiling.

"What gives you that impish little grin?" she said after a pause.

"Do you know how long it's been since I slept on a sheet?"

He took a blanket but no pillow. Then she went to her room. She never knew if he fell asleep. She had the feeling he lay down and rested and never took off his polyesters, just his shirt. When she got up a few hours later, he was up and around.

They were still having coffee when Toni came over to visit, and Gary gave her a big hug, and stood back, and framed her face with his hands and said, "I finally get to meet the kid sister. Man, I've looked at your photographs. What a foxy lady you are."

"You're going to make me blush," said Toni.

She certainly looked like Brenda. Same popping black eyes, black hair, same sassy look. It was just that Brenda was on the voluptuous side and Toni was slim enough to model. Take your pick.

When they sat down, Gary kept reaching over and putting his arm around Toni, or taking hold of her hand. "I wish you weren't my cousin," he said, "and married to such a big tall dude."

Later, Toni would tell Brenda how good and wise Howard had been for saying, "Go over and meet Gary without me." She went on to describe how warm Gary made her feel, not sexy, but more like a brother. He had amazed her with how much he knew of her life. Like that Howard was six foot six. Brenda kept herself from remarking that he had not learned it from any letters Toni had written, since Toni had never written a line.

Before Brenda took Gary over to meet Vern and Ida, Johnny showed a test of strength. He took the bathroom scale and squeezed it between his hands until the needle went up to 250 pounds.

Gary tried and reached 120. He went crazy and squeezed the scales until he was shaking. The needle went to 150.

"Yeah," said Johnny, "you're improving."

"What's the highest you've gone?" asked Gary.

"Oh," said Johnny, "the scale stops at 280, but I've taken it past there. I suppose 300."

On the drive to the shoe shop, Brenda told Gary a little more about her father. Vern, she explained, might be the strongest man she knew.

Stronger than Johnny?

Well, Brenda explained, nobody could top Johnny at squeezing the scales, but she didn't know who had ever beaten Vern Damico at arm wrestling.

Vern, said Brenda, was strong enough to be gentle all the time. "I don't think my father ever gave me a spanking except once in my whole life and I truly asked for that. It was only one pat on the hind end, but that hand of his could cover your whole body."

The mountains had been gold and purple at dawn, but now in the morning they were big and brown and bald and had gray rain-soaked snow on the ridges. It got into their mood. The distance from the north side of Orem where she lived, to Vern's store in the center of Provo, was six miles, but going along State Street, it took a while. There were shopping malls and quick-eat palaces, used-car dealers, chain clothing stores and gas stops, appliance stores and highway signs and fruit stands. There were banks and real estate firms in one-story office compounds and rows of condominiums with sawed-off mansard roofs. There hardly seemed a building that was not painted in a nursery color: pastel yellow, pastel orange, pastel tan, pastel blue. Only a few faded two-story wooden houses looked as if they had been built even thirty years ago. On State Street, going the six miles from Orem to Provo, those houses looked as old as frontier saloons.

"It sure has changed," said Gary.

Overhead was the immense blue of the strong sky of the American West. That had not changed.

At the foot of the mountains, on the boundary between Orem and Provo, was Brigham Young University. It was also new and looked like it had been built from prefabricated toy kits. Twenty years ago, BYU had a few thousand students. Now the enrollment was close to thirty thousand, Brenda told him. As Notre Dame to good Catholics, so BYU to good Mormons.

2

"I better tell you a little more about Vern," Brenda said. "You have to understand when Dad is joking and when he is not. That can be a little hard to figure out because Dad does not always smile when he is joking."

She did not tell him that her father had been born with a harelip, but then she assumed he knew. Vern had a full palate so his speech was not affected, but the mark was right out there. His mustache didn't pretend to hide it. When he first went to school it didn't take him long to become one of the toughest kids. Any boy who wanted to kid Vern about his lip, said Brenda, got a belt in the snout.

It made Vern's personality. To this day, when children came into the shoe shop and saw him for the first time, Vern did not have to hear what the child was saying when the mother said, Hush. He was used to that. It didn't bother him now. Over the years, however, he had had to do a lot to overcome it. Not only did it leave him strong, but frank. He might be gentle in his manner, Brenda said, but he usually came out and said what he thought. That could be abrasive.

Yet when Gary met Vern, Brenda decided she had prepared him too much. He was a little nervous when he said hello, and looked around, and acted surprised at the size of the shoe shop, as if he hadn't expected a big cave of a place. Vern commented that it was a lot of room to walk around in when customers weren't there, and they got on from that to his osteoarthritis. Vern had a powerfully painful accumulation in his knee that had frozen the joint. Just hearing about it seemed to get Gary concerned. It didn't seem phony, Brenda thought. She could almost feel the pain of Vern's knee pass right into Gary's scrotum.

Vern thought Gary ought to move in with Ida and himself right away, but shouldn't plan to go to work for a few days. A fellow needed time to get acquainted with his freedom, Vern observed. After all, Gary had come into a strange town, didn't know where the library was, didn't know where to buy a cup of coffee. So he talked to Gary real slow. Brenda was accustomed to men taking quite a while to say anything to each other, but if you were impatient, it could drive you crazy.

When she and Gary went over to the house, however, Ida was thrilled. "Bessie was my special big sister, and I was always her favorite," Ida told him. She was getting a little plump, but with her red-brown hair and her bright-colored dress, Ida looked like an attractive gypsy lady.

She and Gary began talking right away about how when he was a little boy, he used to visit Grandma and Grandpa Brown. "I loved them days," Gary said to her. "I was as happy then as I've ever been in my life."

Together, Gary and Ida made a sight in that small living room. Although Vern's shoulders could fill a doorway, and any one of his fingers was as wide as anyone else's two fingers, he was not that tall, and Ida was short. They wouldn't be bothered by a low ceiling.

It was a living room with a lot of stuffed furniture in bright autumn colors and bright rugs and color-filled pictures in gold frames and there was a ceramic statue of a black stable boy with a red jacket standing by the fireplace. Chinese end tables and big colored hassocks took up space on the floor.

Having lived among steel bars, reinforced concrete, and cement-block walls, Gary would now be spending a lot of his time in this living room.

Back at her house, on the pretext of helping him pack, Brenda got a peek at the contents of his tote bag. It held a can of shaving cream, a razor, a toothbrush, a comb, some snapshots, his parole papers, a few letters, and no change of underwear.

Vern slipped him some underclothes, some tan slacks, a shirt, and twenty bucks.

Gary said, "I can't pay you back right now."

"I'm giving you the money," Vern said. "If you need more, see me. I don't have a lot, but I'll give you what I can."

Brenda would have understood her father's reasoning: a man without money in his pocket can get into trouble.

Sunday afternoon, Vern and Ida drove him over to Lehi, on the other side of Orem, for a visit with Toni and Howard.

Both of Toni's daughters, Annette and Angela, were excited about Gary. He was like a magnet with kids, Brenda and Toni agreed. On this Sunday, two days out of jail, he sat in a gold cloth-upholstered chair drawing chalk pictures on a blackboard for Angela.

He'd draw a beautiful picture and Angela, who was six, would erase it. He got the biggest kick out of that. He would take pains on the next one, draw it extra-beautiful, and she'd go, Yeah, uh-huh, and she'd erase it. So he could do another one.

After a while he sat down on the floor and played cards with her.

The only game Angela knew was Fish, but she couldn't remember how to say each number. She would speak of 6 as an upper because the line went up, and 9 was a downer. A 7 was a hooker. That tickled Gary. Queens, Angela said firmly, were ladies. Kings were big boys. Jacks were little boys.

He called: "Toni, would you explain something? Am I playing some illicit game here with your daughter?" Gary thought it was very funny.

Later that Sunday, Howard Gurney and Gary tried to talk to each other. Howard had been a construction worker all his life, a union electrician. He'd never been in jail except for one night when he was a kid. It was difficult to find much common denominator. Gary knew a lot, and had a fantastic vocabulary, but he and Howard didn't seem to have any experiences in common.

3

Monday morning, Gary broke the twenty-dollar bill Vern had given him, and bought a pair of gym shoes. That week, he would wake up every day around six, and go out to run. He would take off from Vern's house in a fast long stride down to Fifth West, go around the park, and back — more than ten blocks in four minutes, good time. Vern, with his bad knee, thought Gary was a fantastic runner.

In the beginning, Gary didn't know exactly what he could do in the house. On his first evening alone with Vern and Ida, he asked if he could get a glass of water.

"This is your home," Vern said. "You don't have to ask permission."

Gary came back from the kitchen with the glass in his hand. "I'm beginning to get onto this," he said to Vern. "It's pretty good."

"Yeah," said Vern, "come and go as you want. Within reason."

Gary didn't like television. Maybe he'd seen too much in prison, but in the evening, once Vern went to bed, Gary and Ida would sit and talk.

Ida reminisced about Bessie's skill with makeup. "She was so clever that way," said Ida, "and so tasteful. She knew how to make herself look beautiful all the time. She had the same elegance about her as our mother who is French and always had aristocratic traits." Her mother, said Ida, had a breeding that she gave to her children. The table was always set properly, not to the stiffest standards — they were just poor Mormons — but a tablecloth, always a tablecloth, and enough silverware to do the job.

Bessie, Gary told Ida, was now so arthritic she could hardly move, and the little trailer in which she lived was all plastic. Considering the climate in Portland, that trailer had to be damp. When he got a little money together, he would try to improve matters. One night Gary actually called his mother and talked for a long time. Ida heard him say he loved her and was going to bring her back to Provo to live.

It was a warm week for April, and pleasant talking through the evenings, planning for the summer to come.

About the third night, they got to talking about Vern's driveway. It wasn't wide enough to take more than one car, but Vern had a strip of lawn beside it that could offer space for another car provided he could remove the concrete curb that separated the grass from the paving. That curb ran for thirty-five feet from the sidewalk to the garage. It was about six inches high, eight inches wide, and would take a lot of work to be chopped out. Because of his bad leg, Vern had been holding off.

"I'll do it," said Gary.

Sure enough, next morning at 6 A.M., Vern was awakened by the sound of Gary taking a sledgehammer to the job. Sound slammed through the neighborhood in the dawn. Vern winced for the people in the City Center Motel, next door, who would be awakened by the reverberation. All day Gary worked, cracking the curbing with overhead blows, then prying chunks out, inch by inch, with the crowbar. Before long, Vern had to buy a new one.

Those thirty-five feet of curbing took one day and part of the next. Vern offered to help but Gary wouldn't allow it. "I know a lot about pounding rocks," he told Vern with a grin.

"What can I do for you?" asked Vern.

"Well, it's thirsty work," said Gary. "Just keep me in beer."

It went like that. He drank a lot of beer and worked real hard and they were happy with the job. When he was done, he had open blisters on his hand as large as Vern's fingernails. Ida insisted on bandaging his palms, but Gary was acting like a kid — a man don't wear bandages — and took them off real quick.

Doing the work, however, had loosened him up. He was ready to do his first exploring around town.

Provo was laid out in a checkerboard. It had very wide streets and a few buildings that were four stories high. It had three movie theaters. Two were on Center Street, the main shopping street, and the other was on University Avenue, the other shopping street. In Provo, the equivalent of Times Square was where the two streets crossed. There was a park next to a church on one corner and diagonally across was an extra-large drugstore.

During the day, Gary would walk around town. If he came by the shoe shop around lunchtime, Vern would take him to the Provo Cafe, or to Joe's Spic and Span which had the best coffee in town. It was just a box of a joint with twenty seats. At lunchtime, however, people would be waiting on the street to get in. Of course, Vern told him, Provo was not famous for restaurants.

"What is it famous for?" asked Gary.

"Darned if I know," said Vern. "Maybe it's the low crime rate."

Once Gary started in the shoe shop, he would be making $2.50 an hour. A couple of times after lunch he hung around to get the feel of it. After watching Vern wait on a few people, Gary decided he'd like to concentrate on repair work. Didn't know if he could handle rude customers. "I'm going to have to sneak up on that," he told Vern.

Looking around, Gary decided to get out of his polyesters and buy some Levi's. He borrowed a few more bucks from Vern, and Brenda took him to a shopping mall.

He told her that he had never been to anything like this before. It was mind-stopping. He couldn't keep his eyes off the girls. Right in the middle of goggling at them, Gary walked into the ledge of a fountain. If Brenda hadn't grabbed his sleeve, he'd have been in. "You certainly haven't lost your eye," she told him. He had only been gawking at the most beautiful girls. He was nearly all wet, but he had very good taste.

In the Levi's department at Penney's, Gary just stood there. After a while, he said, "Hey, I don't know how to go about this. Are you supposed to take the pants off the shelf, or does somebody issue them to you?"

Brenda really felt sorry for him. "Find the ones you want," she said, "and tell the clerk. If you want to try them on, you can."

"Without paying for them?"

"Oh, yeah, you can try them on first," she said.

4

Gary's first working day in the shop was good. He was enthusiastic and Vern was not displeased. "Look," Gary said, "I don't know anything about this, but tell me and I'll catch on."

Vern started him on a bench jack, tearing down shoes. The jack was like a metal foot upside down, and Gary would put the shoe on, pry off the sole, take off the heel, remove the nails, pull out the stitching, and generally prepare the top for the new sole and heels. You had to watch not to rip the leather or make a mess for the next man.

Gary was slow, but he did it well. The first few days he had an excellent attitude, humble, pleasant, nice fellow. Vern was getting to like him.

The trouble was to keep him busy. Vern wasn't always able to be teaching. There were rush jobs to get out. The real difficulty was that Vern, and his assistant, Sterling Baker, were used to moving the work between them. It was easier to do it themselves than show a new man how to accomplish something. So Gary had to wait when he really wanted to move on to the next step. If he took a heel off, he wanted to put the new one on. Sometimes twenty minutes would go by before Vern could get back.

Gary would say, "I don't like this standing around and waiting. I feel like a dummy, you know."

The problem, as Vern saw it, was that Gary wanted perfection quickly. Wanted to be able to fix a pair of shoes like Vern could. It just wasn't going to come that way. Vern told him, "You can't learn this immediately."

Gary took it fine. "Well, I know that," he said, but his impatience didn't take long to come back.

Of course, Gary did get on well with Sterling Baker who was about twenty, and the nicest fellow. He didn't raise his voice, had nice looks, and didn't mind talking about shoes. The first couple of days he was there, Gary kept bringing the conversation back to footwear as if he was going to learn everything there was about it. The only time Gary had trouble concentrating was when pretty girls came into the store. "Look at that," he'd say. "I haven't seen anything like that for years."

The girls he liked best, he said, were around twenty. It occurred to Vern that Gary wasn't much older when he said good-bye to the world for thirteen years. He certainly was comfortable becoming friends with a kid like Sterling Baker.

Still, Gary's first date was set up by Vern and Ida with a divorced woman near his own age. Lu Ann Price. When she heard, Brenda said to Johnny, "This has got to be good."

5

Brenda didn't see Lu Ann as a feasible date for Gary. She was skinny, she had a few kids, and she was awful sure of herself. Her eyes had pink lids. That was a piss-poor combination.

All the same, she was a redhead. Maybe Gary would go for that.

The Damicos had decided Lu Ann was worth a try. There was nobody else they could think of right now, and Lu Ann, after all, had heard a little about Gary after Brenda picked up her correspondence with him again. When she heard that Gary didn't know how to meet people and could hardly take care of himself, Lu Ann felt ready to befriend him. "Why not," she said. "He's lonely. He's paid a terrible debt." Maybe a friend could explain things that a family couldn't.

On Thursday evening, therefore, not a week from last Friday night when Gary had been flying from St. Louis to Salt Lake, Lu Ann called to ask Vern if Gary would like to go out with her for a cup of coffee.

"I think that's a super idea," said Vern. Gary, being called to the phone, was quick to say yes.

About nine, she came over. Gary looked stunned when he met her. It was as if he hadn't expected her to look like that. Still, as Lu Ann would tell friends later, she couldn't decide whether he was pleased or disappointed. He stammered while saying hello, and then sat in a chair across the room from her.

He had on a pair of old-fashioned slacks that were not only too short, but without wide bottoms. He wore a jacket that looked like it'd been borrowed from Vern, big in the chest, hiked up at the hips. All the same, he was overdressed for Lu Ann who, on this warm night, was in Levi's and a peasant blouse.

Since he stayed silent in his chair, Vern and Lu Ann kept talking until it got like work. "Gary, do you want to go out for that cup of coffee or stay here?" she asked at last.

"Let's go," he said. He went to his room, however, to emerge with a fisherman's hat that Vern used to wear as a joke. It was red, white and blue with stars all over it. Vern had given it to him after Gary said he liked it. Now he wore it everywhere. "How do you like the hat?" he would ask Vern.

"Well," Vern would reply, "it don't do anything for you."

Lu Ann thought it contrasted abominably with his other clothes.

When they walked out to her car, he neglected to open the door for her. Soon as she asked if he had a particular place in mind for coffee, he winced. "I'd rather have a beer," he said.

Lu Ann took him to Fred's Lounge. She knew the people who ran it and so was sure nobody would hassle him. The way he was dressed, it would not be hard to get into trouble in a strange place. One difficulty was that there were no nice cocktail lounges around. Mormons didn't see any reason for public drinking to take place in agreeable surroundings. If you wanted a beer, you had to get it in a dive. For every car parked outside a bar in Provo or Orem were three or four motorcycles.

At Fred's Lounge, Gary kept looking around the room. His eyes didn't seem able to take in enough.

When the bartender came up, Lu Ann said, "Gary, you have a choice." He looked bewildered. The bartender was a lady, a nice meaty well-set-up lady.

After a little thought, he said, "I want a beer."

Lu Ann said, "You have a choice of beers."

He picked Coors. Lu Ann told Gary what it would cost and he handed over the money. When the bartender brought the change, he looked pleased with himself, as if he'd accomplished a tricky transaction.

He turned around in his seat and started watching the pool table. One by one, he examined the pictures on the wall, and the mirrors, and the little sayings tacked up behind the bar. Although he wanted nothing to eat, he studied the white inserted letters in the dark gray menu-board on the wall. He was taking in the place with the same intensity you would use in a game if you had to memorize the objects in a picture.

Lu Ann said, "Haven't been in a bar lately, have you, Gary?"

"Not since I got out."

The place was practically empty. A couple of people were rolling dice with the lady bartender. Lu Ann explained that the loser paid for the music on the jukebox.

Gary said, "Can I play?" Lu Ann said, "Sure you can." He said, "Will you help me?" She said, "Yes, I will."

They called for the cup, and Gary asked, "Did I win?" Lu Ann said, "Well, I'm afraid you lost this time." He said, "How much do I put in?" She said, "Fifty cents." Gary said, "Will you help me pick out the selections?"

Making their way through the beers, Lu Ann began to talk about herself. She didn't always have red hair, she told him. Used to be a blond, and before that, had tried different shades, a little brown, ash blond, honey blond. Just yuck, she described it. She had settled on red because it suited her temperament. Lu Ann happened to have been, she explained, a honey blond just at the time her first daughter was born with red hair. She soon got tired of people asking how the baby came out that way. So even though her husband objected, she thought she'd try the bright red herself. Talk of a turnabout, she didn't like it, but he did. So she kept it. She had now kept it so many years she would say, "Being a redhead is being me."

She was a Utah girl, she said, and had been bounced back and forth. Her parents moved around the state a lot. When her husband, whom she dated through high school, went into the Navy, she hit both coasts with him: California and Florida. That was her life until she got divorced.

Now, she was back in Utah County again. The desert was at the end of every street, she said, except to the east. There, was the Interstate, and after that, the mountains. That was about it.

She would admit to being curious about his life. "What's it like in prison?" she asked. "What do you have to do to survive?"

Gary said, "I got myself put into Solitary as much as I could so they would leave me alone."

When they were ready to go, Gary asked, "Can I have a six-pack to take home?" She said, "If you want it." Gary said, "Is it all right to drink my beer in your car?" She said yes.

Gary wanted to know why she'd come out to meet him. She said it was simple: he needed a friend and she needed a new friend. That did not satisfy him. He said, "When somebody in prison offers friendship, they want something for it."

As they drove, he kept staring at the road ahead. Once he looked up and said, "Do you normally do that — just drive around?"

"Yes, I do," Lu Ann told him, "it relaxes me."

"It doesn't bother you?" he asked. "No," she said, "it doesn't bother me in the least."

They kept driving. Suddenly he turned to her and said, "Will you go to a motel with me?"

Lu Ann said, "No."

"No," Lu Ann told him, "I'm here to be your friend." She said as forcefully as she could, "If the *other* is what you want, you better go look someplace else."

He said, "I'm sorry, but I haven't been around a girl." He kept staring at the dashboard. After a silence that went on for a couple of minutes, he said, "Everybody's got something, but I've got nothing."

Lu Ann answered, "We all have to earn it, Gary."

He said, "I don't want to hear any of that."

She pulled over. "We've been talking," she told him, "but not face to face. I want you to listen to me." She said that all her friends had all worked superhard to have their homes, their cars, their children.

"You," he said, "all had it easy."

She said, "Gary, you can't expect everything to be handed to you the minute you walk out the prison door. I'm a working girl," she told him, "Brenda works hard at home. She has her kids and husband to take care of. Don't you think she's earned all that?"

He was fidgeting as she spoke. At that point he said, "I'm a guest in this car."

Lu Ann replied, "Yes, you're in my car, but you're not going anywhere, unless you're going on foot." She had the feeling he would get out at this point if he knew where he was.

Gary said, "I don't want to hear any more."

"Well, you're going to."

Suddenly, he raised his fist.

She said, "You want to hit me?" She didn't really think he would. Still, she felt his rage pass over her like a blast of air.

Lu Ann leaned forward and said, "I can hear that switch on the side of your head going click. Gary, turn it back on, and listen to me. I offer you friendship."

"Let's drive home," he said.

She took him back to Vern's and they sat outside in the car. Gary asked if he could hug her. Asked as if he needed a favor. "I'm friendly with a lot of people," Lu Ann said, "but I offer my friendship to very few." He shifted in the seat and put his arms around her and pulled her close. He hugged her very hard. He said, "It's different than I thought it would be."

She felt that he was grabbing at everything. It was as if the world was just out of reach of his fingers. She said, "Don't rush so, Gary. You've got time. You've got so much time." He said, "I haven't. I've lost it. I can't make those years up."

"Well," she told him, "maybe you can't, but you have to put it behind you. If you take one step at a time, you'll find yourself a woman, and some kids. You can still have it all."

"You're not going to see me again, are you?" he asked.

She said, "Yes, I will, if you want me to."

He kissed her, but it was forced. Then he pushed her away and held her by the shoulders and looked at her, one hand on each shoulder.

He said, "I'm sorry. I've messed this up, haven't I?"

She said, "No, you haven't, Gary. I'll see you again." She took a little church key they had been using to open their beers that evening, and now gave it to him and he thanked her. Lu Ann said, "If you need someone to talk to, my phone is open 24 hours a day, Gary."

He got out of the car and said, "I'm sorry. I've muffed it all." Added, "Vern's going to be awful mad at me."

6

Vern, in fact, was up when Gary came through the door, and they talked about the evening. It was Vern's impression that Gary might have been too forceful.

"You just don't," Vern explained, "try to do everything the first time on a date. You find out about each other."

Gary started hitting on the beer in the refrigerator. Vern didn't have to be told Gary had been through a few already.

"Gary," Vern said, "are you going to shape up, or am I going to have to knock you on your ass?"

"What are you going to do?" asked Gary.

"I'm going to have to do it."

"Aren't you afraid of me?" Gary asked.

"No," said Vern, "why should I be?" In his gentlest voice, he said, "I can whip you."

Gary's face lit up as if for the first time he felt like they wanted him in this house.

"Aren't you afraid?" he asked again.

"No," said Vern, "I'm not. I hope that doesn't sound crazy."

They both began to laugh.

Gary looked around the room and said to Vern, "This is what I want."

"Yeah," said Vern, "what do you want?"

"Well, I want a home," said Gary. "I want a family. I want to live like other people live."

Vern said, "You can't have that in five minutes. You can't have it in a year. You've got to work for it."

Gary tried to call Lu Ann in the morning, but she wasn't there, and left a message.

By the time Lu Ann called the shop, he was out.

Sterling Baker took the call. Gary, he told her, had gone up the road to some bar.

"Oh, Sterling," said Lu Ann, "please explain to him that I'm his friend. I really wasn't here when he called. But I did try to get back to him."

Sterling said he'd tell Gary. Lu Ann never did hear from him.

Gary returned to the shop for a couple of hours and seemed sober. It was payday, but Vern had advanced him money, so there wasn't anything due. When Gary said he was short, however, Vern slipped him a ten, and said, "Gary, if you don't think this job is going to be right for you, let me know. We'll find something else."

7

Gary was invited to dinner that night at Sterling Baker's house. He made quite an impression on Sterling's wife, Ruth Ann, by playing with the baby for a long while. Since he liked the music on the radio, he bounced the baby in time to Country-and-Western. Johnny Cash, it came out in conversation, was his all-time favorite. One time he got out of jail and spent an entire day listening to nothing but Johnny Cash records.

How long had he been in prison altogether? Ruth Ann wanted to know. She was small and had long hair that was so light she looked like a natural platinum blond. If she had been a boy, they would have called her Whitey.

Well, Gary told them, if you added it up, he guessed he'd been in, on and off, eighteen of his last twenty-two years. He'd been on ice, and now he'd come out, and he still felt young. Sterling Baker felt sorry for him.

Over dinner, Gary told stories about prison. Back in '68, he had been in some prison riots, and a local TV crew selected him as one of the leaders and had him on television saying a few words. His looks, or something in the way he spoke, attracted attention. He got some mail out of it including a beautiful correspondence with this girl named Becky. He fell in love with her through her letters. Then she came to visit. She was so fat that she had to waddle through the door sideways. Yet he still liked her enough to want to marry her.

It was not uncommon, Gary said. You could always see fat women in the visiting room of a jail. For some reason, very fat women and convicts got along. "Once you get behind bars," Gary remarked, "maybe you need more of an earth mother."

They were going to get married but Becky had to go into the hospital for an operation. She died on the table. That was his prison romance.

He had other stories. LeRoy Earp, who had been one of his best friends as a kid, was sent to Oregon State Penitentiary two years after Gary. LeRoy had killed a woman, picked up a life sentence and didn't have much to look forward to. So he had a bad habit. LeRoy, Gary explained, would stay fucked-up on Valium for months.

"He got in debt to this guy named Bill, who was dealing in prison dope," said Gary, looking at Sterling and Ruth Ann, "and Bill was always fucking with people. One time LeRoy sent word to me, Bill had come to his cell and beat him up, all that shit," said Gary, "put the boots to him while LeRoy was on the floor. Then Bill walked off with LeRoy's outfit, you know, his syringe and needle, his money, everything." Gary took down half a can of beer at a swallow. "Well," he said, "Valium can make you hallucinate, so I wasn't certain LeRoy's story was true. I talked it over with a guy who was going in the hole for seven days and he checked it out for me, confirmed it. The guy wanted to know if I needed any help with Bill.

"I told him I would do it myself. LeRoy was my personal friend. The prison was doing some construction out in the yard, so I went over, stole a hammer and caught Bill watching a football game on TV. I bounced the hammer off his head. Then I turned around and walked off." Gary nodded, studying their reactions. "They took Bill up to Portland for brain surgery. He was pretty fucked-up."

"What happened to you?" asked Ruth Ann.

"There was two or three snitches in the TV room and they saw me do it and told the Warden. But the snitches were afraid to stand up in Court. So the Warden just kept me in the hole for four months. When I got out, this buddy of mine gave me a little toy hammer to wear on a chain, and nicknamed me Hammersmith."

Gary told this story in a Texas accent, very even voice. He was kind of informing Sterling that he had a code. It went: Be loyal to your friends.

Gary now asked Ruth Ann if she knew any girls who would go out with him.

She didn't, offhand.

CHAPTER 3

The First Month

1

Gary went back to visit with Brenda and Johnny for Easter weekend. After the kids went to sleep, they spent Saturday night coloring Easter eggs around the table, and Gary had a fine time and drew beautiful pictures and wrote the names of the kids in Gothic script, and in three-dimensional letters so that, small as they were on the Easter egg, they still appeared to be cut out of stone.

After a while, Johnny and Gary began to giggle together. They were still painting eggs, but instead of saying, "Cristie, I love you," or "Keep it up, Nick," they were printing stuff like "Fuck the Easter Bunny." Brenda exclaimed, "You can't hide those."

"Well," said Gary with a big grin, "guess we got to eat 'em." He and Johnny had a feast of mislabeled hard-boiled eggs.

They spent the rest of the evening drawing maps — Take so many steps; Look under a rock; You can read the next clue only in a mirror; etc. — they were up half the night putting candy, eggs and treats all over the yard.

Brenda had a good time watching Gary climb around in the tree — which was wet for that matter. They were having a wet Easter. Here he was looming through the branches, hiding goodies, and getting soaked right through.

Then he put jelly beans all over his room, especially on the shelf above his couch, so that when the kids got up next morning, they would have to romp over him to get the candies.

Little Tony, who was only four, walked across the front of Gary's chest, up on his face, mashed his nose, and slipped off, squashing his ear. Gary was laughing his head off.

The morning went like that. It was a good morning. When it cleared up a little, they played horseshoes and Johnny and Gary got along fine.

In the kitchen, Brenda said to him, "Hey, Gary, you see this Revere Ware pan? Your mother gave it to me."

"Oh?"

"Yes," Brenda told him, "it was a wedding gift when I first got married."

Gary said, "Boy, that thing ought to be beat up by now."

Brenda said, "Don't get funny."

It seemed the moment for Brenda to ask Gary if he'd been to see Mont Court. Gary said he had.

"Did you like him?"

"Yeah," he said, "pretty good egg."

"Gary," Brenda said, "you work with him and he'll work back with you."

Gary gave a smile. He said a lot of men had been put in charge over him. People who worked in prison, and people who worked for the prison system. He didn't really know anyone who'd been particularly willing to work with him.

Dinner didn't turn out as Brenda had hoped. She'd invited Vern and Ida, and Howard and Toni with their kids, and of course she and Johnny had their own brood present including Johnny's son, Kenny, by a previous marriage. Counting all the noses, they came to thirteen, and they made jokes about that. The main dish was spaghetti Italian style, promised to Gary the way Brenda's Sicilian grandfather used to make it, with mushrooms and peppers and onions and oregano and garlic bread. She had some hot cross buns for dessert with a white X of icing on the top and plenty of coffee, and would have enjoyed the meal if it hadn't been for how tense Gary looked.

Everybody was jabbering back and forth. It was not a quiet meal, but Gary was a little out of it. Occasionally, somebody would ask a polite question of him, or he would say something like, "Boy, this is better grub than what they had at Marion," but kept his head down as he ate, and hid his silence by swallowing food in a hurry.

Brenda came to the glum conclusion that Gary was an atrocious eater. Too bad. Table manners were one of her hang-ups. She couldn't stand to see a man shoveling and slobbering at the table.

From his letters she had expected him to be very much of a gentleman. Now she decided she should have known his manners would be common. In prison, they didn't eat with napkins and place settings. Still, it got to her. Gary had long artist's fingers, small at the tips, nice-looking hands like a pianist might have, but he gripped his fork with his fist and bulldozed it in.

He was, however, sitting at the end of the table by the refrigerator and so the fluorescent light over the sink was shining on his face. It lit up his eyes. Brenda said, "Wow, you've got the bluest eyes I've ever seen."

He didn't like that very well. He said, "They're green."

Brenda looked him back, "They're not green, they're blue."

This went back and forth. Finally, Brenda said, "Okay, when you're mad, they're green; when you're not, they're blue. Right now, they're blue. Do you feel blue?"

Gary said, "Shut up and eat."

After Vern and Ida and Howard and Toni and the children left, and Johnny had gone to sleep, Brenda sat around with Gary having a cup of coffee. "Did you have a good time?" she asked.

"Oh, yeah," said Gary. Then he shrugged, "I felt out of place. I have nothing to talk about."

She said, "Boy, I wish we could get over that hump."

"Come on," he said, "who wants to hear about prison?"

Brenda said, "I'm just afraid of bringing back bad memories. Would you rather we didn't walk so lightly around the subject?"

Gary said, "Yeah."

He told her a couple of prison stories. God, they were crude. Gary could tell an awfully gross story. It seems there was this old boy

Skeezix, who could perform fellatio on himself. He was proud of that. Nobody else in OSP could.

"OSP?" asked Brenda.

"Oregon State Penitentiary."

Gary had taken a small cardboard box, painted it black, and put a tiny hole in it so it looked as if it were one of those lensless pinpoint cameras. He told Skeezix he had film in the box, and it would take a picture through the pinhole. Everybody gathered around to watch Gary take a picture of the fellow going down on himself. Skeezix was so dumb he was still waiting for the photo to come back.

On finishing his story, Gary went off laughing so hard, Brenda thought he'd sling his spaghetti around the room. She was awful glad when he wheezed into silence and fixed her with his eye as if to say, "Now, do you see my conversational problem?"

2

Rikki Baker was one of the regulars in Sterling Baker's poker sessions. Although not heavy for his size, he was tall, very tall, maybe six-five. Gary fixed on him early. He was the only fellow in the game taller than Gary. They kind of got along.

Rikki was Sterling's cousin, and had heard about Gary before he even got out of Marion. Although Rikki had been trained by the Navy to be a diesel mechanic, he didn't get enough experience to qualify for a real job when he got out, and so had to take what came along in the way of day labor or construction. When nothing else was available, Rikki put in time at Vern's shop and Sterling taught him leather work. So Rikki happened to be around when Vern was speaking about this nephew in prison who was getting out soon. Later, Rikki met Gary at the shop, but the guy only seemed like a new worker, uncertain of himself, that's all. It was only when he saw him playing cards that he realized Gary was one hell of a relative.

Sure had a different personality at poker than he did in the shop. Rikki could see right off that Gary wasn't too honest. He had a lot of habits that were just bad manners. Like he would lean over to see what a fellow had in his hand, and was a real lawyer about rules, always interpreting them in his favor. He also kept putting down the other players because they didn't know the poker rules that convicts used. Since it was ten-cent ante, quarter raise, a pot could go to $10.00. Gary's interest in poker was obviously the money. He was making no friends.

After that evening, a couple of Sterling's buddies said they were going to stop coming over. Sterling told them, Fine with me. He was certainly being loyal to Gary. Yet when Rikki was alone with him, Sterling started to put Gary down. Rikki went along. There wasn't too much they would take from him, they agreed. Still, Rikki had a funny feeling about the man. Didn't want to make an enemy of him for too little. He figured if Gary gave trouble, he wouldn't be afraid to just right-out fight him, but he was a little uneasy of what Gary might pull from his pocket.

They agreed, however, that they also felt sorry for him. Gary had a problem. No patience.

The poker games continued. Different people. By the third night, Sterling got Rikki aside and asked if he would take Gary somewhere. The guy was really getting on everybody's nerves.

So Rikki asked if he wanted to chase down some girls. Gary said *Yeah*.

Rikki soon decided this was the horniest guy he had ever met. He was *crazy*.

Rikki had split up with his wife again. He had been with Sue for six years ever since he was 17 and she was 15. They had three kids, and they knew how to fight. So Rikki now started to kid Gary. Told him how beautiful Sue was, big beautiful mean-looking blond yet a nice chick. Now that she was mad at her husband, maybe she'd like to meet Gary.

In fact, Rikki had been so mad at her the last time he left that he took all the money in the house plus the food stamps and the welfare check. It would put her out of her mind for sure if he was to send over a steamed-up dude like Gary. So Rikki had said it, kind of half joking.

Once the possibility was there, though, Gary wouldn't quit bugging Rikki about it. Rikki told him he had only meant it as a joke, it was his wife, man! But Gary kept asking when Rikki would take him

over to Sue's house. When Rikki finally told him, No way, Gary got so
mad they almost did have a fight. Rikki had to get Gary off the subject by saying they could go drag Center Street. Rikki was pretty
good at chasing girls, he let Gary know.

So they went up and down in Rikki Baker's GTO. Would pass
girls cruising in their cars and try to wave them over, then circle
around and go down Center Street again, see the same girls, try to
wave them over a second time, just driving side by side in traffic, part
of a long line of other dudes in their cars, and pickup trucks, and the
chicks in theirs, everybody's radio going real loud.

Gary got bored with the lack of positive results. When they came
to a red light behind one carful of girls who'd been teasing them, he
jumped out and stuck his head in their window. Rikki couldn't hear
what he was saying, but when the light turned green and the girls
tried to take off, Gary wouldn't get his head out of their window.
Didn't care about the cars stuck behind, or anything. After the girls
finally got going, Gary wanted Rikki to chase them down. "Ain't no
way," said Rikki.
"Do it!"
With all the traffic, Rikki couldn't catch up. All the while, Gary
was yelling to make a move and show he was as good as he said.

They had started too late in the evening, however. There were a
lot of cars with guys but only a few with girls, and they were just
fooling around and very cautious. One had to come up on them easy,
not scare them right out of the water. Gary made him promise to go
out earlier next time.

As they were saying good night, Gary had a proposition. What
would Rikki think about teaming up? Make a little money at poker.

Rikki had already heard about this from Sterling. He gave Gary
the same answer Sterling had given: "Well, Gary, I couldn't cheat
against my friends," he said.

For reply, Gary said, "Can I drive your car?" Being a GTO, it was
a fast automobile. This time, he said yes. Figured he'd better. Not
getting his way, bent Gary too far out of shape.

The moment he got the wheel, he almost killed them. Took a corner fast and nearly hit a stop sign. Then he didn't slow down at the intersection and went cata-humping over the drainage ditch that was there to slow you down. Next he almost ran some people off the road, in fact, one car coming toward them had to go onto the shoulder. Rikki kept yelling at him to stop. It felt like an hour with a madman. Gary kept telling him all the while that it was not bad considering how long it had been since he drove, and Rikki was near to having a heart attack. Couldn't get him to stop until Gary popped the clutch without enough gas and the motor conked. Then he couldn't get it started. The GTO had a bad battery.

That's what it took for Rikki to get behind the wheel again. Gary was awful depressed the battery had died on him. Got upset about it the way people can brood over bad weather.

3

Next day around lunchtime, Toni and Brenda picked Gary up at the shoe shop and took him out for a hamburger. Sitting on each side of him at the counter, talking into his left ear and his right ear, they got right to the topic. What it came down to was that he had been borrowing too much money.

Yes, said Toni gently, he'd been hitting Vern for a five-dollar bill here, ten there, once in a while twenty. He hadn't been going to work a full number of hours either. "Vern and Ida said this to you?" Gary asked.

"Gary," said Toni, "I don't think you realize Daddy's financial situation. He's got too much pride to tell you."

"He'd be furious if he knew we were talking to you about this," Brenda said, "but Dad isn't making a whole lot right now. He created a job so the parole board would help you get out."

"If you need ten dollars," said Toni, "Daddy will be there. But not just to buy a six-pack and then come home and sit around and drink beer."

Toni would put it this way. She and Brenda understood it was difficult for Gary to know what to do with his money. After all, he had never had to manage his weekly pay before.

Gary answered, "Well, yeah, I don't seem to know. I go to buy something, and like I don't have enough left. Suddenly I'm broke." Toni assured him, "Gary, I figured once you understand Daddy doesn't have money to keep loaning you, you will never put him in the position of asking him."

"I feel bad," said Gary, "about this. Vern has no money?"

"He has a little," Brenda said. "But he's *hurting* for money. He's trying to save for his operation. Vern doesn't carry on, but that leg gives him pain all the time."

Gary sat with his head down, just thinking. "I didn't realize," he said, "I was putting Vern on the spot."

Toni answered, "Gary, I know it's hard. But try to settle down, just a little. What you spend for beer doesn't sound like much, but it would make a difference to Mother and Daddy if you took five dollars and went and bought a sack of groceries, 'cause, you know, they're feeding you, and clothing you, and board and room."

Brenda now moved to the next topic. She knew Gary had needed time to unwind and work with somebody like Vern, whom he didn't have to regard as a boss all the time. Yet the moment had come, maybe, to start thinking about a place of his own and a real job. She had even been doing some looking for him.

Gary said, "I don't think I'm ready. I appreciate what you're trying to do, Brenda, but I'd like to hang in with your folks a little longer."

"Mother and Dad," said Brenda, "haven't had anybody living in their house since Toni got married. That's been ten or twelve years. Gary, they love you, but I'll be frank. You are starting to get on their nerves."

"Maybe you better tell me about that job."

"I've been talking," said Brenda, "to the wife of a fellow who has an insulation shop. He's Spencer McGrath. From what I hear, Spencer doesn't act like a boss at all. He's right in there with his men."

While Brenda had not met him, she had spent, she explained, an enjoyable few minutes with McGrath's wife, Marie. She was a pleasant woman, Brenda said, kind of heavyset, always smiling or chuckling, a strong Ma Kettle type.

Marie had said to Brenda, "If you don't reach out your hand to someone coming out of prison, they're going to turn right around and be frustrated and start getting in trouble again." Society had to open up a little bit, she had said, if anybody was going to get rehabilitated.

"All right," said Gary, "I'll go meet the man. But," he looked at them, "give me another week."

After work, Gary came in with a sack of groceries. Just odds and ends and nothing to do with putting a meal together, but Ida took it as a happy gesture. It turned back her thoughts to a time thirty years ago and more when she had loaned Bessie $40 because Frank Gilmore was in jail. It took Bessie almost ten years, but she paid back that forty. Maybe Gary had the same characteristic. Ida decided to tell him about Margie Quinn.

She knew this nice girl, Marge, the daughter of a friend. About six years ago, Marge had a baby, but she was living alone now, raised her baby nicely. In fact, she stayed with her sister, and worked as a chambermaid down the street.

"Good looking," Ida told him. "She's a little sad, but she has beautiful blue eyes. They're deep set."

"Are her eyes as beautiful as yours, Ida?" asked Gary.

"Oh, git along, little doggie," said Ida.

Gary said he'd like to see her right now.

The girl who was working the night shift in the Canyon Inn Motel office saw a tall man walk through the door. He came up with a big smile. "Oh," he said, "you must be Margie."

"No," she said, "Margie isn't here this shift."

The fellow just left.

Margie Quinn got a phone call. A pleasant voice said, "I'm Gary, Ida's nephew." When she said hello, he replied that she had a nice voice and he'd like to meet her. She was busy that night, she told him, but come over tomorrow. She knew who he was.

Marjorie Quinn's mother had already mentioned that Ida had a nephew just out of prison and wondered if Marge would consider going out with him. Marge asked what he had been in for, and learned it was robbery. She thought that wasn't too bad. It was not like murder, after all. Since she was just dating one fellow at this time and not going steady, she thought, Well, it can't hurt.

There was a smile on his face as she opened the door. He had a silly hat on, but otherwise seemed all right. She asked if he wanted a beer, and he sat and drank one in the living room, sitting back nicely on the couch. Marge introduced him to Sandy, her sister, who was living with her, and her daughter, and after a while she asked if he wanted to go for a ride up the canyon.

Before they got very far, Gary said, "Let's get some more beer." Marge said, "Well, I don't care."

Halfway up the pass, they stopped by Bridal Falls where a narrow stream of water fell for a thousand feet, but they didn't take the gondola up. It was too expensive.

They sat by the river and talked awhile. It was beginning to get dark and Gary looked at the stars and told her how much he enjoyed them. When he was in prison, he rarely got to see them, he said. You could get out in the yard in the daytime, he explained, and catch plenty of sky above the wall, but the only time you'd ever see the stars was in the winter if you went to Court on some beef or other. Then, you might not be brought back to the penitentiary until late afternoon when it was already dark. On a clear evening, you could see the stars.

He began to talk to Marge about her eyes. They were beautiful, he told her. There was sadness in her eyes but also glints of moonbeam.

She thought he was a pleasant conversationalist. When he asked if she'd like to make a date to see a movie, she consented.

After that, however, a State Police car happened to go tearing up the canyon. His mood shifted. He started talking about cops. The more he spoke, the angrier he got. It came off him like an oven with the door open. She had second thoughts about going to the movies with him.

After the night got really dark, they continued up the canyon to Heber, stopped for more beer, then headed back. It must have been 10:30 by then. As they were coming down the hill into Provo, she said, "You don't mind if I take you home now?"

He said, "I don't want to go there."

Marge said, "I have to get up for work tomorrow."

"Tomorrow is Saturday."

"That's a big day at the motel."

"Let's go over to your house."

She said, "Okay, for a little while. It can't be for long."

Her sister had gone to bed, so they sat in the living room. He kissed her. Then he started to do more.

She said, "I better take you home."

"I don't want to," he said. "They're not there."

She insisted. She got him to go. It took all her powers of argument, but she drove him over. It was just a few blocks and when they got there, the lights were out. He said, "They're not here."

Now, she realized she was drunk. It came over suddenly that she was smashed. She managed to say, "Where do you want me to take you?"

"Over to Sterling's."

"Can't you get in here?"

"I don't want to."

So she took him over to Sterling's. When they got there he said, "Sterling isn't up." She said, "You can't stay at my house."

Still, they went back to her apartment. She didn't want to get picked up for drunk driving, and at least she knew the way to her house.

In the living room, Gary started kissing her again. She was feeling miserable and wondering how to get out of this, when she passed out with her arms folded and her head down. By the time she stirred, he was gone. She woke up remembering she'd made a date to go to a movie with him sometime the following week.

4

Next morning, Gary phoned early. Marge told her sister to say she was not up. He called half an hour later, and Marge said, Just tell him I'm not here. That ended it, she hoped.

By Saturday night, Gary was drunk. Early in the evening he tried to convince Sterling Baker to drive him up to Salt Lake City, but Sterling talked him into going home. Now, Gary tried to warm Vern up for the trip, but got the answer that it was close to midnight and fifty miles one way, and let's forget the idea. Gary answered, All right, just lend me your car. "Well," Vern said, "you can't take it."

Gary gave a look. His eyes at such times had the fury of an eagle in a cage. Those eyes practically said to Vern, "Your '69 gold Pontiac is out in the driveway, and so is your '73 green Ford pickup. You won't lend me either." Aloud he said, "I'll hitch."

Vern could see Gary in a bar in Salt Lake looking for trouble. "Do what you wish," said Vern. "I'd like you to stay here."
"I'm on my way."

After he left, Vern couldn't take it. Before three minutes were gone, he said to Ida, "Hell, I'll drive him." He got into his car, thinking of the look on Gary's face when he would pull up alongside, open the passenger door, and growl, "Why don't you go to Salt Lake with this damn fool?" But Vern couldn't find him. There was a place on West Fifth where you would start hitchhiking, only nobody was there. Vern went back and forth through the streets. Gary must have picked up a driver instantly.

Eight o'clock Sunday morning, Gary called from Idaho. He was 300 miles away. "How," said Vern, "did you get *there?*"
Well, said Gary, this dude picked him up and he fell asleep, and the fellow went right through Salt Lake. By the time he woke up, it was Idaho. "Vern," said Gary, "I'm broke. Could you come and get me?"
"Maybe Brenda will go," said Vern, "but I sure won't." He took a breath.
"You won't come and get me?" Gary sounded real aggravated. A

lot yawned between them. Vern said, "Stay where you are. I'll call Brenda."

"What," asked Brenda, "are you doing up north?"

"I wanted to drop in on Mom," said Gary. "You see, I ran into this fellow in Provo who has friends in Idaho. He said, 'Let's visit my buddies, then shoot you on up to Portland.'"

"Oh, God," said Brenda. He had violated his parole. He had been told not to leave the state.

"Anyway," said Gary, "once we got to Idaho, this fellow got mad at me and took off. I'm stuck at this bar, Brenda, and I better get back. Can you come for me?"

"You poor thing," said Brenda. "You just get your thumb out of your rear end and put it in the air."

A few hours later, a long-distance call reached Mont Court at his home. He was asked to contact Detective Jensen in Twin Falls, Idaho. Mont Court then learned that his parolee, Gary Gilmore, had been arrested for driving without a license. How should they proceed, Detective Jensen wanted to know? Mont Court thought awhile and recommended that Gilmore be allowed to go back to Utah on his own recognizance, and then report in to him immediately.

Brenda got another phone call. Gary was in Twin Falls, he said. Had been hitchhiking and got a ride with a fellow driving a pickup truck. When they stopped in a bar, the guy started making passes. Gary had to fight him right in the bar. Then, they went to the parking lot to finish. He knocked the guy out.

"Brenda, I thought I killed him. God, I really thought I killed him. I put him in his pickup, and drove like a maniac. I figured if I could find a hospital, I'd drop him off there.

"Then the guy went into a seizure. I stopped the car and got his wallet out to see his name — in case he was dying. Then I started speeding for a hospital. Soon as the cops pulled me over, the guy came to. He told the police he wanted me booked for assault and battery, kidnap, stealing his wallet, and taking his truck."

Brenda was trying to follow it all.

"I had some of my week's pay," said Gary, "and that was enough to post bail for driving without the license. Then, I worked it out."

"You did?" said Brenda. "My God, how?"

"Well, you see, the fellow was known as a faggot around here. I guess the cops were on my side, and talked him into dropping the charges. I don't have to go back."

"I can't believe it," said Brenda.

"Coz, there's just one thing," said Gary, "I used up my money to post the bail, I don't know how I'll get back."

"You better," said Brenda. "If you're not here by morning, I'm calling Mont Court. He'd love to give you a free ride back."

"Mont Court knows already," said Gary.

Brenda blew. "You dodo bird," she told him. "You're really dumb!"

It was a long Sunday. A spring snow had started and by evening it was close to a blizzard. In the living room, Brenda got tired of looking at her red rug, her red furniture and her black wrought-iron lamps. She was ready to start kicking a few kids' toys. Kept going over it with Johnny, trying to find some kind of hope for Gary in all this. It was good, she thought, that he hadn't run off from the guy he beat up. That showed some sense of responsibility. On the other hand, had he rode off with him in the truck because the man would be easy to rob that way? And how had he gotten the fellow to drop the charges? By his boyish smile?

It was time to recognize, Brenda decided gloomily, that when you had Gary around, there were questions for which you would not get answers. The snow kept coming down. Out on the roads, the universe would be just one big white field.

5

Around nine in the evening, Gary called from Salt Lake. Now he was broke for sure. He was also stranded in the snow.

Johnny was watching a show he liked on TV. "Well," he said, "I'm not going to get the damn fool."

Brenda said: "It is my side of the family that's acting up, so may I take your truck?" It had four-wheel drive and a CB radio, and her Maverick was too light.

Toni happened to be over and she said she'd go along. Brenda was glad. Toni knew the roads better in Salt Lake.

It was snowing so hard, Brenda almost missed the exit on the Interstate. The bar was out past the airport, and proved to be the dippiest damn dive Brenda ever laid eyes on. Leave it to Gary to find the trashiest place to land.

When they walked in the door, he was chatting with the bartender. It struck Brenda immediately that he had plenty of change on the counter.

Gary gave them a great wide smile. "How's the two foxiest ladies in the whole world?" Oh, was he sopped! So proud: his private peacocks had just come parading through the door. Brenda looked at Toni and said, "What do we do with the drunken sot?"

They had their arms around his neck to steady him. He put his arms around them.

"Are you ready to go, Gary?"

"Let me finish my beer."

Brenda said, "Drink it by the door." She didn't want to stand in the middle of this bar with all these drunks leering at them. Never in her life had she been undressed as many times in 30 seconds.

"Gary, you found yourself a dandy place to stop."

"Well, it was warm," he said. He always had a real explanation for things.

"By the way," he said, his mouth on the glass of beer, "I've got my turn coming up to play pool."

"You," Brenda said, "are planning to stay here and play pool?"

"Well," he said, "I got a good bet in the making."

"You told me you were broke."

They looked at the dollars on the counter next to his glass. He said, "There's been this guy buying me drinks all night."

"You lying turkey," Brenda said. "I'm leaving."

Gary came around then, "All right, all right," he said loudly, "if it'll make my little ladies happy, I'll go now." He made a delicious face of regret at the lost pool game, and gave her a kiss on the nose.

Then a peck on the cheek for Toni. "C'mon, you two foxy bitches," he said loudly, "let's go."

He probably would have fallen in the snow if they hadn't held him up long enough to get to the truck. Suddenly, he looked wiped out. They managed to prop him between them on the front seat, but he said, "Oh, no, I can't stand this. I'm gonna barf."

Brenda shrieked, "Let me out."

They got it rearranged with Toni in the center and Gary on the outside, window part open. The damn fool sang on the way home. He couldn't sing.

"Bottles on the Wall," was the song. There were one hundred bottles on the wall, and something happened to one of the bottles, so there were only ninety-nine. It was like "Roll Me Over in the Clover." They went through one hundred bottles on the wall.

Brenda said, "Why don't you try something you can do? God, you can't sing."

"I can too," he said, and started another verse. Nothing ahead but to suffer.

When they reached Point of the Mountain, it was that snowy on the Interstate, Brenda could not see the taillights ahead, and with no load in the back of the pickup it was beginning to slide. Soon it would be like driving in a barrel of snakes. She got on the CB and tried to pick up a weather report from a truck on the other side of the mountain. If word was bad, she would pull over and let the storm pass.

Gary, however, was upset about Brenda hitting the CB. He had heard of them, but he didn't really know what they did. He got paranoid. Thought Brenda was talking to the cops. "What are you doing?" he asked.

"Getting a Smokey report."

"What," asked Gary, "is a Smokey report?"

"That," said Brenda, "is the name for the police."

"Hey," asked Gary, "are you going to turn me in?"

Brenda said, "For what? Being an asshole? You can't turn somebody in for being an asshole."

"Oh," said Gary, "Okay, I got you."

"No," Brenda said, "I'm not going to turn you in. But that was a dumb thing to say."

"I'm not dumb," he stated.

"Gary, you have a high I.Q., but you do not have a drop of common sense."

"That's just your opinion."

He seemed to think getting into the damnedest situations and finding a way out of them was common sense.

The Smokey report said the weather was less bad on the other side of the mountain, but Brenda didn't know whether to try it. Over the CB, an eighteen-wheeler coming up behind her said the road ahead was treacherous. Then the fellow asked what kind of unit she was driving. After Brenda described Johnny's pickup, the trucker said, "I got you. You're right ahead of me." Then he told her, "I have a buddy behind. We'll escort you."

"Well," said Brenda, "I don't get off till Orem."

"We'll stay with you."

So Brenda drove down the Interstate in line between two large semis. She stayed on the taillights of the fellow up ahead and the guy behind kept close. They moved right along with her.

The lead truck stayed in the lane to the left so she wouldn't slide off toward the island. The other was to her right and just behind. If her back end started to veer out to the shoulder, he could tap the back bumper near her rear right wheel. That would stop the slide. Truckers knew how to do it. It was crucial assistance. Due to the drainage problem, the shoulder on this stretch of the Interstate chopped off sharply into a drainage canal and since it was a spring blizzard, there weren't old snowbanks to protect you. Nothing to the right, in fact, but gravel and the drop-off. So the fellow behind kept talking her in. "Don't worry," he kept saying, "you aren't going over."

This all impressed Gary. He said, "You've got protection." Then he gave a wide smile and said, "But don't you think you need it against me?"

"Why," Brenda said, "what a rotten thing to say. Would you hurt me?"

"That," said Gary, now offended, "was a dumb thing to say."

"No dumber than what you just said."

Toni said, "Children, children, don't quarrel."

So they drove along and got home and Gary went to bed at Brenda and Johnny's house that night.

6

Monday morning, in the wet and slush, Gary went to see Mont Court. He told his parole officer the following story:

He had gone to a party and become somewhat intoxicated. Then he decided to go to Salt Lake to solicit a prostitute. En route, he thumbed a ride with a man who told him that he knew some girls in Twin Falls, Idaho, who would shack up with them. By the time they reached Twin Falls, however, the fellow that made this promise just dropped him off.

He then made telephone calls to Utah and was instructed by his cousin to thumb a ride back. Was able to secure such a ride with a man he met at a bar. En route, the man began to have convulsions and finally passed out. So Gary was obliged to get behind the wheel of the car and try to locate a hospital. At this point he was arrested for driving without a license and had Mr. Court contacted. He, Gary Gilmore, was now reporting in as instructed.

Mont Court didn't feel too happy with the story. Gilmore was sitting in his office, supernice and very polite. But he wasn't explaining an awful lot. Just answering questions. It didn't give a good feeling. All the same, there were a lot of cases where you just had to keep living with them.

Court had about eighty people on parole or probation, and he got to see thirty or forty a week, each for five to fifteen minutes. It meant you had to take chances. He had taken one yesterday by gambling that Gilmore would come back on his own from Idaho.

On the other hand, if he had been kept in jail in Idaho, Court would have had to refer him to the Oregon authorities, which is where his parole originated. It would have been difficult in the extreme to find any members of the Oregon Parole Commission on Sunday afternoon. In fact, it might even take a few days before they could meet to decide on Gilmore's violation. Gary would be sitting in a Twin Falls jail all that time. Right there, a lawyer could spring him on a Writ of Habeas Corpus, and Gilmore could take off. The more he was really in trouble, the more he'd look to get himself lost real fast. Whereas, Gilmore, coming back on his own, would be fortifying the positive side of himself. He would know Court had been right to trust him. That would give a base on which to work. The idea was to get a man into some kind of positive relationship with authority. Then he might begin to change.

Court had been a Mormon missionary in New Zealand and he was a believer in the power of authority to be a change-agent, that is, be able to effect a few real changes in people's personalities. Of course, a person had to be willing to accept authority, whether it was Scripture, the Book of Mormon, or in his case, just accept the fact that he, Mont Court, a probation officer, was neither a hard-nose, nor superheat, but a man willing to talk openly and take a reasonable chance on you. He was there to help, not to rush a man back to an overcrowded prison for the first minor infraction.

Of course, he laid it out. Gilmore had certainly been in violation of his parole agreement. Any more violations would jeopardize his parole. Gilmore nodded, Gilmore listened politely. He was looking old. They were about the same age, but Gilmore, Court was thinking, looked much older. On the other hand, if you put up a profile of what an artist of 35 might look like, Gilmore could fit that physical profile.

Court had seen some of his artistic work. Before he met him, Brenda had shown Mont Court a couple of Gary's drawings and paintings. The prison information he was receiving from Oregon made it clear that Gilmore was a violent person, yet in these paintings Court was able to see a part of the man simply not reflected in the prison record. Mont Court saw tenderness. He thought, Gilmore can't be all evil, all bad. There's something that's salvageable.

After the session with Mont Court, Gary decided to talk to Spencer McGrath about a new job. Brenda took him out to Lindon for the meeting, and took a liking to McGrath. He was really okay, she thought, just a little guy with rough features, a dark mustache, and a down-to-earth manner, who you could think was a plumber when you first looked at him. The kind who would walk around and say to his people, "Okay, guys, let's get this done." She thought he was terrific even if he was short.

A couple of days back, Gary had been to see a man with a sign-painting company but had been offered only $1.50 an hour. When Gary said that wasn't even minimum wage, the man replied, "What do you expect? You're an ex-con." Spencer agreed it wasn't fair. If Gary was doing the same work as somebody else, he should be paid the same money.

It turned out, however, that Gary did not have much experience applicable here. He was good at painting but they didn't do much sign-painting, just covered machinery with a paint gun. "Still," said Spencer, "you impress me as intelligent. I figure you can learn." He would put Gary on at $3.50 an hour. The government had a program for ex-cons and would pay half of this salary. Next day, he would start. Eight to five with breaks for coffee and lunch.

It was seven miles and more from Vern's home in Provo to the shop in Lindon, seven miles along State Street with all the one-story buildings. The first morning Vern drove him there. After that, Gary left at 6 to be sure of getting to work by 8 A.M. in case he wasn't able to find a hitch. Once, after catching a ride right off, he came in at 6:30, an hour and a half early. Other times it was not so fast. Once, a dawn cloudburst came in off the mountains, and he had to walk in the rain. At night he would often trudge home without a ride. It was a lot of traveling to get to a shop that was hardly more than a big shed with nothing to see but trucks and heavy equipment parked all over a muddy yard.

He was real quiet those first few days on the job. It was obvious he didn't know what to do. If they gave him a board to plane, he just waited after he cleaned it off. They had to tell him to turn the plank over and plane the other side. One time the foreman, Craig Taylor, a medium-size fellow with big arms and shoulders, discovered that Gary had been working an electric drill for fifteen minutes with no results. Couldn't get the hole started.

Craig told him he had been running the drill on reverse. Gary shrugged, "I didn't know these things had a reverse," he said.

So the word Spence McGrath got about him was that he was all right, but knew no more than a kid out of high school. Polygrinders and sanders and paint guns all had to be explained. He was also a loner. Brought his lunch in a brown paper bag and took it himself the first few days. Just sat on a piece of machinery off to the side and ate the food in all the presence of his own thoughts. Nobody knew what he was thinking.

7

Night was different. Gary was out just about every night.

Rikki was getting a little in awe of him. He knew he didn't want to mess with Gary. At the poker game, Gary told them about the Idaho fellow he left in a hospital after a fight.

Now, Gary also told everybody about this black dude he killed in jail who had been trying to make a nice white kid his punk. The kid asked Gary for help, so he and another buddy got ahold of some pipes. They had to. The convict they were taking on was a *bad* nigger, and had been a professional fighter, but they caught him on a stairway and beat him half to death with the pipes. Then they put him in his cell and stabbed him with a homemade knife 57 times.

Rikki thought the story was talk. By telling it to everybody, Gary was just trying to make himself look big. Still, that didn't leave Rikki feeling comfortable. Any fellow that wanted to live on such a story could hardly back down if he started to lean on you, and you pushed back.

There were times Gary seemed almost simple, however. Running after the girls in Rikki's GTO, Gary sure hadn't learned much. Rikki kept trying to explain how you talk to girls, soft and easy like Sterling Baker, instead of big and mean, but Gary said he wouldn't play those games. It wasn't no trick for Rikki to get a couple of girls to pull over and talk awhile, but Gary was sure to scare them off.

One night, Rikki started idling next to a pickup with three girls. The truck was on Rikki's left and he just talked through the open window until they could feel he was all right and good looking enough. Then the girls cut down a dark street, and he followed and parked behind. The girl driving came over to talk to Gary, and Rikki got out and walked up to their truck. He was talking nice to the other two girls about moving over to their place for a party, but not a couple of minutes gone, the driver came back looking scared. She said, "You ought to do something with that guy you've got along." She got into her truck fast and took off.

"What happened?"

"Well, I came right out and asked her for it, said, 'It's been a long time and I'd like some right now!' " Gilmore shook his head. "I've had enough. Why don't we just grab a couple of bitches and rape them?"

Rikki chose his words carefully. "Gary, that's something I just couldn't go for."

They drove around until Gary said he knew a girl named Margie Quinn. *"Real* nice." Now, he wanted to go to her place, only to her place. She lived on the second floor of a two-story building with several apartments on each landing. Looked like a small motel.

Gary pounded on her door for ten minutes. Finally, Marge's sister came to answer. She opened just a crack, and whispered, "Marge has gone to bed."

"Tell her I'm here."

"She's gone to bed."

"Just tell her I'm here, and she'll get up."

"She needs her sleep."

The door closed.

"Cunt," Gary shouted.

Then he got mad. On the way down the stairs, said to Rikki, "Let's tip her car."

Rikki was pretty drunk himself. It sounded like it might be kind of fun. Rikki had never tipped a car.

She was just a little old foreign job, but heavy. Put their backs into it, and gave what they had, but couldn't do more than rock her. So Gary grabbed a tire iron out of the GTO's trunk, ran up to Marge Quinn's car and busted the windshield out.

The sound of glass breaking scared Rikki enough to go flying over to his car. It was only as he took off that Gary opened the door on the run, and jumped in. Rikki had to laugh at how Gary would have busted all her windows if they hadn't got moving.

They decided to visit Sterling. On the way, Gary said, "Help me rob a bank?"
"That's something I never done."

A bank was easy, Gary said. He knew how to do it. He would cut Rikki in for 15 percent if Rikki would sit in his car and drive it off when he came out. Rikki, he said, would make a good getaway man.

Gary said, "You wouldn't have to come *into* the bank."
"I couldn't do it."
Gary got inflamed. "You're not supposed to be afraid of anything."
"I wouldn't do it, Gary."
They went the rest of the way to Sterling's house in silence.

Once there, Gary cooled enough to get working on an acceptable story in case Marge Quinn called the cops. They could say they drove up to Salt Lake for the night and didn't get back till morning. The sister had them mixed up with two other guys.

Friday morning, Marge found the window smashed. Gary did it, was the first thing to come to mind, but she hoped it wasn't true. The neighbor downstairs said, "Yeah, that really loud car with those two drunk guys, they pulled up right next to your car. I don't know what happened after that."
She let it go. It was one more unhappiness at the bottom of things.

8

The same morning, Gary called up Brenda. He would be getting his pay that night. His first check from Spence McGrath. "Hey, I want to treat you guys," he told her.

They decided to go to a movie. It was a flick he had seen before. *One Flew Over the Cuckoo's Nest.* He had watched them film it down the road from the penitentiary, watched it right from his cell window. Besides, he told her, he had even been sent over to that very mental institution a couple of times from the prison. Just like Jack Nicholson in the film. Brought him in the same way, with handcuffs and leg irons.

Since the movie was at the Una Theatre in Provo, Brenda and Johnny drove over from Orem and by the time they picked him up at Vern and Ida's, Gary had had about four or five beers to celebrate his paycheck.

In the truck, he smoked a joint. Made him happier than hell. By the time they covered the few blocks to the theatre he was giggling. Brenda said to herself: This is going to be a disastrous evening.

Soon as the movie went on, Gary started to give a running commentary. He said, "You see that broad? She really works in the hospital. But the guy next to her is a phony. Just an actor. Hey!" Gary told the movie theatre at large.

After a while, his language got to be God forbid! "Look at that fucker over there," he said. "I know that fucker."

Brenda could have died. No pain. "Gary — there are people trying to hear the show. Will you shut up?"

"Am I offensive?"

"You're *loud.*"

He spun around in his seat and asked the people behind, "Am I being loud? Am I bothering you folks?"

Brenda slammed her elbow into his ribs.

Johnny got up and moved over a space or two.

"Where's Johnny going?" asked Gary. "Does he have to take a piss?" More people started to move.

Johnny slid down in his seat until no one could see his head. Gary's narration of *One Flew Over the Cuckoo's Nest* continued. "Son of a bitch," he shouted, "that's just the way it was."

From the rear rows, people were saying, "Down in front. Shhh!" Brenda grabbed him by the shirttail. "You're obnoxious."

"I'm sorry." In a big whisper, he said, "I'll hold it down." But his voice came out in a roar.

"Gary, all kidding aside, you're really making me feel like a turd sitting here."

"All right, I'll be good." He put his feet up on the back of the chair in front and started rocking it. The woman who was sitting there had probably been holding out on every impulse to change her seat, but now she gave up, and moved away.

"What'd you do that for?"

"My God, Brenda, do you have to ride herd all the time?"

"You made that poor lady move."

"Her hair was in my way."

"Then sit up straighter."

"Not comfortable sitting up straight."

Going back to Vern's, Gary looked pretty smug. Brenda and Johnny didn't go in with him.

"What's the matter?" asked Gary. "Don't you like me anymore?"

"Right now? I think you are the most insensitive human being I've ever known."

"Brenda, I am not insensitive," said Gary, "to being called insensitive."

He whistled all the way up the steps.

At breakfast, his mood was fine. He saw Vern watching him eat and said, "I guess you think I gobble like a pig, kinda quick."

Vern said, "Yeah, I noticed that."

Gary said, "Well, in prison you learn to eat in a hurry. You've got fifteen minutes to get your food, sit down and swallow it. Sometimes you just don't get it."

"Did *you* manage to get it?" asked Vern.

"Yeah, I worked in the kitchen for a while. My job was to make the salad. Took five hours to make that much salad. I can't touch the stuff now."

"That's fine," said Vern, "you don't need to eat it."

"You're a pretty strong fellow, Vern, aren't you?"

"Just the champ."

"Let's arm wrestle," said Gary.

Vern shook his head, but Ida said, "Go ahead, arm wrestle him."

"Yeah, come on," said Gary. He squinted at Vern: "You think you can take me?"

Vern said, "I don't have to think. I can take you."

"Well, I feel pretty strong today, Vern. What makes you think you can beat me?"

"I'm gonna make up my mind," Vern said, "and I think I can do it."

"Try it."

"Well," Vern said, "you eat your breakfast first."

They got into it before the table was cleared. Vern kept eating his breakfast with his left hand, and arm wrestled with the other.

"Son of a bitch," Gary said, "for an old bastard you're pretty strong."

Vern said. "You're doing pitiful. It's a good thing you finished your breakfast. I wouldn't even give it to you now."

When he got Gary's arm halfway over, Vern set down his fork, picked up a few toothpicks and held them in his left hand. He said, "Okay, my friend, any time you want to say uncle, just quit. If you don't, I'm going to jam your hand right on these toothpicks."

Gary was straining with every muscle. He started giving karate yells. He even got half out of his seat, but it didn't make much difference. Vern got him down on the point of the toothpicks. Gary quit.

"One thing I want to know, Vern. Would you really have stuck me if I hadn't hollered uncle?"

"Yep, I told you I would, didn't I?"

"Son of a gun." Gary shook his hand.

A little later, Gary wanted to wrestle with the left arm. He lost again.

Then he tried finger wrestling. No one beat Vern at that.

"You know," Gary said, "I don't usually take a whipping very kindly."

When Vern didn't look away, Gary said, "Vern, you're all right."

Vern wasn't so sure how he felt about the whole thing.

9

Spencer McGrath had developed a few novel techniques in his field. He was able, for instance, to take old newspapers and produce high-quality insulation for homes and commercial buildings. At present, he was working on a plan to take in all the county garbage for recycling. He had been trying to interest people in such projects for twenty years. Now, the field had begun to open up. Just two and a half years ago, Devon Industries in Orem arranged with Spencer McGrath to transfer his operation from Vancouver, Washington, to Utah County.

Spencer had fifteen people in his employ. They were engaged in building the machinery he would need to fulfill his contract with Devon Industries. It was a large contract and McGrath was working very hard. He knew it had become one of those times in a man's life when he could advance his career and his finances ten years in two years. Or he could fail, and have gained very little beyond the knowledge of how hard he could work.

So his social activities were minimal. Seven days a week, he worked from seven in the morning into the night. Once in a while, in the late spring, he would go water-skiing in Utah Lake, or have friends over for a barbecue, but for days in a row he wouldn't even get home in time to see the ten o'clock news on TV.

Maybe he could have gotten away with less work, but it was Spencer's idea that you gave the time that was necessary to each person who came before you in the day. So it was natural that he not only kept an eye on Gilmore after he hired him, but talked to him quite a bit, and so far as he could see, nobody was trying to downgrade him in any way. The men knew, of course, that he was an ex-con — Spencer thought it was only fair to them (and to Gary for that matter) to have it known — but they were a good crew. If anything, this kind of knowledge could work in Gilmore's favor.

Yet it was all of a week before Spencer McGrath learned that Gary was walking to work whenever he couldn't hitch a ride, and he only found out because there had been some snow that morning and Gilmore came in late. It had taken him longer to walk all the way.

That got to Spencer. Gilmore had never told a soul. Such pride was the makings of decent stuff. McGrath made sure he had a ride home that night.

Later that day, they had a little talk. Gilmore wasn't real anxious to get into the fact that he didn't have a car while most people did. That got to Spencer too. He thought that with another paycheck or two, he could take Gary to Val J. Conlin, a used-car dealer he knew. Conlin sold cars for a little down and small weekly payments thereafter. Gilmore seemed to be appreciative of this conversation.

Spencer felt all right. It had taken a week but Gilmore appeared to be loosening up. He was coming to see that Spencer didn't like his people to think of him as a boss. He did the same work they did, and didn't want any superior relationship. If, as expected, his employees were faithful to what they were all trying to do, that was enough. No need to ride anybody.

Next day, Gary asked Spencer if he was serious about the car. He wanted to know if they could go down that afternoon and look at one.

At V.J. Motors, there was a 6-cylinder '66 Mustang that seemed to be pretty clean. The tires were fair, the body was good. Spencer thought it was a reasonable proposition. The car sat on the lot for $795, but the dealer said he would move it at five and a half for Spence. It beat walking.

So that Friday when Gary got paid, Spencer took him back to the car lot and it was arranged that Gary would put up $50, Spencer McGrath would add another $50 against future salary, and Val Conlin would carry the rest of it in bi-weekly $50 payments. Since Gary was getting $140 a week and taking home $95 of that, the deal could be considered functional.

Gary wanted to know if he could take time off on Monday to get a license. Spencer told him all right. It was agreed that Gary would stop for his license Monday morning, pick up the car, and come to work.

Monday, when he got into the shop, he told Spencer that the Drivers' Bureau said he would have to take a training course unless he had a previous driver's license. Gary told them he had one in Oregon, and they were going to send for it. In the meantime, he would wait on the car.

Wednesday, however, he picked up the Mustang after work. That night, to celebrate, he had an arm-wrestling contest with Rikki Baker at Sterling's house. Rikki tried pretty hard but Gary won and kept bragging it up through the poker game.

Rikki felt embarrassed at losing and stayed away. When, a few days later, he dropped in again, it was to hear that his sister Nicole had gone to visit Sterling one evening, and Gary had been there. Nicole and Gary ended up with each other that night. Now, they were staying out in Spanish Fork. His sister Nicole, who always had to go her own way, was living with Gary Gilmore.

Rikki didn't like the news one bit. Nicole was the best thing in his family as far as he was concerned. He told Sterling that if Gary did anything to hurt her, he would kill him.

Yet when Rikki saw them together, he realized that Nicole liked the guy a lot. Gary came over to Rikki and said, "Man, you've got the most beautiful sister in the world. She's just the best person I ever met." Gary and Nicole held hands like they were locked together at the wrist. It was all different from what Rikki had expected.

Sunday morning, Gary brought Nicole over to meet Spencer and Marie McGrath. Spencer saw a very good-looking girl, hell of a figure, not too tall, with a full mouth, a small nose and nice long brown hair. She must have been 19 or 20 and looked full of her own thoughts. She was wearing Levi's that had been cut off at the thigh, a T-shirt, and no shoes. It sounded like a baby was crying in her car, but she made no move to go back.

Gary was immensely proud of her. He acted as if he had just walked in with Marilyn Monroe. They were sure getting along in supergood shape. "Look at my girl!" Gary was all but saying. "Isn't she fabulous?"

When they left, Spencer said to Marie, "That's just about what Gary needs. A girl friend with a baby to feed. It doesn't look like she'll be too much of an asset to him." He squinted after their car. "My God, did he paint his Mustang blue? I thought it was white."

"Maybe it's her car."

"Same year and model?"

"Wouldn't surprise me a bit," said Marie.

10

Since Spencer lived next door to the work shed in Lindon, Marie could look out the window and see when Gary was there half an hour ahead of time. Some mornings, she would ask him in for a cup of coffee.

While sipping it, Gary would put his feet on the table. Marie would walk over and slap him across the ankles.

"Now, there," Gary said to Brenda, "is a lady who knows her own mind. She's not wishy-washy." He grinned. "I put my feet up just to annoy her."

"If she's such a nice woman, why do you want to annoy her?"

"I guess," he said, "I like an ankle slap."

·Brenda didn't want to hope too hard, but, God willing, Gary might come around the bend.

She wasn't too happy, therefore, when he brought Nicole to her house. Oh, God, Brenda said to herself, Gary *would* end up with a space cadet.

Nicole just sat there and looked at her. She had a little girl by the arm and didn't seem to know the arm was there. The child, a tough-looking 4-year-old, looked to be living in one world and Nicole in another.

Brenda asked, "Where are you staying?"

Nicole roused herself. "Yeah." She roused herself again. "Down the road," she said in a soft and somewhat muffled voice.

Brenda must have been on radar. "Springville?" she asked. "Spanish Fork?"

Nicole gave an angelic smile. "Hey, Spanish Fork, she got it," she said to Gary as if little wonders grew like flowers on the highway of life.

"Don't you love her looks?" Gary said.

"Yeah," said Brenda, "you got yourself a looker."

Yeah, thought Brenda, another girl who pops a kid before she's 15 and lives on the government ever after. One more poverty-stricken welfare witch. Except she had to admit it. Nicole *was* a looker. Star quality for these parts.

My God, she and Gary were in a trance with each other. Could sit and google at one another for the entire day. Don't bother to visit. Brenda was ready to ask the fire department to put out the burn.

"She's 19, you know," Gary said the moment Nicole stepped away.

"You don't say," said Brenda.

"Do you think she is too old for me?" he asked. At the look on his cousin's face, he began to laugh.

"No," said Brenda, "quite frankly I think you are both of the same intellectual and mental level of maturity. Good God, Gary, she's young enough to be your daughter. How can you mess around with a kid?"

"I feel 19," he told her.

"Why don't you try growing up before you get too old?"

"Hey, coz, you're blunt," said Gary.

"Don't you agree it's the truth?"

"Probably," he said. He muttered it.

They were sitting on the patio blinking their eyes in the sun when Nicole came back. Just as if nothing had been said in her absence, Gary pointed tenderly to the tattoo of a heart on his forearm.

When he had stepped out of Marion, a month ago, he said, it had been a blank heart. Now the space was filled with Nicole's name. He had tried to match the blue-black color of the old tattoo, but her name appeared in blue-green. "Like it?" he asked Brenda.

"Looks better than having a blank," she said.

"Well," said Gary, "I was just waiting to fill it in. But first I had to find me a lady like this."

Nicole also had a tattoo. On her ankle. GARY, it said.

"How do you like it?" he asked.

Johnny replied, "I don't."

Nicole was grinning from ear to ear. It was as if the best way to ring her bell was to tell the truth. Something about the sound set off chimes in her. "Oh," she said, extending her ankle for all the world to see the curve of her calf and the meat of her thigh, "I think it looks kinda nice."

"Well, it's done," said Brenda, "with a nice steady touch. But a tattoo on a woman's ankle looks like she stepped in shit."

"I dig it," said Gary.

"Okay," said Brenda, "I'll give you my good opinion. I like that tattoo about as much as I like that silly-ass hat you wear."

"Don't you like my lid?"

"Gary, when it comes to hats, you've got the rottenest taste I've ever seen." She was so mad she was ready to cry.

Less than a week ago, he had come over to apologize for how he had acted in the movie theatre, came over all decked out in beige slacks and a nice tan shirt, but wearing a white Panama hat with a wide rainbow band. That hat wouldn't even have looked happy on a black pimp, and Gary wore it with the brim tilted down in front and up in back like the Godfather might wear it. He'd stood outside on her mat, his body slouched, his hands in his pockets, and kicked the base of the door.

"Why don't you just lift the latch?" Brenda had asked in greeting.

"I can't," he'd said, "my hands are in my pockets," and waited for her to applaud the effect.

"It's a pretty hat," Brenda said, "but it doesn't fit your personality. Not unless you've turned into a procurer."

"Brenda, you're rotten," he'd said, "you're really ignorant." His whole posture was gone.

She had done it to him again. It didn't strike him well that she didn't like Nicole's tattoo any more than his hats. He got up to leave then, and Brenda walked them to the door. Coming outside, she was also surprised by the sight of the pale blue Mustang.

That was enough to restore him. Didn't it have to be fantastic, he told her. He and Nicole had both bought exactly the identical model and year. It was a sign.

She was in all wrong sorts the rest of the day. Kept thinking of the tattoo on Nicole's ankle. Every time she did, her uneasiness returned.

11

The worst story Gary ever told came back to her now. One night in Brenda's living room, he couldn't stop laughing as he told about a tattoo he put once on a convict named Fungoo.

"He was strong and dumb," said Gary, "and he loved me. One time when we were in Isolation, Fungoo was on the cleaning detail, so he was able to walk past my cell. Damn if he didn't ask me to do a rosebud on the back of his neck. I took out my needle and my india ink, and instead of a rosebud, tattooed a real skinny little dick on him and peanut-sized balls.

"Well, his mother and dad was coming next day. When he found out what I'd done, he went crazy. He had to see his folks with a towel wrapped around his neck. It was over a hundred that morning. Told them he liked to wear a towel in the heat," said Gary. Now, he laughed so hard he almost fell off the couch.

"But Fungoo was so dumb he wouldn't get mad at me. Came back and said, 'Gary, I can't go around with a pecker on my neck.'

" 'Okay,' I told him, 'I'll make it into a snake.' Only I got inspired and made it into a big three-headed cock. It had the ugliest warts you ever laid eyes on. I couldn't hardly keep from laughing all the while I was doing it. 'Make sure it's a nice snake,' Fungoo kept saying." Gary was laughing uncontrollably. Right in their living room the memory was still living in his veins. " 'Oh,' I said, 'I believe this is the most beautiful thing I've ever seen.'

"When Fungoo finally got to see it with a mirror, he went into shock. Couldn't even hit me. We'd had some hash smuggled into Isolation, and he decided I was bombed out of my head. He blamed the weed, not me. The last time I saw him, he had tattooed a giant rattlesnake all over his neck to cover the three pricks. He didn't trust anybody by then so he done it with soot and water." Brenda and Johnny's smiles had become as congealed as the grease on a cold steak.

"Guess that's an ugly story, huh," said Gary. "Yeah," he said, "a couple of times I got to feel bad about it. It sure fucked up Fungoo's world. I guess I must have racked up real bad karma on that one . . . but couldn't resist." He sighed.

It was exactly five weeks and two days since he had come to them from prison. Now she could believe the story. "God, how can he be so horrible?" she asked Johnny now. "How could he have done that to a man who trusted him?"

"I guess he was saying a man will do anything in prison to amuse himself. If you can't, you're gone."

She loved Johnny for saying that, loved her big strong whale-heart of a husband who could have compassion for possible rivals, which was more than she could say for herself. "Oh, Lord," said Brenda, "Gary loves Nicole."

PART TWO

Nicole

CHAPTER 4

The House in Spanish Fork

1

Just before the time her mother and father split up, Nicole found a little house in Spanish Fork, and it looked like a change for the better. She wanted to live alone and the house made it easier.

It was very small, about ten miles from Provo, on a quiet street at the start of the foothills. Her little place was the oldest building on the block, and next to all those ranch bungalows lined up on each sidewalk like pictures in supermarket magazines, the house looked as funky as a drawing in a fairy tale. It was kind of pale lavender stucco on the outside with Hershey-brown window trim, and inside, just a living room, bedroom, kitchen and bathroom. The roof beam curved in the middle, and the front door was practically on the sidewalk — that's how long ago it had been built.

In the backyard was a groovy old apple tree with a couple of rusty wires to hold the branches together. She loved it. The tree looked like one of those stray mutts that doesn't get any attention and doesn't care — it's still beautiful.

Then, just as she was really settling in, getting to like herself for really taking care of her kids this once, and trying to put her head together so her thoughts wouldn't rattle when she was alone, why just then Kathryne and Charles chose to split, her poor mom and dad married before they were hardly in high school, married for more than twenty years, five kids, and they never did get, Nicole always thought, to like each other, although maybe they'd been in love from time to time. Anyway, they were split. That would have dislocated her if she hadn't had the house in Spanish Fork. The house was better than a man. Nicole amazed herself. She had not slept with anybody for weeks, didn't want to, just wanted to digest her life, her three marriages, her two kids, and more guys than you wanted to count.

Well, the groove continued. Nicole had a pretty good job as a waitress at the Grand View Cafe in Provo and then she got work sewing in a factory. It was only one step above being a waitress, but it made her feel good. They sent her to school for a week, and she learned how to use the power sewing machines, and was making better money than she had ever brought in before. Two-thirty an hour. Her take-home came to $80 a week.

Of course, the work was hard. Nicole didn't think of herself as being especially well coordinated, and certainly she was not fast — her head was too bombed-out for sure. She would get flustered. They would put her on one machine and just about the time she started getting the hang of it, and was near the hourly quota, they put her on another. Then the machine would fuck up when she least expected.

Still it wasn't bad. She had a nest of a hundred bucks from screwing welfare out of extra money they'd once given her in some mix-up of checks, and put another $75 together from working. So she was able to pay out in cash $175 for an old Mustang that she bought from her next-door neighbor's brother. He had wanted up to $300, but he liked her. She just got a little lucky.

On the night Nicole met Gary, she had taken Sunny and Jeremy for a drive — the kids loved the car. With her was her sister-in-law. While she and Sue Baker weren't tight exactly, they did spend a lot of time together, and Sue was in the dumps at this point, being pregnant and split up from Rikki.

On the drive, Nicole passed about a block from her cousin's house, and Sue suggested they drop in. Nicole agreed. She figured Sue liked Sterling and must have heard that he had also split up with his old lady, just this week, baby and all.

It was a cool dark night, one of those nights in May when the mountain air still had the feel of snow. Except not that cold because Sterling's door was open a little bit. The girls knocked and walked in. Nicole wasn't wearing anything but her Levi's and some kind of halter, and there was this strange-looking guy sitting on the couch. She thought he was just plain strange looking. Hadn't shaved in a couple of days, and was drinking a beer. What with saying hello to Nicole and Sue, Sterling didn't even introduce him.

Nicole made a pretense of ignoring the new fellow, but there was something about him. When their eyes met, he looked at her and said, "I know you." Nicole didn't say anything in reply. For a split second, something flashed in her mind but then she thought, No, I've never met him before, I know that. Maybe I know him from another time.

That started everything off. She hadn't been thinking in such a way for quite a while. Now that feeling was around her again. She knew what he meant.

His eyes looked very blue in a long triangular face and they stared at her and he said again, "Hey, I know you." Finally Nicole kind of laughed and said, "Yeah, maybe." She thought about it a moment more and looked at him again and said, "Maybe." They didn't talk anymore for a while.

She gave her attention to Sterling. In fact, both girls were clustered around Sterling, the easiest man in the world to get along with. Nicole always liked him for he was gentle and warm and very hospitable, and sure sexy. He soothed everything.

What with Sue liking him too, the night was sort of exciting. As they were talking, Nicole finally confessed to Sterling that she had a crush on him for years when she was a kid. He told her right back that he'd always been crazy about her. They just laughed. Cousins with a crush. This other fellow sat in his chair and kept looking at her.

After a while Nicole decided the new fellow was pretty good looking. He was much too old for her, looked like he could be near 40.

But he was tall and had beautiful eyes and a pretty good mouth. He looked intelligent and yet bad at the same time, like an older guy who could fit into a motorcycle gang. She was a little fascinated, even if she wasn't about to admit to much interest.

Sue wasn't saying anything to him either, in fact she pretended he wasn't there. In compensation, Sunny started being a real bad 4-year-old and carried on in front of the stranger, as ornery and bossy as she could. She began ordering Nicole to do this and do that. Soon Sunny got flushed and pretty looking, and now was flirting with the man. Just about then, he looked at Nicole and said, "You're going to have a lot of trouble with this little girl. She could end up in Reform School."

That gave a twinge. It was one remark to get under you. Maybe she had been the kind of mother who could do that to her kids. Nicole knew those words might stick in her like a hook over the next couple of years.

She began to think this guy had some kind of psychic power, and could really see what was going to happen. As if he were a hypnotist or something of that ilk. She hardly knew if she was about to like that.

Anyway, he seemed to think that was enough to start a conversation. Before long, he was talking to her in a very persistent way. He wanted to go to the store to get a six-pack of beer and kept bugging her to go with him. She kept shaking her head. Sue and she had been getting ready to leave and she didn't want to go to the store with this man now. He was too strange. There wasn't any sense to it anyway since the store was just a little down the road.

What worked in his favor, however, was that Sue didn't look ready to leave yet. She was just beginning to get off on talking to Sterling, and obviously wouldn't mind being alone with the guy for a little while. So Nicole said, Okay, and took Jeremy for protection. Sunny was asleep by then.

When they got to the store, it was closed. They continued downtown. Nicole didn't even get out of the car. She stayed while the tall dude went in and got a six-pack or two of beer, and brought back a banana for Jeremy. That was his idea.

It was odd, but he had a Mustang just like hers, same model, same year. Just the color was different. So she felt comfortable in it.

When he returned with the beer, she was leaning against the door, and he put the six-pack on her knee. She joked and said, Oh, that hurts. He started rubbing her knee. He did it decently; not too personal, but it felt pretty good in a nice simple way, and they went on home. When they got to the end of Sterling's driveway, before she got out of the car, he turned around and looked at her and asked if she would kiss him. She didn't say anything for a minute, then said, Yes. He reached across and gave her a kiss and it didn't do any harm at all to what she thought about him. In fact, to her surprise, she felt like crying. A long time later, she would remember that first kiss. Then they went back to the house.

Now Nicole didn't ignore him quite so much, although she still made a point of sitting across the room. Sue obviously couldn't stand the fellow, and was paying even less attention in his direction. In fact Nicole was surprised how indifferent he seemed that Sue disliked him. Sue might be obviously pregnant now, but in Nicole's opinion she was a beautiful-looking blond. Maybe even the more spectacular of the two of them. Yet he didn't care, seemed ready to sit by himself. Sterling was also quiet. After a while, it began to seem as if the evening would all go nowhere.

With the down drift, Nicole and Sue started talking to each other. Nicole often had the feeling that Sue, when things were all right with Rikki, didn't think too good of her because of all the guys she dated, in fact Sue and Rikki told on her when she took a dude into bed once at her great-grandmother's house, and she never trusted Sue completely after that. She certainly didn't want Sue to think she was still that easy. So Nicole got a little stiff when just as she was getting ready to take the kids home, Gary said he wanted her phone number. She certainly felt funny about looking so available in front of her sister-in-law, after all the remarks she'd made tonight about living a new kind of life, so she told him that he couldn't have it. He was amazed.

He said, It just doesn't make any sense for you to walk out of here and never see you again. It would be a waste of a good thing, he said. He even got a little mad when she kept saying no. Sat there and looked at her. She stared into his blue eyes and told him she wouldn't give it to him, and then what with the kids, and Sue saying good-bye to Sterling, it took a while to leave. By the time they were out of the house, Nicole felt like screaming, she had wanted to give him that phone number so bad.

She didn't even have a phone. All she could have given was her address, or the next-door neighbor's number.

On the ride, Nicole didn't like the way she was feeling at all. She took Sue home, drove all the way out to Spanish Fork, pulled up to the house, and didn't move from the car. Then she said, To hell with it, and started back to Sterling's after all. On the way she decided she was an idiot, and the guy wouldn't even be there anymore. Or else, he might be trying to make out with another girl. Sterling could have called one over for him.

2

Nicole was really scared of what she was getting herself into. She couldn't figure out why she was doing it. It was the first time she'd chased after a guy since Doug Brock, and that was the only dude who'd ever sent her away. Brock was a lot older, and she had sure liked him. Nicole had been working at a motel in Salt Lake for a little while, and he lived around the corner, and mentioned something one day about paying her to clean his house. Once he got her in, it turned out pretty terrific and he told her to come over anytime. One night she couldn't sleep and was tired of being by herself, so she walked over. It was two in the morning. He came to the door naked and said, What the hell you doing at this hour? Then he got rude, and mentioned some other guy, and told her he didn't want anything to do with a chick who was going with somebody else. He was just like a foreman when he said it — which happened to be what he did for a living. Right after, he said he was busy with another girl, told her right there at his door at two in the morning. That was gross. Nicole never went back to see him. In fact, she had hardly thought of him until now, going back to Sterling's, when she had to wonder if Gary would still be around.

Then she became really scared of what she might be getting into. In fact her heart was so high, she could have been breathing some strange gas making her half faint, half exhilarated. She had never felt anything so strong as this before. It was as if it would be impossible to let this guy go.

His car was still there and she parked right behind. The kids were asleep in the back seat so she left them. It was safe to leave kids on a quiet street like this. And went up and knocked on the door, even if it was still cracked open a little. She heard him say something just before she knocked. It was incredible but she heard him say, "Man, I like that girl."

When she went in, he came over to her and he touched her, didn't grab her for a big kiss, but just touched her lightly. She felt really good. It was all right. She had done the right thing. They sat on the couch for a couple of hours and they laughed and talked. It hardly mattered if Sterling was in the room with them or not.

After a while, when it was obvious she was going to stay, they went out to the car and picked up the sleeping children and put them in the house and laid them still sleeping on Sterling's bed, and went on talking.

They did hardly anything but laugh. They had a great big laugh about counting her freckles and the impossibility of that because he said you couldn't count freckles on an elf. Then, in the quiet moment that followed a lot of this laughter, he told her he had been in prison for half of his life. He told her in a matter-of-fact way.

While Nicole wasn't afraid of him, she was *scared*. It was the thought of getting mixed up with another loser. Somebody who didn't think enough of himself to make something of himself. She felt it was bad to float through life. You might have to pay too much the next time around.

They got to speaking of karma. Ever since she was a kid, she had believed in reincarnation. It was the only thing that made sense. You had a soul, and after you died, your soul came back to earth as a new-born baby. You had a new life where you suffered for what you had done wrong in your last life. She wanted to do it right so she wouldn't have to make another trip.

To her amazement, he agreed. He said he had believed in karma for a long time. Punishment was having to face something you hadn't been able to face in this life.

Yes, he told her, if you murdered somebody, you might have to come back and be the parents of that person in a future century. That was the whole point of living, he said, facing yourself. If you didn't, the burden got bigger.

It was getting to be the best conversation she ever had. She had always thought the only way to have conversations like that was in your head.

Then he sat on the couch and held her face in his hands and said, "Hey, I love you." He said it from two or three inches away. She felt reluctant to answer him. Nicole hated "I love you." In truth, she despised it. She had said it so many times when she didn't mean it. Still, she supposed she had to get it out. As she expected, it didn't sound right. Left a bad echo in her head.

He said, "Hey, there's a place in the darkness. You know what I mean?" He said, "I think I met you there. I knew you there." He looked at her and smiled and said, "I wonder if Sterling knows about that place? Should we tell him?" They both looked at Sterling, and he was sitting there with a, well, just a funny kind of smile on his face, like he knew it was coming down that way. Then Gary said, "He knows. You can tell. You can see in his eyes that he knows." Nicole laughed with delight. It was funny. This guy looked twice her age, yet there was something naive about him. He sounded smart, but he was so young inside.

He kept drinking the beer, and Nicole got up once in a while and went in to give Sterling's baby a bottle. Ruth Ann was out working — even though Ruth Ann and Sterling had split, they were still living in the same house. It was all they could afford.

Gary kept telling Nicole that he wanted to make love to her. She kept telling him she didn't want to start that night. He'd say, "I don't want to just fuck you, I want to make love to you."

After a while, she went to the bathroom and when she came out, Sterling was leaving. It gave her a funny feeling. Sterling didn't show a sign he'd been forced to leave. He didn't look like he was being ejected. Still, she thought Gary might have been just a little rude. The idea was quite a lot rude, if you wanted to get into it. With all that beer, he was also getting just a little gruff. Still, now that they were alone, there was hardly any logic left to refusing. After a while, her clothes were off and they were on the floor.

3

He couldn't get a hard-on. He looked like he had been hit with an ax but was trying to smile. He wouldn't stop and rest. He had half a hard-on.

He was so heavy on her, and he just kept trying. After a while he began to apologize, and blamed it on too much beer. Asked her to help. Nicole began to do what she could. When her neck was as tired as it was ever going to be, he still wasn't ready to quit. It became straight hard work and it made her mad.

She told him they ought to cool it for a while. Maybe try again later. He asked her then to get on top of him, asked her gently. Now, he said in her ear that he would like her to lay there forever. Asked her if she would be able to sleep that way, on top of him. That would please him. She tried for a long time. She told him he should rest, and not worry. After the heat, and the exhaustion, and the fact that it wasn't going, she still felt tender toward him. She was surprised how tender she felt. She was sad he was drunk, and sorry he was that anxious, and might even have been loving him, but she was also irritated that he was too worked up to let it go and fall asleep. And he wouldn't stop apologizing. Said again it was the beer and the Fiorinal.

He told her he had to keep taking Fiorinal every day for his head-aches.

One time Sterling knocked on the other side of the door and asked if he could come back and Gary told him to get lost. She told him she didn't like at all how rude he was with Sterling. Gary finally pulled a rug over her, and unlocked the door so Sterling could get in, and then Gary came back and climbed under, and bothered her a little more. It went on all night. They got very little sleep.

About six in the morning Ruth Ann came home from where she worked at the old folks home. It was mildly embarrassing to Nicole because she knew Ruth Ann didn't necessarily have a high opinion of her. All the same, it gave an excuse to get up, which was all right with Nicole. She wanted to be by herself for a while.

Yet, before they separated, she gave him her address. It was a real step. He kept asking whether it was truly her house. When she said again it was, he told her he was going to come over after work.

Sure enough, he was there. She had had to go to the store, and left a note. All it said was, "Gary, I'll be back in a few minutes. Make yourself at home." But that note managed to stay around the house all the time they were together. She would stash it, and the kids would get ahold of it, and then she and Gary would run across it again.

On this afternoon, when she came back, he was already standing in the front room, grubby looking. His pants were the kind that look like they were made for a telephone man to carry tools in his pockets, and he had on a T-shirt and was dirty from working with insulation, and Nicole thought he looked beautiful.

Her grandfather, who lived up the canyon in Spanish Fork, came by a little later, just dropping in, and began to give her sly looks like, What the Christ, are you doing it again, Nucoa Butterball? — that had been the nickname he gave her when she was a child. Her grandfather knew the situations she could get herself into. Of course, he could also tell when she wanted the guy to be there, so he didn't stay very long.

Gary seemed uncomfortable to be in someone else's house. While she was busy with the kids, he went outside and walked around. Later, when things quieted, they stayed up late again talking and it made her uneasy at how close this guy was to moving in with her. It truly scared her. Nicole had always thought of herself as phony when it came to love. She might start sincere, but she wasn't so sure she'd ever really been in love with a guy. She'd care about guys, and have a lot of crushes, some of them pretty heavy. Mostly it was because the guy was good looking, or did nice things to her. But when she looked at Gary, she didn't just see his face and the way he looked, it was more like Nicole felt in the right place for the first time. She was enjoying every minute he was there.

Later, she would no longer remember what it had been like in bed on the second night, although it was better. Maybe it set no records, but it wasn't hassled like the first. Then the days and nights began to run together. He didn't move in completely for a week, but he was living with her just about all the time.

4

On the weekend he took her over to meet Vern and Ida, and acted pretty proud. She liked the way he introduced her, and went on about Jeremy's nickname being Peabody. Had they ever heard a better nickname? Nobody was surprised when he said, "Vern, I've decided to move out and live with Nicole." They all knew it was already settled, but he showed how he liked the sound of saying it.

Vern's attitude was fine. What Gary wanted, he said, was what he wanted. Vern allowed that with Nicole also working, maybe by the combination of the two of them, the two compensations, maybe they could swing it. In the meantime, Gary could feel free to keep his room. It wasn't like he was a boarder who lived in the basement and paid weekly rent.

When she saw his room, however, Nicole thought it was a rat-hole. No pictures on the walls, no lamps. It looked like a cubicle in a cheap hotel, and Gary had just a few things, one pair of pants and a few shirts in his drawers. A bunch of pictures in a green folder of his friends in prison. She hardly knew why he had brought her to the room until he got out his hat and put it on, sort of a crazy fishing hat. He looked at himself in the mirror, and acted as if he really looked cool. Then he produced another hat with red, white and blue stripes. That was the oddest thing about him, the absolutely nutty hats he thought looked good.

5

Sue Baker didn't even know Gary was seeing Nicole, let alone living with her. But one day Nicole called and said she had decided to take the day off from the sewing machine factory. Wanted a chance to talk to Sue. So they took the kids to the park for a picnic. It was there Nicole spoke of how she had never felt for anybody what she felt for Gary. She loved him.

About the third or fourth night she knew him, he had gotten drunk, Nicole said, just so drunk on his butt that she was angry at him. But then he sat down and drew a picture of her. Up to then, he had talked about how good he was at drawing, and how he got prizes in contests, but she'd never seen him do anything. Hadn't believed him. She had listened to guys talking about what they could do. She had heard a lot of bullshit. But when he drew that picture, it was really good. He didn't just draw a little — he did it like a real artist.

When it was time to leave the park to pick Gary up at work, there was a light in Nicole's eye. It had come in just at the thought of picking him up. So Sue didn't need anybody to tell her how good Nicole was feeling. If Nicole was that much in love, then, no matter her first impression, Sue was ready to change her mind about the guy.

Of course, now that Rikki and she were split, Sue had no transportation. So she went along with Nicole to Lindon, and, in fact, got to like Gary on the way back. He was sure agreeable. Kept talking about how good he felt to be picked up by two gorgeous women.

It was a compliment. Her belly was big. Sue was still dating once in a while these days, and had even gone dancing once, but she was big and Rikki had sure done it to her. First he complained her IUD hurt him, then she took it out, then he made her pregnant. She was the youngest of ten kids, the outcast at the bottom of her own family, and now Rikki had left her.

If it hadn't been for Gary's compliments, at this minute, Sue Baker would have sunk right into the swamp of misery.

Still, Nicole had had a change of luck. So maybe there was a chance for herself as well. Maybe something terrific could come into your life any night at all.

After they dropped Sue off, Nicole showed Gary a pillow she had brought. To get close to him, Nicole always sat near the hump of the front seat rather than on the seat itself, and that was not very comfortable in the Mustang with its two bucket seats. She had finally gotten smart enough to bring a pillow today. Not only was it more comfortable, but she could sit with her hips raised, and so be tall enough to put an arm around his neck. He drove with his free hand in her lap, holding hands.

This day, as they pulled up to the store for shopping, he didn't get out but began to talk to her of his mother. He hadn't seen her for a long time, he explained, and she had arthritis bad and couldn't hardly walk. Gary stopped talking and tears came to his eyes. Nicole was amazed that he felt something so strong for his mother. She was amazed he could cry. She thought he was harder than that. She didn't say anything but sat close to him and touched his tears. Usually when she saw men cry it was disgusting. She'd had guys cry when she left them. She was good at turning herself off when they got like that, thought it was a weakness to cry over a girl. With Gary, she wasn't thinking about weakness. Wanted to do something for him. Snap her fingers, so to speak, and have his mother there.

They began to talk about going up to Portland for a visit. Maybe they could save a little, and make the drive in her car, or maybe his could last for the ride. Then, they got to talking about islands they could lease for 99 years. Gary said he didn't know that much concerning the subject but was going to get some information on it.

6

On workdays, he had to get up early, but he was used to that. She found it really okay to have him hugging her in the early morning dark and whispering he loved her. They both slept nude but he still had to lay hands on her to be sure she was there. Of course, that could be a problem. Nicole hardly enjoyed to kiss him then. He didn't smoke and his breath was good, but she smoked a lot and her mouth tasted awful at 5:30 A.M.

Before too long, she would get out of bed, go in the kitchen, fix him sandwiches, and set the coffee on. She had a real short little bathrobe which sometimes she wore, or she'd run around nude. He'd sit and drink his instant breakfast of Carnation with a handful of vitamins. He was a vitamin freak and believed them good for energy. Of course, if he'd done a lot of drinking after work, he was tired in the morning. Still, he was good company. He'd sit with her over coffee as long as he could, and keep looking at her, and would tell her she was beautiful, and that she amazed him. He had never believed a woman could be as fresh and sweet smelling as she, and indeed Nicole was willing to hear all of that, for she liked her bath, and no matter how the house or kids might look at times, she really cared about being dainty.

Without makeup, her face was fresh as dew, he told her. She was his elf. She was loveliness, he said. After a while, Nicole got the impression that he was just like her and could hardly comprehend what was happening. The feeling of something beautiful next to you all the time.

Then, just before he was ready to leave, he would get up and lock himself in the bathroom for twenty minutes. Nicole supposed he combed his hair and did his thing. Afterward, they'd spend five minutes at the front door, and she would watch from there while he got in the car. A lot of times he'd have trouble starting it. Sometimes, after slipping on her Levi's, she'd come out to push. Sometimes he would have to take her car. It was dependent on which Mustang had the most gas. They got pretty broke sometimes.

She didn't regret, however, quitting her job. After the day she played hooky from the sewing factory to have a picnic with Sue, she knew she wasn't going to keep working. She needed time to think. It was hard to stay serious about a sewing machine when you wanted to dream all the time about your man. Besides, they had his paycheck, and her welfare, and Gary was just as happy if she quit.

While he was away, she'd piddle around, clean the house, feed the kids. She'd work in the garden a lot, and drink coffee. Sometimes she would sit and drink coffee for a couple of hours and think about Gary. Sit there and smile to herself. She felt so nice she couldn't believe some of the things she felt. A lot of times she would drive over with his lunch just to be with him, and he'd come sit in the car.

She began to visit her mother a lot because Kathryne's house wasn't far from where he worked, and Nicole could have coffee with Kathryne, then leave the kids, and be alone with Gary. She really enjoyed such time. She'd go back to her mother's for an hour or so, then back to Spanish Fork to straighten out the house and wait. It was the first time in her life she felt like a lady of leisure.

One Sunday while she was digging away in her garden, Gary carved their names on the apple tree. He did it with a pocket knife, real nice, really neat: GARY LOVES NICOLE. Nobody had ever done that before.

Next day she had a lot of things to do, and kept wanting to get back. When she finally reached home, she cleaned his car out first, then climbed up the tree to a place above where he had done it, and carved out: NICOLE LOVES GARY. Then she went into the house just in time to meet him.

He came out in the backyard with a beer and she told him to look at the apple tree. He didn't see anything and she finally had to point it out to him. Then he was happy as a kid, and said she had done hers better than his. Told her it was a beautiful heart she had carved around the names.

7

Maybe a week after Gary came to live with her, she found a big yellow folder in his stuff with a bunch of papers about a dispute he had with a prison dentist. The arguments were all typed up in prison language and seemed so funny she just sat there and laughed. All those big words about a set of false teeth. When she told Gary, however, he got upset. He had never mentioned he had false teeth. Bothered the hell out of him that she found out.

Of course it wasn't new to her. She had discovered it the first night. She had lived before with a guy who had a plate and knew how they felt. You could always tell when kissing a man because they never wanted you to put your tongue in their mouth, whereas they were always putting their tongue in yours. She went so far as to tease him about the chompers, but he took it bad. Changed like somebody just turned out the lights. She still kept teasing him, as if to make him see it didn't bother her. She had no desire to compare him to other guys, or rate him in one department or another. She was ready to buy the package, string and all.

Each day she kept coming across the realization that some of the little things he did gave her surprising pleasure. He didn't smoke, for instance, yet when he saw her rolling her own, he brought home a carton of cigarettes. It was beautiful, those little lifts.

They would sit around and drink beer in the evening, and there was hardly time enough together. She could be as honest as she wanted, and tell him anything about her past. He would listen. He would observe everything she had to say. If another fellow would have sickened her with such constant attention, it didn't bother Nicole a bit. She was studying Gary the same way.

All she wanted was more hours with him. She had always appreciated any minute she had to herself, but now she would get impatient with wanting him to be back. When five o'clock rolled around and he was there, the day was made. She loved opening that first beer for him.

Sometimes, he would take his BB gun out to the back, and they would shoot at bottles and beer cans in the twilight until you couldn't

tell anymore when you were hitting except by the sound of the ricochet or a plink of glass. The twilight came down slowly. It was as if
you were taking one breath and then another from a cluster of roses.
The air was good as marijuana then.

In those early evenings, if they stayed home, there were always
kids around. Their baby-sitter was a girl named Laurel, an adolescent
who had a lot of little cousins, and they came with her. Sometimes
when Gary and Nicole got back from a drive, all those kids would be
around and he would play with them. He'd give them piggyback
rides. They'd stand on his shoulders and touch their hands to the
ceiling. He liked to play with the ones who had enough nerve to walk
all the way across the room like that. They just loved the holy shit out
of him.

A lot of the time, though, as soon as he got home, they would get
Laurel over, and take off for a ride alone.

Usually they would eat at a drive-in, and a couple of times he
took her to the Stork Club to play pool. There were afternoons right
after work when they went to the shopping mall and selected sexy
underwear for her, or picked up beer and cigarettes for the drive-in
movie.
Pretty soon after they parked, he'd want her to take her clothes
off. Then they would make it in the front seat. Gary just loved to have
her naked. Couldn't get over the idea he was holding a naked
woman.

Once, watching *Peter Pan,* they got out and sat on the rear deck
over the trunk, back to back, and she was naked then. The Mustang
was parked way in the outfield, but there were other cars around, and
she had nothing on. God, it was the nicest feeling. After all those
years in prison, Gary was insane about watching her walk about with
her bootie exposed and her boobs bouncing. She dug it that he liked
her without clothes. He had her right around his finger and she
didn't mind it a bit.

Yet, he didn't get arrogant. He was so touching when he asked
her to do something. One night, late at night, she even took off her
clothes on the back steps of the First Mormon Church, in Provo Park,
practically the center of town. It was late at night. They just sat there

on the steps, her clothes on the grass, and she danced a little, and
Gary began to sing in a voice like Johnny Cash, although not as good,
unless you were in love with Gary, and he sang "Amazing Grace" —

> Through many dangers, toils and snares,
> We have already come,
> 'Twas Grace that brought us safe this far,
> And Grace will lead us on —

That way she sat beside him naked at two in the morning, on a
hot spring night, with the heat pushing in from the desert instead of
the cold settling down from the mountains.

That night, very late at night, back in bed, they really made it.
Just as the sex was going good, he talked of putting his rough hands
on her soft warm bootie and of breathing into her soul, and she came
with him then, really came for the first time.

In the morning she sat down and wrote a letter to say how much
she loved him, and that she didn't want to stop. It was just a short
letter and she left it out there by his vitamins. He didn't reply when
he read it, but a night or two later they were walking by the same
church off Center Street, and saw a falling star. They both made a
wish. He asked what hers could be, but she wasn't going to tell him.
Then she confessed having wished that her love for him be constant
and forever. He told her that he hoped no unnecessary tragedies
would ever befall them. She had a rush of memories then like falling
down in a dream.

CHAPTER 5

Nicole and Uncle Lee

1

Once, when Gary asked her if she remembered the first time she fucked somebody, Nicole paused in her reply and said, "Vaguely."

" 'Vaguely?' " Gary asked. "What do you mean, 'vaguely'?"

"It wasn't that big of a deal," said Nicole. "I was only 11 or 12."

Of course, she didn't tell him all her stories at once. She told him cute things first like the one about the pet raccoon when she was 6. She used to walk to school with it on her shoulder and think she was hot stuff.

She used, she told him, to play hooky a lot. Sometimes she would just drift on up the hill above the school, sit in the middle of the pine trees and look down on all those little idiots in class. One time Nicole was being smart-ass and instead of keeping to the woods, went walking back by the road. Just then her mother drove around the corner. There Nicole was. She could remember her mother saying, "All right, girl. Get in the car."

Or the time her mother cut her hair so short you could see the skin behind her ears. People used to think she was a boy. One time some kids in the playground said so, and she proved to them she wasn't.

Gary laughed. That sped things up.

She remembered, when she was 10 or 11, writing a pornographic letter to a very nasty little boy who had a very dirty mouth.

Now she didn't know why she wrote it, just that when she finished, she took one look, and tore it up. Kathryne fished it out of the garbage and taped it together. Then her mother told her how horrible she was. Especially since she had written: Okay, you talk about it so much, let's do it.

There came moments when Nicole thought her mother was very intelligent, for Kathryne could pick up on what other people were thinking. Nicole never believed Kathryne listened much to her own soul, but she could sure hone in on others. If you lived around her long enough, you didn't have to think about something before her mother would mention it. That sure gave her a way of bending you out of shape. Kathryne was a tiny woman, but she would tell her big handsome husband with his beautiful black mustache that he was nothing but a slob. Tell him to go fuck the lady he had just been with. When Charley came home from work, which was usually late, because he'd stopped off to have a few at a bar, it wasn't that he walked drunk, or his speech was slurred, but he'd have a half smile on his face like Clark Gable, and Nicole could tell he was feeling good. Then Kathryne would start to fix his mood. She wasn't about to forgive him for a lot.

One time, Kathryne actually caught him coming down the stairs in some motel. He had a girl on the second floor. Kathryne had his Service pistol and threatened to shoot him. But she didn't. In turn, Nicole's father would always accuse Kathryne of adultery, her mother! — Charley Baker was the first man she had, and she never had another one. Didn't stop her father. Once he got home late and nobody was there, and he thought Kathryne'd left forever with the kids and a man. Instead she had just taken the kids to a drive-in movie. When they got home, Charley wouldn't believe it. The kids had to run out of the house and climb in the car, and when Mom leaped in to drive away, Charles tried to jump on as they were all pulling out, and broke his leg. That was when Nicole was around 7 and her father was 25.

There were always fights about money. Her mother's argument was that he was just plain stingy about the family and spent his money on hunting rifles or drinking with his Army buddies. Still, Nicole could remember when she was 10, and her daddy was in Vietnam and her mother was worried that he was going to get killed. They would hear her cry sometimes late at night.

2

When Gary said he would like to meet her mother, Nicole didn't tell him about her last conversation with Kathryne. Her mother had said this new boy friend was a little old, she'd heard. And then there was his having been in prison. That had to be a very good influence.

"I'll go," said Nicole, "with whom I goddamn well please."

Yet when the meeting took place, nothing did happen. Gary was polite and stood at the cupboard holding Jeremy in his arms, and looked at everybody and drank it in and didn't say a thing. It was like he'd been wound up to stay in position and send light out of his eyes. "Nice to meet you," he said to Kathryne when he left, and Nicole knew that an uncomfortable feeling stayed behind.

She cared more because of the things people could do to him. He was stiff as a 14-year-old boy with the wrong people. She understood. She knew what it was like to be in prison. Felt as if she had lived there too. Prison was wanting to breathe when somebody else had a finger up your nose. Soon as they took it out, the air got you crazy. Prison was being married too young and having kids.

She didn't always remember which story she had told him. Just as well. Some of the stories were pretty bad. Still she usually felt as if her thoughts passed over to his head with only a couple of words to help them along. Before she knew it, she was telling him more and more. He listened without getting upset. That was real important.

When she was 8 or 9, she was still ugly in her own mind, a gawky little bird. Then, suddenly, she blossomed. She had the biggest boobs in the sixth grade. In fact, there was a time when she had the biggest boobs in the elementary school. Didn't have to go looking for attention. It came to her. They called her Foam Rubber.

Before she was 11, she wouldn't let anybody put it in. Still, she liked to take her clothes off, and have them look. Then she would let the boys touch her. She liked getting attention from the best-looking boys. That was because she never thought of herself as popular. They didn't ask her out much to parties. The girls from the good Mormon families who went to Sunday School used to spite her a lot.

By junior high, she was making friends with the worst kids. Some were the biggest troublemakers and some were just the ugliest looking. She was stealing a lot, particularly out of other kids' lockers. Even when she didn't get caught, people were always suspecting her, and disgusted with her. Yet nobody was interested enough to want her to be something better. She had the feeling that if she was a good girl and went to church and got good grades, who would acknowledge it?

Then they put her into the nuthouse at 13. There was a far-out lady they sent her to for counseling, and the lady talked her into going. They told her she would only be there for a couple of weeks but after she spilled the beans about Uncle Lee, she stayed for seven months.

Right from when she started school, there was an Army friend of her father's who lived with them. His buddy, her father called him. The kids called him Uncle Lee even though he was no real uncle or any kind of relative, but her dad looked on him as a lot closer than his own brothers. He even looked something like Charley Baker. When they were out together, it was as if Elvis Presley was walking down the street with Elvis Presley.

Uncle Lee was dead now, but he had lived off and on with them from the time she was 6, and Nicole always blamed her mother and dad for Uncle Lee, because he had sure fucked her up. She even thought she became a slut because of him.

When her father would work on the Base at night, and her mother would also work late, and her brother be asleep, Lee would start. When it was late in the evening and her mother was out with her father, Nicole would know it was coming. She'd begin to feel nervous while waiting for Lee to come out of the tub. Soon after, sitting in the living room alone with her, he would open his bathrobe and ask her to play. Called it rubbing pee-pees.

With the lights out, she never really knew if it was touching, or
what he was asking her to kiss. After a while, it didn't even seem that
unusual, she would answer him politely when he asked, Does that
feel good? She would say, Yes.

Nicole was 12 before she told him that he couldn't make her do
it anymore. She was sleeping next to April when Lee woke her up.
Nicole thought April was awake anyway, so she told him no. Then,
Lee said he had caught her in the bathroom. Went into detail how he
had seen a little masturbating. Said, You're such a free spirit, you can
do it with me. She said, I don't care what you saw, you tell the world.
A little while after, he went to Nam and was killed. It made Nicole
wonder if she had left a curse, cause she had enough evil thoughts
about Lee.

She never told anyone in the family what he had done. She was
afraid they might not believe it. Yet, now, they seemed to know.
Maybe the nice lady who sent her to the nuthouse got around to
telling them.

Gary was silent for a long time. "Your old man," he said, "ought
to be shot."
"Are you sure you want to hear all of it?" she asked.
"I want to hear it," he nodded.

So she started to tell him about the nuthouse and her first marriage. And she didn't hide it about the orgy in between. Otherwise, it
would have been too confusing to explain that she met her second
husband before her first.

3

It was really only half a nuthouse and half a Reform School. Kind of a
youth home. It wasn't all that bad, except Nicole felt crazy all the
time because it was ridiculous that she was locked up. Why are they
keeping me here, she would ask herself, when I'm not nuts? It would
get quiet in the night, and she would feel lonely when somebody
would scream.

The first time they let her home for a visit she got to stay at her grandmother's and some dudes next door asked if she wanted to party a little bit. She slipped off to the next house with them for a few days, and got in trouble overstaying her leave. They kept such a watch on her when she went back to the hospital that it took six months before she could go AWOL again.

One time, a real dopy old lady was on guard at the door and Nicole was able to get past her. She took off down the field, climbed two fences, went through a few backyards, found a good-sized road and hitchhiked over to Rikki and Sue's house where she hung around for a few days, and started to go with the guy who became her first husband, Jim Hampton. He claimed to be in love and wanted to marry her from the first date on. She thought he was a big immature clunk. Yet every day she was AWOL, Nicole was with him. She felt very conceited about being superior to him.

Then her father found out where she was, and came over. He wasn't mad or nothing. Thought it was kind of neat she'd run away from the nuthouse. Suggested she get married.

Nicole always felt Mack-trucked into that one. There was a saying they used up in the nuthouse for when you got pushed into a marriage by parties larger than yourself. Mack-trucked. It was obvious to Nicole that her parents wanted her off their hands.

On the other hand, even if she didn't like Hampton's personality, or couldn't be impressed much with his intelligence, she thought he was awfully good looking. Moreover, her dad kept telling her she didn't have to go back to the loonies if she was married. Then Hampton asked Charley for permission, and her father just said, "Let's go." Never did ask Nicole.

He got in the car with Jim Hampton like they were old buddies — her dad wasn't even thirty and Jim was over twenty — put her in the back seat, and the car took off. Nicole knew damn well she wasn't gaining any freedom by marrying Jim Hampton. They drove along, drinking it up in front, and Nicole told herself she'd gotten into this and might as well give it a good try.

Sitting in the back seat, Nicole remembered a time when she was 12 years old and her dad took her to a bar. She thought he was showing her off, but soon found out he had a girl friend in there he wanted to show off, and knew she wouldn't tell her mother. Only, at the door, she stopped. NO ONE UNDER 21 ADMITTED was what the sign read.

Her father pointed to the 2 and the 1 and he said, It says no one under 12. You're old enough. She never was all sure when she was reading numbers backwards and so thought 21 was 12 that day.

Now that she had become 14, it was all she could do to keep from laughing about it.

Charley sure made a sight drinking with Hampton. In fact her father looked a little like her husband-to-be. She began to think they both looked like Uncle Lee, damn him.

Well, the trip turned out to be not too bad. They picked up a friend of hers named Cheryl Kumer, and she drove with them to Elko, Nevada, where Nicole and Jim Hampton got married.

Jim was never rough with her, but kind of sweet, and treated her like she was a precious doll. He was always saying to the rest of his friends who weren't married, Hey, look what I got. You know? He didn't have a job so they were living on unemployment. He wouldn't go to work, but really knew how to use a fingernail file on Coke machines. Even if she didn't wholly like living on dimes and quarters, Nicole thought they were having fun.

After a few months, she was still faithful to him, which wasn't a bad trip. She was trying to unsort her sex hang-ups. They went from too little to too much. She could never come in those days which she knew wasn't all Hampton's fault. Besides Uncle Lee, she had one other big secret in her past she never told Hampton about. It happened the first time she left the nuthouse on a weekend pass and stayed at the party for two days and two nights. That was months before she'd even met Hampton.

The guy that talked her into coming over from her grandmother's house on that occasion was about 28, and there had been booze and dope to smoke. She really liked that dude. He babied her, and paid a lot of attention, and kept her close by. When he made love, it left her feeling kind of mellow. Then he told his buddies there was a sweet little thing in the bedroom, go talk to her. Nicole was really hung up on the guy even when he began to hint to her that she would be befriending him if she would fuck his friends, you know.

Nicole felt a lot of things as it was going on. She took herself off to a distance and watched herself. It was a way to think about things. Think out problems.

Bottom of all, she was proud. Even if, to some degree, the fellows were fucking her over, yet she was into the kind of party her friends would be too chicken to go along on. That was exciting. So she got a little wasted and ended up with just about every guy in the house. Maybe she was there for three days. She just never went out.

In the middle of it, she met Barrett for the first time. He came walking into the bedroom, a skinny little guy she'd never seen before. There she was all alone in bed on the second day, feeling spacey, and he walked in, and spoke to her from the hallway. He said, You know you don't have to do this. You're better than this. Yes, he said, you don't have to waste it all. That was her first memory of her second husband, Jim Barrett. He was only there a few minutes, but she always remembered the way his face looked then.

She didn't see Barrett again until a month later when she was back in the nuthouse, and they threw him in, too. He wasn't the least bit crazy. He had, however, gone AWOL from the Army, so his father signed papers to have him committed. The nuthouse was better than the Stockade. Barrett's father had been a State Trooper, he told her, before he became an insurance agent, so from the point of view of the authorities, the son had to be kind of crazy.

She really fell in love with Barrett in the nuthouse. They were almost the same two people. He was so cunning looking, so really sweet, a real pussycat. All smiles and all sweet, wearing cowboy boots, navy pants, tight shirts, well combed, well groomed, just a little guy. Then they took him back in the Army, and for the longest time she never heard from him. So she went AWOL, and married the other Jim, Hampton.

Months later, Barrett showed up one day. Was waiting for her in the parking lot of the supermarket. They were so happy to see each other. How could she get married on him? Didn't she love him? Hadn't they talked of living in a house of their own where nobody could hassle them? If she was happy with the guy she had married, then he, Barrett, would bow out. He loved her enough to wish her love and luck. But if she wasn't happy . . . it was a beautiful headgame he played. After thirty minutes, she just said good-bye in her heart to Hampton, and ran away with Barrett.

4

They headed for Denver. It was a cold trip. They visited for a week with a friend of his, then came back to Utah and stayed with his folks. Nicole kept trying to say Jim, but that was also Hampton's first name, so she was more comfortable calling him Barrett.

When they got back to Utah, however, Marie Barrett, his mother, was real nice, and took them in every way. Except she wouldn't let them sleep in the house. Get married if you want to stay here, was the way she drew the line. Nicole didn't care. The happiest she'd ever been in her life was when she ran away and slept in an orchard, so she didn't mind spending her nights on the back seat of a Volkswagen. It was Barrett who felt exposed in the street. He found out from his father that while they'd been in Denver, Jim Hampton was over looking for them with Charley Baker. Nicole thought it was stupid how Hampton and her father couldn't mind their own business, but, as Barrett explained to Nicole, he wasn't built to be confronted with a physical challenge. So they found themselves a better hideout.

They found a scrungy little apartment on the main street in Lehi. The stairway leading up to their door was really bad with winos who had staggered out of the bar below. At the end of the street was the desert and the wind whistled in. Their window looked out on that street. Nicole could stand there, and watch her dad enter the bar below.

Then one day Charley showed up at the door. Everybody had been looking, but it took her dad to find out they were not only in the state, not only in town, but, in fact, right above his favorite hangout. Her dad walked right in and gave this shitty smile, asked how she was. Barrett came over, and Charley said, "Boy, I'm gonna cut your goddamn balls off. I'm going to tear them out." He sounded like Clark Gable. Barrett said something kind of mild like "Can we talk about it first?" Then he told her dad that he wasn't evil and loved Nicole very much. Nicole just kept looking Charley in the eye. Before it was all over, her dad broke down and went home peacefully. She could hardly believe it.

A couple of days later, the cops came and busted Barrett for being an improper person. That was the term for poor Jim — Improper Person. She figured her mother learned about it from her father and blew the whistle. Anyway, the guy who supplied Barrett with dope to sell came along and bailed him out. Then it was Nicole's turn. She crashed. She and Barrett sat up one night in a friend's van, eating orange sunshine out of a matchbox. The next day went by all burned out but the next night they all took another hit. Nicole freaked. They were parked on Center Street in Provo, radio on, and Grand Funk came in, the song with the sirens. Suddenly everybody's vibes in the van kind of went in and out. Wham! Nicole felt herself winging down the road, just running, you know. Jim took after her, caught her, dragged her back, but he was feeling too loose himself. Nicole was blowing it and screaming. Barrett took her to the hospital, but even they couldn't handle her. She began to run around telling the nurses they were ugly. She was seeing lions and tigers. So they took her to the Youth Home.

Kathryne wouldn't let her out. She told Barrett that if he wanted to marry Nicole, he had to pay the hospital expense first. Otherwise, she'd be sent on to Reform School. Barrett had to say to his folks, "Just let me marry her. That's all I ever wanted," and he talked them into putting up the $180 that was necessary.

Her mother gave her a black dress to be married in. It was short and slit at the sides. That really affected Nicole. She didn't feel it was appropriate to get married in a black dress at 15. She didn't say anything to her mother, but it bothered Nicole that no one would even take a picture of them. She kept thinking, they must have a camera in the place somewhere, they might want a picture of us getting married. Nobody would take a snap. A couple of weeks later her family disappeared on her. Charley and Kathryne took off with the kids for his new station on Midway.

Living with Barrett, sex was pretty much the same as with Hampton. She was a novice in those days. Wouldn't feel nearly so good as she would make believe. Like she never got her rocks off until a month after she was married. Of course, she would no more start with Barrett than she would flash to that first time with Uncle Lee. In fact, whenever sex went on too long with Jim and she felt sore and burning, or her breasts were tender from a mauling, it would feel the same as when she'd been a child. Still, she was crazy about Barrett. He was a sweet and kindred soul. They swore to be poor but happy all their married lives.

At the onset, however, they just couldn't get that happy. Barrett had one big worry leaning over him. He finally came in with this heavy rap to his father, real dramatic, like a television series. Barrett's father, being an ex-cop, tended to buy it. "Look," Jim told him, "some guys fronted me a little dope, and I blew it all. Now, I can't pay. They're coming down on me and I gotta get out of town." With that, he talked his father into getting a used van, put a mattress in back, and took off. Only a long time later did Nicole decide Barrett had run a line on his father and wasn't in that kind of trouble at all.

They ended up in San Diego in an old wooden hotel called the Commodore, and she found a plump black kitten about to get run over in the middle of the road and went out and got it, only it wasn't a kitten but a little pregnant cat, and had kittens itself in a couple of weeks. She thought that was pretty neat.

It was a funny time. They were happy and miserable at once. She had started to come with Barrett and he started to play with the idea of selling her. It wasn't her so much as that he was a born salesman and needed something to sell. He liked to experiment. So did she. It opened her to a lot of crazy feelings that she couldn't get around to telling Gary about. They were too rough somehow, and besides, she never did get into selling herself. On consideration, she decided she better not mess with Barrett's ego. He was such a jealous person.

Then they gave the cats away and drove back to Utah. When they reached Orem, they left the car parked right near an entrance to the Interstate. Barrett didn't even stop at his folks' house, just mailed them a card telling where he'd hid the keys to the van, and apologized for being unable to keep up the payments. He felt funny, he kept telling Nicole, that his folks would get their card postmarked Orem when they thought their son was in California.

Then they hitchhiked up to Modesto where a weird guy with one eye all screwed up rented them a $50-a-month tiny cabin. It had cockroaches. They would turn off the lights, then turn them on, and kill the cockroaches. She discovered she was pregnant there.

They had a fight about the baby to come. It wouldn't work, he argued. Later, back in Utah, Nicole decided it was a fork in the river. Because she had wanted him to get a job, and he kept promising he would. Saying it and doing it hadn't worked out equal, however. Barrett showed his true talents and talked a woman who was selling a thirteen-room house into renting to them for $80 a month, because that way, she could show it to buyers when she wanted. After they moved in, Barrett didn't work but had his friends over, and began to party, and got back into dealing. By the time Nicole was six months into pregnancy, the party didn't let up.

One day the Chief of Police came over with the landlady, who returned Barrett half a month's rent and the cop evicted him on the spot. He wanted to stay, but they put the money in his hand, told him to go. Nicole was upset at having to live pregnant at her grandmother's while he stayed with his folks. Not only did they owe a lot of money, but Barrett did nothing all day but get stoned with his friends. Life had become a drag.

At that point, her dad came in from Midway on some business. Just joking, he said, "Want to come back with me? See the Islands?" She said, "Damn right!"

5

That was how she left Barrett the first time. Just took off in her seventh month as suddenly as she had left Hampton. On the airplane she kept thinking of early days with Jim when there was so much love she could even feel the things Barrett was feeling. Of course, such thoughts came only after she was able to get on the plane. The onset of the trip didn't go that smoothly. She and Charley spent hours trying to get a military flight to Hawaii, and kept getting bumped. One of the problems was that Charley didn't have her birth certificate, so Nicole couldn't go on his military card as a daughter. Being pregnant, she looked considerably older than usual. Charley, standing next to her, appeared more like a boy friend or husband than a father. That got her thinking about Uncle Lee like crazy. Come to think of it, her dad always treated her with the special courtesy you give a sexy lady.

Maybe her thoughts were tickling his ear because Charley certainly got upset now at the idea of them being stuck overnight. "If I don't get my daughter on this goddamn plane," he swore, "I'm going to hijack the son of a bitch."

He walked out to the Mess Hall, and next thing they knew, four MPs were saying, Would you come with us, Mr. Baker? Took them right outside, and spread-eagled Charley against the wall, shook him down, led him off to the Brig. Left Nicole sitting in the Mess Hall with eighty horny sailors. When she went to look for her father, she saw the largest cockroach ever. Looked as big as a mouse, and it came running out into the lobby where Nicole was waiting. She followed it down the steps, and around the building. With her big belly, she had nothing better to do than run along following that big old cockroach.

Then her dad came out grinning from ear to ear. He had everything all straightened out. Because of the mistake, they were now treating him and Nicole like king and queen. Red carpet was out. She got to Midway in style.

When she walked in the house, Kathryne's eyes almost fell out of her head. Nicole remembered how skinny she was, and how as she hugged her, there was something hollow looking about Kathryne, as if it was all getting too much for her. The teenagers, April and Mike, who had just been kids, were now getting wild. It made Nicole feel so bad she didn't even like to smoke in front of her mother for a couple of days.

When Barrett found where she was, he ran up his old man's phone bill. Got so emotionally worked up, felt so much in love all over again, that he had gone to work. He had, he told her, even started a checking account. Was going to come see her.

Nicole gave her love on the phone. She said not to come. It would get her father in trouble. To save on the fare, Charley had brought her over as his dependent, so everybody thought she was an unwed mother.

Damn if Barrett didn't show up anyway. In Salt Lake, at the airport, he wrote a check which his dad later had to make good, flew over, went to the hospital, found the maternity ward, and sat outside her window. As soon as Kathryne left the room, he was in. Nicole was happy he had come and it made a difference, but not a big one. She couldn't forgive him everything. In a couple of days she made him go home.

CHAPTER 6

Nicole on the River

1

By now, Nicole wanted to hear about Gary's life. Only he didn't want to talk about himself. Preferred to listen to her. It took a while for Nicole to realize that having spent his adolescence in jail and just about every year since, he was more interested to learn what went on in her little mind. He just hadn't grown up with sweet things like herself.

In fact, if he did tell a story it was usually about when he was a kid. Then she would enjoy the way he talked. It was like his drawing. Very definite. He gave it in a few words. A happened, then B and C. Conclusion had to be D.

A. His seventh-grade class voted on whether they should send Valentines to each other. He thought they were too old. He was the only one to vote against it. When he lost, he bought Valentines to mail to everybody. Nobody sent him one. After a couple of days he got tired of going to the mailbox.

B. One night, he was passing a store that had guns in the window. Found a brick and broke the window. Cut his hand, but stole the gun he wanted. It was a Winchester semiautomatic that cost $125 back in 1953. Later he got a box of shells and went plinking. "I had these two friends," Gary told her, "Charley and Jim. They really loved that .22. And I got tired of hiding it from my old man — when I can't have something the way I want it, then I don't really want it. So

I said, 'I'm throwing the gun in the creek, if you guys have the guts to dive for it, it's yours.' They thought I was bullshitting until they heard the splash. Then Jim jumped and hurt his knee on a big old sharp rock. Never got the gun. The creek was too deep. I laughed my ass off."

C. On his thirteenth birthday his mother let him pick between having a party or getting a $20 bill. He chose the party and invited just Charley and Jim. They took the money their folks gave them for Gary and spent it on themselves. Then they told him.

D. He had a fight with Jim. Got angry and beat him half to death. Jim's father, a rough-and-tumble fucker, pulled Gary off. Told him, "Don't come around here again." Soon after, Gary got in trouble for something else and was sent to Reform School.

When his stories got too boiled down, when it got like listening to some old cowboy cutting a piece of dried meat into small chunks and chewing on them, why then he would take a swallow of beer and speak of his Celestial Guitar. He could play music on it while he slept. "Just a big old guitar," he would tell Nicole, "but it has a ship's wheel with hand spokes, and in my dreams, music comes out as I turn the wheel. I can play any tune in the world."

Then Gary told her about his Guardian Angel. Once when he was 3, and his brother was 4, his father and mother stopped to have dinner in a restaurant in Santa Barbara. Then his father said he had to get some change. He'd be right back. He didn't come back for three months. His mother was alone with no money and two little boys. So she started hitchhiking to Provo.

They got stuck on the Humboldt Sink in Nevada. Could have died in the desert. They had no money and had not eaten for the second day in a row. Then a man came walking down the road with a brown sack in his hand, and he said, Well, my wife has fixed a lunch for me, but it's more than I can eat. Would you like some? His mother said, Well, yes, we'd be very grateful. The man gave her the sack and walked on. They stopped and sat down by the side of the road, and there were three sandwiches in the bag, three oranges, and three cookies. Bessie turned to thank him but the man had disappeared. This was on a long flat stretch of Nevada highway.

Gary said that was his Guardian Angel. Came around when you needed him. One winter night of his childhood, standing in a parking lot, snow was all over the ground and Gary's hands hurt from cold. It was then he found new fur-lined mittens on top of the snow. They fit his hands exactly.

Yes, he had a Guardian Angel. Only it left a long time ago. But on the night Nicole walked into Sterling Baker's place, he found his angel again. He liked to tell Nicole this when her legs were up on the dashboard of the car and her panties were off, and they were driving down State Street.

It didn't bother her if somebody looked over. A big truck, for instance, pulled alongside at the light, and the guy up in his cab looked down into their car, but Gary and Nicole both laughed because they didn't give a fat fuck. Gary lit a stick of pot and said it was going to be the best lid ever. As they took a toke, Gary said, "God created it all, you know."

One night they went to the drive-in early and discovered they were the first ones there. Just for the fun of it, Gary began to ride over the bumps between each row. Damn if this fellow from the management didn't come chasing out with a truck and tell them in a rude voice to quit riding around like that. Gary stopped, got out, walked over to the guy and told him off so bad, the fellow whined, "Well, you don't need to get *that* mad."

But Gary was. After dark, he took his pliers and clipped off a couple of speakers. Made a point of picking up a couple more next time they went to the drive-in. Those speakers were good things to have around. You could hook one up in every room, and they would give you music throughout your house. They never got around, however, to installing them. Just left them in the trunk of her car.

Sometimes they went wandering in the grass between the nut-house and the mountains. The idea of being up on the big hill behind the loony bin gave Nicole a charge. What the hell. This was the same nuthouse where they put her six years ago.

Sunny and Peabody didn't always like it too much, and would get scared at night when a funny chill would swoop in like a wind, and the mountains above looked cold as ice. She and Gary would go there alone then.

Once she was running around the place and he called to her. Something in his voice made her tear all the way down and she couldn't stop and banged into him, hitting her knee so hard it really hurt. Gary picked her up then. She had her legs wrapped around his waist, and her arms over his neck. With her eyes closed, she had the odd feeling of an evil presence near her that came from Gary. She found it kind of half agreeable. Said to herself, Well, if he is the devil, maybe I want to get closer.

It wasn't a terrifying sensation so much as a strong and strange feeling, like Gary was a magnet and had brought down a lot of spirits on himself. Of course, those psychos behind all those screened windows could call up anything out of the night ground in back of the nuthouse.

In the dark, she asked: "Are you the devil?"

At that point, Gary set her down and didn't say anything. It really got cold around them. He told Nicole he had a friend named Ward White who once asked him the same question.

Years ago, when Gary was in Reform School, he walked into a room unexpectedly and Ward White was being butt-fucked by another kid. Gary never said a thing about it. He and Ward White were separated for years, and then ran into each other again in jail. They still never spoke of it. One day, though, Gary came into the prison hobby shop and Ward told him he had just received some silver from a mail house and asked Gary to turn it into a ring. Out of a book of Egyptian designs called *The Ring of Osiris,* Gary copied something called the Eye of Horus. When it was done, Gary said it was a magical ring and he wanted it for himself. Never mentioned the old memory. He didn't have to. Ward White just gave him the Eye of Horus.

Nicole always thought of that ring as being taken from the kid who got butt-fucked.

Now Gary wanted to give it to her. He told her that the Hindus believed you had an invisible eye in the middle of your forehead. The ring might help you to see through it. When they got home, he had her lie on the floor. He said she should wait for the third eye to appear in the space between her closed eyes. She had to concentrate until it opened. If it did, she would be able to look through.

Nothing happened that night. She was laughing too much. She kept expecting a pyramid, and saw nothing.

But on another night, she believed she did see something open. Maybe it was the good pot. She could see her life coming back to her through that eye, and remembered things she had forgotten, but they were so far inside she wasn't sure she wanted to tell him all of it. She felt afraid it would bring down more spooks.

So she kept telling him about herself but it wasn't as straight. More and more, she put old boy friends down and made believe they were nothing in her life, and began to keep the best part for herself. After that night at the nuthouse, a lot of her past stayed inside her. It was like seeing a movie of herself floating down the river, and seeing it mostly for herself and just telling him a couple of the sights.

2

Before Sunny was even ten weeks old, Nicole got into a new thing. She began to date guys on Midway that never had been laid right. In part that was because Barrett had convinced her she wasn't any good in bed. Maybe she preferred therefore to go with somebody who didn't know what good was. Of course, Barrett had his own hang-up — he couldn't bet on getting it up with any girl but her. So, in a quiet way, he could get jealous as a maniac. Sometimes they'd be walking through town and a guy would smile at her, and Barrett would be convinced she had fucked the fellow. Only he would hold it to himself. Three or four days later, it would come out. He'd treat her like a slut. Make a point of the number of times she had been tooled before she ever met him. Said the cruelest things about how big she was. She always wanted to reply it wouldn't be so bad if he had something thicker than a finger's worth of dick. So she figured she needed a period where she was just making it with guys who were absolutely grateful.

Before too long, however, Nicole decided to come back from Midway. She had done lots of exercise and was feeling real good and slim, and the baby was beautiful. It was summer and Barrett was there to greet her at the airport. He was moving a couple of pounds a day of the best grass, and looking prosperous himself, wanted her back with him. She had a new rap, however. "I'm not your old lady," she told him. "You're not my old man. I can do what I want." Still, she moved in. That was a summer when they got high all the time on the best THC and Cannibanol. She really felt like sex.

That's when Barrett became the guy she could get her rocks off with consistently. She wondered if that meant he was the guy she was supposed to work it out with. Maybe it was conditioned reflex, but Barrett could turn her on by walking into a room. The THC had mellowed her out and she felt like dancing all the time. (Except she started getting headaches whenever she was straight, and her teeth began to hurt, and her kidneys. Powerful stuff.) Still, it made for some awful good sex.

It was lonely, however. Barrett knew nothing about her head. Just liked to be the big man. Enjoyed walking around like the dealer that people were watching. Karma was a blank to him. Nicole gave him *A World Beyond* by Ruth Montgomery Ford. Later, he said he read it, but that's all he told her. Wasn't much comment for a man as smart as he was. It certainly did no good for Nicole, since she was getting kind of suicidal with the Cannibanol. There was one dream where she thought she'd died, and laid down in a grave dug in the desert. In her last seconds, a soft black night came over all of her, and said, "Come to me."

She was so shook up she told Barrett death had spoken, and she would welcome it. Hey, look, he said, you're much too valuable. But he didn't have anything to give on the subject.

They began to have personal troubles, too. He had a partner, Stoney, that she liked, who was staying with them. One night, feeling as horny as the hot summer night, she went up to Barrett in a sweet little way and said, "Why don't you sleep on the couch and give Stoney a break." It freaked Barrett out, but he had made the deal that she wasn't his old lady no more, so he lay down on the couch, and Stoney got in with her. Barrett was so pissed, he took off in his car, then came back about twenty minutes later and told his partner to get out. That seemed to be the end of that.

A couple of nights later, however, Barrett must have started figuring this is what she really wants, you know, because he took her to a party up the Canyon and went out of his way to share her with a couple of buddies. Then he kind of broke down. They had a big fight and Nicole threw a machete at him which went through the screen door. Then she threw a hammer through the kitchen window. Then they broke it off. She took Sunny, and went to live with Rikki and Sue at her great-grandmother's house.

That substituted one misery for another. She never got along worse with Sue, who was always leaving shitty diapers around. The house stank.

Then Rikki and Sue found Nicole in her great-grandmother's bed with Tom Fong, a Chinaman. He was nice, and made good money ripping off his boss in a Chinese restaurant, and he wanted to marry her. Just another man in her life who wanted to marry. She'd taken Tom up to that room for some privacy — he was giving massages, his specialty, and Rikki and Sue just happened to walk in when she had her top off. After Tom Fong left, though, there was a terrible argument and she gave a lot of lip, and Rikki promised to knock her on her ass if she ever talked that bad again. Then an aunt and uncle came over, and got so mad she'd been in that bed, they wouldn't listen to anything said. Called her a whore. Her uncle actually hit her across the face. She threw a bunch of stuff into a pillowcase, diapers, baby food, bottles, found a backpack, took Sunny, took off.

She was crying. Her great-grandmother was okay, but an active Mormon. It brought back Nicole's childhood when this same great-grandmother would get out of the tub, dry off, and immediately put on her religious garment next to her flesh. A lumpy thing that kept her clothes from looking good. You had to wear the garment next to your skin if you were married in the temple.

Her great-grandmother used to take her to Sunday School. It was kind of boring. They taught outer darkness was your lot if you sinned, and disharmony. If you were a good girl, you would sit at God's knee.

Only trouble was all the good girls didn't like her, and made nasty remarks about Nicole and the boys. They would walk by and sneer. It was all coming back to her now, after that scene in the bedroom. Even as she walked down the highway, she was trying not to cry.

A fellow with a stutter who was driving to Pennsylvania picked her up. She didn't care where she was going. Nicole didn't know if she liked him or not, but he sure needed somebody and she didn't care where she was going. So she took off with him and they ended up living together in Devon, Pennsylvania, where he made a pretty good living in his leathercraft shop. They even talked of getting married. He was a real performer in bed. Worked very hard to please her.

3

This fellow, whose name was Kip Eberhardt, proved difficult to live with, however. He had a lot of paranoia and she made the mistake of telling him about herself. As soon as he went out to work, he would worry that Nicole was with a guy in their very trailer. Nobody ever was, but she couldn't convince him. It really messed her up. What bothered her head was that she did have secret thoughts of bringing in some sweet guy to while away an afternoon. Kip could make love like a fiend, but sometimes he left her feeling like one.

He went to ridiculous lengths. Kip even accused her of going to bed with a fat old man whose face was black from dirt. Occasionally,

Kip would beat her up. Oh, Jesus, she loved him, and he was such an asshole. That hurt more than all the other guys put together.

Considering she gave a year of her life to him, and he almost took her mind away, Nicole got to despise him for hitting her. He was only a little guy, small and wiry and stoop-shouldered, so they had some pretty mean fights. She even came close to winning a couple.

Nicole was 17 when she found out she was pregnant again. The moment Kip heard he was so happy for himself, and so happy for both of them. They were going to have a baby he kept saying. She felt disgusted. She didn't want to spend the rest of her life with this guy.

She had never known how to keep from getting pregnant. In fact, she only found out this time in the Planned Parenthood Association building near Devon where she'd gone to get an IUD. Nicole never took pills, or watched the calendar. She read how at certain times of the month you could get pregnant more than other times, but didn't know when. She'd read about it but they seemed to mention different days in different places. Besides she somehow knew she wasn't going to get pregnant.

This time, though, there was a student nurse who lived next door and she kept after Nicole to make an appointment at Planned Parenthood. When she finally did put in an appearance, they said she was sure carrying something.

Telling Kip made it worse. He sat there with his beautiful black beard and curly hair and loved her enough for both of them. He'd start to say something and get so emotional it would take hours for him to get two words out. She'd have to sit with a smile on her face, wanting to say, I'm not a mind reader, you know. But when she knew what he was going to say, he would still drag it out. That made her want to escape as much as anything.

Plus the paranoia. Every so often he would say somebody was following him, or weird messes were waiting. Trouble ahead. He'd say, See, you know? She couldn't see.

She said good-bye and took the Greyhound to Utah. Twenty-four hours later, she was in bed with a nice guy she met on the bus. No big deal, but she relaxed, and laughed and talked. After all, she wasn't in no big hurry to get back to anything.

She thought about having an abortion. But she couldn't bring herself to kill a baby. She couldn't stand Barrett anymore, but she loved Sunny. So she couldn't see killing a new baby she might also love.

The day after Jeremy was born, Barrett was at the hospital. She couldn't believe the games he played with her. Said that when he saw Jeremy, he felt like it was his son.

Then after she got out, Barrett kept coming around. Jeremy had been so premature, she had to leave him in an incubator and thumb a ride over to the hospital every other day.

Barrett would hitch along. Carried on over the baby. Told her how he really wanted her, new baby and all. It was very emotional for Barrett but just everyday for her. She said, Well, I'll live with you for a while. She had to admit that Barrett really seemed to like going to the hospital, putting on the white shirt and mask, looking at the baby. He had never had that with Sunny.

Up to the time Jeremy was born, Nicole had been working full hours in a motel, changing linen and scrubbing bathrooms. That was about all she'd command, considering she had only finished the seventh grade. Anyway, she finally called Kip. Wanted someone besides Barrett to relate to the fact she had a son. Kip couldn't believe the news. Thought it was still weeks away. Anyway, he didn't stammer a bit, and was so nice on the phone she decided to try again.

For those first few days, it was her best honeymoon with Kip. Lasted until he was back at work in the leathercraft shop. That afternoon she was rushing back and forth, picking things up, sticking them under the couch. He really liked the house clean. If it didn't look right, he always thought she'd been goofing off with some guy — that's how he'd been before. So she was trying to pick up when he came in the door.

She was standing there waiting to kiss him, but he didn't look at her. Instead he began to squint. She had seen that look before.

He kept prowling around the house. Went into the bathroom. When she strolled by, Kip was in the hamper looking her underwear over for gunk. Really gross. She kept trying to find out what made him so suspicious. Finally he told her that just as he drove up, he saw two people walk in front of the window. Since there are two windows to look through, the storm window and the inside window, he probably saw two shadows, she said, but he wouldn't believe it. Swore to God it was two people. Enough to get her screaming.

4

Back in Utah, the family carried on how lucky she was to have a girl and a boy. Nicole didn't see where it was so great taking care of two when she'd never been sure she wanted one. On bad days, her main feeling was that she had missed out on a lot.

Once again, Barrett had been sure to meet her at the airport. They talked about old times and went to his pad and listened to favorite records. He told her he had been getting this house ready for her and wouldn't bother her, so she moved in.

In fact, he had a couple of friends staying there, and they were blowing dope, and he put off leaving. After a few days, he even got mad and said it was his fucking house. Right on. Back with Barrett, and nothing to do about it. No car, no money, no house. Two kids. Kathryne and Charley were home from Midway and offered to let her stay, but she didn't like to come home whipped. Besides they were having their own slew of problems. Charley had to resign from the Navy because April was starting to flip out. It looked like they were all going to be graduates of the nuthouse. In any case, her life was in no shape to listen to her folks fighting.

Right about now, Barrett's business fell in on him. There was a cop in Springville who flagged Jim down every time. Any excuse to search. The cop'd say Barrett's license plate wasn't screwed down properly. One night late, he got stopped for having a taillight out. Just earlier Barrett had shot up 100 wads of speed, done a hit of coke, and made the mistake of thinking he was clean. Before he left the house, however, he picked up a pair of pants lying on the floor and put them on and never felt the core of speed buried way down in the bottom of the pocket. Didn't know till after the cops pulled him over. There he was outside the van, his hands up on the roof of the car for the search, and he was just fine. Clean and high. As he told it to her later, he was looking around, you know, when the cop pulled out his pockets. Barrett now looked down to see this Baggie of 25 whites that the cop held in his hand. Quick as a cat, Barrett let her know, he grabbed it. Should have popped it in his mouth, but threw the stuff away instead, as far as he could. Oliver Nelson, the cop, handcuffed him at that point, and started searching the area, dragging him around by the handcuffs. There was snow on the ground and it was hard to find whites, but he could see Nelson wasn't going to give up. Finally, Barrett got a peek at them near a telephone pole, and as soon as Oliver moved him close enough, he tried to squinch the Baggie into the snow. But when he went to stretch his leg, the cop felt it and saw the whites. They took him down to the station.

Rikki came over and paid the $110 bail and brought him home. It was like two in the morning. Took him back to Nicole, and she wasn't mad at that point. Really understanding. But Barrett was in real trouble. They packed up their stuff in the next couple of days and moved to Verno, Utah. It was the end of business for a while.

5

By now Nicole was letting things slide. Things didn't bother her as much. Barrett was driving oil trucks in Verno, which is to say, he would get a job, lose it, get another. He had a short fuse, and could tell his boss to go to hell without a lot of provocation. Once she got so desperate for a little security that she was walking down the street with both kids and a few belongings when Barrett drove up the road heading home. So they got into a big fight. He seriously tried to beat the shit out of her. Instead she got ahold of Sunny's toy chair and marked him up pretty good. He had black and blue marks everywhere. Therefore, she didn't leave. It felt too good to look at him.

Once in a while, she'd think about going back to school and even wrote letters to a couple of places, but Barrett would say, yeah, yeah, and tell her she didn't need to go to school. He could support her. She decided he saw her as a stupid chick who was nice to call his own.

Then Barrett told her they were moving again. He borrowed a truck and said he would transport their furniture. Before she knew it, he had sold the stuff instead, the stereo, her blow-dryer and the lamps. With the money, he bought some hash to deal with, and took off. Furniture or no, she got registered in school, and picked up $130 a month from welfare and lived in a little trailer court away from everything. Loved her privacy there. With Barrett gone, it was kind of a happy time in her life. Only the rent, $90 a month, bugged her. She didn't have enough left for food and began to get uptight again.

Along came a guy named Steve Hudson, a lot older than herself. Maybe he was only 30, but he seemed ages beyond. She felt more sensible about him than anybody till then. He was straight, and going to church. She only went with him for a few months before they got married. Two weeks later, she left him. They just couldn't get along. It was depressing. She felt so bad she soon picked up with another fellow she met in church, a big slow-talking fellow, Joe Bob Sears. He took good care of himself, worked hard, made love hard, and really liked her kids. In fact, Joe Bob was better with Jeremy than she was. She hadn't been able to love Jeremy so far. When he'd start to cry, she'd pick him up. If he didn't stop, she'd throw him back in his crib. She never hurt him, but still she was thudding him against the mattress. Joe Bob actually treated Jeremy better than she did. Maybe it was because he had a child of his own he'd hardly ever seen.

In Mississippi, Joe Bob's father was dying of cancer, and he wanted to visit, so Nicole left the kids with Charley and Kathryne, and took off. She had hopes for Joe Bob and herself. He gave her real security, yet he was also an exciting guy.

One night in Mississippi Nicole got the shock of her life. Joe Bob's folks had the biggest butcher shop in town, and they kept a few cows for their own use. On this night, Nicole happened to be out in the barn and through the planks, on the other side of an enclosure, there was a calf sucking on her new man.

Once in a while, Joe Bob had talked funny about photos he'd looked at of a chicken being fucked by a dog, and wanted to know if she'd ever seen such stuff, but Nicole just let it slide. Now, she said to herself, "You're going to be a loser forever. Face it."

To herself, she even had to pretend she didn't see Joe Bob with the calf. All the while, he was talking about taking over his father's butcher shop. They'd be surrounded by animals then. Dead ones. It turned out his father wasn't sick the way Joe Bob had let on in Utah, but ready to retire. They would go to Utah, pick up Sunny and Jeremy, then down to Mississippi again. Nicole felt trapped worse than ever.

Back in Utah, fifteen minutes after they came through the front door of Joe Bob's house, there couldn't have been more trouble. Some of Joe Bob's animals were out of their cages and running wild. The house was late being repaired, paneling was still being nailed up, floors were torn, sinks being put in. Worse. His little trailer was gone from the yard. Joe Bob knew immediately who had stolen it because he ripped the thing off the guy in the first place when the fellow wouldn't pay some money he owed. Now it was gone. Joe Bob was out talking to the cops. Nicole was standing at the door. She had a splitting headache. Sunny and Jeremy were crying.

She heard the cop explaining that possession is nine-tenths of the law. Since Joe Bob'd never taken legal possession of the trailer, there wasn't much he could do.

When he came back and started explaining it to her, she said, I know, I heard. I don't want to hear. She swore she was faint, and didn't want to talk. He began to get rude. She got rude back. Must have said something to set it off. Fifteen minutes after they were home, he picked her up and threw her across the room.

Then he came over, picked her up and threw her again. There were mattresses on the floor, but she bounced off a few walls.

He sat on her, and choked her. He said he wasn't having any more of this. Wasn't having any more of that. Started telling her she was his slave now. He was over 200 pounds and most of it in the back and shoulders. He sat on her for hours, smacked her now and again when he felt like it. Kept her in a back room for a few days.

Joe Bob would give the kids a meal or two a day. Allowed them in the room with her once in a while. He didn't lock the door, but she still couldn't leave that room. He wouldn't let her. She cried a lot. Sometimes she screamed. Sometimes she'd sit there for hours. When he came in, he'd cuff her for making noise. Then she wouldn't let any emotion come over her face, or make a sound. She would act like he wasn't there.

He also fucked her a lot — no change in his habits that way — and called her Poopsie and Baby Doll and Honey. Sometimes she'd scream and holler, other times act like it wasn't going on. After a while she remembered his gun and she wondered how to get hold of it. It was a huge handgun, and it kept her going. When she found it, she would kill him. She kept telling Joe Bob that he could wipe her out but she wasn't going to stay with him. Never.

It went on another week. He'd only punish her once a day now, and allowed her to go out in the yard. He even left for work. She suspected a trap and didn't move at first. But after a couple of days, she took off and went to the bus station. It was Jeremy's first birthday. She made a call, and Barrett was over to rescue her once again. He always showed up when there was nobody else in the whole fucking world. Knew it. Loved it. He was the only one who would help her out of the worst situations. Prince Charming.

They lived with the kids in a little tent on the lawn of a friend of his. Then they got an apartment in Provo and had Christmas together. All the while she was trying to make it clear to Barrett she didn't want to live with him, and he was trying to convince her she did. Finally, Barrett split to Cody, Wyoming, with a friend of his also named Barrett, just after she found the house in Spanish Fork that was like something funky out of a fairy tale.

PART THREE

Gary and Nicole

CHAPTER 7

Gary and Pete

1

On the second weekend in June, Gary and Nicole made plans to go up to the canyons and make it in the woods and camp out. But Nicole couldn't get a baby-sitter. Laurel had to go with her parents to visit relatives.

So, Saturday morning, Gary went over to Vern's shop to do some lettering on a sign, and saw Annette Gurney, Toni's daughter, come into the store. She was staying with Vern and Ida for the weekend while Toni and Howard were off to Elko, Nevada, with Brenda and Johnny to enjoy the slot machines and the crap games. Right there, putting eyes on Annette, Gary asked her to baby-sit.

Ida was opposed to the idea. Her granddaughter might look 16, she said, but in fact, she was 12. There was too much responsibility for Annette to look after two little kids by herself.

Gary didn't relinquish the possibility. Later, when the job was done, and he was taking cans of paint from Vern's store out to his car, he told Annette he'd give her $5 to baby-sit. She wanted to, she told him, but she couldn't. She smiled and took a plaque from her pocket. That first Sunday Gary was out of jail, he had given Annette an art lesson when he visited Toni's house, and now Annette had painted the plaque and wanted to give it to him. He was so pleased that he put his arm around her and gave Annette a peck on the cheek. Then they strolled down the street hand in hand. Gary was still trying to talk Annette into coaxing Ida to agree to the baby-sitting.

Peter Galovan, who rented a cottage back of Vern's house, was going into the shop as they were coming out, and he noticed Gary and Annette walking closely together, and stopping. He didn't like it. Gary had Annette leaning against a wall while he talked. He looked like he was trying to make a lot of points as fast as he could. Pete went back into the store. "Ida," he said, "I think Gary is propositioning your granddaughter."

Three months ago, while Annette had been staying with Ida, the child had been struck by a car right in front of their house. The car had hardly been moving and it was nothing serious. Still, Annette was with her grandparents and got hurt. Ida didn't want Toni to think something happened to Annette every time she visited. So she rushed to the window in time to see Gary and Annette strolling back hand in hand.

"I don't know if that was the right thing for you to do," she said. "You stay away from Annette."

Later, Vern said to Gary: "I don't want to see anything out of the way."

2

Next evening, Annette said to Toni, "Mama, we didn't do anything wrong. I gave Gary the plaque, and he gave me a kiss on the cheek."

"Well, why did you walk down the street with him?"

"Because a big red bug — the biggest beetle I ever saw — was flying by. We just went looking at it."

"And you held hands."

"I like him, Mama."

"Did he touch you anywhere? Did he give you anything more than an affectionate kiss?"

"No, Mama." Annette gave Toni a look like she was nuts to ask.

When Toni and her husband talked about it, Howard said, "Gary wouldn't try anything in front of the shoe shop right on the sidewalk.

Honey, I don't believe there's anything to it. Let's just watch, and be kind of cautious."

Monday, Vern told Pete that Gary was saying he would punch him out real good. Pete should watch it. Vern said, "If Gary comes in, and wants a scrap, I don't want it in the store. You go back and fight it out." Pete, however, didn't believe in strife. He had heard all about Gary's trip up to Idaho and the man he put in the hospital.

Back when Gary was taking up Vern's concrete curbing with the sledgehammer and the crowbar, Pete Galovan had been watching from his window, and was impressed with the amount of labor Gary put out in two days. So, Pete, at first opportunity, had invited him then to a church dance.

Pete, as Brenda later told Gary, was more religious than anyone under God. It was like he had come out of the shell a little wobbly. He had a tendency to take people around the neck and get them to pray with him. Since he was also an immense fellow, six-three, heavy, a little blown out around the middle, and had a big dough-faced friendly expression that looked right at you through his eye-glasses, you could hardly say no easily. But when he invited Gary to the dance, he was told immediately to get lost.

Pete didn't want to fight him now. He had too many responsi-bilities. Pete was doing jobs for Vern to take care of his rent, and also working at three other places. He was employed by the Provo School District to maintain the swimming pool, he was a part-time bus driver, and he cleaned carpets on the side. He was also trying to get back in the good graces of the Mormon Church. That all made calls on his time. Moreover, he was doing his best to help his ex-wife Eliz-abeth with the finances of raising seven kids from her first marriage.

Needless to say, he was tired, and that wasn't even mentioning the continuing toll of his various nervous breakdowns, which had required hospitalization in the past for lithium treatment. Just think-ing about getting into trouble with Gary stiffened up Pete's muscles and back.

On Monday, Pete was working in the shop during the late after-noon when Vern said, "Here he comes."

Gary looked just the way Pete had pictured him — all steamed up. The ugliest expression you could expect.

Gary said, "I don't like what you told Ida about me. I want an apology."

Pete answered, "I'm sorry if I upset you, but my ex-wife has girls that age, and I feel —"

"Did you see me do anything?" Gary interrupted.

"I didn't see you *do* anything," Pete said, "but the *appearance* left no doubt in my mind what you were thinking." If that sounded too strong, he added, "I apologize for what I said to Ida. Maybe I should have kept my mouth shut. I apologize for talking too much. But your interest in the girl still didn't look right to me." Pete just couldn't step all the way down when he wanted to be honest.

"All right," Gary said. "I want to fight."

Vern was right there. "Out back," he said. There was a customer in the store.

Pete sure hadn't wanted to get into this. Walking to the rear alley a step or two ahead of Gary, he tried to get himself psyched up by remembering his old feats of strength. He had been a future track star until he shot himself by accident in the foot at the age of 15, so he switched to shot put and still won the high-school state title. He had done construction work and knew his way around weight lifters. Pete was starting to build up to an idea of physical power as large as his own body, when *blam!* he was slammed on the neck from behind. Almost went down. Just as he got himself turned around, Gary rushed, and Pete caught his face in a headlock. Immediately, he dropped to the floor. That position was a lot better than boxing. On the floor, he could bang Gary's head on the cement.

Of course, the grip put a great deal of pressure on Pete's ribs. His glasses broke in his breast pocket. Next day Pete would even have to go to the chiropractor for his neck and his chest. But right now, he had him. Pete could see Vern standing right over them and observing.

If Gary had waited to stand up and punch nose to nose, Vern thought he could have whipped the fellow. But here Pete had the hold and was using all his 240 pounds. That hold was the luckiest thing in the world for Pete. Pete would thump Gary's head on the floor and say, "Had enough?" Gary could hardly breathe. "Oh, ohhh, ahh, ahh," Gary would answer. Mumbling was about all he could manage. Vern waited a minute, because he wanted Gary to get all of what he was getting, then said, "Okay, he's had enough, let him up." Pete undid his grip.

Gary was white in the face and bleeding a lot from the mouth. He had a look in his eye about as mean as anything Vern had seen.

Vern cussed him out. "You asked for it," he said. "That was a rotten thing to do. Hit somebody from behind."

"Think it was?"

"Call yourself a man?" Vern got him by the arm. "Get in the bathroom. Clean yourself up." When Gary just stood there, Vern pushed him directly in. He didn't go too easily, but Vern pushed him anyway. Then Gary turned around and said, "That's the way I fight. First hit counts."

"First hit," said Vern. "But not from the back. You're no man. Get yourself clean and go back to work."

Pete started collecting himself. Felt shook up more than ever now. So soon as Gary came out of the bathroom, however, he was still asking for an apology. Looked ready to fight again. In fact, Gary's face looked ready to do anything. So Pete picked up the telephone and said, "If you don't leave right now, I'll call the police."

There was a long pause. After that, Gary certainly left.

Pete made the call anyway. He didn't like the feeling Gary left behind. A cop came over to the store and told Pete to come to the station and file a report.

Vern and Ida weren't altogether opposed to this. They told Pete that Gary was getting more out of line every day. Pete even got the name of Gary's parole officer, Mont Court, and gave him a call as well, but Mont Court said Gary came from another state, and he wasn't sure he could send him back to jail that routinely. Pete had a feeling the buck was being passed. Gary wouldn't be arrested unless he really worked at it.

That night, Pete went to visit his ex-wife, Elizabeth. "The next time it happens," he said to her, "Gary is going to kill me." Elizabeth was tiny and blond and voluptuous and had a fiery disposition and was very wise as far as Pete was concerned for she had kept her happy spirits through a hundred personal disasters. Now she told him to ignore it.

Pete said no. "It's a certainty," he said. "He's going to kill me. Me or somebody else." He told her he was sensitive to Gary's agitation right now. It was part of the equipment God had given Pete to be that sensitive. But he also knew that when he got too responsive to things he got a breakdown. He tried not to have them anymore. So he told Elizabeth, "I want Gary where he won't harm anybody. Jail is where he belongs, and I'm going to press charges."

3

Next day at work, Gary's mouth was swollen and his face discolored.

"What happened?" Spence asked.

"I was drinking beer," Gary said, "and a guy said something I didn't like. So I took a swing at him."

"Looks like the guy got the best of it," Spence said.

"Oh, no. You ought to see *him*."

"Gary, you're on parole," lectured Spencer McGrath. "If you're in a bar and have a fight, they'll throw your tail in jail. When you can't handle a drink, leave it alone."

Later that morning, Gary came over, "Spence, I thought about it," he said quietly, "and I believe you were telling me for my own good. I'm going to quit drinking."

Spencer agreed. He tried to reinforce the lecture. Suppose that he, Spencer McGrath, went into a bar, had a few drinks, got into a fight, and the police came and threw him in jail. He would be in a fix, right? But that would never be nearly as much trouble as if Gilmore got thrown in. That would be a direct violation of parole.

Gary asked, "Spence, have you ever been in jail?"

"Well, no," said Spence.

Gary was expecting Nicole for lunch but when she did not show up, he sat down next to Craig Taylor, the foreman. They were now friendly enough to eat together time to time. It worked out well because Gary liked to converse and Craig never said a word more than he had to, just flexed his big arms and shoulders.

Today, Gary began to speak of prison. Now and again he would go on about that. This may have been one of those days. Gary got around to mentioning that he knew Charles Manson.

Name-dropping, Craig decided, blinking his eyes behind his glasses. They were sipping beer, and Gary was a lot braver, Craig observed, when he had a few beers. "In prison, I killed a guy," said Gary. "He was black and big and I stabbed him 57 times. Then I propped him up on his bunk, crossed his legs, put his baseball cap on his head, and stuck a cigarette in his mouth."

Craig noticed Gary was taking pills. A white downer. Called it Fiorinal. He offered one to Craig, who refused it. Those pills didn't seem to make much difference in Gilmore's personality. He was sure keyed-up.

Nicole came in just as they were done eating. As soon as she and Gary started talking, Craig could see they looked upset. They were squeezing each other's hands, and gave each other a big kiss and said good-bye. The kiss was Gary's way of showing he had a beautiful chick and everybody better know it, so Craig wasn't impressed by that. But the squeezing of hands looked different. Afterward, Gary acted odd all afternoon.

Craig sent him out in a two-ton truck with a kid also named Gary, an 18-year-old, Gary Weston. They were on a job to insulate a house, and had to blow a plastic coat into the walls, then the insulating material. Dry work for the nostrils. Somewhere along, Gary dropped into a store, lifted a six-pack, and began drinking on the job.

Gary Weston didn't say anything. Being 18, he didn't think it was his place.

While they were working along, Gilmore said, "Let's steal the truck."
"What do you mean?"

"Let's come back tonight and steal it. Then we'll paint it and sell it."

Weston didn't want to get him mad. "Well, Gary," he said, "we insulate for the guy who owns the truck. We kind of know him real well."

"Yeah, can't do it to a friend," said Gary, sipping his beer.

When Weston got back, he told a few of the others. They all had a good laugh. Gary had obviously had a couple of beers. You don't steal a truck.

Before leaving work that night, Spencer asked if he had gotten his license. Gary said that Oregon still hadn't sent it over. Something about how they couldn't find the license. The story was one darn thing after another.

Spencer said that since they couldn't locate the old one, Gary ought to sign up for the driver's training course.

Gary said, "That test is for kids. I'm a grown man and it's beneath me."

Spencer tried to get him over this. "The law," he said, "is for everybody. They're not singling you out." He tried to explain. "If I were in some state and didn't have a driver's license, they would make me take it too. Do you think you're better than I am?"

"Excuse me," said Gary at last, "I've got to call Nicole." As he walked off, he said, "Real good advice. Thanks, Spencer, for the good advice." Quick to get away.

The message Nicole had brought at lunchtime was that Mont Court had gone out to their house in Spanish Fork to tell her that Pete was pressing charges of assault and Gary was in a serious situation if they weren't dropped.

Gary told her not to worry, and they gripped each other's hands.

The moment she said good-bye to Gary, however, Nicole did begin to worry. It was as if a doctor had come to the house and said they were going to amputate her legs. What a weird meeting. Mont Court was a big good-looking Mormon, like captain of the swimming team or tennis team, kind of blond and just a little straitlaced. He was embarrassed terribly by her sister April who had been sitting in Nicole's Mustang when he arrived. April must have liked his looks, or maybe it was just too warm — never knew why April was doing something — but she took off her halter, and was sitting with her bare back up against the car window when he came out. Mont Court made a point of walking around the rear of Nicole's car so he wouldn't be caught staring at April's bare breasts through the front window. Nicole would have loved to be able to laugh at it, but she was sick.

She knew Gary's mind. Don't worry. Don't worry 'cause I'm close to killing Pete. She decided she better talk to Galovan herself.

He lived in a grubby little cottage back of Vern's. She tried to tell him that Gary had his problems and was trying to straighten out. She said the last thing that would do anybody any good was to return Gary to prison. All the while, Pete was dressed in an old sweaty T-shirt and dirty pants. He kept telling her a lot of stupid things. Said Gary hit him pretty good.

She tried to keep calm and sensible. She wanted to explain about Gary and not get upset. Pete, she said, the guy has been locked up a long time. It takes a while to get used to being out.

Pete Galovan kept interrupting. He didn't want to hear. Just a big plain old oaf. "The guy is dangerous," Pete said, "he needs help." Then he added, "I've been working hard long hours, and I shouldn't have to take this kind of thing. He treated me badly. I'm now in pain."

She kept working on his sympathy. Pete would understand what she was saying, she said to him. He could see that she loved Gary, and love was the only way to really help a person.
"Love," agreed Pete, "is the only way to bring the spiritual power of God to a situation."
"Yes," said Nicole.
"But this is a tough situation. Your man is far gone. He's a killer, I believe. He wants to kill me."

At that moment, Galovan was looking so bad to her that she said, "If you press charges, he'll be out on bail. He'll get you then."

She didn't take her eyes away. "Pete, even if they lock him up right away, he's still more important to me than my life. He's a hell of a lot more important to me than your life. If he don't get you, I will."

She had never said anything she meant more. She could feel the shock come over Pete as if he was bleeding inside over every part of him, past and present.

4

In his eighteenth year, Pete saved his money for nine months in order to be a Mormon missionary. At nineteen, he was overseas only four and a half months before he had his first nervous breakdown. During that time, however, he brought nine converts into the Church.

That was two a month. The average rate for young missionaries like himself, working in France, was two converts a year.

He got so carried away with his mission that he started having strange religious experiences. He was convinced he could convert President Kennedy who was on his way to France for a state visit. When the Church told Pete they were taking him home, Pete thought it was because they wanted to make him a general authority on conversions. What a letdown when they put him in a hospital, and gave him lithium.

He was soon out and attributed his recovery from all this super-excitement to prayer, but he didn't feel God had treated him fairly with that breakdown. So at the age of 20 he had his first sexual intercourse. He knew full well that a Mormon missionary was not supposed to have sexual involvement before or during a mission, but he was bitter against God. Right after, he knew he had committed a wrong act, and went to his bishop, and told him. Pete was then chaste for five years. He had a lot of jobs and traveled all over Europe on construction work, but he was chaste.

Later, around 1970, dissatisfied with his life and searchings, he was staying with a friend in Seattle and working as a security guard for Boeing. He happened to be listening one night to a religious station where people dialed in to ask for prayers. Pete didn't know much about the program but when he called, he did mention the Mormon Church and his beliefs, and some Mormons happened to hear the show and informed Pete's Branch President who quickly told him not to phone the program anymore. The Church didn't want Galovan to go public. He was not delegated to that kind of work. It hurt Pete's feelings. He was only trying to help people. So he put in a written request to be excommunicated. Didn't want the Mormon Church limiting his desire to aid.

He worked with the Jesus Movement, and lived in the House of Joshua north of Seattle and went on television and spoke out against the Mormon Church. His father was even called by the prophet, Spencer Kimball himself. "What are you going to do with your son?" the prophet asked. His father said, "Leave him alone. It's the work of God. He'll come back stronger than ever."

Pete went over to Hawaii and met Pat Boone, and tried to live in a commune with about twenty-five people and answered the hot line for addicts. He saw suicides and he saw healings. Worked with all kinds of religions. Decided his mission was to help reform the Mormon Church.

But he crashed. They put him in the hospital and gave him group therapy and lithium. He felt the spirit of Elijah in the heart of his body, and knew the world could come to peace. He returned to Utah and got a job as a janitor. Going back to the Church gave energy to all he did. He ended up running the janitorial shop plus a cleaning business, and it got to where he had contracts to clean a number of grocery stores and as many as twenty people were working for him. Out of the strength of his worldly success, however, he fornicated with a number of women, and was disenfranchised. Then he met Elizabeth.

She had managed to live by herself, earn a living and take care of her seven kids. Pete told her, "I'm a big businessman; I can handle it for you." She kept saying, "I don't feel right." It wasn't, she explained, the overwhelming thing you should have. Finally, she agreed to marry him.

There was tension between Pete and the kids. He had a temper, Elizabeth had a temper, the kids had tempers. The cleaning business was done at night, and in the daytime, Pete slept. The kids couldn't make noise. One day, Elizabeth's son Daryl put his fist through the window. One of the kids said, "Mother, that's it. If you stay with him, we'll take off." She had to explain that Peter was paying for the food.

They got married in July of '75. In October, he threw one of the kids across the room. The police got called. The kids were crying, Peter was crying — they separated.

Since the Church had disenfranchised Pete, his business in Ogden had begun to come apart. His customers had been Mormons in good standing and now he lost them, one grocery contract, then another. He came close to having another nervous breakdown.

He went to see Elizabeth, who had moved to Provo, and stayed the night with her. Next day, he moved into the Hotel Roberts around the corner from Vern Damico. Later, he moved over to Vern's basement. He was hired by the Provo School District, got a bus-driving job, got other jobs, made money enough to help support Elizabeth.

On May 14, 1976, however — the day after Gary met Nicole — Pete and Elizabeth got divorced. They were still friends but she kept saying it wasn't fair. He really wanted to be in love with somebody who would love him, she said, not this circus of working nights and weekends.

5

Now he sat on the bed of his little cottage room feeling dirty and stale from sleep and exhausted from the way he needed his sleep. Before him was the face of this girl Nicole who was saying she was ready to kill him if he pressed charges. Pete felt so miserable, he could cry. This girl, who he judged to have a good heart inside and a hectic rough life on the outside, this girl who was humble and wasn't frivolous, disliked him so much.

He was also scared. He didn't have time to mess with the problem. Yet it didn't scare him at first as much as it hurt him. He felt pricked inside. Nicole loved Gary enough to be willing to commit murder for him. It hurt Pete that no woman had ever loved him that much.

He thought about it, breathing in all the sorrows of these thoughts, and felt sorry for Nicole and touched by her. "Well, relax," he said, "calm down. Maybe the guy deserves another chance." Pete said, "I'll drop the charges."

He got on his knees. "Given your permission," he told her, "I'd like to say a prayer with you."
Nicole said okay.
"It's for you and Gary. You're both going to need it."

He prayed that the Lord have mercy on Nicole and Gary, and bless them, and that Gary get some control of himself. Pete didn't remember all the things he said in the prayer, or even if he held her hand while he prayed. One was not supposed to remember what was said in prayers. It was sacred at the moment, and not really to be repeated.

When Nicole went out the door, there was a calm spirit in the room, and Pete felt happy enough to go over to visit Elizabeth. By the time he got there, however, he was upset all over again. There was horror to feel all over the city of Provo. He sat on the couch, and told what happened with Nicole, and he began to cry. Pete said, "He's a very dangerous man and he's going to kill me." The more upset Pete got, the less Elizabeth would show. She told him to cool it.

Pete told her he was going out and get an insurance policy and put her in as the beneficiary. That made Elizabeth feel terrible. Pete said, "If I can't give you money one way, I'll fix it this way." Then he asked her to marry him. One more time, she said, No.
"I'm dropping the charges," Pete repeated, "I'm not going to press charges." Pause. "Even though I feel I should press them."

Next day Pete went out and got the insurance policy and went over to the Provo Temple and put Gary's name on the list, so people would pray for him.

CHAPTER 8

The Job

1

Early Sunday morning, lying in bed, Gary asked Nicole to shave her pubic hair. He had been talking about that for the last couple of weeks. Now, she said yes. As she climbed into the tub, she was thinking, "It really means something to him."

He helped. They were using a big pair of scissors, and being careful, and smiling a lot. Nicole felt bashful, but also thought it was the thing to do. She was not so much afraid of cutting the hair off as of what it might look like afterward.

He carried her from the bathtub to the bed and for the second time she had an orgasm with Gary. She knew it had something to do with being a 6-year-old pussy once more. Even as her memory had its quick flash of Uncle Lee, so was Nicole carried over the place where she slammed into the wall and stopped.

That shaved little old tooty certainly made a hellion out of Gary this Sunday morning. Ever since the thing with Pete, he had been adoring her twice as much. It was like he was truly mad about her now.

That night, Laurel came over with her cousins and a friend named Rosebeth. Once Gary and Nicole came back from their drive, Laurel's duties as a baby-sitter were over, and she went home. But Rosebeth stayed on. She would sigh just looking at Gary. Nicole laughed. Rosebeth was so young and so cute, and had such a crush on Gary. Next night, she came over all by herself, and before Nicole knew it, she invited Rosebeth to give Gary a kiss. Then they all laughed and Nicole gave Gary a kiss. It got to the point where they had their clothes off, and lay around in bed.

You couldn't call it an orgy exactly. Rosebeth remained a virgin. She was ready, however, for anything else. It got sweet. Nicole really liked the idea of giving this gift to Gary.

Over the weekend, they did it more and more. Once, Rosebeth came over in the daytime, and Gary closed the doors and windows. Since the neighbor kids were used to hanging around, you could feel them getting restless outside. God knows what the neighbors heard. It wasn't all that quiet. Nicole began to feel a little paranoid. If it ever came out that Gary was fooling with minors, he could blow his total case. Then it occurred to Nicole that she wasn't in such a good spot either. They might take her children away.

She began to think of Annette. Nicole didn't have any doubt that Gary might have been having a few thoughts when he gave Annette that peck on the cheek. He did love young girls. But Nicole was also sure he would never have done anything, physically speaking. So from Nicole's point of view, Pete was still out of line. Anyway, Nicole didn't feel ready to stop things with Rosebeth.

In fact, she loved the way everything was new to the girl. Sex had never been new to Nicole. How beautiful if she'd been introduced to the subject like Rosebeth. It was exciting to watch Gary make her blossom. Of course, Gary also could get very demanding with the girl and order her to suck him good, stuff like that. It just turned him on the way the girl had this tremendous crush.

Then Nicole had to face another problem. During the week, when Gary was at work, and Rosebeth came over, Nicole still wanted to get it on with her. She wondered if she was moving into that side of sex a little deeper.

2

A couple of days later, Gary stopped off after work to pay Val Conlin
for the Mustang. He had already missed the first installment and Val
was upset. Of course, it was no big incident. Half the people to whom
Conlin sold cars were sooner or later delinquent in payments. It was
just part of the ongoing hell-of-a-success-story that was Val's life.

    In the last fifteen years, Conlin had gone from being general
manager of Orem Buick–Chevrolet to owning the Lincoln–Mercury
dealership. Then he got into a big dispute with the Ford Motor Company and another with his partner, and before the litigation was over,
he had gone from being the largest new-car dealer in Utah County to
being the smallest used-car dealer. One hell of a success story. V.J.
Motors sold very old cars more often than not-so-old cars, just sold
them off the lot for a little down. The rest when you could get it. People on welfare or picking up a little alimony, ex-cons, stalwart characters who couldn't get credit anyplace else. Those were his clients.

    Val was a tall slim guy with eyeglasses and a keen and friendly
face. He had the build of a golfer — relaxed shoulders and a bit of
paunch. He was dressed this day in polyester red-checked pants and
a pale yellow sports shirt. Gary was grubby with insulation whose
powder coated his face, his nostrils, and his clothing. Kind of a pale
yellow to match Val's shirt.

    Conlin now gave Gary a lecture about missing the payment.
Since V.J. Motors occupied what was once a hole-in-the-wall drive-in
restaurant, its showroom wasn't large enough to show cars. It just
had a couple of desks, a dozen chairs, and anybody who was there.
You could hear everything Val Conlin had to say.
    "Gary," he now stated, "I don't want to go out and start knocking
on doors. I told you how it works. We try to set a rate people can
handle. We agreed you could bring in fifty bucks every two weeks. So
don't give me any manure that you're going to pay a hundred next
week, or two hundred next month. You got to start bringing the
money in on time."
    "I don't like this car," Gary said.
    "Well, it's not a real slick car," said Val.

"It gets left at the intersection by every other heap. It's a bad car."

"Partner," said Val, "let's get it straight. When you buy a car here, I'm doing you the favor. You can't buy from anybody but me."

"What I really want is a truck."

"Get the payments in on time. Once you pay this off, we can swap for a truck. But I want my fifty, Gary, every two weeks. Otherwise, you walk."

Gary cashed his paycheck and gave him fifty dollars.

That night Nicole and Gary had a bad one in bed. It went on too long and once again he was three-quarters erect, half erect, it finally went all bad. Gary got up, got dressed, stomped out of the house, went to sleep in the car. It made Nicole mad as hell that he had walked out, and it didn't help that he woke the kids up en route.

She told herself that if she was going to mellow him out, she'd have to calm herself. There had been other times, after all, when he blew out of the house and sat in the car. Usually when the kids' noise was drilling him. She knew from what he told her that the level of noise in prison was always high, and his ears were oversensitive. Somehow with all the years he had put in, he could never get used to the sound.

Now she managed to get the kids together, gave them warm milk, tucked them in, and went out to his Mustang. He was sitting behind the wheel silent as stone. She did not talk for ten minutes. Then she slipped a hand over.

Once in a while, Gary would talk about a dream. On this night, sitting in the car, he spoke of it again. He believed that once, in another life, he had been executed. Had his head chopped off.

In the dream, there was something about Oldness. Something ugly, old and moldy. As he talked, she had a chill. She was thinking of how he would wake up often in a real cold sweat. Once he had talked about another dream where he was put in a box, then put into a hole in the wall. It had a door like an oven.

3

On the next weekend, Gary ran into Vern. They stared at each other. Good Lord, Vern said to himself, he is giving me one dirty look. "Don't think I'm much of a man, do you?" Gary asked him.

"Maybe I don't," Vern said and turned and left. Afterward, he felt bad.

Same day, while Toni was visiting Brenda, Gary dropped by. Toni certainly didn't know what to say. She wasn't about to accuse Gary — the poor guy had been accused of enough things in his life. On the other hand, she didn't think it was right to let it all ease by unspoken. Annette was a beautiful young lady and Gary could have had intentions.

She went into the kitchen to get a cup of coffee, and Gary chose to come out of the bathroom then. They were obliged to look right at each other.

Gary said, "Toni, you haven't mentioned this thing with Annette." She answered, "Gary, if there's something to say, I'll say it." He took hold of her hand and said, "Hon, I'd never hurt you or your family." There was a silence. Toni believed him. That is, she believed she could accept what he said. Still, she also felt she wasn't going to let Annette be alone with him. There was always the other possibility. "Gary, I go along with you," she answered at last, "but, just remember, I'm a mother first." He smiled and said, "If you weren't, I'd be disappointed in you." He gave her a kiss on the cheek, and walked back to the front room.

Brenda tried to amuse Gary by telling a story about Val Conlin. In the old days when Val had the Lincoln–Mercury dealership, he always acted like a big shot at the Riverside Country Club. Had been the type to snap his fingers at the waitresses. Brenda was working his table once and thought Val kind of brusque, so she said, "How'd you like me to drop this soup on your head?"

"How'd you like me," Val answered, "to get you fired for that last remark?"

"I'd tell my boss you were lying," she said.

Gary laughed. He hugged her and lifted her up in the air with no trouble. Considering that she was 155 pounds at that point in her life, he was awfully strong. How had he ever lost the fight to Pete?

Gary must have been sitting in her brain. "Brenda," he said, "it's not through yet. In prison you don't leave things like that undone."

4

The following Saturday, Gary and Nicole still planned to take a trip into the canyons, but now both Mustangs were giving them trouble. It made Nicole wonder about their luck. All last week, Gary's car had been dead every morning in a row. Having to get it pushed made him late for work. On this Saturday he even decided to visit Spencer McGrath who might know what was wrong.

Spencer said right off he probably needed a battery. "There's nothing wrong with the old one," Gary told him.
Spencer said, "How do you know?" Gary said, "Well, it looks all right." Spencer laughed, "You can't tell by looking."

Spence went over to the shop, got a meter, checked it out. The reading was awful low. "The battery," he said, "has a dead cell in it." Gary said, "Well, what am I going to do?" Spence said, "Buy yourself a new one. They go for twenty to thirty dollars, along in there." Gary said, "Gee, I don't have it." "You got paid just yesterday," Spence said. "I know," said Gary, "but I made the car installment, and there's not much left." Spence said, "How will you last till Friday?" Gary said, "I probably can make it. Just don't have enough to buy a new battery." Spencer loaned him thirty.

Gary was back in half an hour. At K-Mart he found a honey for $29.95. With tax, it was thirty-two. Spence said, "I guess you had to take a couple of dollars out of your pocket?" Gary said, "Well, yes." Spence said, "Gary, how are you going to get through this week?" Gary said he didn't know. Spence gave him another five for gas, and said, "Pay the car off. Then we'll work it out."

The $32 for the dead battery was the beginning of a real run of rotten luck. Monday night, thinking he would surprise her, Gary went to pick up Nicole at driver's training school, and found his lady sauntering down the hall with four guys in tow. As soon as she saw Gary, she rushed right up, gave a big smile, and tried to let everyone know that she was his. But she could feel how the sight went through. On the way home, he said, "I won't tie you down." She knew he was thinking of Uncle Lee, Jim Barrett, the three-day party, a couple of other dudes, and her life.

He told Sterling about it. "She's free. I don't want to lean on her freedom," he said. He crossed over to the cemetery that faced all the houses on Sterling's street, and Sterling went with him. There was one grave that had no flowers. A little boy's grave. Gary went around and took a flower from each of a number of other graves and put them in a rusty little vase by the boy's headstone. Then they turned on to some good pot. Right away, Gary had to get out of the cemetery. Told Sterling he was seeing himself in a tomb.

One night soon after, Rikki was at Sterling's and Gary started needling him to arm wrestle. Bragged to Nicole of how he had beat her brother. They got into it.

Nicole didn't know if Gary was worn out from the night before, but Rikki took him this time. That is, was about to win, but Gary cheated something obvious, and even lifted his elbow off the table.

Now Gary wanted to try with the other arm. Rikki really got him. That left Gary giving dirty looks. On the way home from Sterling's, he dropped by a little store that was open all hours and stalked out with two six-packs.

It was risky to steal from that small a place, but he had technique. Picked up two six-packs, not one. No hesitation in his walk. At the same time, he managed to make his face look unpleasant. Not for too little would you break into such thoughts to ask if he had paid for the beer.

In the beginning it had been fun. By now it was getting on her nerves. Whenever something bothered him, he got brave. Nicole had always been ready to boost if she needed something, and once they got together, she might even have been the first to do it, but Gary showed her how to really walk out with something. It had been a joke for a while. By now she had to notice that if anything went wrong, he'd steal to cheer them up.

Then he'd drink it afterward. Always getting loaded on beer. She came to realize that there had only been a couple of nights he wasn't drinking. She tried to keep up, but didn't like it that much. He wouldn't even let her leave beer. Didn't like to waste it. If she popped a can, he kept after her to finish.

Nicole was kind of irked that Gary was not only ripping stuff off, but letting everybody know. He was even bragging to his uncle. Things weren't right yet, but Gary had to drop by anyway, and offer a case. When Vern noticed that the trunk of the Mustang held two more of the same, he asked Gary how he could afford it.

"I don't need money," Gary said.

"Do you realize," said Vern, "that you're breaking your parole?"

"You wouldn't turn me in, would you?"

"I might," said Vern. "If it persists, I might turn you in."

One day he came home with water skis and that bothered Nicole. It just wasn't worth the risk. He was stealing something he probably couldn't sell for more than $25, yet the price tag was over $100. That meant they could get you for felony. Nicole hated such dumb habits. He would take a chance on all they had for twenty-five bucks. It came over her that this was the first time she ever disliked him.

As if he sensed it, he then told her the worst story she ever heard. It was supergross. Years ago, while still a kid, he pulled off a robbery with a guy who was a true sadist. The manager of the supermarket was there alone after closing and wouldn't give the combination to the safe. So his friend took the guy upstairs, heated a curling iron, and rammed it.

She couldn't help herself. She laughed. The story got way in. She had a picture of that fat supermarket manager trying to hold on to the money and the poker going up his ass. Her laughter reached to the place where she hated people who had a lot of things and acted hot shit about it.

5

For the first time she had a day when she thought she shouldn't be living with Gary so much. A part of her simply didn't like staying that close to a man for so long a stretch, but as soon as she realized how she felt, Nicole knew she couldn't tell him. He expected their souls to breathe together. More and more, however, an old ugly feeling was coming back. It was the way she got when she had to fit herself to somebody. You could put that off only so long. She still felt better with Gary than with anyone else, but that wasn't going to change the fact that when she got into a bad mood, it was like she had two souls, and one of them loved Gary a lot less than the other. Of course, maybe a part of him was the same way. He couldn't be loving her that much when they got into one of those five-hour deals.

It happened the night he brought home the water skis. Next morning, she wondered if it had to do with Barrett. Jim had popped up the other day while Gary was out at the store. Walked through the door cool as you please after being away for months. Maybe it was just conditioned reflex, but she felt a little stirring down there.

After Barrett left, she felt bad at the way she had only kind of told Gary the truth. She had no respect for Barrett, that was right. He was a pussy. But she hadn't let Gary know he could be an eel when it came to wiggling all the way in. So when Gary met Jim this first time, he hadn't acted too heavy. Of course, Barrett just acted like he was the father of Sunny and happy to be tolerated. Still, Nicole felt like she was keeping a rotten secret. Because Barrett could pass a cigarette and make something out of it. Tickle your memory like he was tickling your palm. Hint that you had a gift to offer.

Now, those last couple of nights, she had been tripping a little on good things in the past with Jim to get herself more in the mood for Gary. Barrett's timing had sure been good, just as Gary's — she had to admit — was getting a little crude. Since Rosebeth, Gary had to make love six or seven times a week. Maybe they'd skip a night, but make up for it with two another. It was his idea, not hers. She enjoyed it more a day or two apart, but he kept pressing his damn luck.

This night, from seven to midnight, Nicole and Gary argued first about the water skis, then everything else. Finally she convinced Gary she wasn't going to fuck him. He had gone too far on uppers, downers, and around-ers. If she had a gift, Gary was not exactly bringing it out. Not with his demands to do this, do that. Suck him now. She looked at Gary across their bodies and said, "I hate sucking cock."

The Fiorinal had put a glaze on his eyes, but her words still hit. He took off. Left at midnight and didn't come back until 2 A.M. He was hardly through the door when he was asking her to suck him all over again.

Why? she asked. Like a dunce. Do it because I want you to, he said. It was as bad as the first night. They didn't get to sleep till five. At five-thirty, Gary was up like a maniac, ready for work.

6

Between midnight and two, Gary had been to see Spencer and Marie. When McGrath opened the door, Gary asked if he and Marie would like to play three-hand poker.

Marie was already in bed, but she got up and made a cup of coffee. The McGraths, however, did not want to play poker. Not after midnight. Spencer kept himself from saying, "It's a little rude to come by this late."

In fact, they were used to seeing Gary drunk. There had been a couple of times he came over at odd hours. Once he really needed calming down. Started to talk about what he would do to a fellow named Pete Galovan.

Another time Gary had dropped in when Spence and Marie were having a barbecue in the backyard. He was so drunk he couldn't lift the latch on the gate. Spence had to go over, and bring him in, give him some chow. There were a number of guests around but Spencer gave Gary full attention and made him drink a couple of cups of coffee. Then he talked about things that were wild. Got into reincarnation.

"You really believe that?" asked Spencer.

"Oh, you bet," said Gary.

"A lot of people think we come back as other species, like a horse or an insect," Spencer said. "Seems it would be hard to straighten things out if there's all that shuttling back and forth."

Gary didn't go for Spencer's idea. He was going to come back as a human. If he messed this life up, he'd do a better job in the next one. "Why not a better job in this one?" Spencer thought. Chose not to say it.

Of course ever since Gary had found out that Spencer knew a little about cars, he had begun to come by on Saturday with his Mustang. The muffler fell off once, and Gary didn't know to get it back by tightening the clamp. Hadn't the slightest idea. It wasn't that he was lazy, but a month before he might have tried to figure the situation out. Now, he didn't seem to show any initiative. It was more like he was offended there was something wrong with the car. What he couldn't recognize was that these malfunctions might be due to his inability to drive knowledgeably. One more reason for Spencer to be after him continuously about starting the study program for a driver's license. Talking to the wind. Gary could sure keep you awake. Spence would have gotten as much sleep if he had played poker.

He had to admit it, Gary made him sad. In the beginning, he had always been coming over to ask Craig Taylor or himself to take a look at what he had done. If Gary got the hang of something new, he was pleased when they praised him for it. Swelled up proud. Now that he had been living with Nicole, Spence didn't know if he cared whether he did a good job or not. More like he was putting in his time for the paycheck. Those cutoff Levi's of hers. Gary seemed to be going down to the girl's level.

Unable to sleep, Spencer got mad all over again at the way Gary would now goof off during the day. You had to notice how long he took for lunch. Then, every Thursday he had to leave early to see his parole officer. Plus other time he took for other excuses. Not a week had gone by without asking for extra money, and Spence never deducted the lost hours or his own out-of-pocket from the paycheck. Once, Gary did talk of doing a painting to wipe out the debt, but so soon as Marie and he began to think about it, Gary didn't bring it up anymore.

Next morning, before they were even straightened out on the job, Gary was asking if anybody'd like to buy a pair of water skis. One fellow came up to Spence to inquire if Gary might have stolen them. Spence asked, "Are they brand-new?" Couldn't believe Gary had ripped off water skis. A man might slip cufflinks or a watch into his pocket, but how did you steal those big slats right out of a store?

Spencer looked upon himself as a real simple character, but he was beginning to wonder if Gary was taking marijuana on the job or something. He sure looked awful this morning.

"Gary," Spence said, "let's get down to something basic. Every week you're broke. Why don't you take the money you spend on beer and save it?" Gary said, "I don't pay for beer." "Well, then who in hell gives it to you?" Gary said, "I just walk in a store, and take a six-pack."

Spence said, "Nobody catches you, huh?" "No." "How long you been doing that?" "Weeks." Spencer said, "Steal a six-pack of beer every day and never been caught?" Gary said, "Never." Spencer said, "I don't know. How come people get caught and you don't?" Gary said, "I'm better than they are."

"I think you're pulling my leg," said Spencer.

Gary proceeded to tell about the black convict he had stabbed 57 times. Now Spencer thought Gary was trying to impress him with how tough he was, see if he would scare. "Come on, Gary," he said, "57 times sounds like a variety of soup."

After they finished laughing, Gary broke it to Spence. He'd like to get off early on Friday.

"I don't know if you've noticed," said Spence, "but the other fellows don't take off. They work all day, and take care of things after hours. That's how it's normally done."

Still, he gave him the time. One more time. Spence felt a little uneasy. After all, the government, with the ex-convicts' program, was paying half of Gary's $3.50 an hour. It could account for why Gary was giving him half an hour on the hour.

7

One afternoon, while Nicole was away on a visit to Kathryne, Barrett visited the house in Spanish Fork and found Rosebeth there. By the time Nicole came back, her little friend was no virgin anymore.

At first, Rosebeth merely mentioned that Barrett had been there. Oh, Nicole asked, for how long? About an hour, said Rosebeth, and a half. Nicole began to laugh. If Barrett wasn't feeling bashful, he was in bed. An hour and a half was time enough for Barrett. Seeing that Nicole wasn't upset, Rosebeth began to giggle. She knew now, she told Nicole, why Gary had never been able to put it in. Too big. Nicole and Rosebeth began to have this long laugh waiting for Gary to get home from work.

Gary, however, had dropped in on Val Conlin. The beer he brought was ice cold. After that run-in for not paying on time, Gary made a practice of bringing a six-pack when he went by Val was appreciative.

Gary had his eye on a truck. The one on the lot that was painted white.

"Buddy," said Val, "pay off the Mustang and I'll get you something better."

"I got to have that truck."

"No can do without mucho mazuma," said Val. The truck was up for sale at $1,700. "Listen, pardner, unless you come back with a co-signer, it's too good a truck for you."

Gary thought he could. Maybe his Uncle Vern.

"I know Vern," said Val, "and I don't think he's in shape for this kind of credit. But, if you want, have him fill out the application. We can always see what we can do."

"Okay," said Gary, "okay." He hesitated. "Val," he said, "that Mustang is no good. I had to put a new battery in, and an alternator. It came to fifty dollars."

"What do you want me to do?"

"Well, if I buy the truck, I think you could allow for what I had to lay out on the Mustang."

"Gary, you buy the truck, and we'll knock that fifty dollars off. No problem. Just get a co-signer."

"Val, I don't need a co-signer. I can make the payments."

"No co-signer, no truck. Pardner, let's keep it simple."

"The goddamn Mustang isn't any good."

"Gary, I'm doing you the favor. If you don't want the Mustang, leave the son of a bitch right out there."

"I want the truck."

"The only way you get the truck is by putting a lot of money on the front end of the loan. Or come in with a co-signer. Here, take this credit application to Vern."

Gary sat across the desk, looking out the window at the white truck on the end of the line. It was as white as the snow you could still see on the peak of the mountains.

"Gary, fill out the application and bring it back."

Val knew it. Gary was madder than hell. He didn't say a word, just took the application, got up, walked out the door, wadded it up, and threw it on the ground.

Harper, Val's salesman, said, "Boy, he's hot."

"I don't give a shit," said Val. Around him, people got hot. That was run of the mill. Just his hell-of-a-success-story boiling away.

8

In the middle of making love that night, Gary called Nicole, Pardner. She took it wrong. Thought he was jiving at her for getting it on with Rosebeth. But as he tried to explain later, he often called men and women alike by Buddy or Pal, Pardner, things like that.

In the morning, it was the Mustang. His car would not start. It was as if something in Gary's makeup killed off the electrical system every morning.

CHAPTER 9

In Trouble with the Law

1

Kathryne was getting quite an impression of Gary. It began one day around lunchtime when he came knocking on her door. It startled her. He was so covered with insulating material that he looked like a man who had clawed his way out of the earth.

He had dropped by, he told her, to take a look at the room she wanted done. Kathryne just about remembered that the time Nicole had brought him over to meet her, there was a conversation about insulating the back room. Fine, Kathryne told him now, fine. She wanted to get rid of Gary fast.

Well, he took the look and said he'd have to talk to a boy who worked with him. Then they'd give the estimate. Kathryne said that was real nice. Sure enough, he was back that same afternoon with a kid of eighteen who figured the job at $60. She said she'd think about it.

Three days later, at lunchtime, there was Gary in the doorway again. Talking fast. Said, I thought I'd come and have a beer with you. Got some beer? Gee, she didn't, said Kathryne, just coffee. Well, he told her, I'll come in anyway. Got something to eat?

She said she could make him a sandwich. That was okay. He would run down and get a six-pack. Kathryne just looked at her kid sister Kathy.

Ten minutes later, he was back with the beer. While she fixed the sandwiches, he started talking. What a conversation. If the first time he came to her house he never opened his mouth, now, right off, he told Kathryne and Kathy that he had stolen the six-pack. Wanted to know if they might need cigarettes. No, she said, she had plenty. How about beer? he inquired. Seldom drink it, very seldom.

The day before he had gone in the store, he said, picked up a case, walked out, and was setting it in his trunk when a kid not old enough to drink asked if Gary would buy him a case, and handed over five bucks. Gary started to laugh. "I walked in, picked up the kid's beer, walked out, gave it to him, and took off with the cash."

They were careful to laugh. Weren't you afraid? they asked. No, said Gary, act like you own the place.

He started telling stories. One after another. They couldn't believe him. Told of tattooing a man named Fungoo, and taking a fake photograph of a pervert named Skeezix, then there was a fellow he hit over the head with a hammer, and he stabbed a nigger 57 times. He'd look at them carefully, say, Now did you understand that? His voice got gruff.

They would put on a smile. Gary, the ladies would say, that's something else, you know. They got themselves to laugh. Kathryne didn't know if she was more afraid for Nicole or herself. About the time he'd stayed an hour and a half, she asked if he wouldn't be late getting back to work.

To hell with the job, said Gary. If they didn't like it over at the job, they knew what they could do. Then he told about a friend of his who gave it to the manager of a supermarket with a hot curling iron.

All the while, he watched them real close. He had to see their reaction. They felt they better have a reaction.

Weren't you afraid, Gary? they would ask. Didn't you think somebody would catch you?

He did a lot of boasting. Sounded like he was banging along in a boat from rock to rock. When he left, he thanked them for being so sociable.

2

Nicole heard about the lunch. There was a piece of him, she decided, that liked to tell crazy stories to grown-ups. It must have gotten locked in at the age of eight.

Then she thought of the night up in the hills behind the nut-house when she wondered if he was a magnet to evil spirits. Maybe he had to act that nasty to keep things off. The idea didn't cheer her. He could get meaner and meaner if that was the truth.

Around midnight, Nicole was feeling awfully cooped up with Gary. She found herself thinking of Barrett. It kept working away in her. There had also been a letter from Kip that afternoon but she kept thinking about Barrett and Rosebeth.

She hadn't even wanted to open Kip's letter, and when she did, he wrote that he wanted her to come back. The letter left her feeling crowded. It was like the past was coming back. Hampton, of all people, was going around with her sister April. Everybody, Nicole decided, was fucking with her head.

All the while she was having these thoughts, Gary had been sitting at her feet. Now he had to pick this moment to look up with all the light of love shining in his eyes. "Baby," he said, "I really love you all the way and forever." She looked back. "Yeah," she said, "and so do seven other motherfuckers."

Gary hit her. It was the first time, and he hit her hard. She didn't feel the pain so much as the shock and then the disappointment. It always ended the same way. They hit you when they felt like it.

Soon enough, he apologized. He kept apologizing. But it did no good. She had been hit so fucking many times. The kids were in bed, and she looked at Gary and said, "I want to die." It was how she felt. He kept trying to make up. Finally, she told him that she had felt like dying before but never did anything about it. Tonight, she wouldn't mind.

Gary got a knife and held the point to her stomach. He asked her if she still wanted to die.

It was frightening that she wasn't more afraid. After a few minutes, she finally said, "No, I don't," but she had been tempted. After he put the knife away, she even felt trapped. She couldn't believe the size of the bad feeling that came down on her then.

They had one more marathon. Up all night about whether to fuck. In the middle, around midnight, he took off. Not too long later, he came in with a bunch of boxes. There was a pistol in every box.

She got over it a little. She had to. The guns hung around.

3

Sterling Baker had a birthday party the last Sunday afternoon in June, and the party went on in Sterling's apartment and out in the backyard, fifteen or twenty good people. A lot brought bottles. Nicole had cutoffs on, and a halter top, and knew she was looking good. Gary was sure showing her off. A couple of dudes began to tell Gary what a hot lady he had. Gary would say, "Know it," and grab her by both breasts, or pull her into his lap.

Well, it was Sterling's birthday, and Nicole still had this little crush on her cousin. So Nicole started kidding him about a birthday kiss and Sterling said he'd take her up on it. She asked Gary if it was okay. He gave her a look, but she went and sat on Sterling's lap anyway. Gave him a long kiss that would tell a lot about her.

When she opened her eyes, Gary was sitting with no expression on his face. He said, "Had enough?"

They were keeping a keg of beer out in the back. The fellow upstairs had also invited his friends, and one of them was a guy called Jimmy, a Chicano. He picked up a pair of sunglasses that Sterling had laid on the roof of a broken-down old car out in the back lot while he was tapping a keg. Nicole figured maybe Jimmy didn't know. Just picked them up. Only thing, the glasses were a present from Gary to Sterling

Gary came on strong. "I want them glasses back," he told Jimmy, "they're mine." Jimmy got kind of upset and left. Nicole started shrieking. "You're fucking up the party," she shouted at Gary. "All this horseshit over a stupid pair of glasses."

Jimmy came back to the party with a couple of friends. As soon as he walked in the yard, Gary was on his feet and heading toward him. They were throwing fists before you could stop it.

Maybe Gary was too drunk, but Jimmy split his eye with the first punch. Blood was running all over Gary's face. He got hit again and went down to his knees, got back up and started swinging.

About that time, everybody broke the fight up. Sterling walked Jimmy around the front of the house and got him to leave. Just as Jimmy was walking off, Gary came up holding a gear knob that he'd taken off the beat-up car in the backyard. Sterling stepped in front of him. "Gary, you're through with that, you're not going to hit him," he said. Just talking in a normal tone of voice. But he had a big fellow standing next to him to back what was said. Nicole got Gary out and took him home.

She hated to see her man have his ass whipped. Especially when he started it. She thought he was a fool all the way. A cheater, too. Like when he arm wrestled her brother.

He wanted to go back and find Jimmy. By keeping her mouth shut about how disappointed she was in his fighting, she managed to get him to Spanish Fork. She had hardly ever known a guy who hated to lose a rumble as much as Gary. That softened her feelings somewhat. After all, he had taken a beating from a very tough dude, and hadn't quit.

After she washed him off, Nicole discovered that the cut was bad. So she took him next door to her neighbor Elaine, who had just gotten through taking this emergency course on being an ambulance driver and Elaine said he definitely needed stitches. Nicole started to worry. She had heard that oxygen in the air could enter a cut near the eye, go right to the brain, and kill you. So she did take him to the doctor. Through the rest of the night she kept ice packs on his face and babied him, and kind of enjoyed it, considering how things had been lately. In the morning, when he tried to blow his nose, his cheeks blew up right around his glands and sinuses.

4

Spencer said, "Gary, it doesn't make much sense putting your body up to be abused."

"They can't hurt me," said Gary.

"Oh, no? Your eye is cut and it's turning black, and you've got a lump on your forehead and he gave you a good one on the nose. Don't stand there and put that stuff on me, Gary. I just can't believe you keep getting the best of these deals."

Gary said, "I sure did, you know."

Spencer said, "What's going to happen one night is some little guy about five foot six" — which was around Spencer's height — "is going to stuff a mudhole right in the middle of your face. Because that's what happens. A guy doesn't have to be seven feet tall to be mean."

"I'm Gary Gilmore," Gilmore said, "and they can't hurt me."

In the evening, driving around with Nicole and Sunny and Peabody, he stopped at V.J. Motors to talk to Val Conlin about the truck. Even got to take it out for an hour. Gary was that happy up high behind the wheel with something like a real motor in front of them. All the while she could feel him thinking of the guns. They were shining like $$$ in his eyes.

When he got back, he talked to Val about the size of a down payment. Nicole was hardly listening. It was boring to sit in the showroom with all the freaks and deadbeats who were waiting to get some piece of a car. One girl was wearing a turban and had a big swipe of eyeshadow under each eye, and her blouse just about pulling out of her belt. She said to Nicole, "You have very beautiful eyes." "Thank you," said Nicole.

Gary kept repeating himself like a record with a scratch. "I don't want that Mustang," he said to Val.

"Then let's get closer to the truck, buddy. We're not near it. Come in with a co-signer or with money."

Gary stalked away. Nicole hardly had time to gather the kids and follow. Outside the showroom, Gary was swearing like Val had never heard him swear before. Through the showroom window Val could see the Mustang, and it wouldn't start. Gary sat there pounding the wheel as hard as he could.

"Jesus," said Harper, "this time, he is really hot."

"I don't give a shit," said Val, and walked through the people sitting around with their debts on different cars. Yeah, I'm right on top of the mountain, thought Val, and went outside and said to Gary, "What's the matter?"

"This son of a bitch," said Gary, "this goddamn car."

"Well, now, hold it. Let's get some jumper cables, we'll get it started," and, of course Val did, just needed the boost, and Gary took off in a spray of gravel like he had a switch to his hind end.

By the following night, Gary had a guy who would sell the guns. But they had to meet him. That meant carrying the guns in the car. Gary didn't have a license and her Mustang still had last year's license plates. Both cars had the crappy kind of look a State Trooper would pull over for nothing. So they had quite an argument before they finally put the pistols in her trunk and started out. They brought the kids along. The kids might be insurance against a State Trooper waving them over for too little.

On the other hand, Sunny and Jeremy made her awfully aware of his driving tonight. That definitely got Nicole nervous. He finally swung into the Long Horn Cafe, a taco joint between Orem and Pleasant Grove, to make a phone call. Only he couldn't get ahold of the guy who was to peddle the guns. Gary was getting more and more upset. It looked like the evening was going to get totally squandered. A sweet early summer night.

He came back out of the Long Horn and looked in the car for another phone number, then started tearing pages out of the book.

By the time he finally found the number, his guy was out. Sunny and Jeremy were beginning to make a lot of noise. Next thing she knew, Gary spun out of the Long Horn and headed back toward Orem. He was going 80. She was petrified for the kids. Told him to pull over.

He slammed to the shoulder. A screeching halt. He turned around, and started spanking the kids. They hadn't even been making a sound the last minute. Too scared of the speed.

She started hitting Gary right there, hit him with her fists as hard as she could, hollered for him to let her out of the car. He grabbed her hands to hold her down, and then the kids started screaming. Gary wouldn't let her out. Then this really dumb-looking guy walked by. She must have sounded as if Gary was killing her, but the fucker just stopped and said, "Anything wrong?" Then walked on.

Nicole wouldn't stop hollering. Gary finally wedged her into the space between the bucket seats and got his hand over her mouth. She was trying not to pass out. He had his other hand on her throat to hold her down. She couldn't breathe. He told her then that he would let her go if she promised to be quiet and go home. Nicole mumbled, Okay. It was the best she could get out. The moment he let go, she started yelling. When his hand came back to her mouth, she bit real hard into the flesh near his thumb. Tasted the blood.

Somehow, she didn't know how, she got out of the car. She couldn't remember later if he let her go, or if she just got away. Maybe he let her go. She ran across the street to the middle of the highway divider, a kid in each hand, and started walking. She would hitchhike.

Gary began to follow on foot. At first he let her try to bum a ride, but a car almost stopped for her, and so Gary tried to pull her back to the Mustang. She wouldn't budge. He got smart and tried to yank one of the kids away. She wouldn't let loose, hung on with all she had. Between them, it must have been stretching the kids. Finally a pickup truck pulled over and a couple of guys came over with a chick.

The girl happened to be an old friend Nicole hadn't seen in a year. Pepper, her first girl friend ever. Yet, Nicole couldn't even think of the last name, she was that upset.

Gary said, "Get out of here, this is a family matter." Pepper looked at Gary, just as tall as she could be, and said, "We know Nicole, and you ain't family." That was all of it. Gary let go and walked up the street toward her car. Nicole got the kids into the truck with Pepper, and they took off. The moment she remembered how once she had wanted everything to be good for Gary, she started crying. Nicole couldn't help it. She cried a lot.

5

He got back into her Mustang, drove down to Grand Central Supermarket, picked up a tape deck off the shelf, and started to walk out. At the door, a security guard took one look at his black eye and asked for a receipt.

"Get fucked," said Gary and threw the carton into the guard's arms. Then he ran to the parking lot, jumped in Nicole's car, backed up, and slammed into a car behind him. He careened out of the space he was in, banged another car, and took off.

He zipped through Provo and got out on the back highway to Springville. There he stopped at The Whip. In the parking lot, he hid the pistol boxes under an oil drum, entered the bar, went to the men's room, put Nicole's car keys in the tank over the toilet, and came out to have a beer. While he waited, he called Gary Weston to come and pick him up.

Sirens came along the highway and wound down outside the door of The Whip. Two cops came in, and wanted to know who owned the blue Mustang. They asked everybody. Took down the name on every I.D. The revolving lights of their car kept flaring through the window of the bar. After they took off, Gary left with Gary Weston. Nicole's car, however, stayed behind. The cops had impounded it.

It must have been eleven o'clock. Brenda woke up to hear him knocking on the door. There was Johnny asleep, same as every night, on the couch. He had been there since eight. When she first met Johnny he had been a Class B state champion of archery and had a short pointed beard. Out on the archery range, he looked as handsome as Robin Hood. Today, if dear John didn't get his ten hours of sleep, he couldn't function. Now, Brenda recollected herself falling asleep bored to death.

"I had a hassle," Gary said.

"A hassle."

"I took a tape deck in Grand Central and walked out. The guard stopped me, so I threw it at the guy."

"Then what did you do?"

"I hit a car." He told the rest of it.

He looked so tired, so sad and his beat-up face was such a holy mess that she couldn't stay too angry. Johnny was up and stirring. His expression said the reason he liked to sleep was because it kept him from hearing news such as this.

"Brenda, I need fifty bucks bad," Gary said. "I want to go to Canada."

He had it figured out. "You explain to the police that Nicole had nothing to do with it. That way, they'll let her have the car back."

"You're a man," Brenda said. "Go down, and get the car yourself."

"You won't help me?"

"I'll help you write a confession. I'll see it's delivered."

"Brenda, there's a lot of loudspeakers in the back of the car. I ripped them off in a drive-in movie."

"How many?"

"Five or six."

"Just to be doing something," said Brenda. "Like a little kid."

Gary nodded. There was the sorrow in his eyes of knowing he would never see Canada.

"You have to turn yourself in to Mont Court in the morning," said Brenda.

"Cousin, keep on my ass about it, will you?" said Gary.

6

Nicole spent the night at her great-grandmother's house where he would never think of looking for her. In the morning, she went back to her mother's, and Gary called not long after, and said he was coming over. Nicole was scared. She put in a call to the police, and, in fact, was talking to the dispatcher when Gary walked in. So she said into the phone, "Man, get them out here as fast as you can."

She didn't know if Gary had come to drag her away. But he just stood at the kitchen sink. She told him to go away and leave her alone, and he just kept looking at her. He had a look as if everything inside him hurt, man, really hurt. Then he said, "You fight as good as you fuck."

She was trying hard not to smile, but, in fact, it made her a little less afraid of him. He came over and put his hands on her shoulders. Again, she told him to leave. To her surprise, he turned around and went. He practically passed the cops as they were coming in.

By afternoon, she regretted not letting him stay. She was really afraid he would not come back. A voice in her head kept sounding like an echo in a tunnel. It said, "I love him, I love him."

He showed up after work with a carton of cigarettes and a rose. She couldn't help but smile. She went on the porch to meet him, and he handed her a letter.

Dear Nicole,
I don't know why I did this to myself. You are the most beautiful thing I've ever seen and touched . . .
You just loved me and touched my soul with a wondrous tenderness and you treated me so kindly.
I just couldn't handle that. There's no bullshit or meanness about you and I couldn't deal with an honest spirit like yours that didn't want to hurt me . . .
I'm so fucking sad . . .
I see it in detail like a movie. And it makes no sense. It makes me scream inside.
And you said you want me out of your life. Not that I can blame

you for that. I am one of those people that probably shouldn't exist.
    But I do.
    And I know that I always will.
    Just like you.
    We are both very old.
    I would like to see you smile at me again. I hope I don't have to wait until I reach the place of no darkness to see that.

                                               GARY

After she read the letter, they sat on the porch for a while. Didn't say too much. Then Nicole went in and got the kids, picked up their diapers, and left with him.

On the way, he told her what had happened at Grand Central. By the time they reached Spanish Fork, he got his nerve up and put in a call to Mont Court, who said it was too close to evening to do anything. First thing next day, Court would pick him up and drive him over to the Orem Police. Gary and Nicole slept with their arms around each other. It would be their last night together for they did not know how long.

7

The Lieutenant of Detectives in the Orem Police Department was a pleasant-looking man of average size with a big face, bald head, and a crown of yellow-reddish hair. He wore eyeglasses. His name was Gerald Nielsen and he was a good Mormon who grew up on a ranch and was an Elder of the Church. He was sitting in his office when the dispatcher called and said, "There's a fellow out here wants to turn himself in." That was an event which might happen from time to time, but it wasn't common. The Lieutenant went out to meet him. A fellow could lose his courage during the time it took to walk from Reception to Nielsen's office.

It was early in the morning and the man looked like he hadn't slept too well. "I'm Gary Gilmore," he said. "I want to talk to somebody." He was wearing dark glasses and his eyes were black and his nose was swollen. They had hardly said hello before Gilmore mentioned that he had been in a fight. Considering the number of stitches, you would have supposed it was a car accident.

When they got back to his office, Gerald Nielsen poured him a cup of coffee out of the pot they kept for prisoners — a different expense account — and then they sat there without talking for a little while.

"I stole a tape deck at Grand Central," Gilmore began, "and as I was leaving, I bumped another car. The car I was driving belongs to a friend of mine and they ended up impounding it. I thought about running to Canada, but my girl friend told me to stand up to what I have coming." He said it with his battered face.

"That's all that's involved?" asked Nielsen.

"Yes."

"Well, I'm wondering why you're so nervous about it."

"I just got out of prison."

While they were waiting for the police report of the episode at Grand Central to be brought in, Gilmore recounted how many years he had been in prison. As he spoke, Nielsen got the impression more and more that Gilmore would never have shown up this morning if his parole officer had not driven him to the door.

Gilmore muttered, "Boy, I have a hard time when I drink."

The report came in and the events were as Gilmore described. Nielsen called Mont Court who verified that he had brought Gary over. Since Court had had time to get back from Orem to his office in Provo, Nielsen could see that Gilmore waited more than a few minutes before getting up nerve to announce himself.

Now, he stared at Nielsen through his dark glasses, and said, "I just don't want to go back, you know."

"Well," said Nielsen, "they don't usually return people to prison for misdemeanors."

"They don't?"

"That's a fact of life." It concerned Nielsen a little that the fellow was sufficiently scared, in fact paranoid, to think a misdemeanor was going to terminate his parole. A man with Gilmore's experience ought to know better. The Lieutenant looked one more time at the reports and decided he wouldn't book him. He didn't yet have all the facts in the Complaint, and it would amount to holding the man. That would be counterproductive to the effort Gilmore had made to come in and confess. So Nielsen said, "I'm sure they'll charge you, and there'll be a Complaint filed. But, for now, why don't you go ahead and go to work?" When Gilmore looked confused, Nielsen added, "Have them give you a long lunch hour tomorrow. That'll allow you time to appear before the Judge. I'll tell the officer to have the papers ready."

"You mean you're not going to lock me up?"

"I don't want to jeopardize your job."

"Well, okay, you know." Gilmore was certainly surprised. He sat there for a minute. "Could I make a phone call?" he asked next. "I don't have a ride."

"You bet."

He made a couple of calls but couldn't reach anybody. "Maybe," he said, "I ought to go to Provo and get that car out of impound. I'll hitch a ride."

"Well," said Nielsen, "I'm going there now. I'll give you the ride."

Nielsen drove him to the Provo Police Department, took him to the proper window, and left. Gilmore began to make arrangements to get Nicole's car out. There were complications. The drive-in speakers had been discovered. Since they had not been listed when the car was first impounded, but only on the next day, there was no legal basis for adding stolen speakers to the Complaint. Anyone at The Whip, for instance, could have put them in the trunk.

8

Three hours after he kissed her good-bye and left in Mont Court's car, Gary came driving up to the house in her blue Mustang. He was bright-eyed and talking a streak. Told her they had to get down to court fast. It was a real opportunity. The police Complaint, he had learned, wasn't going to be ready until tomorrow.

If he went over now, he explained to Nicole, there would be no cop around to go into detail over what he had done. He was only up for petty theft. The Judge wouldn't know if it was a dollar or ninety-nine dollars. Besides, he'd also heard the regular Judge was on vacation. There was only a Pro Tem, that is, just a regular lawyer standing in, not a real Judge. He wouldn't know that much. It was made to order. On a misdemeanor, with no prosecutor and no cop to read the Complaint, it could be like coming to pay a traffic ticket.

Even with Gary's explanation, she was surprised by the Judge. He didn't look more than 30. He was a small man with a large head, and he said aloud that he didn't know anything about the case. Gary kept talking to him as smoothly as a salesman making the deal. He was careful to throw in a "sir" now and then.

Nicole wasn't so sure it was working. The Judge had the expression of a man who was not getting a particularly good feeling. One uptight Mormon. When Gary asked what the penalties might be on a plea of Guilty, the Judge said he would make no promises. As a Class B misdemeanor, it could amount to 90 days in jail and $299 for the fine.

She began to wonder. When Gary said, "Your Honor, I think I'm going to enter a plea of Guilty," the Judge asked if he was on drugs or drunk. Did he realize he was waiving his right to a trial and to counsel? The language sounded awful, but by the flat way the young Judge laid it down and Gary nodded, she hoped it was routine.

Then the Judge said he wanted a presentence investigation through the Probation and Parole Department. Now Gary had to explain he already had a local officer. Nicole thought Gary was hanging himself for sure. The Judge frowned and said he would give him until five o'clock to post bail of $100. Otherwise, he could report to the county jail.

Gary said he didn't have any hope of getting that much money before five o'clock. Wouldn't the Judge give him a release if his probation officer vouched for him? The Judge said, "I'm a firm believer that people should not be punished because of lack of funds. Since you walked in of your own accord, I will consider your request. Let your probation officer call me."

Gary came out of the phone booth smiling. Court was pleased he'd turned himself in, so it looked like they wouldn't have to worry for a month. Of course, there would be a presentence investigation, and then he would have to appear on July 24 for sentencing, but maybe it would cool off by then. They walked out of the courtroom together.

Now, after all that had happened, after the fight with the Chicano, and the terrible night on the highway, after two days of being apart and knowing the fear of being separated for a lot more than that, they were together again. For a day and a night everything was better than if they had never been apart. It was as if somebody had hidden sparklers inside her heart in that place where she had expected to find nothing. God, she loved him while his face was mending.

CHAPTER 10

In-laws

1

April came to visit for a couple of days, and didn't stop talking. She was tired, she told Nicole, of their mother. "Man, she's the queen, and I am tired of her power games. She tries to make it look like I'm a rotten defiant child when all I'm trying to do is get away from threats. If I say one damn thing, she threatens me with the hospitals and the doctors. Whereas I," said April, "don't sit around and watch my mother's behavior. She's going to have to go. Queens and princesses don't get along."

Nicole said yes. She was never around April for more than a couple of days before she decided the whole family was crazy. It was just that April was in touch with the heavy strings on the fiddle.

April and Gary, however, really got along. April thought Gary was powerful, witty, and very intelligent. The first night, after a few beers, he began to teach her how to paint. April said he must love Sissy very much and certainly the kids.

Everything Gary painted was sharp as a razor. If he painted a bird, you could see every feather as though under a magnifying glass, but he didn't teach that way. "Just mix the color so it comes out the way you feel," he said. April was looking at Gary like he was her guru.

Nicole never knew what to make of April's looks. She was short and chunky whenever she didn't watch her diet, which was almost all the time, but she would have been beautiful if a girl needed no other features than eyes. April's eyes were purple blue and yet had green in them — a fabulous color. Like one of those transparent stones that change hue according to your mood.

April's hair, however, hung down like crooked spinach, and she had the damnedest mouth. Nicole had put enough time in the nuthouse to know the lips of a disturbed person. April could look in one direction, and her mouth start to quiver in the other, like the rear end of a car going off on its own. Sometimes, her lips would shiver as much as an old faucet just turned off, or her upper lip would relax and her lower lip get stiff. Her entire face could clamp like lockjaw. Most of the time she had a toothache in her expression.

Her voice really got to Nicole. April had an awful big voice for a 17-year-old. You never knew where it came from. She was so goddamn sure of herself. Her voice could grate on you with just how impressive she thought she was. Then she could whine like a brat.

April let them both know that she thought of Gary as a very distinguished person. He was kind of very humble, like a master to his slave. At the same time very tired and sad. He'd been through the same thing a slave'd been through. He was on a much higher level of existence than anybody she knew. Just by focusing on his body, April said, you could feel that.

Before they had been painting very long, April wanted to tell them about Hampton. As far as April was concerned, Hampton was everything. "My nearest past," she whispered. She wanted to hate him for all those nights he had her thinking he went home each morning to his folks. He would get up at 5 A.M., and April thought he loved her because he didn't take off silently in the dark but woke her to say good-bye. Then she found out he was just returning to his steady chick. Had to get back before dawn, like.

There was a space in her stomach that got hungry if she didn't talk. "You've heard the song 'Backstabbers,' haven't you?" she asked, sitting on their floor. "Well, backstabbers wouldn't be in my shoes if you paid them. That's because I have some superfreaky memories." When they did not reply, April said, "Do I sound like a robot tonight?"

"I," said April, "got up this morning and cooked me a two-egg omelet with cheese in the middle and pieces of thin toast, some Tang, and some strawberry milk with sliced banana. Too much. I never tasted anything like that food. Just made me sick. I stuffed myself. Then I dropped my contact lens down the sink. I'm careless." When they didn't say much in return, she said, "I fall in love too easy. It's the kind of love that doesn't wear out. I'm possessed . . . I mean, I was obsessed with my body being so roly-poly." She looked sternly at Gary. "I was not as fat as I am now."

"You're not fat," Nicole said.

"You, Sissy," said April, "were skinny!" She confirmed this with a most definite nod of her head to Gary, and then added, "Sissy was most of my childhood." She said this in a strong voice as though that were the last matter ever to argue about. "Me, Mike, and Sissy would go for walks with Rikki down by the gulch. We picked snails out of mossy logs."

She was remembering the moss and how it was slimy from everything that oozed out of the snails — that was how she felt. You could rub slime between your fingers and never feel a thing but slipperiness. Like you were the center of slipperiness. Making love. "I miss Hampton," she said. She didn't want to talk about him. She was getting to the point where she wanted to be deaf and blind. Sometimes her thoughts came out so strong, April could hear them twenty seconds before they went into her head. Especially before a real strong thought. "I've gone cold turkey," she said. "I've said farewell to the idea of love."

Gary's records were mostly Johnny Cash. Full of the love and sorrow of men at how cruel and sweet and full of grit life feels. It wasn't her trip. The men could love the men. Still, she went on a trip with Gary and was very much in his music, and Johnny Cash, wherever he was now, would be able to feel his song stirring in her. Like he had a magic spoon to stir his soup. People could get down without playing an instrument. It was in the way they put the record on.

"I was crazy about Hampton," April said. "He had so much green in his eyes you knew right away he was going to tell a story."

"He always bored me," said Nicole.

"Good in bed," said April. She sighed. She was thinking of the day last week when Sissy had come over and said to Hampton, "You need a haircut." "*You* want to do it?" he had asked, and Sissy said, "Sure." She had done his hair all right. Like she owned his head. Each time Nicole's scissors cut a lock of his hair, April could feel Hampton's love for herself ending. She could hear it in the sound the hair made when it was cut. Good-bye. Now she could feel Gary hearing the same sound and hating Hampton. "Oh, I loved Hampton," April said to make it right. "He was very spacey."

Nicole snorted. "You loved him 'cause he was spacey?"

April felt truly fierce. "That was 'cause I could live in his spaces."

Next day, the Bicentennial Fourth of July, they went to a carnival and April ran into a couple of boys she knew. Next thing, she was gone. Gary and Nicole turned around and she was gone. No great matter. April was that way.

They got home just in time to pick up the telephone. It was Nicole's father. Charley Baker told Nicole he was up the road at her grandfather's, and Steinie was having a big birthday party for Verna. Would she come?

It made Nicole mad. That big a family party and they couldn't get around to inviting her until it started. She could hear the noise over the phone. "Well," she said, "I'd like to come, but don't get mad when you see my boy friend."

2

Nicole would find out that the Fourth of July party being given by Nicole's grandfather, Thomas Sterling Baker (nicknamed Stein), for his wife, Verna, had been planned in December, back before Christmas, by all of his six sons and two daughters, all coming together from different places to celebrate their mother's birthday on the Bicentennial. Glade Christiansen and his wife, Bonny, came in from Lyman, Wyoming, where Glade was a mine foreman. Danny and Joanne Baker, also from Lyman and the mines, were there, plus

Shelly Baker. Wendell Baker drove in from Mount View, Wyoming. Charley Baker, with his brand-new young woman, Wendy, came over from Toelle, Utah, where Charley now worked at the Army depot, and Kenny, Vicki, and Robbie Baker, from Los Angeles, came in. Boyd, Sterling Baker's father, and his wife, also named Verna, were back from Alaska where they'd been working for some years. Many of the children of all these sons and daughters were present. Some of the grandchildren, in fact, were also grown and married, attending with husbands and wives and kids.

Some began to arrive as early as ten in the morning on the Fourth of July, and the party lasted till eleven that night. Good sunny weather with nearly everybody sitting out in the front yard which was screened from the canyon road by high bushes. The cars went whipping by outside and sometimes would touch the shoulder and throw up gobbets spat-spat against the bushes. That was a sound they knew from childhood.

It was a big yard which wrapped around the front and side of the house, and Stein had gotten the place kind of cleaned up with the lawn swing and lawn chairs in place and all the food set out in the carport on big tables, the barbecued beef, potato salad and baked beans, the potato chips and various jello salads, the soda pop for the kids and the beer, but you still couldn't help but see into the backyard that was to the rear of the side yard, and that was never going to get cleaned up. It had a huge stack of piled-up grass and other cuttings, and a big old rusting billboard laid on top to keep the cuttings from being scattered by the wind, and Stein's old camper that you lifted onto a pickup truck was next to it, and coils of old hose that had gotten half uncoiled, plus the water-soaked swing hanging from the old tackle pulleys in the tree, the overturned wooden dory that needed painting, and a stove-in old red barrel by the rusted sign. There were gardening tools in a leaning shed and a bunch of old damn black rotty tires strewn around an old car body. The farther back you got in Stein's yard, the more you saw a lifetime of living.

Inside the house, Verna must have put every color God gave the world to the furniture — one color for each of her kids was the family joke: yellow, green, blue, purple, red, orange, black, brown, and white in that living room. There was a hi-fi set for the Country-and-

Western, a TV console, couches with different cushions, framed pictures of animals, a BarcaLounger for Stein, and a black leatherette stool with chromium legs for whoever. It probably came out of the bathroom which was white and pink and yellow with big flat rubber flowers pasted to the wallpaper.

It was so large a family, you could hardly count all the members, but nothing compared to the ancestors. On his mother's side, Stein's Mormon grandfather from Kanab, Utah, had been old-style polygamist with six wives and fifty-four children. But you didn't have to go back to Kanab. Stein and Verna had been married since 1929, and there were plenty of memories right here.

It still grated on Stein that starting out as a day laborer and working his way up to be superintendent of the Provo City Water Department, which took 27 years, he still had to quit because the mayor decided to put in an engineering graduate over him. Even had the gall to ask Stein to teach the new boy all about the water business. That was a memory to curdle your good feelings when you give a party to look back over it all.

3

Charley Baker was in charge of the pit barbecue, and he might as well have planned the goddamned party because he had the major share of the job. He'd bought the beef, a big hindquarter, and marinated it three days in a sauce he prepared himself. Then, yesterday morning he'd carried the beef leg over to Spanish Fork, a 100-mile trip from Toelle, after first wrapping it in cheesecloth to keep the moisture in, then wrapped the hell out of it in brown paper, and then in burlap. Of course, he kept it wet all the while he was digging this big goddamn hole in Stein's yard, bigger than a slit trench, and packed it with rocks he had to dig up himself, then got a fire going and watched it burn for hours to get those rocks hot all the way through. You had to get rocks hotter than hell for a pit barbecue to work. The idea was to put the leg in all wrapped up and then — two theories on this — either pack dirt on top, or, as Charley preferred, use a lid so you can get in and spray the burlap every once in a while. That really made for a more juicy tender barbecue.

Now Charley had been planning to stay up all the night before to watch the fire so he planned to take a little nap in the late afternoon of July 3. Went to ask his mother for a room. She had three bedrooms available for company and he'd had the pressure of buying that leg, marinating it, worrying it, trucking it, digging the trench, hefting the rocks — all he wanted was go to bed and take a little nap so he'd be fresh through the night, and his mother said, "You can't go down there and lay on Kenny's bed — you'll sweat on it, and make it stink." Real friendly. It pissed Charley off something terrible. There was his new bride-to-be, Wendy, with him, young as an angel, and Charley was feeling funny enough already because it was the first time he would be seeing all these brothers and sisters without Kathryne — why, if they'd been married a couple more years, everybody would have been coming to Kathryne and his 25th anniversary — but now they were divorced. He was here with Wendy, half his age. And had to sleep in a tent out on the lawn at his mother's suggestion.

His feelings were building. It was too much to ask a man to watch a fire when he was tired and sleepy and had a lot of unhappy memories — nothing to bring out unhappy memories like a fire. Darned if he didn't fall asleep out there. In the early hours of the morning when he woke up, the fire had gone out and the rocks were cold. Well, he kept working to build that fire back, but it was a lost cause. All next day during the party, there was a lot of irritation building because they finally had to hurry the barbecue up on a spit, and that didn't compare in flavor. There was a lot of smoke you couldn't control and soot, and the marinade got charred, instead of there being a juicy tender really deep old-fashioned pit barbecue. Charley couldn't even excuse himself for letting the fire go out. He wasn't about to tell anybody how bad some of those memories had been. Only thing a man could do when memories got *too* bad, was sleep.

It started off because his father mentioned that Nicole was living down the road with a fellow. Of course all through the night Charley was thinking off and on about Nicole. Which got him onto Kathryne and that gave him terrible recollections. Before he got back from

Vietnam, Kathryne used to write loving letters. Things were never better between them. He hadn't been home a week before there was a terrible fight, and Kathryne said, "I wish they'd shipped you back in a box." Hell of a homecoming. It was like the fights they used to have in Germany about him drinking beer, the best goddamn beer in the world for 18 cents, a big stein. How could you keep from getting loaded every night on beer? Then have to come home and face her carping. He was supposed to be a Sergeant. At home, she had him downgraded to fool. He'd still get mad to think of that. Did him no good at all. He could feel that kind of thing getting into his organs and roiling them up.

Then, of course, he would never get over that business of Lee and Nicole. Hell, it was true. They told him as much at the nuthouse when he visited Nicole. The fact of the matter was that he and Nicole were never comfortable with one another.

Watching the flames, deeper woe was coming to him from the fire. April getting raped by three niggers in Hawaii, and nobody to tell him. Going back from Hawaii to Midway, Kathryne had said, April has a real bad case of gas and has to go to the bathroom constantly. Maybe they should wait a day to fly. He told her, We're going to get on that plane. What's a few farts? Made his decision in ignorance, and there was April hurting so bad that he thought he'd have to ask the pilot to turn around and get her to a doctor. When they landed at Midway, Kathryne still kept the news from him. It wasn't until he was out of the Seabees that she admitted being afraid to tell him because there were all those black sailors on the Base. She'd been afraid he'd run amok. It hurt his feelings that she considered him that unstable to go out shooting black people at random. And all that while on Midway, April had been acting unmanageable, and he didn't know why. Had no idea what she'd been through. So he got really hard on her.

April would say she wanted to go out. He'd say, "Did you clean your room?" "Yes." "Okay, go ahead." But when he got around to looking, she hadn't done a thing. So when she came back, he'd tell her, "I'm going to knock the shit out of you." She'd say, "Lay a hand on me and I'll go to the Chaplain." You didn't have to be hot-tempered to kick somebody in the butt for talking back like that. In fact, one time he bumped her pretty hard. She went straight to the Chaplain. Two of them, Catholic and Protestant, both came to the house.

"Well, I understand what you think about me beating her all the time," he said, "and if you want to try socking it to me for child abuse, go ahead. But I haven't been abusing her. I only kicked her, because she threatened me with you." Sad thing was, he had thought she was lying when all the time she was going right out of her head. Told him she'd cleaned her bedroom and thought she did, you know. Didn't know the difference.

Sitting by that big barbecue, watching those rocks heat, these kinds of things were heating up in him. Mike, the sweetest of the kids, also began to go off half-cocked on Midway. He and a little buddy got into the house of the Senior Chief when the man was off the Base on vacation, and dumped all the goddamn food Senior Chief had left for his pet fish into the tank at once. That killed the fish. A real good kid, never been in trouble before, but on Midway he began to go wild.

Then he remembered Sissy living with Barrett up above a bar in Lehi. Kathryne had him half crazy with the idea this fellow Barrett was nothing but a low, dirty heroin pusher who had Sissy strung out. Used to imagine Nicole tied to a bed while Barrett poked needles in her. So he got himself fired up by drinking down in the bar below, figuring his daughter was right above him with a junkie who could be carrying any kind of weapon. Finally, he just walked up the stairs, stepped over a wino or two, and knocked on the door. There was this sweet, pleasant-looking squirt, liked him on sight, but he said all the same, "Barrett, I'm gonna cut your goddamn balls off." Instead the kid just looked at him, smart kid, a lot of potential, cute, with small features, looked just like Sissy, and the kid said, "Well, uh, I know things haven't been going right." Before he got done running himself down, Charley got to feeling sorry for him. Something positive about the boy. Maybe it was the way Barrett looked at him when told there was gonna be a castration party, and said, "If it's going to make you feel better, here I am." Anyway, Charley had to admit once he got a full look at Nicole, "Boy, you don't look bad to me," he had said. "Haven't lost any weight, you know." In fact, Nicole looked terrific. Charley mumbled something about "Your mom said you was here on heroin. Shoot, you're all right." He talked just a little bit then walked down the stairs and left. Felt foolish. Felt double foolish because he turned around at the last and said to Nicole, "Sissy, will you ever forgive me for what I did?" Said that in front of Barrett — he must have been out of his head. But he was brooding over what Lee had told him, and somehow took it personally.

That was when he fell asleep. Woke up in the dawn with the fire out. After that, it was all catch up and lots of smoke in your nostrils.

4

During the morning, tension kept building. Charley finally put the beef on a spit. Everybody was disappointed. Everybody kept telling him how good it was. "Not too burnt?" "No, not too burnt." "Not too sooty?" "Hell, no."

Around this point, his dad mentioned that Sissy was living down the road. Why didn't they invite her? Charley didn't want to, exactly, but he gave a phone call. It took something. He just had never stopped by to see her.

Then he was wondering what kind of hippie she had now. Leave it to Sissy to locate the undesirables. Or should he say the underdogs? Some down-and-out jerk or rotten bastard.

He was getting ready to picture a truly pimply long-haired son of a bitch when Sissy came in with her new guy. Charley thought he looked a little old, but regular enough. In fact, Charley thought they might hit it off if they met in the Army or something.

Right away the Gilmore fellow said he wanted to have a personal talk, so they went to the backyard. Even while Charley was standing there, the boy friend lay down on the grass, put his hands behind his head, and started to talk. First thing he said was real funny. Charley didn't like it. Gilmore said, "You ever feel like killing somebody?"

Charley tried to pass it off as a joke. "Yeah," he said, "I feel like killing my boss all the time, the ignorant son of a bitch." But Gilmore didn't crack a smile. In the silence, Charley felt himself stepping in. "I mean, you're not serious, are you?" he asked. The boy friend said, "Nah, I was just wondering."

It was only when the conversation was over, that Charley started wondering if the remark about wanting to kill somebody had been aimed at him.

This was one evening that just refused to get comfortable. After Sissy came in, damned if one of Charley's brothers didn't point to Wendy and say, "Nicole, meet your new stepmother." Wendy looked embarrassed half to death and Nicole finally said, "*You* are my stepmother?" Wendy said, "I guess so." Nicole looked at her real strange.

Then, Nicole started necking with Gilmore on the grass in front of everybody. Charley saw Verna getting plenty annoyed, she came by pretending to laugh, but said, "Knock it off, you two." It was the way you'd shoo fornicating dogs. Gilmore got up like he'd been shot.

A little later, Charley heard he almost picked a fight with Glade Christiansen who had been sitting under a lilac bush giving a bottle to his youngest boy, a year old. Gilmore came along with a football, asked if he'd like to play catch. Glade said, "I'm trying to get the kid fed." Gary sat down on a stool and started asking questions about what Glade did, but ran out of inquiries. So he looked at Glade and said, "Want to know more about me?" Glade really wanted to be alone feeding the kid. He said, "Not really." Then Gilmore began to act like he was cruising for a bruising. Said to Glade, "You give me the impression you're quite a man." Glade wasn't looking for trouble, and answered, "How do you figure that?" Gilmore said, "Well, you just look like you're a real man." Kept looking him over. Glade didn't see any reason to say anything and Gilmore just walked away.

Then the fellow must have had words with Nicole. He took off suddenly. Charley could hardly blame him. Understood the feeling. Like when you went to church once in five years, and the pewholders looked you over. Enough to make you buy a pew.

Afterward, Charley heard that Gary went in the house, knocked over a stool, fell down in the bathroom and Stein finally had to say, "Your friend looks pretty intoxicated." To which Nicole, just a dreamboat, said, "He'll probably be all right." Anyway, Gary took off. Nicole looked like she didn't care. She was talking away to her relatives for once.

Charley began to feel like he was missing every conversation and that got him to brooding again how he had been pushed out of the Service three years short of his pension. A terrible business to think about 'cause he felt April had done it to him with her mental difficulties, which, after Midway, just got worse and worse. One time she cut her wrists, another night, an overdose. Whenever Charley left the family to go overseas, he had to ask for a leave to come back because April had flipped out again. Then he was out with Battalion, doing rugged duty on Okinawa, and they were kind of depending on him, but he had to go home twice. Emergency leaves. What with the problem looking like it would continue, they recommended he get out. Charley said, "I don't want out." They gave him a discharge. He refused to sign it. Finally they just handed the thing to him and said, "Buddy, get on the plane." Like that. He only had three more years to go. They really slipped it to him.

It was that kind of night. He finally asked Nicole to call Kathryne. Maybe Angel, the youngest child, could come over and stay with him tonight. He always felt upset about Angel. He was away from her just now when she was 6, and she needed him. At that point, Verna started to give him hell. Said there were too many children around. For a woman who had raised eight kids, and couldn't count how many grandchildren, she sure didn't like little ones. Then his father started to get on him. "You ain't staying here. The kids ain't staying here." They got in a fight. His father might be 68, but Charley was tempted to kick his butt if he hadn't been so old. Actually did give him a push. Then he grabbed Wendy and left without speaking.

A true bummer for a Fourth of July Bicentennial celebration.

5

At first, Nicole was hating her relatives and feeling double-loyal to Gary, necking with him on the grass. But she lost respect when he jumped so fast after Verna said, "Knock it off."

In a funny way, Nicole began to feel half-ass proud of her family. So many strong cockeyed people, and there was Gary getting drunk on red wine, and feeding pills to her cousins. He was really looking on the battered side, and the goatee he was starting still looked like the three hairs of a goat. She wasn't that sad when he left.

After all the trouble at Grand Central, she had never loved him more, but that was for a night, and another night. Now he was back on beer and Fiorinal. She just didn't know how loyal she still felt. She was having thoughts about another man.

Mr. Clean was in her life. She hadn't told Gary about him. He was too recent. Roger Eaton was his name, a superclean supersweet executive dude over at Utah Valley Mall and he had come into her life this unbelievable way. She got a letter from some fellow who never signed his name but said he would pay $50 if she slept with him Wednesday night. Could she leave her front door light on for a signal?

She showed the letter to Gary. He tore it up. Said he'd kill the son of a bitch. She forgot about it. Part of the weirdness of things.

But a couple of weeks later, this really good-looking well-built fellow, blue eyes and nice dark brown hair, came up to her at a gas station and introduced himself. He was the one who wrote the letter, he said, and he wanted to buy her a Coke. She talked to him a little that day, saw him for coffee, and then really went to him for help after the fight with Gary on the highway, when she discovered that the scuffle in the car had left bruises all over her body. That got her so upset she went directly over to Roger Eaton's office. He was sympathetic so she went to see him again just yesterday after she went to visit Gary at work and found him drinking beer in place of his lunch.

She had never known a fellow who wore a suit to the job every day, and it tickled her. The first thought to go through her head tonight when Gary had to leave the party, was that Roger Eaton had told her to use his home phone for emergencies. She could call him tonight. But that might spoil whatever little thing was there. It had been so long since she was able to think about one special or sexy quality in a fellow she liked instead of having to live with the whole thing — sweat, habits, gross-out, all. So she didn't call. Just talked to her father awhile, then went home.

Gary came in later. He had gone on drinking at Fred's Lounge with a couple of heavies in the Sundowners and now he was talking of getting a motorcycle. Told them he was going to rip one off. Then he looked kind of sheepishly at Nicole. Admitted they had almost laughed out loud at him. The one thing, they explained, a cop always looked over was a *motorcycle!* A hot motorcycle lasted about as long as an ice cube in your ass. Still, they were real dudes — equal to himself. He looked forward, he said, to doing business with them.

He was like a 19-year-old kid. Into bikes. Happy that bikers liked him. It softened her enough for things to get sweet again. What with meal, drink, and relatives in the flesh, the party had left a little sugar after all. So they started to get it on. Then Gary had a time getting it up. She couldn't think of how she had once been so sure it would improve.

Gary always put the blame on prison. All those years he had to get his rocks off on nude pictures instead of learning on a real woman. She got mad enough tonight to tell him it was bullshit. He was drinking too much, using Fiorinal too much. Gary defended the Fiorinal. "I don't want to make love with a headache," he said. "I have headaches all the time, and Fiorinal relieves it."

She sat there with her anger pushed in like a spring. Dead and wet, he was going to give it a go. Don't start what you can't finish, she told him. Be straight.

The work began. Now they wouldn't get to bed till four, and he'd be up at six. Then he took some speed, and it took effect. He got hard as a horn and wanted to fuck. She was so tired she could only think of sleep. But they were doing it. On and on. He couldn't come.

Lying there, she said it clearly to herself, "He's a bad package."

6

In the second week of July, on a hot morning, she found Jim Hampton over at her mother's house. After the way he had played around with April, Nicole didn't feel too good about him, but he had his little sister and brother in tow, and she kind of enjoyed spending a day with somebody else for once. They just drove around and even stopped at her place in Spanish Fork so she could pick up something for the kids. Then she returned Hampton to her mother's, and drove her own car back. With all that cruising, she must have driven close to a hundred miles that day.

By the time she got in, Gary was already back from work and looking at the motor of his car. She sat down on the front step. There was a silence between them you could push.

He finally asked her what she'd been doing. I, Nicole said, have been sitting on my ass over at my mother's. I didn't have enough gas to come back, so I had to stay there all the goddamn day. "Yes," she told him, "I've been sitting on my ass." Well, he told her, something feels different in the house than when I left this morning. Were you back here today?

Yeah, I got back here today, she answered. I thought you were sitting on your ass over at your mother's all day, he said. She gave a smile and said, That's exactly what I said.

Gary walked over from the car, looking as casual as if he was going into the house, and when he passed, he slapped her front-handed across the face. Pretty sneaky. Her head was ringing like an alarm clock.

Nicole felt like she deserved it. Rudeness that came out of no-where was something he couldn't handle. Still, this was the second time he had hit her. She could feel a lot of ugliness beginning to collect in her.

Next day, she was able to let some of it out. Since she didn't always have money for diapers, or laundry soap, and there wasn't always clean underwear, she liked to let the kids play naked in the summer. Some of the neighbors must have gotten uptight.

On this day, while Jeremy was on the grass of somebody's lawn, and the rest of the kids were sitting on the edge of the ditch between the sidewalk and the street, their feet in the water, a cop car pulled up and hollered something. Nicole couldn't believe what she was seeing. The cop drove no faster than a walking pace right up to her house, and came to her door, and started laying down some unbelievable shit, like you know, your kids are in danger of their lives playing in the ditch down there. Your little boy could drown. Nicole said, "Mister, you don't know what you're talking about. My little boy wasn't anywhere near that water. He doesn't have one drop on his body." He didn't.

The cop started to say the neighbors had been phoning in complaints about her not taking proper care of the kids. "Get off my property," said Nicole, "get your fucking ass down the road."

She knew she could say anything so long as she stayed in her house. The cop stood outside making threats about welfare, and she shut the door in his face. He hollered, I better not see those kids outside. She swung the door open again.

Nicole said, "Those kids are going to play outside all the goddamn day, and you better not touch them, or I'll shoot you."

The cop looked at her. He had an expression like, "Now what do I do?" In the middle of her anger, she could see his side — it was such a crazy situation for a cop. Threatened by a lady. Then she closed the door, and he drove off, and Gary got up from bed. These hot days the bed had been moved up right by the living-room window.

Suddenly she realized what those last couple of minutes must have done to him. She had completely forgotten about the guns. The sight of that cop stopping at their house was going to add up to a lot more beer and Fiorinal.

7

Next morning, he was over at Kathryne's house. She thought he was real abrupt. "Come outside," he said. Kathryne felt scared. "Can't you tell me here?" "No," he said, "outside."

She didn't like the way he was acting, but it was daylight. So she went out and Gary said, "I've got something in my car I want to leave here for a little while," and he went over to the Mustang and took a diaper bag out of the trunk and moved it over to the back of her car. Kathryne said, "What have you got, Gary?" and he answered, "Guns."

"Guns?" she said. "Yes," he said, "guns." She asked where he got them. "Where do you think? I stole them." Kathryne just said, "Oh." Right there on the back deck of her car he started bringing them out for examination. "I'd like," said Gary, "to leave them here." "My God, Gary," said Kathryne, "I don't think you better. I can't keep them here."

"I'll be back," Gary said, "when I get off work. I just want to leave them in a safe place for a little while."

She couldn't believe the way he had set them out on the trunk of the car. If any of the neighbors looked through the window, they wouldn't believe what they were seeing.

Deliberately, he took each gun and described it to her like it was a rare beauty. One was a .357 Magnum this-or-that, another was a .22 Automatic Browning, then a Dan Weston .38 something-or-other. Kathryne just said, "Gary, I don't know much about guns."

"How do you like this one?" he asked.

"Oh, they're nice, they're all nice, you know." She said, "What are you going to do with them, Gary?"

"A couple of dudes are going to buy them," he said.

By now, all the guns were unwrapped. He said, "I gave Nicole one to protect herself. Pretty little over-and-under Derringer. I want you to have this one."

"I don't need it, Gary. I really don't want it."

"I want you to," he said. "You're Nicole's mother."

"God, Gary," said Kathryne, "I've already got a gun."

"Well," he said, "I want you to have this Special. It's just not safe for two women living out here alone like you and your sister."

She tried to explain that she already had her husband's Magnum. But Gary said, "That's too big a gun. You shouldn't even attempt to shoot it."

Now he laid the guns in her car trunk. Kathryne let him know that she definitely didn't want to be driving around with them. So he said, "Let me leave them in the house." Told her he'd return at five o'clock. Well, she declared, she wouldn't be home then.

That was all right, he'd just come and get them. With that, he carried the diaper bag into the house, and put the guns behind the couch, all seven or eight of them. Then he wrapped the Special in an old cloth, and put it under her bedroom mattress.

That evening when she and Kathy got home, they ran to look behind the couch and yes, the guns were gone.

8

During the day, while Gary was at work, Barrett came by in his truck and Nicole drove up with him to the Canyon. Sunny and Peabody left the pickup and went out to play. Before they could even light a stick, his pants were off, hers were off — they were getting it on. She heard herself say, "Gary is crazy. We might end up dead." Then she told Jim, "If anything happens, I want you to know that I love you." She really did as she said it.

Gary came home in a sloppy old windbreaker with the sleeves cut off. His pants were a mess, and he was half drunk. He told her to go over with him to Val Conlin's to examine the truck. She asked him to get cleaned up first. She didn't really want to be seen with him. He looked like he slept out in the yard.

Gary kept talking to that man Conlin as if he had the money. It was a real irritant.

Next, he wanted to stop off and see Craig Taylor. That was the dumbest. Craig's wife, Julie, was in the hospital. Now Nicole's kids and the Taylor kids were carrying on all over while Gary got to play chess with Craig. Whooped when he beat him.

Then Gary started to tee off on Val Conlin for making him wait on the truck. "I'll wreck the place and a couple of his cars too," he said. "I'm going to kick them windows in." It was like opening a bottle that smelled awful.

Craig just listened like an owl. He had the biggest shoulders she'd ever seen for a guy with an owl's face. Never said anything. Just blinked.

Gary said he hated to watch TV. He especially hated the police shows. Nicole yawned.

As they were leaving, Gary asked Craig, "What do you think of me?"
"Well, it seems like you're trying," said Craig. "Just have a few breaks and you'll be all right."

Going up from Craig's to Kathryne's, right on the long road to her mother's house, darn if the Mustang didn't stall again. Gary got so pissed he broke the windshield.

Simply reared back with his feet and kicked the windshield. It cracked.

That got the kids upset. Nicole didn't say two words. She got out and helped him push the car to get it started. It still didn't go. Then somebody came along to give them a shove. They drove in silence for a couple hundred yards.

For a week she had been trying to say that they could live in separate places and see each other time to time. Now, when it came to it, Gary spoke. "I'm taking you to your mother's house," he said, "I don't want to ever see your face again."

He dropped her off with the kids as easily as going down to the grocery for a six-pack. She thought she'd be glad, but she wasn't. It didn't feel like it was over in the right way.

In twelve hours, Gary showed up at Kathryne's house. Just ahead of lunch. He wanted her to come back. He was drunk even as he asked her. She said she wouldn't. She said, I want to think about it awhile.

He didn't want her to think. He wanted her to agree. Still, it amazed her. He didn't force a thing. After he left, though, she decided it had been too easy. By tomorrow he would be coming over every few hours. So she called Barrett and asked if she could stay at his pad. Nicole made it clear she didn't want to hang in. Just wanted a bed for a couple of days.

If she was going to disappear from Gary, there had to be better places than Barrett's. She went looking for an apartment. The next day, Barrett found one in Springville. Hardly anybody knew the address, and she made him swear to keep it secret.

Now she was living five miles from the house in Spanish Fork. If Gary took the back highway to Provo instead of the Interstate, he would pass two streets from her place.

Barrett wanted them to try one more time. One more trip of the mind. When she was young and used to read animal stories, Kathryne had told her about reincarnation. Made it sound like a fairy tale. That was when Nicole made the choice to come back as a little white bird. Now she thought that if she didn't straighten out the way she lived with men, she was going to come back ugly and no man would ever want to look at her.

CHAPTER II

Ex-husbands

1

Barrett had this tendency to think of himself as small. In fact, his mom and dad used to tell him that when he was born, he looked no bigger than a kitten you put in a shoebox. Now he was five-ten and might weigh 145, but he never had the habit of thinking of himself as other than small-sized and self-sufficient. Like a kitten. During the stretch when he had his first romance with Nicole, he remembered spending one week all by himself in a yellow cell in the nuthouse. Painted pale yellow like a kid's nursery, only it was a cell. He remembered taking his socks, rolling them up, and throwing them at the wall, throwing them and catching them. It was the only thing he had to do. He got along.

On the other hand, he wasn't built for the heaviest punishment. Not with his long pointed nose and his fine pale brown hair, soft as a girl's. His hair could pick up bad vibrations from a stranger he passed on the highway. So Barrett had some idea usually what to expect. That was just as well considering the horror right now on his hands of helping Nicole hide out from that old scroungy madman, Gary Gilmore. Here was one love affair caught Barrett by surprise. He was horrified by Nicole's bad taste. Only once before had he seen her exhibit such real lack of judgment.

Barrett had been through everything with Nicole. Seen a lot of dudes come and go, studs, jocks, freaks, animals, characters you could almost call cripples, but they always had something. If they weren't good looking, strong, well hung, then they had something you could relate to, some good trick. Barrett knew Nicole was a beautiful person and really independent, and if you had the misery to be stuck in love with her like Barrett, then you had to live with who she would come up with next. Had to be there when she was ready to quit the guy.

Barrett wasn't built for heavy encounters. That was part of his understanding of himself. Yet the bravest, heaviest things he'd done in his life happened because of Nicole. For example: helping her move out of Joe Bob's house was scary. All those hours with a borrowed truck outside — why, Joe Bob could have come back from work to check on her. Barrett had a gun that day, but Joe Bob was heavy enough to walk through a gun.

Yes, all those hours moving her furniture (which was Barrett's furniture when they had lived together) was some of the tightest time Barrett ever put in, but he got her away, every last lamp shade, and Sunny and Jeremy up in the front seat with them, yes, saved Nicole's buns one more time, and she even went back to living with him when he found the house in Spanish Fork.

He had been working then. Concrete pumping. Had been looking for an occupation to get him out of dealing. Thought concrete pumping might be it, but found it a hard attitude to keep loyal to. Straight people only had to take one look at him and his flowing hippie threads, suede buckskin-style jacket with fringe, long hair, little mustache, and they would categorize him right at the bottom. It was hard to drive somebody else's truck, and get paid a couple of pennies while making the other fellow a couple of hundred bucks. That always got Barrett down. Dealing, you were your own businessman at least.

Still, he had been trying to make a straight living and prove a point to Nicole. Driving from Spanish Fork and working at concrete pumping in American Fork, he was thereby damn well commuting from one end of Utah County to the other, close to 60 miles a day. Commuting in morning traffic was as straight as you could get. That was the point he wished to make. But Nicole and him started hassling about all the things in the past. Her sexual relations with other men bothered him. Couldn't get them out of his head.

Right from the beginning in Spanish Fork their sex life wasn't like it used to be. Not that feeling of love anymore. Times he'd say to her, "You don't even want me." He might just as well have had an open hole in him. To be without Nicole was living in the pits. She didn't realize how he felt — if she could just now and again feel his pain. She didn't know how beautiful it could be with her, if she was in the mood to have it beautiful. Nobody could give you a feeling you were wanted, like Nicole could give it. Like she was the seducer, and it was heavenly places when you got that goodness from her. When she cut it off, Barrett knew the pits.

So even with the house in Spanish Fork — $75 a month — he couldn't help it, he split. Went up to Wyoming for a few weeks, and did what he always did on a split, which is, try to enjoy his free, make the most of life without daily hassles. But he couldn't get on the good side of his free where you could feel kind of dapper. Instead he carried Nicole around like a load. So, first opportunity, he hit her up with a surprise visit from Wyoming, and pulled in front of the house in Spanish Fork about eleven o'clock on a cold February night.

Since another fellow's car was out front, Barrett came in by the back. Nicole and the dude were in the bathroom together naked. The fellow was sitting on the laundry hamper, a weird-looking dirty guy, Clyde Dozier. Barrett knew him in passing. A disgusting nonentity. Barrett didn't get violent, you know, he just went in the kitchen adjacent, and Clyde came and put his clothes on, and started to apologize and say it wasn't Nicole's fault. Barrett said, "Save yourself some problems, Clyde. Get out of here before I get mad." Barrett might not be that tough, but he had a few connections after all. Clyde left, and Nicole started saying, like, "I'm not your old lady. You went to Wyoming and left me, you know. I can do whatever I want to do."

Well, she had a bed made up on the kitchen floor and Barrett got it on. Didn't know why he wanted to have sex at that point, but he figured she gave it to him because he'd get violent if she resisted. Next morning, he wasn't mad. It was just funny more than anything else, you know, there on the kitchen floor with his old lady, saying,

"God, couldn't you pick somebody a little better than Clyde?" He really wanted to get together with her. So he gave up Wyoming and took a place in Lindon. Dropped over two or three times a week until she told him to stay away. One time he went over and another low scroungy dude was there, Freson (what a name!) Phelps. Barrett stayed away a long time before he went over to Spanish Fork again.

On this occasion, different things were around. Different furniture. Somebody new had moved in. He sat and had a cup of coffee with her. Before he could even start talking, Gilmore came in. The first time he heard about the fellow was when she introduced them.

Barrett's impression was that here was one more old scroungy dude. He didn't look right. More bad taste! He was wearing cutoffs and his legs were too white. Gilmore looked a lot older than her. Barrett didn't feel hurt or anything, just kind of disgust, you know, like I don't believe this.

He went on talking with Nicole. Gilmore never said a word, just sat at the kitchen table. He seemed bothered. In a little while he got up and went to the front room. At that point, Barrett nodded at Nicole, and they went outside. Sunny and Jeremy were playing, and they sat near them, and Nicole said Gilmore was an ex-con. Then she went back to the house. Barrett was left outside playing with the kids. Pretty soon, the kids started saying the same things over and over. It was like they had a crowbar in your collarbone and were prying you open. "Pop, poop, pop, poop," they'd say, and giggle.

He went down to his truck, and took off. He could really feel his skinny butt bouncing in the cab.

Then he met Gilmore the second time. Dropped over to visit and Gary was out to the store. While Barrett was talking to Nicole by the apple tree, Gilmore came back. Didn't say, Get the hell out, but he sure acted like his return was the good cue to leave. So Barrett stood up, and Nicole went right into the house. That left Barrett to walk out to the street alone. Just then Gilmore came through the front door to confront him on the sidewalk.

He said, "I want to tell you something. I accept the fact that you're Sunny's father, but Nicole is mine." Barrett said, "Look, buddy, you can have her. I don't want her." These words gave Gilmore a bad look, a real bad-dog look. Gilmore said, "You don't have to insult her."

At that point Barrett got a scared feeling. He was used to seeing Nicole with other men. He'd watched her with other men. What else was there to say? You *can* have her. He certainly couldn't keep them from having her.

Besides, it would do no good for Gilmore to know his true feelings. That would wake Gilmore up. Barrett said, "I wasn't trying to insult her. Nicole don't want me, and I don't want her. I just wanted you to know." He got in his truck, and right there on the road, cruising along, he felt hope. It was the sound of Gilmore saying, "Nicole is mine." They got to talking like that, and they lost her. She didn't want to be owned for long.

After that, riding around, wheeling high off a Thai stick, Barrett might drive by her house. If Gary's car was out in front, he would not stop. If the scene was right, he would visit a little with Nicole, feel her out.

2

One time, Rosebeth answered the door and said Gary was at work, and Nicole was away with the kids. It was the first time Barrett ever saw Rosebeth, but he walked in like it was his house. After all, everything he owned was in there. Gary and Nicole, said Rosebeth, would be gone the whole day for sure. There was nice warm weather in the room.

Jim was sitting in the chair, and the girl was lying on the living-room bed that served for a couch. He thought she was pleasantly plump, had a real sweet baby-fat, but too young and virgin to fool around with. When she got up, however, to lift a blanket off the bed, he decided to get beside her, and they started to kiss. Didn't take a minute for her to say, "Now, let's get undressed." "Okay," he said, "I'll go for that." They took off their clothes and lay on the bed, and she said, "Let me suck it." Barrett said, "Don't let me stop you."

All her doing, you know. Barrett laid back and she spun herself around and popped it right on his face — he had no choice. She didn't really know how, actually hurt him with her teeth. All the same she got pretty warm. But her clit wasn't sensitive, you know, he couldn't make her flinch.

Still, she got pretty warm. He turned her around and she had an expectant look. Only he couldn't get in. She was a virgin, he found out, and he was hurting her.

"Gary only wants me to do things with him, you know," she was saying, "Gary wouldn't like this, you know." Told him how the three of them fooled around. Barrett just kept flicking her clit.

It seemed to open her. He turned around and slipped it in, and it went right in, really good, nice and warm, no movement at all, that's all he needed. That was it, you know.

He put his clothes on and she got up and put her clothes on. Hadn't been in her more than ten seconds. She hadn't really done anything, but she had really nice breasts. He got a phone number from her. A tremendous deal. All free. Did it with his back open to Gilmore.

By the next time he happened to stop, Nicole said she wanted to go for a ride. He took her up to the Canyon and Sunny and Jeremy went out and played. Barrett got seduced right in the truck. That's what happened that day.

He thought it was 'cause she loved him again, because she had special feelings. She told him afterward she still loved him, all that stuff. Then they came down from the canyon, and he took her home.

It sure flared up his love for her. It made him miss her more. Sex was like a sacred thing to him, a way to express a feeling.

The next day, she called him up. "I'm pretty upset," she said, "pretty down." Gary had become very dominating.

When Barrett went over, she was sad and really depressed and he just loved her. He stood naked with her, gave her the attention she needed and told her that he'd get her out of this mess.

Once she was in his dinky little fleabag motel room, it didn't take but one night to know they needed more space. He went to see a friend who owned a couple of apartment houses in Springville and said, Hey, let me work on your swimming pool for the rent. The fellow went for that and moved them into an apartment on Third West in Springville. That same day, while Gilmore was on his job, they got the furniture from Spanish Fork and brought it over.

It was worrisome doing it. Nicole let him hold a .22 Magnum Derringer over-and-under that Gary had given her. This scene was even heavier than Joe Bob. Barrett noticed a piece of paper tacked up against the wall, saying, "Where are you, girl?"

He had the gun in his back pocket, loaded. But he kept thinking of Gilmore's other guns. If the man came home, they would have a shootout right there. Even after they were moved to the apartment, nothing let up. Nicole kept saying, You don't know Gary, he's dangerous. Barrett carried that gun.

This trip, Nicole was giving him sex like a professional. Not taking money, but like she thought he'd done a favor, so he deserved it back. It certainly wasn't one of their good periods. She wasn't into orgasms very regularly. With all he knew about her, it all the same took a few days for Barrett to figure out that Nicole was seeing somebody else.

3

On the Tuesday night that Gary broke up with Nicole, he came back to Craig's house and spent a quiet evening. "She's out of my life," he said. Next morning, soon as he woke up, he talked of getting back with her. Took a Browning .22 Automatic out of his car, and asked

Craig to hold it. Craig did. Wanted to mollify him. Keep him off the deep end.

On the way to work, Gary asked if Craig knew anybody who would buy the Automatic. When Craig said he didn't, Gary said, "You can have it." Craig wasn't certain whether Gary was giving it, or letting him hold it handy.

Spencer asked how the windshield got broke, and when Gary said he kicked it, Spencer asked, "What for?" Gary said he was mad at Nicole. "Well, why didn't you kick *her*?" Spencer said. "You know you got to have a windshield to pass a safety inspection. That kick cost you $50." Gary said he didn't really care.

This got Spence mad. Gary owed him money after all. So Spence asked again if he had the driver's license. When Gary said no, Spence said he must have been lying all along, and they would have to alter their program a little. But Gary's head seemed to be somewhere else. He asked what Spence thought of his buying a pickup truck. He had, Spencer decided, an awfully large ego.

During the day, Gary got the keys to the white truck from Val Conlin and drove it to the shop for Spence to approve.

It was a '68 or '69 Ford. McGrath thought it was seriously overpriced. Gary said he really didn't care, he wanted it. Spencer said, "I do care. You're asking me to lay out $1,700 for a vehicle that is only worth $1,000. It's unfair. You don't have a driver's license. If you wreck that thing, or somebody steals it, if you get into a fight and they arrest you and put you in jail, or if you can't in any way make the payments on it, then I have to pay off. You should think real serious about what you're asking me to do." That didn't bother Gary. There was no doubt in his mind, he told Spence, that he was going to pay for that pickup. He did not think Spence should ever be concerned about losing a cent.

That night Gary went looking in the bars for Nicole and then went home. When he could not sleep, he got in his car and drove all the way to Sterling Baker's new place.

Sterling had moved from Provo to a town called Lark near Salt Lake City. It was late when Gary pulled in. It had spooked him, he explained, to stay in Spanish Fork without Nicole. He had talked to her at Kathryne's today, he told them, and she wanted to stay apart. He couldn't shake off the idea he had lost her. Gary looked so sad that no matter the hour, both Sterling and Ruth Ann had to feel sorry.

Gary began to talk about reincarnation. After death, he said, he was going to start all over again. Have the kind of life he always wished he had. He talked about it as if it was so certain, so real, that Sterling got confused and thought Gary was talking about an actual place like moving bag and baggage up to Winnipeg, Canada.

In the morning, Gary phoned in sick to work, and spent the morning driving around with Ruth Ann looking for Nicole.

They searched a lot of streets in Springville. Somehow, Gary felt she was there. They dropped in on Sue Baker, but she didn't know, she said, where Nicole might be. There was a smell of diapers in Sue's house and she looked miserable. Didn't know where Rikki was; didn't know where Nicole was; didn't know anything. Ruth Ann began to get sorry for Gary. She had never seen a man suffer so much over a woman. He must have checked the laundromat five times.

Toward the middle of the afternoon, Ruth Ann went back to Lark, and Gary showed up at work. He had hardly picked up a tool before there was a call from Nicole.

"Are you drunk?" she asked.
"I'm stone sober," he said.
She was telephoning to tell him that she had just moved her furniture out of the house in Spanish Fork, but he could stay there the next few days until the rent was up. She didn't think they'd rent to him after that.

Could they get together? he asked. She said she did not think so. One of them might kill the other.

4

To her surprise, Kathryne felt like she wanted to cry. Gary came in so pathetic. Just kind of sat. He put a carton of cigarettes and a box of Pampers on the table, and said, "She'll probably be needing these." There was a silence, then he said, "Would you do something for me?" Kathryne said, "Well, yes, if I can." "Will you give her this picture of me? That's the best one I could find. It's not very good, but it's the best I could find." Kathryne looked. Gary was standing in the snow wearing a blue windbreaker. She thought it had probably been taken in prison. He was looking young and tough, and he'd written on the back "I love you." After she lay the photograph down, Gary said, "I've got to be going."

When Sissy dropped by later that evening, she just glanced at the photo, made an *umph* sound, and threw it on the cupboard shelf. Later Kathryne put it at the back of the dish closet where it would be safe from the kids and the jam and the peanut butter.

Toward evening, Gary went to sit with Brenda and Johnny. Their patio wasn't much of a garden spot, more like a shed with pale green corrugated plastic roofing that let light through, and a couple of wrought-iron chairs and dirty old canvas camp chairs. Brenda never tried to fix her yard too much, but it was nice to have a drink there in the dark.

Not only was Gary having his emotional pains but Johnny would soon be hurting. He had to go into the hospital for a hernia operation. It might not take long, but it wasn't going to be fun. Brenda would have liked a joke about the doctor not clipping any extra meat down there, but that, unfortunately, was not Gary's mood.

The white and yellow socks he was wearing looked in better taste than usual, so Brenda remarked, "I like those socks, coz." He stared at her and said, "They're Nicole's." Looked like he was going to cry.

It was awful. Brenda could feel that empty house in Spanish Fork. "I can still smell her perfume," Gary said. It was obvious he was in that advanced kind of suffering where he could hardly keep a thought to himself.

"I've got to find her," he said.

"Honey, this kind of thing takes time," said Brenda. "Maybe Nicole needs a couple of days." "I can't wait," he said. "Will you help me find her?" "It don't work that way," Brenda said. "If a woman don't want to talk to you, she'll kill you first."

Usually no matter what Gary might be feeling, he liked to seem the picture of relaxation. Today he was on the edge of his chair. It was like the air was being eaten by the nervousness he felt. She didn't want to think of his stomach. Shreds. She thought his goatee looked awful.

"This is the first time I've experienced a pain I can't take," he said. "I used to be able to handle anything that came up, didn't matter how bad, but it's tougher out here. Everybody's going about their business. Where is Nicole?"

A dread went into the air with the evening. Brenda could almost hear Gary listening to Nicole with other men. They kept drinking. After a couple of hours he passed out on them. In the morning, he went to work.

"Why look so hard," Spencer asked, "for a woman who doesn't want to get back with you? Leave her alone. She knows where you are."

"I'm going to paint my car," said Gary.

He started to drive the Mustang into the shop, but didn't raise the sliding door high enough. So he banged it going in. Bent it. Spencer didn't even groan. Gary could have had the car painted for fifty bucks, and now it would cost three hundred or more to get the door working right once more. For the present Spence just tied a rope to the stove-in part and winched the dent back to usable condition. The shop door looked like hell.

During lunch, Gary drove to Spanish Fork and walked through the empty rooms. Next, he came back to Springville and visited the laundromat. Stopped to visit Sue Baker. She hadn't heard from Nicole.

"Sissy," said Kathryne, "just doesn't like drinking. She won't put up with it no matter how much she cares about you. She could really love you," Kathryne said, "and I think maybe she does, but you have to make up your mind. What means the most, drinking or Nicole?"

"I'll give up the drinking," he said, "if she'll come back to me. I'll give it up."

They sat there and Kathryne felt close. "Yes, I'll give up the drinking," he said.

He went on to tell Kathryne how brilliant Nicole was, what guts she had. He had never met a girl with such guts. Told Kathryne about the time Nicole went over to Pete Galovan and warned him that Gary meant more to her than life. "She'd have done it too," Gary said.

"Yes," Kathryne said, "she just might."

They sat there and Gary looked at Kathryne in a way to touch her right to the center of her heart. He said, "You know, here I am, thirty-five years old, and I've only known three women in my life. Isn't that ridiculous?"

Kathryne just laughed. She said, "You're two up on me, Gary. I'm almost forty and I've known only one man."

They just seemed to get along. She felt so sorry for him. He said, "I feel left out. Sometimes I don't even understand what people are talking about." Drank a couple of beers and said, "When Nicole gets back, tell her I love her. Will you do that for me?"

"I will, Gary," Kathryne said.

"I promise you, I'll quit," Gary said. "I'll leave the booze alone. I'm a mean rotten bastard when I drink."

A few hours later he called to find out if Nicole had been by. "No," said Kathryne, "I haven't seen her." In fact, she hadn't.

That evening, Gary went by Spencer McGrath's house with the guns. "I want to leave them as security so you can co-sign that truck."

"Number one," said Spencer, "I don't need the guns. Two, I'm not going to co-sign. Take them with you."

"I'm going to leave them," Gary said. "I want you to know I'm real serious."

Spencer decided to ask how he got them. Gary said a friend of his in Portland owed him money, so had given over the guns. He mentioned the guy's name. Soon as Gary was gone, Spence copied the serial numbers, and made a few calls to see if any sporting goods store had been broken into. Couldn't find one. Never called as far south as Spanish Fork, however.

Gary stayed with Sterling and Ruth Ann again, and spent all day Saturday driving between Lark and Spanish Fork. He dropped by to see Kathryne, but the Elders from the Church were visiting, so through the open door he called, "Where is she?" "I don't have any idea where she is," Kathryne said sharply, and knew Gary didn't believe her. You could tell by the way he took off mad.

At midnight, Gary drove out to Spanish Fork one more time to see if Nicole might be there in the house without furniture, and he walked through the empty rooms, and took out a little more of his clothing and put it in the trunk of the Mustang. He was living out of the Mustang by now. Then he drove to the Silver Dollar and had a couple of drinks.

Behind the bar, tacked to the mirror, were some cartoons. One said: HAPPINESS IS A TIGHT PUSSY. It showed a fat woman with breasts hanging out of her halter. She had a big wrinkled belly button and was sitting on top of a mountain of empty beer cans.

Another drawing showed a man with a face of pure misery sitting at a desk. Underneath was printed:

I'M SO HAPPY HERE
I COULD JUST SHIT.

GERMAN SAUSAGES STEAMED IN BEER   50 CENTS
HAPPINESS IS A COLD BEER
NO CHECKS CASHED
NO CREDIT

When he finished his glass, he went out and got into his truck and stopped off at Vern's. They were all asleep so he went down to the basement and found a cot.

Sunday morning he went to the hospital to visit John who was recovering from the hernia operation. John's dad, who was a Mormon Bishop, was there, and he was a little on the straitlaced side. Gary came up wearing a dirty white T-shirt, old slacks, tennis shoes, and, by God, a joke tie that came down to his knees — it had very wide alternating stripes of maroon, gold, and white. On top of his head he had a little hat. He sat around and tried to make conversation with the Bishop. Nothing much got said.

5

The apartment in Springville was not as nice as the house in Spanish Fork. It was just a two-room cinder-block apartment in a two-tier development of cheap apartments on a little old side street. There were kids around, and dogshit on the stairs and in the parking lot. The day she moved in, three rotting mattresses were leaning against the side of the building, and an overturned tricycle was lying in a mud puddle. The doors to the apartments were plywood, and her bathtub had been painted blood red by the last tenant. Still, she had a view from her balcony. Just two blocks away, the town came to an end, and the land went up into the mountains. She was free of Gary. Free to feel a lot of fear. Her breath was heavy.

Without her vacuum cleaner, Nicole couldn't keep the new apartment clean, so on Sunday, she had to go back to Spanish Fork to pick it up. As she came to the house his car wasn't there at all.

Still she had a feeling that Gary was inside, and the Mustang was stashed around the corner, and, in fact, when she walked up, the door was open, and she could hear water running in the tub. Gary's clothes were on the living-room floor right next to her vacuum cleaner which was also placed in the middle of the room as if he had set it out for her. So she picked it up, and carried it to the trunk of her car. Then she came back for the accessories.

She could have rushed but somehow she didn't want to sneak out with the last parts while he was still in the tub. Maybe she would have been more afraid if she didn't have the gun, but she waited. She wanted to see into his eyes. It almost felt good waiting. Like the end of a lot of tension might be near.

He didn't look vengeful when he came out of the tub, just all worn out. Right off, he told her he loved her, and asked if she loved him. She said no. He began to hug her. She tried to push him away. Nicole wasn't really scared, but something nauseating got into her like she was going to pass out if there wasn't some fresh air soon. She said, "I have to sit down."

They rested on the outside steps. She told him she couldn't live with him anymore. They sat. She had to get away. After a few minutes, she took the kids and got into the car. But now he wouldn't let her go. He put his hands through the open window and held her. She opened her purse, took out the gun and pointed it at him.

It was a .22 Magnum and he had told her it was capable of putting a hole in you like a .45. Gary stood there for one minute after another. Just looked at her. He didn't move. She knew if he reached for the gun, she would pull the trigger.

Then he said, "Go ahead and shoot." She said, "Get away from my car." He wasn't about to get away, he told her. Finally she put the gun in her purse. "You left the accessories for the Electrolux," he said. "Come back and get them." That was one thing he had not ripped off — the Electrolux. A long time ago he had missed the first payment on his Mustang to buy her the Electrolux. Now, if she left the accessories, somebody would steal them for sure. Too bad. She started the motor, put the car in gear, and drove off.

6

Roger Eaton wasn't too backward about telling Nicole how he was well liked, and had practically been a movie star at his senior prom in high school. He'd had a nice time dating his wife, who was a sweet smart hometown girl from a good Mormon family. Which was all right with Roger. He didn't practice anything, but he didn't mind having a little religion in the family. What with the salaries he and his wife were making, they could buy a Dodge for her and for himself a nice little Malibu hardtop. It would have been swell, he assured Nicole, but here they'd only been married six months and his wife had developed colitis.

Being a high-school basketball star, Roger had wanted to play college ball, but didn't like to wait all those years to make real money. Wanted it right away, he guessed. So he had gotten this administrative position in the Utah Valley Mall, and there he met his wife who was in administration for the supermarket. He had been at the Mall for a couple of years now, and was into management training. He earned $11,800 a year, he told Nicole. Felt right about life except for the wife's ailment. It certainly had her out of action.

Roger had a friend who lived down the street from Nicole in Spanish Fork, and he got along pretty well with this fellow's folks, and visited them all the time. So he'd heard plenty about Nicole before he ever saw her. Nicole had to stand out in a place like that. His friend's parents were as Mormon as you come, but they were also some of the biggest bullshitters Roger had ever known. One story they told about Nicole was that a fellow drove up to her door one day last winter with a big bag of groceries, got out, handed her the bag, and then, right there on the street, started feeling her breast. Roger didn't really believe the story because, one, it was winter, and, two, concerning sexual things, these people couldn't see straight. But he was fascinated all the same with stories about the girl, and after he got his first look at her, he felt real drawn. There she was, attractive, divorced, and living with a man. Roger found himself traveling up to Spanish Fork just on the chance he'd get another look. He thought it was stupid to get involved with such people, but he wanted to get to know her. The guy she was living with didn't even faze him at first.

Roger wrote a letter. He said if she needed help, in any way, she should turn on her front door light come Wednesday evening. He would get in touch. He didn't identify himself in the letter, but on Wednesday night he went by to visit the bullshitters and there was no light. He tried to forget about it.

A few weeks after he wrote the thing, he was getting gas in Provo, and saw her Mustang pull in. Roger was afraid. If his wife found out, it'd be a catastrophe. He simply didn't understand what was drawing him. Never done anything like this in his life, but he said to her, "Aren't you Nicole Barrett?" When she answered that she was, he said, "I'm the one who wrote that letter." She kind of laughed. "Let me buy you a Coke," he said. She just walked past him into the office to pay for her gasoline.

He waited for her to come out and repeated his offer. Finally she said, Okay, and told him she'd follow his car. So they met at the High Spot, and he told her where he worked, stuff like that. Found out the fellow in her home was an ex-convict. At which point, Roger said, Okay, let's just forget it. He was frankly scared to be dealing with an ex-con.

She said, "Well, you know, I might need your help." Nothing to do then but tell her how to find his office.

Sure enough, she came the very next day, and without the kids. They talked a lot. Before she left, he gave her ten dollars she hadn't even asked for, but was not embarrassed to receive. Just pocketed it.

After that, she'd visit him every other day or so, and they would talk. They were each pretty interested. The other's life was so different. He could really sympathize with her troubles. That ex-convict was someone to be afraid of, apparently. One morning she came to see him, and was a little beaten up. There were a couple of bruises on those juicy thighs.

After a couple of weeks, she got in the habit of meeting him almost every day. Sometimes she would come to the Mall, but usually they met in a park over in Springville after work. Talk maybe an hour. A couple of times they went off in the Malibu and made love. It was interesting, maybe even a little beautiful, although Roger could never tell how special because frankly they didn't have time to do it right, just a half hour or less, and he was in a state somebody would spot him and bring his marriage down around him. So they were always driving on back roads. It was dangerous, to say the least. Then of course her kids were with her, and apart from frustrating any ideas of sex, they didn't always put Roger in the best mood. At times, they weren't too clean. Roger remembered the first time he met her over at the High Spot. The little boy was wearing no pants, and went out in the parking lot and took a shit right there on the asphalt. Of course, he was only two years old, but Roger was awfully embarrassed, Jeez. Nicole didn't care. She just said to Jeremy, Get back in the car where you belong. Put him in with no pants. He started bawling and screaming and went to sleep after five minutes.

One day she came over and laid it on him. She wasn't living in Spanish Fork anymore. Had fled this fellow Gary, and was living in a little apartment her ex-husband had found in Springville. All the while she was talking, it got to him how much she needed new clothes. So he told her to come by after six and he would take her shopping for an outfit. After he bought it, she stayed with him and they really had a night. She was living with this ex-husband now, she told him, but was not afraid of him. They could do this again real soon. The weekend was hopeless, and even Monday was out, Roger said, because his wife's family was coming over, but they agreed Nicole should call him Tuesday morning, July 20. All through Sunday night Roger was thinking of getting through Monday.

7

"Nobody," offered Brenda, "said it was going to be easy out here."

Gary said, "I can't handle it."

"I know," she said. "At the time, it always feels like you can't."

"No," he said, "you don't know. You and Johnny have always been happy."

"John and I," said Brenda, "have come very close to divorce. Gary, I've been through separation and divorce. It can be awful frightening."

Gary looked like he was mulling over his pains. "Hey," he said, "I'm beginning to find that out."

She said, "Nobody is ever really free, Gary. As long as you live with another human being, you're not free."

Gary sat there like he was grinding bones in his mind. When he spoke, it was to say, "I think I'm going to kill Nicole."

"My God, Gary, are you that selfish of a lover?" Brenda's pep talk was bombing out in her face.

"I can't take it," Gary said. "I told you I can't take it."

"Some things in life we can't handle. Okay. Maybe this is yours. But, God, it'll pass! If you kill her, that won't pass. She'll be dead forever. You're damned stupid, do you know that, Gary?" He didn't like to be called stupid.

"When she pulled the gun on me today," he said, "I thought about taking it. But I didn't want Nicole to start screaming." He shook his head. "She was frantic to get away from me."

Brenda was not unhappy when he left. What with Johnny at the hospital, this was too much emotion to be nursing on a hot summer night.

Craig told him that if he couldn't find a place, to come on back. After visiting Brenda, Gary did, in fact, go over on Sunday night and sleep on Craig's couch. He told Craig that he was close to an ulcer now from misery and beer. As of tomorrow, he was going to give up drinking.

PART FOUR

The Gas Station
and the Motel

CHAPTER 12

The Gas Station

1

She had once been told she looked like a Botticelli. She was tall and slender, and had light brown hair, ivory skin, and a long well-shaped nose with a small bump on the bridge. Yet she hardly knew Botticelli's work. They did not teach a great deal about the Renaissance at Utah State in Logan where she was majoring in art education.

It was at Utah State that Colleen was introduced to her future husband, Max Jensen. Afterward they would laugh at how long it took. The few times Max saw Colleen Halling on the campus she happened to be talking to her cousin. Max decided the fellow was her boyfriend, and therefore it never occurred to him to ask her out.

The following year, however, Max happened to be rooming with the guy, and got around to inquiring if he was still interested in the girl he had seen him with. Max's new roommate started laughing and explained that was no romance — just cousins. By now, Colleen was already out of college, but since she was working at the College of Education, she was, in the practical sense, still on campus.

Colleen only became aware of Max when he spoke in church at the beginning of the new school year. He was wearing a suit that day and looked very distinguished, and seemed a little older than the other students, but then he had already finished his two-year mission. That stood out. He spoke on the importance of not tearing other people down but building them up. Managed to show he had quite a sense of humor as he spoke.

He was a tall fellow, six-one, and weighed about a hundred and ninety pounds. With his even features and his hair cleanly parted on the side, he looked real handsome up there in the pulpit. In fact, he created a ripple among the girls. The Ward Colleen belonged to at the University was, after all, a single Ward, that is, single girls and single boys there to meet each other.

Before Max got up to speak, the fellow who introduced him said, Many couples get introduced to each other right here in church and later they get married, but there is one guy who didn't meet anyone last year and that is Max Jensen. "He really wants to get married, you know," said the friend up there in the pulpit.

At that point, since Max hadn't risen yet to speak, all of Colleen's roommates and herself were looking around, and asking, Which one is Max? and laughing about it. Right here was where Max had to stand up. However, he got back at his friend in a real neat way, by telling a story how that fellow, who was a football player, happened to wake up from a dream one night yelling signals, then bashed into the line — except it was the wall. Max now connected that to the subject of his talk by pointing out how it was not enough to devote your life to living by the Scriptures, you also had to know just where you were in life, otherwise you might not relate the teachings properly to your own situation.

2

A few weeks later, Colleen invited her cousin and his five roommates to come over for a little dinner party with herself and her five roommates. Everything was laid out on the table and people walked by to get their porcupine meatballs, that is, hamburger-and-rice casserole. Since they were all strict Mormons, no iced tea or coffee was served, just milk and water. A pleasant meal on regular plates, not paper, and they talked about school, basketball, and church activities. Colleen remembered Max sitting several feet away on a big pillow and laughing with the group. He had a distinctive voice that was a little bit raspy. She learned later he had hay fever and it gave his voice the deep throbbing sound that comes from having a cold. One of Colleen's roommates later described it as being very sexy.

The next day he called. One of her roommates told Colleen she was wanted on the telephone. This was their little trick. If a girl was on the line, they would yell, "Phone!" but should it be a guy, then "*Tele*phone." Colleen was used to hearing the second, so she had no particular idea it would be Max. The night before, she certainly hadn't gotten the feeling he was making any special attempt to communicate with her, yet he now asked her if she would like to go to a show tonight. She told him yes.

Afterward, it was kind of funny when they each admitted they had seen *What's Up, Doc?* before, but hadn't wanted to spoil the other's opportunity to go. Then they went to the Pizza Hut and talked about their ideas on life, and how active they and their families were in LDS work. Max said he was the oldest of four children and his father, a farmer in Montpelier, Idaho, was also a Stake President. That impressed Colleen. There couldn't be that many Stake Presidents in all of Idaho.

He also told her about his mission to Brazil. What got her respect was that he had earned all the money to do that by himself. Missionaries had to pay their own way over, of course, and then also pay for living expenses on the mission, so most of them had to be helped financially by their families. It wasn't easy for an adolescent to earn enough money by the age of nineteen to maintain himself for two years on a mission in a foreign country. Max, however, had done that.

He enjoyed Brazil, his conversion rate had been high. On average, you could hope to convert one person a month over your two-year stretch in that country, but he had done considerably better. He remembered it as a time of great challenge and much necessity to learn how to live with different people.

Naturally, she had heard a lot about missionary work but he explained some of the things that didn't always get mentioned. For instance, he told her how a missionary might have trouble with his companion. It could be tough to live with a fellow who was a complete stranger. You and your companion had to be together all the time in a foreign city. It was closer than marriage. You did your work and you lived together in pairs. Even people who really knew how to get along had to grate on each other a little with their personal habits. Just the noise you made brushing your teeth. Of course, the Church had a practice of rotating missionaries before too much irritation built up.

The most valuable part, he told her, was the way you developed your ability to take rebuff. Sometimes you would really be having fruitful conversations with a possible convert, and the person might even declare they were close. Then one day you'd go over, and, lo and behold, the local Catholic priest was sitting there. He wasn't feeling too friendly to you. There were a lot of such setbacks. You had to learn it wasn't you doing the converting but the readiness of the other person to meet the Spirit.

Colleen's family life wasn't too different from his. Her family did a lot of things that centered around the church, and they expected you to take on things and do well. In high school, she told him, she had been Yearbook Editor, President of the Service Club, and School Artist. She had also done portraits out at Lagoon Resort, which enabled her to save money for college. From the time she entered first grade she wanted her drawings to be better than anyone else's.

All the while, she kept feeling how strong a person he was. Max was strict and wouldn't bend spiritually or mentally. She could see it even in the way he felt obligated to tell her that he was dating another girl. He did take the sharp edge off, however, by describing how things were not going well with the other girl who was certainly not strong enough, in his opinion, about the Church. Then he mentioned that he had a sister who was also named Colleen and really liked the name.

Afterward, he drove her home in his car, a bright red Nova that he kept sparkling clean. Her roommates said the two of them really looked good together as a couple.

3

On their second date they went to hear a speaker on Sunday night meeting in church, a Fireside. On their third date, they saw *South Pacific* put on at the college. Afterward, she got him to go to a dance. He didn't care for them usually, but this was a nice slow one with foxtrots and waltzes, nothing exhibitionistic. She teased him because he didn't like to dance. Hadn't he been told in Sunday School how their ancestors danced their way across the plains when that was the only entertainment?

Now they began dating pretty steadily. Colleen never did think, however, that it was exactly love at first sight. It was more that Max was impressed with her, and she was impressed with him.

Her birthday was on December 3, and he made reservations at Sherwood Hills, about twenty miles from Logan, a special place to go and eat. That evening he also bought her a red rose. Colleen really appreciated his thoughtfulness. She wore a velvet dress and he was in a suit; they spent about two hours at Sherwood Hills eating steak.

On February 1 of 1975, they got engaged. Just that morning he had received a letter from BYU Law School accepting him. In the evening, they went to a basketball game and he kept turning to her and saying. "When we're at the Y next year" — by which he meant BYU. But he hadn't asked her to marry him. So Colleen kept saying, "When *you're* at the Y . . ."

It began to bother him. Later that night, they were driving to Montpelier, Idaho, to hear his father speak at church the next day, and en route, Max stopped at the shores of Bear Lake, on a little road that led to a docking area. Laughing a little, he told her to get out of the car. She answered that she'd freeze to death. "Ah, come and see the beautiful sight," he said. She was shivering in her blue parka with the fur around it, but she left the car, and while they stood on the dock looking at the moon and the water he came right out and asked her to marry him.

A little over a month before, at Christmastime, while washing dishes, her mother had wanted to know, "If Max asks you, will you say yes?" Colleen had turned around and looked at her and said, "I'd be a fool if I didn't."

When they got back to the car, he said they shouldn't let anyone know until after they had the ring. But it only took another fifteen minutes to reach his home and by then they were so excited they told his parents coming through the door.

During their engagement, she only found little things she did not like about Max. He was a perfectionist and occasionally Colleen might say something that wasn't grammatically correct. Max didn't worry about hurting her feelings. It was natural for him to come out and tell her, "You made a mistake," and expect her to correct it.

He was very proud of her painting and drawing, however. Sometimes he would rib her in company by saying that if he wanted her to talk, all he had to do was say, "Art." She'd start like crazy.

They really got along pretty well, however. Before they were married, her mother once asked, "What bothers you about him?" and Colleen answered, "Nothing." Of course she meant nothing that couldn't soon be worked out.

The wedding took place in Logan Temple on May 9, 1975, at six o'clock in the morning before thirty close friends and members of their families. For the ceremony, Colleen and Max were both dressed in white. They were going to be married in time and eternity, married not only in this life, but as each of them had explained to many a Sunday School class, married in death as well, for the souls of the husband and wife would meet again in eternity and be together forever. In fact, marriage in other Christian churches was practically equal to divorce, since such marriages were only made until parting by death. That was what Max and Colleen had taught their students. Now they were marrying each other. Forever.

In the evening, there was a reception at their own church. The families had sent out eight hundred invitations and light refreshments were offered. They had a reception line. Hundreds of relatives and friends walked through.

4

For their honeymoon, they went to Disneyland. They had calculated their money and decided by cutting it close, they would have just enough. They were right. It was a nice week.

Colleen got pregnant soon after, and it was kind of difficult for Max to understand why she didn't feel good all the time. They were both working, but she felt so little like eating that at lunch she would prepare just a small sandwich for each of them. He would say, "You're starving me to death." She would laugh and tell him she had quite a bit to learn about a guy's eating habits.

He never raised his voice and neither did she. If, occasionally, she felt like speaking sharply, she wouldn't. They had decided right from the beginning that they would never leave each other without kissing good-bye. Nor would they go to bed with personal problems unsolved. If they were mad at each other, they would stay up to talk it out. They were not going to sleep even one night being mad at each other.

Of course, they also had fun. Stuff like shaving-cream fights. Throwing glasses of water at each other.

When she'd have morning sickness, he'd keep saying, "Can I help you? Can I help you?" but Colleen would try to keep her discomfort to herself. She saw that he was tired of her saying, "I'm getting fat."

By August, close to the start of law school, they moved from Logan to Provo. That was a good time. Colleen was over morning sickness and had no trouble working. Max was squared away on studies. They found a nice basement apartment with a small front room and a tiny bedroom about twelve blocks from the college for $100 a month, and got along really well.

The week before she had the baby, Colleen typed a thirty-page paper for Max, and he sent her a dozen red roses in return. She loved him for that. They had a little girl born to them on Valentine's Day, a little over nine months from the date of their marriage. The baby had lots of dark hair and weighed seven pounds and Max was real proud of her and took snapshots before she was a day old. They named her Monica. When she got older, he loved to play with her.

Wasn't much time of course. Finishing up first-year law school, Max was really working hard. She'd fix his breakfast and he'd leave; back for dinner at five, out again at six to the law library, home at ten. She was in charge of the baby for sure.

They needed a larger place to live, so they bought a trailer they really liked. It was 12 feet wide, 52 feet long, and had two bedrooms. Colleen's parents loaned the money for the down payment.

The trailer was furnished with a couple of old things her parents gave them, and they had a little lawn. Max also planted a small garden out to the side. Every day he'd water his tomatoes. Maybe there were a hundred trailers in the court, and all kinds of neighbors. Most were their own age with children, and nice enough. There were even several couples they went to church with.

5

He had a construction job promised for the summer, but when it was not yet ready after school, they went up to his dad's farm for a few weeks and Max dug ditches, fed cattle, branded them, planted crops, helped irrigate. It was good to see him physically relaxed instead of worn out from studying.

When they went back to Provo, the man who had promised the construction job to Max said that it had gone instead to the son of one of the men working there already. That job would have paid $6.50 an hour.

Max had a temper and knew how to keep it under control but this got him truly upset. It was the first time Colleen saw Max really depressed. She had to do a lot of talking to turn his mood around. Finally, he said, "Okay, I'll start thinking about another job," and went to the University employment office, but it was late to look for summer work and he only found a listing for Sinclair gas station attendant at $2.75 an hour.

It was a self-service station on a back street in Orem. His work was limited to giving out change, cleaning windows, and taking care of the restrooms from three in the afternoon until eleven at night. The pay, of course, was a lot less than they had counted on, yet for all of June and the first weeks of July he worked without complaint and came home hot and tired. All the same, he was beginning to make friends with some of the customers and the manager liked him. They worshipped in the same Ward.

Two weeks after the Fourth of July, Max and Colleen were asked to give a talk in church. Max spoke of how there were too few people in this world who were really honest. He gave a powerful speech on the importance of being honest. It made all the difference between being able to build on a real foundation or not being able to. Colleen's talk that Sunday was on joy: on the joy she experienced when she met Max, and when they married, and when they had their baby. Afterward, on the way home, he gave her a big hug, and a lot of fine feelings came over her and she said, "We're really beginning to live and love each other more than ever." They went to bed with a real good understanding.

Monday morning, Max was excited about getting some shelves finished for Monica, and spent the morning hammering and sawing and drilling. Colleen had a lot of things to do, the wash, the ironing, fixing dinner. Usually they ate in plenty of time before Max went off to work at 3 P.M., but today they were a little rushed because Max wanted to get the shelves done first. He kept calling her into the bedroom to mark his progress and Monica was also watching. Max was bending over and hammering, listening to the radio, in his Levi's, feeling comfortable and good. Finally he said, "I'm ready to put them up, come help me." She went in and they got them installed quickly, then he kind of backed away, gave a sigh, said, "Well, that's done."

They ate. Being a little late, Max was in a hurry to finish. He was never late to anything, and usually ready one minute before her. So, as soon as he swallowed dinner, he walked down the hall, grabbed some things he needed, and started to walk out the door while she was still sitting at the table. Only then did he realize he hadn't kissed her good-bye and so he turned around, and kind of grinned and said, "Well, I'll meet you halfway."

She walked around the table and he gave her a kiss, and a really good hug and looked into her eyes, things were just going well, and Colleen said, "I'll see you tonight." He said, "Okay," went out, got in the car and drove off.

He was a very conscientious driver, never broke the speed limit, or anything. Fifty-five miles an hour all the time. In her mind, she saw him driving down the road that way. He would be moving along the Interstate at just such a speed until he went around a slow graded turn and disappeared from sight and left her mind free to think of one and then another of the small things she must do that day.

CHAPTER 13

The White Truck

1

About the time Max Jensen was starting work at the Sinclair gas station, Gary Gilmore was in the showroom in V.J. Motors on State Street, about a mile away, coming to terms with Val Conlin about the truck. There wasn't going to be a co-signer, after all. Gary was going to turn over his Mustang on which he'd already paid close to $400 (if you gave him credit for the battery and ignored the windshield) and he would produce another $400 in two days, cash. Then he would come up with another $600 by the fourth of August. Val would let him make the transfer now and he could sign the papers tonight.

Rusty Christiansen could hear them talking, and had to smile. She had come in to work part-time on the books, reconcile Val's bank account, get license plates, and, in general, help. She knew some of the ropes by now.

Rusty's unspoken opinion was that the truck had to be disgustingly overpriced. It was selling for $1,700 and with interest would come to $2,300. Val probably hadn't paid a thousand for that carcass. Now he would have the Mustang to resell, plus a thousand in cash by the first week of August. Otherwise, he would repossess the truck. He wasn't taking that big a chance. Gary could sure have found something better for the money than this white Angel with 100,000 miles on her. He had fallen in love with a paint job.

Now, Rusty watched Conlin tell Gilmore one more time that he, Val, had an extra set of keys with which to make sure Gary would walk if the money wasn't there. It was the same pep talk. Val would make a good coach for a team of mental defectives. "Get the money, Gary," said Val as the truck drove away.

Sterling was taken for a ride and Gary was talking pretty proud. His new engine had a lot more power than the Mustang. For sure, the acceleration was better. Gary didn't abuse it, though. Drove it like a Cadillac. Trundled it for a while. Then they went tooling up the highway.

It was moving toward dark when Kathryne saw him. Some of her family had come over that day. The cherry trees were ripe in the yard, and her mother and a couple of her brothers and sisters were still out with the kids picking fruit, while Kathryne's friend Pat was with her in the kitchen. At that point, Gary came to the back door and said, "Could I talk to you outside?" Kathryne invited him in, but he kept saying, "I have to talk to you outside. It's important."

She went and took a look at his truck, oohed and ahhhed. He looked odd to Kathryne, not drunk, exactly, but made a point of telling her how sober he was. In fact, she couldn't smell alcohol on his breath. He did seem odd, however. She said, no, she hadn't seen Nicole. He said, "As far as I'm concerned, she can go to hell." Then he looked at Kathryne like some nut in him was being tightened right off the threads, and said, "She can get fucked."

That really shocked Kathryne. She could hardly believe Gary would use such words for Nicole. Then he looked at her in that way he had of getting into every little thought you might like to keep to yourself, and said, "Kathryne, I want my gun back." "Gary," she managed to answer, "I don't like to give it to you. Not the way you're acting." He said, "I'm in trouble. I gotta have it. I've got all the guns back now but three. A cop knows, you see, that I done the robbery."

She had the feeling Gary was making it up. "This cop told me if I get the guns back to the store, nothing will happen."

Kathryne said, "Gary, why don't you come back tomorrow and pick it up when you're sober."

He said, "I'm not drinking, and I'm not going to get in trouble. Moreover, if I want to use a gun" — he pulled his jacket open — "this little baby takes care of it all." That was one pistol she recognized. A real German Luger stuck in his pants. "In addition," he said, "I got a sackful." At that point he opened the truck door, and a burlap bag tipped over. By the clanking it sounded like it held half a dozen more guns.

Kathryne said to herself, What does it matter? She took the Special out from under the mattress and gave it to him, and stood with Gary in the twilight trying to calm him down. He was so angry.

Then, April came running out of the house. She was close to hysterical. "Where's Pat?" she asked, "where's Pat?" "She's gone, April," Kathryne said. "Oh," cried April, "Pat promised to take me down to K-Mart to get my guitar string."

At this point, Gary said, "I'll run you over." Quickly, Kathryne told her, "You don't need to go," but April jumped into the truck, and Kathryne barely had time to repeat, "Gary, she don't need to go," when he replied, "That's all right. I'll bring her back." They were gone.

It was in this moment that Kathryne realized she didn't know Gary's last name. Knew him as Gary, just Gary.

They sat in the kitchen among all the boxes of cherries they'd picked. Kathryne wasn't about to call the cops. If the police stopped Gary, he might open up on them. Instead, she waited till Pat got back and went out with her to look for the white truck. They drove till one or two in the morning, going up and down roads. No way they were going to find him, it seemed.

2

April moved in close, turned on the radio, said, "It's hard to get along if you have to wait too long. The rooms get narrow and very often there is a dog." She began to shiver as she thought of the dog. "Every day," she said, "is the same. It's all one day," and nodded her head. "You have to get them used up."

"That's right," he said.

Just before he arrived, she had been lying in the grass, watching others pick cherries. She was playing the guitar with the broken string. It came over her that grandmother was going to die if she didn't fix the string. April was letting her soul run wild as she played, and thought of Jimi Hendrix and Otis Redding dead and that made her start thinking hard about the diseases. The bugs, spiders and flies bring it in, and the fevers give a humming sound until they are aroused, then they make a noise like a breaking string. Death would certainly come to Grandma if she didn't fix the string. That was her thought in the grass. As she looked up, there was a dog in front of her.

This dog started crying. It sounded like a man crying his heart out. The recollection of the tragedy of that sound got April nodding full force in Gary's truck. She didn't like such feelings. When she nodded that way, she might just as well have been galloping on a horse. Her head was certainly being snapped each step the horse came down. It got her to the point where her personal motor turned on again as if Satan was running her body, and pulling in all the people who usually floated around as personalities from Mars and Venus. The black man was staring at her with his cold black eye, and the white man had started acting like he was ecstasy in the worst way in the entire galaxy. The guitar needed a new string to attract more harmonious spirits. "I," said April to Gary, "am the one swinging on the string." She nodded, careful not to do it so hard that the galloping horse would snap her neck.

"Look," she said, "my grandma's washing machine is next to the sewer. That's why those people are floating around. I hate filth." She could feel her mouth twisting from her nostrils to the corners of her lips. "Oh, Gary, I'm cotton-mouthed," she said, "I need Midol. Can you get me a toothbrush?" She could feel him patting her. He said he would get her what she needed.

It was crucial to put it across to people that you didn't go to a store and pull things from the counter, but took a good look at the object you were going to buy and inquired of it. There were all sorts of answers: the object could say, "Go away," or "Please steal me." It could even ask to be bought. The objects had as much concern about themselves as anyone else. Gary just went plink, plink, plunk, got her

Midol, got her toothbrush, got her the hell out of there. He wasn't drinking beer. Boy, he was uptight.

Now they were driving in Pleasant Grove again. "I don't want to go home. I want to stay out all night," she said.

"That's cool," he said.

3

Julie had to stay in the hospital one more night, so Craig Taylor was still alone. He was just putting the kids to sleep, when Gary knocked on the door and introduced this girl as Nicole's sister, April. They looked odd. Not drunk, but the girl was in bad shape. Paranoid. She couldn't sit down. Walked around Craig like he was a barrel or something.

Gary came out of the bathroom, and asked did he still have the gun. Craig said, Yeah. Gary asked to borrow it back. Plus a few shells. "Oh, yeah," said Craig. "Well, it's yours, I'll give it to you." Added, "Why do you want it?" Gary didn't give any answer. Finally he said, "I'd like it." Craig didn't exactly have a good feeling as he passed the shells. Gary seemed awful emotionless. "Gary, I can't refuse you," Craig said, "it's your gun," but he took a good last look. It was a gold-trigger Browning Automatic with a black metal barrel, nice wood handle.

"I don't want to go home," said April when they were in the truck again. "Hell," said Gary, "I'll keep you out all night." He drove to Val Conlin's to sign the papers. On the way, April realized they hadn't gone to the K-Mart after all. She still didn't have the guitar string. It got too complicated to ask again. She felt like she was fighting spiderwebs.

When they came into V.J. Motors, April said aloud, "Hey, that's a show for free." Gary and this fellow Val kept looking at car keys like old magicians studying old dried herbs, weird! She wandered around and the room distorted. Warp was in the atmosphere. So she sat down in a corner. That way you could hold the thing together. They came over, but she didn't know what they were talking about. Just said, "You're the witness. Look at this." Signing a paper.

Rusty Christiansen was bored. By the time they could get Gary out, it would be nine-thirty. She wouldn't be home till a quarter of ten. The interest still had to be calculated, and the payments worked out. They kept going out to the lot to take numbers off the car and the truck. Once in a while, this little girl April in the corner said something in a big voice.

For that matter, Val's voice was pretty good, too. "I'm going to take a chance," said Val, "because you've been good with me. But goddamn it, Gary, you better pay." "Right," said Gary. "Okay," said Val, "I'm going to take a chance."

Gary went to transfer some clothes from the Mustang to the truck, and while he was gone, Val looked at the little broad in the corner and said, "Hey, what are you on?" She looked at him like she had just come in from the next century, and then she honked, "Wha-whaa-wha . . ." Val thought, Whee, she's plain out here in orbit. The girl looked at him steadily and said, "Sometimes I'm not even a girl." She began to cry.

When Gary returned, Val said, "If you don't pay me that first four hundred in two days, I'll take the truck back so goddamn fast you won't even know you had wheels, Pardner. You won't have the truck and you won't have the Mustang. Gary, you don't have that money, you walk, understand?" "Understand," said Gary, "no problem. Okay." He signed the last papers and Val turned the truck over.

When they got in, Gary told April, "Let's go." They drove around looking for Nicole. "Use your radar," Gary said. She didn't want to tell him about interference; he would think she was copping a plea. Interference could keep the most powerful forces of mind from entering a focus. So, they kept driving. April kept hoping she could say something proper. That could regain a lot of force. That was what it took. A word to go out and get everybody in harmony.

"When I was young," said April, "my grandpa put me on the back of a hog in the pigpen and scared me half to death. There was a bunch of wild hogs loose and they was chasing us. I hid in the bathtub. Wasn't much to do that night but I learned to hide. You hide by getting half inside." She snickered. "You see, Gary," April said, "I always wanted to be a pig." She was feeling the force of the pig. Gary pulled the truck over and parked it. "I'm going to go make a phone call," he said; "see if your mother's heard from Nicole."

After he got out, she listened to a group sing "Let Your Love Flow." Two guys, not a sad group. It was all right if she didn't think of Hampton. "Let your love flow, and let your love grow." She was trying to remember going through people's medicine cabinets in olden times when she baby-sitted. "Let your love flow and let your love grow." It used to be like love was flowing through her fingers as she went through cabinets taking out the right pills to get stoned. Oh, to be inside a trance again with black beauties. She loved the way she got on them. Black beauties could be sweet as the harmony of the spring. "I mean," said April to herself, "I can always talk to the radio if I'm that desperate. Disc jockeys realize that people are talking to them."

4

Gary walked around the corner from where the truck was parked and went into a Sinclair service station. It was now deserted. There was only one man present, the attendant. He was a pleasant-looking serious young man with broad jaws and broad shoulders. He had a clean straight part in his hair. His jawbones were slightly farther apart than his ears. On the chest of his overalls was pinned a nameplate, MAX JENSEN. He asked, "Can I help you?"

Gilmore brought out the .22 Browning Automatic and told Jensen to empty his pockets. So soon as Gilmore had pocketed the cash, he picked up the coin changer in his free hand and said, "Go to the bathroom." Right after they passed through the bathroom door, Gilmore said, "Get down." The floor was clean. Jensen must have cleaned it in the last fifteen minutes. He was trying to smile as he lay down on the floor. Gilmore said, "Put your arms under your body." Jensen got into position with his hands under his stomach. He was still trying to smile.

It was a bathroom with green tiles that came to the height of your chest, and tan-painted walls. The floor, six feet by eight feet, was laid in dull gray tiles. A rack for paper towels on the wall had Towl Saver printed on it. The toilet had a split seat. An overhead light was in the wall.

Gilmore brought the Automatic to Jensen's head. "This one is for me," he said, and fired.

"This one is for Nicole," he said, and fired again. The body reacted each time.

He stood up. There was a lot of blood. It spread across the floor at a surprising rate. Some of it got onto the bottom of his pants.

He walked out of the rest room with the bills in his pocket, and the coin changer in his hand, walked by the big Coke machine and the phone on the wall, walked out of this real clean gas station.

5

Just working along, Colleen had accomplished a lot that day. She did the ironing and the cleaning, worked in the garden, picked the beans. She'd been planning to wait up for Max but before it was eleven, she climbed into bed.

On the edge of falling asleep, she felt like somebody was knocking at the door, but when she opened, nobody was there. She thought it was a cat. Still too early for Max to be home. So she went back to bed, fell right into sleep.

Sitting in the truck, on this quiet side street, April thought it was probably quiet. She couldn't tell because the radio was so loud. Except the trees looked quiet. There was a long night just sitting there.

After a while Gary came back. She had been smoking a smoke and waiting. "Come on," he said, "let's go."

As they pulled up to the drive-in theatre, April saw "Cuckoo" in the title so she thought they were going to see *The Sterile Cuckoo* with Liza Minnelli. April had always thought her own looks outside had to be just like the way Liza Minnelli felt inside, so she was looking forward a lot to seeing the movie. But right as they stopped under the light of the ticket booth, she could see that Gary's pants had blood on the cuffs.

They parked. He got shifty in his seat and said he would take a leak. Then she could see him rummaging in the back of the truck. Looked like another pair of pants to her. He went off to the men's room. To herself, April was saying, "The FBI look in on houses to see if people are committing crimes. Through the TV, you know."

She tried to watch the movie while Gary was gone, but it made her think of the night she was raped. That was after walking through the street in Hawaii with the black dudes and the first one of the three black dudes said there was a party going on. Cocaine, and they would all get high. She'd had LSD already, and so was fascinated with the high-class looks of their pad, although the red couches aggravated the problem of her odor. She sweated when she sniffed Lady Snow, and the odor was very bad. The black boy named Warren told her she stunk, and she turned purple inside from those red couches and all these black people. Started to dance around. They asked her if she wanted a shower. She said yes. Then she was in the tub and wet and streaking through the place. She was naked, and she was dancing. "I think I'm a nymphomaniac," she said. "You're a maniac?" they asked. She said it again slowly, and they asked, "Info with a maniac?" She replied haughtily, "You are trying to make myself and my face black."

She danced with them right on the floor and they danced her down to the floor and hurt her pretty bad. She was bleeding all over the place. Like a whore. Warren was forceful on cocaine, awful mean. Even when he relaxed he was hard on her. She was hallucinating so bad that the one called Bob made his face come together at the top and the bottom while his nose wib-wobbled from side to side. One time, two times, three times, intercourse. Then they turned a light on and Bobby was sitting on the floor, and said, "Why don't you sit on the couch? Get high. Don't think of yourself so low, you know?" Then he was on top of her and she was screaming to the song. The twist they gave was vertigo and she was a turntable with the motor started and Satan could dance in the whirlpool the table made.

Suddenly, she could see the movie she had been looking at. It wasn't *The Sterile Cuckoo*. It was *One Flew Over the Cuckoo's Nest*.

All the kooks she had ever lived with in the hospital were on the screen. Jack Nicholson bothered her enormously. He had a numb spot under his nose like the numb spot under her own nose. That reminded her of the blood on Gary's pants — it was in the stiff way Jack Nicholson walked.

Now, Gary came back. She said, "Let's blow this place. I hate the movie. Fucker's freaking me out."

Gary looked disappointed. "This is one movie," he told her, "I want to see again."

"You insane fool," she said, "don't you have any taste?"

At eleven o'clock in the evening, a man drove into the Sinclair service station at 800 North, 175 East in Orem, and served himself twelve gallons of gas and one quart of oil. He couldn't find an attendant so he left his business card with a description of what he had purchased. A little later, Robbie Hamilton, who lived in Toelle, Utah, stopped off. After filling his tank with gas, he went to the open door of the grease room and hollered, "Anybody home?" No answer, so he went back to the car. His wife told him to knock on the bathroom door. When he received no answer there, he pushed the door open a crack and saw a lot of blood. He did not enter. He just called the Orem City Police Department. It took them fifteen minutes to find it. Being from Toelle, Utah, Mr. Hamilton did not know what street he was on, and had to describe the location in general terms to the dispatcher.

6

John was back from the hospital and sleeping on the couch again. Brenda was ready to go to bed. There was a knock on the door. It was Gary with this strange little girl.

"Well, coz," she said, "where you been?"

"Oh," he smiled, "we went to see *One Flew Over the Cuckoo's Nest*." "You didn't see that again?" asked Brenda. "Well," Gary said, "she hadn't seen it yet."

Brenda took a good look at the girl. "It looks to me," she said, "as if she wouldn't know what she's seen."

Gary said, "This is Nicole's sister, January."

The girl got mad. She came alive for the first time.

"It's *April*." Gary chuckled. Brenda said, "Well, April, May, June, or July, whatever your name is, I suppose I'm glad to meet you." Then she said to Gary, "What's wrong with her?" This girl looked awful.

"Oh," Gary said, "April's having flashbacks from LSD. She took it a long time ago, but it keeps catching up."

"She's sick, Gary," Brenda said. "She's awfully pale." At that point the girl said she wanted to go to the bathroom. Following her, Brenda asked, "Honey, are you all right?" The girl said, "I just feel sick to my stomach."

Brenda came out to Gary and said, "What's going on?"

He said nothing in reply. Brenda had the impression he was nervous but careful. Very nervous, and very careful. He was sitting on the edge of his seat, as if to concentrate on every sound in the silence.

April came back and said, "Man, you really scare me when you act like that. I can't take it."

"What scared you, honey?" Brenda asked.

April said, "Gary really scares me."

He drew himself up then. "April, tell Brenda I didn't try to rape you, or molest you."

"Oh, man, you know I didn't mean that," April said. "You've been nice to me tonight. But man, I really get afraid of you."

"Afraid of what?" asked Brenda.

"I can't tell you," April said. There was something so broken-assed about it, that Brenda was getting ill herself. "Gary, what have you done?" she asked. To her surprise, he winced.

"Hey," he said, "let's drop it? *Okay*?"

Gary said, "Can I talk to you in the other room?" When he got her in the kitchen, he said, "Look, I know John is just back, and you guys won't be getting your check right away from the hospital insurance, so, listen, Brenda, could you use fifty?"

"Gary, no," she said, "we've got groceries. We'll make it."

Gary said, "I really want to help."

Brenda said, "Honey, you are generous." She knew what he was up to, but she was moved in spite of herself. Ridiculously moved. She felt like crying at the fact that even in this phony way he could think of her a little. Instead, she said, "Keep your money. I want you to learn to handle it." Saying that, she was suddenly suspicious, and had to ask, "Gary, where in the hell did you get a lot of cash?"

"A friend of mine," said Gary, "loaned me four hundred for my truck."

"You mean you stole the money."

"That's not very nice," he said.

"If I'm wrong," said Brenda, "then it's not very nice."

He took ahold of her face and kissed her on the brow and said, "I can't tell you what's going on. You don't want to be involved."

"All right, Gary," she said. "If it's that bad, then maybe you shouldn't involve us."

"Okay," he said, "fair enough." He wasn't angry. He took April, and went to the truck. Picked April up by the elbows, so to speak, ushered her out.

Brenda found herself following. He had a half gallon of milk in the back of the truck and a bunch of clothes with a rag wrapped around them. She said, "Gary, you'll tip your milk over. Let me fix it." He said, "Don't touch it. Leave it alone!" "All right," Brenda said, "spill your milk. See if I care." After he drove off, she kept wondering what there was about the bunch of clothes that he hadn't wanted her to see.

Gary asked April if she'd like to go to a motel, but she just said she didn't want to go home. So they began driving around and soon got lost.

Just as he discovered he had come all the way from Orem to Provo by back roads, the truck ran out of gas.

It came to a stop on the lonely part of Center Street between the exit from the Interstate and the beginning of town. He got out and plunged into a little ravine off the road and hid the gun, the clip and the coin changer in a bush. Then he headed for the nearest store.

7

Wade Anderson and Chad Richardson were at the 7-11 grocery down on West Center Street when this fellow came up to them. He said if they would take him to a gas station, he would give them five bucks.

He looked all right, except he was kind of tired and certainly in a hurry. He gave up the five dollars as soon as they got in the truck and sat by the window looking out. Kept saying that his girl was sitting alone in the truck and he didn't want no one to hassle her, especially cops, she'd mouth off.

They said, Well, okay, you know, we'll hurry as quick as we can. The trouble was, when they got to a gas station that was open, there was no gas can. Wade then said they could go to his house for one. The guy said, Well, we gotta hurry.

It took a few minutes to get over to the east side of town, pick up the can from his dad's garage, come back to the gas station. Once they returned to the man's truck, Wade started pouring. Since he would soon be a junior in high school and was therefore trying to get a little better at talking to girls, he sprung up a conversation every chance he got and was looking to chat with the one in the truck. Of course he kept his eye on the tall man who was walking around in the little ravine below. The fellow had borrowed a flashlight from Chad's truck, and was beaming around down there looking for something.

Wade said to the girl, "How you doing?" and she looked at him very seriously and said in this big voice, "Are you Gary Gilmore's son?" He said, "Oh, no, ma'am, I'm . . . I never met him before tonight," and about that time the fellow in the field found what he was looking for. Wade saw him pull a pistol out of the bushes, and a clip with it, and a coin changer, then he came walking back to them. Even slammed the clip into the handle of the gun as he did. Put it under the seat with the coin changer. Chad had been standing back a little as Wade poured the gas, and now they just looked at each other. Wow.

After they finally emptied the can, this fellow said, "Thanks a lot" and was ready to take off. Went to start his truck. It wouldn't go. He had wore the battery down. So they gave him a push with their truck. That was it.

Back on the road, Gary said to April, "No more riding around. I want a fancy place to sleep like the Holiday Inn." He turned onto the Interstate and bore down the two miles to the next exit.

"I'm not going to fuck you," April said. "I'm feeling too para-noid."

"I've got to work in the morning," Gary informed her. "We'll get two beds."

8

Frank Taylor, the night auditor at the Holiday Inn, was at the front desk when a tall man carrying a half gallon of milk came in with a short girl who was holding aloft a long Olympia beer can like she was the Statue of Liberty. Frank Taylor thought, Here comes a real case. Since he was not only the night auditor but doubled as a desk clerk, his next thought was that he wasn't going to get his auditing done first thing tonight. The girl didn't look like she'd quiet down too soon. Still, the tall man seemed sober when he came over to register.

The girl kept asking snippy questions of Frank Taylor. Did he like working in a motel for a living? Were there bedbugs? Then she inquired for the ladies' room. The moment Frank Taylor told her it was across the lobby on the left, she started down the hall to her right. Taylor was yelling directions by the time she disappeared. The tall man only smiled. A couple of minutes later she passed across the lobby the other way. The tall man asked for a place to eat, and lis-tened carefully to the answer that the Rodeway Inn, two doors down,

was open 24 hours a day. Then he signed his name in large block letters, GARY GILMORE, gave Spanish Fork as an address, and
reached into his pocket where he pulled out an awful lot of small bills
to pay for the room.

Taylor assumed Gilmore and the girl were shacking up but that
was not really any of his business. You could get in a lot of legal trouble if you were too inquisitive. Just once, suggest to a real married
couple that they were not really married. It was established practice
to accept anybody who was orderly and paid in advance. Taylor
watched them go off together hand in hand with the key.

A while later, they were buzzing the switchboard. Gilmore was
calling down from 212 to say he'd gone out in the hall and put some
money in the machine to buy toothpaste and razor blades and Alka
Seltzer, but the machine had not worked.

It never worked, thought Frank Taylor. He got the items out of
the supply case and walked down long corridors with green carpeting
and yellow-brown walls, past dark brown plywood doors, past an ice
chest and a candy vending machine. He went by an iced-drink machine and reached 212. When Gilmore opened the door, he had on
red slacks and no shirt. He reached into his pocket and took out a big
handful of change, kind of held it down as if to scrutinize it, then
picked out what was needed. Taylor couldn't see the girl, but heard
her giggle as the door closed.

CHAPTER 14

The Motel Room

1

At the far end of the bedroom, to one side of the far wall, was the only window and it looked out over the swimming pool. Since the window was sealed, there was an air conditioner installed beneath. On either side hung drapes made of a green-blue synthetic fabric, and they were drawn apart by white vertical cords that passed around milk-colored plastic pulleys. Two black leatherette barrel chairs and an oc-tagon-shaped synthetic-walnut table sat in front of the window, and next to the table was a TV set on a swivel stand. Its chromium ball feet were set in rubber casters which buried themselves in a blue shaggy synthetic-fabric rug.

A long synthetic-walnut combination desk and bureau was at-tached to one wall. In the interior of the flat drawer of the desk was stationery in a flat wax-paper envelope that bore the Holiday Inn logo: "Your Host from Coast to Coast." A copy of the swimming pool regulations and a room-service menu lay next to a long thin strip of paper that read: PLEASE BE A WATT WATCHER.

The beds on the opposite wall had headboards of synthetic wal-nut and their coverlets were of green-blue synthetic fabric. They gave off the same smell as the room. It was the odor of old air conditioners and old cigars.

Between the beds was an end table with a lamp and an octagonal glass ashtray that carried the green logo of Holiday Inn. A red light for messages kept flashing on the phone. Since it was on by error, it did not go off. Neither did the air conditioner. After a while, its hum vibrated in the bowels.

2

On the door frame of the bathroom was a switch that in the dark glowed like a squared-off fluorescent nipple. Turned on, the overhead light showed white walls and a cement-colored tile floor. A plate-glass mirror was attached above the sink by five plastic glass-clamps screwed into the wall. The sixth had fallen out. Its exposed screw hole looked like a motionless dark bug.

The washbowl was set in a synthetic-walnut top. Along this top, two glasses wrapped in cellophane carried the logo of Holiday Inn, and two small cakes of soap in the Holiday Inn wrappers were placed next to a small tent-shaped piece of yellow cardboard that read, "Welcome to Holiday Inn." There was also a notice that the liquor store would be open from 10 A.M. to 10 P.M. These pieces of paper were damp. The rounded surfaces of the washbowl acted like a centrifuge when you turned on the tap and threw water out of the sink onto the floor.

A strip of white paper was looped around the seat of the toilet bowl to certify that no one had sat there since the strip was placed in position. The toilet paper from the toilet-paper holder in the wall to the left of the toilet seat was soft and very absorbent, and would stick to the anus.

3

"April," Gary said, "are you going to tear that strip off the toilet, or do I have to?" She glowered at him, and threw the paper at the waste-basket. "The world makes you work," she said, "because of the rich. Every organization is rich, you see."

"Man, you sure can talk," said Gary. He walked over and gave her a kiss. She said, "Sissy. Sissy wouldn't like this." He walked away from her and took out a stick of pot. "I want some," said April. He laughed and held it out of her reach. "Give us a kiss," he said.

"I can't kiss you because of Sissy," she said. "Sissy has vampires."

Gary lit the stick, and took a puff. "A toke?" he asked. But when she came near, he held it out of her reach again.

Walking around the room she started taking off clothes. She felt as if they were congesting her. First her peasant blouse, then her Levi's. Walking around in her bra and her panties, she felt better. "Did you ever get up at four in the morning, Gary, and make cookies?" He was lying on the bed and taking his time on the marijuana. He just waved a hand. Then he sat up and burped. A look of pain came over his face, and he reached for the milk and took a swig. "Hey, kid, let's unwind," he said. "I'll give you a massage and you give me one."

"The FBI," she said, "look in on houses to see if people are committing any crimes. They do it through the TV, you know." She lay back on the bed and the room was spinning. It was like a motel room she had gone to with a rich man. She had felt so alive that night because the plastic was so dead.

"Gary," she said, "give me a toke. I'm kind of messed up." He passed her the stick and she sucked in. She must have taken a trip because there was Gary kissing her face, waking her up. "Leave me alone," she cried. When he gave her another kiss, she said, "Gary, you and Nicole were meant for each other."

"Nicole can get fucked."

She started to walk around, remembering the night in Hawaii when she was walking around and Bobby and Warren were massaging her and dancing with her, and then Gary was sort of giving her a massage, walking behind her, right behind her, his legs locked with hers as if they were in prison lockstep, and they walked around the room that way with his thumbs massaging her shoulders and the back of her neck. After a little while she began to feel very close to him and whispered, "It isn't very good for us to do that. Sissy wouldn't think that was very good." She decided to turn on her mind and listen to Paul McCartney. "Open the door and let them in," went the music in her head, and it got to be a carnival. Gary would smack her from behind, or finger her panties, then he would growl in her ear like a lion. She'd think of rich men in motels and knock off his hand with her elbow. "Fuck you," she said. "Let me go to bed."

"We're sleeping standing up," he replied.

They were a king and a queen and she began to get pleased at the thought of them sleeping each in a separate bed, but she knew she would go down into a sleep that gave a very heavy feeling, like pictures she had seen in the Bible of demons coming out of dark space to torment people on this planet and really tear us apart limb from limb. She could picture thousands in the sky coming down like eagles on mice.

All the while he was crawling on her, giving her a back massage. When she closed her eyes, she saw a man flapping his arms. He had about eight limbs on each side and was flapping them, an evil force, bringing disease and everything else like Satan, the strongest, to earth.

Now she knew there was something wrong with the back massage. Gary had changed his personality. Gary, who was always so manly around her, more manly even than her father, had turned female and was crawling on her from behind with this back massage. If she would turn around and look at his face, she would see a woman. He was feeling her in order to feel his own breasts, his own belly. April could feel a woman behind her. That turned her off cold, man.

"Let's go to sleep," she said. He didn't fight. He got into his bed and she got into hers, and he turned out the lights and she lay down in the dark and looked up at the ceiling. The spackled plaster had sparkles of glass embedded to look like a thousand stars. She couldn't stand the smell in the room and turned on the lights. On the wall just back of her was a landscape running all over the wallpaper of palm trees and the ruin of a stone arch, and on a hill, an old Italian house. Long skinny people wearing capes were walking around that countryside. Gary said, "Turn off the light. I need my sleep."

She lay there some more, and he came over to her bed in the dark and tried to make her. She didn't know if he was serious or not. They just scuffled in the dark and he tore her underwear but she held the pieces together, and said, "No." She said, "Gary, I don't feel like doing this." She said, "Gary, you're losing your mind." She said, "Sissy. Sissy. Sissy wouldn't think this is very good." At last he gave up and she lay there in the dark. The room started coming back to her. She saw the room very clearly like she was looking through a magnifying glass. "It's just one more night in a prison cell," she said to herself, "and I've been in prison all my life."

Out in the foyer, as they left, was a small rubber pad on the wall. It kept the knob of the door to 212 from denting the plaster. She didn't know why but it reminded her of the cord to the TV set that was all coiled up and tied neatly by a white plastic wire. In her head that was like a snake strangling another snake.

4

Deep down in sleep, the first thing Colleen knew was that somebody was knocking lightly on her door. It left her startled. She didn't know what time it was until she got up and passed the kitchen clock and saw it was two in the morning and Max was still away. Then she turned on the porch light and looked out the little window that was set in the door. What she saw made her very scared.

Outside the window were five men, and the first of them was President Kanin of her Stake.

He put his arm around her shoulder, "Colleen," he said, "Max won't be home tonight."
She received a feeling that Max might never be home again.
"Is he dead?" she asked.
All five nodded.
She cried for a minute. It wasn't real to her.

At this point, one of the two men she didn't know, said to President Kanin, "Will she be okay with you?" When the answer was yes, these two strangers left. She realized they were plainclothes police-men.

President Kanin helped her dial home. No one answered. She remembered her parents were camping and had left that morning, so she dialed Max's parents. The lady who answered said Mr. and Mrs. Jensen had also gone camping, but she would get in touch with them. President Kanin now asked if there was somebody else one could call and Colleen thought of her cousins who lived across the street from her parents in Clearfield. They were home and said they'd drive right over. That would take an hour and a half.

President Kanin now asked her if there was somebody who could stay with her until the cousins arrived. She said there was a girl in the Ward who lived two trailers down. They called and she came over. The three men left.

The girl stayed nearly two hours. They lay down beside each other on the bed and talked. Monica stayed asleep and Colleen was numb. She had no desire to see where they had taken Max's body. She did not feel like saying "Let me go to him." She just sat and talked to her neighbor and it all seemed unreal. They would talk for a while, and then it would come back. It was a quarter to five when her relatives knocked on the door.

5

April had taken out her earring, and in the dark she was using it to stick herself. She had this dream that one day she was going to take an injection and end it all. She wanted to know what it felt like. So she kept trying the point of the earring post against her neck.

In the morning while it was still kind of dark, Gary moved over to her bed again, and tried one more time. Not that hard. Then he drank more milk. It certainly was love he needed more than sex, but April knew she could not let Sissy down cause Sissy still loved him.

By 6:30 when Monica awoke in the dawn, Colleen was saying to herself that she was still alive, and her baby was still alive, and the baby had to be nursed. It would be terrible to totally upset the baby. So she went in and greeted Monica with "Good morning" and picked her up and loved her and gave her a bath and got her ready for the day.

When the light came through the window, April and Gary dressed and he drove her home. As he dropped her off, he said, "April, whatever last night was like, I want you to remember that you'll always be my friend and I'll always care about you."

She went in the house and nobody was there. Kathryne was off driving Mike to work and April started sweeping the floor. Right in the middle of it she said out loud, "I'll never get married, never."

Kathryne had stayed up all night waiting for Gary and April. By five, she must have fallen asleep, and then the alarm went off not long after. She had to take her son Mike up the Canyon every morning to where he worked for the Forest Service, a twenty-mile trip up twisting roads, and after a day and night of cigarette smoke, the fear in her lungs felt ready to whistle up a storm with every breath. Then she came back down the Canyon to her house, walked in the door, and there was April enthroned like a zombie in the kitchen chair.

"Where in the hell have you been?" April did not answer. She just sat and stared. "Were you," Kathryne asked, "with that dirty crumb all night?" For all the easing of her fear, there was still no relief. She just felt sick. My God, April was in a trance. "Damn it," Kathryne shouted, "Did you stay with Gary all night?"

Suddenly April screamed. "Leave me alone! Can't you leave me alone? I know nothing." She ran in the bedroom. "You're nosey," she cried from the other side of the door.

"I can't do anything about it," Kathryne said to herself. She was just thankful the child was home. It was one more wall Kathryne was holding up with her life.

CHAPTER 15

Debbie and Ben

1

Debbie was feeling a little off one day and Ben kept wanting to take her to the doctor. She was pregnant, after all. But there were eleven kids over from the Busy Bee Day-Care Center, and Debbie didn't have the time. Ben finally raised his voice a little. At which point she told him he bugged her. That was the worst fight they ever had.

They were proud that was the worst fight. They saw marriage as a constant goal of making each other happy. It was the opposite of that song, "I Never Promised You a Rose Garden." They kind of promised each other. They weren't going to be like other marriages.

Debbie was five feet tall and didn't weigh a lot more than a hundred pounds. Ben was six-five and weighed one hundred and ninety when they were married. Two years later, he weighed two-ninety, and looked big and fat and fine to Debbie. He was always going on a diet or splurging. He would lift barbells to try to keep in shape.

For a young Mormon couple, they lived well. They had steaks in the freezer, and loved to go out and get pizzas. They learned to make even better pizzas at home. Ben would cover every square inch with meat and cheese. They also dressed well and they managed to meet a $100 payment each month on their Pinto. Ben could have been the huge man who gets out of the little Pinto in the TV commercial.

They worked hard, however. Ben kept trying to get back to his courses in business management at BYU, but it took two to three jobs a day, plus Debbie managing the day-care center, in order to keep abreast with what they spent living happily with each other. So they hardly needed friends. They had their baby, Benjamin, who was their first priority, and they had each other. That was all of it. It was enough.

Debbie didn't know about matters outside the house. She knew a lot about plastic pants and disposable diapers and just about anything to do with children in the day-care center. She was terrific with kids and would rather mop her kitchen floor than read.

Since she didn't have a driving license, however, she couldn't go to the grocery store, the laundromat, or anywhere without Ben.

She also didn't know their bank accounts nor their debts. She lived in a world of two-year-olds and four-year-olds and took wonderful care of Ben and Benjamin, and their house, and they went out to eat five nights a week. Except when Ben was on a diet, that was their entertainment. They would share one of those deluxe eight-dollar pizzas.

Ben always had to carry two or three jobs. Before Benjamin was born, there was one stretch when Ben used to get up at four in the morning and drop Debbie at the day-care center at five. She would get play materials ready for the children who would start coming in at seven, and by then, Ben would have driven to Salt Lake where he managed a quick-food restaurant. That work began at 6 A.M., and he wouldn't get home until eight at night. Then he got another job where he didn't have to drop her off at the day-care center till 10 A.M., but had to go to Salt Lake for a stint that began at noon in a chain called Arctic Circle. (It later changed its name to Dandy Burgers.) He would get home at 2 A.M. In the winter it was rough when the roads were icy. Ben began to get a bad feeling about doing that forty-five-mile drive in each direction day and night.

Of course, he had other sources of income. He would work at BYU on the maintenance crew, plus whatever cleaning jobs he picked up. In turn, Debbie kept Benjamin with her at the Busy Bee, and even had a crib in the office. Sundays, and whatever spare time

Ben found, he would work as a home teacher for Bishop Christensen. If a widow needed some electrical work or handyman plumbing, if her walk required shoveling, or her windows cleaned, why, Ben would do it. He must have checked on the needs of five or six such families a month.

When the position of Manager at the City Center Motel came open, Ben leaped to take it. The job paid a minimum of $150 a week plus an apartment, but the business might be there for him to build. It was not a large new motel, and not on a highway, but at capacity, he could end up drawing as much as $600 a week. In addition, they could have all the time they wanted together.

Their clientele was mostly tourists, or parents coming up to visit their kids at BYU. Most people who stayed at the motel were quiet. If occasionally a couple looked like they weren't married, Debbie didn't exactly approve of it, and tried to give them a nice, noisy, dirty room.

The busiest time was at 9 A.M., getting the maids out to work. They used to keep four chambermaids who each had a certain number of rooms to do in a given time. If it took six hours but should have taken two, they got paid for two. When they began, Ben and Debbie did a little such work together to learn how long it took. While a lot of other motels paid girls by the hour, Ben did it by the room. Of course, if there was an extra mess, Ben made an adjustment. He was always fair.

After a while, Debbie began to enjoy motel work more than she'd expected. There was lots of time together. Nothing much would happen after the morning rush until evening when the majority of people checked in. Ben began to talk of going back to school.

The work, however, was a little confining. They couldn't, for instance, leave the motel together unless they made arrangements in advance. That interfered with going out to a restaurant. It also rushed their dinner hour. Sometimes they had to eat a little too early.

They never felt any need to mix with other people, and time went by well. Ben got what social life he needed by going around town to drum up business. He wanted to get the name of the City

Center Motel well known, so he worked out special arrangements with a few of the larger motels. He had an understanding where the clerk would receive a dollar for each overflow guest sent Ben's way. City Center was always the first small motel to put out a NO VACANCY.

Nor were they ever afraid of being robbed. Once in a great while, they talked about what they would do if they had to face a gun, and Ben would shrug. He said that a little bit of money wasn't worth, you know, risking your life for. He would do what the robber asked.

2

Craig Taylor heard about the service station murder on the radio next morning while driving to work. His first thought was that Gary had done it. Then he thought he heard the announcer say Jensen had been killed with a .32. That gave him hope. The Browning Automatic was a .22.

At work, Gary seemed normal. It wasn't that he was relaxed, but he had been on edge since the day he broke up with Nicole. This morning he was just normally on edge.

Later that morning, Spencer McGrath got a call from a lady who said she had an apartment in Provo for Gilmore. If he was going to take the place, he had better come by around noon and give a deposit. Spencer felt that if there was any chance left for the guy, it was to get out of Spanish Fork and learn to live by himself. So he told Gary to take the afternoon off. It was the sad truth, Spencer decided, that he was happier when Gary wasn't around.

Craig didn't have a chance to talk about anything until right before the lunch break. But as they were slowing down about a quarter to twelve, Gary said, "Want to pitch pennies?" With that, he pulled out a handful of change. It sat there in his palm, a mountain of change. After Gary left, Craig couldn't help but wonder if that was money from the service station murder.

Gary stopped at Val Conlin's to thank Rusty Christiansen. She had pretended to be the landlady with an apartment for Gary. Val took the opportunity to remind him that he had to get the money for the truck.

Gary went by Vern and Ida's to ask if he could take a shower. Ida and Vern, however, were just leaving the house, and Ida wanted to be able to lock up. It got complicated. Gary had a funny wild-eyed look, and so Vern suggested they lock the house and let Gary take his shower in the basement, which had a separate exit. Gary agreed but looked a little hurt that they were shutting doors on him.

Soon after lunch, Val Conlin got a call. Gary had lost the keys to the truck. He was down at the University Mall, and needed somebody to come over and take his stuff, since he couldn't lock the cab.

Val sent Rusty Christiansen. When she pulled up in the parking lot, Gary was sitting there grinning. "Got the boss's car?" he asked.

Rusty didn't like Gilmore's assumptions. She was driving her own blue Thunderbird and it wasn't all that new. Still Gilmore tried to make up for the bad start. He got almost too gallant opening car doors for her.

He had a great big pair of rainbow-colored slalom water skis sticking out of the window of his truck with a price tag from Grand Central still on them. Now he explained he wanted to lock the skis in the trunk of her car.

Next, they went looking for the keys. He retraced his steps through various stores and in the health-food shop he found them — a great big bunch.

Going back through the Mall, Rusty stopped in front of Kiddy Ville. Her little girl collected Madam Alexander International Dolls and she could see they had a new one in from Spain. So Rusty said, "Have you got a minute?" and he said, "Hey, you know, sure."

Two old salesladies were clear down the other end. Rusty waited and waited — must have been five minutes. Nobody acknowledged they were in the place, and Gilmore was getting nervous.

She could feel how painful it was for him to wait. Finally, he said, "Which one do you want?" She told him. He said, "Don't worry about it," and opened the case, took the doll, took her elbow, and before she could protest, he had her out of the store. There was a bright red satin dress on the doll and Gary was saying, "Well, you know, it's really cute."

Rusty didn't know if he was showing off, but at this stage of her life, nothing was going to shock her. She just wanted to get out of the Mall.

As they went around the long way in the parking lot, Gary said, "You know, you're a pretty cool lady. You handle everything really good. You don't fall apart." When she nodded, he said, "I've been looking for someone to work with."

"Oh, that's nice," Rusty said. She was in one hurry to get to the car. She'd already decided he was unbalanced, so she certainly didn't want to insult him. "I'm glad you think I can handle things," she said.

"You're not bad looking," he said, "but you're too old for me." Looked at her critically. "How old are you?" he asked.

"Twenty-seven," Rusty said.

"You don't have a little sister, do you?" Gilmore asked.

Rusty thought, Lord, if I did, she'd be locked in the basement!

Gary said, "It's really too bad but you're just a little too old. I like younger girls."

"Well," Rusty said, "that's my loss."

Gilmore stopped to pick up a couple of six-packs so she got back to V.J. Motors before him. "Hey," she said, as she came in, "don't do this to me anymore, Conlin. You go next time." And told about the water skis.

Gary came in with the loot. "I don't want those slats," Val Conlin said. "They're worth," Gary told him, "$150."

"Hey, Gary, I don't have a goddamn boat. What do I want water skis for?" When Gilmore set them down in a corner, Val said, "When are you going to take your personal shit out of the Mustang so I can sell it?"

"Take a look at these water skis," Gary said.

"Hot?" Val asked.

Gary said, "What difference does it make?"

Val said, "I'm not a hock shop. I don't want hot merchandise. I sure as hell don't need new problems."

"Well," said Gary, "it's a good buy."

"Not a worth a turd without a boat," said Val. "Where's the boat? Just remember you owe me $400 as of tomorrow."

"I'll have it."

"Gary, you son of a bitch," said Val, "you better understand this and understand this good. If I don't have the goddamn money, you walk. You won't even know you had wheels."

"Val, you've been good to me, and don't worry. I'll have it."

"Okay," said Val. "Fine."

In the silence, Val picked up a newspaper and began reading. After a bit, he put the paper down and exploded. "Judas Priest, can you believe this murder?" he asked. "What kind of idiot would do it? Guy gotta be nuts, just shooting a guy in a gas station. For nothing." It really upset him. He slammed the paper on his desk. "You know, I can understand a son of a bitch shooting somebody if you can't get the money. But anybody that would take the cash, and then put the kid in the back room and lay him on the floor and shoot him in the head twice, has got to be a psychomaniac son of a bitch! They ought to string up that bastard." Conlin heard himself raving even as he was saying it, and Gilmore looked him back in the eye and said, "Well, maybe he deserved to be killed."

The expression on his face was so blank that Rusty decided Gary knew something about the killing. Had he sold a hot gun?

Val was yelling, "Oh, Gary, come on, for Christ's sakes, to shoot a kid in the head? You got to be crazy, man. Nuts!" Gary just said, "Well . . ." He got up and asked if Val wanted another beer. Val said, "No, we got some. Take it with you, Gary." Maybe it was drinking all that beer so early, but there was definitely a pall on the afternoon.

3

On Tuesday afternoons Gary had his weekly session with Mont Court. Their meetings, since Gary had stolen the tape deck at Grand Central, took longer now, but on this hot Tuesday in July, it lasted for over an hour. Gilmore had finally begun to confide, and the parole officer saw it as his opportunity to reach him. In a few days, Court would have to make a recommendation on the presentence investigation, and he had about decided to propose a week of jail. It would give Gary a taste.

Court didn't look forward to that, however. Gilmore was using every opportunity to manipulate his environment but still it was hard not to feel sorry for him, particularly on a day like this.

Gilmore was talking about drinking, and how much he wanted to cut it out. As he saw it, that was the only way to get back with Nicole. He had to get back.

They talked, and Court found out that Nicole had left because she was frightened. That disturbed Gilmore. He didn't want her to think he was a violent person. Court listened politely, but he thought Gary was being unrealistic. You couldn't turn somebody's fear around by your desire that they not be afraid. Court did think, however, that Gilmore was being realistic in understanding how much he needed Nicole, and that his chances of getting her back might be better if he cut out drinking.

Of course, he hardly looked like a teetotaler now. His goatee was on the way to becoming a beard and his clothing looked sloppy.

It was the nearest they had ever come to a real talk. Gilmore sat there forlornly, saying in a flat sad voice that he thought he had problems as a lover. That carried their relationship a step forward, Court thought.

Gary spent the next few hours looking for Nicole around Orem and Provo, then in Springville and Spanish Fork. While he was driving on one road, Nicole and Roger Eaton were moving along another.

4

Nicole was in a state. Before long, Roger Eaton was in the same state. The Tuesday afternoon he had been looking forward to wasn't turning out well.

First, she told him about seeing Gary on Sunday in Spanish Fork. Showed Roger the little Derringer. Seeing the way Nicole pulled it out of her pocketbook, Roger was pretty sure she could use it. He said, "Put that away." He never knew anybody who began to live the way Nicole had to live.

While driving around, Roger told her about the murder last night at the gas station. That was the first she had heard of it. If she had known, she wouldn't have left her house, she told him. "I'm scared," said Nicole.

After a little while, she murmured, "I think Gary did that murder." "Are you kidding me?" he asked. "No, I think so," she repeated. "But you don't know for sure?" Roger asked. She wouldn't answer.

He took her to the Utah Valley Mall and bought her a pair of jeans that ran around $25 and a shirt that cost $35. Then he took her back to her apartment in Springville quickly as he could and let her off about a block away. Before she got out of the car, she warned Roger that Gary had seen the letter he sent.

Roger began to think that Gary might find Nicole, and beat her up until she gave away his name. Then Gary would come over to the Mall to look for him. When that thought went through Roger's mind, he said to himself, "My ass is grass."

As they were saying good-bye, Roger couldn't help himself. He said, "Nicole, I'm afraid Gary might find me." She said, "He'll kill you if he does."

"What did you *do* to him?" Roger asked.

She said, "Nothing. He just wants me."

Roger said, "He must want you a lot worse than I do, because I don't want to get killed over you."

She said, "I can understand that."

He said, "I want this thing to end if it's going to mean my damned life or yours. Let's just forget this crap."

It was getting dark when he said good-bye to her.

That evening over the newspaper, Johnny said to Brenda, "Hey, they had a shooting over here." He waited for her to read the account, and then said, "It has all the earmarks of Gary Gilmore."

Brenda said, "I know he's an asshole, Johnny, but he's not a killer."

Johnny said, "I'm afraid he is."

5

All day at the motel, Debbie Bushnell had been nervous. All afternoon, she kept calling her friend Chris Caffee. That was most unusual. She and Chris usually talked to each other about once every two weeks, and Chris would drop in at the motel now and again. Chris had used to work for her at the Busy Bee, and they got along well, but they weren't exactly close friends. Debbie was so restless this Tuesday afternoon, however, that she kept calling. Chris finally said, "Debbie, I have five hundred things to do. I don't have anything more to say." Debbie couldn't help herself; she phoned two hours later. "What are you doing?" she asked. Chris said, "Nothing. Why are you calling?"

Debbie had been having a strange feeling from Sunday on. It continued all day Monday and was worse on Tuesday afternoon. Same with Ben. They had gone to visit his best friend, Porter Dudson, up in Wyoming on Sunday, a rare Sunday off from the motel, and Ben couldn't sit still all day. Rushed poor Porter and his wife, Pam, through the meal and everything. Now, he was over whatever was bothering him. He had spent part of Tuesday afternoon working on his weights and then he took a nap. It was Debbie at this point who didn't know what to do with herself.

When Ben got up, she fixed him a steak and a salad and they sat down to dinner. Benjamin was already bathed and asleep and finally it got dark. People started coming in for rooms and Ben turned on the TV in the office and began to watch the Olympics. After a while Debbie left him alone to handle incoming guests and went back to cleaning the house. But this stupid fear just kept crawling in her stomach.

Gary stopped at a gas station on University Street and Third South, a couple of blocks from Vern's house. Gary knew a fellow named Martin Ontiveros who worked there, and in fact, had put in some time that week painting Martin's car. Now he stopped off to ask Ontiveros if he could borrow $400, but was told by Martin's step-father, Norman Fulmer, who ran the gas station, that they'd just bought 6,000 gallons that day, and didn't have a dime to their name. Nothing in the station but credit-card slips. Very little cash. Gary drove off to Orem.

Around nine o'clock he started to go back to Spanish Fork to look for Nicole, but on the way he stopped at a store, and the motor wouldn't start. The truck had to have a push. So he pulled in again at Norman Fulmer's gas station to complain. Not only did he have trouble starting, he told them, but in addition, the motor was overheating. "Well," said Norman, "just put it in the bay. We'll change the thermostat." Gilmore asked how long it would take and when Fulmer said twenty minutes, Gilmore said he would do a little visiting.

As soon as Gilmore was gone, Martin got into the truck, turned the key and pressed the starter. The motor turned over with no trouble.

In the middle of washing the couch cushions, Debbie Bushnell went out to the front office and asked Ben to go to the store and get some low-fat milk. She was also hoping he would bring back some ice cream and candy bars, and began to giggle at the thought she must be pregnant again. She had certainly felt telltale cravings. Ben, however, didn't want to go. He was interested in the Olympics.

Washing the couch cushions proved to be a job. She couldn't get it done to her satisfaction with a damp cloth. So she decided to unzip the covers, wash them, dry them, put them on again. In the mean-while, she was planning to vacuum out the corners of the couch, but when she started to turn on the Kirby, she couldn't bring herself to press the switch. Three times in a row she just kept looking at the label — Kirby — on the vacuum, and not turning it on.

Then she heard Ben talking to somebody in the front office. She thought maybe there was a child there, because she heard a balloon pop. So she went out to talk. No reason. Just felt like talking to a kid.

As she went through the door from the apartment to the office, a tall man with a goatee, who had been about to leave, turned around and came back toward her. The craziest word went through her head. "There's poopy-doo," she said to herself. Quickly, she turned around and went back to the apartment.

She actually retreated into the farthest corner of the baby's bedroom. In her mind, she kept seeing that man looking her square in the face from the other side of the counter. She had an ice-cold feeling on her heart. That man was after her.

Then she got herself together, and walked through the living room into the kitchen and peeked into the office through the narrow space between the television set and the square hole in the wall that separated the kitchen from the office. You could sort of squint into the office through that space. She got there in time to watch the strange man walk out the door. Then she walked in.

Ben was on the floor. He just lay there face down, and his legs were shaking. When she bent over to look at him, she saw his head was bleeding. She had had first-aid courses once and they told you to put your hand to a wound and apply pressure, but this was awful heavy bleeding. A wave of blood kept rising out of his hair. She put her hand on it.

She sat there with the phone in her free hand ringing the operator. It rang five times, and ten, and fifteen times, and a man came into the office and said he had seen the fellow with the gun. The phone was ringing the eighteenth, and the twentieth, and the twenty-second, and the twenty-fifth time. There was still no answer. She said to the man, "I need an ambulance." The new man didn't speak very good English, but he held the phone, and the operator still didn't answer. The man went out to call the police.

Now she called Chris Caffee. It was easy to remember that number after calling her four times that afternoon. Then Debbie just sat there with her hand on Ben's head and time went on for a long time. She couldn't tell how long before help came.

CHAPTER 16

Armed and Dangerous

1

Peter Arroyo was coming back to the City Center Motel from the Golden Spike Restaurant where he had gone with his wife and his son and two nieces for supper around nine-thirty that evening. It was now close to ten-thirty and they were returning to their rooms.

As they passed the front window of the motel office, Arroyo could see a strange sight. He had noticed, while registering, a large motel attendant with a small wife. Now neither of them was visible. Instead, a tall man with a goatee was stepping around the counter just as Arroyo came along the street. The man had a cash drawer in his hand. Arroyo could see that he also had a pistol with a long barrel in the other hand.

The kids observed nothing. One of Arroyo's nieces even wanted to go into the office to get stamps. Arroyo said, "Just keep going." Out of the corner of his eye he could see the man turn around and go back to the counter. Arroyo looked no more, but continued walking to his car. He kept hoping that what he had seen was somebody fooling around with a gun. Maybe there was a simple legitimate explanation.

When he reached his Matador which was parked about fifty feet from the office, he sent the girls upstairs. Then he started unloading the car carrier on the roof. Two men came down from the balcony, and he wondered if they were going to the office, but they just happened to be looking for ice, and went right upstairs again.

Now the man with the gun came out of the door, turned left, and went up the street on foot. Arroyo headed right to the office.

He could see the motel manager on the floor, and the man's wife next to him with a phone in her hand, and blood all over the place. The man on the ground didn't say anything, he just made noises. His leg was moving a little. Arroyo tried to help the woman turn him over, but the footing was slippery. The man was very heavy and lying in too great a puddle.

2

Walking away from the motel, Gary put the money in his pocket and discarded the cash box in a bush. About a block from the gas station, he stopped to get rid of the gun. Took it by the muzzle and pushed it into another bush. A twig must have caught the trigger for the gun went off. The bullet shot into the soft meat between the thumb and the palm.

Norman Fulmer took a bucket of water and threw it over the walls of the bathroom. He took a big sponge and washed the tile and scrubbed the floor. Then he went out to see how the work was going on Gilmore's truck. Instead, he saw Gary walking real fast right past him to the men's room that Fulmer had just finished cleaning. There was a trail of blood following Gilmore. "I don't know," Norman said to himself, "I guess he ran into something." And he just mopped up those big drops right there on the bay floor.

The scanner box was overhead, and Fulmer heard the police dispatcher talking about an aggravated assault and robbery at the City Center Motel. Norman began to listen real hard. He was in the habit of paying attention to the scanner anyway. It was more interesting than music. The dispatcher was now saying that a man got shot and another left on foot.

Fulmer went back into the bay and saw with one look that Martin Ontiveros had also heard the scanner. He hadn't even removed the old thermostat, but right now he started putting a bolt back in, and Fulmer screwed in the other, and soon as that was done, they slammed down the hood even as Gary came back through the men's room door, and said, "Got it done?" Fulmer said, "Yep. I got it all done."

Gilmore went in from the shotgun side and slid all the way over to the driver's seat. He was hurting, Fulmer could tell. Had to lean all the way over to the left of the steering wheel in order to get the key in with his right hand. When he finally got it started, Fulmer said, "Hey, take care," and Gary said, "All right," and backed out, and sure enough, he slammed into the concrete pole that was there to prevent people from hitting the drinking fountain. "Oh, God," said Fulmer to himself. Gilmore wasn't moving the truck now, and Fulmer was thinking Gilmore still had a gun, but he went back out and slapped the side of the door, and said, "Hey, looks like you're a little wasted. You ought to get some Z's." Gilmore said, "Yeah, I'm gonna go crash." "All right," said Norman, "see you tomorrow."

As he drove away, Fulmer got the license number, and wrote it right down. He noticed that Gilmore turned west on Third Street, and so was probably going to drive directly past the City Center Motel. Fulmer put a dime in the phone, called the police, told them what kind of a truck Gilmore was driving. The dispatcher said, "How do you know it's the right man?" He told her about the bloody trail Gilmore had left. Then she asked how Gilmore parted his hair. Fulmer said, "Down the middle. He's got a little goatee." The girl said, "That's him." Somebody else must have given a description already. Then Fulmer could hear the dispatcher telling the police that the suspect was heading west from University Avenue. At that moment, one of the patrol cars came screaming through the intersection going east. Fulmer called the dispatcher back and said, "Hey, lady, one of your friends just went the wrong way with the siren on," and had the pleasure of hearing her yell, "Turn around and go the other way."

3

That night Vern and Ida had been sitting in their living room next to the motel and never heard a sound. "Perry Mason" had been on television, then "Ironside." After which, the sirens began to sound right in front of their house. Naturally they went out in the street to see what was happening. Vern was wearing slippers, and Ida, an orange robe. She was actually barefoot. That's how sudden the police were.

Ida had never viewed a scene to compare with it. Patrol cars were coming in every moment with their blue lights turning and that awful siren going. Loudspeakers kept making different kinds of noises. Some were blasting orders to the cops, others kept droning the same remark over and over to the bystanders, "WOULD YOU KEEP THE SIDEWALK CLEAR, PLEASE? WOULD YOU KEEP THE SIDEWALK CLEAR, PLEASE?" Ida could see blazes of light, and pools of light, and now an ambulance came up, and paramedics started running out. One great big white light was circling as if to look for the guilty party. It wasn't hard to feel under examination each time the light turned past your face. The sirens were frantic. Every thirty seconds a new police car came screaming into the motel compound. People were even running in from Center Street three blocks away. There was more noise than if the town of Provo was burning down.

SWAT arrived. Special Weapons and Tactical Team. Two teams of five, one after the other. Moving around in dark blue two-piece fatigue uniforms, with black high-laced jump boots, they looked like paratroopers. Except the word POLICE was spelled out in big yellow letters on their shirts. They were certainly carrying heavy stuff — shotguns, .357 Magnums, semiautomatic rifles, tear gas. The night had turned cool after a hot day, but they were sweating plenty. Those armored vests under the fatigues were hot to carry.

In the courtyard of the motel, one guest kept shouting, "I saw somebody run in there." He was pointing to a downstairs room, 115.

It wasn't easy to break in on an armed killer. The police were sweating plenty as they axed the door down. Then they maced the hell out of the interior. Put on their gas masks, and jumped through the mess of broken plywood. Nobody was in the room. The smell of Mace, so close to the odor of vomit, drifted out into the courtyard of the motel. For the rest of the evening, everything smelled of vomit.

Outside, people kept rushing up to the office window. Kids would come tearing along, look in, take off. At one point, a crowd got to gather in front of the picture window of the office, and stood there looking at paramedics pounding away on the chest of Benny Bushnell. He was on a stretcher in front of the counter now. Ida had one nightmarish glimpse of the gore. The office looked like a slaughterhouse.

Paramedics kept running back and forth between the office and the ambulance. They wouldn't let Chris and David Caffee inside. Chris still felt half unconscious. When the phone rang, she and David had been asleep, and woke up to hear the sound of Debbie screaming, "Ben's been shot." Chris had said out of her sleep, "You know, this isn't a real good joke for late at night. This isn't funny." Half asleep, after being completely asleep, nothing made sense. They had rummaged around the house trying to find what to wear, then rushed over to the motel. Hours later, she would notice they put things on so fast, David's zipper was still down.

Chris worked her way to the front door of the motel and yelled, "Debbie, I'm here." She could see that Debbie, whose head barely came over the top of the counter, had heard her voice, for she left the office to go back into her apartment, then emerged from the private door. Debbie had little Benjamin wrapped in a blanket and was carrying a large plastic bag of diapers. Debbie now *threw* the baby on her. Just dumped him over. Like he wasn't real. Debbie wasn't screaming, but she looked weird.

Debbie said, "Ben's been shot in the head, and I think he's going to die." Chris said, "Oh, no, Debbie. Remember when my mom fell down the steps in D.C. and cracked her head open? Her head bled a lot but she's all right now. Ben'll be just fine." She didn't know what to say. How many times did somebody get shot in the head? She really didn't know what it meant.

Debbie went back in the house, and David looked at Chris and said, "If he's been shot in the head, he's already gone."

About this time, Chris began to notice that the baby was acting very odd. Benjamin usually recognized her. Chris had worked so often with Debbie in the day-care center that little Benjamin had seen Chris nearly every day of his early life. He was usually very lively and perky with her. Now Benjamin lay there like he was dead.

His eyes were completely still. Just flopped in her arms and didn't move.

4

Vern had known Bushnell slightly. They would chat while Vern sprinkled his lawn and Bushnell watered the motel flowers. One evening a pile of scrap lumber got left in the Damico driveway and had to be brought to Bushnell's attention. He apologized and said he'd get after the carpenters. Next morning the mess was gone. It gave Vern the impression of a conscientious man.

Now, Martin Ontiveros came up to Vern and said, "Gary did it." Vern said, "Gary who?" The kid said, "Gilmore." Vern said, "How do you know Gary did it? Did you see him do it?"

"No," said Martin Ontiveros.

"Then, how do you know I didn't do it?" Vern asked. "You didn't see it happen."

Vern said, "Go tell an officer. If you think it was him, go tell." Ontiveros now said Gary had just been up at the station, and there was blood all over his pants.

Vern thought, "Well, it has to bear looking into." He grabbed a cop who was married to a niece of Ida's, Phil Johnson, and asked him to check. Some talk went back and forth on a police radio. Then Phil came back and said, "It must have been him, Vern."

"Do you think he did it?" asked Ida.

"Yeah, he did it, the stupid shit," said Vern.

Glen Overton, who owned the City Center Motel, had just finished listening to the TV news when Debbie called. He lived in Indian Hills at the other end of Provo and came over fast in his green BMW, running every red light on the way.

When he arrived, the street was in chaos. Nothing but police and spectators jamming the sidewalk and all over the road. There was an unheard sound in the air like everybody was waiting for a scream. Glen didn't know if it looked like a disaster or a carnival.

Before he even tried to get into the office, he saw Debbie standing all alone outside her apartment. She seemed to be in total shock. He put his arm around her and held her. She kept asking, "Is Ben going to die?" Since they didn't want to let her back in the office, Glen finally asked her to wait outside a minute.

After Glen identified himself and got in, he watched the paramedics working over Ben. The police were making chalk marks on the carpet, and photographing an empty cartridge on the floor. When he saw a paramedic giving Ben heart massage right there, the heel of the man's hand thumping in brutal all-out rhythm against Ben's chest, he knew Ben was dead, or near it. Heart massage was a last resort.

Now a detective asked Glen to count the receipts and estimate the loss. Glen told them straight out that they never kept much more than one hundred dollars in the cash box. Any greater amount would be concealed in the apartment.

At this point, the medics got ready to take Ben to the ambulance. Glen Overton found Debbie and as soon as the ambulance took off, he put her in his BMW and followed.

On the drive, Glen sat behind the wheel trying to digest the irony that Ben had wanted this job because it would safeguard his life.

On the day Glen first interviewed him, Ben had said he was working in Salt Lake but hated the drive. Said he had the feeling he was going to be killed on that drive. Somehow, Glen felt Bushnell's conviction. There had been a number of good applicants at Ben's level, but the intensity of his feeling that he had to get off the road got him the job. Glen didn't regret it. In fact, he had never known a manager who was so anxious to do more. Ben had kept talking to him about getting his life in order. Didn't know when he'd be leaving. It obsessed Ben a little that he hadn't finished college yet and a new baby might be on the way.

Ida was on the phone to Brenda. "Honey, somebody shot that dear Mr. Bushnell next door." Ida started to cry. In between sobs, she said, "Somebody seen Gary running away. They've identified him."

"Oh, Mom." Brenda had been walking around all evening with a sense of disaster.

Ida said, "He'll come to you. He always does."

Brenda knew the police dispatcher in Orem, so she called, and said, "This is nothing more than a suspicion, but I think I'm going to need help with my cousin. Catch Toby Bath before he goes off duty."

Toby was her neighbor. It was like having your own private police force.

Then they locked the doors, and Johnny got out his .22 rifle. They had no more than done this, when the phone rang. It was Gary. "Brenda," he said, "is Johnny home? Can I talk to him?" Brenda thought, "That's different. He usually wants to talk to me first."

"Johnny," he said, "I need some help."

"What's the matter?"

"I've been shot," said Gary. "I'm hurt real bad, man. I'm over at Craig Taylor's, and I need your help."

At the hospital Glen Overton was trying to keep Debbie's mind on other things, so he got her to call her uncle in Pasadena. It seemed to give her a desire to inform other people, for when Chris and David Caffee walked in with Benjamin, Debbie asked Chris right off to contact Ben's bishop, Dean Christiansen. That took some doing.

There were a slew of Christiansens in the Provo-Orem phone book, and they all had different spellings. It was one super-Mormon name. Besides, Chris didn't know if Dean was the first name or the title.

They finally put Debbie in a little office. She sat there thinking she had to believe in something. So she kept thinking Ben was going to be all right. Then she realized that the doctor had come into the room with Bishop Christiansen, and they had both been sitting there. Why wasn't the doctor with Ben? Then another doctor came in. They were all sitting there. It came in on her slowly. They were waiting to get up their nerve.

Bishop Christiansen looked at her, and whispered gently. She didn't hear it. She kept looking at his silver hair. The doctor said that if Ben had lived, he would have been a vegetable. That thought went all the way in. That thought cleared her head. Debbie said, "If Ben had lived, he would have been warm, and I could have fed him and taken care of him." She had never felt more certain about what she knew. "At least," she said, "I would have had him with me."

5

She had met Ben at the Mormon Institute at Pasadena City College when she was twenty-one. She had never dreamed of going out with him. He was big and very good looking with a high pompadour of nice dark hair, and she was just a pint-sized ex-tomboy with a big broad turned-up nose and a slightly receded chin. Still, she made a point of sitting behind him. She wanted to keep her eye on him.

It took a while for Ben to ask her out, but on Christmas Eve of 1972, he did, and they went to church. Debbie didn't remember any of the Bishop's talk, she just sat by Ben. They saw each other every night after that. Took their happiness from looking at each other. They hadn't been going together a week before they decided to get married.

Glen Overton happened to be with Debbie when they brought her in to see Ben. That was the hardest part of the evening for Glen. He was looking at a person he had spoken to three hours previously. Now that person was stretched out, face blue, mouth open. Glen had seen a boy killed in an avalanche. This was worse.

A sheet covered Ben up to his neck, but Debbie walked forward, put her arms around him and hugged him. She really threw her arms around him. They had to sort of pull her away. She held on. They let her stay for thirty seconds more before they asked her to come out. Then they had to pull her away after all.

A doctor took Chris Caffee aside. "Would it be all right if Debbie went home with you? She doesn't have anyone in Provo."

Chris said, "Well, yeah, if the police'll check my house every minute on the minute all night long." They certainly hadn't found the murderer yet.

On the way out of the hospital, a nurse followed them to the car and handed over a paper bag with Ben's bloody clothes, his valuables and his watch. The nurse said, "Do you want his wedding band?" Debbie looked at them and asked, "Do I want it?" David said, "Well, why don't you take it?" Chris said, "If you decide you don't want it, you can have it put back on him." They stood there waiting while the nurse went in, and came back out, and said, "We can't get his ring off. He's too fat. Do you want us to cut it off?" She was *terrible*. They said, "Leave the ring." Debbie was getting wimpy now. She wasn't crying hysterically or anything, but she kind of collapsed.

6

Julie Taylor had come home from the hospital that day, and was sleeping with Craig in their double bed, when the knock came. Craig went to the window and looked. Gary was standing on the porch. Just like that, he said, "I've been shot." He made a point of showing a bleeding hand to Craig, and said he was in a lot of pain.

Gary didn't ask if he could come in the house and Craig didn't feel exactly ready to let him in. Didn't know why, just didn't want to ask him. Julie being out of the hospital he didn't want blood all over the house, and her having to clean it.

Gary, however, didn't seem to care. Just said he needed help. He had to have a set of clothes. He wanted Craig to take him to the airport.

"I'll take you to the hospital if you like," Craig told him.

"No," Gary said from the other side of the screen door, "I can't do that." He wasn't the least bit boisterous. Just moved his mouth, then said, "Call Brenda, then."

When Craig heard her voice, he passed the phone out the window to Gary on the porch. Julie was really tired. From the corner of his eye, Craig could see that she had already gone back to sleep.

While Johnny was talking to Gary, Toby Bath and his partner, Jay Barker, drove up and motioned for Brenda to come out. Just as she reached the patrol car, she heard an All-Points Bulletin on their radio. A voice said, "Gilmore is considered armed and extremely dangerous. Be prepared to shoot on sight."

She started to bawl. "Come on in," she managed to say, "Gary's on the phone."

Johnny needed a pencil to write down the address that Gary was giving him, so he handed the phone to Brenda. She got herself together and said, "How are you doing, Gary?"

He told some story about a man robbing a store and there was he getting shot in the attempt to prevent it. It was a shitty story and he was a shitty liar. He really was.

"Will you come to me?" Gary asked.

"Yeah," she said, "I'll come to you. I've got some codeine and I've got bandages. Where are you?" He gave the address. She said it out loud for Johnny to write down. Toby Bath and Jay Barker stood there in their uniforms and also wrote it down.

It hardly improved matters that Gary was at Craig Taylor's. Craig had a wife and two children. Brenda could see the shoot-out. But as soon as she hung up, the cops proposed that Johnny go in his truck. They would hide in the back.

If Gary discovered he had brought the cops with him, everybody was going to get wasted. Johnny found himself lighting one cigarette right after putting the previous one, just lit, in the ashtray, and he said, "I don't want to go over." It was about as good a fear as Johnny ever felt. On reconsideration, the police agreed it was too risky.

Brenda said, "I'll go. I don't think Gary will hurt me. Just let me take care of his hand."

Johnny said, "You're not going."

The cops said no. Flat-out.

Brenda didn't know if she were relieved or miserable.

Johnny went down to Orem Police Headquarters with Toby Bath and Jay Barker to see what the plans might be. Meantime, the Orem Police Chief called Brenda and said, "Stall Gilmore as much as you can. We need time." They agreed that Brenda would communicate with the police through her CB, and so be able to keep her telephone line open for Gary.

Before long, Craig was calling again. He said, "Hey, Gary's getting kind of nervous. How long has Johnny been gone?"

"Tell Gary," Brenda said, "that as usual, Johnny's out of gas again." This might pacify him for a few minutes. Johnny was famous as the family character who always delayed everybody while he got gas. On the street outside her house, police cars were screaming around the corners.

Craig called again. Brenda told him she hadn't heard from Johnny but he'd probably gotten lost. People who lived in Orem, she explained, only had to deal with a checkerboard arrangement for their streets and that was easy. It got them spoiled. They didn't know what to do with the weirdly curved roads in Pleasant Grove where Fourth North didn't mind getting its ass skewed around Third South.

She called the police to tell them that Gary was getting impatient. Brenda felt like a traitor. Gary's trust was the weapon she was using to nail him. It was true she wanted to nail him, she told herself, but she didn't want, well, she didn't want to have to betray him to do it.

Craig had gone outside to be with Gary. They sat out in the dark on the bungalow porch. Having been asleep, Craig didn't know about any killings this night. He was still worrying over last night's, but didn't feel ready to ask Gary outright. Did say, "Gary, if I knew you had anything to do with that fellow Jensen's murder, I'd turn you in right now."

Gary said, "I swear to God I didn't shoot the guy." Looked him straight in the eye. He had a powerful knack of staring right into you.

Again, Gary asked him to call. Craig went inside, picked up the phone, talked to Brenda once more. She was nervous. Craig could more or less sense she had called the police. She didn't say anything such to Craig, she just asked if he and his family were all right, and if Gary was being decent, and Craig said, "We're all right. He's fine."

He went back to the porch.

Gary said he had friends in Washington State, and he believed he would go underground. He mentioned Patty Hearst. Said he could connect with her old network. Craig didn't know if Gary really knew her, or was bragging. Craig asked once more if he wanted to go to the hospital. Gary said he was an ex-con, and the hospital wouldn't understand.

They sat out there half an hour. Gary spoke about April. Said she was a slick chick. Said she was *"Real nice."* The longer they sat out there, the calmer Gary got. He almost got despondent. Then he said that when he was settled, he would send Craig a painting. He also said, "I'll write you my new address. You can mail my clothes and stuff." He had brought his paintings, his poems, his manila envelope full of snapshots and his other belongings over from Spanish Fork. He said, "Send me all them things when I get settled."

To himself, Craig kept saying, "Come on, Johnny, you son of a bitch, get here."

7

When the Caffees got home, they discovered that Debbie was covered with blood. Chris had to take her into the other room to change. Then Debbie wanted to make phone calls. She telephoned her mom, and Ben's sister, and all her own brothers and sisters, and Ben's friend, Porter Dudson, up in Wyoming. She just called and called. She would start crying and say, "Ben's been shot and he's dead." It was like a recording.

Chris opened their sofa bed in the living room, and she and David lay there while Debbie sat in the rocking chair and rocked Benjamin.

Now, it was Gary on the phone. "Where's John?" he asked.
"He should be there by now," said Brenda.
"God, man," said Gary, "he's not."
"Well, honey, calm down," she said.

"Cousin, is Johnny really coming out?"

Brenda said, "He's coming, Gary."

She had a flash. "Gary, what was the house number, 67 or 69?"

Gary said, "No, it was 76."

"Uh-oh," said Brenda, "I gave him the wrong one."

"Will you get it right this time?" he snapped.

"Okay, Gary," she said meekly. "Johnny's got the CB in the truck, and I have one here. I'll plug him into the right address. Just hang tight." She took a breath, "If you feel kind of faint," she said, "or kind of badly from the wound, why don't you go out on the porch where the air is cool and take some deep breaths. Turn the light on so Johnny can find you."

"How stupid," said Gary, "do you think I am?"

Brenda said, "Excuse me, stay inside."

"All right," he said. He still must trust her.

Soon as she hung up, she began to bawl again. It seemed so wrong to do it this way. But she called the police department, and told them, "He's getting very impatient."

To Gary, who soon called again, she said, "Listen, I know you're in pain. Hang loose. Just stay put."

Brenda was now patched in with the Provo, the Orem, and the Pleasant Grove Police Chiefs, and she could tell from what the dispatchers were saying that the houses around Craig Taylor's were being quietly evacuated. The police were moving into position. One of the Police Chiefs wanted to know which room Gary was in and she told them, she thought he was in the living room. Was the light on? he wanted to know. She said she didn't think so.

Just then Gary called back again. "If John ain't here in five minutes I'm splitting."

"My God, Gary," she said, "are you on the run or something?"

Gary said, "I'm leaving in five minutes."

She said, "Be careful, Gary. I love you."

He said, "Yeah." Hung up.

To the police, she said, "He's coming out. I know he's got a gun, but for God's sake, try not to kill him." Brenda added, "I mean it.

Don't fire. He doesn't know you're there. See if you can surround him." She didn't know if she was reaching anybody.

After the last call, Craig just talked to Gary through the screen in the window, until finally Gary said, "Stick your head out through the screen and let me see your face."

Now, Gary shook hands with Craig and said, "Well, they're never coming, so I'm leaving." They shook hands, thumbs up, pretty good handshake, Gary still looking Craig in the eye. Then he went out to his truck. Craig turned the porch light off, and watched him go down the road.

For a while, Brenda got the play-by-play. Over the special channel on the CB a voice said, "Gilmore's leaving. I can see the truck. He's pulling out now. He has the lights on." Then she heard he was heading down to the first roadblock. She didn't know what happened next. He seemed to have driven around that first roadblock. He was out. He was loose in Pleasant Grove.

She heard somebody from the police say, "I've got to cut you off now." Cut her off, they did. For an hour and a half. It was all of that before she knew what had happened.

Craig called Spence McGrath and said Gary was in trouble and might try to get over to his place. Craig thought the police were after him. Spencer said, "Wow, that's kind of wild," and got out his deer rifle, and had it lying right next to the door.

Lights shone through the window, and the cops were shouting at Craig Taylor, "Come out with your hands up." They searched the house. Julie appeared in her bathrobe, but the cops weren't all that courteous. They found Gary's clothes, told Craig to drive down to Provo and give a statement. He was up all night.

8

A SWAT team from Provo, five officers from Orem, and three from Pleasant Grove, a couple of County Sheriffs and some Highway Patrol had all met at the Pleasant Grove High School where an impromptu command post was established. Since there was every chance of a shoot-out, they had started cleaning out the area around Craig Taylor's house. It meant tiptoeing from door to door, waking people up, leading them out of the neighborhood — it took time. In the meanwhile, they set up roadblocks.

When the word came down that somebody was driving away from Craig Taylor's in a white truck, everybody expected a vehicle to come barreling through. What fooled them was that the white truck drove at a moderate rate of speed, slowed down, and went right around. It hadn't been that heavy a roadblock. Just a barrier across one-half of the two-lane, with a police car parked to the side. After the guy in the white truck had gone past, it was reported that he had a goatee. Then it registered. That was him. Two of their vehicles took off.

A couple of the cops stayed right where they were. They were thinking this fellow might have been a decoy passing the roadblock in hopes everybody would chase him. Then Gilmore could walk right on out.

One trouble with a roadblock is that it could start a lot of guns firing. So Lieutenant Peacock, who was running the operation from the command post at the Pleasant Grove High School, had told his people that if there was any doubt, they were to let a white vehicle go through. Next thing, he got the news. The driver in the white truck did fit Gilmore's description. Then Peacock could actually see the truck, just a few hundred yards away from the high school, driving east toward the mountains on a street called Battle Creek Drive. Going along at no great speed, in fact. Maybe five or ten miles over the speed limit, which was only 25 miles an hour there. Peacock radioed for a car to follow the truck, but when he heard that all vehicles in the vicinity were tied up, he got into his unmarked patrol car, a plain four-door '76 Chevelle, and proceeded after Gilmore. Within a few blocks he got near enough to see the truck again. Since he had been radioing in his position, another car driven by Ron Allen fell in behind.

The white truck made a right-hand turn and started going west down an empty country road at the edge of Pleasant Grove. There were just a few houses on either side, but he was heading back toward population. At that point, still another patrol car had gotten in line, and Peacock decided he now had sufficient assistance to make a stop on the truck. While the road they were on was not real wide, it would still be broad enough for three cars to get abreast. So, at that point, he radioed for the other two to come up on his left-hand side, and soon as they did, all three turned on their spotlights at once and their overhead revolving red lights.

On the PA system, Peacock cried out: "DRIVER IN THE WHITE TRUCK, STOP YOUR VEHICLE, STOP YOUR VEHI-CLE." He could see the truck waver, slow down, come to a halt. Peacock opened his door. He had a Remington .12-gauge shotgun in the front seat, but, instinctively, he came out with his service weapon.

The white truck had stopped in the center of the road. Peacock stood behind the protection of his open door. He could hear Ron Allen commanding Gilmore to put his hands up. Right there in the driver's seat he was to put his hands up. Lift them so he could be seen through the rear window. The man hesitated. Allen had to give the order a third time before he finally raised his hands. Next Allen told him to put those hands outside the driver's window. The driver hesitated again. Then he finally obeyed. Now he was told to open the door by the outside latch. Once that door was open, he was told to get out of the truck.

By now, Peacock had walked around in back of his Chevelle, and was standing behind the headlights, on the right-hand side of the road where it was dark. He had his weapon ready. He knew the suspect couldn't see him. The man's eyes would be blinded by the lights of the car. In turn, the other officers were standing back of the open doors of their patrol cars.

On command, the man took two steps away from his vehicle. He hesitated. They told him to lie down on the road. He hesitated again. At that moment, his pickup truck started to roll away. He kept hesitating. He didn't know whether to run after the truck and set the emergency brake or to lie down. At this point, Peacock hollered, "LET THE TRUCK GO. LAY DOWN IMMEDIATELY. LET THE TRUCK GO." The man finally did as he was told and the white truck rolled farther and farther away from him and picked up speed going down that road which sloped all the way into town.

Slowly, gently, almost thoughtfully, it coasted off the shoulder, broke through a fence, ran through a pasture, and came to rest in the field.

Now all three officers, weapons out, moved forward along the blacktop. Peacock and the next officer were holding Service weapons. The third had a shotgun.

When they reached the man, Peacock put his gun away, and frisked him right there on the ground. Simultaneously, Officer Allen began to read off the Miranda.

"*You have the right to remain silent and refuse to answer questions. Do you understand?*" asked Allen. There was a nod. The man didn't speak.

"*Anything you say may be used against you in a court of law. Do you understand?*" asked Allen. A nod.

"*You have the right to consult an attorney before speaking to the police and to have an attorney present during any questions now or in the future. Do you understand?*" asked Allen. A nod.

"*If you cannot afford an attorney, one will be provided for you without cost. Do you understand?*" asked Allen.

The man nodded.

"*If you do not have an attorney available, you have the right to remain silent until you have an opportunity to consult one. Do you understand?*" asked Allen.

The man nodded.

"*Now that I have advised you of your rights, are you willing to answer the questions without an attorney present?*" asked Allen.

All the while, Lieutenant Peacock was putting handcuffs on him.

"Be careful of that hand. It's been hurt," said the man.

Peacock fastened the restraints, turned him over, and began to go through his pockets. The fellow had upwards of $200 in change and small bills in various shirt pockets and pants pockets, and he certainly had a wild look in his eye. "What am I going to do now?" said his expression. "What's my next move?"

Peacock had the feeling that the prisoner did not make any move without looking for the possibility of escape. Even though he had him handcuffed, Peacock remained on guard. It was as if he was still capturing the fellow. There was such resistance in the way this man hesitated whenever a command was given. He looked like a wildcat in a bag. Temporarily quiet.

A number of people had begun to come out of nearby houses and they stood in a circle staring at the captive. Lieutenant Nielsen arrived then in another police car and at that point, the prisoner spoke up suddenly. "Hey," he said, pointing at Gerald Nielsen, "I'm not going to talk to anybody but him."

They put him in the back seat of Peacock's car and Nielsen got in and said, "What's going on, Gary?" Gilmore said, "I'm hurting, you know? Can you give me one of those pills?" He pointed to the plastic bag where they had everything they took from his pockets. Nielsen said, "Well, we'll take you down, get you taken care of." They drove off.

9

For hours before this capture, Kathryne was spending a fearful evening. April had taken off again, and the weather had been hot beyond belief all day. They left the doors open, and the windows, and kept waiting for April to come back. Watched television. The tension in the house got so great they couldn't even go to sleep. Nicole had come over with the kids and bedded down with them on the floor of their room because it was cooler, but Kathy and Kathryne were too keyed-up and just sat around talking, scared to death.

Then all of a sudden, a floodlight went right across the windows. My God, they didn't know what was happening. A huge loudspeaker boomed in, a *huge* loudspeaker. "YOU IN THE WHITE PICKUP," it shouted. Two words, "Crazy Gary," jumped instantly into Kathryne's mind. "Oh, my God, it's that crazy Gary." Then they heard the loudspeaker say, "AT THE COUNT OF TWO, PUT UP YOUR HANDS,

PUT UP YOUR HANDS." A quieter voice said, "Get ready to open up, if he doesn't obey."

At those words, Kathy and Kathryne hit the floor. They could have been soldiers, they did it so instinctively. The bedroom flared with light. A police beacon was turning in a circle. When they dared to raise their heads they could see three policemen walking up the road carrying guns. Then someone yelled, "They got him."

Nicole woke up out of a crazy dream, and started screaming. Kathryne was holding onto her, shouting, "Sissy, don't go out there. You can't go out," which was all Nicole needed to break loose and she was out and in the crowd that was standing on the road staring at Gary on the ground. With all those lights on him, he didn't seem to know what was going on.

The police wouldn't let Nicole up close. She stood a distance away looking at him, and one of the cops began to question Kathryne who had just come out and asked, "Do you know him?" When Kathryne said, "Yeah," the cop said, "Well, he was right about up to your driveway when we got him. You were lucky." Then another cop said, "We think he killed the fellow last night too." That's when panic hit Kathryne. They still hadn't found April.

Nicole didn't know whether she wanted to go up to him or not. She just stood there, watching them point those rifles. There was nothing in her.

Back inside the house, however, she was shaking and screaming and crying. She took Gary's photograph and threw it in the garbage. "That crazy son of a bitch," she shouted, "I should have killed him when I had the chance!"

Later that night, she went through all kinds of changes. She lay there and words went through her mind like a broken record. Things they had said, over and over.

Toby Bath called Brenda. "We've got him," he told her. "Is he okay?" asked Brenda. "Yes," said Toby, "he's fine." "Anybody else get hurt?" asked Brenda. "Nope, nobody got hurt. Did a good clean job."

"Thank God," said Brenda. She had never been in a more shattered state. She couldn't even cry. "Oh," she said, "Gary's going to hate me. He's not too happy with me anyways. But now he's going to hate me." She was more worried about that than anything.

10

Chris Caffee couldn't sleep at all and Debbie kept saying, "I can't believe Ben's dead. I can't believe it."

They were all feeling pretty paranoid. Chris got up once to take a shower but started shaking when she realized there was a window in the bathroom and the killer could come through it. While the water was running she wouldn't hear a sound. It was like the movie *Psycho.*

Then she got back in the living room, and almost gave a yip. Some big person with a flashlight was walking in the front yard. But it was only a policeman. He had noticed their car door was open, and a cat had taken up abode in the back seat. They invited the man in, and that was how they learned a suspect had been caught. They didn't know if it was really the killer, but at least the police had somebody.

Debbie kept saying things you couldn't answer any more than you could talk back to your TV set. "When I was a kid," she announced, "I used to play touch football with the boys. I liked to swing off the roof on ropes." She said that, sitting in the rocking chair, holding Benjamin. "Yeah, that's great," said Chris from the studio bed.

"Ben took a lot of classes in bookkeeping and business administration, but his main interest was working with people," Debbie said, "and advising them."
"That's true," said Chris.

Debbie said, "We never had any time to play tennis or water ski because there was no recreation time. We were working all the way."

Holding Benjamin and rocking in the chair, she looked straight ahead. She had dark green eyes but they looked flat and black now. "It was Ben," she said, "who wanted to have the baby by natural childbirth. I went along because we always had the same idea about things."

"Yes," Debbie said, "Benjamin weighed seven pounds when he was born. The delivery presented no problem at all. Ben was with me at the hospital. He had a doctor's white outfit on. I could feel," she said, "his presence all the time. That was a nice time." She paused. "I wonder if I am pregnant now. Yesterday, I told Ben I thought I was. I think he's happy about it."

Debbie was in the rocking chair all night and Benjamin was in her arms. She kept trying to get the new thing together, but there had been too many breaks. Seeing the strange man in the motel office was a break in her understanding. Then the instant when she saw Ben's head bleeding. That was an awfully large break. Ben dead. She never went back to the motel.

Next afternoon, Debbie's mom came, and people from the Ward, and the Bishop. Things never stopped moving. Debbie stayed with Chris and David for three days before she went back to Pasadena. It was the first time she traveled on an airplane in her life.

CHAPTER 17

Captured

1

After the arrest, on the drive to the hospital, Gary said to Gerald Nielsen, "When we get alone, I want to tell you about it." Nielsen said okay.

It alerted him to look for a confession. Most of the time they were silent, but Gilmore did say again, "I want to talk to you about it, you know."

At the hospital, Gerald Nielsen stayed close while they doctored him. The Provo police had already called to say they wanted a metal detection test on his hand, but Gilmore refused. He said, "I want to talk to an attorney first." Gerald said, "Well, we'll get you an attorney, but he can't help you there. That's legal evidence."

Gilmore said, "Do I have a legal right to refuse it?" "Yeah," Gerald said, "you can. And we always have the legal right to do it by force." "Well," said Gilmore, "you're going to have to force me." He swore a couple of times and cussed and hollered and said he wasn't going to do it, and a couple of times Nielsen thought it might end up in a brawl, but finally he consented. The tests revealed he had held metal in his hand. Gilmore replied, "Yes, I had to do some filing today at work." It must have been four in the morning before they got to the Provo City Jail.

While the doctors were setting plaster of paris on Gilmore's hand, Nielsen decided to take a gamble and said, "Put a ring in it, will you, so we can get the handcuffs on." Gary said, "God, you have a polluted sense of humor." Nielsen felt it got them started.

2

Noall Wootton, the prosecutor for Utah County, was a small guy with light hair, a high forehead, and a large nose that looked like it had been flattened. He was usually a bundle of energy. When he got stoked up, he was like a tugboat chug-chug-chugging at any big job assigned to him.

In Noall Wootton's opinion the best lawyer he ever met was his father. Maybe for that reason he could never go into a courtroom without a stomach tied in knots. He won cases and still felt badly because they hadn't been up to what they should have been. For that reason he was more than careful to observe all the legal amenities on the night they brought Gilmore to the Provo City Police Station.

Tuesday night, or, rather, Wednesday 1:00 A.M. when the call came in to Wootton's home that the police had a man in custody for the motel murder in Provo, Noall sent a deputy to the hospital, and himself proceeded to the murder scene at the City Center Motel, where he spent an hour and a half directing the search for a gun. Having talked to Martin Ontiveros, and learned that Gilmore had come in bleeding, he backtracked up the street from the gas station following the trail of blood to its source near a bush on the street. They looked into the twigs and found a Browning Automatic .22.

Wootton was sitting on the desk in the detectives' room at the Provo Police Station, wearing his boots and Levi's, and not looking very official, when Gilmore was brought in. The prisoner looked pretty messed up. His left arm was bandaged in a cast and his hair was unruly. His Vandyke goatee looked wild. He was glaring. Seemed pissed off about the whole deal.

Gilmore acted particularly angry that he had chains on his feet. It made Wootton glad there were a number of cops around. Chains and all, he would not have wanted to be alone in that room with Gilmore.

Just so soon as Wootton learned that the only man Gilmore would talk to was Gerald Nielsen, he took the Lieutenant aside and told him what strategy to use: calm Gilmore down; get him into a befriending type of thing; be sure to advise him of all his rights. Also make sure he was not under the influence of alcohol, knew where he was, what he was doing. Most important, don't put pressure on him.

Wootton was taking care not to get into a dialogue with Gilmore. Such a conversation could easily become evidence, and then he might have to get up on the stand. Since he was going to prosecute the case, he didn't wish to be in Court wearing a second hat. So he listened through a speaker to the conversation Nielsen conducted in another room.

3

July 21, 1976 5:00 a.m.

GILMORE   What am I being held for?

NIELSEN   I don't know except I suspect armed robbery. I'm almost sure that's what it is.

GILMORE   What robbery?

NIELSEN   The one here in Provo tonight at the motel, and the one last night in Orem at the service station.

GILMORE   You know, I can account for last night real well, and I can account for tonight . . .

NIELSEN   Not too well, Gary.

GILMORE   Yes I can. . . . I went and had some work done on my truck down at Penney's. You'll see the receipts in the glove box, and I did some drinking. The truck kept stopping so I took it down here . . . and told them, "Listen, I'll leave my truck here and I'll pick it up in the morning and go to work and go down here and rent a room." I walked in and this guy had a gun on this guy. I grabbed it and he tried to shoot me in the head, and I pushed the gun up, and it got me in the hand. By that time, we was about outside, so I just went back down and got my truck and went out to Pleasant Grove . . .

NIELSEN   That's your story?

GILMORE   That's the truth.

NIELSEN   I don't believe it, Gary, I really don't believe that, and I know that you know that I don't . . .

GILMORE   I'm just telling you what happened . . .

NIELSEN   You know that story doesn't convince me, okay? I can't understand why those people got shot. Why did you shoot them, Gary? That's what I'm wondering.

GILMORE   I didn't shoot anybody.

NIELSEN   I think you did, Gary. That's the only thing I can't understand.

GILMORE   Listen, last night I was with that girl all night.

NIELSEN   What girl?

GILMORE   April Baker.

NIELSEN   April Baker? Where's she from, how can I get in touch with her?

GILMORE   She lives in Pleasant Grove. She was with me every minute. Her mother will tell you that I went over there and picked her up pretty early in my truck. See, I was going with her big sister, you know, who used to live out in Spanish Fork and we busted up, so I went over to show them my truck and April said, "Take me down here to get something for my brother," and I said, "Do you want to drive around and drink some beer?" and she said, "Yeah." She don't get along with her mother. She said, "Okay," so we drove around and drank some beer, smoked some weed, and I said, "Let's get a motel, I have to work in the morning." She said, "Go out here to American Fork." Well, I couldn't find one, so I ended up coming back to Provo.

NIELSEN   Which place?

GILMORE   Holiday.

NIELSEN   At the Holiday? Did you sign in on your own name?

GILMORE   Yeah, we stayed there until about seven. I took her home.

NIELSEN   Seven this morning?

GILMORE   Yeah, then I went to work.

NIELSEN   What time did you pick her up?

GILMORE   Seven. Five. Seven, I don't know. I don't have a watch. I don't like to wear watches.

NIELSEN   Was she with you when you stopped at the service station out there?

GILMORE   I didn't stop at any service station.

NIELSEN   Gary, I really think you did.

GILMORE   I didn't.

NIELSEN   You saw that .22 Automatic out there on the way in?

GILMORE   I seen a gun laying out there.

NIELSEN   Have you ever seen it before?

GILMORE   No.

NIELSEN   Well, if it's registered to you, you're sunk.

GILMORE   It ain't.

NIELSEN   Okay. I don't know, Gary. I can't . . .

GILMORE   Hey, that's what happened. I know you don't believe it.

NIELSEN   I really don't, Gary. I really don't, I really don't. I think you did 'er, and I can't understand why you ended up shooting the people. That's what I can't understand.

GILMORE   Listen . . .

NIELSEN   Gary, that's really the way I feel.

GILMORE   Do you think I'd shoot a person with that girl?

NIELSEN   I don't know. If you left her in the car down at the corner or she didn't know, that's another matter.

GILMORE   You can talk to her . . .

NIELSEN   How do we get ahold of her? . . .

GILMORE   She lives with her mother . . .

NIELSEN   Can you tell me how to get there? . . .

GILMORE   I can give you a phone number. She might be kind of hot that I had her daughter out all night . . .

NIELSEN   April Baker.

GILMORE   She was with me all the time.

NIELSON   How old is she?

GILMORE   Eighteen.

NIELSEN   She's of age then. I don't know, it just looks bad, Gary. . . . Can you describe the robber?

GILMORE   He had long hair, dressed, you know, in Levi's, a brighter jacket, you know, a Levi's jacket.

NIELSEN   I'll check that, I'll check it, but I don't believe that. I think as it stands, especially with your past record, I think they have a good case of robbery against you. I still can't understand why they were killed, I can't understand that.

GILMORE   Can't understand what?

NIELSEN   Why they were killed. I can't understand that. Gary, why were they killed?

GILMORE   Who?

NIELSEN   The guy in the motel and the guy out there . . .

GILMORE   I didn't kill anybody.

NIELSEN   I don't know, I think so.

GILMORE   Like I told you, I knew just where I was at every minute.

NIELSEN   What if I go check with these people and they say, "He's feeding you B.S."?

GILMORE   They won't.

NIELSEN   You sure? Everybody will say that?

GILMORE   They might tell you a little different times or whatever.

NIELSEN   What will April say if I ask her about 10:30 last night . . .

GILMORE   I don't know; she's a little spacey. When she was young, some guys took her out and gave her some acid without her knowing it and raped her. I don't know what she'll tell you. April was with me every minute last night. . . . I got lonely for Nicole, so I just went by and got her little sister. April wanted a ride. We got to necking and laughing and giggling, and I kept her all night. Well, look, that's it.

NIELSEN   I'll check it, I'll check her.

GILMORE   I ain't going to tell you nothing else without a lawyer. That's all, can I eat?

NIELSEN   It's getting close to breakfast time, you hungry? I'll tell them.

GILMORE   My hand still hurts too . . .

NIELSEN   Without an attorney and off the record, you wouldn't answer what I asked you a while ago?

GILMORE   What was that?

NIELSEN   About why they were killed when you left.

GILMORE   I don't know why they were killed. I didn't kill them.

NIELSEN   I hope that's true because that just worries me, that part. I can't understand it. I can understand the other. I can understand the stick-up thing.

GILMORE   I didn't stick nobody up, and I didn't kill nobody.

NIELSEN   Is it all right if I come back this afternoon to talk to you after I check on some of this?

GILMORE   I ain't killed nobody, and I ain't robbed anybody.

NIELSEN   Gary, I hope not but I have a hard time believing otherwise. At this point I have a hard time believing otherwise . . .

GILMORE   I'm hungry, and I'm in pain.

By the time Wootton got home on Wednesday morning, he had about decided to charge Gilmore with First-Degree Murder on the motel case. While the only print on the gun was too smudged to check out, they had the paraffin test and a witness, Peter Arroyo. He had seen Gilmore in the motel with the gun and the cash box. It looked promising to Wootton.

4

Around three-thirty that morning, Val Conlin received a phone call. A voice said, "This is the police. We have impounded a car of yours."

Val was so drowsy, he said, "Well, okay, fine."

"We want to let you know we have the car. There's been a homicide." "That's fine," said Val and hung up and his wife said, "What was that all about?" He said, "They've impounded a car. There's been a homicide. I don't know why, I don't know why, gee, you know." He went back to sleep. In the morning he'd forgotten about it.

When he came into the office next morning, Marie McGrath was there waiting to tell him.

"You got to be kidding," said Val. "Did he kill that guy the other night?"

Marie said, "What do you mean, the other night? Last night."

"Last night?" said Val. He was bringing up the rear in every heat.

"Yes," said Marie, "they caught him on the one he killed last night." That was when Val heard about the motel murder. The call at 3:30 A.M. came back to him.

A little later, the police were out examining the Mustang. Started taking out clothing and looking for blood. Val was asked, "Did he ever trade any guns with you?"

"Not to me," said Val, "I don't like guns. *I don't like guns.*"

"Well," said the cop, "he stole a bunch of guns. We're looking for them." "Hey," said Val, "not me."

The police were there an hour. After they left, Rusty took some trash out to the back. She came in saying, "Look what I got."

The wind had been blowing everything around. She had discovered a sack stuffed under an old soft-drink chest. Opening it, she found several pistols wrapped in newspaper.

When Val saw them, he shouted, "Hold it, wait a minute. JUST DON'T TOUCH THAT STUFF! Get on the phone. Call a detective!"

When the police came out, they again asked whether Gilmore offered any guns. Val said, "No. If he had, I would have shit. I don't like guns."

5

At 9 A.M., Gary was on the phone. "Where are you?" Brenda asked. He kind of snickered. "It's all right," he said, "I'm in custody. I can't get to you."

She said, "Oooh, God, thank goodness." Her voice sounded awful in her ear. She was as strung out from lack of sleep as she'd ever been. "Hey, really," Brenda said, "you okay?"

"Why," asked Gary, "didn't you come?"

"I was scared," said Brenda.

"What about John?" Gary asked.

"They wouldn't let him come, Gary."

"You betrayed me," he said.

"I didn't want to see you smeared all over Highway 89. I didn't want to see policemen I knew getting sent out and their wives left as widows. They're my neighbors." She added, "You're alive, aren't you?"

"It would have been a lot simpler if they'd wasted me out there."

"I really didn't want you to get blown away like some common criminal," she said. "To me, you're very uncommon. You're crooked, but you're not common."

"You could have taken me," he said, "to the state line."

"Gary, that's good dreaming, but it isn't real."

"I'd have done it for you," he said.

"I believe that," she said, and added, "Gary, I love you very much, but I couldn't've done that for you."

"You betrayed me."

"I didn't know any other way to round you up," Brenda said. "I love you."

There was a long pause, and then he said, "Well, I need some clothes."

"Why did they take yours?" she asked.

"Evidence."

"I'll bring some."

"I gotta have them by ten o'clock."

"I'll be there," she said.

"Okay, coz," he said, and hung up.

She went down to the Provo City Center where they had the new modern jail with the dark brown stone. It looked a lot like the modern Orem City Center with the dark brown stone that also had a jail. She took some of John's old work clothes. Since she couldn't get them back, no reason to give away his best things.

When she arrived, they had him in some cell downstairs. Told her he hadn't been arraigned yet, so she couldn't see him.

"Goddamn," said Brenda, "the man can't go into court naked."

"We'll take it to him," they said.

Now, while Brenda was still in the lobby, a TV crew arrived, and the hall became jammed with cables and minicameras, and people she'd never seen before in her life. She didn't have any makeup on, her hair was in a dumb ponytail, she had a pair of shorts on, and must have looked as overweight as she felt. She just wasn't about to get on camera.

Gary was being brought up the stairs, however, so she stepped behind a TV rig and a big cameraman, and watched as he went down the hall. She could see he was looking for her. To herself, she said, "I guess I really hate facing him." She thought she probably shouldn't feel ashamed, but she did.

6

Mike Esplin, the court-appointed defense attorney, looked a little bit like a rancher. In fact, he came from a ranching family. He was of reasonable height, pleasantly built, and wore a small brush mustache. His eyes were a watery blue-gray as if he had been staring into harsh sunlight for too long. He was, however, dapper in his dress, real dapper: a gray shirt, red tie, a gray plaid suit with a red stripe.

The first he heard of Gary Gilmore was when the Clerk in the City Court of Provo called that morning to say the Judge had asked Esplin to come over, if he could, for the arraignment.

It was no problem. There was hardly a lawyer in Provo who didn't have offices within a block or two of the Court. But things were moving so quickly, Mike Esplin didn't have an opportunity to discuss anything with his new client. In fact, he only met him in the courtroom.

Of course, there was nothing unusual about that. A Court-appointed lawyer didn't even have to be there for the arraignment. They had called him in this early only because it was a First-Degree Murder case. Esplin found himself standing with Gilmore in front of the Court one minute after he had introduced himself.

After the charges were read, they went to an anteroom, and that gave a brief opportunity to chat. But the scene was confusing. What with four or five officers and several news people, they were hardly alone, and Gilmore seemed ill at ease. He immediately said to Mike, "I'm new in the area and don't know any lawyers." Then he said he had no funds.

Since Esplin wanted to interview him a little more agreeably than this, they were moved down to the holding room in City Jail, a small cell with two bunks. Gilmore seemed paranoid that someone might be listening in on a bug, so they whispered, therefore, in low voices, and Gilmore said he had gone down to City Center Motel and happened to walk right into the robbery.

When Esplin asked Gilmore why he didn't go to the police after he was shot, Gilmore said being an ex-con, he was afraid they wouldn't believe him. To the lawyer, the story sounded like a bunch of bullshit.

In First-Degree Murder cases, the defense was allowed two attorneys, so, after the interview, Esplin went back to his office and called a few people. When two other lawyers told him that Craig Snyder, whom he knew slightly, did good defense work, he phoned and asked Snyder if he wanted to be involved. While he, Esplin, would be doing this as part of his regular salary, $17,500 a year, a Court-appointed attorney like Snyder, Mike explained, would be paid $17.50 an hour for legal work and $22 an hour for Court time. Snyder said that would be agreeable.

Esplin then went back to the jail around noon, and told Gilmore the name of his new attorney. He also mentioned that they would charge Gary with the Jensen murder. Gilmore looked him in the eye and said, "No way, man."

7

After the police had driven off, Nicole kept saying that Gary was crazy and she should have left him a long time ago. "That crazy bastard, that crazy bastard," she was still telling herself in the morning. When the Orem police called, however, a little before noon, to say they wanted Kathryne and Nicole to come down, she was pretty deliberate and cool about it. Even kind of flat.

She told Lieutenant Nielsen that she had had fights with Gilmore, and left because she was afraid of him. One time, she said, she had to get out of the car and run down the highway because he started to choke her. Then she told Nielsen that Gary had stolen the guns from Swan's Market in Spanish Fork. Added, "I can't tell you much more than that." "Look," said Nielsen, "I'm not going to prosecute you." So she told him that Gary had given her a Derringer for protection, but that after a while she felt she wanted protection from him.

When the interview was over, Nicole said, "Please don't tell him I told you these things because . . ." She paused and her mind seemed to slide away from all of them. It was as if she was looking for something a distance away, and then she murmured, "Because I still love him." A little later Lieutenant Nielsen drove her to the apartment in Springville and Nicole turned over her gun and a box of bullets. Nielsen couldn't get over how depressed she was about it all. He was used to taking the depositions of people who were real down, but Nicole would equal any of them.

After he came back to the station, the Lieutenant began to look into what evidence had accumulated. Two casings had been found under Jensen's body, and one in the blood by Bushnell's head. Those were useful, because an Automatic's markings were easy to identify. It looked like Provo would have authentication for Bushnell, and Orem for Jensen. If they could tie the gun to Gilmore, the case was solid.

Nielsen went over to see Gary about five in the evening. They had moved him already from Provo City Center to County, and that was one old jail. It was dirty. It was noisy. A real slammer. Nielsen had a real interview.

He brought along a briefcase on which you could flip the handle, and a tape recorder inside would start functioning unseen. He didn't dare take it, however, into the cell. Gilmore would have the right to inquire what was in that briefcase, and whether he was being recorded. Nielsen would then have to open it up. That would destroy all confidence Gilmore might have in him. So he left it turned on in the hall just on the other side of the bars. It would pick up what it could.

The county jail had to be one of the oldest buildings in Utah County. By July, it was hot enough inside to offer a free ticket to hell. With its windows open, you had to breathe the exhausts of the freeway. The prison sat on the edge of the desert in a flat field of cinders midway between the ramp that came off the freeway and the one that went up to it. The sound of traffic was loud, therefore. Since a spur of railroad track also went by, boxcars rumbled through the interview. When Nielsen tried listening to the tape recorder in his office, the sound of traffic on a hot summer evening was the clearest statement he could hear.

The detective had hopes for the interview. He felt Gilmore would talk ever since the moment right after the capture in Pleasant Grove when Gary asked for him. Nielsen had a strong feeling then that there would be a chance to get his confession. So he moved quickly and not at all unnaturally, into the role of the old friend and the good cop.

In police work, you had to play a part from time to time. Nielsen liked that. The thing is, for this role, he was supposed to show compassion. From past experience, he knew it wouldn't be altogether a role. Sooner or later, he would really feel compassion. That was all right. That was one of the more interesting sides of police work.

He had had his experiences. Years ago, when a patrolman, Nielsen did some undercover work in narcotics. There was a working agreement then with the Salt Lake City Police. Because Orem was still small, its police were well known to the locals. To get any effective undercover work, they had to import officers from Salt Lake City. In turn, Orem paid back the debt by sending a few of their own cops. That was how Nielsen first got into it.

His personal appearance, however, presented a problem. He had been a scoutmaster for seven or eight years and looked it. His substantial build, his early baldness, his eyeglasses and red-gold hair gave him the appearance of a businessman, rather than a fellow who might be dealing in drugs. For cover, therefore, he had pretended to be a Safeway meat-cutter, a job he knew something about, since he had done a little of that while working his way through BYU. He even had a union card.

In Salt Lake City he became known for a time as the meat-cutter who was always looking for dope on the weekend. That worked. A lot of meat-cutters weren't known as the straightest people. Nielsen even used to wear working clothes that showed bloodstains on the chest of his white smock, and below the knees of his white slacks where the apron gave no protection.

8

On this hot July evening, Nielsen began by saying that Gilmore's story, unhappily, was full of holes. They were checking it out, but it did not add up. So he wanted to know if it would be all right if they talked. Gilmore said, "I've been charged with a capital offense, and I'm innocent, and you're all screwing up my life."

"Gary, I know things are serious," Nielsen said, "but I'm not screwing with anybody's life. You don't have to talk to me if you don't want to, you know that."

Gary walked away and then came back a little later and said, "I don't mind talking."

Nielsen was with Gilmore about an hour and a half. There, in a Maximum Security cell, the two of them locked in together, they spoke. Nielsen came on very light at first. "Have you seen your attorney?" he asked, and Gilmore said he had. Then Nielsen asked him how he was feeling. "How's the arm?" Gilmore said, "Hey, I'm really hurting. They only give me one pain pill, and the doctor said I was supposed to have two."

"Well," Nielsen said, "I'll tell them I heard the doctor say two."

Nielsen tried to be as easygoing as he could. He inquired if Gary liked to fish, and Gilmore answered that with the time he'd spent in jail, there just hadn't been much fishing. Nielsen began to talk a little about fly casting and Gilmore showed interest at the idea that you had to get good enough to guess under different circumstances, what a trout was likely to accept in the way of a fly. The detective told him of taking overnight camping trips with his family up in the canyons.

Gilmore, in turn, talked about a few of his experiences in prison. Told of the fat girl who died, and the time they gave him too much Prolixin, and he swelled up, and couldn't move. Spoke of how prison demanded you be a man every step of the way. Then he asked a little more about Nielsen's background. He seemed interested that Nielsen had a wife and five children.

Was his wife a good Mormon? Gilmore asked. Oh, yes. He had met her at BYU where she had gone to get away from Idaho. What did she major in? asked Gilmore, as if he were truly fascinated. Nielsen shrugged. "She majored in home economics," he said. Then he grinned at Gilmore. "Her interest was to — you know, maybe, you know, kind of find a husband." Now they both laughed. Yes, said Nielsen, they had met in freshman year and were married the next summer. Well, said Gilmore, that was interesting. How did Nielsen become a cop? He didn't seem much like a cop. Well, actually, Gerald explained, he had planned on being a science and mathematics teacher when he went up to Brigham Young University from the family ranch at St. John's, Arizona, but he was an active Mormon and in his church work he met a detective on the police force whom he liked and so got interested and took a job as a patrolman.

Now he was a lieutenant, Gilmore remarked. Yes, in a little more than ten years he'd risen to be a detective, then a sergeant, now a lieutenant. He didn't say that he'd taken courses at the FBI Academy at Quantico, Virginia.

Well, that was interesting, said Gilmore. His mother had been a Mormon, too. Then he paused and shook his head. "It's going to kill my mother when she finds out." Again, he shook his head. "You know, she's crippled," said Gilmore, "and I haven't seen her for a long time."

"Gary," said Nielsen, "why did you kill those guys?"

Gilmore looked him right back in the eye. Nielsen was used to seeing hatred in a suspect's eyes, or remorse, or the kind of indifference that could lay a chill on your heart, but Gilmore had a way of looking into his eyes that made Nielsen shift inside. It was as if the man was staring all the way to the bottom of your worth. It was hard to keep the gaze.

"Hey," said Gilmore, "I don't know. I don't have a reason." He was calm when he said it, and sad. Looked like he was close to crying. Nielsen felt the sorrow of the man; felt him fill with sorrow at this moment.

"Gary," said Nielsen, "I can understand a lot of things. I can understand killing a guy who's turned on you, or killing a guy who hassles you. I can understand those kind of things, you know." He paused. He was trying to keep in command of his voice. They were close, and he wanted to keep it just there. "But I just can't understand, you know, killing these guys for almost no reason."

Nielsen knew he was taking a great many chances. If it ever came to it, he was cutting the corners on the Miranda close enough to send the whole thing up on appeal, and he was also making a mistake to keep talking about "those guys" or "why did you kill those guys?" If any of this was going to be worth a nickel in court, he should say, "Mr. Bushnell in Provo," and "Why did you kill Max Jensen in Orem?" You couldn't send a guy to trial for killing two men on two separate nights in separate towns if you put both cases into one phrase. Legally speaking, the killings had to be separated.

Nielsen, however, was sure it would be nonproductive to question him in any more correct way. That would cut it off. So he asked, "Was it because they were going to bear witness against you?" Gilmore said, "No, I really don't know why."

"Gary," said Nielsen, "I have to think like a good policeman doing a good job. You know, if I can prevent these kinds of things from happening, that makes me successful in my work. And I would like to understand — why would you hit those places? Why did you hit the motel in Provo or the service station? Why those particular places?" "Well," said Gilmore, "the motel just happened to be next to my uncle Vern's place. I just happened on it."

"But the service station?" said Nielsen. "Why that service station in the middle of nowhere?"

"I don't know," said Gilmore. "It was there." He looked for a moment like he wished to help Nielsen. "Now you take the place where I hid that thing," he said, "after the motel." Nielsen realized he was speaking of the money tray lifted from Benny Bushnell's counter. "Well, I put the thing in that particular bush," he said, "because when I was a kid I used to mow the lawn right there for an old lady."

Nielsen was trying to think of a few Court decisions that might apply to a situation like this. A confession obtained in an interview that was conducted without the express permission of the man's attorney would not be legal. On the other hand, the suspect himself could initiate the confession. Nielsen was ready to claim that Gilmore had done just this today. After all, he had asked Gary in their first interview at 5 A.M. this morning if he could come back and talk to him after the story was checked out. Gilmore had not said no. With the present Supreme Court, Nielsen had the idea a confession like this might hold up.

9

Nevertheless, Nielsen wasn't forgetting the Supreme Court decision on the Williams case. A ten-year-old girl in Iowa had been raped and murdered by a mental patient named Williams, who had been picked up in Des Moines and taken back to the place where he was to be charged. Williams's attorney in Des Moines told the detectives transporting him, "Don't question him out of my presence," then told his client, "Don't make any statements to policemen." All the same, on the way back, one of the detectives accompanying the suspect started playing Williams on his Christian side. The old boy was deeply religious and so the detective said: "Here we are, just a few days before Christmas, and the family of that little girl doesn't know where the body is. It sure would be nice if we could find the body and give the little girl a good Christian burial before Christmas. The family could at least have that much peace." He went on in such a low-key way that the old guy finally told them where the corpse could be found, and got convicted. The Supreme Court, however, had just overruled. They said once a guy has an attorney, the police could not interview him without permission.

Yet here he was, talking to Gilmore while his attorneys were not aware of it. Still, a couple of technicalities could be argued. Gilmore had already, out on the road, in Nielsen's presence, been read his Miranda rights. Also, the attorneys had been appointed for the Provo case, not for Orem. He might still be, therefore, on legal ground. Besides, the key thing was not to get a confession but a conviction.

What would be good about a confession, even if they couldn't use it, was that it would produce information they could then employ to dig up further evidence against the guy, and get a good solid case. If they never used the confession in Court, they would have no trouble with the Miranda.

Besides, it would be good for morale. Once the police knew their man was guilty, they could feel more incentive to keep plugging hard on detail work. It would also avoid any power conflict with officers who wanted to work other leads. The confession would integrate the case, make it a psychological success.

They went through the cycle again. Nielsen talked about the Church of Jesus Christ of the Latter-Day Saints and what his kids contributed on family night each week. Gilmore was interested in the details, and mentioned again that not only was his mother a Mormon, but all of her folks, and he talked about his father who had been a Catholic and drank like hell, and they stayed off the real subject as if they had earned a rest.

Then they would get back to it. Nielsen would ask one question, then a couple of questions. So soon as Gilmore began to assume a look that said, "No more questions," Nielsen would talk of other things.

Jensen's coin changer had been missing from the service station, and the police had spent much of yesterday going through garbage at the Holiday Inn with no results. Casually, Nielsen now asked about that. Gilmore stared at him for a long time, as if to say, "I don't know whether to answer you or not. I don't know if I can trust you." Finally he muttered, "I really don't remember. I threw it out the window of the truck, but I can't recollect if it was in the drive-in or on the road." He paused as if searching into his recollection of a movie and he said, "I honestly don't remember. It could have been at the drive-in."

"Would April know?" Nielsen asked.

"Don't worry about April," Gilmore said. "She didn't see a thing." He shook his head. "For all practical purposes, she wasn't there."

When Nielsen began to wonder whether April had any idea of the murder, Gary repeated, "Don't worry, she didn't see a thing. In her head, that little girl was never there."

He gave a turn to his mouth that was almost a smile. "You know," he said, "If I'd been thinking as straight the last couple of nights as I am today, you guys would not have caught me. When I was a kid I used to pull off robberies . . ." He had a look on his face like a pimp bragging of the number of women who worked for him over the years. "I guess," he said, "I must have pulled off fifty or seventy, maybe even a hundred successful robberies. I knew how to plan something and do it right."

Nielsen then asked him if he would have gone on killing, if he hadn't been caught. Gilmore nodded. He thought he probably would have. He sat there for a minute and looked amazed. Not amazed, but certainly surprised, and said, "God, I don't know what the hell I'm doing. I've never confessed to a cop before." Nielsen thought he probably hadn't. His record was certainly hard-core all the way. Egotistically speaking, Nielsen felt bolstered. He had gotten a confession out of a hard-core criminal.

"How many guns did you steal?" Nielsen asked. "Nine," Gilmore told him. "Where did they come from?" "Spanish Fork." "Then we've recovered all but three." That left three unaccounted for. Where might they be? "They're gone," said Gilmore. Nielsen didn't bother to follow up. The way Gilmore said that made it obvious they had been sold, and he would never tell who he sold them to. "I'm responsible," said Gilmore. "Don't blame other people."

Then he asked, "Did Nicole tell you about her gun?" "No," Nielsen said, "I asked her." Gary said, "I don't want her to get in any trouble about those guns." Nielsen assured him.

Nielsen tried to get a few more facts about the homicides themselves. Gilmore would give details up to the point where he entered the service station and then he would talk of everything after he left. But he did not wish to describe the crime itself.

Nielsen was trying to determine what went on during the act. Gilmore had asked Jensen to lie on the floor. He must then have told him to put his arms beneath his body. No one would ever be found lying face down in such an uncomfortable position of their own choice. Next Gilmore had fired the shots right into Jensen's head. First with the pistol two inches away, then with the pistol touching. It was the surest way to kill a man and cause him no suffering. On the other hand, ordering those arms to stay under the body was the surest way to be certain the victim didn't grab your leg as you were putting the muzzle to his head. He could not, however, get Gilmore to talk about this.

"Why'd you do it, Gary?" Nielsen asked again quietly.
"I don't know," Gary said.
"Are you sure?"
"I'm not going to talk about that," Gilmore said. He shook his head delicately, and looked at Nielsen, and said, "I can't keep up with life."

Then he asked, "What do you think they'll do to me?"
Nielsen said, "I don't know. It is very serious."

"I'd like to be able to talk to Nicole," Gilmore said. "I've been looking for her and I'd really like to talk to her."
"Hey," Nielsen said, "I'll do anything I can to get her here." They shook hands.

10

About five o'clock that afternoon, while Nielsen was talking to Gary, April came home. She had heard about the murders on the radio and said it wasn't true. Gary hadn't done it. She also said she wasn't going to no police station.

Charley Baker had come in from Toelle when Kathryne phoned to say April was missing. Now, so soon as April saw them together, she got hostile and began shouting that if they tried to take her to the police station by force she would call on her protection to stop them. Then, all of a sudden, she seemed to give in. Said she would go.

Now, Kathryne did not want to bring April over on her own. Didn't know if the child would open the door of the car and jump out. So she begged Charley to come along, but he was hesitant. Said, "If she changes her mind even halfway over, then to hell with them. Turn around and bring her back." No way did he want to go.

July 21, 1976

NIELSEN   What time did he get gas?

APRIL   When we were at the service station in Pleasant Grove.

NIELSEN   Was it after dark?

APRIL   It was dark, it was past sundown.

NIELSEN   After that did you drive around for a while?

APRIL   He said he was taking me home and he wasn't going to put up with any of my smart-ass crap telling him where to go and he said he wanted a classy place like the Holiday Inn, so we went there and I was going to go to sleep because I was really tired. I didn't really know why, I felt like I was running from somebody — ever since somebody broke the windows in our bathroom at home, and I can't really sleep well since then.

NIELSEN   And then you stayed there for that night until what time the next morning?

APRIL   About 8:30 or 9:00.

NIELSEN   I don't mean to imply anything or to pry into your personal life, but did you sleep with him that night?

APRIL   I almost did, but I changed my mind.

NIELSEN   Did he get mad at you then?

APRIL   He was mad at me for acting like a kid half the time, but I just lost my love for him, only I never did sleep with him or anything.

NIELSEN   Did you tell your mom that?

APRIL   She didn't ask me because she knows I have my private life and if I wanted to blow it, I could . . .

NIELSEN   April, Gary is in very serious trouble. I know that, I have talked to him about it and there is no question about it. He already told me you were with him at the time and so I know that you know about it. I am not interested in you telling me so that I can charge you. I don't intend to charge you with it, but I do intend to see that you tell the truth.

APRIL I am a split personality. I am controlling it pretty good today. A lot of time I like to just let go and let the other person creep on out . . .

NIELSEN Where did you go last night, when you left home?

APRIL I went riding around with a couple of friends.

NIELSEN Did they know him?

APRIL No.

NIELSEN Do you mind telling me who they were?

APRIL One is Grant and one is Joe.

NIELSEN Where did you stay last night?

APRIL I didn't sleep all night, rode to Wyoming, and just went in the mountains and down this road and came home.

NIELSEN What time did you get home?

APRIL 4:30 or 5:00.

NIELSEN Don't you worry about your mom worrying about you?

APRIL I don't think she worries about me. I'm not afraid of no guns and I am not afraid of no dudes with knives. They don't scare me. I have learned self-defense.

NIELSEN I want to ask you one more time about the service station. April, I think it would be best if you tell me what you know.

APRIL I don't remember the service station in Orem.

NIELSEN Do you remember seeing him pull a gun at the service station?

APRIL We went into a service station right before we went to the Holiday Inn and I am sure there were no guns attached. They may have been carrying them, but that's all.

NIELSEN Who are "they"?

APRIL Any of the dudes that were around.

NIELSEN Do you know any of them?

APRIL I recognize all of them, but I don't know some of their names. One of them works with him at the insulation place.

NIELSEN Insulation?

APRIL Where he works at the Ideal Insulation. I am pretty sure it was the friend we visited.

NIELSEN At the cafe?

APRIL It may not have been.

NIELSEN Are you about ready to go back home?

APRIL Yes. I am wondering why I am here.

NIELSEN I will be glad to help you if I can.

When April came out of the interview, she said, "Mama, they told me Gary killed two men. Do you believe that?"

Kathryne said, "Well, April, I guess he must have."

"Gary couldn't kill someone, Mama."

"Well, April," Kathryne said, "I think Gary told them he did."

CHAPTER 18

An Act of Contrition

1

Next morning, Gilmore was brought from Provo to Orem, and Nielsen saw him in his office, and apologized about the crowd outside. There were TV lights and a lot of reporters and city employees in the hall, but what really embarrassed Nielsen was that half the police force including off-duty officers had also come out. People were even standing on chairs to get a look.

Nielsen had his secretary bring a cup of coffee. Then he said, "Lieutenant Skinner is going to sign a complaint charging you with the homicide of Max Jensen." After a short pause, Gary said, "Hey, I really feel bad about those two guys. I read one of their obituaries in the paper last night. He was a young man and had a kid and he was a missionary. Makes me really feel bad."

"Gary, I feel bad too. I can't understand taking a life for the amount of money you got."

Gary replied, "I don't know how much I got. What was there?"

Nielsen said, "It was $125, and in Provo, approximately the same amount." Gary began to cry. He didn't weep with any noise but there were tears in his eyes. He said, "I hope they execute me for it. I ought to die for what I did."

"Gary, are you ready to?" Nielsen asked. "It doesn't scare you?"

"Would you like to die?"

"Criminy," said Nielsen, "no."

"Me, neither," said Gilmore, "but I ought to be executed for it."

"I don't know," said Nielsen; "there's got to be forgiveness somewhere along the line."

2

A little later, Gary made a private call to Brenda.

"How," he asked her, "did the cops know I was at Craig Taylor's house?"

"Gary, you might as well know, I don't want you hearing it from somebody else. I called the police."

"I see."

Brenda said, "You're probably going to be bent real out of shape with me. But, Gary, it had to stop. You commit a murder Monday, and commit a murder Tuesday. I wasn't waiting for Wednesday to roll around."

"Hey, cousin," said Gary, "don't worry about it."

Brenda said, "Gary, you're going to go down hard this time. You're going to ride this one clear to the bottom."

He said, "Man, how do you know I'm not innocent?"

"Gary, what's the matter with your head?"

"I don't know," Gary said, "I must have been insane."

Brenda asked, "What about your mother? What do you want me to tell her?"

He was quiet for a while. Then he said, "Tell her it's true."

Brenda said, "Okay. Anything else?"

"Just tell her I love her."

Craig Snyder, Gary's other lawyer, was shorter than Esplin, about five-seven, with broad shoulders, blond hair, and pale eyes. He had eyeglasses with pale frames. Today, he was wearing a blond-colored suit with a tie that had several shades of yellow, green, and orange, and a yellow shirt.

On this morning in Orem, Snyder and Esplin didn't even know Gary was being interviewed by Gerald Nielsen until he was brought up to be arraigned. Afterward, they sat down with him, and he said he had committed both murders, and had told Nielsen.

They were certainly upset. Gilmore had been informed of his Miranda rights when arrested, but he had not been given full Miranda down at the jail. Any confession Gilmore offered had to be worthless, the lawyers decided. It was infuriating. They had been kept waiting forty-five minutes while a Lieutenant of Detectives was grilling him.

In reply, Gary seemed more interested in the fact that Nielsen had promised he could see Nicole at the jail. He wanted his lawyers to make sure Nielsen kept his word.

3

Nicole was in Springville with Barrett when the police came. They didn't phone or anything. Just a cop to ask her to get ready. A little later, Lieutenant Nielsen was there in a car. He would drive her over to see Gary.

She didn't know how she felt, and she didn't know if she cared how she felt. It had been a real hang-up listening to Barrett. The last couple of days he had been coming on as the wise man. Her judgment, he kept saying, was so goofy. Like she had picked a middle-aged murderer for herself.

On the way, Lieutenant Nielsen was nice and polite, and he laid it out. They were going to let Nicole talk to Gary, but she had to ask if he had done the murders. Nicole was about to get mad at the suggestion, except she figured out Nielsen needed a reason to justify bringing her over. She was sure he wasn't so dumb as to think Gary was going to answer her question while a bunch of cops was listening.

That was how it turned out. Nicole walked into this funky one-story jail, went down a couple of short corridors, passed a bunch of inmates who looked like beer bums, then a couple of dudes who whistled as she went by, twirled their mustaches, showed a bicep, generally acted like the cat's ass. Two cops and Detective Nielsen were right behind her, and she came to a big cell with a table in the middle of it, four bunks she could see, and thick prison bars in front of her.

Then she saw Gary come toward her from the back of the cell. His left hand was in a cast. It was only three days from the night she had seen him arrested and lying on the ground, but she could feel the difference. He said, "Hello, baby," and, at first, she didn't even want to look at him.

With her head down, she muttered, "Did you do this?"

She was really whispering as if, should he say yes, maybe the cops wouldn't hear the question. He said, "Nicole, don't ask me that."

Now, she looked up. She couldn't get over how clear his eyes were. There was a minute where they didn't say any more. Then he put one arm through the bars. She wanted to touch him, but didn't. However, she kept feeling the impulse. More and more she had this desire to touch him.

It was close to a spooky experience. Nicole didn't know what she was feeling. She certainly wasn't feeling sorry for him. She wasn't feeling sorry for herself. Rather, she couldn't breathe. She could hardly believe it, but she was ready to faint. That was the moment when she knew that it didn't matter what she had said about him these last couple of weeks. She had been in love with him from the moment she met him and she would love him forever.

It wasn't an emotion so much as a physical sensation. A magnet could have been pulling her to the bars. She reached out to put a hand on the arm he extended through, and one of the officers stepped forward and said, "No physical contact."

She stepped back, and Gary looked good. He looked surprisingly good. His eyes were more blue than they had ever been. All that fog from the Fiorinal was gone. His eyes looked into her as if he was returning from all the way back and something ugly had passed through completely and was gone. All through these last couple of bad weeks, it was like he had been looking a year older every day. Now he looked fine. "I love you," he said as they said good-bye. "I love you," she said.

In the same hour that Nicole was going to and from the jail, April went berserk. She began to scream that someone was trying to blow her head off. Kathryne could do nothing. First she had to call the police and then she decided to commit her to the hospital. It was horrible. April had flipped out completely. Kathryne even had to keep the children out of the house all those hours while it was being decided.

4

The Sheriff, Ken Cahoon, was a tall man with an easygoing manner and white hair. He wore metal-rimmed glasses, had a large nose, a small mouth, a small chin, and a little potbelly. He liked to believe he ran a reasonably good jail. His main tank had bunks for thirty men, but he never went over twenty if he could help it. That kept the fights down. The trustees who worked in the kitchen were given a cell to themselves, and there was also Maximum Detention, with room for six. That was the tank where Gary now sat by himself. Plus another cell for six down the same hall to hold prisoners on work release. Altogether, Cahoon's jail could carry forty people without busting the seams of anyone's patience.

A while after Nicole left, Cahoon decided to look back in on Gilmore.

"I have blisters on my feet," Gilmore told him.

"From doing what?" asked Cahoon.

"Why," said Gilmore, "I've been jogging in place."

"Well, dummy, quit jogging in place."

"No," said Gilmore, "give me some Band-Aids. I'll put them on, and I can jog some more."

Next day, he asked the same thing. Said he wanted Band-Aids because his feet were sore. "Why, let's see," said Cahoon, "if you got an infection."

Gilmore said, "Just give me some Band-Aids. It's not that bad."

"No," said Cahoon, "if you got blisters, I want to see them."

"Oh, hell," said Gilmore, "forget it."

Cahoon decided he was pulling a bluff. There was no telling what he might use the Band-Aids for, unless it was to tape contraband to the bottom of the bedsprings or something.

Next morning, Gilmore said to a guard, "I want out of here today. I've got a Writ of Habeas Corpus. Let me see the head man of the jail."

Cahoon decided Gilmore must have the opinion they were back-woodsy in this little old humble place. Now Gary said to Cahoon in a nice confidential voice, "Look, I'm in for five days. I'm not being held for nothing but a traffic violation. So I would like out of here right now. You see," he said, "I've got to be under a doctor's care. As you may know, I came in with this cast on, and things of this nature want attention. I'd like to be taken to the hospital. The hand has to have its medication, and if you can't get me out, you see, there could be complications."

Cahoon thought Gilmore was a pretty good con man, considering the odds, and he didn't exactly laugh at the idea that Gilmore might get loose in some simple but crazy way. A while back, they'd had a man in the tank named Dennis Howell, and another prisoner happened to come in also named Dennis Howell. The same day, word came to release the first Dennis. So the jailer on duty who was new on the job went down the list, went back and said to the new arrival, "Howell, your wife is outside, you can go now." The wrong Dennis walked out the door, trotted right past the woman, took off like a whistle.

Gilmore sure kept trying. A little later, he wanted to get ahold of his attorney. Said he was going to sue the jail for not giving attention to his hand. He was really in sympathy with himself over that hand.

After it all failed, Gary said, "I know Utah County is poor in spirit, and full of hard feelings toward me, but Sheriff, you can let me go home now. I'm not mad anymore."

That was a pretty good sense of humor, Cahoon decided.

It made it easier for him to put up with Gilmore decorating the walls. Cahoon liked to eliminate any drawing of obscenity pictures but Gary was not doing that. Pictures he drew were nice pictures. They were also something you could erase. One day he'd do a drawing, and next day wipe it out, do another, so Cahoon never made an issue of it.

They really got along all right until Gilmore learned that they wouldn't allow him to see Nicole on visits. It seemed she wasn't family. That left Gary not speaking to anybody.

5

About the second time that Brenda went down to the jail, which was on Sunday, a week and a half after his arrest, Nicole had also shown up. When Gary heard she was outside, the expression on his face, Brenda had to admit, was beautiful. "Oh, God," he said, "she promised to come back and she did."

However, he explained, it didn't mean he could visit with her. She wasn't allowed on his list just yet. Brenda said, "Let me see what I can do." She went up to a big tough Indian guard at the door, a confident-looking fellow, and said, "Alex, could you put Nicole Barrett in for the last five minutes of my time?" "Well, now," he said, "we really shouldn't break the rules." "Bullshit," said Brenda, "what's the difference if it's me or Nicole? He ain't going to go nowhere! Why, Alex Hunt, you mean to tell me," she asked, "you can't take care of this poor man with a busted-up hand? What's he going to do with one hand? Tear you apart?" "Well," said Alex, "I think we can handle Gilmore."

While Nicole was visiting, Brenda walked over to Nicole's sister-in-law, who had also come. It was hot that day, and Sue Baker was holding her newborn baby and perspiring in volumes. "How is Nicole doing?" asked Brenda.

The sun didn't stir on the black cinder gravel back of the jail.

"She's pretty broke up," said Sue.

Brenda said, "Gary's not going to get out of this one. If Nicole gets all hung up, it's going to ruin her."

"She won't quit," said Sue, "we already tried."

"Well," said Brenda, "she's in for a lot of hurt."

When Nicole came out, she was weeping. Brenda put her arms around her and said, "Nicole, we both love him."

Then Brenda said: "Nicole, why don't you think a little about giving up the ship? Gary is never going to get out. You'll spend the rest of your life visiting this guy. That's all the future you're going to have." Now Brenda began to cry. "Tuck those beautiful memories in your heart," she said, "tuck them away."

Nicole muttered, "I'll stick."

She was feeling an animosity toward Brenda she didn't even understand. Nicole heard herself thinking, "As if I owe her a million dollars for giving me five minutes of her visiting time."

6

There was a Preliminary Hearing on August 3 in Provo and Noall Wootton was determined to ram it through as hard and fast as he could. He had a lot of witnesses so his problem was to keep the case intact. When the defense asked for delay, Wootton objected.

He was reasonably confident of the conviction, or to put it more precisely, he was confident that if he did not get a conviction, it would be his own fault. He was, however, not at all sure of getting the death penalty. So he was feeling the usual tension he had before a case began. His stomach was right with him that morning.

At the Preliminary Hearing, Gilmore didn't take the stand, but Wootton did talk face to face with him in the recess. They got on well. They even joked. Wootton was impressed with his intelligence. Gilmore told Wootton that the prison system was not doing what it was designed to achieve, that is, rehabilitate. In his opinion, it was a complete failure.

Of course, they avoided talking about the crimes themselves, but Noall did detect that Gilmore was doing his best to soften him up. Gary certainly kept flattering him about what a fair and efficient prosecutor he was, what a basic sense of fairness he had. Said he'd never seen another prosecutor with that kind of fairness.

Not every con knew enough to run that line. Wootton expected Gilmore was working up to a deal. He must have heard they were going for the death penalty, and thought if he was nice enough, Wootton might feel encouraged to return from so far out a stand, far out at least from the defendant's point of view.

Sure enough, Gilmore got around to asking what Wootton thought would happen. Noall looked him in the eye and said, "They might come back with the death penalty." Gilmore said, "I know, but what are they really going to do?" Wootton repeated, "They might execute you." He had the impression that took Gilmore aback.

Snyder also approached Noall, and suggested they plead guilty to Murder One, and accept a life top. Wootton kind of dismissed it. "No way," he said.

He had made up his mind to go for Death after looking at Gilmore's record. It showed violence in prison, a history of escape, and unsuccessful efforts made at rehabilitation. Wootton could only conclude that, one: Gilmore would be looking to escape; two: he would be a hazard to other inmates and guards; and, three: rehabilitation was hopeless. Couple this to a damned cold-blooded set of crimes.

7

Nicole drove down to the Preliminary Hearing in Provo on August 3, but they let her visit with Gary for only a moment. It made her dizzy to see him in leg shackles. Then they only gave her time for one hug and a tremendous kiss before pulling him away. She was left in the hall of the court with the world rocketing around her. Outside, in the summer light, the horseflies were mean as insanity itself.

On the drive back to Springville, she was dreaming away and got in a wreck. Nobody was hurt but the car. After that, all the way home, her Mustang sounded like it was breaking up in pain. She couldn't shift out of second.

It became a crazy trip. She kept having an urge to cross the divider, and bang into oncoming traffic. Next day, when the mail came, there was a very long letter from Gary that he had begun to write as soon as they took him back to jail from the hearing. So she realized he had been saying these words to her at the same time she had been driving along with the urge to smash into every car going the other way.

Now she read Gary's letter over and over. She must have read it five times and the words went in and out of her head like a wind blowing off the top of the world.

August 3

Nothing in my experience, prepared me for the kind of honest open love you gave me. I'm so used to bullshit and hostility, deceit and pettiness, evil and hatred. Those things are my natural habitat. They have shaped me. I look at the world through eyes that suspect, doubt, fear, hate, cheat, mock, are selfish and vain. All things unacceptable, I see them as natural and have even come to accept them as such. I look around the ugly vile cell and know that I truly belong in a place this dank and dirty, for where else should I be? There's water all over the floor from the fucking toilet that don't flush right. The shower is filthy and the thin mattress they gave me is almost black, it's so old. I have no pillow. There are dead cockroaches in the corners. At nite there are mosquitoes and the lite is very dim. I'm alone here with my thoughts and I can feel the oldness. Remember I told you about The Oldness? and you told me how ugly it was — the oldness, the oldness. I can hear the tumbrel wheels creek. So fucking ugly and coming so close to me. When I was a child . . . I had a nightmare about being beheaded. But it was more than just a dream. More like a memory. It brought me right out of the bed. And it was sort of a turning point in my life. . . . Recently it has begun to make a little sense. I owe a debt, from a long time ago. Nicole, this must depress you. I've never told anybody of this thing, except my mother the nite I had that nitemare and she came in to comfort me but we never spoke of it after that. And I started to tell you one nite and I told you quite a bit of it before it became plain to me that you didn't want to hear it. There have been years when I haven't even thought much of it at all and then something (a picture of a guillotine, a headmans block, or a broad ax, or even a rope) will bring it all back and for days it will seem I'm on the verge of knowing something very personal, something about myself. Something that somehow wasn't completed and makes me different. Something I owe, I guess. Wish I knew.

Once you asked me if I was the devil, remember? I'm not. The devil would be far more clever than I, would operate on a much larger scale and of course would feel no remorse. So I'm not Beelzebub. And I know the devil can't feel love. But I might be further from God than I am from the devil. Which is not a good thing. It seems that I know evil more intimately than I know goodness and that's not a good thing either. I want to get even, to be made even, whole, my debts paid (whatever it may take!) to have no blemish, no reason to feel guilt or fear. I hope this ain't corny, but I'd like to stand in the sight of God. To know that I'm just and right and clean. When you're this way you know it. And when you're not, you know that too. It's all inside of us, each of us — but I guess I ran from it and when I did try to approach it, I went about it wrong, became discouraged, bored, lazy, and finally unacceptable. But what do I do now? I don't know. Hang myself?

I've thought about that for years, I may do that. Hope that the state executes me? That's more acceptable and easier than suicide. But they haven't executed anybody here since 1963 (just about the last year for legal executions anywhere). What do I do, rot in prison? growing old and bitter and eventually work this around in my mind to where it reads that I'm the one who's getting fucked around, that I'm just an innocent victim of society's bullshit? What do I do? Spend a life in prison searching for the God I've wanted to know for such a long time? Resume my painting? Write poetry? Play handball? Eat my heart out for the wondrous love you gave me that I threw away Monday nite because I was so spoiled and couldn't immediately have a white pickup truck I wanted? What do I do? We always have a choice, don't we?

I'm not asking you to answer these questions for me, Angel, please don't think that I am. I have to make my own choice. But anything you want to comment on or suggest, or say, is always welcome.

God, I love you, Nicole.

PART FIVE

The Shadows
of the Dream

CHAPTER 19

Kin to the Magician

1

Shortly after Gary got out of Marion, and was living in Provo with Vern and Ida, he sent Bessie an eleven-pound box of chocolates for Mother's Day. Then, a letter arrived. "I didn't know I could be this happy. I have the most beautiful girl in Utah. Mom, I'm making more money than I could take in stealing."

Bessie wrote back, "This is what I always wanted for you. I'm glad you have this girl. I hope someday to meet your beautiful Nicole."

Then she didn't hear any more, and phoned Ida, who told her Gary had gotten in a little trouble by walking out of a store with a few things. Bessie asked Ida to tell him to call, and began to worry. Gary never got in touch when he was in trouble.

The day she found out about the murders, she had been out on the porch of her trailer taking the sun. Her phone rang and it was a woman. Quick as she heard the tone of voice, Bess said, "It's you, Brenda. Something's happened to Gary." She thought he had robbed a bank.

Brenda told her they were holding Gary on Murder One. "I don't believe that, Brenda. Gary wouldn't kill anybody." "Oh, yes," said Brenda, "he killed two people and shot one of his thumbs off." That was how Bessie got it.

She said, "Well, there has to be a mistake. Gary did not do this. No matter what else, he is not a killer." She hung up, and the phone rang again, and it was Ida to tell her that the blood kept spurting out of Mr. Bushnell and she and Vern had seen it. Bess felt she would never get over that description. Then Vern got on the phone and said, "They have a death penalty here. They're going to kill Gary." It was all Bess could take. Execution had always been a phobia to her. She couldn't go near the thought. When she was a little girl growing up in Utah, she would hide if she heard they were having an execution.

After Vern's message, she kept the news to herself. She told Frank Jr., when he came into town, but not Mikal, her youngest son. One morning he called, and said, You sound like you've been crying, and Bess said, I have a cold. He said, I'm going to come out and spend the day with you. She said, You read about Gary, and he said, Yes, he had heard about it.

She kept thinking of the time in the fall of '72 when they let Gary out of OSP to study in art school. He was going to live in a halfway house up at Eugene, and be given furloughs. The first day, right out, Gary dropped in on Bess for the afternoon, and spent the evening. The next morning he went to the store to get eggs for breakfast, and asked her if it was all right to bring back a six-pack. She said sure. So he sat there and talked through the morning while drinking the beer. They felt very close. She fixed his breakfast and said, "That's the first time we spent the night under the same roof for a long time, Gary." He said, "Sure is." In fact, it was close to ten years. He drank his beer and said he had to leave. Had to get to the art school in Eugene.

After he was gone, she remembered that last time ten years ago in 1962 when they had been alone together. She and Gary were Johnny Cash fans, and so he brought all his records down from upstairs and they listened all day long. Now the records made her too sad, and she would turn off the radio when a song by Johnny Cash came on.

A few nights later in that same fall of '72, Gary pulled in with a car, and said he'd like to take her to dinner. She told him she was not dressed and it was pretty late, so he stayed and talked a long time. A couple of nights later, she noticed the police were sitting outside her trailer, and wouldn't say anything to her. That was when she knew a lot had gone wrong.

Next morning, a neighbor gave a buzz and asked, "Was that your son they picked up for armed robbery?" "No," Bessie replied, "but what paper was it in?" The woman told her and Bess said, "I'll look it up." When she found the story, she cried till she was sick. One more river in the million tears she had cried over Gary.

Now, in the summer of '76, it was a nightmare. She kept thinking that if she had been able to get to Provo, Gary would never have killed those men. That first night in April when he called from Ida's house he had said, "I'm going to get a car, Mom, and get up to Portland, and bring you back." Bess had laughed, "Oh, Gary," she had said, "by now, I'm such a decrepit piece of work that they play the band when I get out to the street."

A few months before, while Gary was still in Marion, she had been sitting one night with her son Frank Jr., and started to cough up blood. They came for her in an ambulance and took her to surgery. Half of her stomach was removed. The aspirin she took to relieve her arthritis had perforated her ulcer. "The faster I fixed one end," she told a friend, "the more I was scraping on the other." Now she never passed through her door unless it was to walk the few steps to her landlady's trailer and pick up the mail. Still, she let Gary speak of how nice it would be to keep house in Provo, and she dreamed of it, until he wrote her about living with Nicole.

It had all been, she decided, part of the pleasures of thought, no more. She couldn't even keep the trailer in order. It looked as old and moldering as herself.

Just a week ahead of the murders, she had written a letter to Gary. He must have received it just a day or two before those Mormon boys were killed. She had mentioned the house on Crystal Springs Boulevard that he liked living in when he was nine years old. That was the year he kept saying he wanted to be a priest. In the letter, she told him that they had torn down the house and put up an apartment building. One more memory you would not find.

Still, it was in the house on Crystal Springs Boulevard that Gary developed his fear of being beheaded. He was a daring kid, but he had this fear. There was a bedroom in that house he shared with Frank Jr., and the previous occupants must have put luminous paint on the wall because something would shine out pale green at night. Gary would holler, "Mom, I see that thing again." She would try to explain that it was paint and all right but they finally had to do the walls over. Then his dreams of being executed had begun. They had caused such fear. "He's been a frightened man," Bessie said to herself, "all his life."

Yes, Gary was a sad and lonely man, one of the most sad and one of the most lonely. "Oh, God," thought Bessie, "he was in prison so long, he didn't know how to work for a living or pay a bill. All the while he should have been learning, he was locked up."

It was hot in the trailer. Living with her news at the end of July, she felt she was breathing in a steam bath. One could sit still in Portland and lose weight. "When it's real hot in my trailer," she said aloud, "I can lose five pounds an hour." Of course, she only weighed 110. This shouldn't be Portland, she told the walls, but Africa. She felt like Portland would soon overgrow itself and wipe it all out. The heat was strong and terrible, a jungle. "I always knew it was too green when I first came here," she said to the walls.

There was a suction-type feeling inside the trailer. If anybody made the wrong move, it would all disintegrate.

2

One day when Gary was 22, in the year after his father had died, in that brief half-year of freedom and liberty when he was out of Oregon State Correctional Institute but not yet in Oregon State Prison to serve the twelve and a half years he would be sentenced for armed robbery; in that same brief half-year when they had spent a day listening to Johnny Cash, Bess came back to the house one afternoon, the house on Oakhill Road with the small circle driveway that Frank had bought when their life was prosperous and settled, and there was Gary rooting in her desk. "I want to show you something," he said. He had found his birth certificate. His mother's name was on it, and his own birthdate, but he and his father were there in plain sight as Fay Robert Coffman and Walt Coffman.

It was ironic because Frank had given the name to Gary. Fay for Frank's mother and Robert for Frank's son by an earlier marriage. Coffman came from not being born in Frank Gilmore territory, but rather in Walt Coffman land, which in this case was Texas; McCamey, Texas. Crossing certain state lines, Frank used to change his name. Bessie never knew if that was to get rid of an old trail or pick up a new one.

Of course, Bessie didn't allow Fay Robert for long. The people in the hotel suggested they rename him Doyle. Bess liked that, but Gary was better. She loved Gary Cooper. She and Frank had arguments over it. Gary was a name to remind him of Grady, and Grady was an ex-brother-in-law who had cheated him once.

Now, she and Gary didn't even raise their voices, but when he started to get unpleasant, Bessie said, "Don't you dare! You were in my desk without permission."

Gary said, "I never would have gotten this news with permission, would I?" When he said next, "No wonder the old man never liked me," Bessie replied, "Don't you ever, ever intimate that you are illegitimate."

It was only years later that Bessie found out Gary had known about his birth certificate for a year and a half before she found him sitting at the desk in her green leather chair. His institutional counselor at Oregon State Correctional (for boys too old for Reform School and too young for prison) had asked why his birth record in Texas showed his father's name to be Coffman not Gilmore. It got him pretty upset. Two weeks later, they gave him an electroencephalogram for severe headaches. He kept receiving write-ups for refusing to work and provoking fights. He complained to his psychiatrist of strange dreams. He had a hell of a time controlling his temper. Thought people were saying derogatory things behind his back. Then his father died. He was in Isolation at the time and they wouldn't give him a furlough for the funeral.

All this had happened before the day Gary sat at her desk and handed his birth certificate over.

She did not like to think of how that ridiculous misunderstanding ate at him. Gary had been getting in enough trouble for enough years not to blame it on a birth certificate, especially when he knew his father had traveled with a number of names. Still, she could never be certain that piece of paper had nothing to do with the armed robbery he did next and the terrible sentence of fifteen years at the age of twenty-two. Soon after, Bess's gall bladder went so bad, it had to be removed. What with complications in her convalescence, a few months went by before she could even visit Gary at the prison. It was the longest she'd ever gone without seeing him. She was shockproof by then or she would have screamed when he came into the visiting room. There he stood at the age of twenty-two without any teeth, but for two in his lower jaw — looked like fangs. "They're working on the plates," he said.

By the next visit, he told her that he liked his new set. "I can pick up an apple and really eat it without getting a toothache," he stated. His headaches seemed better too.

"Well," she said to herself then, "I am the daughter of the very first people who settled in Provo. I am the granddaughter and great-granddaughter of pioneers on both sides. If they could live through it, I can live through it." She had to say it to herself again after the phone calls from Brenda and Ida and Vern.

3

Bessie could see the old blacksmith shop down by the creek where she grew up. Smell it, too. She could sniff the steam of horses when the manure flew out of them in fear, and catch again the bottom-rind stink that came up from the parings of the horses' hooves. That was worse than an old man's feet, and the awful reek of charred hooves on the hot horseshoe followed — she always knew what hell was planning to offer. It was so bad that she almost liked the strong air of red-hot iron when it mixed with the odor of burning coal. She thought it had to be the way a tomb would smell if a strong man was buried in it.

Outside the blacksmith shop, there was grass and some fruit trees, and the fall-into-heaven of a fresh breeze. Of course, there was also the desert that had no smell at all, but was dry in the nose and left you for dust. In the background were the mountains high as a wall when you stood next to a wall and looked up.

She lived in a big family of seven girls and two sons that came out of two big families. Her mother was the eldest of thirteen children; her father of nine. The mother's family name was Kerby, like the vacuum cleaner company, but with an "e" not an "i," and at one time Kerbys owned the Isle of Wales, so they would tell her, but her great-grandfather joined the Mormon Church in 1850, and was disowned by his family, so he came to America without a cent, and moved on to Utah with the Goddard Handcart Company, pushed a cart across the plains with all his belongings, one of an army of Mormons pushing their little wagons up the canyons of the Rockies because there was not enough money in the Church that year for prairie-wagons, and Brigham Young had told them, Come anyway, come with handcarts to the new Zion in the Kingdom of Deseret. Hardy, healthy people, Bessie always said, and knew what they were doing.

Her great-grandmother was Mary Ellen Murphy, the only Irish in the Kerby family. The rest was English and one dot of French. Bessie was 98 percent English and could never understand why Gary told people he was Irish. He was about as Irish as Texan, considering that he was not only born in Texas but lived there for six weeks.

Bessie had seventy-eight cousins. They couldn't move. They were the kings and clods of Provo, everybody cut out of the same pattern. Later, she would say to people, "Do you know how we are raised? You can't even believe it. If the head of our Church says, Walk on the right-hand side of the street, then you would in no way walk over on the left, even if the rain was pouring down . . . we are almost ridiculous."

That childhood might exist no longer, but she tried to live in it now. It was better than floods of misery that a son of her flesh had killed the sons of other mothers. That burned in her heart like the pain which flared in the arthritis of her knees. Pain was a boring conversationalist who never stopped, just found new topics.

Bess had an early memory of Provo in World War One. She was five years old and there was no telephone, no electricity in their house, and a telegram was rare. The roads were dirt paved carefully with dust. Newspapers had to be a week old by the time you read them. Their house held two rooms with a lean-to on the back, and they used to go over the hill to the spring and carry water back two buckets at a time, in summer on a small wagon, in winter by sleigh. One November, she remembered, the sky looked like snow, and they heard terrible whistles blowing in town two miles away. Her mother kept saying in a small dark fearsome mood, "Oh, the Germans are coming, the Germans are coming," but instead her dad came up on a horse over the hill, and that was how they received the news that war had ended.

She thought Bessie was the ugliest name. People named cows and horses Bessie. She told everybody to call her Betty and told it to them again while picking potatoes, picking cucumbers, picking bush beans, and taking turns pushing the washer handle back and forth. At night around the table, their mother would read to them by the illumination of an oil lamp. "Betty," Bessie would say when her name was called. She would feel the same way fifty years later. When she had the name Betty, which was what Frank always called her, they had money. Somehow it was Bessie again after he died, and she felt poor as a church mouse.

She sat in her chair in that superheated trailer, breathing the heated air, hot as the blacksmith shop, and the old smell of a frightened horse was in her heart and lungs forever. Thinking of Ida's voice on the phone, describing the blood she had seen on the face and head of Mr. Bushnell, Bess felt vertigo at the fall through space of all those years since Ida was born with her twin Ada.

Those twins had been ten years younger than Bessie, and Ida was her favorite. Bootie, Bess would call her. Little Bootie, like little boots. Now she was married to a man with fists as large as horses' hooves, and he had worked all his life on shoes and boots. It tore through Bess like a treachery, for she had always liked Vern, that he had chosen to say to her on the phone, "They're going to kill Gary." She tried to think instead of the extra room her father built on the house when the twins were born, and the tin tubs on Saturday night.

She felt so raw that agreeable memories were more than agreeable and felt like salve on a small wound. So she thought of the dancing teacher who came down from Salt Lake every Friday to teach ballet. In high-school gym, Bessie would never play basketball, or march, and even had the nerve to sit there and say, Give me Grade E, no excuse. They all talked about her already. She was a farm girl who wouldn't work in the sun and wore large sun hats and long gloves.

The dancing teacher changed everything. Bessie started getting A+ for Dance, and the teacher moved her up to the front row, said she was a natural-born ballerina. Wish I could have gotten hold of her when she was four, said the teacher.

Bessie also listened to the radio and tried to sing, but nobody in the family could even hum. All used the same tune for everything. Later, it was worse when Frank and she and the boys would try. Every Christmas Eve, Frank would get into "Giddyap, Napoleon, it looks like rain." Every Christmas Eve they would suffer through that. Gary would say aloud, "It's enough to make you give up Christmas." When it came his turn, however, Gary had a worse voice. Nothing but grunts and a girlish soprano. He sounded like a Country-and-Western singer who had swallowed a brick.

Now it came over her that Gary would spend the rest of his life in jail. If he was not executed.

4

Maybe she couldn't sing, but she was Queen of the Golden Green Ball at church. There were fifteen girls eligible from the ten or twelve families in Grandview Ward north of Provo, south of Orem, but Bessie was chosen, and college students came out from Brigham Young to teach them ballroom dancing. It was like a film.

Bess never liked the movies, however. She would walk in with her parents, and the picture would flicker over her eyes like a moth in a closet, except it was high up on the wall at the end of a long dismal hall, and an organ was racing away in the dark. You had to become a speed reader or you'd miss what the actors were saying. Being rushed gave her the shivers.

The darkness of the movies would remind her of the long-gone Christmas when her sister Alta was killed after her horse bolted and her sleigh hit a tree. They buried Alta with the snow deep on the ground, and had to leave her up in the cemetery under the snow. The family never really did have another happy Christmas. Melancholy kept coming into the celebration like memories out of the ground.

That was the worst Christmas, until she thought of the one in '55 when Gary was away at MacLaren, and they tried to get the juvenile authorities to let him home for a couple of days. First they said they would, then he had an infraction and they wouldn't. Since Bess and Frank couldn't get out to MacLaren Christmas Day because of the other kids, there was Gary with nothing. On December 26 they took over his gifts.

The only thing to be said for these present hours under the heat of the sun and the airless night of the trailer was that heat never made her feel as alone as the winter damp. Winter was the time when she felt so cold she had need of all the life she had lived. But now at the age of 63, Bessie could feel old as 83 in the cold snowbound cemetery of all those feelings that had frozen in the middle of July by the word that Gary had killed two boys. She kept seeing the face of Mr. Bushnell whose face she did not know, but it did not matter, for his head was covered with blood.

"Oh, Gary," whispered the child that never ceased to live in the remains of her operations and twisted joints, "Oh, Gary, how could you?"

Yes, the memory of one's life might be one's best and only friend. It was certainly the only touch to soothe those outraged bones that would chafe in the flesh until they were a skeleton free of the flesh.

So she thought often of sweet evenings in the past and breezes along the hill on warm summer twilights, thought of how she loved Provo once, and could sit for hours looking at the beautiful peak she called Y Mountain because the first settlers had put down flat white stones on its flank to make a great big white "Y" for old Brigham Young. Once, when she was a child, she was looking at Y Mountain and her father came over and Bess said, "Dad, I'm going to claim that for my very own," and he said, "Well, honey, you've got just as much right as anyone else, I guess," and walked off, and she thought, "He gave me his consent. That mountain belongs to me." Sitting in the trailer, she said to the good friend who was her memory, "That mountain still belongs to me."

5

Bessie studied dresses in the rotogravure before sewing her own, and went ballroom dancing at the Utahma Dance Hall in Provo when they brought orchestras in. She had a girl friend, Ruby Hills, and Ruby's brother drove them in a Model A Ford. He drove carefully. The roads had ruts as deep as the cracks in a rock.

She had girl friends whose names after marriage would become Afton Davies Atkins and Eva Daball Brickey. Bess dated a boy who went to Brigham Young and gave every promise of being the big boat to catch, but she couldn't stand him. Bess was interested in whatever else it was.

Others saw her as restless. She was on her way. She went hitchhiking with girl friends to Salt Lake City and beyond. She went hitching, at last, to California. She would go and work awhile and then come back. Her parents did not ask that many questions, there were so many girls. You were raised to know what was right, and then free to do wrong. Since you were a Mormon, you had been taught exactly how to act, but Christ gave you free will to work out your destiny. Bess would do what she wanted to do, and she left home more and more.

Those were years that belonged to her, and she would never tell anybody about them. It irked her that she became the subject of gossip in Grandview Ward, where they would talk of how she came back from long trips with fine dresses and jewelry. It gave her no pleasure that most of those fine dresses had been cut and sewed by Bessie Brown herself, and if she had a little jewelry, it was on the strength of her fine fingers that could model rings. So she told them.

She was in love with a man, and lived in Salt Lake because he lived there, and did housework for an old lady who kept a large house, and lived in a small hotel room by herself. When the love affair was over, she didn't date. It was a year when she lived alone and was still too young to suffer from being alone. She rather liked it.

She had a friend named Ava Rodgers who drank too much and lived around, and was staying with a man she called Daddy. Daddy sold ads for *Utah Magazine* for $100 a page and got 25-percent commission. Ava was very much in love with him, she said. He had something that sure got women.

"Daddy bought me a new typewriter today," Ava told Bessie, and invited her to their room. Bessie didn't drink — "one of those," she would always say — but Ava had a couple of beers while waiting for Daddy. Then she tried to pick up the typewriter, only it slipped, and bounced on the floor, and of course it broke. A brand-new typewriter. This happened just as Daddy walked in. He was not tall, but he was rugged, and he wore spats. He sure had confidence, and he sure had a temper. Poor Ava. It was not her typewriter, Bess soon learned. Just another lie, just another sob. Daddy had a look on his face like Ava had ninety-five items on her unpaid bill, and this was the ninety-sixth. "Pack your things, and get out," he said.

The next time Bess met Daddy was on the street and his name, she learned, was Frank Gilmore. "I'm getting married tomorrow," he said.
"Congratulations," she said.

When she saw him next in the street, she asked, "How's married life?"
"It's over with," he said.

She liked him. He was worldly-wise, and she was just a farmerette. He always knew where he was going. They could shop in a dime store or an expensive place, they could even have stood in a soup line, what with it being '37, but she felt comfortable. Even felt comfortable when she was yelling at him.

He was a very factual man and tough. He told her he had been a lion tamer and had scars on his face. Had been an acrobat and a tightrope walker, he said, and had a limp. Once, in vaudeville, he told her, he had been so drunk while doing his act that he fell into the orchestra pit from a height. Broke his ankle. Now he was in his late forties, and had gray hair but he still had a look that seemed to assume every woman he met was carrying his mattress on her back. Betty loved the way women were attracted. First man she ever wanted to chase.

She never knew that he really proposed to her. One day they were walking out of a movie, and he said, "Let's get married." To get down on his knees would have killed him. He would have died right there. So he asked her coming out of *Captains Courageous*.

He was sober, too. The kind of man who stayed that way until he decided to take a drink. Then he went on until petrified. A few years later, in their travels, he would get kicked out of a hotel or two.

For their wedding, they decided to hit Sacramento. It turned out he had a mother lived there who had been in show business all her life.

When Betty asked what his father did, Frank also said show business.

Before they left Salt Lake, they stopped in Provo to see her folks. Having seven girls, her mother and dad weren't going to sit down and cry when they heard the news. On to Sacramento.

6

Frank hadn't told anything about his mother being beautiful. Betty was surprised. Fay had a scintillating smile. She was petite, her hair was white, and her eyes were so blue you couldn't believe it. Her skin was flawless. Her teeth were to perfection. She had no wrinkles.

Even at her advanced age, which must have been close to 70, she acted like a most regal queen.

Her stage name had been Baby Fay. Now she was a medium and rarely left her bed. Just lived in it, in the big bedroom of a big house in Sacramento, and ordered people around. She would command them like she was waving a wand. Never tried it with Betty, however.

All the same, Fay could carry things off. She let it drop that she was connected by blood to a very large and royal family in France. The Bourbons. "When you have children," Fay said, "the royal blood of France will flow in their veins."

Fay's maiden name was another matter. Betty never learned it. She had been in vaudeville around the turn of the century and when she hadn't used Baby Fay, she was Fay La Foe. That was it. Miss La Foe didn't tell you what she didn't want to.

Maybe once a week, Fay would give a séance. Sometimes forty people would gather in chairs around her bed, and pay $5 apiece. Betty didn't go. She didn't want to get too near such things. For that matter, you could be talking to Fay, and there would be a knock on the wall, or a thump on the ceiling. At night, Betty could feel presences walking over her bed. When they were married by Fay (who had a clergyman's license and was called a Spiritualist) Betty always wondered which spirits were in and around Fay's bed.

She and Frank began to travel. At the time she met him, Frank had lived in Salt Lake for more than a year, but that wasn't common. He liked to go state to state selling space in special magazines. They were as-yet-unpublished magazines that often did not get published.

He had different names. Seville and Sullivan and Kaufman and Coffman and Gilmore and La Foe. Once he told her that his father's name was Weiss and he was Jewish on that side although he thought of himself as a Catholic since Fay had put him in Catholic schools and brought him up that way. Nonetheless, he had a Jewish wife in Alabama, and wives in other places. They were named Dolly and Nan and Babs and Millie and Barbara and Jacqueline and there was one who had been a famous opera singer. So far as Betty knew, he was divorced from them all.

But he sure had been in show business. Theatre people recognized him everywhere. They had free theatre tickets everywhere they traveled. One day they even drove across Salt Lake City. Never stopped. Just a quick minute across the wide, wide, forever wide streets. They must have traveled over the years through every state but Maine and New York. Stayed in hotels with names like Carillo Hotel and Semoh Hotel, Semoh for Homes spelled backwards. He had several birth certificates, but she never asked why they lived that way. He would have said, "If I thought it was any of your business, I would have told you years ago." Still, she was probably as strange to him as he was to her. She had been raised so root straight down that they never understood each other. No matter. She never tried. She thought you had to love people as they were. If you could change them, you would probably leave them anyway.

Frank drove a big car. Always put his short burly body in clothes where everything was big and loose and comfortable. If he didn't use suspenders, his pants were sure to hit the floor. She thought he looked like Glenn Ford. Years later, considering how chewed up his face had been by the lions, she decided he looked more like Charles Bronson. Short of the devil, he was certainly afraid of no one.

He also spoke the Jewish language. Had a knack for making friends with Jewish people. Spoke their language. He could Jew them down and they loved it. One time Betty was in this place and bought something expensive. When Frank found out what it cost, he said, "You mean he charged you the full price?" "Well, of course." Took Betty over to the owner and the Jewish man apologized because he didn't know Betty was Frank's wife.

7

That visit where Fay married them was the first Frank had seen of his mother in twenty years. Now, he and Betty would go back to Sacramento once in a while. On such trips, Betty couldn't help noticing how often Frank and Fay got to talking about Houdini. He was a favorite topic. They sure hated the man, and could get their blood up calling him ugly names. He had been dead for more than ten years,

but they labeled Houdini a pip-squeak and a cheap tramp. It didn't
upset Betty. She had never enjoyed reading about Houdini in the
newspapers anyway. In fact, when Houdini had pulled his favorite
stunt of escaping from a sealed casket underwater while wearing
handcuffs and chains, it had given Betty an uncomfortable, even a
frightening feeling.

Fay and Frank talked about the man, however, like they knew
him intimately. Listening to their conversation, Betty had to conclude
that Houdini had given Fay the money to send Frank to private
school. Then she remembered that Houdini was killed by a boy who
hit him in the stomach with a baseball bat, and Frank had told her
that his Jewish father, whose name was Weiss, had been killed by a
blow to the belly. Then she learned that Houdini's original name was
Weiss, and he was Jewish too.

By then, Fay didn't bother to conceal it. Frank was out of wed-
lock, of course. Before Fay died, she showed Betty where a lot of
papers were locked in her desk, and said they would prove Frank's
parentage. Of course, she didn't take them out and show them. Just
told Betty to be sure to be around her deathbed. "I don't want anybody else to get them," Fay said mysteriously.

They were in San Diego, when Fay passed away in Sacramento.
Somebody back east was notified. The papers went east. Before
Frank and Betty even received the news, the funeral was over.

The boys grew up, however, knowing something of the subject.
Gaylen, the third son, didn't like Houdini exactly, but he sure was
fascinated, for he used to celebrate the anniversary of his death on
October 31, Halloween. He lit candles and had a little ceremony. It
always came the day after Frank Jr.'s birthday on October 30. Frank
Jr. became an amateur magician and, at 15, belonged to the Portland
Magician Society. Gary never made much of it.

Sitting in the trailer through the heat of July and August, Bessie
could hear Brenda teasing him. "Well, cousin, here you are in jail.
Houdini should have taught you how to escape!"

CHAPTER 20

Silent Days

1

Cliff Bonnors, who worked at Geneva Steel, dropped in at the Silver Dollar one night after work. A little later, Nicole and Sue Baker came through the door, and that made Cliff's night. He started talking to Nicole.

About the time Cliff figured they were going to hit it off pretty good, he asked if Nicole wanted to ride over to his house while he cleaned up. He was feeling extra dirty because she was looking so neat. She didn't really have a lot of fancy clothes on her back, but what she had was fresh and cool. It made him feel the grease on his own self even more when she didn't want to go along. He only talked her into it by agreeing to drive her to the jail. She had a letter to drop off there for Gary.

That kind of bothered Cliff. He'd heard about Gilmore on the news, but hadn't known the dude was connected with this girl. Then Cliff said to himself, "What the hell, he can't do nothing. He's locked up." So they rode the truck over to Cliff's house and he took a shower, and then went down to the jail and stopped in the dirty old cinder lot by the railroad siding. She knocked and gave the guard a letter to pass on to Gary. Then they rode around for a while in the foothills before they parked.

Cliff thought she really knew how to enjoy it the first time. It was no short quick thing but pretty liberal. They were there for a while. Then he took her back to the Silver Dollar, and got her address.

After that, Cliff would go to her place in Springville every few nights and stay over. Being divorced from his wife hadn't ended his marriage altogether. Some of the roots were cut but not all. Even if he was seeing a few girls, there were still a lot of twinges in his feelings. It was all the nicer, therefore, what he and Nicole had, since they didn't ask too much of each other. He could see whoever he wanted to see, and Nicole had her friends — in fact, once or twice when he knocked on the door, she had to tell him there was company.

He always said: "I'm not going to butt into your business." Never really questioned her. On the other hand, there were times he went over and didn't make love or nothing, just talked out what she was bothered about. Nicole would say she liked somebody with her. Anybody could see she hated to be alone.

It was a nice friendship. If she was out of cigarettes, he'd get her a pack. If she had her period, he'd ride to the store, bring Tampax back. Wasn't really rich, but tried to help her. Besides, he never got too curious about the guy with the motorcycle — on those times Cliff came and there was company, the same bike always sat in the parking lot.

2

Same story as Cliff. Nicole met Tom while out with Sue. One night, she was feeling so depressed she actually fell asleep in the car and Sue drove her to a truck stop, dragged her in fact, and there was Tom eating in the next booth. Tom Dynamite, who worked in a gas station. He was coming down off acid, and they got to talk a little. Although they never had much to say, he took her home on his motorcycle, and they became very good friends. Never talked too much, but close. Quite a closeness.

Sometimes, when Cliff would go over, she'd be sitting in the dark. Meditating, she said. There were letters on the table in front of her. It would look like she had been reading before she turned off the lamp. Gary was writing her two letters a day, she would explain, and they were long letters. Looked to be five or ten pages on long yellow sheets.

Did she read all of them, Cliff wanted to know.

Well, nearly all. He wrote so much. Maybe she didn't read every last word religiously if you got down to it. There were a few she just scrounged through.

Then she shook her head. No, she said, she really read all of them.

August 4

Will you send me a picture of you. I want one real bad. In color 'cause you have such beautiful color to you. Hope I see you again. I get choked up sometimes when I look at you. The last few times I've seen you that's happened to me. I kind of lose my sense of time and place. It's like shifting into another awareness almost sorta going blank and being aware only of a Love (capitol L) that can't adequately be put into words. I look into your eyes and I can see for at least a thousand years. I see no evil in you, or menace. I see beauty and strength and love that doesn't have any bullshit to it. You're just you and you're real and you're not afraid, are you? I haven't seen you show any fear. That's remarkable. Fear is an ugly thing. I haven't seen any in you. It's like you've passed your test in life and know it. Like you've been up to the edge. And looked over. You're precious, Nicole. These things I write here are things I know are true and they make up part of the reason that I love you so utterly. I love that vein in your forehead. And I love the vein in your right tit. Didn't know I loved that one, did you?

Saturday, August 7

I can hear a radio in the background and they're playing "Afternoon Delight." We had a few afternoon delights, didn't we? I made you come one time in the afternoon and we were both covered with sweat. I could have held you forever then.

When I thought I had lost you — Nicole, that Monday nite, the next day, and the days that followed, I felt like a man whose flesh had been stripped. I've never felt such pain. And it kept building. I couldn't drown it and I couldn't shake it. It shadowed all of my hours. I once thought that I'd really been through some rough things, that I was immune to pain. One time I was chained to a bed for two weeks spread-eagled hand and foot, flat on my back. When they came in to laughingly ask me how I was doing, I spit on them and got punched out for it. And they shot me with that foul drug Prolixin and made a zombie out of me for four months. I was virtually paralized. I couldn't stand up without help and when I was raised to my feet I'd wonder what the fuck I wanted to stand up for and I'd sit back down. When it was driving me the worst I went for three weeks without sleep. I just sat on the corner of the bed — I hallucinated to the edge of insanity. I wondered if I'd ever be the same again, if I'd ever be able to draw and paint again. I lost about 50 pounds. I just couldn't get the food to my mouth. Getting up to take a piss was a major effort, I dreaded it, it would take me about 15 to 20 minutes — I couldn't get the pants buttoned. After a while I could barely see; my eyes had filled with some kind of white discharge that dried real thick on the lashes and I couldn't reach up to wipe it away and I couldn't see through it. Every 3 days or so they'd take me out of my cell to shower and shave. I hated that, it was such an effort! They'd hand me this electric razor and stand me in front of a mirror. I'd just stand there. There was no way on earth I could get that razor to my face. Sometimes they'd talk bad to me, say: "well, you're one of them tough guys, huh? Can't button your pants . . ." shit like that. I just had to look at them and take it. Sometimes I'd reply: "Fuck your mother, you pig." They'd get pretty pissed about that but it wasn't really much consolation to me. . . . I never begged them and I never cried not even when I was alone and I was completely alone. I knew that it would pass, eventually, and it did. I was able to shake it.

That was a bad experience. I've had others — unpleasant experiences of a long duration. I've always shaken them off and felt strong for it.

But I've never felt the kind of pain I felt when I thought I'd lost you. I couldn't shake that off — I only wanted you back, that's all I knew. I stayed at your house a few nites, and it was so lonely, Nicole. I was depressed. I'd walk those rooms and wonder where you were. When you called me that Thursday at work to tell me you were moving I felt my heart breaking. Really. It's a physical pain — it's not just in the mind. It was something I could feel. And it felt bad. Friday I looked for you but I didn't know where to look. Your mother wouldn't tell.

I felt so alone and depressed. Like I was a void. And it didn't lessen any. I had lost the only thing of real value I'd ever had or known.

My life had lost meaning, it had become a gulf, empty and void but for the shadows and the ever-present ghosts who have followed me for so long.

I don't ever want to feel that pain again. I am so completely in love with you, Nicole. I miss you so much, Baby. When I read your two letters and picture your pretty face the darkness rolls back and I know that I am loved. And that's a beautiful thing. The hurt stops. We were together for only two months but it is the fullest two months I've known in this life. I wouldn't trade it for anything. Just two months but I believe that I have known you, that we've known each other, for so much longer — a thousand, two thousand years? — I don't know what we were to each other before, I will know, as you will also when it becomes ultimately clear one day — but I feel we were always lovers. I knew this when I saw you that first nite, May 13th, Thursday, at Sterlings. There are some things you just know. And it went so deep so fast — it was a recognition, a re-newal, a re-union. Me and you Nicole; from a long time ago. I have always loved you Angel. Let's don't ever hurt each other again.

3

Cliff Bonnors was great because he always brought his mood around to meet hers. They could travel through the same sad thoughts never saying a word. Tom, she liked, for opposite reasons. Tom was always happy or full of sorrow, and his feelings were so strong he would take her out of her own mood. He wasn't dynamite but a bear full of grease. Always smelled full of hamburgers and french fries. He and Cliff were beautiful. She could like them and never have to worry about loving them one bit. In fact, she enjoyed it like a chocolate bar. Never thought of Gary when making love to them, almost never.

It certainly wasn't like sex had been with Gary. The moment something good happened with him, when it did, why it traveled to her heart and started to build, as if she was some goof-ass bird making a nest. When she went to visit Gary, therefore, she never thought of Tom or Cliff, or Barrett, or any incidental party. One life on Earth, another on Mars.

It wouldn't have been the worst way to live if not for those horrible depressions. Sometimes it would get real what she had done to Gary, and what he had done. Whenever she let herself think of the death penalty, everything started to get unreal.

Death would sit in her thoughts. Except it was more as if she was sitting in death, and it was a big armchair. She could sit back. The chair would begin to go upside-down, but slowly, until she felt the kind of nausea you get on one of those twisty carnival rides where you can't tell if you're excited or ready to throw up. Even when the thoughts stopped, she still felt as if she was spinning.

Sure I miss the sunlite and the air! I'm already losing my tan. Before long I'll be paler than a ghost. In fact, before long, I may be a ghost.

4

After a couple of weeks, they began to move Gary back and forth from the jail to the mental hospital. It was a two-mile transfer. He would be taken from the west end of town up Center Street past the hardware stores and clothing stores, and ice-cream parlors, to the east end, where you got nearer to the mountain, and the road came to an end in those foothills in which Nicole had run naked in the grass. Now he was at her old nuthouse, Utah State Hospital. A different ward, of course.

One thing was better there. They could have contact visits. Not the way it was at the jail, where he was taken to a little room and she stood on the other side, trying to see him through a thick mesh tough enough to keep minks and raccoons from breaking out. Their fingertips could hardly touch through the tough mean little holes. All the while they were talking, every noise of the jail was going on behind her. She would stand right out in the dirty old entrance with guards and trustees and delivery men and what-all yelling back and forth, straining to hear Gary's voice, a loud radio or TV always on. One prisoner or another was usually shouting in the main tank. It was like you had to fight for what you could hear.

At the hospital, it was different. They were in a little room together. She would sit on his lap and he would grip her, and they would kiss for five minutes, far out on the other side of sex, as if it was her soul taking the trip rather than any juice starting to flow. They were kissing from one heart to the other — not sex, but love. Right on the wing.

Then they would land. They were in a bare room, cement-brick walls painted yellow, four inmates looking at them. Trying not to look at them. That was the posse, Gary would explain. He would say it in a clear voice, his snottiest voice, clear enough for the inmates to hear, say that they had put him among a flock of sheep who were hell-bent on policing each other. "A herd mentality," he would say. "The posse can't even talk to you unless there's two of them around. One to snitch on what the other just said."

The four fellows in the posse took it different ways. One might grin like an asshole, another would look as if he was measuring Gary for some lumps, the third was depressed, and the fourth real eager, like he wanted to explain to Nicole how the patient program worked in this hospital.

She picked up on that bit by bit. There was a crazy system. Different from when she was here. They called it the program. A bunch of dudes were facing prison sentences, and were mixed in with real psychos and zombies. These kids, right out of prison and Reform School, had been put together with the true nuts, and they all wrote a constitution and had elections and a patient-run government.

Gary explained, right in that yellow room, with these four dudes monitoring Gary's hand every time it touched her tit, he spoke out on this hospital system where the doctors let the patients control everything, why they could even elect their own President of all the patients. It was the hottest kind of horseshit. That was what the patients controlled. The horseshit.

Gary had always told her stories about prison, but now he got into the nitty-gritty. Spoke of the way prison was supposed to work. It was a war. It was supposed to be a war. Convicts might do a job on other convicts, convicts might even kill other convicts, but they were on the same side. They were against the guards. It was a war where there was nothing worse than a snitch.

The guards and the Warden did everything they could to build an intelligence system. So they depended, for what they knew, on snitches. A snitch, said Gary, would even suck your cock and then run to the Warden with what you said. So the convicts did all they could to wipe out such inmates. In a good prison where the convicts had it down, there weren't too many snitches. Prison, after all, was a city where convicts lived, and had the real control. Guards just passed through for eight-hour shifts. That was the way it should work.

Here they had it inside out. There were no guards. Just a few aides. The inmates *supposedly* had the power. But the inmates who got elected to the posse became the new guards. They worked for the doctors. "They are in the throes of brainwash," said Gary, pointing at the posse. She wanted to giggle at the way he told them off right to their faces. "Self-seeking snitches," he said. "Not a spark of life in them. Nobody looks at anybody. They just have *agenda* meetings."

He would say this while she sat on his lap, say it while he was feeling her, and the four dudes were looking, boiling, hurting, from what he said. Then he and she would just hold each other and whisper and talk of other things. He would want to know how Sunny and Peabody were getting along. He would speak of how sorry he was that he used to yell at them and let them get on his nerves. In fact, they were remarkable children. Right in front of the posse they talked.

Then he would get mad again. The way they worked this hospital, he said, was worse than student government. Everybody was always taking everything up at a meeting. Committees for everything. A committee to sweep the hall. A committee to pick up the straws from the brooms of the fuck-up committee who swept the hall. Each committee ran around snitching on the other committee for doing a bad job. A punk could go into a real prison, Gary announced, and if he had balls, he could come out a convict. In this hospital, men came in as convicts, and got released as punks. "This place sucks. I've never seen the like." The posse listened.

After a few visits, Gary gave up riding them. It was as if the hour was too valuable for such talk. They would sit and hold hands and be silent. They would think of places they used to go to, and live in the breath that went back and forth. Sorrow would visit from one to the other. Not a flood of waters, not the way she would cry on Tom Dynamite's naked shoulder for what she had done to Gary, or cry with Cliff because the high-school sweetheart he had married wouldn't even let Cliff's son talk to him now, no, sorrow lifted out of her heart and passed into Gary's chest and returned with the breath of his sorrow. It was as if they stood on a ledge and sorrow was as light as all the air below the fall.

Then they would feel loving again and he would grope her until she wouldn't have minded taking off a thing or two. Something new for the posse! Then, time up, feeling truly horny for Gary, she would get ready to go out in the street and start the long walk down to a part of town where she could hitch a ride.

Sometimes, the doctor who seemed to be the head guy around the ward, a fellow named Dr. Woods, would ask her into his office. He would talk about her feeling that she was to blame for Gary's acts. Nicole would wonder if the posse had reported what she said to Gary. Anyway, Woods would try to tell her that she didn't have to keep that thought in her head. Gary was a complex individual, and not the sort to say, I care for Nicole, so I'm going to kill somebody.

Nicole would listen. Dr. Woods had the power to say Gary was insane, and then they wouldn't give him the death penalty. In fact, if Gary could get to a mental hospital, he might be able to escape. So she wasn't going to insult the doctor. Still, he was the weirdest for a psychiatrist. He was tall and very well built, and looked like Robert Redford in *Downhill Racer,* except he was maybe better looking and maybe even bigger — he was one of the best-looking men Nicole had ever seen. Yet she thought he was kind of wimpy in his manner and never came down hard on one side or the other. She certainly felt funny talking to handsome Dr. Woods, when she was horny as hell from being with Gary and the posse.

She would leave John Woods's office and hitch a ride, and the world that was outside Gary and herself would come slowly back to her, and she would feel a little less like a space ship, and begin to think of supper for the kids, and annoyance that her car was on the blink, and Barrett had not yet fixed it. Her problems would start living again, and so by the time she got home, it would be truly weird to find a letter from Gary describing the very nuthouse she had just seen him at. It was like waking up from a dream to answer a knock on the door but the knock came from the person you had just kissed in the dream.

5

August 10

A posse member's supervising me because I have a pencil — they broke it in half then tore the eraser out — I asked them what the fuck that was for and they told me so that I wouldn't stab anybody. Unbelievable! . . .

Nicole, what the fuck kind of journey am I on?

Three nuts are having an argument outside my door because one of them emptied my urinal an hour ago and forgot to chart it. The first loony is accusing the second loony of gross negligence and dereliction of duty in his failure to properly chart on the log hanging outside my door the time of day that he emptied my urinal. The third loony is bouncing from foot to foot trying to get a word in edgewise. The second loony is becoming quite excited and is trying to appeal to me to settle this national disaster. I don't know what the fuck to say but I'd hate to see this poor buffoon lose his T.V. privileges or something — he's the same chap who sat so patiently outside my door the other day while I wrote a letter — so I tell 'em "Hey, it's okay man, everything is really cool, this guy is on the ball. Didn't spill a drop and brought that urinal back clean as a whistle!" Now they don't know what to say but it appears to have settled the argument. They're getting a pen to make the required chart entry.

Oh, Nicole, I'm so lonesome. I miss the life we had. I miss being in the same bed with you, holding your pretty face in my hands looking into your charming alarming eyes. Coming home to you at nite — how slowly the days went when I was at work!

God, Nicole! You're the most important person in the world.

I remember one time when we were fucking and we were really bucking up against each other. Hard. Wild. How I'd love to do that.

August 14

The drinking fountain is across from my cell and it is really funny the way some of these guys drink water. This one dude sucks up the water for 2 or 3 minutes at a time! He 'bout got in a fight cause of it yesterday — this other cat got impatient, pushed him and said, "You don't need to drink so long." Another dude really slurps, I've never heard anything like it, he sounds like a sump pump. A truly startling noise.

What a bum life.

There's a one man band parading up and down the hall making strange tuneless lip farts.

August 17

Man, I'm sitting here really feeling like an idiot! It's about 7:30 in the morning. I missed a nice opportunity yesterday, didn't I? Would you believe that it just now became clear to me? I missed a swell chance to touch you on your sweet little cunt. You said something like 'you won't get another chance' but I didn't quite hear you, like I sometimes don't. Now this morning it fell into place — the fucking posse had momentarily turned their heads and I just sat there like a bump on a log. God, Baby, my mind was elsewhere . . . I'm really kicking myself in the ass right now. I'm so dumb.

August 18

There's a guy washing his face in the drinking fountain — I hope nobody sees him; I'm sure that must be some kind of offense. A couple women from the ladies side just came over to the office here asking for a plunger. This one dude told 'em: "I got a plunger, pucker up." I thought that was pretty cute.

August 19

These are some of the most silent days I've ever spent.

August 20

What a bunch of punks. I'll bet I could take any one of them posse punks and fuck him in the ass and then make him lick my dick clean.

I was interviewed by a couple of psychiatrists today. They wanted lurid details . . .

CHAPTER 21

The Silver Sword

1

After the accident, early in August, Nicole's car was a mess. First, it would only go in one gear, then something slipped into place again, and she had all three forward gears operating, but reverse was out. Sometimes, none of the gears would shift. The clutch was acting crazy.

She had stopped sleeping with Barrett about the time of this accident. Barrett never said a word but moved up to Wyoming, and came back every week or so to the room he kept in Springville. Once in a while, he would drop around and ask if she needed any help. If he had money, he sure wasn't showing it, but one day he did offer to fix the car. Considering she still wouldn't go to bed with him, he couldn't have been nicer about it. So she did give him something that night.

Next day when she came back from visiting Gary, the car was gone. Barrett had towed it away. His rooming house wasn't that far from her place in Springville, so she walked over, and there he was working on the car in the back lot with friends. She kind of had fun helping get it up on the blocks. Then progress stopped. There was something, the bell housing, or whatever he called it, that was welded together from her driving it too hot. Then, after Barrett got the transmission out, sitting on the ground, he discovered she needed a new main clutch plate. There was no money for that. It was a problem she could resolve, but she did not like to think about how.

Nicole went and saw Albert Johnson who was the manager of a food store in the area. He was about twice her age, just a pleasant-looking family man, and she used to shop at his store a couple of years ago and buy a couple of things she would pay for, while shoplifting with the other hand.

One day they stopped her out front. She was caught with a pound of margarine and some jars of baby food in her purse. When they brought her up to the office, she said she was stealing 'cause her kids were hungry, but he let her think he was going to call the police, anyway. She sat and sweated it out, and got scared real good, began to cry. She had been picked up on something like that a year before in another store. This time she thought for sure they would send her away.

After fifteen minutes, however, of hearing her story, Johnson told her she was a nice young girl, with all kinds of bad breaks, and that she'd never had an opportunity really to climb the ladder. He was going to let her go. They got friendlier and he explained to her that his store might look like a shoplifter's paradise because it was long and narrow with short aisles across, but the losses got so big, they had put a walkway up in the attic with one-way mirrors looking down. Tell her friends to beware.

He talked quite a bit. He noticed, he said, she was on food stamps, and he told her he wasn't always that fond of such people. He thought food-stamp people were extravagant and didn't shop the bargains. The guy that had to earn the dollar was going to look for the steak on sale, but kids like herself just picked up the $2.79 cut, and ate too many convenience foods, potato chips, soda pop. Then they'd get irate and damn the government if their welfare checks didn't come in on time one week. He liked her, however, he said, and went out of his way to explain he had a daughter her age and could understand her problem. If she ever needed anything, let him know.

Next time she came into the store, he said he'd like to trade with her, you know? Said it in a nice way and told her how pretty she was, and that he really liked her. She joked back. "Nothing to trade this week," she said. Then, after a while, she moved out of Provo to Spanish Fork and rarely got to shop there.

Now, about a year later, she started seeing Albert Johnson again. He was the only store manager she knew who would give her cash for her food stamps. To get him to agree, she had had to tell him about Gary and her new troubles but he sympathized enough to trade eighty bucks for that much worth of stamps. This time, however, she was out and told him she just needed fifty. He gave it to her without conditions. She heard herself saying that she didn't like leaving debts unpaid.

Afterward, Johnson said he wished to Christ he hadn't done this to her. Begged her not to turn professional. She wasn't that way. He was a family man, and felt real bad.

She told him not to worry. It was only because she was without a car and needed wheels so desperately. It was really an incredible story in her own ears, all that stuff about the transmission out, and hitching to see Gary.

Albert Johnson hadn't been bad to her, but it was an ugly experience. With all she had mentioned to Gary about her life, she could never tell him about the store manager.

Anyway, she had the cash, fifty dollars. And gave it to Barrett. He got in his car and went off to get the main clutch plate. She went home. Next thing she learned Barrett had split for Wyoming. Must have been a week before he returned. Then she went over to look at her car, and he still hadn't done a damned thing. The Mustang was sitting wide open with the parts on the ground starting to rust, and the body on blocks like a corpse. She could feel how angry Barrett was. So she did no more than leave word she'd been there. Sure enough, three in the morning, he showed at her apartment, stoned out of his head.

2

It had been one of those days when Nicole was getting to Barrett on the sentimental side. He kept remembering the first time he had brought her home to his mother and dad. When his mother had said they'd have to sleep outside in the Volkswagen until they were married, Nicole had answered, "I don't care where we sleep. We're going to be happy." He could never get that out of his head. Every time he was sure that he was free of Nicole, no love left whatsoever, he would think of that remark, and all over again would be nothing but a man with a wound.

He had been on so many hits the last week in Wyoming that he could hardly remember what he had taken and with whom — couldn't even remember who first said Nicole was seeing Gary again. Then everybody was telling him. They all knew but Barrett. He went on a self-pity cruise. Couldn't help thinking of all the times he had come in to rescue Nicole, taken his lumps, dared his life if you get down to it, and she had rewarded him with a trip to the bedroom. Not love, just the bedroom. It was an unhappy situation when screwing your nearest could bend you out of shape.

Full of self-pity, he decided it was still all right. At least, self-pity let the good memories come back. Like the time Hampton found him after he first stole Nicole, and wasted him, and yet that was still a good memory after all these years.

He had been over at a friend of his selling drugs, a little crystal, some speed, toked a couple, got blasted. He drove down a Technicolor road from Lehi to Pleasant Grove to pick up Nicole at high school. She was staying with her parents then.

Well, just as Nicole walked out the school door, Hampton drove up in a '58 DeSoto and jumped out. Barrett got on the street also, figuring, I know Nicole. If I sit here and lock the doors, she's going to say I'm chickenshit. So Barrett stepped up, hoping Hampton wouldn't punch him, just eat him out, but Hampton went right over to meet him, looking three heads taller, and as Barrett smiled and said "How are you doing?" Hampton knocked him down.

Having smoked those two joints, Barrett was pretty loose. Everything went black. He couldn't see. He'd been cooled. Tried to get up, and then he did get up, and Nicole came on at that point and called Hampton a fucker. Everybody could see Barrett wasn't able to defend himself. After they pulled Hampton off, Nicole and Barrett got in the car and drove up to the river. They sat by the water and he told Nicole how the windshield was turning yellow and melting. All kinds of shit, you know. Between the blow he'd taken and the pot he'd smoked, he might as well have been flying an acid trip. But it was over and he felt fine. Full of colored streams. Nicole was sitting next to him. If he had to take a couple of bumps, big deal. He felt like heaven thinking she loved him and took his side.

Then there was the day when Sunny, Jeremy, Nicole and himself were getting into a car, and Joe Bob Sears, the animal — Barrett could still hear the whistle in his ears — came, zoom, right from across the street, his car pulled across theirs, so they couldn't go. Joe Bob Sears in a black Maverick. Barrett's heart hiccuped out of his chest. Joe Bob opened their door, jerked Nicole out, grabbed Sunny, jerked her out, grabbed Jeremy, hit his head on the car, picked them all up, threw them in his Maverick, and all the while Nicole was calling Joe Bob every rotten name. Barrett got out to see what he could do, and Joe Bob grabbed a knife, pointed it at Barrett, said, "I'm going to cut you open." At that, Jim jumped in his car, backed up and came forward to run Joe Bob over, but Sears jumped away, got in his car, and took off down the road with Nicole and the two kids. Just then a cop came along, Barrett flagged him, said, "That guy just kidnapped my wife, you know, my girl friend." The cop gave chase, gave Joe Bob the red light, pulled him over.

Nicole and the kids were standing on the grass, Joe Bob was saying, "She's my woman, she's coming with me, you know," and the cop was saying, "She doesn't have to go with you if she doesn't want to." Nicole was saying, "I ain't going with you, you bastard." Finally, the cop said, "Listen, young lady, you better knock off that language, or I'll lock you up too." Finally, Sunny, Jeremy, and Nicole got back in the car with Barrett and he took off and that's the last they ever seen of Joe Bob. They went back to living in the tent.

3

All this was in his head when he went over to see Nicole on this occasion at three in the morning. She was sitting there, writing a letter to Gary and did not want to be interrupted, but Barrett came in, and announced right off he wanted to fuck. She wasn't into it, she said.

As she started to walk away, he sat her down. Didn't throw her, but sat her hard enough she knew she wasn't getting up in a hurry. "Oh," he said, "you are writing a letter to your murdering sweetheart." Why, he started to say, if she knew the things going on in him, she would be scared right now. "Nothing," said Nicole, "scares me anymore."

Barrett took the picture of Gary that she had taped on the wall, and started to rip it. But it was some kind of tough Polaroid that was hard to tear, and it struck her as comical. He was so stoned he was having difficulty. Then she got mad, and said, "Give me that son-of-a-bitching picture." But Barrett held it away, took his lighter out, started burning it. She picked up an ashtray, and hit him in the head.

He started throwing her all over. He might just as well have been Joe Bob Sears, except he wasn't hitting her so much as slapping her, picking her up, pushing her down. She knew she was in trouble, yet she felt no fear. Which was interesting. She'd always had the idea she could handle Barrett if it came to it, but tonight he was awful strong in his anger. She didn't even try to hit back.

Then Sue Baker came to the door. She had left her baby with Nicole and was taking the night off, but happened to drive by, and saw Nicole's light on, so she came up to see. Jim told her and her boy friend to get lost, and Sue didn't say a word, just left, but Nicole knew she would call the police.

They got there pretty fast. When the uniforms showed at the door, Barrett hid in the hallway. It was like the movies. He kept motioning to Nicole not to let them know he was there. Threatening gestures, like you fucking well better not. Nicole just opened the door, however, and said, "Will you get him out of here?"

The cops walked in, asked what was going on, and Barrett said, "Nothing." Nicole said, "Nothing, my ass! That motherfucker's been knocking me around for the last hour. Excuse my language, officer, but he's been terrible." They handcuffed him, and read his rights, and took him away. About that time, she began to realize they had been looking for him on something else and had a warrant. Barrett spent the night in jail.

It was only when the police were gone that she understood how crazy Barrett had made her. After they'd handcuffed him, one of the cops went down to his car to answer the patrol radio and the other happened to turn his back. She saw a knife on the kitchen sink. There was one moment when she wanted to cut Barrett's throat. Do it right while he was handcuffed. Quick as that. They could have given her the cell next to Gary.

4

After he got out of jail, Barrett sold her car. It was logical. He needed some money for his legal problems, and Nicole had ripped him off for a lot more than money. So he sold the transmission to a neighbor and towed the rest over to a wrecking yard in Mapleton where he signed a bill of sale. It was all done. She would never have her Mustang again.

When Nicole found out, she decided to smash the windshield of Barrett's pickup.

It was a cool August night and she put on a jacket with baggy sleeves and stood outside his motel room holding a borrowed hammer. Even with two Valiums to mellow her out, she felt crazy inside every time she thought about Barrett selling her car, so kept waiting for the Valiums to take effect, but they didn't. Besides she had a problem. The moment she went to work on the windshield, he would hear the noise. His truck was parked just outside his door. Maybe she should put dirt in his gas tank.

She thought she'd try a different approach, however, and walked up. Through a locked screen door, she said, "I want to talk to you, Barrett." He wouldn't open, however. He was cooking a steak, which she could smell, and she said, "Come on out, I want to talk to you," and he kind of laughed a little. "No," he said, "talk to me here." "I'd rather," Nicole said, "you come outside." He laughed again. "I don't know, Nicole, I don't trust you," he said. "You got a strange look." Then a friend of his came up, and Barrett felt a little more safe, cause he opened the door and said, "Come on in." At that point, Nicole decided to have it out on the basis alone of the money. "You owe me for my car," she said. They started talking, and Barrett said he couldn't believe what he had done. He didn't have the right.

She wasn't going to buy too much of that. Nicole didn't shout, but she did threaten him in a nice quiet way. Said, "Barrett, you screwed me up pretty bad this time. I'm tired of messing around. You owe me $125."

"There's no way," said Barrett, "I'm going to come up with that much." He paused, however, and said, "I can get you sixty tomorrow, forty a few days after."

She believed him. In fact, he came by the next day with $40 and told her that was all he had. Nicole was really rude, and said, "I want the rest." Finally he came with another sixty. That was about it. He just trailed off, like with everything else. She had no wheels and finally had to spend the hundred for other things. Food. Rent.

5

Gary received a letter from a woman in Nevada who wrote she was 27 years old, divorced, five feet five inches tall, a little on the plump side. "*Please feel free to ask me anything that is on your mind, because I am quite broad minded, and nothing will shock me either. I am a red-blooded American female, and definitely enjoy it too, and of course, I like sex, attention, a lot of affection, and like to do just about anything that is connected with the opposite sex for sure!*" Gary sent the letter to Nicole who wrote him back right away to say it was like a slap in the face.

She couldn't believe how angry she became at this woman. Underneath all the talk of how much she loved Gary, she had to be really crazy about him. Never felt jealousy like this for another man. It was so bad, she decided she had to see him right that minute.

Only it was a bummer. Hitchhiking over to the nuthouse, the whole day got lost. First, she couldn't find a sitter for the kids. Then, when she finally got a ride to the hospital, they told her he had been returned to the jail that very morning. It wouldn't be visiting day over there. Nicole wanted so much to hear his voice, however, that she walked all the way across town from the nuthouse, and stood outside by the wire fence in back and hollered, "Gary Gilmore, can you hear me!" She shouted it loud as she could. Just about, she heard a voice call back, "Yeah, babe."

"YEAH!" she cried out.

Then she screamed for all the world to hear, "Gary Gilmore, I love you!"

A cop came around the building and told her she'd have to leave. She could be arrested for doing something like that. It surprised her. She didn't know they could keep you from expressing yourself that way. She hollered out to Gary that she had to go, and took off. But she felt a whole lot better.

Aug. 20

Hey baby the most beautiful thing just happened to me. I just heard a magic elf's voice holler: "Gary Gilmore, can you hear me? I love you!" Well I love you too! Boy, oh boy, do I love you! Nicole — you amaze me. You are absolutely wonderful. I just don't have words to say how great you make me feel. You make me cry happy tears.

6

Sat. Aug. 21

I went to sleep for awhile this afternoon and I woke up feeling that clear cold thing that I hate so much. It's more than a feeling — it's a sort of knowledge. Like a total awareness of being in a box and it's bright daylite outside and the whole world is going on without me.

August 24

What will I meet when I die? The Oldness? Vengeful ghosts? A dark gulf? Will my spirit be flung about the universe faster than thought? Will I be judged and sentenced, as so many churches would have us believe? Will I be called to and clutched at by lost spirits? Will there be nothing? . . . Just an end? . . . I can't even picture the concept of nothing — I don't think that "nothing" exists. There is no such thing as "nothing." There is always something — some energy. But how long a journey is death? Is it instantaneous? Does it take minutes, hours, weeks? What dies first — the body of course — but then does the personality slowly dissolve? Are there different levels of death — some darker and heavier than others, some brighter and lighter, some more and some less material?

Nicole, I believe we always have a choice. And I choose, that when I die, or change form, or whatever best describes this thing called death, I choose that I wait for you, that I meet you, that I find you — the part of my heart and soul I have sought for so long — the only real love I've ever known. Then we will know. We'll know everything that we know now but can't consciously recall.

You said that girl's letter was like a slap in the face — Baby, Baby, I didn't mean anything like that when I gave it to you! I just thought I'd let you read it. Guess I wasn't thinking, huh?! I'm not gonna write to her. You're the only girl in my life Angel. I wouldn't take a thousand girls for you.

August 25

Maybe when you get your next check you could get me a couple things, okay? What I would like to have is a couple "Flair" felt tip pens, one brown and one blue with fine points — and a fairly decent watercolor brush: a Grumbacher Sable Round No. 5 watercolor — and a decent pad of paper. If you can't afford it, it's okay honey, 'cause I know they don't give you much on that fuckin welfare and I don't want you to be broke again like you was this month.

I got into a search for Truth real heavily at one time. I was looking for a truth that was very rigid, unbending, a single straight line that excluded everything but itself. A simple Truth, plain, unadorned. I was never quite satisfied — I found many truths though. Courage is a Truth. Overcoming fear is a Truth. It would be too simple to say that God is truth. God is that and much, much more. I found these Truths, and others . . .

I found a lot of Truths. But I was still hungry — and it's true that hunger teaches many things. So I kept looking. And one day I was fortunate. I saw a simple, quiet Truth, a profound, deep, and personal Truth of beauty and love.

It came down on Nicole what an expression like "horrible loss" really meant. It was throwing away the most valuable thing in your life. It was knowing you had to live next to something larger than your own life. In this case, it was knowing that Gary was going to die.

She began to think there was not even a minute when she stopped loving him, not for a minute. Not a minute of her day in which the guy was not in her mind. That she liked. She liked what was inside of her. But it was spooky. She would take in a breath and recognize that she was falling more and more in love with a guy who was going to be dead.

7

One night Tom Dynamite came over, but she couldn't bring herself to screw him. That surprised her. Sex had nothing to do with Gary. It was just that this night she had been thinking about him so hard she didn't want to separate herself from the pleasure of continuing to think about him. Somehow, she got Tom to sleep on the floor next to the couch where she always lay down, and Nicole even put her hand on Tom's shoulder in gratitude while they slept. He left in the morning without waking her.

On opening her eyes, she remembered that even while falling asleep, she had decided to kill herself in the morning. She awoke with the same thought. She sat as quietly as a bird not moving in its nest.

If she died first, Gary would soon be with her. He had told her that. She didn't know where she would be then, or what else might happen, but she would be with him on the other side. His love would be so strong that she would be attracted to him like a magnet. It would be like the magnet that pulled her to him the day she first saw him in jail.

She didn't have any decent razor blades, and considered going next door to borrow one, but thought that might be too suspicious. So she broke open a Daisy Shaver, a kind of disposable plastic dingus, cracked it with a steak knife and got the blade loose. Then wrapped it in some notebook paper, and put it in her bra. She thought if she didn't move around too much it would be safe and not cut her. She felt strange leaving the kids over to a friend's house, but set out to hitchhike to the jail. A couple of guys picked her up.

One was an ex-con, and he was really foulmouthed. Kinda cute. He talked real rough, and kept asking if she wasn't worried that he and his buddy would take her up in the mountains, rape her, cut her throat. Nicole kind of laughed at them. Here she had this blade in her bra, all set to take care of the job herself.

Anyway, they dropped her off by the jail without further ado. Of course, when she told them she was going to visit her boy friend, and the ex-con recognized the name, he had to make a smart-ass remark. "Well," he said, "he's going to get a little lead poisoning." That cracked Nicole up. She didn't feel bad laughing about Gary. She knew he would have laughed over it too.

She went over to the back, and hollered a couple of times and somebody else finally answered her and said Gary was in another cell. Then she heard him, so faintly, trying to holler back. The cops came and threatened to arrest her. Of course, she didn't give a fuck.

This time, they took her around to the front and kept her inside for a half hour, and she made herself right at home, using the floor for an ashtray, laughing at their threats, she didn't give one shit. They could let her go, or lock her up. Without female cops they couldn't shake her down, and she still had the razor.

After a while, they let her go. On the way out she noticed a small cement tunnel that went under the freeway. It was just a few feet in width and dark enough so you couldn't see far. She crawled in, and it was sure dark. Her sleeves were rolled up over her biceps, but she pulled them up further, and then cut herself as hard as she could right across the vein and the artery. It was a good feeling. Really warm, really bleeding and splashing on the cement. She could feel blood running down her arm and it was hot, and good. She liked the way it felt, kind of soothing. There was so much going on. Like the ocean was coming into the tunnel. She could see the opening where she had come in, and all the light Nicole could see in the world was in the circle of that hole.

She sat there, and the nice warm feeling changed. She began getting sick. Then she was nauseated. Started shaking all over. She wasn't cold but she was shaking. There was blood all over the cement. Every nice long slow thought faded, and now she didn't feel as if she was slipping into something warm, but as if everything was getting colder. She didn't like that. But she made herself sit. Even made herself lie down and try to go to sleep. Then she tried to talk herself into not moving. Just stay there until it was over.

Finally, she thought, I got to get to a doctor. At least, I got to try. That's the best I can do, is give it a good try. Then I can handle dying.

She got up, and couldn't even walk straight, and kept feeling she was going to pass out. She would walk a few steps, and spots would come in front of her eyes, and she'd squat. But it was just a little way from the jail, and she made it back over, and there was a cop washing a truck, wasn't even in uniform. She told him she'd been climbing a chain-link fence and slipped and showed him how her shirt was bloody. He took her down to the Utah Valley Hospital.

The doctor didn't believe her shit about climbing a fence. He said, Looks like a pretty sharp thing did the job. Asked her how much she bled, was it a pint or a quart. She said, well, she didn't know what a pint or a quart was. Not when it was running out of you. They took her blood pressure, and she began to feel better, and hitchhiked home. By the time she got back, she was sick to her stomach again, couldn't really stand up without getting dizzy. Slept a lot. In the morning she found out they were mad out at the jail and had lifted her right to visit.

August 29
Fucked me up that I couldn't see you today — these chickenshit pricks. Give a motherfucker a little authority and they think they have to start taking privileges away from people . . . bunch of slack-jawed jizz-gurgling come-drunk punks.

8

Nicole went to bed with Cliff Bonnors the night after she got home from the hospital. Her arm was stitched and it hurt like hell. All the time she was making love she kept thinking that if she didn't watch out it would start bleeding again. Night after, she found herself in bed with Tom Dynamite. Same damned thing. Her arm hurt like a fucker, and it got to her. She had to stop making love.

Sometimes she was convinced Gary could hear her think. It wasn't that she thought it was right or wrong to be doing this while Gary was in jail, it's just that it came over her how it might seem peculiar to be in love with a man and still make it with guys on the outside. She had never experienced this feeling before. That it was important to be faithful. Something she had to ponder.

She finally decided to test the water, and say something in a letter. She decided to use Kip as an example. Kip, of all people, had dropped in on her almost a month ago. He had changed so much, she told Gary in the letter, that she couldn't believe it. Kip had become a Mormon. Now he would get naked and play with her, but he wouldn't go to bed. It was like he had become the cock-teaser, not her. That was really freaky.

One morning, for instance, Kip went to an LDS church right down the street, and came back all dressed up in his Sunday pants, all fired up with religion. He was planning to go to the evening services but she started fooling around with him. Before she was done she made Kip cream his pants. That messed him up. The pants were so wrinkled and wet, he couldn't go to church.

Well, she told Gary a little of that in her letter. Wanted to see what sort of reaction she would get. After all, it had happened weeks ago, and wasn't important. But Gary simply ignored it.

9

Sheriff Cahoon wasn't surprised when Gary asked if he could come out and talk. Cahoon even took him into the front room and they sat by the desk. Had a nice friendly conversation. Gary said he agreed with Sheriff Cahoon on the way the place should be run and wanted to come to some agreement on what was expected from him and Nicole. Well, said Cahoon, he wanted Gary's lady to come and act ladylike, not create no problems. Come decently dressed. When he saw the spark in Gary's eye he remarked that, of course, her dress wasn't that far out. Her attitude was creating the problem. Gary agreed they could arrive at an understanding. Cahoon said they were having a good one, and he would permit Gary a phone call to Brenda to notify Nicole she was reinstated.

On the next visit, she told Gary about using the razor blade in the underpass. She had tried and couldn't do it. Scared of dying. He told her it was very hard to bleed to death. Most people who tried it got sick. It was one of the hard ways to die.

She had a bandage on, but he finally asked her to show him the stitches. Then said, "That's a fucking deep cut," and the tone went through her like praise, as if he had said, "Baby, you did that for me."

He never did mention Kip.

Having agreed to these visits, Cahoon got concerned all over again. Gilmore and his girl friend were having the damnedest correspondence. One letter actually talked about how she cut her arm and felt the warm blood dripping. Heard it make a puddle on the ground. The guard who brought it to Sheriff Cahoon said, "What kind of message is this to be writing to a guy on First-Degree Murder?"

Cahoon sure read it carefully. Nicole kept talking about the silver sword and life after death. How they would have a better kind of life with the silver sword. She wrote about going up to the spot where she had been bleeding and the rain had washed most of the blood away. Since she was always bringing him books, Cahoon inspected one of them, and it was all about the hereafter. How to get jubilant.

It made the guards so nervous that next visit when Nicole turned around from talking to Gary and went to reach into her purse for a cigarette, the officer on watch was so jumpy he actually grabbed her wrist. It was that silver sword she kept talking about.

Cahoon was debating whether to stop her visits again, but all of a sudden, she stopped coming to the jail. Her letters also stopped.

10

Nicole had decided to take the plunge. At the end of a long letter to Gary that had been full of love, she put in a couple of sentences at the end to say how pointless it was that she spent so much time — and she wrote it right out — "getting fucked." Had to know what he thought.

> *September 5*
>
> *I just read your letter. It's a long and beautiful letter and full of love. But on page 5 you said "it's such an ugly thing to do. I spend so much time either getting drunk or getting fucked." I felt like I had been hit or something — a cold numbness moved thru me and I couldn't go on reading the letter for a few minutes. Nicole, don't ever tell me anything like that again unless you want to hurt me. I don't want anybody to fuck you and I try not to think of that — I do pretty good until you write and tell me.*

She felt as if somebody had socked her right on the side of the head. She could hear his voice ringing in her brain. It spoke in a terrible anger, as if he was capable of biting his teeth clear through his tongue. He didn't want her ever to get with a guy again. Didn't want to have those thoughts in his head. *"Everybody fucks Nicole,"* said his voice in her head. *"Don't fuck those cocksuckers. It makes me want to commit murder again. If I feel like murder it doesn't necessarily matter who gets murdered — don't you know that about me?"* Way inside, a part of her felt extraloving. It was that important to him.

After all, it had never been important to her. Easier to let things happen than tell a guy to leave you alone. It was kind of a relief now to have a reason for saying no. Of course, it wasn't that easy to turn away Cliff or Tom Dynamite. She would explain, "I'm not here with you anymore, I'm with somebody else." They understood, Cliff particularly. That didn't keep them from still trying to get it on. She did need company.

Once or twice it was really hard to tell them to go home. Besides, other people kept dropping over. Dudes out of the past. It wasn't that she couldn't say no, it was that they were expecting it to be like the last time. She didn't want to stand in front of them and scream, "Get out of my life." They hadn't done her any harm.

She had to figure it out. So she didn't visit the jail, or write. She wanted to wait until she could tell him she loved him enough to be able to do what he asked.

CHAPTER 22

Troth

1

Gary was so quiet over the next few days that it got ominous. Cahoon decided he was too morbid and needed company, so he moved over a prisoner named Gibbs from the main tank. They had both done so much time, they might get along.

Cahoon noticed that soon as he shut the bars, they started a conversation in jail talk. It was that gibberish talk. Use a word like figger to say nigger. Show the other fellow how many years you put in by carrying on a whole conversation. Cahoon didn't try to get it all. If they said lady from Bristol, that meant pistol, and he would have to get concerned, but Gilmore was talking of ones and twos, and those were shoes. "Yeah," said Gilmore to Gibbs, "A nice pair to go with my fleas and ants."

"You still got to think," said Gibbs, "of your bunny and boat."

"Fuck the goat," said Gilmore, "let me stroll in with a dickery dick."

"That's right, it could juice the chick."

Cahoon left. They were just doing time. He thought they made a cute couple. Both had Fu Manchu goatees. It was just that Gilmore was a lot bigger than Gibbs. Like cat and mouse. Hell, like cat and rat.

2

There were only three things in the world Gibbs could honestly say he had any feeling for: children, kittens, and money. Been on his own since he was 14. When 17, he wrote and cashed $17,000 worth of checks in a month and bought himself a new car. Always had new cars.

By the time he was 14, Gilmore said, he'd broken into 50 houses. Maybe more.

First time Gibbs went to prison out here, he was behind a 2½-million-dollar forgery. He took, Gibbs said, 21 counts. Next time he went back was when he blew up a cop's car in Salt Lake. Captain Haywood's car.

Gave him 15 years when he was 22, Gilmore said. Did them at Oregon and Marion. Gibbs nodded. Marion had the credentials. Flattened 11 years consecutively, Gilmore told him. Probably 4 years altogether in Solitary. Gilmore showed real pedigree.

He was in for rubber rafts, Gibbs told him. Stole forty of them in two weeks out of J.C. Penney's in Utah Valley, Salt Lake Valley, $139 apiece. Chain saws same way. Made two or three hundred bucks a day. Just couldn't manage his money, that's all.

My problem, too, allowed Gilmore. He had also done a little boosting at J.C. Penney's.

"Yeah," said Gibbs, "the only difference between you and me is when I do it, I have two shoulder men to run interference. If they come after, my big boys say, 'What are you chasing this guy for?' "

Gibbs could recognize that Gilmore didn't know any heavies out of Salt Lake. Didn't know the Barbaro brothers, Len Rails, Ron Clout, Mardu, or Gus Latagapolos. "You're talking heavies, then," said Gibbs.

Gilmore spoke of the Aryan Brotherhood and his connections there. Gibbs could recognize some heavy names out of Oregon and

Atlanta, Leavenworth and Marion. Not legends, but still heavies. Gilmore carried himself like he was well regarded. Of course, Murder One gives a man standing. When they ask you, "What do you get for killing?" the answer is "self-satisfaction." Clears the mind.

His ring, Gibbs told Gilmore, had done outboard motors, inboard motors, house trailers, and trailer homes. Don't get nervous when they see you carrying the stuff. They had a laugh over this. "Half a million dollars' worth," said Gibbs, "going right down the Interstate."

3

"If you get out before me," said Gilmore, "can you bring back some hacksaw blades?"

"Anybody would, I probably would," said Gibbs. In fact, thought Gibbs, he might. He had as much loyalty in one direction as in the other. He was the man in the old saying. "You got blue eyes, one blew north, one blew south." Except it was Gilmore had the blue eyes. He liked Gilmore. A lot of class.

"Hey," said Gilmore, "if you could figure a way to get me out of here, I'd pull any job you want. Just keep enough money for me and my old lady to leave the country, and I'll give you the rest."

"If I wanted out of this jail," said Gibbs, "I'd have people come take me out."

"Well, around here, I don't know people," said Gilmore.

"If anybody would, I would," repeated Gibbs.

The cell they were in was divided into two parts, a small dining area with a table and benches, and to the back, away from the bars, a toilet, a sink, a shower, and six bunks. On the other side of the bars was a corridor that led to the next tank. That was used as the women's cell. When no women were there, it was the pen for drunks. Their first night, they had a drunk next door who kept yelling.

Gilmore answered as if he were the jailer. "What do you want?" he bellowed. The drunk said he had to make a phone call. Had to get bond. Gilmore told him no Judge would give it. Why, the little boy he had hit in the trailer court died. What little boy, said the drunk? Those are your charges: drunk driving, auto homicide, hit and run. Gibbs loved it. The drunk believed Gilmore. Spent the rest of the night crying to himself, instead of yelling for the jailer.

Gilmore began to do his exercises. That was something, he told Gibbs, he did every night. Had to, in order to tire himself out enough to get a little sleep.

He did a hundred sit-ups, took a break, then did jumping jacks, clapping his hands over his head. Gibbs lay on his bunk and smoked and lost count. Gilmore must have done two or three hundred. Then he took another break and tried push-ups but could only get to twenty-five. His left hand was still weak, he explained.

Then he stood on his head for ten minutes. What's the purpose of that, asked Gibbs. Oh, said Gilmore, it gets the blood circulating in your head, good for your hair. He wanted, Gilmore added, to try to keep as much youthfulness in appearance as possible. Gibbs nodded. Every con he knew, including himself, had a complex about age. What the hell, the youthful years were all lost. "My personal opinion," Gibbs said, "is that you are a young-looking person for 35 years old. I am five years younger, and look five years older than you."

"It's your coffin nails," said Gilmore, sniffing the smoke. He had picked a top bunk as far away as possible from Gibbs, who was sleeping in the bottom bed across.

"You don't smoke?" said Gibbs.

"I don't believe in supporting any habit you have to pay for," said Gary. "Not if you spend your time in lockup. They had a cell in Isolation named after me."

The drunk in the next tank was whimpering piteously. Gilmore said, "Yeah, the Gary M. Gilmore Room," and they both laughed. Listening to the drunk cry was as comfortable as lying in bed on a summer night hearing trees rustle. Yes, Gilmore told him, he had put in so much time in Segregation that he almost never earned money from a prison job. And there sure wasn't money coming from outside. Any luxuries allowed in the can, he had learned to do without. "Besides," he said, "smoking is bad for your health. Of course, speaking of health . . ." He looked at Gibbs.

Speaking of health, he expected the death sentence.

"A good lawyer could get you Second Degree. They parole Second Degree in Utah in six years. Six years, you're on the street."

"I can't afford a good lawyer," said Gilmore. "The State pays for my lawyers." He looked down at Gibbs from his bunk and said, "My lawyers work for the same people that are going to sentence me."

4

"They keep taking me," said Gilmore, "to be interviewed by psychiatrists. Shit, they come up with the stupidest questions. Why, they ask, did I park my car to the side of the gas station? 'If I parked in front,' I said to them, 'you'd ask me why I didn't park to the side.'" He snorted at that. "I could put on an act, have them saying, 'Yeah, he's crazy,' but I won't."

Gibbs understood. That offended a true man's idea of himself.

"I am telling them that the killings were unreal. That I saw everything through a veil of water." Now they could hear the drunk moaning again. "'It was like I was in a movie,' I say to them, 'and I couldn't stop the movie.'"

"Is that how it came down?" asked Gibbs.

"Shit, no," said Gilmore. "I walked in on Benny Bushnell and I said to that fat son of a bitch, 'Your money, son, *and* your life.'"

They both cracked. It was funny as hell. Right there in the middle of the night, in this hot fucking two-bit asshole jail, with the drunk slobbering in his shit and counting his sins, they couldn't stop laughing. "Pipe down in there," said Gilmore to the drunk. "Save your crying for the Judge." The drunk was one wet sorrow. Like a puppy first night in a new house. "Hell," said Gilmore, "the morning after I killed Jensen, I called up the gas station and asked them if they had any job openings." Again they cracked.

Gilmore, tonight, would break off his arm if he could make a good joke. Cut off his head and hand it to you, if his mouth would spit nails. "What's your last best request when they're hanging you?" he asked, and answered, "Use a rubber rope." Pretended to be bouncing on the end, he put his face in a scowl, and said, "Guess I'll be hanging around for a while."

Gibbs thought he'd piss his pants. "What," asked Gilmore, "is your last request when they put you in the gas chamber?" He waited. Gibbs wheezed. "Why," Gilmore said, "ask them for laughing gas."

"That is enough," said Gibbs, "to choke you up."

For that matter, he was almost strangling on his own phlegm. Smoking gave him a dozen oysters every meal. The kid with the phlegm-pot. Gilmore asked, "What do you say to the firing squad?"

"I," said Gibbs, "ask them for a bullet-proof vest." They laughed back and forth like an animal going in circles and getting weak. "Yeah," said Gibbs, "I heard that one."

Gilmore had a quality Gibbs could recognize. He accommodated. Gibbs believed he, himself, could always get near somebody — just use the side that was like them. Gilmore did the same. Around each other tonight, they were like boiler-plated farts. Filthy devils.

No sooner did he think this, than Gilmore got serious. "Hey," he said to Gibbs, "they're figuring to give me the death penalty, but I have an answer for them. I'm going to check into the State of Utah's hole card. I'm going to make them do it. Then we'll see if they have as many guts as I do."

Gibbs couldn't decide if the guy was a bullshitter. He couldn't visualize doing something like that.

"Yes," said Gilmore, "I'll tell them to do it without a hood. Do it at night if it's outside, or in a dark room with tracer bullets. That way I can see those babies coming!"

The drunk was screaming, "I didn't mean to kill the little boy, oh Judge, I'll never drive again."

"Knock it off," shouted Gilmore.

Yeah, he said to Gibbs, the only legitimate fear a man in his position could have while facing the firing squad was that one of the marksmen might be a friend or relative of one of the victims. "Then," said Gilmore, "they might shoot at my head. I don't like that. I have perfect twenty-twenty, and I want to donate my eyes."

This guy was a roulette wheel, decided Gibbs. Just depended which number came up. "I've made a lot of mistakes in my life," said Gilmore from the upper bunk, "and a great many errors in judgment the last couple of months, but this I will say, Gibbs. I am in my element now. I have never misjudged a person who has done time."

"I hope you have a favorable impression of me."

"I believe you are a good convict," said Gilmore.

On that high praise, no higher praise, they went to sleep. It was three in the morning. They would bullshit until three every morning.

5

September 9

I'm not a weak man. I've never been a punk, I've never been a rat, I've always fought — I ain't the toughest son of a bitch around but I've always stood up and been counted among the men. I've done a few things that would make a lot of motherfuckers tremble and I've endured some shit that nobody should have to go thru. But what I want you to understand, little girl, is that you hold my heart and along with my heart I guess you have the power to crush me or destroy me. Please don't. I have no defense for what I feel for you.

I can't share you with any other man or men Nicole. I'd rather be dead and burning in some hell than have any other man be with you.

I can't share you — I want all of you —

I have to go without fucking, you can too. Sorry to be crude but that's true. We love each other and belong to each other let's don't ever hurt each other Nicole let's don't ever hurt each other.

This pain paralyzes me. I keep thinking of you being with somebody. I can't help it. I have to chase the ugly pictures out of my mind. I don't want anybody to kiss you or hold you or fuck you. You're mine I love you.

You said on the last page of your letter that I will not have reason to hurt that way ever again — I'm 35 fucking years old been locked up more than half my life. I should be a tough son of a bitch, all the things that have happened to me.

But I can't take being away from you — I miss you every min-ute.

And I cannot stand the thought of some man holding your naked body and watching your eyes roll back sleeping in your arms.

I can't share you — I won't. You've got to be all mine. I don't care that you say you have this crazy heart that won't let you refuse any request to make another happy. I have a crazy heart too. And my crazy heart makes a request of your crazy heart — don't refuse my request to be only mine in heart mind soul and body. Let me be the next and only man to have you.

God I want you baby baby baby
fuck only me
don't fuck anybody else dont dont it kills me dont kill me
Am I demanding too much??
Write and tell me —
TELL ME   **TELL ME**
'GODDAMN IT
                TELL ME
Fuck shit piss God Nicole
Tell me.

Wednesday and Sunday are too far apart ———— why don't you write me more!?

Nicole don't be with anybody else dont dont dont dont
                d o n t
I'm really fucking this letter up

I've got to come to a conclusion and this is it. I've got to hava all of you! With nobody can I share you. I love you.
I LOVE YOU   **I LOVE YOU**   **I LOVE YOU**
            I LOVE YOU

No, I ain't drunk or loaded or nothing this is just me writing this letter that lacks beauty — just me Gary Gilmore thief and mur-derer. Crazy Gary. Who will one day have a dream that he was a guy named GARY in 20th century America and that there was something very wrong . . . but what was it and is it why things are so super shitty, to the max, as they used to say in 20th century Spanish Fork. And he'll remember that there was something very beautiful too in that long ago Mormon mountain Empire and he'll begin to dream of a dark red haired sort of green eyed elfin fox whose eyes rolled back

*and could swallow all of his cock and who laughed and cried with
him and didn't care that his teeth were fucked up forever and who
taught him how to fuck girls again instead of his hand and pictures
in Playboy.*

Next night, they put a girl in the same tank where the drunk
had been. She was also crying and Gary hollered over, Hey, sister, it
can't be all that bad. She immediately quieted down.

Gary found out her name was Connie, and when she inquired if
he had a cigarette, Gibbs slid a pack down the hallway to her cell and
Connie thanked them.

They kept trying to talk but you had to holler loud, so Gary wrote
a note and slid it over. Told her he was rather handsome, liked young
girls, western music, and yodeling. Especially, he liked to yodel. She
wrote back that she'd seen his picture in the newspaper and agreed
he was good looking. Thanked him for being kind, and asked if he
would yodel.

"Well, Tex," said Gibbs, "crank up." Gary could no more yodel
than Gibbs could knit. So Gary just hollered over shucks he was
lying, couldn't oo-lay, oo-lay-oo to save his butt. All three began to
laugh. They had a good night sending notes back and forth. In the
morning, she got out. Gary's depression was back.

6

September 11

*I could not sleep for the third nite running. Somethings happen-
ing to me. I dozed briefly last nite and awoke in the middle of a
dream about a severed head. I can hear the tumbrel wheels creaking
again and the swift slide of the blade — in my dream I was being interviewed by a female Mont Court parole officeress or whatever,
dreams take their own course, and pretty soon a doctor or the male
Mont Court, or somebody, came back.*

I've told you that I haven't slept lately — the ghosts have descended and set upon me with a force I didn't believe they possessed. I smack 'em down but they sneak back and climb in my ear and demons that they are tell me foul jokes, they want to sap my will, drink my strength, drain my hope leave me derelict bereft of hope lost empty alone foul demon motherfuckers with dirty furry bodies whispering vile things in the nite chortling and laughing with a hideous glee to see me toss sleepless in durance truly vile they plan to pounce on me in a shrieking mad fury when I leave with their hideous yellow long toe and finger claws teeth dripping with rank saliva and mucous thick yellow green. Dirty inhuman beasts jackals hyena rumor monger plague ridden unhappy lost ghostly foul ungodly things unacceptable creeping crawling red eyed bat eared soulless beasts.

They won't let the ol' boy have a nites sleep. God-damned lost motherfuckers.

I need our silver sword against them. They're slippery motherfuckers.

The demon ghosts
trick tease tantalize
bite and claw scratch and screech
weave a web of oldness oldness pull in harness
like oxen a wood creaking tumbrel a gray wood
tumbrel through the cobbled streets of my
ancient mind.

They've attacked me before we have had several bouts they humped on me like fiends when I was on Prolixin for four months I endured a constant onslaught of demon fury —— oooooooOOOOOOOOOOOOOH!

Left me drained and 50 pounds lighter but stronger than they will ever be.

they like it when I hurt
And I have been burning lately

I hate to say it but in the last week they almost got me they came the closest they ever have and they ever will.

Gibbs had a habit of waking up in the middle of the night for a cigarette. There, in the endless wee hours, he lit up and lay back to do some quiet thinking about his private situation. All of a sudden,

Gary said, "You actually did it, didn't you, Gibbs?" He replied carefully, "Did what?" Gary said, "You actually lit that motherfucker, didn't you?"

In the morning, Gary said, "You talk in your sleep, Gibbs. You say a few words and then you start playing with your teeth. Sounds like you got a dice game going on down there." Gibbs got a little paranoid. He wasn't altogether happy about saying things in his sleep. If it was the wrong thing, Gilmore might decide to separate his heart from his lungs.

All that day, Gary's depression got worse, and the next night about 3 A.M., when Gibbs woke up again, Gary said, "Are you okay?" Gibbs replied, "I think so. I'm not sure." Made a point of trying to laugh even though he was gasping and coughing from his cigarette. "You going to be all right, man?" asked Gilmore, "need an iron lung maybe?"

Gibbs was silent. He was just trying to control his wheezes. Out of the silence, Gilmore said, "In the morning, we'll tell the guard we can't get along. That way he'll move you."

"Oh, yeah?" said Gibbs.

"Yeah," said Gilmore, "I think I'm going to hang it up. If I do, you're better off out of here. They might just try to drop a murder rap on you." He nodded. "They're going to be a mite disappointed if they don't receive the self-satisfaction of trying me on my two hot ones."

Gibbs nodded. "If that's what you want," he said, "I'll go so far as spitting at the guard or throwing something, and take the hole." "Yeah," said Gary, "I appreciate that. I really might have to ask you to leave tomorrow."

"Yeah," said Gibbs, "I'll do it."

In the morning, however, Gilmore said to hold off. He wanted to see if word would come from Nicole that day. In the afternoon, sure enough, a letter did arrive. He read it and said, "'Never mind. I've decided to wait." Gibbs couldn't get over how jubilant he was.

Gary spent the afternoon going through her old mail, picking up this one and that one, finally he said, "Here's one to read if you like." Gibbs noticed it had little spots of blood on the pages. He felt embarrassed and just skim-read it, but couldn't help taking notice of one part where Nicole said, "how warm and nice it felt, my life being drained from my body."

Gibbs was careful not to say anything or show any emotion, but to himself he thought, "She's either the most sincere broad I ever heard of, or one of the dingiest, ding-a-ling chicks in the world." Gilmore said, "What do you think?" Gibbs replied, "I can't really say because I've never been in your position, but evidently she's dedicated to you."

Now that Gilmore was out of his depression, Gibbs decided to keep him out of it, and started talking about how easy it would be to escape. Just get a hacksaw blade. The jail was old and the bars didn't have a stainless steel core inside. In fact you could see where somebody had already cut a couple and they'd had to weld them back in place.

Gary decided to send word to Nicole to tell Sterling Baker. He could do the job right at the shoe repair. Gibbs said you had to separate the outer sole from the base, insert two blades, then carefully restitch the shoe by hand, using the same holes. Any shoemaker could do it.

Gary approved of the idea one hundred percent. Started a letter to Nicole explaining how to go about it. Since he didn't want any jailer to look over what was written, he gave it to Mike Esplin to mail for him after the lawyer dropped by to discuss his case.

September 12

Dearest Fairest

I have something I want you to do. If you will do this and do it right I believe that I will soon take you away — to Canada, perhaps — the Pacific Northwest — somewhere. Away. Together me and you and your kids. Here is what I want: a carbon steel high quality hacksaw blade. They sell them in hardware stores. I need a pair of shoes size 11. Sterling can put the hacksaw blade inside the sole of the shoes. It would be cool if perhaps Ida, she's above any suspicion, were to bring the shoes along with some clothes to me on a visiting day or the lawyer Craig or Mike — this is a hick town mickey mouse

jail — they don't x-ray shoes, they don't have a metal detector — I
could be out of here that very nite.

Do this for me Angel. I will come and get you and we will go.

And I don't want to find any man with you when I get there.

Get me that blade. I'll come in the nite and take you away and
for whatever its worth for as long as it can last before I am caught —
or killed we will live laff love sing be together come together.

Like we're supposed to be.

September 13

I stayed so fucked up on that beer and Fiorinol I'm afraid I never re-
ally gave you a good fuck — makes me feel bad — wish I could fuck
you now when my body is on the natural, clean and pure and not full
of booze and Fiorinol. I would lay you on your back and put some
vasalene in your bootie and fuck you there until we both came — and
then take you to the bath tub and frolic in the water with you for a
while and scrub each others back and butts and arms and legs and
balls and cock and pink cunt and tell you a story while we both
soaked and you smoked a cigarette.

Baby we've got each other — that's all that matters my fair
freckled angel. The bringer of the silver sword. Baby hold me tonite
against your naked body wrap it all around me and fuck me in your
mind and in your thoughts and in your dreams come to me when you
leave your fair body in sleep and enter my heart and soul my mind
my body take me into your soft warm wet love into your beautiful
mouth into your heart your soul your very essence put my hands on
your bootie and go wild with me abandon it to me so that in sleep
and in all that is we may be as one something beyond imagination.

Once again she decided she had never been loving him more.
His sexy letters got her so excited, it was playing hell with her decision to be true. "You're so full of bullshit," she said on her next visit,
"I bet you can't even get a hard-on, and here you are writing things
like this." He just grinned back. She was loving him.

Nicole spoke of the hacksaw blades. She had tried a little hardware store and asked for carbon steel. The old guy behind the
counter saw she didn't know the size and didn't seem to care 'cause
she bought the two kinds in stock. He gave her a funny look, and

said, "Who are you trying to break out of jail?" She had a hard time keeping a straight face.

Now, she had taken the blades over to Sterling. He wasn't, she told Gary, too enthused. First, he said he would, then decided he'd have to think about it. A couple of days had gone by. He was still thinking.

7

Gilmore owned the best sense of hearing Gibbs had ever come across. If there was a case of a man with bionic ears, it was Gary Gilmore. While it was at least ninety feet from their cell out to the front office, ninety feet of turning down three different halls and walkways, nonetheless Gilmore could listen to them book somebody, and tell you the name and the charge. It sure kept him from sleeping. Gibbs had noticed that Gilmore would only average two to three hours out of the twenty-four. He didn't seem to need more.

Cahoon would have breakfast at 6:30, and Gibbs would still be in a drowse, but Gary would be up and eating. Then he would write a letter to Nicole, or read one of his books. He did this in the morning while it was peaceful through the jail.

From time to time Gilmore would speak of how unusual it was to find a man who had done as much time as Gibbs and didn't like to read. Gibbs figured he had gotten through three books in his life: *The Godfather, The Green Felt Jungle, Vendetta*. Now, Gary handed him *The Reincarnation of Peter Proud*. Said it would give Gibbs a clue to the hereafter. Gibbs read it to make Gilmore feel good, but that didn't turn him into no believer in reincarnation.

They got into a discussion about Charlie Manson. Manson had psychic powers, Gilmore explained. "I know he made Squeaky Fromme take a shot at President Ford."

"You actually believe such stuff?" asked Gibbs.

"Yeah," Gilmore said, "you can control people with your mind."

Gibbs felt apologetic. "I don't believe in nothing I just can't see."

"Well," Gary said, "Manson put her up to it."

"How?" asked Gibbs. "They didn't let Manson have a visit from the girl."

"No," Gilmore said, "Manson was using psychic powers."

Gibbs didn't see it.

Later that evening, Gilmore was heating water for coffee. They would roll toilet paper into a doughnut shape and light the middle. It produced a steady flame that lasted long enough to get the water to boil. Their heating pot was made out of a Dixie cup with the aluminum foil from their baked potatoes wrapped around it. For a handle, they tied the ends of a piece of string to two holes on the rim, and held the cup above the flame.

Gibbs was lying on his bunk watching Gary do this when he had the thought: "I'd sure laugh if the string broke." Just then, the string did catch fire, the cup fell, the water spilled. Gibbs let it out. He laughed so hard he rolled up in his bunk like a potato bug, and pop-popped a string of farts. Gilmore looked at him with disgust, then threw the cup, string and all, into the toilet.

"You are," said Gilmore to Gibbs, "the fartingest motherfucker I ever saw."

"I," said Gibbs, "can fart at will." He laughed his ass off at the remark and gave another. Always laughed like a maniac after a fart.

"Well," said Gilmore, "they don't stink. I'll say that for you."

"I've always been a toot-tooting son of a bitch."

"Why don't you save 'em for a week," said Gilmore, "and make an album?"

After Gibbs caught his breath, he told him, "Hey, Gary, I wasn't being ignorant about your misfortune. It's just I was thinking it was going to happen. Right before it did."

Gary lit up. "That," he said, "is psychic powers." Gibbs wanted to say, It will take more than a broken string to give me religion, but he kept his mouth shut.

Still, Gibbs did have a kid sister living in Provo who was married to a fellow named Gilmore. When Gibbs heard of Gilmore's arrest, meaning Gary's, he wondered at first if it was his brother-in-law, whom he had never met.

Gary, hearing that, said, "Did you ever think how much we have in common? Maybe we were meant to meet." Gibbs thought, "Here we go with reincarnation again."

Gary made a list: they had both spent a lot of time in prison, Gibbs in Utah and Wyoming, himself in Oregon and Illinois. Prior to prison, they had each gone to Reform School. Both were considered hard-core convicts. Both had done a lot of time in Maximum Security. Both had been shot in the left hand whilst in the commission of a crime. Neither of them cared for their fathers. Both fathers were heavy drinkers and dead now. Gilmore and Gibbs both loved their mothers, who were religious Mormons and lived in small trailer courts. Neither Gilmore nor Gibbs had anything to do with the rest of each immediate family. On top of that, the first two letters on both their last names were "GI" although neither had ever seen the armed services. Their first experience with drugs was in the early '60s and they both used the same drug, Ritalin, a rare type of speed not in common use.

"Had enough?" Gilmore asked.

"Hit me," said Gibbs.

Well, Gary would point out that prior to their arrests, they had both been living with 20-year-old divorcées. Each of them had met the girl through her cousin. Each of the girls had two children. The first was a 5-year-old daughter, brunette, whose name started with an S. Each girl had a 3-year-old son by another marriage. Both little boys were blonds and their names started with a J. Both Nicole and Gibbs's girlfriend had mothers whose first name was Kathryne. And each of them had moved in right after he met the girl.

After comparing these coincidences, Gibbs did stop and think. He even started to wonder. Maybe there was sense in what Gary was saying.

Of course, Gary hadn't hit the difference. Gibbs's girl was nothing to look at, and Nicole was beautiful. After Gibbs saw the way she put herself out for Gary, he decided she must also be beautiful inside. Why, when she didn't have money for stamps, she would hitchhike down to the jail to bring Gary a letter. If they needed coffee, Tang, writing paper, pens, whatever, Gibbs had only to tell the jailer to release money from his account and Nicole would go right out and buy the things and bring them back.

One time, making up the list, Gibbs asked if there was anything that had not been mentioned, and Gary said, "Do you like that instant hot chocolate?" "Yeah," Gibbs replied, "it's all right." Actually he preferred cold drinks like Tang but said, "Have Nicole get a carton of those packets of hot chocolate." He could see how embarrassed Gary was to want something or need it. Got all choked up. "Gibbs," Gary said now, "you are one of the best sons of bitches I ever met in twenty years of lockup. Mark my words, somehow, someday, you'll be repaid for being so good to others."

Gibbs could see that Gilmore was really looking for some way to repay these favors. He even began to speak of fixing Gibbs's teeth, which rattled in his sleep. "Well," said Gibbs, feeling uncomfortable, "I like to play with them." He had a full upper plate, but he had sure broken it in two. Shortly before he came to the slammer, he had been driving along in his Eldorado, drunk as a skunk, got sick and had to puke. Too lazy to stop. What the hell, he was doing 80 on the Interstate. He just opened the window, heaved, and must have gone another 100 yards before he realized his teeth had gone out with the cakes. Slammed to a stop on the shoulder and ran back in the dark, until he found a stream of vomit. The false teeth were in two pieces in the middle of it.

Now he played with them. Made a clickety-click sound like castanets. Sometimes Gibbs would poke the whole job out at people just to watch their expression when his front teeth split apart in front of them.

He wouldn't kid this way around Gary, however. Gilmore was too self-conscious about his own teeth. It even took him a couple of days to get around to telling how he worked in the dental lab at Oregon State. If Nicole could buy a kit in a pharmacy, Gilmore could repair his denture. Gibbs released the money right off.

After her visit, she sent back a box of Denture-Weld, which contained a bottle of liquid, tube of powder base, eyedropper, plastic cup, a stick to stir it all, sandpaper, and instructions. Gilmore threw the instructions aside and went to work. In fifteen minutes the teeth were back together and fit like new. It made Gibbs worry. With his plate fixed, Gilmore might be able to hear the words he was saying while asleep. Gibbs just hoped those words wouldn't embarrass him.

Later that night, Gilmore sat up and began to work at little adjustments on his own plates. Gary was really looking for a privacy trip with those teeth. In the silence of the night, Gibbs pretended to be sleeping and watched Gary, intent and alone at his work, old as his age and more, his lips fallen in on his gums.

The four trustees were petty criminals just serving a little county jail time. So they were all deathly afraid of Gilmore when they came back at mealtime. They would stand as far as they could from the slot in the door when they slid their trays through. A man could hardly reach out and grab you through that little space, but the trustees had a lot of caution. They had heard the jailers talk of how Gilmore made his victims get down on the floor, then, *splat!* Anytime a fellow in one of the other tanks started a tough-guy role, the jailers would now tell him to quit or he could go live with Gilmore. That man, they would point out, did not have a hell of a lot to lose by killing another man.

They took Gibbs out of the cell one day to let Gary be alone with a psychiatrist, and the jailer took Gibbs to the kitchen for coffee. The trustees couldn't be nice enough. Fixed Gibbs a sandwich, the works. Finally one of them asked why he was out of his cell. "Oh," Gibbs said, giving a wink to the jailer, "we're being pulled one at a time for a shakedown. Gary will be here just as soon as I go back." Gibbs had never seen four guys wash trays so fast. They planned to be done for sure before The Great Gilmore arrived.

Just then the jailer had to walk to the front office to answer the phone. Soon as he did, Gibbs took every package of punch he could see on the table, stuffed them in his pants, said to the trustees, "If one of you punks say a word about this, you'll *hate* it."

Soon as the jailer took him back, Gibbs started unloading his stolen goods. Gary said the nut doctor was going to recommend that he was sane and competent to stand trial. "What do you expect?" said Gilmore. "He's paid by the same people who pay my lawyers. The State of Utah. I can't win for losing." Then he said, "What are we waiting for? Let's mix up that punch before the Man comes looking," So they got busy and made up a gallon.

PART SIX

The Trial of
Gary M. Gilmore

CHAPTER 23

Sanity

1

Esplin and Snyder had been offered a crack at distinguishing themselves in a big case, in fact, the most prominent case either of them had yet taken on. They certainly thought they were working hard. The legal community that met informally each morning and afternoon in the Provo Courthouse coffee shop in the basement hall across from the foot of the marble stairs was a group to pay attention to the upcoming trial. It was some time since Provo had had a case of Murder in the First Degree, and a young lawyer could do service or injury to his reputation among colleagues.

So they were eager to put their skills to work, and not without awe at the responsibility. A man's life would depend on their presentation. It was frustrating, therefore, to discover they had an uncooperative client.

He wanted to live — at least they assumed he wanted to live — he talked about getting off with Murder in the Second Degree, even being found Not Guilty. Yet he would not offer new material to improve a weak defense.

The prosecution had circumstantial evidence that was tightly knit. If perfect evidence could run from A to Z without a letter missing, then here, perhaps no more than a letter or two was smudged, and only one was absent. The fingerprint on the automatic was not clear enough to be established as Gary's. Everything else brought the case together — most particularly the shell casing found beside Benny Bushnell's body. That could have come only from the Browning found in the bushes. A trail of blood led from those bushes to the service station where Martin Ontiveros and Norman Fulmer had seen Gary's bloody hand.

There was direct evidence as well. At the Preliminary Hearing on August 3, Peter Arroyo testified to seeing Gary with a gun in one hand and a cash box in the other. Arroyo made a perfect appearance. He was a family man who spoke in a clear and definite voice. If you were filming a movie and wanted a witness for the prosecution who could hurt the defense, you would cast Peter Arroyo. In fact, after the Preliminary Hearing, Snyder and Esplin ran into Noall Wootton in the coffee shop, and they joked about the witness's talents the way rival coaches might talk of a star who played for one of them.

The confession Gary gave to Gerald Nielsen had also hurt a great deal. Snyder and Esplin were not concerned Wootton would try to bring such a confession into the trial. If he did, they thought they could show Gerald Nielsen had violated the defendant's rights. In fact, Esplin delivered a pretty potent plea at the Preliminary Hearing. "Your Honor," he said, "the police can't lay out a case before a suspect and say this is the evidence we've got, and wait for him to make a statement, and then say we didn't actually ask him anything. Why, the inflection of one's voice can lead one to believe he's being asked a question."

The Judge came close to agreeing. He said, "If I was sitting as a trial judge, I'd exclude it . . . but for the purposes of a Preliminary Hearing, I'm going to admit it."

Wootton would probably not even bring the confession into court now. It could taint the case sufficiently to have a conviction overthrown on appeal.

Even so, the confession had done its damage. Much of the promise was out of the defense. A lawyer without a reputation for probity might be able to ignore the fact that half the legal community of Provo now knew, after the Preliminary Hearing, that Gilmore had confessed, and the other half, via the coffee shop, would soon find out. That was bound to inhibit any really imaginative defense. It would not be comfortable before the fact of such a confession to work up the possibility that Bushnell's death was an accident in the course of a robbery.

The most telling evidence against Gary was the powder marks that proved he had put the gun to Bushnell's head. Otherwise, you could argue the murder took place because Benny Bushnell had the bad luck to walk into the office just as Gary was robbing the cash box. That would be Second-Degree Murder, a homicide committed in the heat of a robbery. It was hardly as bad as ordering a man to lie down on the floor, then pulling the trigger. That was premeditated. Ice-cold.

Nonetheless, you could still work up a defense from those facts. Automatics had the most sensitive triggers of any handguns. Since Gilmore, a few minutes later, would shoot himself by accident with just such a sensitive trigger, you might still argue that he had been surprised by Bushnell and had taken out his gun. Trying to decide what to do next, he told Bushnell to lie down. When Bushnell started to say something, he threatened him by putting the gun to his head. Then the gun, to his horror, went off. By accident. It might have been a defense. It could have created some reasonable doubt. It would, at least, tone down the most powerful detail, emotionally speaking, in the prosecution's case. Yet, that argument could now be employed only as one of several possibilities during a general summation to the Jury. You could not build your case on it, not when many a lawyer in Provo, given the existence of the confession, would see such tactics as sleazy.

2

A trial for murder in Utah was conducted in two parts. If the defendant was found Guilty in the First Degree, a Mitigation Hearing had to be held right after. One could then introduce witnesses who were there to testify to the character of the accused, good or bad. After such testimony, the Jury would go out a second time, and decide between life imprisonment and death.

If Gary was found guilty, his life would depend on this Mitigation

Hearing. Yet here he became uncooperative. He would not agree to calling Nicole as a witness. They tried to discuss it. There, in the little visitor's room at County Jail, he did not listen to Snyder and Esplin's argument that they had to be able to make the Jury see him as a human being. Who better than his girl friend could show he was a man with a good side? But Gilmore would not allow bringing her into the case. "My life with Nicole," he seemed to be saying, "is sacred and sealed."

He was not forthcoming. He did not suggest witnesses. When he gave up a few details of how he lived in Provo, the details were dry. He did not offer the names of friends. He would say, "There was this kid I work with, and we had a beer." He sat on his side of the visiting room, remote, soft voiced, not unfriendly, hopelessly distant.

On the other hand, he did show some curiosity about his lawyers' backgrounds. It was as if he preferred to ask the questions. In the hope of priming him, Snyder and Esplin were ready, therefore, to talk about themselves. Craig Snyder's father, for instance, had run a nursing home in Salt Lake, and Craig had gone to the University of Utah. While there, he made head cheerleader, he told Gary with a self-effacing grin. His wife had been president of a sorority. He was still an avid football and basketball fan. Played golf, paddle ball and tennis, gin rummy and bridge. After law school, he moved to Texas and worked in the corporate tax department of Exxon, but came back to Utah because he liked being a trial attorney more.

"Any kids?" asked Gilmore.

"Travis is six, and Brady is two." Craig's expression was round and serious, friendly and cautious.

"Yeah," said Gilmore.

Esplin had wanted to be a sports hero, but suffered hay fever as a child. He grew up on a ranch, and went to England on a mission. When he came back at twenty-one, he got married. Long before, by the time he was thirteen, he had read all the Perry Mason books he could find. Erle Stanley Gardner made Mike Esplin a lawyer, but private practice seemed to consist of bankruptcies and divorce cases. So, for the last year, he had worked full time in Provo as a Public Defender.

Gilmore nodded. Gilmore took it in. He did not give a great deal back. Did not think there was anything they could use from his prison years. Only the prison record and that wasn't written for him but for the institution. His mother might make a good witness, he allowed, but she was arthritic, and could not travel.

Snyder and Esplin got in touch with Bessie Gilmore. Gary was right — she could not travel. There was the cousin, Brenda Nicol, only Gary was angry at her. At the Preliminary Hearing on August 3, he had waved to her across the Court. Thought she was there to see him. Soon learned that Noall Wootton had called her. On the stand, Brenda told of the phone call Gary made from the Orem Police Station. "I asked him what he would like me to tell his mother," Brenda had said on the stand. "He said, 'I guess you can tell her it's true.'" Mike Esplin tried to get Brenda to agree Gary meant it was true he had been charged with murder. Brenda repeated her testimony, and took no sides. Gary found that hard to forgive.

Still, the lawyers tried. They talked to Brenda on the phone. Snyder thought she was flippant and more than a little frightened of Gilmore. He had told her, she said, that he would get even with her for turning him in. Lately, there had been an orange van following her car. She thought it might be a friend of Gary's.

She said she had gone out on a limb to get Gary out of prison, and felt he'd kind of stabbed her in the back. She loved him very much, she said, but thought he was going to have to pay for what he had done.

Later, the lawyers phoned again. On the Monday night that Gary came to her house with April, did he seem to be under the influence of drugs or alcohol? Those were mitigating circumstances. Brenda repeated what April had said, "I'm really afraid of you when you get that way, Gary." She liked Gary, Brenda repeated, but he deserved what he was going to get. At best, Brenda would be a dangerous witness, decided Snyder and Esplin.

They called Spencer McGrath, and he said he liked Gary, but was very disappointed over the turn of events. The mothers of a couple of young fellows he had working for him were indignant that he had hired a criminal. He was now catching about all the trouble he needed. People would stop him on the street and say, "How's it feel, Spencer, to have had a murderer on your payroll?" That wasn't helping his projects any.

They never talked to Vern Damico. Gary kept saying that his relationship with his relatives had not been that good. Besides, the lawyers received a report of a conversation with Vern from Utah State Hospital:

Mr. Damico gave me the following information regarding Gary Gilmore:

He doesn't like to be defeated, and when he is, he will not forget it and won't forgive. He is also very revengeful and has Mr. Damico's family very frightened as they were the ones who turned him in. He has written a letter to his cousin and told her he hopes she has nightmares for turning him in. The family is also a little concerned that he will break out of jail or the hospital as he has a history of that in the past.

3

They were down to searching for a psychiatrist who would declare Gilmore insane. Failing that, Snyder and Esplin were looking to find a paragraph in one of the psychiatric reports or even a sentence they could use.

PSYCHOLOGICAL ASSESSMENT

Dates of Assessment: August 10, 11, 13 and 14, 1976

Assessment Procedures: Interviews with patient
Minnesota Multiphasic Personality Inventory
Bipolar Psychological Inventory
Sentence Completion
Shipley Institute for Living
Bender-Gestalt
Graham Kendall
Rorschach

Mr. Gilmore said at one point, "All week long I had this unreal feeling, like I was seeing things through water, or I was watching myself do things. Especially this night, everything felt like I had this unreal feeling, like I was watching at a distance of what I was doing . . . had this cloudy feeling. I went in and told the guy to give me the money, and I told him to lay down on the floor, and then I shot him. . . . I know it's all real, and I know I did it, but somehow or other, I don't feel too responsible. It was as though I had to do it. I can remember when I was a boy I would put my finger over the end of a BB gun and pull the trigger to see if a BB was really in it, or stick my finger in water and put it in a light socket to see if it really would shock me. It seemed like I just had to do it, that there was a compulsion for me to do these things."

Intellectual Functioning:

Gary is functioning in the above-average to superior range of intelligence. His vocabulary IQ was 140, his abstraction IQ was 120, and his full-scale IQ was 129. He said that he had read an awful lot in his life, and indeed, he missed only two words on the vocabulary test. . . .

Personality Integration:

On the paper-pencil personality test, Gary shows himself to be an individual who is very hostile, socially deviant, currently unhappy with his life, and insensitive to the feelings of other people. He has a high hostility component toward the establishment. . . .

Summary and Conclusion:

In summary, Gary is a 35-year-old Caucasian single male . . . of superior intellect. There is no evidence of organic brain damage. Gary is basically a personality disorder of the psychopathic or antisocial type. I think, however, that there may be some substance to his talk about the depersonalization symptoms that he experienced during the week that he was separated from Nicole and during the shooting of these two people. It is clear, however, that he knew what he was doing. . . . I see no alternative other than to return him to court for further legal processing.

ROBERT J. HOWELL, PH.D.

18 August 1976

Neurologic Consultation

He indicated he occasionally has jagged lines across his visual fields, especially on the right, followed by inability to see for about 10 minutes followed by severe headache, which is occasionally accompanied by a dizziness. Headache lasts an hour or so, then goes away. The headache always follows a visual experience, but he also has other headaches which are sometimes "real bad," which come without this and may occur at any time. These occur with considerable variability, and at times he has used Fiorinal almost every day because this usually stops it, whereas aspirin, Tylenol, and other things have not seemed to help. He has been struck in the head in some fights, but has not been knocked out. A few months ago he suffered a laceration in the left eyebrow region, which has healed well. As a youth, his brother tended to hit him on the back of the neck and he thinks he may have a vertebra out of place, and has recurring neck aches.

He reports that from his youth he has had a tendency towards compulsive behavior. He would get a thought in his mind and not be able to keep himself from doing it. He gives as an example going out to the middle of a train trestle and waiting until the train came to the end of the trestle before starting to run in the opposite direction to get off the trestle before the train caught up with him. While in the penitentiary on a fifth tier, he would get a compulsion to stand up on a railing and touch the ceiling above, with the possibility of falling 50 feet to the floor below. . . .

His unusual behavior in response to a sense of compulsion and his alleged spotty amnesia will require further appraisal from the psychiatric point of view, but at this point it seems quite unlikely that they represent any sort of seizure manifestation.

MADISON H. THOMAS, M.D.

August 31, 1976

Staff Presentation:

DR. HOWELL   How many ECTs did you get?

ANSWER   Well, they told me they gave me one series of six . . . the doctor they had working there at the penitentiary, the psychiatrist, that was his cure-all for everything. If you got violent or got out of line or whatever, or he figured you needed to be a little more passive, he would, you know, hook you up to Bonneville Dam.

DR. WOODS So a lot of guys got hooked up to Bonneville Dam.

ANSWER Yeah, while he was working there. One hell of a lot of guys.

DR. LEBEGUE Now why did you get the Prolixin? What happened there?

ANSWER Well, there was another riot. It happened in the hole and it took them about 11 days to contain it. I was chained for two weeks, and during that time they came in and shot me with Prolixin. They were giving me 2 cc's twice a week, and I had lost 50, maybe a little bit more, 50 pounds by the time they finally let me up out of that nightmare.

DR. HOWELL About how many would you guess you had?

ANSWER They were giving me two shots a week for four months.

DR. KIGER You have got clean psychiatric reports eleven out of twelve. The whole time you have been in the prison system except one. One report . . . said you had a paranoid psychotic state. Do you recall when that one was?

ANSWER God, it's so easy to be accused of being paranoid in prison. I mean maybe I had a disagreement with somebody and they were in a position to say I was paranoid and thereby dismiss whatever the thing was. I don't know.

DR. HOWELL During that time you don't see yourself as having been mentally ill.

ANSWER A lot of those guards are mentally ill.

DENNIS CULLIMORE, MEDICAL STAFF WORKER Was there anything either of the evenings of the murders about your mental state that was different than usual?

ANSWER Well, I didn't have — all of the strings had been cut, like I didn't have control of myself. I mean I was just going through motions. I wasn't planning anything. These things were just occurring . . .

DENNIS CULLIMORE, MSW At what point did you know that you were going to shoot him?

ANSWER When I shot him. I didn't know it before then . . . it just seemed like it was the next move in a motion that was happening, you know.

DR. KIGER Have you had other emotionally charged episodes where you didn't remember all that happened at that time?

ANSWER I'm not really excitable, you know, I don't get emotional. Some things I let weigh on me pretty heavy, but it's not the sort of thing that mounts and builds, you know. It's not a spur of the moment thing.

DR. LEBEGUE That feeling that you described to several of us about somehow things being unreal like seeing through water, has that happened to you before this summer?

ANSWER Not, not really . . . only there have been times when life seems to slow down and you can watch movement more intensely. Like if you get in a tight situation, a fight situation, or something like that, the feeling there is somewhat similar to this.

DR. KIGER Anything similar to when you are on grass?

ANSWER When you are on grass, you just trip along and everything is fine, but when you're in a tense situation, I don't know. No, I can't say that I have really experienced that feeling before.

DR. LEBEGUE So, it was something new to you.

ANSWER Yeah, I would say so.

DENNIS CULLIMORE, MSW Does anyone have anything else? OK.

DR. WOODS Thanks for coming in, Gary.

ANSWER All right.

Comprehensive Treatment Plan

A report will be made to the court stating that the patient is both competent and responsible.

BRECK LEBEGUE, M.D.
Resident in Psychiatry

Formulation:

This is a 35-year-old white male who is here for psychiatric evaluation. There is no evidence of thought disorder or psychosis, amnesia, organic brain damage, seizures, or any other behavior of pathology which would prevent him from conferring with his attorney and standing trial on the charges. He is aware of the circumstances and of his actions. He does describe some symptoms of depersonalization during the actions, but it is not uncommon for those who murder to undergo a temporary process of dehumanization. I feel that he was responsible for his actions at the time of the incident.

Staff Diagnosis:

Personality disorder of the antisocial type.

BRECK LEBEGUE, M.D.
Resident in Psychiatry

4

Gilmore gave off no aura of the psychotic. The more Snyder and Esplin searched these staff reports and transcripts, the less they encountered madness, and the more he appeared grim, ironic, practical. There was hardly a wall in the law you could not climb if you could get onto some little thing, some legal grip with which to raise yourself to find another hold. There were cracks in many a block of law, but in the Gilmore case, these psychiatric walls offered nothing.

They took the problem to Dr. Woods, who had seen a lot of Gary at the ward level, and John Woods went over it with them. The lawyers came up so often to his office that he began to worry about it. Woods was young to be Director of the Forensic Program, and he liked his job, and was intellectually stimulated by the therapeutic ideas of his superior, Dr. Kiger, whom he thought was one hell of an innovator. So, Woods didn't want to get the hospital in any trouble, and worried a little over the correctness of all these visits. On the other hand, he didn't mind helping the defense lawyers and enjoyed contemplating the problem. Finally, he told himself, Well, if the prosecuting attorney wants to talk about these things, I'll help him too. I'm here to give any information I can.

Woods thought that if Gary's defense was to be based on his mental condition, then Snyder and Esplin had to come up with an argument that would connect the psychotic to the psychopathic. Not easy. The law recognized insanity. You could always save the neck of a psychotic. Psychopathy, however, was more a madness of the moral reflexes, if you could begin to use such a term (which you couldn't) in a Court of Law. Woods pointed to one interview where Gary, speaking of the moment he shot himself, said, "I looked at my thumb and thought, 'You stupid son of a bitch!' " That was hardly a psychotic reaction. Morally self-centered, yes. Criminally indifferent to the mortal damage just done to others, yes, but there was no psychological incapacity to grasp his practical situation. If you were practical, then you were liable.

Of course, Gary did fit into a psychiatric category. There was a medical term for moral insanity, criminality, uncontrolled animality — call it what you will. Psychiatrists called it "psychopathic personality," or, same thing, "sociopathic personality." It meant you were antisocial. In terms of accountability before the law, it was equal to sanity. The law saw a great difference between the psychotic and the psychopathic personality.

In psychosis, Woods said, there was little connection between the event and the personal reaction. If Gary, after he shot his thumb, had said, "They are poisoning hot dogs in Chicago," you could assume he was psychotic. Instead, Gary had said, "You stupid son of a bitch," just like anyone else.

A certifiable psychosis usually depended on thought disorder. Gilmore did not exhibit that. Of course, it wasn't always a simple question. If a man came up to you and said, "My mother just died," and he giggled, you would think psychosis was present. If the man, however, was a hardened criminal, his pride might be that there was no feeling he would not laugh at. So his attitude would be sociopathic, not psychotic. Of course, that example was small use to the lawyers. They needed something that might appear psychopathic but would prove psychotic.

Woods had pondered this question before. A psychopath could certainly become a psychotic. The average psychopath lived, after all, in a dangerous world. A reasonable amount of paranoia was even necessary. You had to be sensitive to trouble in the environment. Under stress, however, what had been a serviceable paranoia could become magnified. If you were asleep, and the alarm went off, and you were under such tension you thought it was a fire siren, and saw imaginary flames and leaped out of a high window into eternity, well, it hardly mattered then whether your normal label had been psychopathic, manic, melancholic, or obsessive-compulsive, you could be sure to be called psychotic as you went through the window. The psychopath had fantasies. The psychotic had hallucinations.

Maybe they could attack the problem here. The line between fantasies and hallucinations would certainly not be precise. The trouble, however, remained that in the observations made of Gary over these weeks, there just hadn't been any behavior that was excessively paranoid. They had to recognize, Woods warned, that the law wanted to keep psychopathy and psychosis apart. If the psychopath were ever accepted as legally insane, then crime, judgment, and punishment would be replaced by antisocial act, therapy, and convalescence.

CHAPTER 24

Geelmore and Geebs

1

Gary had propped up a photograph of Nicole, and made a sketch with a ball-point pen, then took an old refill and broke it in half. Using a toothpick, he dug out a little of the coagulated ink. With a watercolor brush and a few drops of water, he shaded the drawing. Gibbs always enjoyed watching him.

Sept. 20

Wish I had taken more pictures of you naked. No kiddin — Nicole I think you should never have to wear clothes. There is something about nakedness and you that just go together. I don't mean anything crude, baby, you know that — although you are tremendously sexy. You are just so natural naked — innocent, playful, happy, pretty, like a sprite in the forest. Just something that belongs.

I was surprised to get this flick back — I bet those cops in Orem looked this picture over pretty good, huh? Bastards — pisses me off to think that some fuckin pig — or anybody — saw such a personal picture of my love.

Sept. 21

I would really like you to see a picture of that sculpture "Ecstasy of St. Therese." I believe the sculptor is Bernini. I've never seen any great works of art in person but I guess I'm familiar with most European Art through books I've studied. I once saw a picture of Christ by a Russian artist that really haunted me for a long time. Christ didn't look anything like the popular beaming Western Chris-

tian version of the kindly shepherd we're used to. He looked like a man, with a gaunt, lean, sort of haunted face with deep set large dark eyes. You could tell he was pretty tall, angular, rangy, a man alone and I guess that was the most striking thing about the picture. No halo, no radiant beam from heaven above. Just this extra-ordinary man — this ordinary human being who made himself extra-ordinary and tried to tell us all that it was nothing more than any of us could do. Loneliness and a hint of doubt seemed to fill the picture. I would like to have known the man in that picture.

In the Salt Lake pokey, just before Gibbs had been transferred to Provo, a jailer told him about some student who'd been in law school with Jensen. The dude had actually tried to get into jail to kill Gary. He had planned to tell the guards he was a working lawyer, but would smuggle in a knife.

Gilmore said he could sympathize. What was a dead man worth, if he didn't have friends to avenge him? Then he looked at Gibbs and said, "You know, this is the first time I've ever had any feelings for either of those two guys I killed."

Sept. 22

I'm the only one in my family who feels the pull of the Emerald Isle. It's a land of magic.

I got something I want to give you and I hope you won't think its silly. It's something I do and it's kind of magic. It's a force, a pull, that I've tapped and it works. Just a little sort of chant:

GOOD THINGS COME

TO ME NOW.

Lately I have revised it to: GOOD THINGS COME TO US NOW. Just a personal prayer spoken softly, quietly in my mind, aloud if I'm alone. I hope this don't seem silly to you. I know the power of things like this, the rhythm, the repetition of a soft harmonic chant sets magic in the air, pulls, draws, gives the believer power to attract and power to receive.

2

In their tank, labeled by Gilmore The Stinking Dungeon, they had a cracked porcelain toilet, now nicotine yellow in color. You flushed it by pressing a button on the wall. But in order to get enough leverage, you had to grab on to the side of the shower, and lean for two full minutes on the button. Only that way could you build sufficient pressure.

Then, once the waters started, you had to hold the toilet plunger to the base of the bowl until the level came up to the rim. That was the only way to have enough liquid to force a load down. All the while, a leak would be oozing around the seal at the bottom. The Open-Pit Sulfur Mine, they called it.

One afternoon, needing fuel for coffee water, they tore down the cardboard sign that gave instructions on how to flush the pot, and Gary replaced it with words of his own, written with a Magic Marker on the wall.

Important Notice!!!
To Flush this Chitter
You keep Butt on Bowl
Press Button Firmly with Tongue
Good Luck Motherfucker

Then he fell in love with the Magic Marker. "After I'm gone, they'll really think a nut was in here," he said, and on all the walls, he wrote, "WALL," wrote "CEILING" on the ceiling, "TABLE" on the table, "BENCH" on the bench, "CHOWER" in the shower. Then he numbered each bunk "BUNK ONE," "BUNK TWO." Finally he printed on Gibbs's face and his own: "FOREHEAD," "NOSE," "CHEEK," "CHIN."

When the jailer arrived to serve the evening meal, he asked "Vy you do thees?" He was a wetback named Luis. Thickest accent, "Vy you do thees?" "Oh," said Gilmore, "they told me to get ready for Court."

They looked forward to getting the wetback. One time Gary asked to phone his lawyer, and since Luis never wanted to stir ass for a prisoner, he said, "Geelmore, ees thees important?"

"Yeah," said Gary, "it's a matter of life and death." They howled. Old Luis just stomped away.

Now, the trustee who did the haircutting was afraid to be in the cell with Gary. So Gary asked Gibbs to do the job. Gibbs told him, "Never in my life," but Gary said he was a master barber, and would give the instructions step by step.

Luis brought them a big pair of scissors. The propped up a sheet of polished aluminum to make a mirror, and Gary would run his hand through his hair and stop with the amount he wanted cut off above his closed fingers. It took about an hour. Gibbs was real cautious. When they were done, however, Gary asked Luis if they could use the electric clippers. "No," said the guard, "no outlet." He wasn't about to go to the trouble of running an extension cord. Gary threw the scissors as hard as he could at the tray slot where Luis was standing. It hit the steel door and shattered into pieces. Luis said, "You zon of a beech, Geelmore." Gary started toward the bars. "What did you say?" he asked. The Mexican took off for the front office.

About an hour later, he came back with a deputy and a plastic Zip-Lok bag. Luis handed it through the window and told Gary, "Put broke pieces een sack." Gary did it. He had cooled down quite a bit. "I've probably blown Nicole's visits," he said, "that's all that really has any meaning to me." Gibbs said, "Wait until six when Big Jake comes on." "They can put me in the hole," Gary said, "just so long as they don't stop me from seeing Nicole."

When Big Jake came over, he was laughing. "You scared Luis so bad with them scissors," he said, "that he shit tacos clear out to the front desk."

Big Jake and Gary got along. He and Alex Hunt were the only jailers Gary had respect for. Because they had no fear. Shortly after Gary came to the prison, a couple of big dudes in the main tank tried to jump Jake and pull an escape. Jake beat them halfway to death. One good-looking, well-built Swede from Montana. He was confident, all right. There was an order put out by Captain Cahoon that when Nicole came to visit Gary, a call was to be put in for a patrol car. That way a couple of extra cops would be around the jail. Every guard did this but Jake and Alex. Neither of them needed extra help.

Now Gary explained in a real sincere tone of voice what had happened. He told Big Jake he was in the wrong for losing his temper.

Went on to say he would accept his punishment, but hoped they wouldn't take away his visiting privileges. Big Jake said it was up to Captain Cahoon, but he would talk to him personally. Maybe replacing the broken scissors would be sufficient. Gibbs spoke up. "If that's what it takes to mend things," he said, "use some money from my account."

"Gibbs," asked Gilmore, "have you ever heard of Ralph Waldo Emerson?"

"No."

"He was a writer, and he made a statement you and me live by. Emerson said, 'Life is not so short that there is not always time for courtesy.'"

3

They put in a big fellow with them. He was an ex-paratrooper about six-three, 210 pounds, named Bart Powers. He had walloped a kid in the main tank that morning.

When Powers entered the cell, his first words were "Which one of you guys is Gilmore?" It popped out so loud and so tough that Gibbs thought Powers had come to sell a Wolf ticket. He got off his bunk immediately, and went over to the toilet in order to get behind him.

Gary's eyes lifted from the letter he was writing, and he said real cool, "I'm Gilmore. Why do you want to know?"

It could have been hypnosis. Gary must have given him a dose of psychic powers. Gibbs could see Bart Powers lose his peace of mind. In a meek tone, Bart said, "The guys in the main tank said to tell you 'Hi.'" It was all Gibbs could do to keep from snickering. Powers said "Hi" like a kid in school.

The new arrival stayed good. Kept to himself, read a book, made no trouble. Gibbs could see Gary getting agitated, however. There had been a deal talked about with Big Jake to bring Nicole in for a night. Jake had seen a saddle he wanted to buy. It would probably cost $100, but Gibbs thought he might be able to get the sum together. The deal was still very much in the unmade stage, but they had been thinking on it. Now, the presence of Powers would kill it.

Luis came by, and said through the bars, "Pow-ass, vy you heet a choovenile? He vuz justa keed, Pow-ass." Then he left.

Gilmore and Gibbs cracked up. They started to look at Powers and then they would laugh. "He vuz justa keed, Pow-ass," they would say, "justa keed." Then they would laugh again. Bart Powers looked like he hated it. Only he wasn't about to speak up, Gibbs noticed.

Powers had no cigarettes, so Gibbs flipped him a pack. "You don't owe me nothing," said Gibbs. "You could never pay me back, therefore I'm giving it to you."

"You've met a generous man," said Gilmore, looking Powers over, and added, "That's a nice-looking shirt you're wearing."

"Thanks," said Powers.

"I'd like to buy it," said Gary.

"It's the only shirt I got."

"Well, man," said Gary, "I'm going to trial soon, you see, and man, I want to appear in Court in proper attire, you know."

"I couldn't sell this shirt, why, it's a gift from my girl friend."

"I'll give you mucho cigarettes for it," said Gary. There was a nod from Gibbs. It would be Gibbs's carton.

"The shirt's all I got," said Powers.

"Give back the pack I just threw you," said Gibbs. Powers did. Quickly.

"He vuz justa keed," said Gilmore.

They roared in Powers's face.

That evening, Gary said, "Nothing personal, but this cell is too crowded for three. I think it's in your best interest, Powers, to tell the man you can't get along in here." Gary looked as serious as a heart attack. "Tell him if he don't move you out tonight, I'll kill you."

Powers started yelling for Big Jake. "Nothing personal," Gary whispered.

"Oh, you want out?" said Big Jake. "Ready to go to Isolation? What's the matter, Powers? Can't smack these two around, huh?

Can't say, 'Go back to your bunk 'cause I'm tired of looking at your face'? They don't play around, do they?" He nodded at Gilmore and Gibbs. "All right, I'll move you to the hole, Powers. Gary, here, has two murder charges. He don't need no more."

"Just get me out," said Powers. "Just put me in the hole."

After the transfer, Big Jake said, "I'd like to bring him here some night, and have you guys work on him. We can't do it, and he could sure use it."

Gibbs knew Gary didn't want to say no. It would hurt future negotiations for getting Nicole into his cell. Still, Gary said, "I won't, Jake. Powers is a prisoner like me. I can't work for you guys."

"Well," said Big Jake, "that's cool."

Next morning, they took Gary over to the nuthouse for a psychiatric, and he came back late for lunch. Big Jake gave him a Ding-Dong extra from the kitchen consisting of a double sandwich and a couple of pickles, plus a piece of fresh fruit. Gary said, "Hey, I really appreciate that."

Big Jake said, "Don't bother, Gary, it's not mine to do you a real favor."

They got playful that afternoon. A nothing-to-lose kind of mood. Some pats of butter were left from Gibbs's midday meal, and they decided to flip the stuff through the bars. The idea was to see who could make the biggest splotch on the corridor wall.

Luis came back to investigate the laughter. "Geelmore and Geebs," he said, "you mees meal!" He got two trustees to clean up, and Geelmore and Geebs laughed so hard they got stomach cramps. "Luis," said Gary, "is a tad bit retarded."

No dinner was served that evening. Around eight-thirty Luis came back with a pot of coffee looking like he felt a little sorry for them.

Gary asked, "Luis, are you married?"

The guard nodded.

"Do you have any naked pictures of your wife?"

Luis was shocked. "No," he answered.

"Well," said Gary, "do you want to buy some?"

It took a couple of seconds. Then Luis shouted, "Geelmore, Geebs, I tired of your chit!" He slammed the door in the corridor.

Goddamn, thought Gibbs, that wetback is the only toy we got.

CHAPTER 25

Insanity

1

Would he, at least, testify for Gary in the Mitigation Hearing, Snyder and Esplin asked.

Yes, said Woods, he could find his way clear to doing that. But, he warned, with the best will in the world, what could he offer in good professional conscience that the District Attorney would not be able to reduce?

They did not ask him if he liked Gary, and if they had, he might not have replied, but the answer he could have given was, Yes, I think I do like Gary. I may even like him a little more than I want to.

Woods felt he understood a few of Gilmore's obsessions. Getting up in the middle of the trestle and racing the train or standing on the railing of the top tier in prison were impulses familiar to Woods. He sometimes believed he had gone into psychiatry so one hand could keep a grip on the other.

Hell, if Gilmore were a free man, Woods might have taken him on a rock climb. That is, he might have, if he were still doing it. Woods felt again the swoop of his last long fall on an ice face. That had ended climbing. The guy with him had almost been killed in a crevasse. So Woods knew the depression that came when you ceased making crazy bets. He also knew the logic to making them in the first place. No psychic reward might be so powerful as winning a dare with yourself.

If you were really scared, and went through it, and came out on the other side intact, then it was hard not to believe for a little while that you were on the side of the gods. It felt as if you could do no wrong. Time slowed. *You* were no longer doing it. For good or ill, *it* was doing it. You had entered the logic of that other scheme where death and life had as many relations as Yin and Yang.

That was the identification Woods felt. Gilmore had also felt compelled to take a chance with his life. Gilmore had been keeping in touch with something it was indispensable to be in touch with. Woods knew all about that, and it depressed him. Looking back on the times he had seen Gilmore at the hospital, he felt uneasy at the reserve he had maintained between them, even felt shame that he had never had a real conversation with the man.

After a while, he did get Gilmore to talk a little about the murders, but it was no help. Gilmore seemed genuinely perplexed over his behavior. Kept going back to his feeling of being under water. "Lot of strange things," he would say. "You know, it was inevitable."

This vagueness impressed Woods as pretty straight. A convict trying to convince you he was insane would give more of a picture show. Instead, Gilmore gave the impression of a man who was quiet, thoughtful, cornered, and living simultaneously in many places.

On the other hand, Gilmore had been in seclusion all the way. That had been altogether against Woods's ideas of treatment, for it cut off interaction with the other patients. They had a new brand of therapy to offer at this hospital and he was all for giving Gilmore some of it. The prison authorities, however, had only agreed to transfer Gilmore from County Jail for these two- and three-day visits if he were kept in lockup all the way. So there you were. A man who had spent nearly all of his last twelve years locked up every night in a cell the size of a bathroom, was still being locked up.

In addition, they had all been concerned, himself included, that no error be made with the guy, so they kept seeing him in pairs. Later, he heard Gilmore had said, "One thing I have against Woods

is that he never talks to me alone." Yes, Woods thought, I really
kept my distance.

Of course, he knew why. Becoming a psychiatrist had left Woods
in a funny place, philosophically speaking. He did not like to stir his
doubts. His own contradictions, once set moving, had a lot of mo-
mentum. Woods hadn't had, after all, the kind of upbringing that
tended to land you in the psychiatric establishment.

2

Woods's father had been a hell of a football player in college, and
tried to raise his son to be more of the same. Woods grew up on a
ranch, but his father made sure there was a football around, and he
was one son who spent his boyhood running out for passes. As soon
as his hands were large enough, he was pulling them in over his
shoulder. When he got through high school, there was an athletic
scholarship at the University of Wyoming.

At Wyoming, the real talent seemed to be imported from the
East. Woods got the idea that just as the greatest potatoes grew in-
digenously in Idaho, so football players came naturally from Pennsylvania and Ohio. Woods had always thought he was pretty good and
pretty big and pretty crazy until those eastern football players came
in from the mill towns. Six of those Polacks, Bohunks, and Italians
shared the same girl all freshman year. It wasn't that they couldn't
have others, it was that they liked keeping it in the family. It was better that way. One of those monsters, right out of the middle of defensive line, got so tired one night of being turned down by a new date
that he proceeded to urinate on her.

Another night, with a lot of snow on the ground, a group of them
took off in two cars for a ride through the mountains. A bottle of
booze for each car. On the way back, in a snowstorm, the lead vehicle
came around a curve, went into a skid, and smashed into a snowbound Chevvy by the side of the road. There were only two football
players in the first collision, and they jumped out into the middle of
the highway. Woods, in the second car, following at high speed,
came around the same turn and went into the ditch to avoid hitting

them. The two from the first car and the three in the second got together and lifted Woods's car onto the road again. That felt so good that the fellows from the first car now ripped their license plates off, and pushed the vehicle over the mountain and into the ravine. It struck on rocks with the great noise of thunder, and made soft deep sounds like the wind when it plowed through deep snow. They watched with the awe attending large events.

Of course the car they had smacked into was a mess. So they decided to roll it down the highway. Woods tried to talk them out of that. Right in the middle, he could not get over the fact that he, with his own big reputation to maintain, was being the peacemaker.

He failed. They set that wreck rolling. A police car coming up the grade just avoided a head-on collision. Some rich alumnus settled the cost. One did not lose five talented sophomores for too little.

Woods never starred. After a while he was too scared. You could get maimed out there. The coach he liked moved on, and the new coach disapproved of the hours Woods had to give to pre-med labs. Told him to switch to Phys. Ed. Woods didn't. He never starred.

Nonetheless, he didn't have any illusions about the scope of the problem. There were two kinds of human beings on earth and maybe he had been placed to know both kinds. The civilized had their small self-destructive habits and their controlled paranoia, but they could live in a civilized world. You could tinker with them on the couch. It was the uncivilized who caused the discomfort in psychiatric circles.

Woods had long suspected the best-kept secret in psychiatric circles was that nobody understood psychopaths, and few had any notion of psychotics. "Look," he would sometimes be tempted to tell a colleague, "the psychotic thinks he's in contact with spirits from other worlds. He believes he is prey to the spirits of the dead. He's in terror. By his understanding, he lives in a field of evil forces.

"The psychopath," Woods would tell them, "inhabits the same place. It is just that he feels stronger. The psychopath sees himself as a potent force in that field of forces. Sometimes he even believes he can go to war against them, and win. So if he really loses, he is close to collapse, and can be as ghost ridden as a psychotic."

For a moment, Woods wondered if that was the way to build a bridge from the psychopathic to the insane.

But he always came back to the difficulty. The speech was of no legal use to Snyder and Esplin. You could not appear in court with spirits from other worlds.

3

There did remain one legitimate possibility. In the record from Oregon State Penitentiary was Dr. Wesley Weissart's psychiatric entry for November 1974:

IT IS MY IMPRESSION THAT AT THIS TIME GILMORE IS IN A PARANOID STATE, SO THAT HE IS UNABLE TO DETERMINE WHAT HIS BEST INTERESTS ARE. HE IS TOTALLY UNABLE TO CONTROL HIS HOSTILE AND AGGRESSIVE IMPULSES. . . . I FEEL COMPLETELY JUSTIFIED IN GIVING GILMORE MEDICATION AGAINST HIS WISHES AS HE CREATES A SERIOUS PROBLEM TO THE PATIENTS AND TO THE ENTIRE INSTITUTION.

That was the *unclean* report to which Dr. Kiger referred when the staff interviewed Gilmore. "Why," asked Woods, of Snyder and Esplin, "don't you get that doctor down here to testify?"

Gary didn't want him, that was why. Gary had said: Of all the dirty, mean, rotten sons of bitches. He did not want to be evaluated by that man.

Woods said even if they had to go to Oregon and rope the fellow, they ought to get him for the trial.
It was very hard, they replied, to get a person to respond to a subpoena if he lived out of the state. Woods said, "Man, that seems critical to me."

Snyder and Esplin called Weissart, but he told them he did not wish to be involved. They received the impression that, if he had to get on the stand, he would say that Gilmore might be four-plus paranoiac, but was not, in the legal sense, psychotic. Another dead end.

Woods had seen the difference between experienced trial lawyers and young attorneys. It was a hell of a difference. He said to them as diplomatically as he could, Why don't you get somebody else in on this who can pull some shots? He couldn't get across. They kept on trying to get some evaluation of Gary as a victim of mental illness.

Actually, Woods did hate Prolixin. He saw it as incarceration within the incarceration. One morning he even woke up exhausted from the ardors of a dream that had him conducting a cross-examination:

QUESTION What was his dosage?

ANSWER Fifty milligrams a week, that's pretty much an average, standard dose.

QUESTION But he swelled up under it, didn't he?

ANSWER Well, they get side effects from all these antipsychotic drugs. The more potent the drug, the more apt they are to develop side effects. Prolixin causes many more side effects than Thorazine.

QUESTION What would be the advantage then of using Prolixin?

ANSWER You'd only have to give him medicine one time a week, rather than try to give it to him every day.

QUESTION It's really a matter of administering it.

ANSWER That's right.

QUESTION If you have a saddle a bad horse, you want to be able to do it once a week, not twice a day.

ANSWER That's right. Prolixin is the only drug out now that we can give at infrequent intervals. Everything else has to be given hourly, two or three times a day, or daily.

QUESTION What were Gilmore's side effects?

ANSWER He had a real severe reaction. Oh, as I recall, he had swelling in his feet and it was difficult to get his shoes on, he had trouble walking and his hands swelled, he really had a severe reaction.

QUESTION How long did it last?

ANSWER Well, let me put it this way, that's a long-acting drug, Prolixin, you give a shot today, probably there will be some of that same shot in his system maybe six or eight weeks from now. That's why, if they develop a reaction it takes them two or three months to get over it.

QUESTION   Well, what did you use for medication after that didn't work, the Prolixin?

ANSWER   I don't think I used any medication after that at all.

QUESTION   So he was just a problem then. . . .

ANSWER   Just talking, we just talked.

QUESTION   How did Gilmore himself respond to the Prolixin? I mean, when the side effects had hit him, how did he respond in his relationship with you?

ANSWER   Well, he was very unhappy with me, naturally.

QUESTION   He got paranoid about you, wouldn't you say?

ANSWER   Oh, yes, yeah.

QUESTION   He thought you were out to get him.

ANSWER   Uh-huh, yes.

QUESTION   Did you feel bad about the Prolixin, sort of like oh, Lord, you know, what have I done?

ANSWER   Well, I don't like to see that type of reaction on anybody, and I certainly didn't on Gary. The way it developed, though, I thought that we got along reasonably well after that.

QUESTION   Aren't you worried about Prolixin in the sense that you don't really know? You've got a machine, which has two levers sticking out of it. You walk up and push one lever in, and the other lever comes out at the other end of the machine. What goes on in the machine, you don't know. Is that a fair description of its effects? That you can't name the inner process that goes on?

ANSWER   Well, there . . . well, I guess maybe you're right. Really, we don't know the direct effects of these antipsychotic drugs on the brain cells. . . .

Woods wasn't at all certain that the Prolixin hadn't done a real damage to Gary's psyche. Whole fields of the soul could be defoliated and never leave a trace. Yet how did you convince a Jury? The medicine had been accepted by a generation of psychiatrists. Once again, Woods wished for some absolute dazzler of a lawyer who could handle a Jury like a basketball and take them up and down the court.

CHAPTER 26

Stone in Love

1

Nicole asked Gary if there wasn't a chance to get a real good lawyer. Gary said big leaguers like Percy Foreman or F. Lee Bailey sometimes took on a job for the publicity, but in his case there were not special elements. A big man would want money.

Of course, one of the really good ones, he said, might be able to get him acquitted. Or bring in a short sentence. Without money, however, they had to forget it.

She had no idea what a big lawyer would cost, but that was when she got the idea of selling her eyes. She never told Gary, and in fact felt a little dumb about it. She really didn't know how it came into her head. It could have had a lot to do with those commercials where they told you how much your vision was worth. She thought if she could get $5,000, maybe that would pay for a good lawyer.

Gibbs got a little excited by the idea. There was a fellow in Salt Lake who happened to be the biggest criminal defense man in Utah, Phil Hansen. In the past, Phil had been Attorney General and everything. Had more volume of cases going through his office than anybody in the state. He could perform miracles. Once, he even got a guy off who shot a Sheriff in front of another Sheriff. Sometimes, Gibbs said, Hansen would take a case for free. Gary lit up.

Gibbs now said he wasn't going to pull any punches with Gary when he knew how jealous a man could get, so he also wanted to tell him that Phil Hansen was reputed to have a yearn for attractive ladies.

Gary sat right down and wrote Nicole what Gibbs had said, then remarked it was up to her if she wanted to hitch a ride to see Hansen. But "If the guy makes any suggestive motions, get up and walk out."

Same night, a guard gave him a note from Nicole, *"He didn't ask for my bod, but will meet me at 2 o'clock Saturday at the jail and talk with you."*

She had seen Hansen in a big office and he did treat her like she was sure attractive, only he didn't put any pressure on. He was middle-aged, kept smoking a cigar, and liked to laugh a lot. After a while, he told her a story. Said the last man executed in Utah was named Rogers, and he had been asked to defend him, and told Rogers to get some money together. Phil was informed there'd be no problem. Rogers had a sister in Chicago who was well off.

Well, no telling about the sister, Rogers never called back. Hansen let it slide. Then the man was executed.

The lawyer never knew if it was coincidental, but the morning Rogers met his death, Hansen bolted out of bed. Didn't even know it was the day. Just woke up in a cold sweat.

Hearing about the execution over the radio, he swore he would never turn another person down for lack of funds if a life was involved.

Look, Hansen said, even if there was no money, he would represent Gilmore. Then he made the arrangements to meet Saturday afternoon at the jail.

Before she left, he put his arms around her, and gave a nice hug and said, "Don't worry. Don't look so sad. They're not going to execute him." He told Nicole he had never seen a case yet, didn't matter how bad it looked when you first took it, as you got into the story, you could explain it to the Jury.

For instance, he said, even a person who would swear by capital punishment might have to change their mind if it was their own mother on trial. "My mother's not like that," they would say. "Something went wrong." People were ready for capital punishment only if they were sentencing a stranger. The approach was to get the Jury feeling they understood the criminal.

Saturday came. Even though Hansen had said two o'clock, she was there at one-thirty.

She waited until three, but Mr. Hansen never showed up. Christ, she made an idiot of herself waiting. She called him later that afternoon, but it was Saturday, and his office didn't answer. While visiting Gary, Nicole began to cry. She couldn't help it. She had really been counting on getting a good lawyer.

She was even more depressed when she received Gary's next letter:

Sept. 26

All Snyder and Esplin want to do is leave themselves a good case for appeal. Thats the way they're paid by the state to think. I'm not saying they are paid to sell me out, I'm not paranoid about it. But they are court appointed lawyers, they don't have the resource to do a proper job. I'll get no more than a token defense from them.

2

Sept. 27

I can't sleep in the daytime. Sometimes I try but I always wake up in a cold sweat and I hear the cars on the hiway and see the light coming brightly thru the bars and know how far away I am from it all.

I know that dying is just changin form. I don't expect to escape any of my debts, I'll meet them and I'll pay them. I want to quit racking up such heavy debts though!

I fucked you all night in my mind Nicole. I sent love over all the distance to Springville, which is not at all a ball o'chalk, I could run that meagre distance without stopping! I loved you so hard and wet and long last nite Angel and I held you to me tite tite tite and you felt good. I kissed your forehead your nose your eyes, your cheeks and long and wet on your lips your neck I fucked your ears with my tongue and heard you cry out oh oh oh ooooh baby I kissed all down your body, put your tits in my mouth all I could get in there and I put my face between them sucked your big nipples fucked your belly button pushed my tongue in your mouth in your cunt in your ass your pretty fuckin ass. God I love your pretty pretty ass. Whew! You got ass that won't quit! You got a blue ribbon first prize ass. You got an elf ass.

You're an elf. And I'm stone in love with you.

Your honesty astounds me. I've thought long and hard of you, little elf, of your experience — the men who have known you, have loved you, been loved in return, have used, abused, and hurt you, made you love — I've thought of Uncle Lee. I understand as well as I can Nicole.

I don't want you to live like a hermit without friends. I don't give you any order or impose my restrictions.

But I don't like the idea of all those guys coming to see you.

Because somebody gives you a ride hitch-hiking, does he have to become a friend, come and see you again and again, every few days———? Fuck that.

I felt something yesterday that I didn't like. Vague, haunting———you smelled of beer . . .

I know the guys that come to see you must want more than company. I don't doubt you, but I know the flesh is weak.

You have always been so very honest and open with me, you are just Nicole and you present yourself just as you are, without pretense.

Something jarred me yesterday and made me feel something I don't want to feel. Your face your tears, it reminded me of another time not long ago———

Baby I guess I'm just an insanely jealous son of a bitch and a selfish motherfucker.

I don't like those friends of yours that come again and again for your company. Jesus Christ I've never heard of any men like that. Baby I'm a man — I know what guys want.

I don't want you having all of them men friends.

Nicole had been living with true intentions, but she still went to bed with Cliff and Tom a couple of times in that long month of September, and it was hell afterward to visit Gary and shy away from the subject. Finally she decided that the only way she'd be able to find out if she loved Gary enough to be able to break through these fucking sloppy habits was to tell him one more time. So when she read, "you smelled of beer," Nicole got her nerve together, and bought some stationery in Walgreen's and wrote him a long loving letter with everything rich and sweet she could put into it, and then at the end, as if she didn't want to spoil the good stationery, she picked up a paper napkin from the soda counter, and added a few words. Tried to say, When I get into situations, it isn't anything. Nothing is happening. Finally, she wrote, *"Why not just say what I mean? Gary, nobody is ever going to fuck me but you."*

Sept. 28

Baby the jailer just brought me your letter. You're always writing and telling me about getting fucked, getting fucked, getting fucked, getting fucked. Everybody fucks Nicole. Everybody. Everybody picks her up hitchhiking or sees her 3 or 4 times a week just for the vibes the beautiful vibes feel the beauty just friends just company don't even have to know her just sit and listen to her talk about how much she loves Gary then fuck her. Goddam motherfuckin son of a goddam bitch.

That was a neat napkin you wrote. "But man Baby you must understand what I mean by friends these friends are those that come to see me again and again for company and have not once demanded physical or mentally my physical attentions."

You write me that goddam motherfuckin lie . . . just sat down and wrote me that fuckin lie and signed it love. If you feel so much motherfuckin sympathy for someone that you'll fuck him why oh Jesus Jesus Jesus fucking Christ Goddam Goddam fucking damn

Baby Jesus Christ help me to understand. I don't look at life like that. I've never been in love before I've been locked up all my fuckin life I guess I'm emotionally crippled or something cause I'm one person that can't share his woman. Other people might be able to do that, might not give a fuck if somebody fucks what is theirs but I'm Gary. Somebody fucked you. Somebody kissed you. Somebody kissed you saw your eyes roll back, well, I guess its your bod and your life. Fuck everybody in Utah if you want to. What do I care? What do I care? I care all. I care everything.

Nicole — is my love not enough to suffice for even one small lifetime — my love for you can it not be enough? Do you have to give your body, your self? Your love to other men? Am I not enough? I can't fuck. I'm locked up. Why can't you go without too?

Don't fuck those "lovely" cocksuckers that want to fuck you. They make me want to commit murder again and I hate to feel that kind of thing. Get those bastards away from our life. Get rid of those motherfuckers. If I feel like murder it doesn't necessarily matter who gets murdered. Don't you know that about me? Murder is just a thing of itself, a rage and rage is not reason — so why does it matter who vents a rage. That's the first time I've consciously acknowledged that insane truth. Perhaps I'm beginning to grow . . . grow with me. Love me. Teach me. Learn from me. Softly grow stronger with me. O Fair Nicole.

Jesus what a letter. I guess them ghosts will attack me tonite. I can't stand the thought of some son of a bitch fucking you. You know what hurts so bad? Not only the thought of you getting fucked sucking some motherfucker's cock all the way down your throat but they kiss you too. And you would have to kiss them back, put your arms around them AND FUCK GODDAM THAT SHIT MOTHERFUCKER JESUS CHRIST makes me wish I could erase the whole world. Cause all creation to cease to be. My Nicole? My Nicole? Who's Nicole? Take your life? Thats what you wrote you said you fucked one guy twice. I think that's what you said I ain't gonna read it again. Why not just fuck everybody all the time its the same thing to me. You know Lonny the red haired jailer here who gave you a ride one day. Was it him that you fucked? Does he look at me and think "I'm fucking Gilmore's girl?" Oh Jesus. I can't stand this. I can't take it. Fuck this shit. Fuck you. Goddam mother fucker can't you break your fuck habit? Nicole, Nicole, Nicole. Them are ugly ghosts aren't they? Jesus. Ugly ugly. OOOOOH GODDAM! Fuck. I think I got it under control and it gets away again. Nicole I ain't trying to do anything. Probably shouldn't let you read this.

Goddam. Your letters both of them that I got today smell so good they smell like you. Baby this is an ugly letter. It goes from reason to rage.

Honey when you read this letter know that I love you. That I don't understand this thing as well as I thought I did, that I hurt immensely, go back and cross out the parts that hurt you. don't want

*to hurt you Angel Angel Angel Fair Angel. I can't decide to give you
this letter or not am I just sitting here writing words that won't be
read? OOOOH Baby. You'll read this. You knew before you got it that
you would be reading this right now. You can read it over and over.
But you'll never get another letter like this from me again. I know the
emotion here and if you want to feel this you'll just have to read this
letter over. Cause I'll never tell you again of my hurt.*

NOTHING IN THE WORLD, NOT BLINDNESS, LOSS OF MY VERY
EYES, LOSS OF MY ARMS OR LEGS, BEING TOTALLY PARALYZED, PUT ON
PROLIXIN, NOTHING COULD HURT ME WORSE THAN TO KNOW YOU GIVE
YOUR BODY YOUR LOVE TO SOMEONE ELSE.

His letter had more pain in it than she had known anyone could
feel. She felt modest in the middle of her own sorrow, as if some
quiet person in heaven was crying with her too. So she wrote to him
that she would never again do any of the things that tore his heart.
She told him that she'd rather be dead than cause such pain again.
That she would want her life taken away if her eyes ever lied to him
again. She left the letter at the jail.

*Sometime toward dawn this morning I felt love returning — it
flowed warm and tenderly . . . it had never left, of course, was just
waiting for me to become acceptable to it again. I hurt you again but
in a different way and I think it will hurt you for a long time.*

Oh, Nicole.

I wrote you an unneccesarily ugly letter. You're a good girl.

*You get by on very little money and love and raise your kids to
the very best of your ability. I'm not blind to any of those things.
You're a beautiful girl. I love you utterly.*

*Right now I hurt again. It is something that I didn't ever want
to feel again. But it's here once more, my darling, and it's coupled
with a rage that is blinding my reason. Please try to know what I
feel. A voice in me tells me to be gentle — to go slow, to understand,
to love and know my angel, my elf. Know her many hurts — the
things that have happened to her through her young life. But more
than that — know of her love for you. Her trust in you, shown by the
fact that she doesn't lie to you, that she is able to bare her soul and
trust you — Know GARY that you too have habits that are not so
easy to break. That you GARY are not perfect — that you GARY will*

*be a fool if you do not now understand this woman who loves you.
But instead I wrote that ugly letter I gave you yesterday — Oh,
Angel. Please have more faith and strength than I had in my mo-
ments of weak blind rage.*

*I have lain on the bed all day in a fog, a miasma, a senseless
stupor. I'm sorry I'm sorry I'm so fucking sorry. All my body feels
leaden and heavy. I barely answer Gibbs when he talks. I guess he
can sense something is wrong. He keeps the radio turned off because
he knows I can't stand to hear it.*

3

On the last day of September, just before dawn, four cops brought a
stocky-built dude with a neatly trimmed beard into the Maximum
tank. He smelled of booze. When he saw Gilmore and Gibbs watching, he said loudly, "You guys know Cameron Cooper?" Neither answered. So the fellow said, "Well, my name is Gerald Starkey, and I
just killed the motherfucker."

Gibbs said, "If there were doubts, you just eliminated them.
Man, there are four policemen listening to your statement." Even
Gary started laughing. But Starkey was too drunk to care. He put his
mattress and blankets on the bottom bunk and lay down with his
head two feet from the toilet bowl. Quickly, he passed out.

In a while, breakfast came. They split his share. He'd be out for a
few hours.

Around nine-thirty that morning, Big Jake told Starkey to get up
for Court. Afterward, Big Jake explained that Cameron Cooper was
from a real Founding Family in Utah, knew everybody. Right now,
four or five of his friends were in the main tank, so Starkey would
have to stay with Gilmore and Gibbs.

By the time the fellow came back from Court, he was sober and
asked if he could read any of the pocketbooks on the table. All afternoon, he lay on his bunk and read. Had a habit of sneezing right onto
the pages. Gary would mutter, "Doesn't he have enough sense to
turn his fat head?"

Later, he told them he was the cook at Beebee's Steak House in Lehi, and had been a friend of Cameron Cooper's, but they got in an argument. Cameron took his belt off, wrapped the tongue around his hand, and started whaling the buckle at Starkey, who ducked, came up, and stuck a chef's knife right through his heart. "Well," said Gary to Starkey, "I think he got the point!" They had a laugh on that.

Then it came out that Brenda and John had walked into the cafe just as the fight began. Soon as Starkey stabbed the dude, Cameron fell up against Brenda and got blood all over her clothes. "Can you believe it," said Gary to Gibbs, "she's going to be the star witness in his trial too. That bitch is having a busy year in the Courts." He got out a letter of Brenda's and read it aloud: "Gary, you just don't know how badly I feel inside. When I was at the Preliminary Hearing, testifying against you, it really hurt." He shook his head, "Can you believe she is a blood relative? I understand better now," he said, "how she's been married and divorced so many times. Anybody with an I.Q. of 60, which is moron level, could tell she's a backstabber. Mark my words, Geebs, retribution will get her in the end."

4

Saturday Oct 2

I been jackin off so much in these past few weeks thinkin of you and the things we did — well, I got to feelin like I was jackin off too much, 2, 3, 4 sometimes 5 times a day. Now they give me a little Fiorinal and that sleeper Dalmine at nite now and downers down me, and I don't jack off so much no more.

Aw, baby, it's just always bothered me cause I never felt like I really gave you a great wild sweating all controls gone down to earth honest to gosh fuck. Sigh! I was just so hooked on that booze and Fiorinal and I knew all the time that it was fucking me up sexually and I was robbing myself of something so much sweeter and neater. Guess I've mentioned that enough times that you see it bothers me. Plus, Baby Nicole, I was just a little shy around girls, around you. I mean really, it had just been so damn long since I was with a chick. I don't mean that to sound like I ever messed with punks in the joint,

I didn't except the time or two I told you I kissed a couple pretty boys and even once fucked one young pretty boy in his bootie. But it weren't nothing and I didn't dig it. I've always dug chicks but I was away from them for so damn long that I was downright shy about even being naked with you. You were always so beautiful gentle and patient and understanding about it. I think in the first week or so you had me relaxed and feeling purty natural again. I had been locked up for 12½ years. I ain't offering excuses or nothing but that amount of time made a difference that I wasn't even aware of.

When I was a teen-ager pussy was tight. I mean it was hard to get. Girls didn't have the sexual freedom they do now. They even talked different. I never heard a girl say fuck. Just wasn't done. You've seen Happy Days on T.V. — well, things weren't quite that dumb but not far from it, really.

Man, if you got in some chicks pants when I was a kid you were doing something. I got pussy now and then but you had to work at it, morals were different. Girls were suppose to remain virgins till married. It was like a game, ya know? Lots of flirting and teasing. When a girl finally decided to let you fuck her she'd always put on this act like she was being taken advantage of and 9 times outa 10 the girl would say "Well, will you still respect me?" Some goof-ball shit like that. Well the cat was always so hot and ready to go by then that he was ready to about promise anything, even respect. That always seemed so silly, but it was just the way the game was played. I had a chick ask me that once, a real pretty little blond girl, everybody really was hot for her ass and I had her alone one nite in her house. We was both about 15 and necking pretty heavy both getting worked up and I was in and I knew it and then she came up with that cornball line: "Gary, if I let you do it would you still respect me?" Well, I blew it. I started laffing and I told her: "Respect you? For what? I just wanta fuck and so do you, what the fuck am I sposed to respect you for? You just won a first place trophy in the Indianapolis 500 or something?" Well, like I said I blew that one.

Oh well. There's still 2 or 3 weeks. If Gibbs makes bail — but the time is right <u>right</u> now. This is the best time. That fool wetback Luis is on at nites now and he never comes back here to check on me. He don't check the bars for cuts. He just sets out there watching cop shows on the boob tube. Also this is the perfect time for me to get the shoes — just before I go to court it would be so natural for Snyder or Esplin to bring me a pair of ones and twos.

Sterling finally said he wouldn't sew the hacksaw into the shoes. A lot of precious time had gone by. Nicole decided to try it herself. She bought a pair of brogans at the thrift store, and cut a little slot in the sole with a razor. With a lot of work, she was able to push the blade in, but it was too long and so she took a chance and broke the blade in half. She could get that much in. But when she tried to sew up the slit, it looked a mess. They would never pass those shoes.

CHAPTER 27

A Prosecution

1

The District Court of Utah County had jurisdiction for the trial. It would take place in Judge Bullock's courtroom, 310 in the Utah County Building, largest edifice in downtown Provo, a gray, massive, old lion of a legal temple reminiscent to Noall Wootton of a thousand other government buildings that had a Greek pediment supported by stone columns at the top of broad steps.

Having been born in Provo and grown up in Provo, Wootton kind of liked going to Court there, and this was going to be the biggest murder case he had yet tried.

Like a lot of other lawyers in the area, Wootton had gone to BYU and transferred to the University of Utah for law school. Did it with no great desire, not in the beginning anyway, just that his father had a successful practice, and Noall figured, hell, he could take the course, and try business afterward. When he got out he was offered a job with the FBI and a position with United Airlines, but turned them down because his father offered to take him in. That worked out well. Wootton, Senior, taught him a great deal.

Noall soon decided, however, that being in an office all day was not his idea. He enjoyed a courtroom. Even felt contempt for classmates who went to Salt Lake or Denver or L.A. to work. They just ended up in back rooms preparing cases for big-city trial lawyers. Whereas Noall was where he wanted to be. Right in the courtroom against those big lawyers.

He started by doing defense work, but came to the conclusion most of his clients were punks. His duty, as he saw it, was to make certain his client was not convicted if innocent, or not overcharged if guilty. The punks wanted to get off at all costs, guilty or not. Noall couldn't buy that. He began to think prosecution was the way to go.

One case brought this home. It was a man he defended who had much the same background as Gilmore. The fellow, Harlow Custis, had spent eighteen years in prison, and had now been charged with a simple forged credit card. They were going to send him back to jail for that. Wootton thought Custis was being screwed over. He fought for nine months to get him out of prison. Finally succeeded.

On the day Custis was placed on probation, he came over to Noall's house and demanded some tires back that he had given in payment. When Wootton told him he wouldn't return them unless paid in cash, he was called every name in the book.

Three weeks later, Custis got drunk and wrecked his car. Killed a man. No driver's license. At that point, Wootton decided he'd made a mistake and shouldn't have tried to fight the case so hard. That was the moment he decided to move over to the prosecutor's side.

Preparing for Gilmore, Wootton thought often of his other big case, which had been prosecuting Francis Clyde Martin, who had been forced to get married because his girl was pregnant. Martin took his new wife in the woods and stabbed her twenty times, cut her throat, cut the unborn baby out of her body, stabbed the baby, went home.

In that case, Wootton had decided not to go for the death penalty. Martin was a nice-looking eighteen-year-old high-school student with no criminal record. Just a kid in a terrible trap who ran amok. Wootton had gone for a life sentence, and the boy was in prison now, and might be brought around eventually.

In fact, Wootton didn't see himself as a terribly strong advocate of the death penalty. He just didn't know that it had a deterrent effect

on other criminals. The only reason he was looking for the maximum
sentence with Gilmore was risk. Gilmore alive was a risk to society.

2

On October 4, Monday, the day before the trial would begin, Craig
Snyder and Mike Esplin had a long conference with Gary. After a
while, he asked, "What do you think my chances are?" and Craig
Snyder replied, "I don't think they are good — I don't think they are
good at all."

Gary answered, "Well, you know, this doesn't come as a big
shock."

They had, they told him, made a special effort with the psychiatrists. Not one would declare Gary insane. For that matter, Gary
agreed with them. "Like I said," he remarked, "I can get on and convince the Jury that I'm out of my head. But, man, I don't want to do
that. I resent having my intelligence insulted."

Then there was the business of Hansen. Snyder and Esplin
agreed they would be happy if Phil Hansen came in. They said no
lawyer was going to be so egotistical as to take a position that he
didn't want or need the best professional aid available. But Hansen
hadn't gotten in touch.

They did not say to him that they didn't feel ready to pick up the
phone and call Hansen. There was nothing, after all, but Nicole's
story to go by. It could prove embarrassing if she misunderstood what
Hansen had promised.

Once more they asked Gary about putting Nicole on the stand. "I
don't want her brought into it," Gary said. They could sense his objection. She would have to say she had provoked him unendurably.
Specify a few sordid details. He wouldn't have anything to do with
that. In fact, he was furious that Wootton was calling Nicole as a witness. He told Snyder and Esplin that he didn't want them to exclude
the prosecution's witnesses from the courtroom because it meant that
Nicole, having been listed by Wootton, would also be kept out. Gary's

lawyers said this had to give Wootton an advantage. His witnesses would be able to hear what the ones before them said. Everything in Wootton's presentation would come out smoother. Didn't matter, Gary told them.

Snyder and Esplin tried to change his mind. When witnesses, they said, were not able to hear each other, they felt more nervous on the stand. Didn't know what they were stepping into. That was a great deal for the defense to give away just so they could have Nicole in the courtroom. Gary shook his head. Nicole had to be there.

3

The first day was spent in selecting a Jury. On the second day, it was Esplin's disagreeable task at the real commencement of the trial to ask the Judge to send the Jury out since there was a matter of law to discuss. He then told Judge Bullock that the defendant, against their advice, did not wish any of the prosecution witnesses to be excluded. It was a poor start. Many a Judge lost respect for a lawyer who could not show a client his best interest.

MR. ESPLIN   Your Honor, Mr. Gilmore has expressed to me the reason for his decision and it's based upon the fact that Nicole Barrett, who is the defendant's girl friend, is listed as a witness for the State, and he does not want her excluded from the courtroom. I think that's the sole basis for his decision.

THE COURT   Is that so, Mr. Gilmore?

MR. GILMORE   Well, yes. I seen that she wasn't on the list until just, you know, yesterday or so, and it appears to me that the reason was so that she would have to be excluded from the courtroom. And I don't want her to have to sit out in that uncomfortable hall all day.

THE COURT   Well, she may have to be in the hall, but certainly we'll have chairs and other comforts there.

MR. GILMORE   Well, it's my decision that she not be excluded, Your Honor.

THE COURT   Is that all there is?

MR. ESPLIN   That's all we have, Your Honor.

THE COURT   That's the law matter? All right, you may bring the Jury back in.

Gary, as if to recoup what he had given away, now spent time glowering at Wootton.

The irony of the whole thing, Esplin decided, was that Nicole, so far as he could see, wasn't even in Court. All morning Gary kept turning around to look for her. She didn't show up. She didn't get there, in fact, until lunchtime, and then Gary couldn't have been happier to see her.

4

Wootton began by explaining his witnesses to the Jury. "Each one," he said, "will give you a small piece of the overall story. They will tell you about how the defendant, Gary Gilmore . . . walked down the street with the motel cash box in one hand and the pistol in the other hand . . . abandoned the cash box at the end of the block . . . and abandoned the gun. They will tell you how shortly thereafter he was seen at a service station on the corner of Third South and University Avenue where he picked up his truck, at that time bleeding rather profusely from an injury to his left hand. The witnesses will tell you how they traced the blood trail from the service station back up the sidewalk to where it stopped at a Pfitzer evergreen bush that was planted along the side of the sidewalk. They will tell you how they found a .22 automatic pistol that appeared to have been discharged in the Pfitzer bush, because it had weeds and leaves in the automatic portion of the gun. They will tell you that they found a shell casing there. You'll also hear testimony that the investigators at the motel office where Mr. Bushnell was killed found another .22 shell casing. You'll hear expert testimony to the effect that the slug in his head was in fact a .22-caliber slug fired from a gun with the same type of markings inside the barrel, as the .22 pistol that was found in the Pfitzer bush."

As the exhibits and witnesses were presented during the length of that day, Wootton's case came forth much as he had announced it, solid and well connected. Snyder and Esplin could only raise doubts on small points or try to reduce the credibility of the testimony. So Esplin got the first witness, Larry Johnson, a draftsman, to admit that his plan of the motel, drawn to order in this last week before trial, could provide "no idea as to what plants or vegetables were growing on the 20th of July" around the motel windows. It was a detail, but it dissipated the authority of the first exhibit, and so kept the Jury from becoming impressed too quickly by the sheer quantity of exhibits. Wootton, after all, was going to produce eighteen.

The next witness, Detective Fraser, had taken a number of photographs of the motel office. Esplin got him to agree that the drapes might have been moved before the photographs were taken.

So it went. Small corrections and small adjustments on the case Wootton was making. When Glen Overton came to the stand and described the appearance of Benny Bushnell dying in his own blood, and the demeanor of Debbie Bushnell as he drove her to the hospital, the defense was silent. Esplin was not going to intensify the vividness of those scenes by cross-examination.

The fourth witness, Dr. Morrison, was the Deputy Chief Medical Examiner of Utah, and had performed the autopsy on Benny Bushnell. Dr. Morrison testified that the absence of powder burns on the surface of Bushnell's skin dictated that the murder weapon had been put in direct contact with his head.

Esplin had to make some attempt to discredit him.

MR. ESPLIN   At the time that you examined the decedent did you examine the weapon that was allegedly used in the commission of this offense?

DR. MORRISON   No, sir. . . .

MR. ESPLIN   And I take it at the time that you examined the decedent, you did not know the type of ammunition that was used?

DR. MORRISON   That's correct.

MR. ESPLIN   And yet you say these things were all things which do make a difference in making your determination?

DR. MORRISON   They could make a difference. . . . In this particular case, in my opinion, it did not make a difference. . . . I did not feel that the type of ammunition or the specific type of weapon would enter into or present a problem as far as the determination went. However, I was informed at the time I did the autopsy the weapon was a handgun.

MR. ESPLIN   But you didn't examine it?

DR. MORRISON   But I did not examine the weapon? No, sir.

The defense had to gamble. If nothing else, the vigor of Esplin's cross-examination could confuse the Jury. So, even as Dr. Morrison was saying that he did not need to know the gun nor the ammunition since, in this case, neither affected the result, so Esplin gained the admission that Dr. Morrison had not examined the weapon. That might bother some of the panel.

Martin Ontiveros came next and established that Gary had left his truck at the service station two blocks from the motel and went away for half an hour. When he returned, Gary had blood on his left hand.

Ned Lee, a patrolman, had found the gun by retracing Gilmore's trail of blood from the service station to the bushes. "Anything liquid has a tendency to flow in the direction you are traveling," he said, so he had been able to determine that Gilmore's movements had been from the place in the bush where the gun was hidden on eastward to Fulmer's gas station. Again, there was little for the defense to do with his testimony.

Detective William Brown received the cartridge case and gun from Patrolman Lee and had them photographed in the position they were discovered. Wootton offered the photograph as Exhibit Three.

MR. ESPLIN   Officer Brown, did you take that photograph?

OFFICER BROWN   No, sir.

MR. ESPLIN   Do you know who took it?

OFFICER BROWN   No, sir. I don't.

MR. ESPLIN   We object, Your Honor. Improper foundation.

MR. WOOTTON   I've laid a foundation. . . . Your Honor, I don't have to establish when or under what circumstances it was taken. All I've got to establish is he was looking at the bush and he looked at the photo and it's the same.

Still, it was a small gain. One more exhibit slightly tainted. You never knew when a few small gains could contribute to the final effect.

MR. ESPLIN You did dust the weapon for fingerprints, is that correct?

OFFICER BROWN Yes, sir.

MR. ESPLIN Did you find any prints?

OFFICER BROWN I found one.

MR. ESPLIN Did you transmit that to the FBI laboratory?

OFFICER BROWN I did . . .

MR. ESPLIN What were those results?

OFFICER BROWN They needed a better comparison.

MR. ESPLIN In other words they couldn't make a determination?

OFFICER BROWN Right.

MR. ESPLIN No further questions.

When Gerald Nielsen came on, Wootton did not ask him about the confession. Nielsen merely testified to the existence of a fresh gunshot wound on Gilmore's left hand at the time he was arrested.

Gerald F. Wilkes, a Special Agent with the FBI, was an expert on ballistics.

MR. WOOTTON Would you tell the Jury, please, what your conclusions were?

MR. WILKES Based on my examination of these two cartridges, I was able to determine that both cartridge cases were fired with this weapon and no other weapon.

Esplin had no recourse but to ask questions that might bring back damaging answers.

MR. ESPLIN Is there a certain number of marks which must be on a particular item of evidence . . . before you are able to say beyond a reasonable doubt that the cartridge was fired by the same gun?

MR. WILKES   No, sir. I fix no minimum number of microscopic marks to effect an identification.

MR. ESPLIN   Do you have any idea of how many marks, similarities or points of similarity you found between Exhibit No. 12 and the test cartridge which you fired in the laboratory?

MR. WILKES   The marks of similarity were contained around the entire circumference of the cartridge case. It's so many microscopic marks in fact that it left no doubt in my mind as to the conclusion I reached.

Peter Arroyo testified to seeing Gary in the motel office.

MR. WOOTTON   How far away from him were you at that time?

MR. ARROYO   Oh, somewhere near ten feet.

MR. WOOTTON   Was he inside the office?

MR. ARROYO   Yes.

MR. WOOTTON   And you were out in the driveway?

MR. ARROYO   Yes.

MR. WOOTTON   Did you observe anything in his possession at the time?

MR. ARROYO   Yes.

MR. WOOTTON   Tell us what you saw.

MR. ARROYO   In his right hand he had a pistol with a long barrel. In his left hand he had a cash box from a cash register.

MR. WOOTTON   Are you able to describe the pistol for us?

MR. ARROYO   Yes.

MR. WOOTTON   Tell us how you observed it.

MR. ARROYO   He actually stopped when he saw us. I looked right at him, I looked at the gun, and I looked up at his face to see what he was going to do with the gun. I thought he worked in the office and he was fooling around with the gun. I was concerned about that. So I looked right at his eyes. And he just stopped and looked at me. And after a few seconds he turned around and walked back around the counter.

MR. WOOTTON   What did you do?

MR. ARROYO   We kept on walking right to the car. . . .

MR. WOOTTON   Mr. Arroyo, do you see the individual in the courtroom now that you observed with the gun and the cash box at that
time?

MR. ARROYO   Yes.

MR. WOOTTON   Would you identify him for the Court and the Jury,
please?

MR. ARROYO   The man with the red jacket and the green shirt. (Indicating)

MR. WOOTTON   Seated at the counsel table opposite me?

MR. ARROYO   Yes.

MR. WOOTTON   Your Honor, may the record reflect that the witness
is identifying the defendant?

THE COURT   It may so show.

MR. WOOTTON   Your witness.

MR. ESPLIN   Sir, could you describe the individual that you observed
in the motel office that night?

MR. ARROYO   Yes. He appeared to be a little taller than I am. . . .

MR. ESPLIN   What other characteristics would you describe?

MR. ARROYO   He had a Vandyke-type beard and long hair.

MR. ESPLIN   What other distinguishing characteristics do you recall?

MR. ARROYO   His eyes.

MR. ESPLIN   What do you recall about his eyes?

MR. ARROYO   When I looked at his eyes, it's kind of hard to describe.
I'd never forget those eyes.

MR. ESPLIN   Did you see the color of his eyes?

MR. ARROYO   No. Just the look.

Not hard to comprehend what Arroyo meant. Gilmore had been
glaring at Wootton throughout the testimony.

After Arroyo stepped down, the prosecution rested its case. Esplin stood up and said the defense would also rest.

THE COURT   You do not intend to put on any evidence?

MR. ESPLIN   No, Your Honor.

THE COURT   Very well. Both sides having rested, then it would be the duty of the Court to instruct the Jury. . . . I am ready but it would take half an hour and require us to again go into the evening quite late. My understanding is that there are the great debates on tonight.

The Judge was referring to the second scheduled debate between Jerry Ford and Jimmy Carter.

THE COURT   In the interests of everyone I will instruct in the morning rather than tonight and then we'll complete the case tomorrow.

5

October 6

I just got back from court.
Wow!
I had told you that I didn't expect much from Snyder and Esplin but I was not prepared for the fact that they intended to put up absolutely no defense at all.
To say I was surprised when Esplin rested the case would be a hell of an understatement.
They never told me that they were gonna do that — offer no defense at all.
I couldn't believe it!
I figured on some sort of defense — no matter how meager.
I thought they would at least try to get a second degree conviction.
Its a dead certain cinch right now that I'll be convicted on first degree — and Esplin and Snyder knew this when they rested today.
They never told me they were gonna pull that shit.
They acted guilty and defensive as a motherfucker when I confronted em about it after the trial.
They didn't even try.
All they want to do is leave theirself a case for appeal and they haven't even done that.
That's the way it is with court appointed lawyers.

As soon as Court had adjourned, there had been a conference, and Gary let them know he was not happy.

"I thought you'd call a psychiatrist or something."

They explained again. They would call one at the Mitigation Hearing tomorrow. There had been no point to do it in the trial itself. No doctor would say he was legally insane, so they'd only be making it easier for the Jury to convict. This way, a few of the jurors might have their own questions of his sanity.

"Couldn't we have called somebody?" he asked, "just for appearance's sake?"

They laid out their strategy. His situation might not be as bad as it looked, they said. Number one — the prosecution hadn't tested Gary's blood against the blood found on the trail. If it had come out O, which was Gary's type, that would have been another nail in. Two, said Craig Snyder, they didn't have fingerprints off the gun. Therefore, the gun had not been attached to his hand beyond a shadow of a doubt. Three: the prosecution had neglected to put in the money from the robbery as an exhibit. They had the money, but hadn't introduced it. Fourth, Wootton hadn't dared to use Gary's confession to Gerald Nielsen. The Jury, said Craig, his eyes getting serious behind his glasses, still had to cross the bridge to find him guilty.

Not easy to sentence a man to death, was their unvoiced remark. Who could speak of what it would do to your dreams? A Jury really had to get itself up to go across the bridge. So, if the case could be conducted with decorum, and the proceedings kept calm, the atmosphere might give a Jury pause. It would be hard to sentence a man to death if no strong feelings were flowing.

At this point, Gary said he wanted to make a statement to the Judge. He wanted to testify.

It was against their advice. This way, said Craig Snyder, he was 99 percent convicted. If he testified, it was 100 percent.

Gary looked gloomy for a moment. "I did it," he said, "that's it." He insisted again on taking the stand.

They tried to think of what it would be like to reopen the case. Messy. Once more they thought of calling Nicole, but had lived so long with the idea of not calling her that the thought of having her on the stand was unsettling. It could boomerang. If it ever came out that Gary had guns in the car and was driving with children. No, Nicole was also a bad gamble.

Any decision was left up in the air. Each of the three men slept by his own best means.

CHAPTER 28

A Defense

1

Nicole hadn't been in Court that morning for good cause. She was still feeling sick over the way Gary had acted the day before.

She thought the first day of the trial would be the whole trial, but instead, the first day was spent picking a Jury. There weren't any witnesses called. It was just one long dull stretch and she didn't even get to speak to Gary until the second recess when they let her sit on the other side of the railing from him. All of a sudden, he brought up the letter she had written a week before, the one where she told him she would rather be dead than cause him pain by being with other men. Now, out of nowhere, he was nasty about it. "You talk about dying, but it's just words, baby," he said, and gave her a look as if to say she was safe on her side of the fence.

Then she told him that if he wanted to, he could kill her right there in the courtroom where she stood. In fact, she said, trying not to cry, it was killing her that he could think the way he did. Real sarcastically he said, "How would I go about killing you right now? With my arms in handcuffs and my legs in shackles?" She felt foolish. Later, he winked at her. It didn't seem to mean anything to him. Like he'd had a vicious spasm and it was gone.

But she didn't sleep all night. In the morning, after leaving the kids with her neighbor, she dozed some, and woke up feeling dopey, and her body out of sorts.

426 / THE EXECUTIONER'S SONG

Sure enough, when she got to the courtroom, he couldn't have been happier to see her. He had completely forgotten the day before. Nicole just sat there in a trance. She didn't even know what was going on. At the end of the day, she felt further away from Gary than at any time since their worst days in Spanish Fork.

That night Sue came over and announced she would take Nicole out and get her drunk. Cheer her up.

Nicole realized she really wanted to get loose, really wanted to dance. It wasn't all that good of an idea, but there was Sue. Nicole let herself be taken out.

They passed through the Silver Dollar and went on to Fred's Lounge. Nicole liked the tension in the place. A lot of Sundowners were around, and she danced with a couple of them and liked them. Dapper, the way they stroked a pool ball.

One fellow who was real together told her that he was an ex-president of the Sundowners in Salt Lake. A sweet talker. He was good looking, and fun to dance with. But she kept going back to her own table, and sipping on her vodka and grapefruit juice.

Then Sue disappeared, and Nicole was left alone with all her own business to mind. That was when the ex-president started talking about going over to Salt Lake. Nicole thought she would like to see what that club was all about. For years, she'd been hearing about the Sundowners' house in Salt Lake. Maybe she'd get a little bit loose and meet the people.

She tried to think clearly about where this might end. It was already two in the morning. It would take nearly an hour to get to Salt Lake, then there would be more of a party there. She figured daylight would arrive before there'd be trouble.

Sure enough, when they got to Salt Lake, she just sat around and listened to people, talked a little bit, lit up, drank beer, just got wasted in a nice quiet way. She felt sleepy, sitting on the sofa, an old beat-up ragged sofa. It was all right at that clubhouse, a place to enjoy the vibes, sort of like a bar set up right in the living room, and a bunch of motorcycles in the living room too. Their beat-up old carpet had a little gas and oil on it. She just closed her eyes a few times and maybe nodded off. It must have been five in the morning when she said, "I want to get some sleep."

The ex-president talked her into going downstairs, and that felt kind of safe. It was just a big room with mattresses, and people crashing all over. Maybe some of them were getting it on. Too murky to see. She started to wake up a little, and wonder how the hell she was going to get out of Salt Lake by herself. Then the guy got down on the same mattress, and there was no way she could make him understand that she had no desire. Whatever she tried to say bounced off. He just kept asking why she had her clothes on and he didn't. She tried to compromise her way out of it, but he had had too much grass. Couldn't get off that way. She finally had to let him in. She really blew the idea that she was going to be faithful to Gary in life and in death.

When she woke up, she felt as raw as she had ever felt. She wasn't scared that Gary would find out, she was just scared, period. She was living in this awful place inside herself where everything was shitty. She would have cried but it would have made the most awful crappy moaning sound.

That was a long morning. She had to get the ex-president of the Sundowners waked up to take her back to Court, and she didn't get in until it had started. Riding from Salt Lake to Provo on the back of his bike, she knew that she would never lie about this to Gary if he asked, but she didn't want to tell him. She shivered at the thought he would ask.

Riding behind this strange guy's back, she decided that she would never sleep with another guy for the rest of her life.

She never would let herself get into anything again that would make her feel this uneasy personally. One of these days, on one of her visits, Gary might look her in the eye and ask if she had made it with anybody. She did not know if she could tell him the truth. She didn't want to think of the damage it would do inside to him and to her if she actually lied point-blank while looking right into his face. She had enough worms right now.

2

MR. ESPLIN   Your Honor, we request that the courtroom be cleared for this matter. It's a matter of some delicacy.

THE COURT   Mr. Gilmore, do you request that the courtroom be cleared?

MR. GILMORE   Yes.

THE COURT   I will do so. I'll ask everyone to leave except Court personnel, security people.

(Whereupon, the courtroom was cleared at 9: o'clock A.M.)

MR. ESPLIN   Your Honor. The defense rested its case yesterday. . . . At that time it was our opinion and our advice that Mr. Gilmore not testify in this case, that he exercise his right to remain silent throughout this trial. . . . After discussing the matter last night and becoming aware of his desire to take the stand, again we . . . both gave our considered opinions . . . that he not take the stand . . . and put the State to its proof. But again we assured him that was his decision and . . . he had a right to take the stand against our advice. We advised him to consider his decision overnight. We met with him again this morning. . . .

THE COURT   Mr. Gilmore, do you desire to take the stand at this time?

MR. GILMORE   It isn't that I have such burning desire to take the stand, but I was simply unprepared for counsel to rest the case at the point they did yesterday. I mean, I'm on trial for my life and I have been expecting all along to present some sort of a defense. And when they rested yesterday, man, it appeared to me to be in effect tantamount to a plea of guilty to a First-Degree Murder charge, because I don't see where the Jury could return any other verdict at that stage. And why have a trial? I mean I —

THE COURT   What evidence do you have that you want to present?

MR. GILMORE   Apparently I don't have any, according to my lawyers.

THE COURT   Do you have any or do you not?

MR. GILMORE   God, I don't know . . . I have feelings and beliefs and I guess these doctors don't concur with them.

THE COURT   Now, Mr. Gilmore —

MR. GILMORE   You have to let me finish.

THE COURT   Yes. Yes. Go ahead.

MR. GILMORE   I feel myself that I have a good insanity defense or at least a basis of it. But apparently the doctors don't concur. But the conditions that I talked to the doctors under were adverse. There were inmates present. The whole thing was not right. It wasn't fair to me, really. And it blew my whole defense off. I don't want to just plead guilty to First-Degree Murder and accept a First-Degree Murder conviction. It will take them less than a half an hour to find that, the way I see it right now. That's what I'm saying. That's what I feel, man. I mean I have been expecting all along to present some sort of case even if it's meager. And I think that probably the best thing I could possibly do would be to talk to them myself. I could do that at the Mitigation Hearing, but that's after they find me guilty. I'd like them to at least consider what I have to say before they go out.

THE COURT   You can take the stand, if you care to. But if you do so you should understand fully the consequences of it.

MR. GILMORE   Man, I'm not, you know, telling you I'm burning to get on the stand. I just would like to present a defense. That's been my expectation all along.

THE COURT   Do you want to take the witness stand and testify?

MR. GILMORE   I want to present a defense. I just don't want to sit here mute and be —

THE COURT   My question to you is: Do you want to have the Court reopen the case —

MR. GILMORE   Right.

THE COURT   — be sworn as a witness and testify?

MR. GILMORE   Yeah. Yeah. Right. If that's the way you've got to ask me, okay.

THE COURT   Now and I want you to fully understand that if you do that then you are subject to cross-examination by the State's attorney. Do you understand that?

MR. GILMORE   Yes.

THE COURT   And you'll be compelled to answer the questions that he asks.

MR. GILMORE   Yes.

THE COURT   And those questions and your answers may be incriminating to you. Do you understand that?

MR. GILMORE I understand it. You know. I understand all that you are going to say. I understand all that you've said.

MR. SNYDER Your Honor, my I make one other statement?

THE COURT Yes, you may.

MR. SNYDER I want Mr. Gilmore to understand perfectly that Mr. Esplin and I have contacted Dr. Howell, Dr. Crist, Dr. Lebegue, Dr. Woods, we have discussed with them in detail their examination and findings and we have reviewed their entire file at the Utah State Hospital, which is approximately three inches thick. The very best that they really can do is that they will testify that he has a form of mental disorder known as a psychopathic or antisocial behavior. We have discussed that with the defendant. We have told him in our opinion and according to the law that that is not a defense, as far as insanity is concerned. And we have advised the defendant that we have no witnesses that we can call in the line of expert witnesses, doctors, psychiatrists, psychologists who would help the defendant in that regard; and that without that type of expert testimony the Court will not give an instruction even for the Jury to consider on the sanity plea. And I want to make the record clear on that, and I want to advise Mr. Gilmore of those items.

MR. GILMORE I'll withdraw my request. Just go ahead on with it like it was.

THE COURT You what?

MR. GILMORE I withdraw my request to reopen it.

THE COURT You do?

MR. GILMORE Yeah.

THE COURT All right. Will you bring the Jury back in, please? Yes, and the others may come in.

They were bewildered. The defense attorneys, the prosecutor, the Judge, conceivably the defendant himself. It was as if a resignation had come over him as he argued, a gloom, and he now saw the case as Snyder and Esplin had seen it weeks before.

3

On this morning, as Gary was making his statement, Noall Wootton was at a loss to figure it out.

He liked to go at a case as though he were the defense lawyer. Sometimes it gave him a few inspirations on what the others would be up to. In this situation, he had been looking for the defense to find a better motive for Gilmore than robbery when he went to the City Center Motel. Going, for instance, to get a room, or dropping by to resume a dispute. Maybe Bushnell had once refused to rent to Gilmore because he was intoxicated. In that case, having come in with no intent to rob, he could have shot Bushnell without premeditation. The robbery would have been an afterthought. That would be Murder Two. Wootton expected such a defense as a matter of course. He had not really known what he could do to refute it if Gary got on the stand and told a convincing tale.

Only later, did Wootton find out that Gary wouldn't cooperate with his lawyers. At this point, he could hardly understand why they had rested, but decided the reason they didn't put Gilmore on the stand had to be his personality. He must have an explosive temper. So, this morning, as soon as Gary said he wanted to testify, Wootton decided yes, might as well have him there. It could be a way to get in the fact that Gilmore had ordered his victim to lie down, then shot him.

Maybe Gary saw the look in his eye, maybe Gary felt his confidence. Wootton was twice flabbergasted after Gary changed his mind again. It was like dealing with a crazy pony who was off on a gallop at every wind. Then wouldn't move.

Wootton kept his closing statement short. Reviewed what his witnesses had established the day before, laid out the chain of evidence, and put emphasis on the testimony of Dr. Morrison.

"In his opinion," said Wootton, "Benny Bushnell died of a single gunshot wound to the head. But he told you something much more important than that. He told you that the gun had been placed directly against Benny's skull when the trigger was pulled . . . this tells you that it was not a wild shot fired across the room, it was not a shot fired to intimidate or frighten, it was a shot intending to kill and kill instantly. Okay." He took a breath.

"Think about the case deeply," he said in conclusion, "and judge it fairly. But when I say judge it fairly, I don't mean just judge it fairly from the point of view of Gary Gilmore, although that's important; you judge it fairly from the point of view of Benny Bushnell's widow and his child and the child yet to be born." The State was done.

Mike Esplin began by complimenting the Jury. Then he went looking for weak places in the evidence Noall Wootton had put together.

MR. ESPLIN   Consider the lateness of the hour. Seems reasonable to infer that the motel manager wasn't even in the office to start off. It's possible . . . he was back here in his living room and whoever was in the office, maybe he was in the act of taking money from the box and the manager came upon him and was shot. That is not robbery, it's a theft. So I submit on that question there is a reasonable doubt. The State has not proved that. Now they have witnesses they could have called and established that . . .

He was making a reference to Debbie Bushnell.

. . . but they have not done so. Again, they indicated $125 missing, and they also indicated they arrested the defendant for this offense later on the same night. They haven't produced one bit, one cent of that money. They haven't indicated that they searched him. This defendant is charged with taking money. Where is it? Another matter: this gun, whoever placed it in the bush, when they placed it in that bush it went off accidentally, it discharged. Doesn't that place a possible inference in your mind that there's a gun going off accidentally? They have to show an intentional killing. These things have not been answered. There is no one that actually saw the incident. The only thing that Mr. Arroyo could testify to is that he saw a person who he identified as the defendant in the office with a gun similar to this one. He said that he couldn't testify that that was the same gun. . . . All he could say was he remembers his face and remembers seeing a gun in his hand.

Couldn't make much of the testimony of Martin Ontiveros. He said that Gary Gilmore arrived at the service station to have his truck fixed. It seems kind of ridiculous. I submit if Mr. Gilmore's intention was to go down and rob the City Center Motel he would not have left his truck there at the service station where he could easily be placed at the scene or near the scene of the crime.

Esplin was feeling emotion. This closing argument became, to his surprise, the most emotional thing he had ever done. His voice cracked in several places. Afterward, people said to him in the recess, "How did you put on an act like that?" "It wasn't fake," Esplin added. He had noticed, and he felt some hope, that several jurors were in tears.

As you go to the jury room take the questions that you have, consider them, and if you do have doubts about it, any reasonable doubts, then I suggest that your obligation is either (1) find the defendant guilty of the lesser included offense of second degree criminal homicide, Murder in the Second Degree, or (2) to acquit the defendant. Thank you.

MR. WOOTTON   We'll waive rebuttal.

(Whereupon, the Jury retired to deliberate at 10:13 o'clock A.M., October 7, 1976.)

After the Jury had left, Esplin stood up again.

MR. ESPLIN   Your Honor, there is one point: we would object to the comment made by the prosecutor in his closing arguments where he referred to doing justice for Benny Bushnell and his widow and so forth as being prejudicial to this Jury, and would at this point move for a mistrial based on that reasoning.

THE COURT   The motion for mistrial is denied. Anything further? All right. Then we'll be in recess until such time as the bailiff notifies us that the Jury has reached a verdict.

The Jury had recessed at 10:13 A.M. An hour and twenty minutes later, they brought back a verdict of Guilty in the First Degree. Since it was close to lunch, Judge Bullock recessed the trial until 1:30 in the afternoon, when the Mitigation Hearing to determine whether Gary would receive life imprisonment or the death sentence would begin.

CHAPTER 29

The Sentence

1

Until now, the courtroom had been half-empty, but during the lunch recess word must have passed through the coffee shop, for the Mitigation Hearing was crowded. A legal process would decide a man's life — that had to be an awesome afternoon.

As Judge Bullock explained, the aim of the Mitigation Hearing was to discover whether the defendant, having been found guilty of First-Degree Murder, would now receive the death sentence or life imprisonment. For that reason, hearsay evidence, at the discretion of the Court, would be admissible.

Since hearsay could prove injurious to Gary, Craig Snyder (who was doing the Mitigation Hearing even as Mike Esplin had handled the trial) was trying his best to lay grounds for appeal. Snyder objected often, and Judge Bullock overruled him almost as often. Let one ruling by the Judge be declared in error by a higher Court, and Gary could not be executed. So Craig Snyder was counting as much on the strength of future appeal as on his chances of avoiding the death sentence now.

He took, therefore, a continuing objection to the testimony of Duane Fraser who had just made a long-distance call during the lunch recess to the Assistant Superintendent of Oregon State Penitentiary. Duane Fraser testified that he had been told in this phone call how Gilmore "assaulted someone with a hammer," and "on another occasion, assaulted a dentist" and therefore "was removed from Oregon State Prison and taken to Marion Prison in Illinois." Snyder had a continuing objection to all of that as inexpert and imprecise.

Albert Swenson, a professor of chemistry at BYU, testified that a sample of Gary Gilmore's blood, obtained after arrest, showed less than seven-hundredths of a gram of alcohol per hundred grams of blood. That was not a high level. He would be well aware of what he was doing. Since the sample, however, had been taken five hours after the crime, Professor Swenson told Wootton the content at the time of shooting might have been thirteen-hundredths. That, he testified, was a level at which the defendant would still know what he was doing, but would care less.

On cross-examination, Snyder succeeded in getting Professor Swenson to admit the level could easily have been as high as seventeen-hundredths, which was more than twice the level at which the State found a man guilty of driving under the influence of alcohol. Taken in combination with Fiorinal, such a man's intoxication would be greater.

On balance, Swenson's testimony might prove a plus for Gary.

The next witness was Dean Blanchard, District Agent for Adult Probation and Parole. He was appearing in place of Mont Court who was away on vacation. Mr. Blanchard said, "I don't know where he's at." Blanchard then said that he had had "very little direct contact with Mr. Gilmore." At this point Snyder said he had a continuing objection to his testimony.

Detective Rex Skinner took the stand. Then there was a long argument between Snyder and the Court. Skinner's testimony, said Snyder, "would be entirely prejudicial to the defendant."

MR. WOOTTON   Mr. Skinner . . . did you assist in the investigation of . . . the shooting death of one Max Jensen?

MR. SKINNER   Yes, sir. I did. . . .

MR. WOOTTON   Where did that take place?

MR. SKINNER   At the Sinclair service station on 800 North in Orem.

MR. WOOTTON   When you got there did you observe the body of Max Jensen?

MR. SKINNER   Yes, sir. I did.

MR. WOOTTON   Would you describe where it was, sir, and how it was lying as you observed it?

MR. SNYDER   Your Honor, I'm going to object.

THE COURT   Objection sustained.

MR. WOOTTON   Did you observe any injuries about the body?

MR. SNYDER   Objection, Your Honor.

THE COURT   Objection sustained.

MR. WOOTTON   Do you know whether it was a homicide?

MR. SNYDER   I'd make the same objection, Your Honor.

THE COURT   He may answer.

MR. SKINNER   Yes, sir.

MR. WOOTTON   How do you know?

MR. SNYDER   Your Honor, I'm going to object to any testimony beyond that point.

THE COURT   I think that is so. If he knows it's a homicide— He said yes. Proceed.

MR. WOOTTON   Mr. Skinner, did you cause anybody to be arrested in connection with that incident?

MR. SKINNER   Yes, sir.

MR. SNYDER   Your Honor, I'm going to object to that.

THE COURT   He may answer.

MR. WOOTTON   Who did you arrest?

MR. SKINNER   Gary Gilmore.

MR. SNYDER   No questions.

THE COURT   No questions? Very well, you may step down.

MR. WOOTTON   Call Brenda Nicol.

Brenda was in misery. She had asked Noall Wootton not to call her. He had, he said, a subpoena for her, and she better get her ass down to Court. So she came, and all the while she was testifying, Gary glared at her. He gave the Kerby look that made your blood clabber on the spot. If a look in somebody's eyes could kill you, then you had just been killed. Wiped you out like an electric shock.

"Oh, Gary," said Brenda in her heart, "don't be so angry with me.

My testimony means nothing," and once again she told how Gary had asked her to call his mother. "Gary, she's going to be upset," she testified to saying, "Your mother's going to ask me, are these charges true?" And she told how Gary had said, "Tell her that it's true," and once again Esplin got her to agree, even as she had agreed in the Preliminary Hearing, that she couldn't be certain whether Gary meant it was true that he committed murder, or true that he was charged with murder. All the while she felt Gary glaring at her as if this mild testimony, which wasn't going to move things one way or the other, was the most heinous crime she could ever have committed.

She was also worrying what Nicole might do if Gary got angry enough to sic her on. To please Gary, there was nothing at which Nicole would stop, Brenda had come to believe.

2

Wootton rested the case for the State. John Woods now testified for Gary.

MR. SNYDER   If you had an individual who was a psychopathic personality, would that person have the same capacity to appreciate the wrongfulness of conduct . . . as a quote-unquote "normal person" would have? . . .

DR. WOODS   He would have the capacity but would most likely not choose to.

MR. SNYDER   And if you added at that point alcohol and medication such as Fiorinal, would that increase or decrease this person's capacity to appreciate and to understand the wrongfulness of his conduct?

DR. WOODS   Hypothetically, it would impair his judgment and would loosen the controls on a person that already has very poor control of himself. . . .

MR. SNYDER   Dr. Woods, did the defendant relate to you any childhood experiences which were particularly considered in the course of your evaluation?

DR. WOODS   Yes. He related some childhood experiences, and I would say that I would think that some people might think that they were peculiar.

MR. SNYDER   For example, would you give us an example of one of those?

DR. WOODS   The one that comes to mind was the experience in which he would walk out on a train trestle and wait for a train to come, and then he'd race to the end of the train trestle to see if he could beat the train before the train would knock him off the train trestle into the gorge below.

Wootton was next:

MR. WOOTTON   Sir, you prepared and filed in the Court on September 2nd of 1976 a summary of your report.

DR. WOODS   Yes, sir.

MR. WOOTTON   Was it an accurate summary, in fact, of your analysis of this man?

DR. WOODS   Yes, sir.

MR. WOOTTON   Part of that report indicated that, I'm reading from it: "We do not find him to be psychotic or 'insane.' We can find no evidence of organic neurological disease, disturbed thought processes, altered perception of reality, inappropriate affect or mood, or lack of insight. . . . We do not feel that he was mentally ill at the time of the alleged acts. We find that at the time of the alleged act he had the capacity to appreciate the wrongfulness of the act and to conform his behavior to the requirements of the law. We have carefully considered his voluntary use of alcohol, medication (Fiorinal) at the time of the act and do not feel that this altered his responsibility." Is that still your opinion?

DR. WOODS   Yes, sir.

MR. WOOTTON   You go on to say: "We have likewise considered his alleged partial amnesia for the alleged event on 7/20/76 and feel that it is too circumspect and convenient to be valid." Is that still your opinion?

DR. WOODS   Yes, sir.

MR. WOOTTON   Thank you. That's all.

The defense had one special possibility. It was to call Gerald Nielsen to the stand. In the notes from which Nielsen had read at the

Preliminary Hearing was testimony that Gary had said, "I really feel ba*," and there had been tears in his eyes. "I hope they execute me for it," he had said to Nielsen. "I deserve to die." Such contrition might influence the Jury.

Still, they did not think long or hard of calling Nielsen. He knew too much. Nielsen could testify to how Gary had abused the clemency of police officers, probation officers, and judges. Then Wootton could make the point that Gilmore's repentance came after he was caught. On balance, it was too great a risk. The defense, therefore, brought Gary to the stand. His best chance today would come with his own testimony.

3

MR. SNYDER   Mr. Gilmore, did you kill Benny Bushnell?

MR. GILMORE   Yes, I guess I did.

MR. SNYDER   Did you intend to kill Mr. Bushnell at the time that you went to the City Center Motel?

MR. GILMORE   No.

MR. SNYDER   Why did you kill Benny Bushnell?

MR. GILMORE   I don't know.

MR. SNYDER   Can you tell the Jury how you felt at the time these events were occurring?

MR. GILMORE   I don't know. Just how I felt, I don't know for sure.

MR. SNYDER   Go ahead.

MR. GILMORE   Well, I felt like there was no way that what happened could have been avoided, that there was no other choice or chance for Mr. Bushnell. It was just something that, you know, couldn't be stopped.

MR. SNYDER   Do you feel like you had control of yourself or your actions?

MR. GILMORE   No, I don't.

MR. SNYDER   Do you feel like— Well, let me ask you this: Do you know why you killed Benny Bushnell?

MR. GILMORE   No.

MR. SNYDER Did you need the money?

MR. GILMORE No.

MR. SNYDER How did you feel at the time?

MR. GILMORE I felt like I was watching a movie or, you know, somebody else was perhaps doing this, and I was watching them doing it. . . .

MR. SNYDER Do you feel like you were seeing someone else do it?

MR. GILMORE A little, I guess. I don't really know. I can't recall that clearly. There were spots that night that I don't recall at all. Some of it is sharp and some of it is totally blank.

MR. SNYDER Mr. Gilmore, do you recall a childhood experience such as the one that Dr. Woods described, standing in the middle of a railroad track with a train coming towards you and then you would run across a trestle to beat the train?

MR. GILMORE Yes. I didn't tell him that to be traumatic or anything. I was trying to give him a comparison to the urge and the impulse that I felt on the night of July 20th. I sometimes feel I have to do things and seems like there's no other chance or choice.

MR. SNYDER I see. And is that similar to the way you felt on the night of July 20, 1976.

MR. GILMORE Similar. Very similar. Yeah, it would be. Sometimes I would feel an urge to do something, and I would try to put it off, and the urge would become stronger until it was irresistible. And that's the way I felt on the night of July 20th.

MR. SNYDER Felt like you had no control over what you did?

MR. GILMORE Yes.

It was possible his testimony had helped. They had put him on the stand in the hope he might say he was sorry and appear remorseful, or at least would lead the Jury away from the idea that he was a heartless animal. He had hardly accomplished that task, but maybe he had served himself. Maybe. He had been calm on the stand, probably too calm, too solemn, even a little remote. Certainly too judicious. He might just as well have been one of many experts at this trial. Snyder gave him over to Wootton.

The transformation was abrupt. It was as if Gilmore would never forgive Wootton for trying to keep Nicole out of the courtroom. Hostility came back with every speech.

"How did you kill him?" Wootton began.

"Shot him," said Gilmore.

"Tell me about it," said Wootton, "tell me what you did."

"I shot him," said Gilmore with contempt for the question and the man who would ask such a question.

MR. WOOTTON   Did you lay him down on the floor?

MR. GILMORE   Not with my own hands, no.

MR. WOOTTON   Did you tell him to get down on the floor?

MR. GILMORE   Yes, I guess I did.

MR. WOOTTON   Face down?

MR. GILMORE   No, I don't know if I went into all that much detail, Wootton.

MR. WOOTTON   Did he lay down face down?

MR. GILMORE   He laid down on the floor.

MR. WOOTTON   Did you put the gun up against his head?

MR. GILMORE   I suppose I did.

MR. WOOTTON   Did you pull the trigger?

MR. GILMORE   Yeah.

MR. WOOTTON   Then what did you do?

MR. GILMORE   I left.

MR. WOOTTON   Did you take the cash box with you?

MR. GILMORE   I don't recall taking the cash box with me.

MR. WOOTTON   But you saw it in the courtroom, didn't you?

MR. GILMORE   Yes, I saw what you said was the cash box sitting there.

MR. WOOTTON   You don't ever remember seeing that before?

MR. GILMORE   No.

MR. WOOTTON   Did you take his money?

MR. GILMORE   I don't recall that either.

MR. WOOTTON   Do you remember taking any money?

MR. GILMORE   I don't recall that either, I said.

MR. WOOTTON   Do you remember having some money on you when you were arrested later that night?

MR. GILMORE   I always had money on me.

MR. WOOTTON   How much did you have on you?

MR. GILMORE   I don't know.

MR. WOOTTON   You don't have any idea?

MR. GILMORE   I don't have a bank account. I always just carry my money in my pocket.

MR. WOOTTON   You don't know where it came from?

MR. GILMORE   Well, I got paid Friday. That wasn't too long before that.

MR. WOOTTON   You said you were pushed out of shape that night over a personal matter. Why don't you tell us about that?

MR. GILMORE   I'd rather not.

MR. WOOTTON   Are you refusing?

MR. GILMORE   Right.

MR. WOOTTON   Even if the Court tells you that you have to, you won't?

MR. GILMORE   Right.

Walking away, Wootton thought Gilmore had certainly been damaging to his own chances. He had come across as very cold. Wootton wanted to be objective, but he was feeling pretty good. He thought his cross-examination had been very effective, particularly that first question, "How did you kill him?" and the answer, "I shot him." No remorse at all. Not the smartest way to fight for your life.

Wootton took another look at the Jury now and knew he'd be surprised if Gilmore didn't get death. Wootton had been watching that Jury all the way, and while they had not been looking at Gilmore before he testified, which to Wootton meant they felt uneasy at sitting in judgment on him, they were now staring at him like crazy, almost stunned, particularly one of the two women Wootton had selected to work on all through the case.

In talking to a Jury, Wootton's strategy was to pick one member who was strong and intelligent and one who, in his opinion, wasn't. You tried to present your case in story form to the juror who was not intelligent, whereas you argued the contradictions before the one who was. This latter lady was now really watching Gilmore. The expression on her face was all Wootton could have desired. It said: "You are as bad as the prosecutor says you are."

4

After that cross-examination, Wootton was careful not to make his summation too long.

"Benny Bushnell did not deserve to die," Wootton told them, "and it's hard for me to get across to you the real grief that this kind of behavior on the part of Gary Gilmore has caused to Benny's wife and his children."

MR. SNYDER Your Honor, I object to the introduction of that kind of prejudicial statement in the argument by counsel. . . .

THE COURT All right. I'll reserve a ruling on your motion. I'll ask Mr. Wootton to omit any further reference to that matter.

MR. WOOTTON Let's look at the kind of man the defendant is. For the last twelve years he's been in prison. All rehabilitation attempts apparently have been a total dismal complete failure. Now if you can't rehabilitate somebody in twelve years, can you expect to ever rehabilitate them at all? He tells you he killed Benny. He tells you he doesn't know why. He tells you how. He told him to lay down on the floor, put a gun to his head and he pulled the trigger. That's pretty cold-blooded. Now he's been convicted on two prior occasions of robbery. He served time for those. And he's learned something because of that time. Do you know what it is? He's going to kill his victims. Now that's smart. If you are going to make your living as a robber, that just makes sense, because a dead victim's not going to identify you. He'd have gotten away with this most likely free and clear except for some dumb bad luck. He accidentally shot himself. Those things happen, I suppose, when you have been drinking a little bit, and fooling around with guns. Now he's also got a history of escape, three times from some sort of Reform School and once from the Oregon State Penitentiary. Now what does that tell you? If you people tell us lock Gary Gilmore up for life, whatever that means, we can't guarantee it. We cannot guarantee that he won't escape again. He's got a history of it. He's apparently pretty good at it. If he's ever free again, nobody who ever comes in contact with him is going to be safe, if they happen to have something that he happens to want. Now he's got a history of violence in the prison. Even the other prisoners, if you tell us to send him to prison, cannot be guaranteed safety from his behavior. What then is the point at this time of allowing him to continue to live? Rehabilitation is hopeless. He's a danger if he escapes, he's a danger if he doesn't. Obviously, nothing can be done to save this man at this point. He's an extremely high escape risk. He's an extreme danger to anybody. Without even considering all these factors, however, I submit to you this: for what he did to Benny Bushnell and the position that he's put Bushnell's wife in, he has forfeited his right to continue to live any longer and he should be executed, and I recommend that to you.

Wootton sat down, and Snyder came toward the Jury to give his final remarks. He spoke with considerable emotion.

MR. SNYDER I suppose that nobody feels worse about what happened to Ben Bushnell and to his family than I do. This has been a very difficult case for me personally to even try. I think that it puts the Jury in a position that I would not want to be in, because in spite of the fact that this type of crime was committed in this particular case, what we are dealing with here is human life. Mr. Gilmore is a person, too. And although Mr. Gilmore has a history of prior conduct which hopefully we can all learn something from and which hopefully none of us will have to come in contact with again, he is a person and, in my opinion, he has a right to his life. I don't think there's anything more personal to any individual than his right to live. And you are in the position at this point where you have to decide whether to take that life from Gary Gilmore or whether to let him live. I don't excuse what Mr. Gilmore did, I don't even pretend to try to explain it, but I think he does have the right to live and I would ask that you give him that opportunity. I think the sum of what Mr. Wootton says is well taken. I think that Mr. Gilmore's history is certainly something that he's not to be proud of. I don't think any of us are. . . . Mr. Gilmore does have something maybe he can't cope with, but it's not something that we ought to take his life for. . . . Mr. Gilmore is the type of person that needs treatment more than he does to be killed. He needs, I think, to be punished for what he does, and the law provides for that by a term of life imprisonment. And I don't think that Mr. Wootton's fears about rehabilitation or that if he ever gets out again, that type of thing, are founded. Mr. Gilmore's thirty-six years old.

MR. GILMORE Thirty-five.

MR. SNYDER Thirty-five years old. He is going to be incarcerated, if you will, for life. That's a long long time. And though I suppose at some point in the future after many years he may be eligible for parole, that's a long long ways away. I think he deserves the same opportunity really that Benny Bushnell should have had. And I think and I would strongly recommend to the Jury that you award Mr. Gilmore his life. I would point out to you as is indicated in the Instructions that in order to impose the death penalty it does require a unanimous vote of all twelve of you. If one of you does not vote to impose the death penalty, then the sentence will be life imprisonment and will be imposed by the Court as such. I would ask each of you to search your own conscience and to impose in this case life imprisonment.

THE COURT Mr. Esplin, do you care to make any comments?

MR. ESPLIN I think Mr. Snyder has accurately portrayed my feelings.

Now, Judge Bullock asked the defendant if there was anything he would like to say to the Jury. It would be his last opportunity to speak of repentance.

Gilmore replied, "Well, I am finally glad to see that the Jury is looking at me." When this remark was received in silence, he added, "No, I have nothing to say."

"Is that all?" the Judge asked.

"That's all."

5

Now that the Mitigation Hearing was over and the Jury had gone to the jury room, Vern and Ida went outside and milled around the courthouse with other people waiting for the verdict. They had not planned to be in Court at all, but Gary had called Ida days ago and asked her to be there, and after that, nothing could have kept them away.

Inside the courtroom, Mike Esplin arranged with the guards for Nicole to be able to sit near Gary. That way, he was able to talk to her across the railing. While they waited, they joked. They even held hands. It impressed Mike Esplin. The fellow was waiting to find out whether he was going to be executed or not, yet he was acting like a cavalier.

Craig Snyder got curious what Gary and Nicole might be talking about, and got near enough to hear Nicole say, "My mother wants you to paint her a picture." "Oh," said Gary, "I didn't think your mother really liked me." "Well," replied Nicole, "she doesn't. She just wants it so she can say, 'Gary Gilmore painted that picture.'" Gary laughed. Craig couldn't get over it. To have Nicole near seemed more important to Gary than anything in the trial. He looked so happy.

A little later, he wanted to go to the bathroom, and so the two guards got up with him, and they filed off slowly, Gary in lockstep, the shackles keeping his feet from moving quickly. Brenda came up. "Gary," she said, "don't be such a sore-ass. Just because I turned you in, and testified against you, is no reason to be mad, is it?" He arched his neck and looked down at her. It was awful to see him chained. She reached out and touched his handcuffs tenderly, but he pulled his hand back, and gave her a look that ate at her for a long time and never stopped bothering her.

For weeks to come, she would be standing at the sink doing the dishes, and she would start to cry. Johnny would walk over and put his arm around her and say, Honey, try not to think about it so much. All she could see was Gary behind bars again, deeper than he'd ever been.

6

Word came that the verdict was ready, and they all returned to the courtroom. The Jury walked in. The Bailiff read the verdict. It was Death. The Jury was polled. In turn, each one of the twelve said: Yes, and Gary looked across at Vern and Ida and shrugged. When the

Judge asked him, "Do you have an election as to the mode of death?" Gary said, "I prefer to be shot."

Then Judge Bullock replied, "Very well, that will be the order." The sentence was set for Monday, November 15, at eight o'clock in the morning of this year, and Gary Gilmore would be remanded to the Sheriff of Utah County for delivery to the Warden of Utah State Prison.

The news lived in the air of the courtroom. It was as if there had been one kind of existence in the room, and now there was another: a man was going to be executed. It was real but it was not comprehensible. The man was standing there.

Gilmore chose this moment to speak to Noall Wootton. This was the first time he had addressed him in weeks. Gary looked over calmly, and said, "Wootton, everybody around here looks like they're crazy. Everybody but me." Wootton looked back and thought, "Yes, at this moment, everybody could be crazy, except Gary."

Noall had this bothersome feeling now. It was in the impression he had had all the way that Gilmore was more intelligent than himself. Wootton knew damned well that Gilmore was more educated. Self-educated, but better educated. "Jesus Almighty," Wootton said to himself, "the system has really failed with this man, just miserably failed."

After that, people were going out and Nicole was crying in the corridor, and Nicole and Ida met, and they embraced, and broke down, and Nicole said, "Don't worry, everything is going to be all right." Vern was walking around in a state of shock. He had expected it all, but he was shocked.

A girl, a young reporter, came up to Gary and asked, "Do you have any comments?" He said, "No, not particularly." She said, "Do you think everything was fair? Is there anything you'd like to say?" Gary said, "Well, I'd like to ask you a question." She said, "What's that?" He said, "Who the hell won the World Series?"

7

The State Patrolman who would escort Gary back to jail and then take him up to the prison was named Jerry Scott, and he was a big, good-looking man. He had a personality clash with Gary right from the start.

When he went into the courtroom to pick him up, Gilmore didn't have leg shackles on, or handcuffs, so Scott knelt and attached the stuff, and asked him to stand so the restraining belt could be locked. Scott thought it was easier and more comfortable for the prisoner if you could put on a restraining belt and hook the handcuffs through the hole in front rather than pinion a man with his arms behind his back. But when Gary stood up, he said, "You've got the leg irons too tight. I'm not going anywhere."

Jerry Scott reached down. He could move the irons back and forth a little, so he knew they were not binding. "Gary," he said, "they're okay." At which point, Gilmore replied, "Either get those shackles off me, or you're going to carry me out."

Scott said, "I'm not carrying you anywhere. I'll drag you out." Scott was disgusted. Everybody around Gilmore had been saying Yes, Sir, and No, Sir, as if committing the murder made him a special person. You had to be firm with prisoners was one thing Scott had decided a long time ago, and here was everybody hovering over backwards to be extra nice to this fellow. Maybe it was because he was always staring you right in the eye like he was innocent or something.

Gilmore was really starting to act up now and using profanities in the courtroom. Scott didn't want to fight him all the way down the stairs and into the elevator with everybody watching, so he loosened the cuffs and shackles after all. Gilmore complained again, and now Scott had them really loose, and Gilmore was still complaining. Scott got suspicious, especially when Gilmore repeated, "You're going to have to carry me out of here."

"I'm not loosening them any further," Scott said. "Just get your ass in gear. We're going down whether you like it or not, and if you don't, I'll drag you, but I won't carry you. The decision," Scott said, "is up to you."

At this point, Gilmore started walking out with him. They had to go real slow, because he only had about ten inches of movement with the leg shackles on, and Gilmore was mad all the way down to the car, and all the way across Center Street to the jail. Scott put Gary in the front seat next to himself and had two deputies in the back. After they arrived, they took off the leg shackles, and the handcuffs, and brought Gilmore to his cell and listened to him talk to his cellmate while he gathered his personal items for transport up to Utah State Prison.

Well, they gave me the death penalty, Gilmore said to his cellmate. He shook his head, and added, "You know, I'm going to eat first." His cellmate said he had a money order which he hadn't cashed yet, and he got $5 from one of the guards in exchange for it and gave it to Gary who said, "You're too much. I'll never be able to repay you." "It ain't no big thing," said the cellmate. "Listen, do me a favor," said Gilmore, "get these books back to the Provo Library, so Nicole won't get into any trouble. They're checked out in her name." "No sweat," said the cellmate. Then as Scott watched, Gilmore handed him a blue western shirt and said, "Nicole made this for me," and then he handed over a Schick Ejectable Razor and said, "I want you to have this as a remembrance." They shook hands and wished one another good luck, and the jailer undid the lock and chain on the door and Gary walked out, turned around with his thumb to his nose and wiggled his fingers. The cellmate did the same. Sheriff Cahoon came by and shook hands with Gary.

Scott took him down the corridor, and made him strip for a shakedown. That got Gilmore upset all over again. He was being very protective about his person and his personal items. This last was just a bunch of letters and some books, but he wouldn't let them out of his sight and acted like the skin shake was a personal attack. Scott didn't feel that way at all. The fellow had just been given the death sentence. There had to be tight security.

Once he was stripped, they ran their fingers through his hair to make sure he hadn't glued anything in there. His hair was long enough to hide a nail file. They checked behind the ear lobes, and made him hold his arms high, checked through the hair under his armpits and in the navel. They had to lift up his testicles to see if there was something taped under his sac and then had him bend over and spread his cheeks to make sure nothing was extending from the rectum area. Policy was not to give finger waves down there anymore. Finally they checked the bottoms of his feet to make sure something wasn't being held between the toes. All the while, Gilmore kept using every four-letter word he could find.

Then they put the shackles back, and Scott made sure they were secure. Jerry Scott said, "Gary, I don't like you, and you don't like me, but let's forget that. I'm going to take you to State Prison and I don't want you trying to get away. Deputy Fox is going to be sitting right behind, and if you give any trouble, or make any fast movements, or any aggressive movements, he's going to snap your neck, snap it." Even after a skin search, you never knew what a prisoner could hide. A flat bobby pin could be slipped up under the cuffs and get them loose. Why you could open handcuffs with the refill from a ball-point pen if you knew how to do it. So, there was always a lot to worry in moving a prisoner. Scott told him to just sit in the car and they would go straight to prison and it would be all right.

He moved in his slow shackle-step out of the jail and into the vehicle, and sitting the same way as before, they took off. For protection, Jerry Scott had arranged to have two detectives follow in another car three hundred yards behind. They would watch for any driver who might pull in behind the lead car to commence an escape plan. They were also watching for any vehicle driven by a kook who might decide he wanted to assassinate Gilmore.

Anyway, the trip went quietly. Gilmore said something about how the air felt good and the scenery did look good out there in the evening, and Scott answered, "Yeah, the weather is fine." Gilmore took a real deep breath and said, "Can I have my window down a little bit?" Scott said, "Sure," and then said over his shoulder to the officer behind him, "Lee, I'm going to bend over and open his window some." So Deputy Fox leaned forward to cover as Scott leaned over with one hand and rolled it down. That seemed to cool Gilmore. He didn't say any more for the rest of the way . . . but he also seemed to relax.

When they got to the State Prison, the officer in charge ushered them through different gates into the Maximum Security area. There they took the foot braces off, and the shackles, and the handcuffs, and shook him down again, and took him to his cell, and he never said another word. Scott didn't say good-bye. He didn't want to agitate him, and such an attempt might seem like heckling. Outside the prison, night had come, and the ridge of the mountain came down to the Interstate like a big dark animal laying out its paw.

That night, Mikal Gilmore, Gary's youngest brother, received a phone call from Bessie. She told him that Gary received the death penalty. "Mother," Mikal said, "they haven't executed anybody in this country for ten years, and they aren't about to start with Gary." Still, nausea came up on him as he put down the phone. All he could see for the rest of the night were Gary's eyes.

PART SEVEN

Death Row

CHAPTER 30

The Slammer

1

Soon after high school began in September, another teacher told Grace McGinnis of a story he read in July about a fellow from Portland, arrested for killing two men in Utah. The name, as he recollected, was Gilmore. Didn't she have a friend by that name? Grace really didn't want to hear more. Certain kinds of bad news were like mysterious lumps that went away if you paid no attention.

Now, the story was in the Portland papers again. The killer certainly was Gary Gilmore, and he had been sentenced to death in Provo, Utah. Grace thought of calling Bessie. It would be the first phone call in years. But she could hear the conversation before it took place.

"I cannot believe," Bessie would say, "that the Gary I know, killed those two young men. He couldn't have. He had a natural sweetness to him."

"Yes," Grace would say, "he really did."

"I never saw that kind of cruelty in Gary," Bessie would say, and Grace would again agree, and know she was not telling the truth. Gary had never done anything cruel to her, certainly not, but she had seen something awful come into him after his Prolixin treatments, a personality change so drastic that Grace could honestly say she didn't know the man named Gary Gilmore who existed after taking it. It was as if something obscene had come into his mind. She was not very surprised he had killed two people. After the Prolixin, she had always been a little afraid of him.

Grace's hand was on the phone that day, but she could not call Bessie, not yet. "I am a coward," said Grace to herself, "I am a devout coward," and thought of all of them, of Bessie in her trailer, and Frank Sr., dead before she ever met him, but known to her by each and every one of Bessie's stories, and Bessie's sons, Frank Jr., who never said a word, and Gaylen, who had almost died in Grace's car, and Mikal, and Gary. A feeling of love, and misery, and anger hot as bile, plus all the woe Grace could carry in her big body, came flooding down, memories as sad as rue, and the horror that told her once to step out of Bessie's life came back, and she thought of Bessie in her trailer.

2

Mikal was the first Gilmore that Grace met. In the school year of '67–'68, she had him as a senior in Creative Writing, and he was one of the best students she ever had. Grace's maiden name was Gilmore, Grace Gilmore McGinnis, although when she and Bessie traced it out, there was no relation, but names aside, Grace was impressed with a long, intelligent conversation she had with Mikal about Truman Capote. She had assigned In Cold Blood to the class. Mikal showed a lot of insight in talking about that book.

The first time she and Mikal became close, however, was when Grace was asked to do a World Affairs Council Program for local Channel 8, and pick four students she thought could handle a topic like the Chinese Cultural Revolution. She chose Mikal first.

At that time, his hair was long. Milwaukie, a working-class suburb of Portland, had its share of red-necks among the teachers, and they thought no student with long hair ought to represent the school on a television program. Grace went to the principal and asked for a faculty meeting to decide the issue. She accused a few teachers of being absolutely warped. She knew she'd never win any contests for being the slenderest middle-aged lady in town, but Grace could use her height and her bulk and her voice — which was not small — to get a little liberal scorn across. Mikal went on the television program. He performed beautifully.

Once in a while, Grace had a student she didn't have to teach at, as she would put it, but could teach to. Mikal was that kind of student. Grace would look up things she thought would take his interest. She would frankly confess to a bit of prejudice in his favor. It didn't seem exceptional to her, therefore, that he came to her one day and said his mother was going to lose her home for back taxes, and he didn't know anybody to go to for advice. Would she talk to them? Grace went over to Oakhill Road one Saturday and her first thought when she saw the house with the circle driveway was, "My God, this place is haunted." Something about the vegetation in the back creeping up.

It was just a first impression, but she had been interested in psychic phenomena for quite a while, so the thought caused no great agitation. Grace just went in to a large dark living room, furnished sparsely in what Grace called Portland Gothic. A collection of nice postwar Philippine mahogany pieces.

3

Bessie was slight, with dark gray hair tied back in a bun to show the most interesting face, the kind you wanted to know more about. She looked like a woman who, at the least, would have made an excellent housemother in a sorority. But then Grace thought Bessie really belonged in a mansion. She could have been the widow of the president of a utility company who dressed all the way down in grays as if she wouldn't give an inch to money. Grace loved her on sight. All that class and dignity, all that quietly accumulated reserve.

Loved her more when they started to talk. The moment Grace mentioned that her maiden name was Gilmore, it commenced a conversation that went on for three hours. They covered a lot of the universe.

After a while, Bessie got into her problems with the house. Frank had bought it outright, and there was no mortgage, but it was still hard to keep up. He hadn't left insurance and she was earning less than $200 a month working as a bus girl at a tavern called Speed's. She couldn't advance up to waitressing, because she was getting too slow and arthritic. At present, she was in her sixth year of arrears on taxes, and the city was going after her property. She had received a notice they were going to foreclose. Well, she didn't want to lose the house while Mikal was in school. Indeed, she wanted to keep it as the place for her boys to come back to. She wanted them to have the home they had known before they left. So, she was hoping to get the Mormon Church to pay the taxes, and she, in turn, would deed the house to the Church after she died. She hoped they would consider it a worthy investment.

Grace couldn't help her with that. Grace knew little enough about Mormons, and the solution here had to do with the local Bishop and his attitude. So they moved on to other matters. Bessie proved a delightful conversationalist.

She told how at the restaurant where she worked, they only gave her a little time to eat. "We have thirty minutes to order our food from an ornery chef, run to the back and try to get it swallowed. They could see I wasn't finishing, so the chef said, 'I'm going to cut you way down.' 'Please do,' I said, 'I can't eat all you give me unless you give me another thirty minutes to eat it.' Besides, I like," she said, "to leave food on my plate. I cannot clean up a plate. Never have in my entire life. The day I clean a plate will take me right out to the other side. It'll send me home — wherever home is."

Yesterday, Bessie had said to the bus driver, "Do you know there was a dead possum right in front of my gate?" The bus driver said, "Why didn't you pick it up and make stew?" She said, "You know, Glen, I'm never going to speak to you again." He said, "The possum couldn't hurt you if it was dead." She said, "It could me. It might have fleas."

Grace enjoyed her more and more. They talked of how they both disliked synthetic fabrics, yet who could afford wool or cotton or silk anymore? "I just go on year after year with no clothes," said Bess. "Not exactly nude, however — that would be enough to cure the country of sex."

She came to tell Grace about Gary. At Speed's, nobody knew she had a son in the penitentiary. One lady even said, "You are a fortunate person to have lived as long as you have, and haven't had one heartbreak in your entire life."

Grace thought Bessie had a remarkable voice. It was not exactly cultivated or grand, but it sure was unusual. Bette Davis playing a pioneer woman. Grace asked to see a picture of Bessie when young, and thought she was beautiful then. Grace decided that what had rubbed off on Bessie over the years was stoicism.

Their conversation only ended when Bessie had to go to work. She left wearing a white blouse and dark skirt and navy blue sweater. Carried an apron over her arm. She was wearing flats, and did not walk like a woman who had once been told she would make a good ballet dancer. The arthritis was already in her hands and in her knees and ankles.

Grace drove her, and had a cup of coffee, and watched her picking up plates at Speed's. She was appalled that Bess had to do such work.

The woman stayed on her mind. Bess, living in that haunted house, and wanting to keep it. Grace would visit Bess from time to time and talk to her about taxes and the Church. Later, after it was all lost, other stories came out, and Grace would wonder why Bess ever wanted to keep the place. "The house *was* haunted, Grace," she told her once, "No one but me would have stayed so long. If you were to go upstairs, you would have felt it. One night when my husband was very sick, just a few months before he died, he got up and started down the hall to the bathroom and fell down those stairs with a terrible sound. It was almost as if something grabbed him and hurled him to the very bottom. His long years of acrobatic training is all that kept him from getting killed. I screamed as I went past, and I was banging on every one of the boys' doors. 'Get up, your father's fallen down.' They came running out, and Frank Jr. picked him up and carried him back. Then, after Frank Sr. died, I and Mikal got ready to go to bed one night, and in the hallway on the ground floor, between the bedroom and the kitchen, I heard the worst noise ever in my life. It was a frightening place to live, really."

Of course, Grace only heard those stories after Mikal was in college, and Bess was in the trailer she had bought with a little help from the Church and the sale of her Philippine mahogany furniture.

4

Bessie mentioned that on Sunday, the only day she was free from work, there was no round-trip bus service between Portland and Salem. Grace said, "There's no reason why I can't take you over to the prison." The visits were only twice a month and Grace's kids were married. She had no heavy family obligations. Besides, Grace loved to read. She took along a book to enjoy in the car while waiting through the visit, and they had a fine time driving there and back, and talked about witches. Bessie said she was only a step away from being a creature of the woods. She respected witches, she said, and didn't want to be in their powers. "Do you know," she said, "I'm frightened of riding in a car next to someone who has dealings with them, because I believe they can wreck your car. One has to be on guard against every strong and evil vibration that comes along."

Grace sat in the car for a couple of hours that day and read her book while Bessie was inside the prison. Afterward, Bessie said that Gary had put Grace's name on the visiting list. Grace had no particular interest in meeting him, but thought, Well, if Bessie wants this, okay.

The visits went on for two years. They went almost every other week. Sometimes they would get there and the authorities would say, You can't see him today. He is in the pokey, all locked up. They would never tell Bess before she came.

The first time that Grace went into the prison itself, she was overcome with the power of the echoes. Otherwise, it was not as bad as prisons she had seen in movies. There was a big gray stone wall around it, and that was depressing enough, but the place was situated casually enough across a field from a heavy-trafficked road on the edge of Salem, and the administration building was only two stories high. Its entrance was through a small door. The reception room looked like the shabby lobby of a small factory or a supply-parts house. There was a big circular desk for information, and on the walls were paintings of deer and horses done by convicts. There was also a sliding barred gate to a small room with a second gate on the other side. Given word, the visitors would all crowd into this space, then the gate behind them would slam, there would be a pause, and the gate in front would open. Those gates would send out echoes. Down the long stone walls those echoes went out as loud as boxcars slamming into one another. Then everybody would pass into the visiting room.

That looked like a conference area for PTA meetings at the high school. Lots of pale orange, pale blue, pale yellow and pale green stack-up plastic chairs were placed around cheap blond wood tables. Cigarette machines were along the wall, Coke machines, candy machines. Just a guard or two, and thirty or forty people talking across the tables, often two or three visitors for each convict.

Grace saw all kinds of visitors. Sad working-class fathers and mothers, harried-looking wives with babies on their arms, a little curd on the corner of the babies' mouths. A considerable number of very fat women waddled in through the gates. They were usually having a heavyweight romance with a very thin convict. A few young well-built girls would be there with a look Grace came to recognize. They wore a lot of lipstick and had the look of belonging to a special culture. They obviously had boy friends in the prison, and Grace came to learn from Gary that a lot of them also had boy friends on the outside who had been in prison, were now out, and would doubtless soon be back. It was perfectly possible those girls were more in love with the man they were visiting here than the fellow they were living with outside.

There were also the prisoners. Some looked like the downtrodden, to say the least. They were simpleminded, or misshapen in body or posture, furtive, or stolid, or cowed, or stupid. They were men who looked like they had grown up in barnyards and had the logic of louts.

Then there were men who carried themselves as if they were true figures of interest. They looked as if they belonged to an exclusive society. They would have a little smile on their faces as if they knew more about life, living, and the world, than the people who came to visit. They were usually lithe in appearance or downright powerful. Moved with the skill of tightrope walkers. They were arrogant as hell in the mocking way they had of looking at visitors and tourists. It was as if they were accustomed to being looked at, and were worth being looked at. They would keep such expressions on their faces until they sat down with their visitors. Then other looks might appear. Half an hour later, one could see vulnerability, or tenderness, or just plain misery.

Later, when she got to know Gary better, he explained carefully that there were two kinds of prisoners: inmates and convicts. The way he said it indicated that the second category was the superior one and he belonged to it. Grace would have put him there herself. He wore his clothes that way. Very neat in his pale blue shirt and light blue prison dungarees. Convicts, as opposed to inmates, wore their shirts as if they were tailored. After a while, the difference in the two groups was apparent. She could compare it to a high school where all the class leaders, athletes, and attractive kids always formed an in-group. Then there was the general population.

Gary, however, was never arrogant around his mother. He would talk to her with great seriousness. They would be so deep in their conversation that Grace would look around the room so as not to be too much on top of them. Then Bessie or Gary would say something funny. They would both laugh in absolute merriment. They laughed an awful lot in that visiting room.

He always devoted a few minutes to Grace. He would be gentle in his talk, but with a touch of irony. Would always want to know which spook Grace had met in her thoughts this week, and then they would talk about spooks. He would also ask Grace's opinion of the books he was reading. The one he liked most was *The Ginger Man* by J. P. Donleavy. Once she bought Gary a subscription to *Art Today*. She thought his pictures of children were worthy of superlatives.

The only time she saw him get angry was on the day Bessie told him she had definitely lost the house. He was so angry at the Mormon Church that even the recollection of his wrath years later made

Grace think, "I'll bet a nickel he knew those boys were Mormon before he killed them."

He would also ask how Mikal was getting along in college. Mikal the Mysterious, he would call him, because he never came to visit. Grace could hear him say, "I just don't know Gary," and that was true, considering that Mikal had only been four years old when his brother went to Reform School. Grace also thought Mikal's long hair might have something to do with it. He would be uncomfortable in that visiting room under the eyes of the convicts.

At such times, Bessie would divert Gary with funny stories of his father. It was impossible not to recognize that the father and son never got along, but now, somehow, it was funny stories about Frank Sr. that would make Gary laugh the most.

5

Frank had been bragging of the somersault he used to do off the top of some piled-up chairs into the orchestra pit, and once in Denver, Frank decided to show her. Bess told him she didn't think he should try it. He was too drunk. "I've done this all my life," he told her, "I know how." He got up, and the chairs fell, and he knocked the wind out of himself so badly she thought he was dead. "I kept trying to give him mouth-to-mouth whatever-you-call-it."

Or the time with the sheep. Gaylen had a black sheep, and Mikal cried, "I want one." What Mikal wanted, Mikal got. "Sure, sure," she said, "sheep, horse, cow, whatever, get it for the kid." Frank came back from the stockyards with a white sheep who had a black face and pulled it out of the back of the station wagon. Bess was angry. She didn't like animals, and the back of the car would have to be cleaned. That damned sheep.

The lady next door had three yapping dogs. As Frank came around the corner, the sheep turned unmanageable. All the boys began to scream, "Help Father get the sheep in the pen." It went on for a half hour. Bess stayed up on the porch. She cried out, "Twist his tail, Frank, and he will go right ahead of you," but Frank couldn't hear what she was saying, and told Gaylen, "Kick the damned thing in the ass." Gaylen would go to launch his foot, the sheep would turn around and get kicked in the face. Frank would say, "Don't you know the goddamn face from the butt?"

All at once the animal turned. Frank got his foot caught in the rope, fell, and the sheep began to drag him. That sheep laid a slide of green diarrhea, while Frank was pulled across the lawn, the sidewalk, and the gravel in the shoulder of the road. Before they got Frank up, he had one sore bottom. "Look at me," he said, brushing himself, "grass all over."

"Frank," Bessie said, "it isn't grass."

Between her sobs of laughter, she would say, "That was the one funniest thing I ever watched."

"Remember," said Gary, "how Dad was the worst driver in the world?" He turned to Grace. "My father caused more wrecks. When people would start honking at him, he'd put his thumb to his nose. Or he'd let go of the steering wheel and wiggle all of his fingers next to his ears like Bullwinkle the Moose. They'd go crazy till he put his hands back on the wheel. We kids used to think he was hot stuff. We'd wiggle our fingers at the other cars, too."

After the laughter, in all the thought that followed on memories, Gary said, "I wish Dad was still alive. He would have gotten me out of here years ago."

"I know that, Gary," Bessie said, "but I can't get you out. I don't have the money and the know-how. I don't have the bearing your father had."

"Well," said Gary, "I have laid awake a lot of nights wishing my dad was still here."

"They were two bulls locking horns," Bessie said to Grace on the way home, "but, Gary is right. His dad would never have let him stay in prison. Frank would have known the people to see and what to say. I just grew up on a stupid farm back in stupid Utah. All I ever knew was cows, pigs, chickens, goats, horses, and sheep, so I'm no use to Gary." She sighed. "I just wish Frank had gotten closer to that boy while he was living."

They would take the drive forward and back, forty miles each way, every other Sunday, and the echoes of the past would reverberate like the slamming of the steel doors. Bessie had a fund of stories and passed them out like confections. It was as if she naturally preferred tasty little stories to the depth of those echoes that came up from the past.

6

She explained to Grace how she and Frank had been traveling through Texas by bus when Gary was born on an overnight stop at the Burleson Hotel in McCamey. They couldn't move until he was six weeks old. Enough to make him think of himself as a Texan forever.

"Did you like to travel with two babies?" asked Grace.

No, she didn't, but her attitude remained: she would love Frank as he was. Not try to change him. So they traveled. She kept waiting for trouble.

In Colorado, Frank got arrested for passing a bad check and was sentenced to three years. Bessie went back to Provo and waited. There was no money to go anywhere else.

She thought it was the end of everything. Her family was not friendly. She had been away a couple of years and came back with two kids and a husband in jail. But she waited. She never thought of another man. It was a long wait, but it wasn't the end. Frank got out in eighteen months and took her to California and worked in a defense plant and then they traveled again. By the time the boys were six and seven and Gaylen was born, she managed to talk Frank into buying a house on the outskirts of Portland. That was a lot better than letting the boys sleep nights in bus depots and feast on hot dogs.

Frank started rewriting the Building Code digests of cities like Portland and Seattle and Tacoma. He would put them into clear language so that by buying his manual, people could understand how to build or renovate their house in accordance with the city codes. Then he sold advertising for the manuals. Over the years it got profitable. There was a time when Frank had checks rolling in every day.

The boys went to Our Lady of Sorrows parochial school, and Gary thought he'd be a priest. Bess loved their house on Crystal Springs Boulevard. It was small but she did her best cooking and sewing there. Then Frank had to move to Salt Lake for a year. That was the time, she told Grace, when an apparition attached itself to Gary.

She blamed it on the house in which they lived. Even Frank agreed it was haunted, and he was not a man partial to such ideas, but one time they were in the bedroom feeding Mikal, who had just been born, and they could hear somebody talking and laughing in the kitchen. When they ran down, nobody was there.

Then a flood came, and the safety valve in the basement heater failed to turn off after the fire went out. Gas started bubbling up along the walls. Frank said, "That's it. We're getting out." It was as if they saw a picture of themselves in the newspapers. Father, Mother, Four Sons Dead.

She had been happy to say good-bye to the house, but not to her neighbor, Mrs. Cohen, who was a sweet old lady. Bess met her because Mrs. Cohen's bedroom window was right across from the boys', and Gary would shoot his water pistol right through the window — *pssst*. Mrs. Cohen talked to him and said: Don't you do this. I'm an old lady, and you shouldn't be doing this. Finally, she said to her brother, Well, I'm going to tell his folks. Mrs. Cohen's brother said, "They're Gentiles. Stay away." She said, "I'm going over." When visited with the complaint, Frank said, "I can tell you, they will never do it again." At that point, Mrs. Cohen made him promise he wouldn't spank the boys. The kids fell in love with her for that, and Mrs. Cohen stayed over at their house for so long on this visit her brother came over. "He thought we'd killed her," said Bess, "and put her in the basement. I said, 'No, no, we're too busy to kill people.' Oh, I really liked that lady. She said, 'I'll never forget you. You're my only Gentile friends.' "

The day they left, Mrs. Cohen and she cried as they said good-bye, and Mrs. Cohen said, "You're lucky not to stay in that house. It's an evil house."

7

Frank was never good with the boys again, and Gary certainly changed, and later they would fight all the time.

Back in Portland, Gary used profane language in abundance. It came out of him in a sulfurous streak. It sounded to Bessie as if some foul and abominable demon was just walking out of his mouth. So she started a family game. "You won't have to use such language," she told the boys, "if you have a big vocabulary."

One of them would open the dictionary and pick a word. Then another would give the meaning and spell it. Through the years they developed a knowledge of words to stump their teachers.

She was a lenient mother. If she promised they could go to the show, on Saturday they got to go, even if they had knocked the house down. Their father was the opposite. Tip over a glass of milk, that did it. So they lived under two systems.

Of course, more than half of Frank's business was in Seattle. He would come back only every other weekend to fight with Gary.

It would start over nothing. Shut the door behind you, Frank would say. Shut it yourself, Gary would reply. They would be up and yelling. You could cut the air with a knife. Bess knew the meaning of those words.

Yet the first time Gary got in trouble, Frank was there to bail him out. Hired a private detective a couple of times to prove that Gary hadn't done what Bess knew very well he had done. She spoiled Gary on his good side, and Frank on the bad.

After Gary was caught stealing a car, they put him in Reform School. Once a month Bessie and Frank went to visit, and would picnic on the grass. MacLaren didn't seem any worse from the outside than a couple of private schools she'd seen on her travels, nice red tile roofs and yellow stucco two-story buildings. A large green campus.

He had been a bad boy when he went in; he was a hard young man when he came out. It was like a void had entered the house. His teachers reported that he had no interest in studying. Slept through the days.

At night, Bessie would ask him, "Where are you going?" "Out to find trouble," Gary would reply, "find some trouble."

Once or twice he came back badly beaten up. He had a very bad temper, and it screeched right at you. She just prayed he would learn to curb it. He got so scarred in his fights she couldn't stand it. Came home one night at dawn and collapsed on the doorstep. His eye was almost out of his head. They had to take him to the hospital.

He was twenty years old before he came close to being actually violent with his father. By then Frank was too sick to pursue it. Bess had to ask Gary to leave the house for the night.

8

One year, there were riots in Oregon State, and Gary took part in them, and was interviewed on TV. A girl saw the show, started corresponding, and liked him enough to visit. According to Gary she was 26, her name was Becky and she was very fat. Nonetheless, she wrote beautiful letters. He told Bessie he was going to marry her and adopt her little boy.

Becky, however, had an ulcer, and went into surgery, and came home from the operation, and died.

The prison would not let Gary go to the funeral. He was not a relative. Bessie sent flowers in his name.

Not too long after this, Gary and four other convicts in Isolation slashed their wrists. The next time Grace saw him, he was on Prolixin. Looked as if he had left his body, and come back in the hulk of a stranger. His jaw dropped, his mouth hung open, his eyes were blank as glass. He walked as slowly as a man with shackles on his legs.

Bessie took one look and burst into tears. The visiting room stopped. There wasn't a sound. Prisoners kept calling out, "Hang in there, buddy."

All through that visit, prisoners kept saying, "Steady, boy!" Gary kept trying to talk to Bessie and Grace, but his lips moved like a man with stones in his mouth. Grace could only think of getting Bessie out of there, but she would not leave until they saw an Assistant Warden.

"How could you have done this to my son?" asked Bessie.

He looked unhappy but said Prolixin was the best drug they had found for violent and psychotic people.

Grace wanted to say, "Bullshit." Didn't.

The prison took him off Prolixin, and the symptoms went away, but he was a different man to Grace. There was something in him now she did not trust. His talk turned shabby. His view was nasty. It was as if they were on different islands.

9

Gaylen Gilmore came into Grace's life. Gaylen, whom Bessie had talked about for two years. Gaylen who, of all the boys, wanted most to be a writer. He wrote beautiful poetry, Bessie said. Also wrote checks. When he was 16, he began to drink. Then he would go down to the bank and write a check with her name on it. His downfall, said Bessie, was that he was handsome. In Bessie's mind, she had never seen a more handsome boy. She laughed even more with Gaylen than with Gary.

The worst thing Gaylen ever did was cash a check at Speed's for $100. When it bounced, she said to Speed, "I'll turn over my next check," and he said, "No, it's not your fault." Bessie said, "I have to." When she told Gaylen about the conversation, he got in his car and was gone for five years.

Called from Chicago and said, "Mother, this is the first time I've been away from you at Thanksgiving and I wish I was there." Bess said, "If I send the money, will you come?" Said he would, but he didn't.

Years later, he came back with Janet, his wife, and a bleeding stomach. Bess didn't know that it was not an ulcer. He had been stabbed with an ice pick. Bess was going to take him to Gary for a visit — he hadn't seen Gary for years — but Gaylen said, "I'm hung over." Bessie said, "What did you do to get so drunk last night?" He said it was the anniversary of Harry Houdini's death, and he always celebrated that.

Then one night, close after midnight, Janet called Grace to say that Gaylen was very ill, and had no money for a cab. Could she drive them over to Milwaukie Hospital? Grace did, but Gaylen could not get admitted. He had neither a welfare card nor a doctor.

On the hospital's suggestion, they went on to Oregon City. There, Gaylen was told the same thing again. It was now two in the morning. The next hospital said no. Grace said she would sign for his treatment, whatever it cost, but they said he needed a doctor to admit him. Grace thought: This boy is going to die in the back seat of my car.

At the Medical School, they were told to wait, and my God, they sat there until a quarter after five. Gaylen, in considerable pain, finally stood up and told the women he would wait no longer. Grace said good-bye at the motel. Grace said, Call me if I can help you, and went home thinking they could lay her out next to a basket case and little to choose.

A day later, Grace got a letter from Gary. There was $50 enclosed as partial payment for $100 she had advanced for a new set of teeth, but the rest of the letter was terrifying. His hatred for the prison seemed uncontrollable. He spoke of violence with a gusto she could not comprehend. It was altogether outside every conversation or understanding they had ever had of each other.

At this point, Grace said to herself, "I only have so much energy. I have children and grandchildren. I can't carry this. I am a devout coward."

She called Bessie and said, With all the love in the world, and I will not stop the way I feel for you, I just have to pull out.

Bessie understood. There was no bad-mouthing. Grace just very gently pulled out, and that was it. She had not seen any of them since.

Later, she heard that Gaylen had died, and Bessie took on the costs of two guards' bringing Gary to the funeral. The officers were decent and dressed in regular clothes and stood way back. Nobody knew Gary was in custody. Afterward, Bessie went over personally, and paid the guards while she was thanking them.

CHAPTER 31

Wild Wind Blowing

1

October 7th

Angel Nicole,

I'm at the joint now. Just got here. I seem to be in the hole. A single cell with a fucked up mattress, no pillow and somebody else's dirty paper plates on the floor. . . . They gave me a pair of white coveralls to wear and I hate to wear coveralls. Too tite in the crotch.

October 8th

This morning they brought me a pillow. Wow! I'm shittin in tall cotton now!

I was given a brief rundown on the place by a lieutenant and a caseworker. I asked them about visits and they said that you would be able to see me. Even though we are not legally married you will be able to visit me. One hour a week on Friday morning between 9 and 11 o'clock. Listed you on the visiting form as NICOLE GILMORE (BARRETT) and under "Relationship" I put common law wife — fiancee. I would like you to use my name but of course your identification says Barrett — and they will probably ask you for I.D.

October 9th

I don't know if I've told you of my feelings of the Civil War before — I probably have. You won't be surprised anyway to know that all of my sympathies lie with the South. And its as strong a pull as that I feel for the Emerald Isle.

Right or Wrong, they Believed — toward the end that's all they had to fight on; belief and courage. They were out of supplies — out of food and ammunition and the things it takes to fight a war. But they almost won. They came within a hair of winning that most bloody of wars.

> "When Honest Abe heard the news about your fall,
> The folks thot he'd threw a great victory ball,
> But he asked the band to play Dixie, for you
> Johnny Reb — and for all that you believed —
> You fought all the way Johnny Reb, Johnny Reb,
> You fought all the way."

Oh well, its one of the things in history that appeal to me, like also the Alamo.

What is to become of us Nicole? I know you wonder. And the answer is simply: By love . . . we can become more than the situation.

Nicole my inclination is to let them execute me. If I were to drop the appeals they would be forced to either commute the sentence or carry it out. I don't think they would commute it.

The decision is not really mine alone to make. I cannot ask you to commit suicide. I thot at one time that I could but I can't. If I am executed and you do commit suicide well to be simply honest I guess that is what I would want.

But Im not going to put it on you by asking you to do that.

October 11

I wrote to my mother Friday after she called me here. I have never before spoken to my mother in the way that I talked to her two days ago. Although the feeling between my mom and I runs deep it has always been expressed in surface tones. Anyhow, I told my mom of the love you and I have for each other. I told her that I can't and don't want to explain just what happened that resulted in this. I did tell her that thru a lifetime of lonely frustration I have allowed weak bad habits to develop that have left me somewhat evil. That I don't like being evil and that I desire to not be evil anymore.

Oh, Nicole, there comes a time where a person must have the courage of their convictions. You know I've spent about 18 years of my 35 *locked up. I've hated every moment of it but I've never cried about it. I never will. But I am tired of it, Nicole. I hate the routine, I hate the noise, I hate the guards, I hate the hopelessness it makes me feel, that anything and everything I do is just to pass the time. Prison maybe affects me more than most people. It drains me. Everytime I've been locked up I guess I've felt so hopeless about it that I've allowed myself to sink so fully into it that, well, its resulted in me spending more time in jail than I've probably had to. If that makes sense.*

You are a very strong girl, a very strong soul. You know that, and you know that I know it. You had to get that strength somewhere, you're not simply born with it. I mean you can bring it from an earlier life, but you had to originally earn it by overcoming something hard. We are only stronger than the things we overcome.

October 12th

My bills are all due and the babies need shoes
  And I'm busted.
Cotton is down to a quarter of a pound
  And I'm busted
Got a cow that went dry and a hen that won't lay
A big stack of bills that get bigger each day
The county will haul my belongings away
  I'm busted.
I went to my brother to ask for a loan
  I was busted.
How I hate to beg like a dog for a bone
  but I'm busted.
My brother said "There ain't a thing I can do
My wife and nineteen kids are all down with the flu,
And I was just thinkin of callin on you —
  I'm busted."

The bravest people are those who've overcome the greatest amounts of fear.
  I just hate fear. I think that fear is sort of a sin in a way. . . .
  I may shortly, next month, be faced with more fear than I've ever known before . . . I can't say what I will feel when and if that time comes . . . I sort of feel that all my life has been building to this.

October 15th

If you come to see me and they won't let you in, go to the Warden, his name is Sam Smith. Don't argue or get angry with him — people in his position don't have to listen to arguments, they are a power unto themselves, just explain that we are engaged to be married and that the visits, and our letters, mean an awful lot to both of us.

It's a dull motherfucker back here. I ain't got conversation. All these two Mexicans talk about is pimpin bitches and how sharp they are. Little greaseball turds. I've heard all this conversation for years — it never varies from penitentiary to penitentiary. Pure bullshit — essence of bullshit.

I'm not saying its right to break the law. I'm not talkin about that — but these prisons as they exist are wrong.

October 17th

I ain't had a nite's sleep since I been here. They keep the lites on outside the bars 24 hrs. a day. I hang my towel up at nite to shut out some of the lite and they wake me up when they count and threaten to take my fuckin mattress if I don't take the towel down. It's insane.

2

Kathryne was in a state about Nicole. Things were bad enough when Gary was at the County Jail, but then Nicole was just going from Springville to Provo. Now, it was different. Hitchhiking to the prison took Nicole through Pleasant Grove, and she would often leave the kids with Kathryne and stop off on her way back.

Kathryne tried to talk about Gary, but it wasn't very successful. "How's he seem?" she would ask, and Nicole would answer, "How? How could he seem?" Then, Kathryne found out through Kathy that Gary was saying he wanted to die. Nicole was very quiet about this. Kathryne really got scared when Nicole said that her kids would be better off without her.

They got into a big fight over that. Kathryne said a lot of mean things she didn't even feel. To begin with, she was afraid of hitchhiking, so she got on Nicole's ass over that. Then, Gary. "He's no good," Kathryne would say. "He's nothing but a damned killer and he deserves the death penalty. No," she would correct herself, "that's too good for him."

"You don't understand him," Nicole would say. "No," Kathryne said, "I don't, but why don't you try to understand those two poor women who have to raise those kids who don't have a father now, while you are running up every cockeyed day to see that damned killer."

Kathryne wasn't really feeling as angry at Gary as she pretended. Secretly, she might even feel bad for him, but she had to find a way to stop Nicole from hitching to the prison. All Kathryne could see for the future was that when they executed Gary, Nicole would go to pieces.

It was one big argument. At the end, Nicole was yelling. That, at least, was better than silence. "Fine, isn't it," Kathryne said. "Go and blow a man's head off." "I don't care," said Nicole, "I don't want to hear a goddamned thing you got to say."

"Oh, Nicole, why, why," asked Kathryne. "Why in the hell are you going there?"

"Because he has nobody else. I'll go every single day until they execute him. In fact," said Nicole, "I'll go and watch it."

"How could you?" shrieked Kathryne.

Then it wore itself down to simpler stuff. "If you need a ride," said Kathryne, "for Christ's sake, if you need to get up there, call one of us." "Well, you work," said Nicole, "and I don't want to bother you." "Dammit," said Kathryne, "it don't make any difference if I'm working. I don't want you hitchhiking." "Well," said Nicole, "I can't waste the time to drop off here."

Even Mr. Overman, for whom Kathryne was working, told Nicole, "Listen, girl, if you need a ride, call us at work. It don't matter if you want to go at eight o'clock in the morning. Your mother can take off to go with you. I don't like hitchhiking." Nicole just laughed. She said, "Oh, you all worry too much."

3

October 17

I was once deprived almost totally of my dreams for about 3 weeks. It was when I was on that Prolixin and couldn't sleep. Luckily, I knew the importance of dreams.

So, I compensated the best I could. I would let my mind wander into the hallucinations that were imposing themselves on me but never enough that I couldn't pull out of it. I believe I learned something that few people could ever really understand: what a terrible thing it would be to be insane.

It is a fact that I was on trial for my life and my lawyers simply did not defend me. It's true that they didn't have a hell of a lot to work with — but they were never curious either. They never really tried to look beneath the surface. They assume that like everybody else who ever gets a death sentence, I will allow them to keep me alive with appeals.

I mean they simply don't know a lot of things — those two puppets Snyder & Esplin. Fuck them.

I s'pose they got paid pretty good. They earned it. The State paid them and they did what they were s'posed to do for the State.

October 18th

The lieutenant . . . said we gonna have to cool it a little with the "lovemakin" in the visitin room. I told him we was just glad to see each other (an understatement). He said he can understand that — he's human, too, I didn't know, but rules are rules and he don't wanna have to warn us too many times.

Here's some verses from The Sensitive Plant. It's by Percy Bysshe Shelley.

> *And the leaves, brown, yellow and gray, and red*
> *and white with the whiteness of what is dead,*
> *like troops of ghosts on the dry wind passed;*
> *Their whistling noise made the birds aghast.*
>
> *I dare not guess; but in this life*
> *Of error, ignorance, and strife,*
> *Where nothing is, but all things seem,*
> *And we the shadows of the dream.*

October 19th

    I ain't got anything against Sue but you said in one of your letters that she's always tryin' to get you to go out with her boyfriend's boyfriend and that fucking Hawaiian probably came over because of Sue. I don't know why you even let that Hawaiian even stay in your house that long — Jesus, baby, fuck that. Just make it clear to the motherfucker that he's gotta go. And I wish you'd make it clear to Sue that you don't need boyfriends.

    You don't have to let some asshole set in your living room while he's waiting for his friend to come get him — let him go sit in the gutter.

    The reason you couldn't find the word in the dictionary is because you read it wrong — or I didn't write it right — anyhow it's TAUTOLOGIC not TANTOLOGIC. Look again.

    I've considered outright asking you to commit suicide. I've thot of telling you that I would assume all the debt, if there were any to be paid if you did commit suicide. I would if I could. But how can I make an offer like that when I don't know what it would cause if you were to do that. Angel, are we now being given a chance to relive something that we've fucked up in an earlier life???

    That could easily be what is happening as anything else.

    Look, I've told you I ain't much afraid about any of this — well, I am afraid of making the wrong choice. I'm afraid of hurting us. I don't want to hurt us.

October 20th

    Fuck me in your mind and in your dreams Angel come to me and wrap it around me warm and wet and hot and sticky and sweet and take my cock in your mouth and in your cunt and in your bootie and lay on me and lay under me and lay beside me with your head so close and your pretty legs so high and tite around me and put your cunt in my mouth for me to kiss and lick and probe and suck and love and feel you explode and moan and sigh and run wet and warm into my mouth.

4

Sue was seeing all the changes in Nicole. In the beginning, when Gary had first been in the county jail, Nicole really wanted to go out. Maybe she was in love with Gary as much as she said, but she was also enjoying that nobody was on her all the time, nobody. She and Sue started going out together. Sometimes, after Sue had the baby, they'd party at Nicole's house.

Then it started. Nicole didn't want to see guys anymore. After the trial, Nicole would read letters all night long. Or else, the girl was constantly writing. That impressed Sue Baker. One time Sue even saw her writing at four in the morning. She couldn't stop. It was like smoking.

Sometimes Nicole would laugh at the funny things in his letters. Some would make her cry. She would try not to let Sue know she was crying, but you could see her reading with red eyes. Tears would come down her cheeks. Then she would sit up, stop crying, and go on with her letters.

A couple of weeks after the trial, Nicole became really excited. "Yes," she said to Sue, "he's not going to fight it. He wants to die." Sue started to say what she thought of that and Nicole said, "If he wants to, he's got the right." You couldn't tell Nicole otherwise.

One day, hearing Sue talk about her Valiums of which Sue had one hundred, 10 mg. each, Nicole asked, "How many do you take if you want to kill yourself?" Just asked it one night calmly as hell. Sue never thought nothing of it. Said, "Well, I don't know. I don't want to try, so I don't know." Never gave it thought, but as the days went by, and Nicole got moodier, Sue began to worry now and again.

October 20
I am reminded constantly of the almost awesome unreal situa-
tion we are in. I have to accept it — I have no choice — you choose to
accept it. You amaze me, the utter strength and beauty you show. It
would be so easy for me to die; I have but to fire those two idiot
lawyers drop all appeals walk out of here Monday Nov. 15 at 8 AM

and quickly and easily be shot to death. If you choose to join me it would be much harder for you would have to do it yourself by whatever means you decide on: sleepin pills, gun, razor blade whatever — it would have to be by your own hand — and that's hard, I know. I'm also not blind to the fact that you believe a heavy debt is incurred when a person commits suicide. I'm also not unaware of Sunny and Peabody. Oh, Jesus! There's no reason why you should acquire a debt that I may not if I am simply shot to death. Baby I'm not asking or telling you to go with me. I just can't do that. But I've told you that's what I want — if that's a contradiction well, I can't help it. I'm just trying to be honest.

October 21

I've felt fucked up and shitty all day. Depressed. Down. This fuckin cell is too small.

When I was a little kid I used to sing all the time. I'd go down to Johnson Creek, this was in Portland — and this was a real neat creek, all woods and swimmin holes where I used to swim naked and when I was alone I'd sing my little ass off!

October 22

Oh Baby. You said in your letter that sometimes you can't _feel_ my love. Baby it's here! It's there every second, every moment, every hour of every day. I send it all to you —

I want to give you all that I am. I want you to know all of me. Even the things that I don't particularly like about myself and have always sort of hidden or altered, changed a little, in my own mind so they wouldn't seem so bad — I would willingly show to you.

Goddam, this is a noisy place. Some fool ass fool is in the background screaming, screaming for no other reason than to scream. I'd like to put one of my size 11's right in his ass. This is football season and there seems to be a game on every nite. I hate football and I hate to listen to these nuts screechin everytime some sonofabitch gains a couple yards.

Well, fuck that. I just never was one to make a lot of noise and I can't understand how other dudes can make all that noise all day and nite. I don't even like to talk from these cells — it's weird carryin on a conversation with someone you can't see — think of a *whole gang of motherfuckers locked in cells all day and nite and about 10 different conversations going on at once — some of them clear from one end of the building to the other.*

I was hopin' it would stay quiet in here for a while. But it never does. These doors, Jesus, how they clang and bang. The motherfuckin' TV blasts all day. I hear those guys all day long takin' votes about what to watch — it takes five or ten minutes — some fool reads the whole TV Guide hourly, loud as he can, then they vote on each idiotic show. Insane. The Boob Tube.

I've done a lot of time — and it ain't never been any different than it is now.

Nicole wrote Gary about a girl hitchhiker who was raped and then knifed twenty or thirty times by some guy in a white van. She wrote how she wasn't afraid of that creep or any other. If she was ever in such a situation, nobody was going to make it with her body, unless she was not in it.

Gary didn't say much in answer, and Nicole was glad. She realized it was her way of trying to apologize for the ex-president of the Sundowners.

Sometimes while hitchhiking, she would have a flash on her death. In her mind she would see the car she was in jumping off the freeway. She would wonder then what would happen in the next moment when she was dead. The thought was like an echo. She would keep seeing the car going off the freeway. Then she would feel the worry, What if death was a mistake? What if in that last moment, just as it was happening, she realized her action was truly a mistake? It was the only concern she had. That she might not have the right to die.

Now in the visits, Gary began to talk about pills. You faded out under them. It was peaceful, he said. Not at all like the nausea she felt, and the cold in the tunnel. Pills were gentle.

She still didn't know if it was okay to die. All through this month, she couldn't come to a decision. She went back and forth in her mind about the kids, and finally decided she would do it rather than be without him. Sooner or later she would have to take a shot at it. That was cool.

Of course, Gary kept writing to her about it. A couple of times she got mad and told him he pushed the subject too much. Then he would get apologetic and say he was only expressing how he felt. But his talking about it would get her wondering if she wanted to go ahead.

5

Gary woke up in a panic, and sent word to the Mormon Chaplain in the prison, Cline Campbell, that he had to see him. Campbell came by a little later, and Gary told of a dream he had. Pure paranoia, he said. Nicole was hitchhiking and the driver started to molest her. It was crucial that he see her today. Would Campbell bring her to the prison? Campbell would.

The first time Cline Campbell visited Gary, he mentioned that years ago Nicole used to be his student in seminary class. He had spent hours counseling her. The news seemed to go well with Gary. After that, they got along. Shared a few conversations.

Campbell believed the prison system was a complete socialist way of life. No wonder Gilmore had gotten into trouble. For twelve years, a prison had told him when to go to bed and when to eat, what to wear and when to get up. It was absolutely diametrically opposed to the capitalist environment. Then one day they put the convict out the front door, told him today is magic, at two o'clock you are a capitalist. Now, do it on your own. Go out, find a job, get up by yourself, report to work on time, manage your money, do all the things you were taught not to do in prison. Guaranteed to fail. Eighty percent went back to jail.

So he was curious about Gilmore. Looked forward to counseling him. Took the first opportunity, in fact, a few days after the man came to the prison. One evening Campbell just walked into his cell and said, "I'm the Chaplain, my name's Cline Campbell."

Gilmore was dressed in the white clothing they wore in Maximum Detention, and he was sitting on his bunk engrossed in his drawing. He had a pencil in his hand and a half-finished pencil portrait before him, but he got up, shook hands, said he was happy to meet Campbell. They got along fine. The Chaplain saw him often.

Until now, Cline Campbell had never been involved with counseling a person who was going to be executed. The men on Death Row were always there, and Campbell had chatted with them, and joked with them, but did not have serious counseling sessions. Those men were not close to being executed — their appeals had gone on for years — and their conditions were depraved. But then all of Maximum was a zoo, a flat one-story zoo with many cages.

At right angles to the main hall were the regular units. Behind a gate would be a series of five cells facing another five cells. Each prisoner had a full view therefore of the prisoner across from him, and partial views of the remaining prisoners on the other side. Sometimes all ten men could be speaking at once. It was a bedlam of cries, and sound reverberated from steel and stone. Echoes crashed into one another like car collisions. It was close to living on the inside of an iron intestine.

Most men were in Maximum Security for three months, no more. But prisoners on Death Row were there forever. Other men could leave their tier at mealtime to move to the cafeteria, or go to the yard. On Death Row, your meals were served in your cell. You never went to the yard. One at a time, each man could leave his cell for a half hour a day and walk up and down the tier. You could talk to the other men, take out — as Campbell had seen — your God-given penis, or invite the other man to stick his through the bars. You could be threatened — and Gilmore was the man to issue such a threat — to get away from the bars, or you'd catch a cup of urine in your face. That was exercise on Death Row.

Compared with other convicts there, Gilmore was relaxed. In fact, Campbell marveled at this ability. Campbell would make a point of going to the kitchen first to bring him a cup of black coffee, and Gilmore would grin, "How you doing, preach?" and speak in a quiet voice.

Sometimes they would talk in Gilmore's cell. More often, Campbell would have him called out, and they would go into a counsel room in Maximum Security in order that nobody overhear their conversation. Several times, Gilmore would say, "I really appreciate rapping with you. I can't talk with anybody else here."

Once in a while they got into deeper conversations. Gilmore would say, "This is stuff I wouldn't even tell the shrinks," and mentioned a time when he first went to MacLaren and a couple of boys held him and he was raped. He hated it, he said, but would admit that as he got older, he participated in the same game on the other side. They nodded. There was the old prison saying, "In every wolf is a punk looking for revenge."

One time, Gilmore made a statement Campbell did not forget. "I've killed two men," he said, "I want to be executed on schedule."
Then he added, "I want absolutely no notoriety." His voice was emphatic. He told Campbell he didn't want news coverage, TV, radio interviews, nothing. "I just believe I ought to be executed, I feel myself responsible."

Campbell said, "Well, that can't be all of your motive for wanting to die, Gary, just responsibility?" Gary answered, "No, I'll be honest with you. I've been in eighteen years and I'm not about to do another twenty. Rather than live in this hole, I'd choose to be dead."

Campbell could understand that. Generally, the LDS Church did believe in the death penalty. Campbell certainly did. He thought to watch a man become more debased, more hateful, more resentful and mean, both to himself and to others on Death Row, was absolutely cruel. The man was better off, and would change less, and be more himself after he was executed, than right here. It was wiser to pass into the spirit world — and await resurrection. There a man could have a better chance to fight for his cause. In the spirit world, one would be more likely to find assistance than degradation.

6

Campbell had been an LDS missionary in Korea, then a Chaplain in the Army with an airborne outfit. He taught seminary for six years after he got out. Also worked as a weekend cop. He would pick up a patrol car at six on Friday night, and turn it back in Monday at 8 A.M.

Since he had grown up in the boonies on a Utah ranch, he never needed any training in firearms. He had carried a gun as a boy, and was pretty quick with it. From the hip, he could hit a gallon can fifty feet away in a quarter of a second. Grew up thinking of himself as a second Butch Cassidy.

He was not too tall, but he would have considered it on the side of sin not to be in good shape and well groomed. He stood real straight, shoulders back, and looked like a marksman. He had the patina of finely machined metal. During those weekends when he used to work as a cop, he was on for 24 hours a day, taking all calls. Of course, it was a small town, and he usually had time to go to church, but he carried a beeper so he could always be contacted and actually made more arrests in Lindon City than the other two officers put together, since on the weekend you had to handle every drunk and fracas.

The last time he had seen Nicole was one of those weekends, at two o'clock in the morning. He was driving down a road in Lindon and there she stood hitchhiking. He said, Get in the car, what are you doing out here? It's dangerous.

He had heard she had a child, and now she was obviously loaded on drugs. He had every reason to take her to jail, but she trusted him, and he saw that she got home. He kept thinking of all the times he had counseled her once a week from five to thirty minutes, and knew what a bad situation she had at home. She had told him about Uncle Lee. It was a touchy thing, however. He could not really get her to go into it. Sometimes she would sit in his seminary class looking dreamy, and have no idea she was there.

Now, on this morning that Campbell went over to find Nicole for Gary, she was asleep on the couch and her two children were asleep on the floor with a blanket over them. After she kind of combed her hair a little, she let Campbell in. Didn't even know who it was.

Cracked the curtain. Didn't recognize him. He said, "How are you, Nicole, do you remember me?" She looked hard and she said, "Sure, come on in." He said, "I'm Brother Campbell." She said, "Yes, of course, come in." They exchanged a few courtesies, and he said he'd come because Gary wanted to see her.

She dropped the children off with her ex-mother-in-law, Mrs.

Barrett, and on the way out to prison, Campbell discussed her situation. She just said to him without any particular ado, that if Gary died, she might also.

It was quite a remark for Campbell to keep to himself, yet he could hardly turn it in. His life at the prison consisted of holding secrets.

Sometimes a convict would come in and say a particular man was after him. Campbell wouldn't go to the Warden and discuss what the man had said. The action taken would enable other inmates to pick up that the man was snitching. They'd be after him even more.

So Campbell didn't disclose a thing unless it was a matter of life and death. Then he would get the man's permission.

Now, even though he knew Gary and Nicole were thinking of suicide, he could not speak. That would only increase the pressure. There'd be a guard sitting in Gilmore's cell every minute after that. He could hardly pretend his mind was easy, however. The quiet way Nicole had discussed it worried him most of all. Except for those occasions when he was angry, Gary had the most relaxed eyes Campbell had ever seen — they looked at everything with no strain, graceful as a good outfielder sitting under a fly ball he would never fail to catch. Nicole's voice had something of the same. It never stumbled when she told the truth.

7

October 26

Remember the nite we met? I had to have you, not just physically but in all ways, forever — there was a wild wind blowing in my heart that nite.

It will remain forever the most beautiful nite of my life. I love you more than God. I'm glad you understand the way I mean that Angel. It still feels a little awkward to say. But I mean no offense to anything by a statement like that. I just love you more than anything — I think God would smile. In one of your early letters you talk of climbing in my mouth and sliding down my throat with a strand of your hair to mend the worn spot in my stomach. You write good.

Last Friday you told me you would like us each to think of the other at a certain hour of the day, that we might become closer. But I never know what time it is here. I can't see a clock and I just have a general idea of the time. I know they feed at about 6 or 7 or so in the morn and about 11 or 12 for lunch and around 4 for dinner but I don't even know if that's always the same — they might rotate and feed one section first one day and another — the next. Fuck, in short I just don't know what time it is.

Now darlin we come to something that can't be avoided discussing. The rest of your life. I don't want any man to have you. I don't want any man to have you in any way but especially I don't want any man to steal any part of your heart.

If I was to look from the other side and see another man with you I can't say right now what I would do.

I believe that I would seek a way to have my soul, my very being, extinguished forever from existence.

If a thing like that is not possible I would consider hurtling my soul into the center of the planet Uranus, that most evil of places, that I might become forever such that I could not change.

October 28

Baby I would love to be able to meditate. I already can to some degree. I do, but not real deeply, you know? Even when it's quiet there's always the expectation of noise. I know you can get the right answer to anything through meditation, but I ain't, because of my surroundings, very deep into it. It's more than the noise, you just can't let yourself go in a place like this — there is an atmosphere of tension, a climate of violence, in prison — all prisons — and it's in the air. Lot of paranoid motherfuckers in these places and they walk around putting out negative, hostile paranoid vibes.

I like it a lot that you meditate. I don't know if I'm too crazy about the automatic writing. I think with things like automatic writing, Ouija boards, it's possible to open doors that are better not opened. I think that there are many lonely lost forlorn spirits seeking an inroad into a human mind. All spirits are not benevolent. Many are merely lonely, but many are malevolent, too.

Baby, if you mess with spirits you must beware. I ain't trying to sound dark and foreboding and I don't know just how I know this as certainly as I do, but I do know that you got to remain in control. You gotta be stronger than the thing that you are communicating with. Weigh carefully the "Messages" you receive, and if after a while you begin to feel a pull, something that ain't right, if it makes you feel sad or strange or in some way not good — then you should back off. Like about everything else in life, you gotta remain in control. Be strong, don't fear.

Baby, I don't know just what happens when you die except that it will be familiar. It's just an awful strong feeling I have — it's something I've thought of, known really, for years. The thing about dying is that you gotta remain in control. Don't be sidetracked by lonely forlorn spirits who call to you as you pass by — they may even reach and clutch.

Whenever this does occur to us we must each keep the other in mind. Somehow, Angel eyes, this is one of those things that I KNOW. When you die you will be free as never before in life — be able to travel at a tremendous speed just by thinking of some place you will be there. It's a natural thing and you adjust — it's just conscious-ness unencumbered by body.

Hey, this guy next door to me lets the goddamdest farts I've ever heard. I thot that Gibbs was a fartin motherfucker — but he don't hold a candle to this fool! Loud, harsh, rumbling, angry sounding farts — Never heard nothin like it. Sounds worse than startin a lawn mower.

8

Snyder and Esplin had a couple of postmortems with Noall Wootton over the case. They would run into each other in the corridors or the coffee shop, and sometimes bring up questions they had about the other side's strategy: having won, Wootton did needle them a little, but didn't think he was too bad about it. His tone went: "Are you sure you suckers got all the cooperation you could from your client?" Or, "Why in Christ didn't you put his girl friend up there?" "He wouldn't let us," they would answer. All agreed it was quite a question. As long as a defendant was sane and competent, he probably had the right to run his defense.

Since Gary had been at Utah State, Snyder and Esplin had had little communication. They talked to him on the phone a couple of times, and in the beginning, made arrangements for Nicole to get in, but they didn't actually go themselves until a couple of days before the Appeal Hearing on November 1. That day, however, they were given physical contact in the visitors' room at Maximum. Enough space to pace the floor, maybe 15 by 20 feet.

They were coming as the bearers of good tidings. Their chances of getting the death sentence reduced to life were, they thought, pretty nimble. Number one, as they laid it out for him, the Utah statute on the death penalty passed by the last Legislature did not provide for mandatory review of a death sentence. That was serious. Probably, it was constitutionally defective. This criticism, "constitutionally defective," was about as strong as you could get in such areas of the law. A lot of lawyers felt the Utah statute was almost certainly going to be overthrown by the U.S. Supreme Court. So it was Snyder and Esplin's opinion the Utah Supreme Court would now be very hesitant about enforcing a death sentence on November 15th. That Utah Supreme Court would certainly look bad if shortly after they let a man be executed the Supreme Court came down against them.

Besides, they had another good legal vein to work. During the Mitigation Hearing, Judge Bullock had admitted evidence of the Orem murder. That had to have a big effect on the Jury. It certainly was easier to vote for a man's death if you heard about an additional murder he had committed; therefore, Snyder and Esplin were feeling optimistic. The brunt of their defense had been to maneuver onto these good appeal grounds. Now, they were feeling, in fact, a little excited. Some of this would be brand-new legal stuff for Utah County.

Gary listened. Then he said, "I've been here for three weeks, and I don't know that I want to live here for the rest of my life." He shook his head. "I came with the idea that maybe I could work it out, but the lights are on 24 hours a day and the noise is too much for me."

The lawyers kept talking about their grounds for appeal. Wootton's closing argument with his comments on the suffering of Debbie

Bushnell could easily be called prejudicial to Gary. The prospects were good, even excellent.

Gary paced back and forth, and looked a little nervous. He repeated the difficulties he felt with living in Maximum. Finally, he said quietly, "Can I fire you?"

They replied that they guessed he could. However, they said, they thought they might have to go ahead with the appeal anyway. It was their duty.

Gilmore said, "Now, don't I have the right to die?" He stared at them. "Can't I accept my punishment?"

Gary told them of his belief that he had been executed once before, in eighteenth-century England. He said, "I feel I've been here before. There is some crime from my past." He got quiet, and said, "I feel I have to atone for the thing I did then." Esplin couldn't help thinking that this stuff about eighteenth-century England would sure have made a difference with the psychiatrists if they had heard it.

Gilmore now began to say that his life wouldn't end with this life. He would still be in existence after he was dead. It all seemed part of a logical discussion. Esplin finally said, "Gary, we can see your point of view, but we still feel duty bound to go ahead on that appeal."

When Gary said again, "What can I do about it?" Snyder answered, "Well, I don't know."

Gary then said, "Can I fire you?"

Esplin said, "Gary, we'll make the Judge aware that you want to can us, but we're going to file anyway."

They parted on pretty good terms.

9

Noall Wootton was up in San Francisco at a national homicide symposium. Went there, as he put it, to learn how to prosecute murder cases, and they even gave him a certificate. He was going to have his wife join him for a few days and have a little fun, but word from his office took care of that. Wootton's secretary phoned to say that Gary Gilmore was going to withdraw his motion for a new trial. He was not going to appeal. He wanted to be executed and Snyder and Esplin were damn upset. Didn't know what their ethical position was supposed to be. Wootton concluded he had better get back. Who knew what con's trick Gilmore had come up with? Wootton couldn't remember a ploy like this before.

The courtroom on November 1 offered a quiet scene. There were not many people seated, and Gary's speech to the Judge, everything considered, was, Wootton thought, kind of open and courteous. It was still off the wall. Wootton got permission from Judge Bullock to make a few inquiries:

MR. WOOTTON   Mr. Gilmore, has your treatment in prison thus far at the Utah State Prison influenced your decision in any way?

MR. GILMORE   No.

MR. WOOTTON   How about your treatment at the Utah County Jail?

MR. GILMORE   No.

MR. WOOTTON   Now you have been represented by two attorneys who are paid by Utah County. Do you understand that?

MR. GILMORE   Yes.

MR. WOOTTON   Are you satisfied with the counseling they have given you and the representation that they have made for you?

MR. GILMORE   Not entirely.

MR. WOOTTON   In what way, sir?

MR. GILMORE   I'm satisfied with them.

MR. WOOTTON   So the way they have represented you hasn't necessarily had any influence on your decision, is that correct?

MR. GILMORE   That's my own decision. It's not influenced by anything other than the fact that I don't care to live the rest of my life in jail. That doesn't mean this jail or that jail, but any jail.

MR. WOOTTON   Has anyone else influenced your decision other than your own thoughts, sir?

MR. GILMORE   I make my own decisions.

MR. WOOTTON   Are you under the influence of any alcohol or drugs or other intoxicants at this time?

MR. GILMORE   No. Of course not.

MR. WOOTTON   Have you been under the influence of any such thing, sir, in the course of your thoughts concerning this decision?

MR. GILMORE   No. I'm in jail. They don't serve beer, whiskey, or anything.

MR. WOOTTON   Sir, in your own judgment, do you feel that you are mentally and emotionally competent to make this decision at this time?

MR. GILMORE   Yes.

MR. WOOTTON   Do you make any claims of being insane or mentally disturbed at this point?

MR. GILMORE   No. I know what I'm doing.

MR. WOOTTON   Sir, would you request that the Court extend the execution date beyond the normal appeal time in order to give you additional time to think this decision out?

MR. GILMORE   I'm not going to think differently about it at any time.

DESERET NEWS

Slayer Wants To Keep Death Date

Provo (AP) Nov. 1 — Unless he changes his mind and appeals, or the courts and the governor intervene, a 35-year-old parolee convicted of murdering a hotel clerk will keep his Nov. 15 execution date.

"You sentenced me to die. Unless it's a joke or something, I want to go ahead and do it," Gilmore said yesterday.

Fourth District Court Judge Bullock told Gilmore he could still change his mind and appeal, and an attorney for Gilmore said he would prepare appeal papers just in case Gilmore decides to appeal.

DESERET NEWS

Houdini Didn't Show

Nov. 1. . . . Halloween was a disappointment to groups trying to make contact with the spirit of escape artist Harry Houdini who died on Halloween 50 years ago.

Several magicians gathered Sunday in the Detroit hospital room where Houdini died, hoping for a message from the master. All they got on a video tape machine brought to record the event, was interference from a local rock station.

"It's not even very good music," said one magician.

CHAPTER 32

Old Cancer. New Madness

1

By the second day of November, after all the phone calls came in, Bessie began to hear echoes again. The past rang in Bessie's ear, the past reverberated in her head. Steel bars slammed into stone.

"The fool," Mikal screamed at her. "Doesn't he know he's in Utah? They will kill him, if he pushes it." She tried to calm her youngest son, and all the while she was thinking that from the time Gary was 3 years old, she knew he was going to be executed. He had been a dear little guy, but she had lived with that fear since he was 3. That was when he began to show a side she could not go near.

One time, in that endless year when Frank was away in the Colorado jail, she sat in her mother's house and watched Gary play in the yard. There was a mud puddle she had told him to stay away from. Two minutes after she went inside, he then sat down in the middle.

It put a fear through her. Would he always be so defiant?

Now, the walls of the trailer closed in again. Somebody asked her once if it had been difficult to learn to live in the trailer, and she said no, not difficult at all. That was because she had never lived there, but died the day she moved in.

It was an ugly place, and she hated ugly places. Her health went down. She had only, she thought, inherited enough art from

Uncle George, the painter, to know how to decorate a home, but she had done that much for the last house. It had been nice. Now, she lived in a narrow room, and her arthritis got worse as she sat through the days and years at a table in the kitchen end of the thing with the radio stacked on the telephone books and the sore bones of her pelvis installed on a pillow.

Everything was shades of brown. One poverty after another. Even the icebox was brown. It was that shade of gloom which would not lift. The color of clay. Nothing could grow.

Outside were fifty trailers in this lot off the highway they called a Park. It parked old people. At little expense. Had her trailer cost $3,500? She could no longer remember. When people asked if it had one bedroom or two, she would say, "It's got one and a half bedrooms, if you can believe it." It also had a half porch with a half awning.

Sometimes she didn't get out for weeks at a time. The arthritis got worse. At Speed's, she couldn't keep up with her work. Those twisted fingers ached with every plate she lifted from a table. Each move felt like the beginning of a disagreeable transaction. Sometimes she had to figure out in the middle how to shift her course so that the repercussion of the pain would not freeze her spine. Finally, the boss said he had to let her go, and gave her final pay. She was making $70 a week. Once she stopped working, the arthritis got worse. One knee started to bother her, then the other.

A doctor said he could operate on her arthritic knees and put in plastic ones. She said no. She had a picture of living in this plastic house with plastic knees. The long hair that fell to her waist turned gray, and she kept it in a bun. What with the difficulty of raising her arms, it usually stayed in the bun. "I'm ugly," Bessie would say to herself. It was as if, in losing the house, she must also lose her looks.

She moved in the year Mikal graduated from high school. He went to college in Portland, and put himself through. He was bright and got good marks, and had to think of his own life. There were periods when he would visit less. The day she lost the ten-room house with the marble-top furniture, Mikal went north, she went south, and they never lived under the same roof again.

She had only moved a little farther south on McLaughlin Boulevard in Milwaukie south of Portland City line, moved farther down that four-lane avenue of bars and eateries and discount stores. One gas station even had an old World War II Boeing bomber stuck up in the air above its gasoline pumps. That was about as surplus as you could get. Since she stayed in the trailer more and more, she passed that silly airplane on beat-up old McLaughlin Boulevard less and less.

Mikal was gone. They were all gone. She did not know how much was her fault, and how much was the fault of the ongoing world that ground along like iron-banded wagon wheels in the prairie grass, but they were gone. Gary was away forever, and in her dreams, the wind still whistled through the vent in Gaylen's belly that the ice pick made, and Frank Jr. was often gone, and when she saw him on weekends, he lived deep in his own thoughts and rarely spoke, and practiced magic no more, and Frank Sr. was dead and long gone.

The sorrows of the family had begun with Gary, and now he wanted to be dead. When he departed, would they all descend another step into that pit where they gave up searching for one another? She lived again through the days when Frank Sr. died.

His bad look, she was fond of saying, was strong enough to push a man across a room. He had been in show business so long his muscles rippled. He was a strong and powerfully built man and she watched him go down to nothing and die.

He had always been very afraid of cancer. His mother died of it, and Frank never said a word, but Bessie knew. There was a straight-out fear. The sound of the word could change the day for him.

She watched him linger in the hospital. He wasted as he went. Once she had been very much in love with him, but there had been so many fights over the boys, over Gary most of all, that toward the end, there was not much feeling. But, oh, it was hard to watch him die. She almost loved him very much again.

To herself she wept when she thought of the first time Gary was brought before a Judge, because that was the first time Frank could be found on Gary's side. "Don't admit a thing," he kept saying to Gary. The wisdom of his life was in the remark. If nothing was admitted, the other side might not be able to start the game of law and justice.

The Judge found Gary guilty anyway.

Now Gary was playing at the other end of the field. "Kill me," he was saying.

2

When Frank Sr. was in Colorado Prison, she lived for a time with Fay. One night a bat flew into Fay's house. She called the police to get it out. No question of the evil in that bat. Then, a year to the day after Frank died, a bat entered the house with the Philippine mahogany furniture and the turnaround drive. She ran upstairs and called the police again, shivering with a fear twenty years old. It happened near to the day Gary was sitting at her desk holding the birth certificate with the name of Fay Robert Coffman. That was the moment she knew no matter how many years it took, she would lose the house. There was too much hatred in Gary. You did not keep a house on hatred such as that.

Still, she did try. Tried through the years, and the thickening fingers, the stiffening knees, the slow twisting of her limbs. If the Mormon Church would pay those back taxes, $1,400, no fortune, she would sign the deed over until she repaid the Church in full.

It would be simple, she thought, but the outcome produced new voices in her ear. Real voices. She could hear every ugly thought. The Bishop said, We'll send a man to appraise the property, but when he came, he set the worth at $7,000. She told him that her husband had paid twice the sum ten years ago, and her husband was no fool. He said, "They asked me to appraise it low," and talked of the deterioration of the grounds.

Soon the voices began to ask why she didn't agree to live on a lesser basis. Did she have to stay in a big house now? She could always work for one of the rich ladies in the Church, and have her bed and room free.

It didn't seem wise, the Bishop explained, to keep a home she could not maintain physically. As it was, the city threatened suit if she didn't take care of the weeds in the rear. She had four sons, but the rear of the house was a thicket of tall grass, tin cans, cat briars. The Church sent young people over to try to clear it, but that was a large job. Couldn't Mikal help?

He had, explained Bessie, his studies. After this reply, there was a crevasse of ice between the Bishop and herself.

She heard the voices talking of the financial situation. The home, if you included the expense of keeping it up, would not be worth what it would cost to buy back the arrears on the taxes. They told her again that the grounds to the house were ill kept, and choked with weeds, and her sons had not kept it up. She felt able to kill. She didn't like someone telling her what her sons ought to do. Nor those voices saying that the wise course was to find a mobile home she could live in and handle.

Of all the people, she said to herself, who ever hurt me, it's been only Mormons, nobody else ever could. She remembered the terrible hatred in Gary's face on the day she told him in the visiting room at Oregon State that the Church never helped her to save the house. There was a look in his eyes then as if he had found an enemy worthy of his stature.

Now, she was in the trailer sitting in the dark, TV not on, radio not on, her legs in wrapping, and her nightgown looking like it was a hundred and two years old. She could hear the boy from the Mormon Church rapping on the door, breaking the silence, the boy who came over to help her. He would do the dirty dishes that were all over the table and all over the sink, pick up after the trail of the immediate past of the day before, and the five days before, all that record of living from day to day through the twisting of her limbs. Sometimes she would sit and not reply to the boy's knock, sit in the dark, and feel him looking through the panes of the door to see if he could find her shadow sitting there. Finally, she would say, "Go away."

"I love you, Bessie," the Mormon boy would tell her through the door, and leave on his rounds to help another old lady even as Benny Bushnell once had done.

"Gary cannot want to die," she would say to herself in the dark.

Nov. 2 — 76
Milw. Oregon

Gary Gilmore
No. 13871
Dear Gary:

I heard the news at noon, and Gary, my dear, I could hardly stand it. I love you & I want you to live.

Gary, Mikal loves you and he is your friend & you know I wouldn't lie to you. He took this real hard but he will try very hard to help you.

If you have 4 or 5 people who really love you, you are lucky. So please hold on.

Here is a picture of me and Mikal taken in Salt Lake City years ago.

I love you,
MOTHER

3

Mikal had never told Bessie how much rage Gary aroused in him by his murders. It could've been *me,* was his thought back in July when he first heard the news.

Mikal worked in a record store. While he was the envy of his friends for being able to pick up new releases at 30 percent off, he also had to throw dope peddlers and ass peddlers out of the store. He wasn't necessarily ready for that. One time, a shoplifter pulled a knife on him. Another time he almost got wasted by a big drunk who was urinating in the doorway. The violence of Portland licked right up to the edge of the store and left a spew like that yellow foam on city beaches where old rubber dries out with jellyfish and whiskey bottles and the dead squid.

If Mikal's life was seen by some as the attempt of one Gilmore boy to get out from the family hex, that was not necessarily Mikal's attitude. He had a simpler view. He had just been afraid of Gary for years. Mikal, reading the headline on that one terrible July night, OREGON MAN HELD IN UTAH SLAYING, felt shame. "It could have been *me*." He could have been the same victim of the same mindless robbery. He hated his brother then. His brother had no respect for the horrors of waste. His brother did not know that when you robbed a house, you ruined it for the people who were living there.

Next day, Bessie had said to Mikal, "Can you imagine what it feels like to mother a son whom you love, when he has deprived two other mothers of *their* sons?" Mikal did not know how to tell her he was frightened of the violent and capricious impulses of his brother, did not know how to face them, and had been glad, ever since 1972, that he did not have to see him again.

That was when Gary had been granted what they call a "school release" from Oregon State Penitentiary to a halfway house in Eugene. They were letting him out to study art. Mikal had been told of this coming event by Bessie, but was nonetheless startled to see Gary turn up at his college room on the day after his release in the fall of 1972, six-pack in hand, and the happy information that he could still register tomorrow. The school at Eugene was a couple of hundred miles away, but Gary seemed in no hurry. Just wanted to see how Mikal was getting along.

Next day, Gary was at the door again. Wearing the same clothes. His blue eyes stared at Mikal out of a bloodshot field of white, and there was yellow in the corners. He was ready to take Mikal to lunch, but only in a cab. He did not want to be seen on the streets.

Mikal began to feel steeped again in the dread he had always felt on those rare occasions he visited Gary in prison. It was not only Gary but the lost lives of the other prisoners in that visiting room, the depression, the apathy, the congealed rage, the bottomless potential for violence in those halls. After a while, Mikal stopped visiting. It created too much disturbance when he walked in wearing his long hair. It was like protesting the war in Vietnam in front of a barracks of Marines.

On this day, for lunch, they went to a topless bar. Mikal thought Gary was in a trance. He just kept studying the breasts of the girl on the dance floor. After a while, Mikal got up his courage and said, "It's obvious you're not going to school."

Gary answered in a slow deliberate countrified way. Phony as hell, Mikal always thought, more Texas than Oregon. "Man," said Gary, "I'm not cut out for school. They can't teach me anything about art I don't know already." Then he changed the subject. He needed a gun. A friend in Oregon State Penitentiary was going to be brought out for dental work next week. Ward White was his name. He wanted to spring him.

Mikal protested. "You're throwing away your life."

"It's a matter of dignity," said Gary and looked at Mikal's eyes. When he took in the knowledge that there was no gun forthcoming, Gary said, "I'd do it for *my* brother."

He dropped Mikal off in a taxi, and went on.

Mikal only saw him twice more that month. Once Gary stopped by to hear some Johnny Cash records. He was charming and sober. Another day, Gary picked him up at school, took him to a rich friend's house, showed him the swimming pool, then showed him a pistol. "Think you could ever use one of these?" he asked.

It was like a bigger dude squeezing your machismo to see if it leaked. "I could use a gun if I had to," said Mikal, "but I hope you're talking about survival."

Gary put the gun away and ruffled Mikal's hair. "C'mon," he said, "I'll drive you home."

On the way, Gary started to honk at a car that was going too slow, and when the driver slowed down a little more, to spite him, Gary whipped around a turn on the wrong lane and went right into the path of an approaching van. At the last instant, he escaped collision by driving their car up on the sidewalk.

"You almost got us killed," Mikal shouted.

Gary was breathing deeply. He lay his forehead on the steering wheel. "Sometimes," he said, "you have to be able to face that."

4

A couple of nights later, Mikal heard over the news that Gary had been arrested for armed robbery. Back he went to prison. Months later, Bessie and Mikal attended his trial. Just before sentencing, Gary made a speech to the Court. Mikal never forgot it.

"I would like to make a special appeal for leniency. I've been locked up for the last nine and a half calendar years and I have had about two and a half years of freedom since I was fourteen years old. I have always gotten time and always done it, never been paroled. I have never had a break from the law, and I have come to feel that justice is kind of harsh, and I have never asked for a break until now. Your Honor, you can keep a person locked up too long just as you can keep them long enough. What I am saying is there is an appropriate time to release somebody or give them a break. Of course, who is to say. Only the individual himself really knows, it's more a matter of just convincing somebody. There have been times when I felt if I had had a break, right then I would probably never have been in trouble again, but like I said, I don't feel that I have ever had a break from the law. Last September, I was released from the Penitentiary to go to school in Eugene at Lane Community College and study art, and I had every intention of doing it. One day I'm in the pen for nine years, and the next day I'm free, and I was kind of shook. I had a couple of drinks and I realized that this was a pretty stupid thing to do. I just got out, and I was afraid to go to the halfway house with booze on my breath. I thought I would be taken back to the pen immediately and to be honest, I guess I kind of wanted to continue drinking, it tasted kind of good. Well, anyway, I split. It wasn't long before I was broke, and I spent a couple of days looking for a job, but I couldn't find one. I didn't have any work background. When you are free, you can afford to be broke for a few days, and it doesn't matter, but if you are a fugitive you can't afford to be broke at all. I needed some money. I am not a stupid person, although I have done a lot of stupid and foolish things, but I want freedom enough to realize at last that the only way I can have it and maintain it is to quit breaking the law. I never realized it more than I do now. If you were to grant me probation on this sentence, you wouldn't be turning me loose right now. I still have additional time, but like I said, I have got problems, and if you give me more time, I'm going to compound them."

The Judge sentenced him to nine additional years. "Don't worry," said Gary to his mother, "They can't hurt me any more than I've hurt myself." Mikal shook hands with him through the hand-cuffs, and Gary said, "Do me a favor. Put on some weight, okay? You're too goddamned skinny." Mikal would not hear his voice again for close to four years, not until he made a call to Utah State Prison in the middle of November 1976. By that time, Gary Gilmore was a household name to half of America.

BOOK TWO

EASTERN VOICES

PART ONE

In the Reign
of Good King Boaz

CHAPTER 1

Fear of Falling

1

On November 1, the day that Gary Gilmore first stated in Court that he did not wish to appeal his conviction, Assistant Attorney General Earl Dorius was at his desk in the Utah Attorney General's office, in the State Capitol, Salt Lake City. It was a monument of a building with a golden dome, a rectangular marble palace whose interior had a parquet marble floor from the center of which you could look up to the stories above with their polished white balustrades. Earl liked working in all that marble. He was not averse to working there for the rest of his responsible life.

That afternoon, Earl received a call from the Warden of Utah State Prison. Since Dorius was legal counsel for the prison, the Warden talked to him frequently, but this time Sam Smith seemed nervous. His transportation officer had just taken an inmate, Gary Gilmore, to Provo for a Court hearing, and Gilmore apparently told the Judge that he didn't want to appeal his death sentence. So the Judge confirmed the execution date. It was only two weeks away. The Warden was concerned. That didn't give a lot of time to get ready. Could Dorius verify the story?

Earl called Noall Wootton and they had quite a conversation. Wootton said it was not only true, but he was trying to figure Gilmore's angle. The statute called for execution in not less than thirty and not more than sixty days. Now that Gilmore had no appeal in, what would happen if they didn't execute him by December 7, sixty days after October 7, the last day of his trial? Gilmore could ask for an immediate release. The only sentence he had received, after all, was death. That was not a prison term. Technically, they would have nothing to hold him on. He could get out on a Writ of Habeas Corpus.

Of course, Gilmore wasn't going to get loose that easy, the lawyers agreed, but it sure could prove embarrassing. The State would look ridiculous and incompetent holding him in jail on one pretext or another while the law was straightened out in the Legislature and the Courts.

Earl Dorius called Sam Smith back and said, "You better start preparing for an execution." The Warden was awestruck.

Nonetheless, Sam Smith started asking some good questions. How many members of the firing squad would there be, he inquired? From where could he draw them — out of the community at large or from the ranks of police officers?

The Warden had also looked up the appropriate statutes and they left something to be desired. They didn't, for example, tell the Warden whether it was possible to conduct the execution outside the prison walls. They were not precise on a host of matters. A lot would have to be decided. Gilmore, for instance, wanted to donate a few of his body organs to the University Medical Center. Could Earl look up the law on that?

Dorius was excited. He realized he was sitting on a very hot case, and started going around the office telling people, "You won't believe this, but we have a potential execution on our hands." He went down to the Attorney General's office, but the A.G. was out, so he had to tell the secretaries. Earl was a little disappointed with the reaction. It was as if they really didn't get the import of what he was saying. First execution in America in ten years! You couldn't exactly shout that at people.

November 1

Hi Baby
   Just wrote a letter to Warden Smith asking for a little more visiting time. I told him it meant a great deal to both of us. It would probably help if you would talk to him too. I don't know what kind of guy he is, and I didn't know how to approach him in my letter. I

simply told him I expect to be executed as scheduled Nov. 15 and that the only request I have to make is that I be allowed to see you more. . . . I told him that you and me have a real good understanding and that we don't depress each other with our visits in spite of the circumstances I'm in. I sorta felt it mite be good to say that cause you know how these people sometimes think —

Baby you said in a letter a couple of days ago that no woman ever loved a man more than you love me. I believe that. I feel blessed with your love. And Angel no man ever loved a woman more than I love you. I love you with all that I am. And you keep making me more than I am.

Early on the morning of the 2nd, Election Day, Earl got a telephone call from Eric Mishara of the *National Enquirer*. He had called the Warden who referred him to the prison's legal counsel. Mishara said he wanted to interview Gilmore right away.

He was too forceful for Dorius's taste. The moment Earl tried to slow him down, Mishara began to talk about what he was going to do to the prison if they attempted to keep him out.

A case came right into mind: *Pell v. Procunier.* It was a United States Supreme Court decision which said that members of the news media had no special right of access to inmates. The prison, Dorius told Mishara, would be taking that position — Gary Gilmore could not be interviewed.

Immediately, Mishara said, "I'll sue." He started to talk about high-powered attorneys in New York. Dorius said, "I don't care where your attorneys are from. You have them look up *Pell versus Procunier.* I think they'll agree with me."

Earl didn't hear from Mr. Mishara for some time after that.

DESERET NEWS

Carter Wins Election

Judge Orders Test of Convicted Slayer

Utah State Prison, Nov. 2 — . . . If Gilmore gets his way he will be the first person executed in Utah in 16 years.

2

On November 2, the day he was driving to Utah, Dennis Boaz read in the papers about Gary Gilmore, and soon afterward, had this experience with death. That seemed a little synchronistic.

He was moving along in the left lane and thinking about the course he was going to give at Westminster College in Salt Lake City. Dennis was into alliteration these days, so he was going to call it: Society / Symbolism / Synchronicity. Just as he said the last word to himself, a trailer truck slammed to a stop just ahead and he had to take his car around on the right. After he passed, there was this incredible sight in the mirror: a torso of a man hanging through the windshield, arms outstretched to the ground.

Then another sight!
A rear-mirror view of a second truck driver running toward the first truck. Dennis didn't stop. There were too many cars behind. But just before it happened, he had been thinking of the date, November 2nd. In his mind, he was writing it as 11/2. That, of course, added up to thirteen. In the major arcana of the tarot, thirteen was the card for death.

So the word had been running through his mind even as he saw the dead man. He thought, "Wow! God! I bet the next road sign will be another indication." When the exit came up on the shoulder, it said: *Star Valley and Deeth.* That had to be as much synchronicity as anybody's synapses could take.

On the evening of the second, he got to Salt Lake early enough to vote for Carter on the Independent line. Then, on the morning of the third, he woke up thinking about Gilmore. "God, here I am," Dennis thought, "right in the juncture of something really important." He could see the possibilities extending out. "It's a tremendous opportunity for a writer," he thought, "and I ought to send Gilmore a letter!"

Boaz did. A few years ago when he had been a young prosecutor, Dennis had actually been against capital punishment, but now he had come to believe that even in an ideal society, we might still need the death penalty. Capital punishment, properly applied, could say a lot about being responsible for one's actions, and the thing was to get back to responsibility. Boaz didn't put all this in his letter, but did say he supported Gilmore in his right to die.

3

On those evenings that Timber Oaks Mental Health would let April out, Kathryne would take her to Nicole's apartment for a couple of hours. Sometimes April would say, "Sissy, are they really going to shoot Gary? Why doesn't Gary want to live, Sissy?" Nicole would be real calm about it. "Oh, I don't know," she'd say. Real calm. Like it didn't even bother her. It bothered Kathryne so bad, she'd bawl at night. Couldn't stand seeing the announcer on TV talking about it. There, right in the middle of the commercials. It made everybody on TV look crazy.

Sometimes, Nicole would come to Kathryne's with the kids and sleep over. She would never talk. Not even to her aunt Kathy. She would put Sunny and Jeremy to bed and then write poetry. That was all. Writing and writing at poetry. She was never abusive to the kids, just didn't pay much attention.

Right in the first week of November, Kip died. Killed in a fall down a mountain. Rock-climbing. Kathryne was getting ready for work on November 4, when she heard a name on the radio, Alfred Eberhardt, and said to herself, "Oh, my God, that must be Kip." All day at work, she worried how Sissy might be taking it. In fact, she went straight over to Springville from her job, and there was Nicole with her little lamp off, writing, writing. Kathryne went in and said, "What are you doing in the dark?" Nicole said, "Oh, I hadn't noticed." She turned on the light, got coffee, was laughing and joking around. Kathryne didn't know how to ask her if Alfred Eberhardt was Kip. Finally had to pop it. Nicole just said, "Yeah, yeah." Kathryne said, "That's what I was afraid of." Nicole said, "Yeah." Kathryne didn't think Nicole was showing what she ought.

A little later, however, Nicole looked up and said she'd like to call Kip's folks. Soon as Kathryne was all for it, Nicole said, "I don't know. What would I say to them?"

It did hurt, Kathryne said to herself. She does care.

Nicole was remembering back to that day years ago when she left Barrett and went out with all she owned in a pack on her back, and Sunny, an infant, on her arm. When Kip picked her up hitchhiking, their romance started right that night. He had been a stud in the beginning. A real first night.

The next day they found themselves driving in the Colorado Rockies, and Kip stopped the car and took Nicole and Sunny on a mountain trail. At one point they could see a fellow who was trying to climb a rock wall up a cliff. There was a little ledge about three feet off the ground that this fellow kept stepping onto, but then he would lose his nerve about going higher, and step back.

A couple of hours later, when they came down the trail, the fellow was still there. "He's stoned," said Kip, trying to laugh, but looked bothered. There were other fellows high up on the rock wall now with ropes, maybe as high as the eighth or tenth floor of a building, just hooked into the wall. Kip couldn't take his eyes off. Nicole could see him get depressed. It was like here he was with a new chick, a super chick, and these dudes were showing him up. In fact, Nicole wouldn't have minded meeting one of them. They looked superdaring.

The radio report said Kip was a novice climber. Nicole began to wonder if he had been doing it with ropes, or was like that poor stoned fellow stuck at the bottom of the ledge getting nowhere.

November 3
Just listen — and don't become rebellious or stubborn or independent as is often your immediate reaction when told to do or not to do a thing. Okay. What I am telling you is this: You are not to go before me. You mention this in your letter and I always take you serious. I don't like to tell anyone, but especially you, to do or not to do anything. Without giving them a reason. The reasons are this: I desire to go first. Period. I desire it. Second, I believe I may know a bit more ABOUT THE TRANSITION FROM LIFE TO DEATH than you do. I just think I do. I intend and expect to become instantly in your physical presence — wherever you are at the time. I will do all in my power to calm and soothe your grief, pain, and fear. I will wrap my very soul and all of the tremendous love I feel around you. You are not to go before me, Nicole Kathryne Gilmore. Do not disobey me.

A letter also came to Vern. In it Gary wrote that neither Vern nor Ida had come to visit him after his death sentence, *"so that's self-evident that you're ashamed of me."* Then Gary added, *"You haven't even put a frame on the portrait I gave you. I want you to take that picture and give it to Nicole. I don't want to have anything to do with you."*

When Ida got her bearings, she wrote, *"I cherish the drawings you gave me. That's the only thing I have of you. As far as me giving them up and giving them to Nicole, you can just go sit on it, I won't do it. They're mine."*

Vern added a note to Ida's letter, *"I don't know what's gotten into you. We tried to see you down at the jailhouse and the only person you wanted to see was Nicole, so we gave up. That's a true fact. I'm going to back Ida all the way. We're not giving the pictures up."*

Nicole, I hope it didn't develop into a hassle or a bad scene. I got a letter from Vern and Ida today — Ida would have you picked up if you "caused any trouble." (Her words, not mine.)

Jesus, baby, I'm sorry. I'm sorry I got relatives like that. I hope you did not have to go thru an unpleasant thing with either Vern or Ida. Fuck them. Forget it, let them keep the pictures. They know they ain't welcome to them but I ain't gonna have you go thru a hassle with them. I'm embarrassed about it.

Gary also wrote Brenda to give Nicole his oil painting, and she asked Vern what to do. Vern told her to follow her conscience. She sent Gary a letter: *"I don't want to, but if you insist I will. If it doesn't mean that much to you, it sure don't mean that much to me. Up your bucket. I don't want it. If that's how nasty and selfish and childish you want to be about it, I'll take it and stuff it over Nicole's head. Then she can really wear it and enjoy it."*

4

On the 3rd of November, Esplin got a letter from Gary. It read: *"Mike, butt out. Quit fucking around with my life. You're fired."*

PROVO HERALD

Nov. 4 — Despite being dismissed, the two defense attorneys later Wednesday filed a notice of appeal — in their names — with Fourth District Court Judge J. Robert Bullock.

They said it was "in the best interest" of the defendant.

That story produced numerous phone calls for Earl Dorius. The press kept asking what position the Attorney General's office intended to take on Gilmore. Dorius replied that Snyder and Esplin could try to file an appeal without their client's consent, but he thought they would lack standing.

Earl had the feeling "standing" was soon going to be a big legal word in the office. Even if Snyder and Esplin moved off the case, he figured other groups — whether Gilmore wanted it or not — would soon try to appeal. Then, standing — one's right to take a case to Court — was going to be very important.

November 4

Hi Baby.

Today when I was going to talk to Fagan about extra visits, this dude who was dressed sorta like a girl called to me from one of the other sections as I passed by . . . this cat's on Max for beating the shit out of a guard lieutenant. I guess he's a man in most respects, a solid convict from all I hear about him, but also a sissy, queen, or whatever you wanta call 'em. Tonite at chow he sent over this little note I'm enclosing for you to read — thot you might get a kick outa it.

Hi, Gil,
I have been reading about you in the paper and I must say that you are an exception to all rules. People just don't know what to think of you, hell they just don't know us Texans, do they, for we can handle anything in this fucking world, huh.

I made the remark this morning, that I was wanting to talk to you, to see what made you tick!

Sugar, don't pay any attention to some of the shit that I come off with, for you know how a dizzy bitch is.

What do you do over there all the time besides a lot of thinking? I guess that I shouldn't be asking you a lot of old foolish questions, but you know how a whore is, always wanting something!

Under it, Gary wrote:

Hey Baby Nicole — don't go getting any kind of jealous feelings now!

Jimmy Carter is the new Pres. Ain't that somethin! I didn't believe Ford could lose — I think it's only the second time in history of the entire universe that an incumbent president lost an election.

DESERET NEWS

Nov. 5 — Utah officials of the American Civil Liberties Union (ACLU)' and the NAACP said they will try to have their attorneys assist in the appeal process.

ACLU spokesman Shirley Pedler said, "Our stance is that the state does not have the right to take his life regardless of his choices or decisions."

I met an Indian today who I've known for years. His name's Chief Bolton. He was a guard in the Oregon joint when I knew him several years ago. He's a great big fucker. 300 pounds or so, a purty good man, even if he is a guard, and . . . he told me he can easily understand my feelings — Indians understand death more easily than white people I think —

November 5

I also got a letter from a Dennis Boaz in Salt Lake. He's a former lawyer from California. He seems to fully understand my situation and feels I have the right to make the ultimate decision without interference from any legal source. This guy Boaz is now a free-lance writer and wants to do an article for national publication. He said he would split any money he receives for his story with anyone I choose.

Well I reject that outright . . . I simply refuse to capitalize on this in any way . . .

This is a personal thing, it is my life Nicole. I can't help getting some publicity but I'm not looking for any.

Warden Smith asked me today what I might like for a last meal.
I always thot that was somethin they just did in the movies. I told
him I don't know but I would like a couple cans of Coors, he said he
didn't know about that — but maybe . . .

5

Some bug caught up with Earl, and he had to stay home from work.
It was the same day, November 5, that Gilmore phoned the office! In
the evening, Earl watched a couple of newscasts where Bill Barrett,
his associate — no relation to Jim or Nicole Barrett, Earl would yet
have to tell people — got interviewed with respect to Gilmore's phone
call. Earl was discouraged that he had not been in the office to take it
himself. Barrett might be his best friend at work, and they had made
a good team this last year — what the heck, they always joked, Barrett being tall and thin next to Earl who was short and well built, how
could they help but bring separate points of view to a problem? Still,
it was frustrating to be legal counsel to the prison, do all the work,
and yet miss a high spot like Gilmore calling up.

Barrett only spoke to Gary for four or five minutes, but as he later
told Earl, it was one of those things in his life that he didn't know if
he'd ever get over.

The call came in from Deputy Warden Hatch. A little later, Maximum Security was on the line with Lieutenant Fagan who introduced the convict. Barrett heard this soft-spoken man who
sounded very rational. He didn't rant, rave, yell or scream. In fact he
kept saying, Mr. Barrett.

First thing he asked about was getting a new lawyer.
"Mr. Gilmore," said Barrett, "I believe I understand your situa-
tion, but this office can't do anything. A new appointment is up to the
Court."
"Well, Mr. Barrett," said Gilmore, "it is not a spur-of-the-moment
decision. I have given a lot of thought to this, and I feel I should pay
for what I have done."
"The difficulty, Mr. Gilmore," Barrett said, "is that it may not be

routine to convince a lawyer that he ought to help you get executed. However, if there are any developments that I feel you should know about, I'll keep you informed. I am sympathetic to your position."

Actually, Barrett felt helpless. It was all so incongruous. His job was to see that the man got executed, so they were working on the same side, yet they weren't.

A reporter hanging around the office picked up the story. After it was printed, Barrett got calls from all over the country. ABC correspondent Greg Dobbs rang in from Chicago and said, "I'll be out this weekend, can I interview you? Can I come to your home?" Before it was over, they set a time. Radio stations in the Deep South interviewed him by telephone. In Utah!

Work hit Earl like never before. In the criminal division of the Attorney General's office, there were only two full-time attorneys, Barrett and himself, plus a few law clerks and secretaries. That was not much staff to take on all that was coming in. Right next day, for instance, Dorius ran into two well-known Salt Lake lawyers named Gil Athay and Robert Van Sciver, and they were holding a press conference out in the hall of the Utah Supreme Court a floor above the Attorney General's office. Earl heard them saying to the cameras that they intended to request a Stay of Gilmore's execution on behalf of all other Death Row inmates at Utah State Prison. Athay's client was one of the "hi-fi killers."

The hi-fi killers had been convicted of killing several people in a record store. First they poured Drano down their throats, then pushed ball-point pens into their ears. Those were the most gruesome killings in Utah for many years, exactly the kind to bring capital punishment back in one big hurry. Gilmore, by asking for his execution, wasn't going to sweeten public opinion toward the hi-fi killers.

Yes, it was heating up fast. Too fast. Dorius had been looking forward to a conference in Phoenix for corrections officials that he and Barrett were going to attend, but this was a poor time to leave the shop. Earl was being interviewed like crazy by members of the media. They caught him in his office, at home, on the street — everywhere.

CHAPTER 2

Synchronicity

1

No sooner had Earl Dorius and Bill Barrett arrived at the correction officials conference, than they noticed that Gary Gilmore was hot news in Phoenix too. TV reports every night. In fact, they even saw the interview Greg Dobbs did with Bill Barrett on the ABC evening news. To be actually seeing Barrett on national network!

Then Earl and Bill met two Assistant Attorney Generals from the State of Oregon who talked about what a problem Gilmore used to be in the Oregon prison system. It seems he was never satisfied with his false teeth. Every time they made a new set, he would flush them down the toilet. The prison finally said that if he sent any more choppers that route, he'd be gumming his food for the rest of his penitentiary life. These Assistant Attorney Generals now said jokingly that after Gilmore was executed, Utah ought to return the plates to the Oregon Department of Corrections.

Next day, new developments. If you jacked up an old plaster ceiling, you couldn't have more fast-developing cracks in a situation. The Utah Supreme Court had just ruled on Snyder and Esplin's petition for an appeal and had given Gilmore a Stay of Execution whether he wanted it or not. Now, nobody knew when it would come off. Same day, Gilmore sent a letter back to the Court. The papers naturally printed it. Earl thought he could hardly believe what he was reading.

Don't the people of Utah have the courage of their convictions?
You sentence a man to die — me — and when I accept this most ex-
treme punishment with grace and dignity, you, the people of Utah
want to back down and argue with me about it. You're silly.

Right after that, Warden Smith called. Another Gilmore letter to
him:

Sir, I do not wish to see any members of the press. However
there is a man named Dennis Boaz, free lance writer, and former
attorney, who I do desire to see. Mr. Boaz is the only exception to my
no-interview rule.

Who, wondered Earl, is Dennis Boaz?

2

On Sunday night, Gary said to Cline Campbell, "I need your help. I
have no lawyer and I figure to be in Court in a few days. I can always
go up there and represent myself, but it would look more serious if I
have an attorney." He handed a letter to Campbell. "This man says
he's a lawyer. Will you contact him?" When Campbell promised he
would, Gilmore added, "You got to do it quick."

The letter gave no telephone number. Monday morning, Campbell drove to the address on the envelope, and ran into a fellow just
leaving the apartment. He turned out to be Boaz's roommate, and
said, "Dennis is in bed, but I'll get him up. He's been writing all
night."

After Campbell told Boaz why he had come, both took a good
look at each other. Campbell had to squint toward the ceiling. Boaz
was as tall as a basketball player, six-four at least, and, like a tele-
scope, seemed to go up in extensions. At the top, he had a pleasant
serious face, dark hair, and a dark brush mustache. To Campbell he
looked as much like a tall skinny doctor or dentist as a lawyer.

3

Since Dennis had been living rent-free in the basement his first thought when Campbell arrived was that the fellow might be a creditor. Campbell looked like a tough clean little soldier. He had a no-nonsense look, straight as starch. Of course Dennis had this new Saab he was out on a limb on. What the hell, he was broke. In fact, he owed ten grand. Under such circumstances, he naturally thought Campbell had come to repossess the Saab. The moment he found out Cline was instead the bearer of good tidings, he was able to take a liking to him. A gentle soft-spoken man, he decided, courteous and concerned.

The place was looking a mess. Everson, his roommate, was a little disorganized at the time, and so there were books and papers all over, and this big double bed in the front room, somewhat chaotic, right. Campbell wasn't going to be impressed unless he could see that the place had decent atmosphere. Everson was a good dude for letting him stay there, since it certainly interfered with Everson having any ladies around. Yet being such a good person about it, Everson's attitude mellowed out the chaos. Besides, Boaz felt he was now in the positive channel of the flow. He could carry off worse appearances than this.

He told Campbell it would only take an hour to get ready but then he had to get batteries for his tape recorder, and check in on his legal job for the bus drivers' union. That was supposed to pay him a nominal retainer but hadn't yet. With it all, he didn't get out to the prison till two o'clock, three hours later.

The prison was at Point of the Mountain, twenty miles south from Salt Lake City, halfway to Orem and Provo, and just opposite the place on the Interstate where the mountain came down to the road. To the right, at the exit, you got a good look at all the barrens stretching west, and then a view of the prison right at the edge of the desert, a compound of low yellow stone buildings behind a high wire fence.

Boaz parked his Saab, walked under the guard tower and into the Administration Building. It had a small entrance and no lobby, just two narrow hallways intersecting at right angles and an information window to one side of this cross. It was like the dinky office you might find inside the door of a large warehouse. The guards wore maroon blazers that were too short in the back for those who had big asses, and Boaz could see them strolling down the hall, or going in and out of the crashing double gates that led into Medium Security. A trustee standing by a glass museum case was selling convict-made tooled leather belts to a group of tourists. Compared to California prisons he'd seen, Dennis thought it was old and funky for a state penitentiary. Still, it didn't have the worst vibration, but was kind of farmlike. Simple faces on the guards, and sly, like they'd been out in the hay. Yet nothing invidious or technologically corrupt. Why, some of the older guards had bellies sticking out large as wheelbarrows, yes, a simple place relatively speaking, country people as they should be. Some very tough dudes among the guards.

Outside the Warden's office was a typed message tacked to the wall:

> *I hate guys*
> *Who criticize*
> *Vigorous guys*
> *Whose enterprise*
> *Has helped them rise*
> *Above the guys*
> *Who criticize*
> *Sam Smith*

Then the office. Small for a Warden's den, and awful small for Sam Smith who was even taller than Dennis and had a big numb hulk of a body. He looked kind of a cross, Dennis thought, between Boris Karloff and Andy Warhol, and wore big light-shelled plastic-frame glasses. In fact, he spoke in a soft voice.

"I think," said Dennis, "you have some knowledge of my coming here."

"No," said Smith, "I don't know anything about it."

Awful cautious man, thought Dennis. Smith, he decided, was in a frozen space, expression-wise. Leaned back in his chair and looked at his visitor with circumspection.

Dennis explained that he was there as a writer. Gilmore wanted to discuss the possibility of doing an interview with him.

"Oh," said Smith, "we can't let any writers in."

"Well, Gilmore wants to see me. He sent the Chaplain."

Smith shook his head. These were very Warden-type energies, Dennis decided. Many layers of control over fear — didn't want anything to interfere with that control.

"What is this?" said Dennis, starting to get angry. "The man's going to die soon, and no one's getting any access to him. He wants to see me. He wants to *talk*."

"I just can't let any writers in," said Smith. Man, his body was rigid. For a big man, Smith moved all right, but he sure was tightly controlled. Dennis didn't like him, not the way he'd sit in his chair, cold, worried, not smiling.

Sam Smith sat there thinking for a long time. His next remark surprised Dennis. "Well," said the Warden, "you *are* a lawyer."

He sure knows, thought Dennis, a lot more about me than he has let on up to now.

From California, Dennis told him. Well, murmured Sam Smith in reply, we couldn't interfere with Gilmore's right to see a lawyer.

Now Boaz was beginning to get it. Could it be that Smith wanted him around instead of Esplin and Snyder? Even if they had been fired, they were still the only Gilmore lawyers in existence. Already, they had caused a delay. Of course! The Warden wanted the execution to take place on time.

Sam Smith still wasn't friendly. In fact, you might say he was physically intimidating. But now he said in that quiet voice, never looking at Boaz, that the only way Mr. Boaz could get in was as a legal counselor. Something would have to be put in writing to that effect.

Dennis drafted a note to say he wouldn't do magazine or newspaper articles, and was in the prison as a lawyer. He added, however, that he was writing this at the Warden's request, and made a point of saying, "Our agreement is illegal." The Warden was angered. It came off him like the radiation from a heated iron skillet. Obviously, these procedures all meant a great deal to Sam Smith. The man had something to prove.

Boaz was let in, but without his tape recorder. A guard took him outside the Administration Building and they walked in the November air about a hundred yards over to Maximum Security, one ugly squat building by itself. There Boaz was put in a fairly large visiting room, maybe 40 by 25, with only a guard in a bullet-proof glass cage to keep an eye on him. That guard was controlling the door to get in and out, but probably couldn't hear much inside his booth. He was half asleep. Stupor on top of old woe was the sad vibration Dennis was getting from Maximum.

4

Dennis's first impression was that an intelligence had just come into the room. Gilmore showed a quiet indrawn face. Dennis thought he might not have noticed him on the street unless they made eye contact. Gilmore had smoky gray-blue eyes with a lot of light in them. Startling. A direct clear gaze. Since he was wearing the loose white coveralls of Maximum Security, and had come into the room barefoot, Dennis could see him as a holy man in New Delhi.

They got off to a good start. Boaz laid an awful lot down real fast. Told of his law background, Boalt Hall at Berkeley — Gary's nod showed he knew these were worthy credentials — and of the time he had put in as assistant prosecutor in the D.A.'s office of Contra Costa County a little northwest of San Francisco. He had been a pot-smoking prosecutor, he made a point of telling Gary. While he had dealt in the punitive side of the law, his sympathies were more to the defense. That was probably because of listening to Ginsberg and Kerouac back in the late fifties when just a college freshman — he and Gilmore must be about the same age, they agreed — and then later giving his sympathies to people like Mario Savio, Jerry Rubin, and the Berkeley movement in general. He pinpointed his life with these names — Gilmore knew the names.

Lately, he had not practiced much law, Boaz said. Too restricting. He was interested more in the consciousness movement, encounter groups, meditation, Sufi, the process called Fischer-Hoffman. He had come out of that process so moved by the transformations in himself that he became a Fischer-Hoffman counsellor. Still he came to find that restricting. So, in his mind at least, he had moved on to Findhorn. He liked the idea that there was a place where twenty-pound cabbages could be grown in an inch of topsoil way up in Scotland, and even flowers could bloom in the winter through your attunement to the plants and your ability to guide the energies as they came down.

Gilmore took it all in, and came back with good questions. Boaz was kind of blown out of it. Gilmore was offering the best intellectual conversation he'd had since coming to Salt Lake City. Bizarre.

They were rapping about books, a fast heavy rap, and Gary was talking about *Demian* by Hermann Hesse, and *Catch-22*, Ken Kesey, Alan Watts, *Death in Venice*. He called the author Tom Mann, and said, "the pretty boy knocked me out." Finally he said, "I like everything that wild Irish maniac, J. P. Donleavy, ever wrote." It wasn't so much a discussion as a sharing of taste. He also liked *The Agony and the Ecstasy* and *Lust for Life* by Irving Stone.

Dennis wasn't hearing ideas that were new to him, hell, by comparison to most, he was pretty cultivated in these matters even if, by his own measure, a dilettante. Still he was conversant, and so was impressed that Gilmore was actually this familiar with the consciousness stuff. While, essentially, Gary had nothing new to contribute, still he had done a good deal of thinking on the subject. "You cannot escape yourself," Gilmore said. "You have to meet yourself."

Dennis was all for that. You *were* responsible for your actions. But he thought Gilmore was a little dogmatic about reincarnation. In that area, Boaz had no intense belief himself — reincarnation was just one possibility among others. "Look, Gary," he said — he had decided to play devil's advocate — "I've been with a person who said he'd take me back into my past lives, and we did some exercises. I can play that game. I was supposed to have died on the rack in the fourteenth century, and then I was Pan at another time. I looked down and saw those cloven feet — right? Could have been nothing but my creative imagination. I don't know. I'm open, but I don't find it relevant. I think one can have ethics without getting into reincarnation."

Gilmore shook his head. "There is reincarnation," he said, "I *know*."

Boaz dropped it. No matter how you might love a discussion, you had to sense when to give way.

They got into numerology. Gilmore's birthday added up to 21. In tarot, that was the card for The Universe. 2 and 1 also made 3, a fortunate number, The Empress. In turn, Boaz's birthday summed up to The Emperor and The Fool.

"We're balanced," said Boaz, giggling.

"Yeah," said Gilmore, "we're good partners."

If you assigned numbers to the letters in the name, however, Gary added up to seven, and Gilmore to six. Thirteen was the card for death. Boaz could feel that vibration going right through Gilmore. What a waste, he thought, what a shame. He's down to the last week of his life. It made him sad that he was one of the very few people to realize Gilmore was serious about dying with dignity, and he told him so.

Gilmore nodded. "I'm ready to give you the interview," he said, but added, "I'd like some help. Will you be my lawyer?"

If he agreed, thought Dennis, a lot of people were sure not going to understand. It was going to be awfully difficult professionally. But what an experience!

"God," said Dennis, "do you know the kind of reputation I'm going to get for this?"

"You can handle it," Gary said.

Boaz nodded. He could handle it. Still, he had to say, "I feel like Judas helping you get executed."

"Judas," said Gary, "was the most bum-beefed man in history."

Judas knew what was going down, Gilmore said. Judas was there to help Jesus tune into the prophecy.

Now that they had agreed to work together, Boaz began to ponder the tougher side of Gary. Macho to a certain extent. Of course, he had had to use a gun to prove his power. Lived in ultimates. Must have been a very sensitive child.

At this point, Gary said, "It's like I'm the Fonz and you're Richie." That made Dennis think of his eighth grade in Fresno and the element in school who got girls and smoked and looked at porno photographs and drank illicit booze, all the while that he was still naive about it.

On the way out, Gilmore said, "I want you to come every day." Boaz promised he would. He had been there close to three hours.

Sam Smith wanted to know how it had gone. Came up to Dennis in the hall and gave a smile. "Well, Mr. Boaz," asked Sam Smith, "are you really with us?" With Us?

It brought in response, a grin to Dennis's face. The Defense Attorney buddying with the Warden. "Yeah, I'm with you, Warden." Yeah. All the way.

5

Even though they got to California years after the Okies migrated from the dust bowl, Boaz's folks were touchy about coming from Oklahoma. All through the Depression and the Second World War, Okie had been a bad word in Fresno. It didn't matter that Dennis's stepfather was a Staff Sergeant in the Army, it was still a stigma. As a kid, Dennis would say things like "my brother, he . . ." and in elementary school they made him take a remedial English course. He would make up for that by getting good grades in high school, and working on diction and making friends with kids from middle-class parents. Wanted to establish himself as a Californian.

When he was older, however, he could appreciate his heritage. A part of him never did get won over by all this middle-class ethos. But he had worked at it. He got elected student body president in the ninth grade, played basketball, and was captain of the tennis team in high school, yet he always knew he was being an overachiever and all through college and law school, he had this big division in himself. Would he opt for that job as Assistant D.A. up in Contra Costa

County, or go for an underground thing about the right to play, and the pursuit of happiness?

A third of the Prosecutors in the Contra Costa office, the younger ones, smoked pot all the while they were working under bosses with narrow attitudes and that FBI mentality — white short-sleeved shirts and skinny black ties.

In one party at a two-story bungalow a half-dozen young Prosecutors, including Dennis, drifted up to the attic for a toke, while down below their bosses were imbibing alcohol in the living room. The true juxtaposition between booze and grass. The bosses — you could say, the boozers — were down in hell, and Dennis and all his associates upstairs in heaven.

About then, Dennis got married to a beautiful woman, and helped raise her son. Dennis had been brought up by a stepfather and had ended as a stepfather. Good symmetry helped to maintain good emotion. It was a good marriage for a while. He left the D.A.'s office, did criminal defense, and enjoyed that. It was more dramatic to fight in Court for someone's liberty than to protect their money. He and his wife, Ariadne, during that time, also took a taste of the sensuous aspects of the right to play. The selfish things, good cars, French food, trips to Europe.

Then he and Ariadne went off in different directions. Divorce was a shock point. Dennis got less interested in his practice. Law was dealing with property problems, and here was he with psychological problems. He moved over into consciousness raising, and hung in with a Hindu named Harish. In orbit around the guru were physicists, poets, artists, physicians, musicians, and theatre people. A group of them formed Maya Modulation. They all put money into a sound film that was going to be made in India, but one of the members died over there. The whole thing kind of collapsed.

By '75, Dennis was flat-out broke, and determined to live as a writer. Flopped in Ariadne Street in East Oakland with an old handball-playing partner, and a mad jogger. The house smelled of track shoes and sweat socks. Dennis slept on a couch in the front room for six months. There were dog's hairballs all over the house on Ariadne

Street. Still, it was the name of his ex-wife. Good vibes in that synchronicity. He also had a couple of lady friends who took pity on a struggling writer and gave him nurturing.

But by '76, he was on a yo-yo. A couple of weeks of free room and board with his mother meant living with her annoyance that a successful young lawyer had let it all go. A couple of months with a buddy who ran an after-hours club meant no sleep and no writing. Next he painted a house for his real father. Dennis was living by his wits. Of course, he loved brinkmanship.

But he decided to go back to the law. He also cared about responsibility. His real father was a pipe fitter, and Dennis never wanted to lose his identity with the working class. In fact, he'd even worked in college as a teamster. So now he took up this retainer for the bus drivers' union in Salt Lake and got ready to prepare a lawsuit against the bus companies who were not allowing bus drivers to use CBs. As Dennis saw it, CBs could save lives in emergencies. He was, therefore, commuting by Saab between California and Utah, when, on the last of these swings, he saw the dead man on the highway while coming back to Salt Lake to vote for Carter.

6

Now, one week later, his life was on the brink of great change. He was going up the hill to the State Capitol with its beautiful dome that he had looked at so often, for it was visible just about anywhere below in Salt Lake. Dennis was certainly feeling up for the occasion. Today he was going to lay his calling card on the Attorney General's desk, and declare that Gilmore wanted Dennis Boaz to be his lawyer tomorrow before the Utah Supreme Court and there argue his right not to have any delay of execution. It was going to be no ordinary meeting, and Dennis took his time going through the building. He was trying to pick up the aura of these old Mormons. The piety in the air was like the heavy piety you could find in all courtrooms and governmental buildings, except without the old stale cigar smoke. Maybe there was less payola in this piety. It sure smelled of reverential air. Like we will all be present on Day One when the Lord makes His appearance.

Dennis had already visited Temple Square and looked at the building where the Mormon Tabernacle Choir sang, and in the Visitors Center he had listened to the guide tell the story of God coming to Joseph Smith with the golden plates of the Angel Moroni. Dennis couldn't help it, he had a big reaction: there were these angels Mormon and Moroni, two angels directly under God, just as important as Peter and Paul in Mormon circles, and their names had something to tell him.

It was only after he had walked up to the Capitol Building and was standing on the steps, looking down the hill and out across Salt Lake City, that it came to him. From here, on a clear day, you could see across half of Utah. Only today it was not clear. There never was that clear a day in Salt Lake anymore. Once, the desert of Utah had been as beautiful as the deserts of Palestine in the Old Testament, but now it looked no better than the outskirts of Los Angeles. Shacky ranch houses stretched as far as the smog would allow the eye to see, and off to the west were the smelters of Anaconda Copper pouring up into the pollution of the sky. Dennis really got it then. Those angels, Mormon and Moroni, meant More Money. No wonder the Mormons were getting to be the richest church in America. All that sanction to make More and More Money. Dennis giggled. His consciousness was now raised to deal with the Attorney General.

Intrigued with the similarity of the names, Dennis knew nonetheless that the A.G. elect, Robert Hansen, was no relation to Phil Hansen, former Attorney General and best-known criminal lawyer in Utah. No, this Hansen, Robert Hansen, had been elected just last week from Assistant A.G. to Attorney General.

He did not look bad in Dennis's eyes. Kind of friendly and curt. A well-built good-looking right-winger, dark hair, glasses, sort of Republican cabinet material — a Clark Kent character. They talked about law schools right off, and Boaz knew he had gotten to a good place in Bob Hansen's mind when he said Boalt. Hansen replied that he had gone to Hastings. Right. Right. It was all so neat and formal in this big walnut-paneled office with blue rugs, dark blue velvet drapes.

The media, Hansen explained, were assuming that his office was cooperating with Gilmore's desire to die, even piggybacking on it. However, the Attorney General's office would insist that Gilmore was not going to die because he wanted to, but because it was the lawful proper sentence for what he had done.

That said, Hansen got cooperative. Boaz, he explained, would need a Utah attorney as sponsor before the State Supreme Court. It happened that the Deputy Attorney General, Mike Deamer, had a classmate named Tom Jones right in his office at this time. Tom Jones, called in, quickly agreed. It was all full of teamwork and smooth.

Preparing his case that night, Dennis was trying to take into account the Utah Supreme Court he would appear before. They had a reputation of being to the right of Barry Goldwater. Those Justices were probably all Mormon, and just about the closest thing you could find on the Bench to a theocracy. Dennis decided he would be most effective, therefore, if he were a little emotional in his argument. While he hadn't done any criminal law since the spring of '74, he didn't feel lax. To the contrary, he felt highly competent. There was, after all, no need to do research here. Hansen, with his assistants, could handle five or six times the output he could muster at this late hour. So he would try, Dennis decided, to give the Judges sympathy for Gilmore's desire to die with dignity.

7

MR. HANSEN   The State of Utah is not here to urge Mr. Gilmore's rights, the State is here to urge the rights of the people. . . . I submit that the Stay of Execution is . . . contrary to the rights of the victim and his family, and contrary to the public interest as has been set forth by the laws of this state.

JUSTICE HENRIOD   Thank you. Which one of you gentlemen wants to address the court? You may proceed.

MR. BOAZ   Your Honor, the Supreme Court of the State of Utah . . . I have reviewed the case set by the Attorney General and agree with their opinion. . . . This is not a case where my client makes some kind of suicide pact with the State, or has some kind of perverse death wish. He is a man who is willing to accept the responsibility for his act, and he has asked that there be speedy and just execution . . . as opposed to the lingering death that would accompany an imposed automatic appeal that might stretch into days, months, conceivably years. It is not for us to judge. None of us here have spent more than 90 percent of our adult life in the cages where the animals are. He has made an intelligent decision whether he wishes to continue his life or be executed. He is here acting in that capacity as a sane, responsible man who has accepted the judgment of the people, who has made peace with himself, and wishes to die like a man with self-respect and dignity. . . . That is all he is asking of the Court, that the motion for appeal be set aside and that the Stay be vacated, and that he be allowed to die with self-respect next Monday. I now have some questions for Mr. Gilmore. . . . Gary Gilmore, do you realize you have an absolute right to appeal the conviction and sentence rendered in this case?

MR. GILMORE   Yes sir.

JUSTICE HENRIOD   Mr. Gilmore, will you speak as loudly as you possibly can so that everyone can hear you because I can hardly hear you myself.

MR. BOAZ   Did you previously indicate to your attorneys of record that you did not wish an appeal taken in this case?

MR. GILMORE   I told them during the trial and perhaps before that, that if I were found guilty and sentenced to death that I would prefer to accept without any delay. I guess perhaps they didn't quite take me literal because when it became a reality and . . . I still felt the same way, they wanted to argue with me about it . . . told me they were going to file appeals over my objections. Now I wasn't able to fire them in front of a Judge and make the matter record simply because I don't have access to Judges in Court because I am in prison. But I fired them and they understand that.

MR. BOAZ   Gary Gilmore, are you in fact at this moment ready to accept execution?

MR. GILMORE   Not at this moment, but I am ready to accept it . . . next Monday morning at 8:00 A.M. That is when it was set. That is when I am ready to accept it.

JUSTICE HENRIOD   I think in the interest of justice we should ask Mr. Snyder to state his position. I want this to be very brief.

MR. SNYDER For the record, I have talked to Mr. Gilmore far more and far longer than Mr. Boaz has. It is my opinion that this type of decision facing Mr. Gilmore has placed tremendous emotional stress and strain upon him. . . . What Mr. Gilmore, in my opinion, is attempting to do in this case is tantamount to suicide. He does not have to die. . . . I think it would be a shame if this Court at this point withdrew the Stay of Execution, and allowed Mr. Gilmore to be executed on November 15th without having reviewed and considered the substantial matters which are raised both by the trial conviction and the subsequent proceeding.

JUSTICE HENRIOD Thank you.

JUSTICE MAUGHAN . . . Your concern then, as I understand it, is to make sure that as a matter of fact due process has occurred. . . .

MR. SYNDER That is exactly correct. . . . We were appointed by the Court to insure that Mr. Gilmore got a fair trial and that there was no error and the process of the trial ought to have been reviewed by this Court.

JUSTICE ELLETT You are no longer in it. You have been relieved, you have been supplanted. . . .

MR. SNYDER I understand that. . . .

JUSTICE ELLETT Why won't you accept in good grace his firing you, like he is willing to accept in good grace the sentence of the Court?

JUSTICE CROCKETT I think that counsel has done what they conscientiously think they should do and I think we should not criticize them for what they have done. But, we have a different situation now and we all appreciate it.

JUSTICE HENRIOD Mr. Gilmore, is there anything that you would like to say at this time without being asked any questions?

MR. GILMORE Your Honor, I don't want to take up a lot of your time with my words. I believe I was given a fair trial and I think the sentence is proper and I am willing to accept it like a man. I don't wish to appeal. I don't know exactly what the motives are of Mr. Esplin and Mr. Snyder . . . I know they have professional careers to consider — maybe they are catching some criticism they don't like. I don't know. But I desire to be executed on schedule, and I just wish to accept that with the grace and dignity of a man and I hope you will allow that to be. That is all I have to say.

8

Gary and Dennis were in a room together when the result was brought in. The Utah Supreme Court had lifted the Stay by a vote of 4 to 1. Monday, November 15, the execution would take place.

Gary was elated with the result. "It brings him peace," Dennis said to himself, "to know he's leaving all this." In a few minutes, he would say as much at a press conference.

"You can have," Gary said now, "everything you make off the writing." "Oh, no," Dennis said, laughing, "I figure fifty-fifty. It just seems fair."

It was the first time they had discussed terms. Fifty-fifty it would be. They didn't even bother to draw up a paper. Just shook hands.

DESERET NEWS

Salt Lake, Nov. 10 — Handcuffed and his feet shackled, Gilmore was led into Court chambers in the State Capitol Building. Security was tight. When he departed, a crush of spectators and national and local news reporters and cameramen engulfed the man.

That night, over dinner, Bob Hansen's wife and the children all wanted to hear about Gilmore. In private practice, Hansen never discussed his cases, but the Attorney General's office was constantly involved in public issues. It was like practicing law in a fish bowl. So Hansen's kids were not only curious, but knowledgeable. They virtually researched his cases in the newspaper.

Now, over the dinner table, he told his family that Boaz had been articulate, even impressive, and Gilmore had struck him as being on an intellectual par with the Court. In fact, Hansen could not think of another case in which the accused person seemed to be able to understand and deal with lawyers and Judges as peers. Yet Gilmore had never presented himself as a lawyer. Hansen thought that was impressive, too. You never had the feeling he was contemptuous of the Judges or of the lawyers' right to argue for him, or against him. That added dignity. In fact, Hansen remarked he certainly hadn't acted like a disoriented or depressed person, but on the contrary, seemed altogether sane. That had impressed him, he said. The family ate thoughtfully.

November 10

Dear Gilroy,

He vuzz justa keed! I've been debating wether or not to write, but I decided just to drop a few lines and enclosed a few dollars, I'm sure you can put it to good use.

I've heard a lot concerning you on the news; you know you've got more style, class, and guts than anyone I've ever met.

There is something I want to say and as you know I'm not good with words such as you, so I'll just come out and say it.

I don't know what kind of funeral arrangements your family, relatives, & Nicole have made, but if there is anything I can do to help out financially just let me know who and where you want it sent.

GEEBS

DESERET NEWS

Gilmore Story Is Front Page News

November 11, Salt Lake. . . . The decision by the Utah Supreme Court to allow Gary Mark Gilmore to die before a prison firing squad was front page news today in the New York Times, the New York Daily News and the Washington Post.

NEW YORK TIMES

Nov. 11, 1976 — Detective Glade M. Perry of the Provo Police Department was one of the volunteers for the firing squad. "Somebody's got to do it," he said, "and we've got the guts to put our lives on the line every day."

A gray-haired, elderly man, who refused to give his name, said: "The parents of the boys that Gilmore killed should be given the chance to shoot him."

Sheriff Ed Ryan of Ogden said that in the past he

received dozens of requests from people who wanted to serve on a firing squad, but he added:

"They'd have buck fever if the time ever came to do the job. One of the men on my force participated in an execution nearly 20 years ago and he swears he's sorry he ever did it — it still bothers him late at night."

LOS ANGELES HERALD EXAMINER

Nov. 17, Salt Lake — . . . Gilmore let it be known that his choice for the condemned man's traditional last meal was a six-pack of cold beer.

"Gary's on a real macho trip, that's for sure," Boaz said, "but he's not that cold-blooded. He believes in karma, and that he will suffer pain for what he's done. He also believes that the soul evolves and there is reincarnation and that the manner in which he dies can be a learning experience for others."

CHAPTER 3

The Sob Sister

1

About the time that all the reporters were finding out they couldn't get an interview with Gary because of those darn prison requirements, Tamera Smith, of the *Deseret News,* noticed a lot of interest beginning to focus on Nicole Barrett. The word was out that Nicole was seeing Gary every day, so everybody was trying to get to her. Nobody had been successful, except for a fellow on Channel 5 who talked with Gilmore's sweetheart for a few minutes one night on the air. Tamera thought Nicole was not at her best there. In fact, she looked peaked and worried, like a drenched little bird.

Anyway, a fellow reporter on the *Deseret News* named Dale Van Atta happened to be complaining how hard it was to get to Nicole, and Tamera said, "I've met her before. Would you like me to try?"

Van Atta looked at her for what she was, girl reporter out of college, and said, "I don't think it will do you any good," but she called the prison, and Nicole happened to be in the Maximum Security visiting room. Tamera wasn't expecting to talk that quickly, and hardly knew what to say, except that Nicole remembered right off who she was, so Tamera said, "I wonder if you'd like to get together and talk a little."

Even on the telephone, Tamera felt the thought go in. Nicole always received things you said very seriously. Even the most casual remark she would take all of the way into herself. It was as if she only trusted herself to give the right answer if she got *all* of what you laid on her. Now, after a pause, Nicole said she really wouldn't want to talk, but there was something about the way she answered that was encouraging, so Tamera asked if they could do it off the record. Again, there was the pause, and then Nicole said, *off* the record, that would be okay, like a hand was taking the record off the turntable. Tamera said she'd pick her up at the prison.

Out in the parking lot, Tamera was stomping around in the early November snow and shivering, when Nicole came down the walk from Maximum, saw her, gave a nice smile and came over. On the drive, however, Nicole started looking sad again. Soon she mentioned that her grandfather had died, and his funeral was going to be in two days, and then there was this ex–boy friend Kip who had also died just a day or two ago. Now Gary was excited because just this morning he had won in front of the Utah Supreme Court and was probably going to face a firing squad on Monday. It surprised Tamera that Nicole didn't appear upset. She just sat, still and calm, smoking away quietly, one of those people who looked like they really enjoyed a cigarette.

Tamera stopped in Provo to buy Nicole lunch, and they must have talked for a good two hours there at J.B.'s on Center Street, eating Big Boys, and milkshakes. J.B.'s was usually jammed with college kids, but this was the middle of the afternoon, and it was pretty empty. Tamera could feel Nicole getting off on talking to her.

2

Back in August, they had met at Gary's second Preliminary Hearing. Tamera was working then as a Provo stringer for the *Deseret News,* a job she got on the basis of her work at BYU on the *Daily Universe.* Having done college journalism, she was used to a police beat, but in Court, Nicole sure captured her attention.

When they brought Gilmore into the room, shuffling along in leg shackles, there was this girl sitting in the front row and he stopped in front of her, and kissed, and Tamera knew it had to be his girl friend. She even heard him say, "I love you." Tamera found herself having this immediate empathy with the girl. Gilmore didn't look anything really overpowering right then, just a regular criminal, hard looking, almost sleazy, with a marked-up face. Tamera felt humiliated for him in leg manacles, walking in short jerky steps like he was a spavined monster or something, but it was the girl who drew her, in fact, absolutely fascinated her by those looks. She had a kind of mystique about her, a sky glow, Tamera thought, like an old movie star. The drama of it came right over Tamera. There's another woman in the story besides the widows, she said to herself.

After Court, Tamera hung in the background and watched Gary kiss Nicole good-bye. Then, on the street, she watched Nicole wave until he was completely out of sight. You could tell she'd gotten herself all fixed up for him because she was wearing a long dress that was kind of old-fashioned and demure. Tamera, watching, felt so tall and gawky and dirty blond that she kept going "Oh, oh," to herself, you know, at how beautiful Nicole was. She even waited until Nicole was clear into her car. Then Tamera couldn't stand it anymore. Just had a compelling need to talk, and ran across the street to do it.

At the time, it had nothing to do with a story. Gilmore was a routine case. Tamera just wanted Nicole to know somebody cared. In a town like Provo, everybody took the side of the victims.

At the car, she said, "My name is Tamera Smith and I work for the *Deseret News* and I'd like to talk. Not for a story, but as friends. I wonder if you'd like to get some coffee. You must have a lot on your mind right now." Nicole hesitated, then said, yeah, she'd like that, so they got in her car, which drove in the most awful way, never knew which gear it would go into, and Nicole mentioned it had been in an accident two days ago, and they went down to Sambo's and talked.

The girls told each other about themselves, in fact, Tamera found herself rattling away at a great rate. She was amazed how soon she told Nicole that her father had died years ago and it had left this hunger inside herself ever since, this terrible empty space that kept her restless all the time. Then she told how she used to write to a guy in prison, and her brothers and sisters, who were all as active Mormons as you could find, had been terribly upset. But the fellow had been wonderful, and she'd even gone to visit him in a Kentucky prison. That certainly opened Nicole up.

All the while Tamera was enraptured. It wasn't that Nicole was a striking beauty, yet she was. She had such an air of calm. It was like sitting on the back porch for all of a hot July afternoon, just that long calm feeling. From the stories Nicole was telling, Tamera figured she had to have a big temper, but she was so serene that day.

When they said good-bye, Tamera passed over her telephone number, and said, "If you ever need help, I'd be glad to see you." That was it. The newspaper didn't assign her to the trial in October and she had no more to do with the case. Went her separate way. Almost forgot.

3

Now, at J.B.'s, hey, wow, maybe there was nobody near to her that Nicole could trust, but she sure let the floodgate go. Right over those milkshakes, she told Tamera she was planning suicide. Told it straight up with all those deaths hanging on her, Kip, her grandfather, Gary soon. Tamara could see she was afraid.

What made Tamera want to cry was that Nicole was waiting out her death date just like Gilmore. When she was around him it was all right, she said, and she wasn't afraid because Gary had a vision of what life would be like after death, but when she got away, it was frightening again. The on-again off-again must be hideous, Tamera thought. Every time Gary got a Stay, Nicole did, too.

It was mind-blowing for Tamera. Her friends were always kidding her for being such an emotional person, and Tamera always thought she had to be one of the most divided people in existence. So active and true-believing a Mormon on the one hand, such crazy impulses on the other. Why, to anyone but herself, she would have been a mess. To grow up with the Doctrine of Covenants, and believe all of it to this day, yet go hog wild over the Rolling Stones. Her roommates at BYU used to say that if she didn't gush, she'd overflow — such lava inside. Now, to get handed this story. It was the biggest story she'd ever come near, yet at the same time she was worried stiff over Nicole.

Tamera hadn't planned on prying. But now she had to ask questions. "What about the kids?" she wanted to know.

Nicole looked like she would cry. She didn't, she confessed, treat them nearly as good as she wanted to. Tamera asked if she and Gary talked a lot about this suicide, and Nicole said, "That's all we ever talk about."

Tamera was burning to do the story.

On the street, outside Nicole's little apartment building, they could see a van from a Salt Lake TV station. Sure enough, no sooner did they get on the stairs that led to the second floor, when a reporter rushed out of a waiting car. "You Nicole Barrett?" he asked. "I'm her sister," Nicole said. "No, you're Nicole," the reporter insisted. She looked back calmly. "I'm her sister. She's up at the prison." "I recognize you," the reporter said. "No, I'm the sister." She and Tamera walked away, strolled down the balcony and into her apartment. The moment the door was shut, they began to laugh. It emboldened Tamera to ask a little later if she could write the story after all.

The way it happened was that Nicole had gotten out some of Gary's drawings, and Tamera thought they were awfully talented. She said people ought to know more about Gary's life. It was a good argument to use, and Tamera believed it. In fact, looking at the pictures, she felt he must have an intense inner life. Those drawings were so sorrowful and so controlled.

Sitting there, she told Nicole about the convict who had been her boy friend. Tamera had interviewed him at Provo City Jail while she was still at BYU. Had walked in and here was this guy in a cell, nice, warm and good looking. All he'd done was steal a bunch of credit cards and cameras and stuff. She had fallen in love right off the bat, and when they sent him to Kentucky, she got truly nailed. He wrote magnificent love letters. She corresponded with him for a year and a half. Sometimes she got as many as seven letters a day. It was the nearest thing to filling the space her father's death had left. Those letters kept saying, Wow, you're so beautiful, and I've never met anyone like you, your understanding and your patience has overcome me. Wow, wow, wow, went his letters.

She told Nicole how she'd even taken a bus to Kentucky after he sent her money, and for a week spent six hours a day visiting him. Her family thought she was off her rocker, but that had been precious time.

It was a Minimum Security prison, and they sat on the lawn and read together out of books, and she had never felt as close to anybody in her life. Her roommates were agog when she got back. They fixed her up with a nice guy for her birthday, but after she returned to the apartment and said good night to the date, all seven of her roommates jumped out of the bedroom. They were all wearing T-shirts with her boy friend's prison number across them. They flashed water pistols, kidnapped her, and took her out to this restaurant. She guessed she was kind of a legend at BYU. Her roommates even took pride in the way they had learned how to handle it. "Never know what's going to happen next to Tammy's life," they learned to say smugly.

When her boy friend got out of prison, he came back to Provo and got a job as a carpenter. About three weeks later, he took Tamera's car, loaded it up with everything he could take out of her house and the house of the fellow he was living with, and drove off. Tamera hadn't seen him since.

Having it end in such a way, she wondered how close she had ever been to the boy. His whole life had to be a con. He had told so many lies she wondered how she could have felt so close. They hadn't been sharing the same truth, she said to Nicole. Yet, all the same, there had been some kind of truth, she said.

4

Now in the silence that followed, Tamera couldn't hold back any longer. She was so excited. "Please," she said, "let me just —" She gulped. She said, "Look, I'm going to find a typewriter, write a story, and bring it back and let you read it. If you don't like what I do, we'll just forget about it, you know. Because, after all — I said it'll be off the record," Tamera went on, "so if you still want it that way, it will be. But I got to try."

She went over to an old roommate's apartment and told her what was going on and sat down and started. It felt weird. There were so many constraints it took a couple of hours to write a couple of pages and when she brought them back, Nicole read, and took it all into herself, looked up and said, "No, I don't feel good about it." Tamera said, "Okay, that's it, then."

She felt disappointed, but, big deal — she'd just have to wait. She wasn't going to violate the agreement.

The disappointment must have been marked right into her face, because now Nicole felt bad too. Tamera said, "Don't worry. That was our agreement." But Nicole got up and went over to a cabinet, and said, "I'm gonna show you something I never showed before. Would you like to read Gary's letters?"

That was one more heavy thing in what had sure been a heavy day. Tamera said, "Sure." Nicole took this full drawer, and dumped it on the table. There were so many envelopes Tamera just started reading at random. Couldn't believe it. Right off, first one she picked had some really good quotes. "Nicole," she said, "would you mind if I wrote down a couple of these sentences?"

They came to a kind of agreement: Tamera wouldn't do a story now, but after Nicole was gone, Tamera could write anything she wanted. So they both sat there at the kitchen table and read letters, and Tamera copied quotes as fast as she could. Finally left about eight that night. They'd been together since noon.

On the drive from Provo to Salt Lake, Tamera usually took it fast, went along with her radio full blast, and got a lot of tickets. On this night she poked along at 50, and tried to think. She didn't know what to do, couldn't sleep, and by morning, decided to tell her editor. It all seemed too big. In his sanctum, strictly off the record, she told how Nicole was planning to commit suicide when Gilmore went, and her editor remarked he had heard as much from other reporters. There were a lot of rumors going around. This new information, however,

had convinced him to alert the authorities. That made Tamera feel
better.

She got to thinking that what Nicole needed most right now was
a friend. Tamera was going to be that. Get her out doing things, and
out from under the huge burden of living with Gilmore in her mind
all the time.

5

*Today you kissed my eyes, you have blessed them forever. I can
see only beauty now. Oh, fair Nicole Kathryne Gilmore. You're a little
elf sweet and neat and fun to eat. I'm not a great poet ——— But if I
had you naked on a bed or on the grass beneath the stars I'd write
such a love song all over your fair freckled body with my tongue and
my hands and my cock and my lips and whisper softly of your
beauty, make you feel and soar and sail and sing to dance around
the sun and moon and become as one and come as one and come and
come and make you moan soft sighs wild eyes rolled back abandoned
lusty sweaty wet and warm wrapped tite around mouths locked in
sweet wet kisses kisses kisses — look at you naked love to look at
you naked or just in knee socks pull your panties up in the sweet
crack of your little bouncy elf bootie loved to watch you walk around
the house without your clothes on . . . sexy elf girl, I love you —
Your Gary*

Gibbs also received a note that day:

*So far, I've gotten a letter from Napoleon, one from Santa Claus,
several from Satan, and you wouldn't believe how many postmarks
and return addresses Jesus Christ himself uses. . . . People think
I'm crazy. Ha ha ha.*
*You'll never guess who I got a letter from. Brenda! First she
helps them catch me, then she helps them convict me, now she wants
to write and visit. She's got more balls than a bull elephant.*

Next day, Thursday, soon as Tamera came into work, she received a call from a correspondent for *Time* magazine. Heard she'd

been with Nicole. Wanted to know if she had a little information to pass along. Pressure was coming down on her editors as well. They were having to stall old newspaper acquaintances. It was the first time Tamera had seen how the newspaper business was like a swap shop. "I'll give you a piece of my story today, if you take care of me tomorrow." She had always thought it was closer to the movies: you went out by yourself and brought it back alive.

At this point, the news editor took Tamera off other assignments, and said, "You're on Nicole. Do what you have to do." She looked blank, and he added, "I don't care if you bring her up to Salt Lake, and have her stay at your house. If you have to, take her out to dinner. I don't care what it costs. Do anything, but don't lose that story." Well, this was more like what she had thought it would be. Then the guy from *Time* magazine called back to say he wanted quotes. When she said, "This is between me and Nicole," he said, "She's just given an interview to the *New York Times*." Tamera just thought, "WHAT??"

Later that morning, Tamera was waiting as Nicole came out of prison. Soon as she brought up the interview with the *Times*, Nicole said, "That's ridiculous. I'm not talking to anyone."

"I just want you," said Tamera, "to understand my position. I'll keep the secrets you told me so long as you also keep them." She looked real straight at Nicole. "But as soon as you start talking to other media people, I don't feel bound to honor our agreement. If you want to earn some money on this thing, you're totally justified. Somebody wants to pay you, that's great. But I want you to know I'll write a story too when that happens."

Nicole just said, "Agreed." Acted like they were still friends. All of Tamera's anger went away. She just loved Nicole again and started making plans for what they could do on Saturday, her day off. Maybe go up to the mountains. A good idea to get out. Nicole agreed.

6

Then they drove over to Kathryne's house and had whole wheat toast, and talked, and in the middle of that, Nicole whispered that she wanted Tamera to keep Gary's letters. Didn't want her mother to see them after she was gone.

Next, Nicole and Kathryne got into the most impossible conversation. "I'm going," Nicole said, "to the execution Monday morning." Kathryne said, "Sissy, I don't want you there."

"Well," said Nicole, "I'm going."

"If you are," said Kathryne, "I'm going too."

"Gary didn't invite you."

"I don't care whether he did or not. I'm not going to see him. I'm there to wait for you."

"No," Nicole said, "I'll go myself."

"Get it straight, kid," said Kathryne, "I'm taking you."

Then the news came over the radio. None of them could believe it. Gary's execution had been delayed again. Governor Rampton had just issued a Stay. The radio announcer kept repeating it in an excited voice.

Tamera was sure glad her editor had said to stick with Nicole. Otherwise, she might have run back to the newspaper to see if they needed her. Instead, she could now offer to take Nicole over to the prison. On the way, Nicole gave her the key to the apartment in Springville. Told her she could pick up the letters, and hold them.

During that twenty-minute trip to the prison, Nicole still looked calm, but Tamera knew she was stunned. What came off was one clear message: Gary would now have to commit suicide. That was bringing it very near to Nicole.

She started telling Tamera about her mother-in-law, Marie Barrett. Really liked Marie, she said, liked her a lot better than Jim Barrett. Marie was a groovy lady and loved Sunny and Jeremy. Nicole said she would have always gotten along great with her, if Marie hadn't been such a super housekeeper. Nicole liked to keep the house clean, but her mother-in-law had to do it her way. Other than that, she was terrific. Nicole had about decided Sunny and Jeremy ought to grow up with Marie after she was gone.

Then she told Tamera about the last time she saw Marie. It was just after Kip had been killed.

"Now, it will happen to Gary soon," Nicole had said to Marie Barrett, "I don't know what there is about me."

She had been feeling miserable all over. Marie said, "Nicole, maybe next time, you'll find a fellow you can have a good relationship with. Just be more careful. Check him out a little more before you get married."

Nicole said, "There won't be another time."

"You're through with men?" Marie asked.

Nicole said, "I don't know what I mean, but there won't be another time." She almost gave it away. "If something happens to me," Nicole said, "would you take the kids?"

"Sure, I would," Marie said, "you know I would. Only nothing's going to happen to you."

"Then, that afternoon," Nicole said to Tamera, "the cops came around to Springville and knocked on the door and kind of looked me over." Just made polite conversation at the door, but she knew Marie had sent them. Nicole would still trust her with the children, only she didn't know about confiding in her personally. Tamera took it as a message.

Soon as she dropped her at the prison, Tamera returned to Nicole's apartment, picked up the letters, put them in a grocery sack, and searched the place for a gun or sleeping pills. Didn't know what she would do if she did find something, but made the search.

PROVO HERALD

Nov. 11, 1976 . . . Salt Lake City (UPI) — Utah Governor Calvin L. Rampton asked the Utah Board of Pardons to review Gilmore's conviction at their next meeting on Wednesday, November 17, and decide if the death penalty is justified.

Gilmore said he was "disappointed and angered" by the governor's action. "The governor is apparently bowing to pressure from various groups who are motivated by publicity and their own egotistical concerns rather than concern for my 'welfare.' "

CHAPTER 4

Press Conferences

1

Out in Phoenix, Earl Dorius was bombarded with the news. Everybody was stopping him in the lobby to ask, "What's going on in
Utah?" Earl felt as if the conference were totally destroyed for him.
He couldn't listen to anything. Kept racing back to his room to catch
the news. If he wasn't on the phone, he was flipping stations on the
TV set. "What do you think of the Governor's action?" everyone asked
him. "I haven't had a chance to research it," he would say, "but
it's my impression the Stay was improper because it was granted at
the request of outside parties."

He realized he was closer to the office at this point than to the
conference, and decided to check out of Phoenix and get back to
work.

2

SALT LAKE TRIBUNE

Nov. 12, 1976 — Boaz signed an agreement with Utah
State Prison Warden Samuel W. Smith that he would
serve only as an attorney for Gilmore, then talked freely
about his intentions to "serve as a writer first, a lawyer
second."

"We have no power to censure him. He is not a member of the Utah bar," a member of the Utah State Bar's executive committee explained.

PROVO HERALD

Provo, Nov. 12, 1976 — Boaz said he plans to "make some money" from Gilmore's story and split it 50–50 with the condemned man's family and any charities he may choose.

Just as Dennis was coming into the prison, Sam Smith called him over and said, "I heard Gilmore had an interview with a London newspaper this morning. Do you know anything about that?"

Dennis was in a real state of excitement. David Susskind had just called from New York. He was interested in doing a movie on Gary's life. There could be large money at the other end. Dennis's mind was racing.

"The London newspaper?" he said to Sam Smith. "Oh, sure, I set it up."

The Warden's face got red, unusual color for a pale man. Then he shouted. Everybody at that end of the hall popped their heads out of offices. For that matter, Dennis was startled too. Nobody was used to Sam Smith yelling.

Smith said he was going to file suit. Dennis said, "I couldn't care less, Warden." He was beginning to take personal pleasure in looking for statements to rile Sam Smith. There was something about Sam's skin that inspired you to get under it.

Dennis even laughed when they strip-searched him, just to be vindictive. It was a comedy. The guards came up to his armpits. Why, two days ago, they'd been so impressed with the way he acted before the Utah Supreme Court, they let him bring his typewriter into the talk with Gary.

After Boaz got through the strip-search, he met Nicole. There was a slitted window along the south end of the visiting room, and there she was sitting on Gary's lap, right at that end window, both of them looking out at Point of the Mountain. She didn't pay much attention to Dennis. Necking with Gary was all she was heeding.

Still, when she came out of it, Dennis thought she had a sweeter, more innocent-looking face than he had anticipated. She was looking tired, even washed out, and that gave her a melancholy wistfulness he definitely liked. But, Gary glowered. Didn't approve of the budding friendship whatsoever. Looked like he thought Nicole was flirting, when all she was saying was that her grandfather's funeral would be starting in an hour or so.

Once she left, and Dennis was alone with him, Gary hardly offered a chance to talk about Susskind's offer. He was too fired up over Governor Rampton. The subject proved infectious. Dennis loved the way Gary could pass you his steam. In fact, Dennis felt like a boiler, all fired up himself at what he could soon say about the Governor:

3

From the beginning, Dennis was looking to give out thoughts that would bring people face to face with stuff they had never pondered before. Dennis was looking to make a few shocking statements about public executions and get the people thinking. Make them ask themselves, "Why do we have executions behind locked doors? What are we ashamed of?" Just that morning one of his zingers had been printed:

PROVO HERALD

Provo, Nov. 12, 1976 — "I think executions should be on prime time television," Boaz said. "Then we would get some deterrent out of it."

He'd been having press conferences practically twice a day since he and Gary won at the Utah Supreme Court and over and over he

kept telling the press that he was there to represent free and open
dealing and would present his life as an open book. He might get
roasted, but his responsibility was to be very Aquarian and even report things about himself and his feelings that might seem strange.
At least the people would be getting open treatment, not manipula-
tion. The press could misquote him, misrepresent him, take his remarks at random and distort them. It didn't matter. He wasn't going
to flatten his personality. In fact, right after he came out of the Utah
Supreme Court, he told the reporters he was in Salt Lake because it had a higher percentage of beautiful women than any city
he'd been in. Plus the fact, he told the press, that a lot of these
women like to meet Californians. For the taste of evil. There were
millions to be made here, he said, importing California consciousness. Really, he said. Of course, they never printed a word of it.

The press responded by asking about his financial affairs. "I
have nothing to hold back," he told them. "The fact is, I owe $10,000,
actually about $15,000, if you include not only what I owe creditors
but friends. I have no shame about this. I made a bad investment
once, and immediately found the whole thing bellied up, money
gone."

The word in response, he soon learned, was that he was playing
Gilmore for the money. He didn't care. The word would turn around
when they realized he wasn't.

"Do you think," asked one reporter, "that your experience as a
Deputy District Attorney has given you a certain lust for Gilmore's
blood?"

"Get it straight," replied Dennis, "working in the D.A.'s office
gave me more power to help people than being a Public Defender. I
could reduce charges, take pleas. I cleared nine people in a row on
the polygraph before I left the office. That, you see, is part of the
game too." With it all, they listened to him. Dennis had had this concept for years that the media was restless and didn't really want to be
surfeited with handouts and crap. One honest man with no impediment between his impulses and his tongue could turn the world
around.

"I'm into this in part because of numerology," Dennis would say.
"I'm not a numerology nut, of course. I believe in free will too much

for that. But numerology can keep you sensitive to patterns. Every spiritual discipline reveals a pattern, after all. Then you choose your route through the patterns. That's where free will comes in."

"You say you have a great many debts?"

"I announce my debts," said Boaz. "I also owe $2,100 to Master Charge, but I won't pay that. A friend embezzled them with my Master Charge card. That's Master Charge's affair, not mine."

They wanted to know what he had published. He had not published yet, he said. Did he write under his own name? He wrote under K. V. Kitty, under Lejohn Marz. Another pen name was S. L. Y. Fox. Fox, he told them, meant 666, the sign of the beast. Of course they had never heard of Aleister Crowley.

They brought him back to the subject. What did he think of Governor Rampton's decision? *Monstrous.* They could quote him. He was always surprised at how little they quoted him.

Nor would they print what he said next, but he would tell them. "Gary lives," he said, "in a cell so narrow he can touch both walls. The light is on 24 hours a day. Guards beat on the bars. The noise confounds a man's last thoughts. Gary puts a towel on the bars to keep the light out. 'Take it down,' they tell him, 'or we'll come in and remove your mattress.' "

It did not matter if they got a tenth of what he said. Let them miss the ironies. When you start to open a door, the pressure has to be greatest in the beginning, yet the door moves the least. "Gary is cramped in his cell," he said. "That's why they have to give him Fiorinal. Most prisoners take drugs to survive. It lifts some of the oppression." They asked him if the officials knew. "Of course. The officials want convicts to be on dope. That way they don't riot."

Dennis could sense the reactions. He heard a reporter whisper, "The guy is totally hyper."

He was not here to defend himself. The opportunity was to attack. "The Warden," he said, "wants to close this execution down. We want it open. In the Middle East, at an Arabian execution, crowds are welcomed. The crowd gives the victim a lift. It makes him feel like they are there together in a ceremony. It reminds everybody that we are all sacrifices to the gods. Whereas here, at a condemned man's last moment, there is nobody but executioners. I think that's wrong, really."

"What do you and Gary talk about?"

"We talk," said Boaz, "of the evolution of the soul. Gary knows a lot about Edgar Cayce and the Akashic Register. We discuss karma and the need to take responsibility for our deeds. Gods and goddesses have total freedom because they have total responsibility." They never printed any of this.

A reporter read aloud a statement by Craig Snyder: "Boaz never contacted us. I was in Utah Supreme Court, and we argued opposing viewpoints, but I was not introduced, and I've never spoken to the man. To my knowledge he has never examined the record or found out what happened at the trial. His publishing agreement with Gilmore flies right in the face of the Canon of Ethics." "Where did he give the statement?" asked Dennis.

"At the Adelphi Building, where his office is, in Provo."

"That's a place with yellow shag carpets and brown and yellow walls, right?" asked Dennis.

"You ever see it?" asked the reporter.

"No," said Boaz, "but I know crypto-corporate vibes."

"Come on, Dennis," said the reporter, "why didn't you get in touch with Esplin and Snyder?"

"Gilmore doesn't want to appeal, do you understand that? I'm representing Gilmore, not the fucking appeals system."

"But, what if you read the transcript?"

"There is no transcript."

"That," said a reporter, "is because nobody ever asked for one. A transcript is easily obtained."

"There is," said Dennis, "no money to pay for a transcript. Besides," added Dennis, "it wouldn't do any good. Gilmore doesn't want his sentence reduced to life."

"But what," asked the reporter, "if it turned out he didn't get a Miranda warning, or the Judge's instructions were wrong? If he had a chance for a new trial, that would be another thing, right?"

"No," said Dennis. "Gary's dead on the facts. He'd be convicted again. Look, you have to understand Gilmore," said Dennis. "He may be a vicious killer, but he's *just*."

"He wasn't," said the reporter, "very *just* with those two guys he killed."

"No, definitely," said Dennis, "really, he's *just*."

That was how his interviews went. Now, on this day, on these steps, fresh with the rumor that Warden Smith had gone hog wild with rage, the reporters wanted to know what Dennis had done to get him that way. Dennis had an impromptu press conference right on the steps of the prison.

Well, he said, Sam Smith was mad because he had sold two interviews. One had gone for $500 to the *London Daily Express,* and another for $500 to a Swedish labor-union newspaper. The Swedes were probably attracted by the historical coincidence, Dennis suggested. Joe Hill, the famous Swedish immigrant who organized the Wobblies, was executed in Utah in 1915. Didn't they remember, *"I dreamt I saw Joe Hill last night, alive as you and me?"* Why, Joe Hill had even asked his best buddy to carry his remains across the state line into Wyoming. "I don't care," said Joe Hill, "to ever spend another night in Utah."

"What was the other sale?" they asked.

"Bryan Vine for the *Daily Express.* 'I Talked With A Killer' is what he's going to call it. He was the first to offer me money," said Dennis. "Came right out front with it."

"What did you get?"

"I told you, $500!"

"Don't you think it was cheap?"

"I didn't want to make too much and look like I was greedy. $500 for a ten-minute interview! That's good money for your time." So he would talk, and they would write, and then the news stories would come out. They made him look relatively responsible in the newspaper stories, like a controlled nut, Dennis thought.

4

Tamera had gone to work at 5 A.M. and spent six hours Xeroxing Gary's letters. She knew some of the reporters were raising their eyebrows at how she protected the stuff, but Tamera didn't want anyone reading over her shoulder, and making the sort of cynical non-chalant comments newspaper people could make. Still, nobody seemed that excited.

In fact, at Friday afternoon meeting, the Executive Editor said, "I don't think we're interested in love letters." Just brushed it off like that.

The paper was famous, of course, for being the leading Mormon daily in the world, and was owned by the Church, so it tended to be a little starchy. Tammy had certainly heard enough complaints from the non-Mormons on staff. The *Deseret News* had rules you wouldn't believe for a paper. Since it was located in a Church-owned building, you couldn't smoke in the newsroom, or drink coffee at your desk. Had to go to the lunchroom. A lot of the reporters would make frantic trips all day to the bathroom. It wasn't like the *Deseret News*, therefore, to get excited about having these love letters in the house. Except, two days ago, they'd been frantic to obtain them. Now, the story was on the back burner. Even Tamera had to feel skeptical. The whole thing could end up being just another account of a con and his girl. With the execution being put off again, Gary's death could be in the distance.

November 12

Boaz was all excited 'cause a movie producer and famous newsman named David Susskind had just offered him 15 to 20 thousand dollars cash as a down payment for rights to this fuckin story — plus 5 percent of the gross on movie rights and shit — could run to hundreds of thousands, says Boaz.

Baby, I don't like that — it's getting way outa hand.

Boaz is my lawyer but he's acting now more in the role of an agent, press agent.

Its all become like a circus.

Oh baby wish we was just back in Spanish Fork tending your little garden, making love.

Nicole arrived at her grandfather's funeral a little late. Kathryne thought she looked real sad, standing in the front with the family, and noticed that she didn't go up to the coffin for a last look. Kathryne kept thinking, "Oh, God, she's brooding about Gary and his turn." Afterward, Nicole asked if she could take Kathryne's car. Wanted to run down and visit Gary once more. Kathryne tried to complain that Nicole had already been up there today, and didn't have a driver's license but kept getting for an answer, "I won't get in no accident," until Kathryne finally said, "Oh, my God, take it."

Nicole didn't get home until evening, and by then Kathryne jumped on her. Said, "You didn't even go to the prison." Nicole said, "I know. I called, and they said I couldn't come in, so I just drove around. It felt good looking at everything."

5

Now David Susskind was on the phone to Dennis and really talking contract. Dennis liked Susskind's approach. The flow was suave and stimulating. A lot of energy running around but well schooled.

Then there was this fellow Larry Schiller who called and said he was a former photographer for *Life* magazine and now a producer of motion pictures for theatre and television release. Dennis didn't like his voice. Too intent on the importance of getting his point across. A super hard-sell salesman. Very professional sounding. Dennis was uneasy.

When they met downstairs in the coffee shop of the Hotel Utah, they didn't get along too well. Dennis just felt distrustful. The coffee shop was in the basement and big and empty and gloomy.

Schiller had a full black beard and a mustache that grew into the beard, vigorous curly black hair, handsome head. He could have looked something like Fidel Castro, but much too overweight, Dennis thought. It was as if you'd taken the head of Fidel Castro and plugged it into a wide body. While he didn't know much about Schiller in advance, he'd asked a couple of reporters and heard that the man had picked up the rights to Susan Atkins's life in the Charlie Manson case, plus the last interview Jack Ruby ever gave. A guy to watch yourself with, somebody warned Boaz. Gets in when people are dying.

Still, Boaz was entertained by the conversation. For one thing, Schiller was offering more money than Susskind. He kept talking about all the projects he'd brought off. Boaz made a point of being flippant in return. "Gary isn't Susan Atkins," he would say. He really enjoyed being arrogant these days. What did he care if Schiller disliked his guts? It wouldn't cut down the bid for Gary.

"You better get an agent," Schiller said in conclusion.

It brought Dennis short. He had to admit he was enjoying the feeling of going back to Susskind with a higher offer. How did this relate to his nature as The Emperor and The Juggler? Could he handle all the bones that would be thrown in the air?

6

Saturday morning, Nicole called and said she needed the letters back. Sounded distrustful. Tamera couldn't understand. They'd left on such friendly terms. She wondered if Gary or Boaz had told her to get them returned. Anyway, Tamera informed Nicole it was no problem. It wasn't. She had her Xerox. So, she asked the fellow she was dating to drive her to Springville that night and by the time they arrived, Nicole was apologetic at the trouble it caused.

They stayed a couple of hours and had a real good time. The boy Tamera brought along was from Philadelphia and Italian, not Mormon, a real character at BYU. His last name was Millebambini and nobody ever got to hear his first name, since he translated Millebambini as A Thousand Bastards, said that was the true meaning, and they just rolled on the floor with shock out at school. Some student started calling him Milly from Philly. Just wild. That was his name thereafter. Milly from Philly. He was an intense person and had so many funny stories to tell, and was into so many weird things. Tamera really liked him.

Nicole was fascinated with Milly that night. Tamera had told him, Don't talk about Gilmore, but try to cheer Nicole up. Milly really had her laughing. Tamera began to realize that Nicole, in a funny way, was kind of sheltered and didn't know a lot about certain aspects of life like music and backpacking in Oregon, or even rap sessions like this. She just listened all night as if they were feeding her, and Tamera left with an optimistic feeling. Told Milly on the way back, "Maybe if we keep hanging around, we can change her attitude about life a little bit." Tamera felt it was going to be a while before Gilmore was executed, if he ever was. She had about concluded they could discount a suicide.

CHAPTER 5

Testaments

1

SALT LAKE TRIBUNE

Church Leaders Air Capital Punishment Views

Nov, 13, 1976 — Msgr. McDougall said the majority of modern theologians oppose capital punishment, believing the death penalty tends to work against the socially and economically disadvantaged.

The Rev. Jay H. Confair, pastor of Wasatch Presbyterian Church, 1626 17th East, said "The Old Testament idea of 'an eye for an eye' was replaced by the New Testament concepts of love and rehabilitation."

But the Gilmore case presents a different problem, Pastor Confair said. "The man wants to die. He doesn't want to be rehabilitated," and pointed out it is similar to the case of a person being kept alive by machines in a hospital who wants the "plug pulled."

Many here, although saying they believe in the death penalty, especially for crimes as brutal as Gilmore's, say also that they cannot stomach taking part in the execution itself.

"You couldn't drag me up there," said Noall T. Wootton, the county attorney who prosecuted Gilmore. "I've done my job, I asked for it and got the death penalty — and I believe in it. But execution is a dirty, messy job and I don't want to be part of it."

SALT LAKE TRIBUNE

Old Rifle Ready Again If Needed

Nov. 13, 1976 — A gun at present in a rifle shop, and used in previous Utah executions, will be among the five loaned to the Salt Lake County Sheriff's office if and when convicted murderer Gary Mark Gilmore is executed.

Leo Gallenson, one of the corporate managers of the shop, estimated that the unsold rifle has been used in 6 to 12 executions.

LOS ANGELES TIMES

Former Boss of Utah Killer
Would Serve on his Firing Squad

Nov. 14, 1976 Provo, Utah — . . . Spencer McGrath gave Gary Mark Gilmore a good job and an extra $10 to $20 a week out of his own pocket. He fixed Gilmore's car and kept Gilmore on the payroll even when the ex-convict took to drinking and showed up late for work.

Now McGrath, a kindly sort of man who runs an insulation factory and who has helped many former convicts, says he would willingly serve on the firing squad Gilmore wants to have execute him, "just to show Gary that laws do apply to him."

November 14

Honey, I'm becoming very famous.

I don't like it — not like this, it's not right.

Sometimes I think I know about fame and how it feels because I was famous in a previous life. I seem to understand it. But I don't want to get to the point where we're enjoying fame and not being ourselves anymore. We are just GARY AND NICOLE and we've got to remember that.

November 14

Hey Geebs

He was just-a-keed.

Nice to hear from you ——— you know you got a little class yourself.

If at some time you are flush and have a few dollars to spare, I'm sure my mother could use it. She's old, crippled, and on welfare. Or if even now you'd care to write her a letter to help ease this thing a bit.

Thanks for the ten spot.

A friend
GARY

Gibbs thought to himself, how do you write to someone's mother you've never met?

Dear Mrs. Gilmore, it's going to be alright. Only 4 of the 5 rifles are really loaded.

He asked Big Jake to pick him up a nice card and Gibbs enclosed $30 and mailed it off to her.

LOS ANGELES TIMES

Death Lawyer's Lively Career

Nov. 14 — Only last January Boaz became a self-styled crusader against what he called the "hypocrisy of the system," as he unsuccessfully tried to get himself arrested for smoking marijuana in the lobby of the Federal Building here.

Now he has turned up at Utah's state prison at Draper as both a lawyer for the condemned Gary Gilmore as well as his biographer.

This double role is one he cannot play and still observe the canons of the Utah State Bar, Craig Snyder asserted. The canons demand a lawyer represent a client and not one's own pocketbook. "If that execution takes place," Snyder said, "Boaz stands to profit from it."

Although Boaz has been criticized for exploiting his client in this manner, he is nevertheless remembered in a kindly way by the Assistant Dean of Boalt Hall, James Hill.

"He's a shy, modest, tender guy, a hell of a good guy," recalls Hill who says he has seen Boaz occasionally since his graduation.

SALT LAKE TRIBUNE

Nov. 15, 1976 . . . Utah — Condemned killer Gary Gilmore wanted to die at 8 A.M. today. Instead he breakfasted on sweet rolls, cereal, oranges, milk and coffee and returned to his cell on Death Row.

Gilmore will be visited today by Nicole Barrett, 20, a divorcee and mother of two.

"He thought a lot of that girl and she must have thought something of him or she wouldn't be doing what she's doing now (visiting Gilmore)," his uncle Vern said.

Boaz, who spent 3½ hours with Gilmore Sunday night, said his client would like to meet singer Johnny Cash.

"There is no greater Johnny Cash fan," Boaz said. He dispatched a telegram to the singer informing him of Gilmore's wish.

2

Vern hadn't seen Gary in close to six weeks, not since the last day of the trial. Going to visit him, he felt awkward. Vern had just gotten out of the hospital after an operation on his bad knee, and walking, even with a cane, felt like hammering a nail into his bone. It was one painful stretch from where he had to leave his car near the prison gate all the way out to Maximum Security. A real jaw-grinder putting each step in front of the next all that hundred yards and more of walking between two parallel fences of barbed wire.

Yet, in the visitors' room, there was Gary looking stronger than Vern had ever seen him, and right away, bringing up the angry letter Ida had written.

Vern said, "Well, you wrote a bad letter first. You didn't want to have anything to do with us anymore."

They looked at one another, and Vern said, "Gary, we're not mad. We want to help you."

"All right," said Gary, "I feel bad about writing that letter to Ida and I want to apologize."

"Ida wants to apologize to you," said Vern. "She wants you to tear up her letter, just as she tore up yours. Flush it down the toilet." That was the end of that. Gary looked relieved, and they talked back and forth a little while. Wasn't a bad visit at all.

By the time Dennis got to the prison on Monday morning, Vern had finished. It didn't take Boaz long to figure that old Uncle Vern was back in the picture, all right. Gary was speaking of his uncle in praiseworthy, loving terms.

Dennis had not heard him do that before. A lot of resentment had been aired up to now. All of a sudden, Gary was nurturing this whole change toward his uncle. It was obvious to Dennis that Gary really wanted to be loved by his family. Didn't matter what had gone down before.

Yesterday, Dennis had a funny hassle with him. On Saturday, Gary had kept saying he wanted Dennis to smuggle in fifty Seconals. At first Dennis even promised he would, but found he couldn't fall asleep on that. By the next day, he had to tell Gary he couldn't do such a job under any circumstances, but it left him shaken. Sunday night going back to Everson's house, Dennis could practically smell suicide coming up from the day. The moment he turned on the radio, he heard Blue Oyster Cult. They had been on the radio like crazy these last two days, and now he was actually listening to the words of "Don't Fear the Reaper." It could freeze your synapses. "Come on, baby, don't fear the Reaper," Dennis heard himself humming. "Romeo and Juliet are together in eternity." My God, you could go crazy getting off on synchronism, thought Dennis, feeling the great linking-in of all the little things. It was awful. The mind could undulate like a jellyfish.

Monday, after Vern's visit, Brenda got a call from Gary who asked the name of the doctor that was taking care of her daughter. He wanted the doctor to make certain his pituitary gland would go to Cristie after the execution. Since Johnny and Brenda were always broke trying to keep Cristie in pituitary extract, which was the most expensive thing on God's earth, this call from Gary, out of the blue, telling Brenda he wanted the doctor to credit his pituitary after death to Johnny's account, was like handing over a thousand bucks. It was a crazy conversation. Brenda didn't know if they were now friends. "Take care, Gary," she said at the end. He just hung up.

3

That same morning as Tamera came into the newsroom her editor said, "We're getting a lot of calls about Nicole. Your story won't hold till Gary is executed. I want you to get permission from Nicole to run it."

Driving over to Springville, Tamera didn't know how to ask. When she laid her predicament on Nicole, however, there was a smile and Nicole said, "Well, I got to tell you something, too. I decided to give an interview for $2,000." Some kind of affiliate for NBC out of Boston — at least as Nicole understood it — had sent over this good-looking tall fellow, Jeff Newman, with curly hair, blue eyes, and a beard. He had talked her into it. She would be giving the interview this Friday. Later Tamera found out it was really the *National Enquirer,* not any Boston affiliate of NBC. But for now, her only reaction was that Nicole had told her to go ahead. So, Tamera left on real good terms. Went back to the office, and spent the rest of the night working on the story.

Over the last week, Nicole had gone to several doctors she had picked from the phone book and told them she was from out of state and had trouble sleeping. The only thing that worked were reds. Seconal was what did it.

She managed to collect fifty of them and twenty Dalmanes. Now, with Gary on her case about it, she decided Monday morning was the time to pass them over. So she split the stuff down the middle, twenty-five Seconals and ten of the Dalmanes for Gary, same for herself, and put Gary's capsules in a kid's balloon, two balloons, in fact. Both yellow, one inside the other. Then she inserted the balloons up her vagina.

She felt afraid all the way over to the prison that Gary would scold her. He had kept telling her to get more. Pushed her and pushed her to go to more doctors, but she had the feeling none of those doctors trusted her, and if she went to even one more, it could blow the whole thing. Those doctors might even be calling the cops ten minutes after they wrote the prescription. She really sweated it out all day Sunday. Now, here she was inside Maximum with those balloons inside her.

They gave her a skin search, but the matron didn't put her fingers anywhere, just looked under her armpits and in her cheeks, went through her long hair. It wasn't an indecent search, and, in fact, the matron would have had to have a long finger, the balloons were pushed up that far.

In the visiting room, there happened to be nobody else, just the guard in the glass booth, and she and Gary went to the chair by the window and she sat on his lap. Sometimes they allowed you to do that, sometimes not, but this day the guard wasn't bothering them. They could do some heavy petting. It was really lucky. Sometimes as many as four or five people could be in the room, or a couple of lawyers, but she and Gary were the only ones this time.

As she sat on his lap, Gary made a pass with his finger for the balloon, but got nowhere. It was too far up. Finally Nicole had to stand by the window with Gary hugging her from behind so the guard couldn't see her body. In that position, with his arms around her shoulders, she reached down under her skirt to get the balloon. It was a real sweat. She had shoved it up so high, there was nothing to touch with her fingers, and she got to the point where she had to try to push it down as if she were pushing a baby out. In fact, she pressed so hard in her gut, while reaching up so far with her fingers, that before she finally got ahold of it, her head hurt. She was seeing stars. They kept rocketing off. Her head, in fact, felt like it had just broken, or some blood vessel had certainly shattered. Gary didn't know what she was going through. He was just making sweet and encouraging remarks.

After she gave him the balloon, Gary sat down and reached through the front of his big, wide, floppy, loose pants, big baggy things, to push the balloon up his rectum. It was a slow, tricky business, not at all easy, and took over a minute. When it was done, he just said, "Yeah, they're there. I know." Then she sat on his lap and kissed him.

She felt fine. She realized how worried she had been. Nicole had been sure the prison had gotten word from the doctors and would check her. So she was feeling proud of her accomplishment now, and Gary was very proud of her. The visit went on for at least another hour. They necked like crazy. It was the most beautiful of their visits. When they weren't kissing, they were singing to one another. Neither of them could sing, but it was beautiful all the same. She had never felt as near to anyone's soul in her life.

4

That evening, Marie Barrett got a call from Nicole asking if she would pick her up. Nicole wanted to visit with Sunny. They sat around the living room watching *Sybil* on TV, and Nicole said the girl sure reminded her of April. She went into the bedroom and read Sunny some stories, and listened to her prayers, and then visited in the front room with Marie and her ex-father-in-law Tom Barrett who she also liked, and finally went home, although she kind of drug her feet about leaving.

Then, she went night shopping with her neighbor, Kathy Maynard. The center was open till 9 P.M., and Nicole went on a splurge and bought coloring books and crayons for all of Kathy's kids. When they returned, she handed $10 to Kathy and said, "Come on, if you don't take it, you're going to make me feel bad." Kathy just looked at her. Kathy wasn't that big, and had ash-blond hair and round eyes kind of, and a sweet simple face. It just looked bewildered now. Nicole said, "You enjoy it." "See you in the morning," said Kathy. "In the morning," said Nicole.

Alone in the apartment, with Jeremy sound asleep, Nicole was waiting for midnight. That was the time she and Gary had picked for the pills, only it took a long time to get there. It kept coming over Nicole how Gary had worried that the amount was not enough. He had explained that if you took enough to put you out, but not enough to die, you could become a vegetable. That was truly something to worry about. Yet, they'd agreed to go forward. Either it would work or it wouldn't. Nicole now got out her Last Will and Testament. She had spent all day Sunday writing it, and she went over it again for spelling errors. She was pretty sure, in fact, a couple of mistakes had been made. It was a long Last Will and Testament, and there were probably errors she didn't catch, but she felt all right about it.

5

Nicole K. Baker
Sun. Nov. 14
1976

TO WHOMEVER IT MAY CONCERN:
I, Nicole Kathryne Baker — have a number of personal requests I would desire to have carried out — in the event that I am at any time — found dead.
I am considering myself of a strong, logical, and totally sane mind — so that which I am writing should be taken serious in every respect.
At the time of this writing I am going through a divorce from a man named Steve Hudson.
By my own standards — the event of death should disolve all ties with that man and the divorce be carried through and finalized AT ALL COSTS.
I wish to legally be returned to my maiden name which is Baker. And have none ever acknoledge me by any other name.
My daughters birth certificate states her name as Sunny Marie Baker, even thoe, at the time of her birth, I was then legally married to her father — James Paul Barrett.

My son's birth certificate states his name as Jeremy Kip Barrett. Because I was at that time still married to James Paul Barrett, who is not Jeremys father.

Jeremys father is the late Alfred Kip Eberhardt.

So Jeremy does have legal grandparents by the last name of Eberhardt who may wish to be notified of his whereabouts. They are residing in Paoli, Pennsylvania, I think.

As to the care custody and welfare of my children — I am not only desireing but <u>demanding</u> that the responsibility of them and any decisions concerning them — be placed directly and immeadiatly into the hands of <u>Thomas Giles Barrett</u> and/or <u>Marie Barrett</u> of Springville, Utah.

If the Barretts so wish to adopt my children — they have my willing consent.

If they wish to place the responsibility of one or both children into the hands of another responsible party of their choice — they again have my willing consent.

That is of course — until the children are of legal age to make their own choices.

I have a pearl ring in hock in the bowling alley in Springville. I would really like for someone to get it out and give it to my little Sister — April L. Baker.

Also I have made arrangements for a sum of money to go for April's mental health problem. My mother should not spend that money for anything other than to pay a good Mental Hospital for helping April back to her sanity.

Now, as to the decision as to what should be done with my dead body — I ask that it be cremated. And with the consent of Mrs. Bessie Gilmore I would have my ashes mixed with those of her son — Gary Mark Gilmore. To be then — at any future convenient date scattered upon a green hillside in the State of Oregon and also in the State of Washington.

If my own mother and father — Charles R. Baker and Kathryne N. Baker are not agreeable to this request — so be it. Let them decide as they choose.

I would ask that they arrange for at least three songs to be sung at my funeral. . . .

A song written by John Newton called (Amazing Grace), also one by Kris Kristofferson titaled (Why me) and lastly a song titaled (Vally of Tears) which I know not the author of.

If any other persons, friends or family wish to sing or have sung

*any more songs at my funeral on my behalf or on behalf of those who
grieve, resent or are indifferent to my passing — why . . . I would be
grateful.*

Now going through it, Nicole realized she had more to say, just a
little more. She had not really disposed of her belongings. In the
quiet of her apartment, she sat at the table before a piece of paper:

> Nicole K. Baker
> Mon. Nov. 15, 1976

*I do not feel much like writing this day. Thoe I suppose there are
a couple of things left I should take care of.*

No, jest this.

*Everything in my apartment of course — my mother can decide
what to do with.*

*I have nothing here of great value except the painting of the two
little boys gazing at the moon. It is Sunny Marie Barretts painting
now. It is to be hung in her room at Tom and Marie Barretts house,
until or unless she asks that it be removed — and I would rather she
never sell it — but the choice should be hers when she reaches the age
of 18.*

*Again I state; the painting of the two little boys gazing at the
moon, done by Gary Gilmore — now belongs to Sunny Marie Baker
Barrett.*

*My mother has my every consent to take all or any of my letters
and do with them what she pleases. If they can in any way bring her
some money — then I'll be all the gladder. But I would desire her to
share the money as she sees fair — with all my brothers and sisters
and also my Aunt — Kathy Kampman.*

*Since there are so many people trying and being successful at
makeing money on the story of Gary Gilmore and I, I would jest as
soon it was someone I love and care for and trust — to have part of
that success. So . . . the letters are my Mothers, Kathryn N. Baker's.*

If she wishes to burn them — so be it also.

*My Mother probably has little use for any of my house-hold
belongings — which are of no value — so I would truely like for my
good friend Kathy Maynard to have any of my furniture she chooses
and any of the things hanging on my walls — jest anything in this
apartment that my Mother would not feel too reluctant to part with.
I do hope Mom is reasonable about it. Kathy M. has helped me*

*through many a long hard day — she has little furniture and that
sort of stuff . . .*

> *That's it.*
> NICOLE K. BAKER

6

There were a lot of pills and she took them slowly, swallowing one or
two at a time, being careful not to gag. If she threw up, the whole
thing would be blown. In the middle, she started having a lot of
thoughts. She remembered the guy from the television station in Bos-
ton who was going to pay the $2,000 and worried whether he would
honor it now when she was gone. Without it, where would April get
the money for her hospital? She was also thinking that he had said
he would be here in the morning and what if she didn't answer his
ring? Would he come in? If she wasn't departed by then, they might
revive her. So she had to decide whether or not to lock the door.

She didn't want anybody to be able to walk in. Yet if they had to
break the door, that noise could terrify Jeremy. On the other hand, if
the door wasn't locked, Jeremy could open it with no trouble and
wander out in the morning. Kathy Maynard might pick him up, carry
him back and discover her too soon. Finally, Nicole turned the latch.
Still, that made her miserable, thinking of Jeremy moping around
tomorrow looking at her.

Now she was taking three or four Seconal at a time with water,
and Gary was sitting with her. There weren't even seconds these
days that she did not think of him. But, now he was very near and
she began to think of how soon she would be with him and how she
trusted him and was not afraid. Then she thought of lying down
without her clothes on, and wondered what to do about that. She did
not want to die with her clothes on, that was for sure. But she did feel
strange about taking them off. Reporters might come in the morning
and look at her body.

As she got into bed, she took a picture of Gary and put it under
the pillow and held on to it with her hand, and felt a little extra naked

tonight. Then the pills started to feel good. She felt it really coming on. Got out of bed and walked around a little just to have that good feeling of her legs moving in one nice floating feeling after the other. It was awful nice, as if she were learning to walk for the first time, and her legs started to get heavy. She lay down and held onto the picture of Gary again, and thought of the letter she had written in the ten minutes before she took the pills. Reading over the Last Will and Testament and the letter how to dispose of her furniture, she decided there had been nothing very personal, truly, to her mother and family. So she'd written an additional letter, and she was thinking of that, and of Kathy Maynard next door who was the nicest neighbor she'd ever had, an angel and a stand-up neighbor. Then that very last letter began to swim around her mind and Nicole went to sleep.

Mon. Nov. 15, 1976

Mom, Dad, Rik, April, Mike, Angel

—Everybody knows that i Love and Care for You.
Please do not resent my leaving this life.
I'm not trying to hurt anyone — if I could spare you all any pain — i surely would.
But i just go. Because i <u>want</u> to so bad.
Wanting a thing like that — and not granting it to myself — would surely turn me into some bitter ugly old maid in just a matter of time — or possibly I would lose my sanity.
I think you all pretty much understand about me and Gary. if you don't — well time wil tell all.
i Love him. More than life and more than that.

And i Love you all very much. i could never have asked for a better family. We've been over a few rough spots a time or two — but i hope that any wrong i've done anyone will be forgiven me as easy as i forgive.
i don't want to talk anymore. i'm sorry i should have written this sooner. i had so much to say.
Well, all will ultimately be clear and right just know that i love you all today and i will love you always.
Please try also not to greive for me — or resent Gary.

i Love him.

i made my own choice.

i'll not regret it.

Please Love my kids always, as they are part of the family.

Never hid truths from them.

When any of you need me, i will be there to listen for i and Gary — and yourselves — are all a part of a wondrous good understandin God.

May this parting bring us closer in Loveing, understanding and expeting of one another.

i Love You All
SISSY

PART TWO

Exclusive Rights

CHAPTER 6

Wake

1

Four months after the morning that Kathy Maynard found Nicole in bed with an overdose of Seconal, journalists were still coming around with tape recorders. Their interest in Nicole was great, and curiosity about Kathy herself was small, but it is a technique of some interviewers to begin by asking each witness, important or unimportant, many questions about their life.

INTERVIEWER   How old were you when you got married?

KATHY MAYNARD   Sixteen.

INTERVIEWER   Why did you get married at sixteen?

KATHY MAYNARD   'Cause my other friends did.

INTERVIEWER   And who did you marry?

KATHY MAYNARD   Tim Mair from Heber City.

INTERVIEWER   How old was he?

KATHY MAYNARD   (snickers) Seventeen.

INTERVIEWER   Seventeen, well what was he doing?

KATHY MAYNARD   He was working at a lumber mill.

INTERVIEWER   And where did you meet him?

KATHY MAYNARD   Out in front of the school. On a lawn.

INTERVIEWER   How long did you go with him before you married him?

KATHY MAYNARD   'Bout a month.

INTERVIEWER Where did you get married?

KATHY MAYNARD At his house in Heber.

INTERVIEWER Why did you get married at his house and not yours?

KATHY MAYNARD Because my mom was living in a motel.

INTERVIEWER Was your mother happy about you getting married or what?

KATHY MAYNARD No, she was pretty shook up — she didn't want me to.

INTERVIEWER He's got the peanut butter jar, is that okay?

KATHY MAYNARD *Kevin, put the peanut butter up! Come on!*

INTERVIEWER How long were you married?

KATHY MAYNARD Ohhhhh, let's see — three months.

INTERVIEWER Had you slept with him before you got married?

KATHY MAYNARD Oh yeah. (snickers)

INTERVIEWER Right. And uh, what happened to that marriage?

KATHY MAYNARD He killed hisself.

INTERVIEWER He killed himself?

KATHY MAYNARD Uh huh.

INTERVIEWER While you were married?

KATHY MAYNARD Uh huh.

INTERVIEWER Why — I mean what happened — what's the story surrounding it?

KATHY MAYNARD Well, he was drinking and we was going to Provo, we was Christmas shopping . . . and he stopped on the way out of Provo and bought a hunting knife, and I didn't think nothing of it. . . .

INTERVIEWER Right.

KATHY MAYNARD And coming back we was arguing 'cause he kept rolling the window down and it was cold so when we got back to mom's . . . he started arguing with me again and my mom was asleep, she was working graveyard, and I just asked him if he would be quiet you know . . . if he'd keep his voice down so it wouldn't wake Mom up and he got mad and walked out the door. I was in bed. And then he turned around and come back and he flipped the light on, had his knife out and said, "Watch," and he stabbed hisself.

INTERVIEWER   Right in front of you?

KATHY MAYNARD   Uh huh. *Kevin put the peanut butter up!*

INTERVIEWER   Do you have any idea why he did it?

KATHY MAYNARD   I don't know — He shot hisself in the foot once.

INTERVIEWER   When you were married?

KATHY MAYNARD   Before we was married — because I was with another guy.

INTERVIEWER   Right.

KATHY MAYNARD   *Kevin, go play for a minute.*

INTERVIEWER   Did you blame yourself?

KATHY MAYNARD   Ohh, I did for quite a while 'cause it kinda shook me up 'cause I thought well, if I hadn't been fighting with him . . .

INTERVIEWER   Uh huh.

KATHY MAYNARD   I don't know, after talking to quite a few people I realized he was sick and needed help.

INTERVIEWER   Where did he stab himself?

KATHY MAYNARD   Well, it was in the stomach. They couldn't get the bleeding stopped to tie his arteries so he got into shock and loss of blood . . .

INTERVIEWER   Did he die in the — in the apartment?

KATHY MAYNARD   Oh no, he died in the University of Utah . . . in Salt Lake . . . two days later.

INTERVIEWER   Two days later?

KATHY MAYNARD   Uh huh.

INTERVIEWER   And uh, you weren't pregnant at that time or anything?

KATHY MAYNARD   Well, I was pregnant — my twins were Tim's.

INTERVIEWER   And did you know you were pregnant at that time?

KATHY MAYNARD   No!

INTERVIEWER   How long after he died did you know you were pregnant?

KATHY MAYNARD   Ohhh, *Why don't you bring me the peanut butter and the lid, okay?* Uhhh, let's see I had missed one period but I wasn't worried about it because I had messed up before so . . .

INTERVIEWER   So you found out about it two months later then?

KATHY MAYNARD Yeah.

INTERVIEWER You say that with a sigh —

KATHY MAYNARD Ohhh, kind of messed me up. Like I say, I married Les Maynard two weeks after Tim died so . . .

INTERVIEWER You mean you got married right after Tim died?

KATHY MAYNARD I met Les at Tim's funeral.

INTERVIEWER Did you know Les Maynard before or what?

KATHY MAYNARD Didn't even know who he was.

INTERVIEWER How come he was at the funeral?

KATHY MAYNARD He was one of Tim's friends. He knew Tim.

INTERVIEWER Right. So you met him at the funeral? What happened after that?

KATHY MAYNARD Uh huh. (pause) Well, I was staying with my cousin and her husband and Les came down — I stayed drunk for two weeks after Tim died . . .

INTERVIEWER Stayed drunk?

KATHY MAYNARD I did. (snickers)

INTERVIEWER On beer, whiskey or what?

KATHY MAYNARD Oh, you name it — we had it. I took all the money from Tim's funeral and just bought booze with it and Les stayed down there with me for two weeks and then we got married . . .

INTERVIEWER Why did you marry Les?

KATHY MAYNARD Lonely. I guess I was scared.

INTERVIEWER And why did he marry you?

KATHY MAYNARD I have no idea — maybe 'cause he felt sorry for me.

INTERVIEWER You never discussed it with him?

KATHY MAYNARD No.

INTERVIEWER And how was your marriage with Les?

KATHY MAYNARD Awful.

INTERVIEWER From the very beginning?

KATHY MAYNARD Well, after I sobered up and realized what I had done I couldn't stand him to touch me and I — I would sit up at the cemetery by Tim's grave all the time and I threw my wedding ring on Tim's grave. So, I was pretty messed up — for a while I took off for a couple of months, which caused a lot of problems, started jealousy and stuff like that . . .

INTERVIEWER   When you took off, did you start to make it with other guys?

KATHY MAYNARD   Oh no.

INTERVIEWER   You just took off to be by yourself?

KATHY MAYNARD   Yeah.

INTERVIEWER   So you were never in love with him.

KATHY MAYNARD   It wasn't love. It couldn't have been. But I think it kind of grew to that. After we had the kids.

INTERVIEWER   The first two?

KATHY MAYNARD   Hmmm, hmmm [yes].

INTERVIEWER   And how long did you live with him?

KATHY MAYNARD   Couple of weeks.

INTERVIEWER   You only lived with Les a couple of weeks, too. When was the last time you saw him?

KATHY MAYNARD   Les? Ha, ha, day before yesterday.

INTERVIEWER   So you see him periodically?

KATHY MAYNARD   Hmmm, hmmm, he's with my best girl friend.

INTERVIEWER   When he comes back, and sees you, does he make it with you or what?

KATHY MAYNARD   Oh no.

INTERVIEWER   Did you and Les ever get a divorce?

KATHY MAYNARD   We're going through it now.

INTERVIEWER   What does he do now?

KATHY MAYNARD   Works at a service station out in Spanish.

INTERVIEWER   Spanish Fork?

KATHY MAYNARD   That's it.

2

Kathy had been waking Nicole up every morning. In order to get out early to see Gary, it was necessary for Kathy to come by. Most days, Nicole just couldn't wake herself.

On that special sunrise, Kathy took the coffeepot over, and knocked, and rang Nicole's bell, then looked through the window to see Nicole asleep. She was lying stomach down on the couch. You could see a little of her bare back. After Kathy had rung awhile, she tried the door. It was locked, which kind of bothered her. She returned the coffee to her own house, went back, and started calling Jeremy's name until he finally woke up and came out of the bedroom. He was still half asleep and just flopped down on the couch beside Nicole. He was wearing a little pair of green pajamas and all he wanted was to get back to sleep. Finally, after fifteen minutes, she got Jeremy to open the door, but when Kathy went in and shook Nicole and turned her over, she didn't respond.

Nicole had fallen asleep on top of a picture of Gary in a little gold frame, just a color photo in a blue jacket in prison, but he was looking good. Next to the picture was a letter, and Kathy saw at a glance that it was an old one, written early in August. She noticed the date because Nicole had often talked about how much his first long letter meant to her. Then Kathy tried to wake Nicole up again. All the while, Jeremy was looking at both of them.

Finally, Kathy called on Sherry, another neighbor, and both women went over to shake Nicole, and stood around on the balcony in their Levi's and bare feet, looking worried. About the time they decided to ring the doctor, there came along that reporter, Jeff Newman, heading right toward Nicole's door, and Kathy hollered out, "She's asleep. Nicole's asleep."

Jeff Newman stared at them kind of funny, and said, "Is she all right? I'm supposed to take her out to the prison this morning." Kathy said, "Yes, she's just tired." He said, "I'll be back in half an hour," and went away. Then they called Sherry's doctor. The moment he heard Nicole's name, he told them to call the hospital.

The cops were running around the apartment trying to find pill bottles, and the ambulance men worked fast, checked her out and had Nicole on a stretcher, and Kathy went looking for Jeremy, who was now over at her apartment with her kids. They were all eating jello out of the fridge. Just then, Jeff Newman came back. Kathy said, "I don't know whether Nicole appreciates you being here." "Well, I'm not leaving," he told her.

Kathy decided with people like Jeff poking around, she'd better get Nicole's letters. So she took a brown paper sack, stuffed them in, and carried it all back to her apartment. Then Les came by and Kathy went out to get milk for the kids, and, while she was gone, a couple of police showed, and told Les they wanted the letters. Maybe they had been watching the apartment. Told Les that Kathy could get in real trouble. Les said, "Okay, take 'em back." Later in the day, Kathy tried to visit Nicole at the hospital, but the authorities weren't letting anybody in, only family. In fact, Kathy never got to see Nicole again.

3

Conversations with Gary over the weekend had been full of literary and philosophical questions on the nature of prison, and this Tuesday morning, Dennis was looking forward to talking about the murders. Naturally, he had a lot of curiosity. It hit hard when the reporter phoned to ask what Mr. Boaz thought of Gary and Nicole's double suicide attempt. Dennis had completely forgotten "Don't Fear the Reaper." He said to himself, "I'm not in touch with anything." To the reporter, he said, "Are they alive?"

"Hanging in," said the reporter.

Only yesterday, a friend had suggested to Dennis that he get an agreement in writing from Gary. He hadn't wanted to. In unusual circumstances like these, a contract would suffocate any possibility for decent human relations. He had had, however, to admit that Gary was getting businesslike. Yesterday, he had shown a little interest in Susskind, and was talking about Schiller, who had sent him a telegram. Dennis had heard a new interest coming into Gary's voice. That was why the suicide attempt surprised him so.

Then the day got worse. Another reporter called to say, Mr. Boaz, you have been put on Sam Smith's list of people who could have slipped the drugs to Gilmore. Dennis felt sick. What if, unknown to him, the prison had been recording his conversations with Gary? They might have taped the one where he talked with Gary about bringing in fifty Seconals but not the next visit where he told Gary he certainly wouldn't and couldn't. At that moment, Dennis knew something about the cold, clammy hand of fear when it takes possession of your guts. No cliché. His guts were being handled by an outside force.

Out at the hospital, a man from *Newsweek* gave the same news. Boaz was the Warden's number-one suspect. Then Geraldo Rivera of ABC said as much. Dennis thought, I don't need this a bit.

It became a day of catharsis for him and much emotion. At the thought of Gary dead, or Nicole gone, Dennis felt such a sense of loss that he began to wonder if he could keep asking in good conscience that Gary be executed.

At just that point, Geraldo Rivera suggested an interview, and they went up to his hotel suite to discuss it. To protect Gary, Dennis had stayed away from pot this last week, and had none on his person, but he figured Rivera might know somebody to turn him on, and, in fact, there was a reporter in the hotel with some high-quality Thai. Dennis took it into his lungs like love. But then there was always the reasonable premise that a portion of God's love had been put into grass. Of course, Dennis had also run into a fellow who had the interesting counterhypothesis that what came into your lungs as love was a facsimile offered by the devil. An interesting argument, but all Dennis knew right now was that fine grass affected him emotionally. Went right to his heart.

As he sat in the hotel room, talking with Geraldo Rivera, he started to have this overwhelming feeling of the great hopelessness of the situation, and began to cry. Dennis couldn't help himself. He just began to sob aloud in front of Geraldo. It was all so much sadder than he had conceived.

4

Afterward, Tamera would be the first to say that it sure sounded like she was stupid, but at the time, she had no idea her piece was going to be put on the front page.

A couple of months back, when she first started at the *Deseret News,* she actually got a front-page by-line for a story on the break in the Teton Dam. That was terrific for a cub reporter. She thought the Teton Dam piece was going to be her one and ever, and she wasn't even thinking of something as big as that again. So Monday afternoon, after she left Nicole, she returned to the paper, read through the letters, and worked on her story all night without thinking once where they'd put it. Yet by the time she finished, 7 A.M., she should have known. There were other people working with her now including a couple of editors. She just assumed the story might be sensitive to the readership, and so they wanted to take a look. Still, everybody was gathered at her desk, helping with last-minute corrections, and it even became one of those pull-it-out-of-the-typewriter, get-it-to-the-printer jobs. They went to press at eight in the morning and Tamera hung in helping write cut lines, and about eight-thirty or nine, she was ready to go to bed but felt like seeing her story in print first. So, she went for a walk while waiting for the first edition.

Tamera ended up over at the Visitors Center at Temple Square and went up the ramp. It was a large spiral walkway that curved up through the air so you felt as if you were ascending into the universe or the galaxies. A dark blue ceiling was overhead and at the summit was a huge statue of Jesus. A beautiful place. Tamera had gone there other times to be alone and ponder. Very gentle peacefulness was out there. You could feel powerful bodies hovering around you, almost, and she prayed that her story would count and things would somehow work out for Nicole.

Then Tamera came back to the paper, and never had she seen a newsroom so electric. She knew something immense had landed right on top of their deadline. A story was being put together so fast, they were putting it right into the terminal that went to typesetting. Really wild. Her editor came up, and said, "Nicole and Gilmore tried to commit suicide. They are in Intensive Care. Start writing a little story." Tamera said, "Wow." Sat down at her typewriter, not even knowing what she was supposed to do.

Death and suicide, Tamera began, *were the main topic in convicted killer Gary Mark Gilmore's conversations with his girlfriend Nicole Barrett in the week preceding suicide attempts by both.*

Nicole confided these conversations to me. In a series of intimate talks we had in the tension-filled week, she shared her many letters from Gilmore, spoke of how he had encouraged and reassured her about suicide, and discussed candidly her own feelings about dying.

Now my friend lies near death in a Provo hospital while all the world watches. . . .

She kept writing for page after page of all that had happened to her and Nicole.

I had a source no one had been able to reach up to that point. My emotions were mixed. I cared about her as a person and like anyone in my profession, hoped for a story from her. But I didn't want to pressure her or nudge her into a corner where she didn't want to be.

As I saw her come out of the prison, levi-clad, sweater in hand and smoking a cigarette, I asked about her visit and our conversation began. As we got in my Volkswagen, I left the radio off so that it would be silent if she wanted to talk — and it seemed she did.

"There are knots in my stomach when I first go to see him," she said, "but I feel better afterwards. He is so strong, so much stronger than I am, and he always reassures me and makes me feel better."

It was one piece of work Tamera carried out like a robot. Actually took her news story over to the terminal and started putting it in, before any feeling began to come. Then she really did have a slew of mixed emotions. She had had no idea Nicole was going to do it today, none on earth.

By the time she calmed down one way, she was getting angry another. Gary was just a manipulator of the worst kind. It was one thing, Tamera thought, to try to talk someone into going to bed with you, but to manipulate them to die with you, that was totally selfish. All those letters, where he was so insanely jealous. Couldn't stand the thought of her meeting another man or something. Boy, Tamera thought, just boy!

Exactly then, her brother Cardell came walking into the news-room. He worked downtown but this was the first he had ever done that. Heard the story on the radio and figured Tamera would be need-ing him. She just hugged Cardell and cried. They might both be thinking of her old boy friend, the convict. Later that night, her brother up in Vancouver, Washington, called to congratulate her and say how proud he and his wife were of her. They were making copies of the stories to send to the family. She found out later she had been syndicated all over. The AP carried her heavily and the *London Observer,* a Scandinavian service, some paper in South Africa, a Paris syndication, *Newsweek,* and the West Germans. The paper made each of those sales at $750, which more than made back Tamera's salary to date. That was really neat.

5

Wayne Watson and Brent Bullock, from Noall Wootton's office, went over to Nicole Barrett's apartment after a call came from the police about the letters. They thought there might be admissions therein that could prove useful for the Max Jensen case if they ever had to try Gary on it.

Back in Noall's office, Watson and Bullock started going through the stuff, but by the time they'd read the first ten, they got pretty disinterested. The guy was obviously an intelligent individual, but the letters, from the standpoint of uncovering new evidence, were boring. Wayne Watson did come across a paragraph that made sense if you knew how to translate rhyming slang, for it referred to pills as Jacks and Jills, and he contacted a man in the Sheriff's office at Salt Lake who was doing the prison investigation on how the drugs got smuggled in, and told him Nicole might be the one.

Actually, the best part of the whole deal was that Brent Bullock and Wayne Watson had their picture taken by a press photographer in Nicole's little living room. There they were, each squatting on one knee while looking at the letters on the floor, both of them appearing as big as professional football players, and handsome as all get-out with Brent showing his six-inch handlebar mustache. After that came out, they took a ribbing from their wives and friends. Supersleuth, stuff like that.

6

Kathryne was at work at Ideal Furniture when her mother, Mrs. Strong, called. "Have you heard the radio?" she asked, "do you have the radio on?" Then she blurted out one word, "Nicole!"

Kathryne went to pieces. Started screaming, "No! No! No!" She just assumed the worst. The big stereo in the back of the store was on, but it had been turned low and she'd not been listening. Now her ears came right into focus, and she heard the words, "Gilmore's girl friend . . . suicide." Kathryne went hysterical. Her mother had to keep yelling over the phone until she heard what was being told her. "She's not dead, you know," said her mother, "she's up at Utah Valley. I'll be right over to pick you up." Time passed for Kathryne in lost minutes, like she was in concussion. Then her mother was outside the store in the old Lincoln, the stinking Lincoln, their old family joke, picking her up. Next, they were in the emergency door of the hospital, and the lady at the desk was sending them to the second. When she entered Nicole's room, Kathryne went through the horrors. That dreadful machine was there once more. Not seven days ago, her father had had the same machine on him. Now he was dead and they were working on Nicole.

They gave Kathryne a little Valium, and a doctor came by. He talked out of a tight little mouth and couldn't even give Nicole a 50-50 chance. "Could go either way," he said, then added, "We don't know if there was brain damage or not . . . question is if the machine can keep her lungs working . . . can't guarantee that either." Sure wasn't offering hope. "I can't," he said, "guarantee anything until all medication is out of her system." There was a police officer sitting outside the door.

Kathryne would go to Nicole's room for fifteen minutes, then go out and sit in the hall, while they let her mother in. Then she'd go back. This went on all afternoon. Rikki had come back from Wyoming for her father's funeral, and was still here, and now he stayed in the Intensive Care Unit waiting room and kept journalists away. The reporters were all being held downstairs, but one girl snuck up to Intensive Care, and sat there all day with a knitting bag on the floor.

They never knew she was a reporter. After three hours, she said to Kathryne, "Are you Nicole's mother?" Kathryne just looked at her and paid no mind. The girl then said to Kathy Kampman, "Are you Nicole's family?" Kathy said, "Please don't bother us." But the girl asked, "Does Nicole have any brothers and sisters?" That was when Kathy got it. She said, "You're a TV reporter." She had noticed that whenever any of them started to talk, the girl would lean down to her knitting bag and turn on something. Kathryne went berserk. They got the girl right out.

At first, Charley wasn't going to come, but then, to Kathryne's surprise, he popped over around three in the afternoon while she was over to Nicole's apartment. The nurse said Mr. Baker had been there and went all to pieces when he saw Nicole, and left. Later, Kathryne found out Charley had gone to Pleasant Grove and stayed there with Angel and Mike for the rest of the day and night.

Kathryne hung in. She couldn't remember eating anything. A little after midnight, she called some Elders she knew in the Church and they came over and prayed with Kathryne by Nicole's bed, anointing her head with oil, putting hands on her forehead. Prayed to God to bring her through. They could not do it in the name of the Church due to the fact she had tried to take her own life, but did ask the Lord to hear her on the basis of the faith of all the rest of the family.

About 4 A.M., Kathryne's mother took her home and she stayed up with Charley until ten when he took her back to the hospital. In all those hours, she had no rest. Kept calling the hospital to see if there was any change.

By the next day, so many reporters were downstairs that Kathryne was obliged to go in and out with a long, blond wig.

DESERET NEWS

Nashville, Tenn. (AP) Nov. 16 — Country music star Johnny Cash says he tried to call Gary Gilmore at the

Utah State Prison to urge him to "fight for his life" only minutes after the convicted murder was found unconscious in an apparent suicide attempt.

"I don't know what I would have told a man who was planning to take his life," Cash said. "Sometimes it helps, sometimes it doesn't. But I would have tried to talk him out of it."

The singer said his first impulse was not to get involved. "I told him (the attorney) I wasn't looking for any publicity. I thought I had better mind my own business. Who needs that kind of publicity?"

When Boaz persisted, saying his client wanted to see Cash or visit him, Cash said he decided to call the prison.

7

The moment Brenda heard the news, she began to call every hour, but all they would say at Gary's hospital in Salt Lake was that he was still alive. Brenda would ask, "If I go over, will you let me see him?" They would reply, "You better be walking in with the Governor if you want to get through." She asked if she could talk, at least, to one of the nurses taking care of him, and they finally put a woman on. "Would you please tell Gary that Brenda called and I'm thinking of him dearly," she said. "I'd love him to fight for his life." It was a mind-blower. She never knew if the nurse passed on the message.

Up at the hospital, they had about decided Gary had not made a real attempt to kill himself. By their best calculation he had taken half of a lethal dose, twenty capsules, about two grams. Three grams represented a 50-percent-lethal dose, that is, half the people who took such an amount died. Since Gilmore was a big man, his chance of doing the job with two grams was small. Besides, he had taken the pills just before morning check. That was suspicious. Nicole seemed to have swallowed the same amount many hours earlier and was in much worse condition. After all, she hardly weighed one hundred pounds. He weighed nearly twice as much.

Warden Sam Smith was being interviewed.

INTERVIEWER   Any ideas as to how he may have gotten the substance?

WARDEN   Well, there's a number of possibilities. He could have accumulated his own medication, saved it up, ingested it; he could have obtained it from possibly other inmates living in Maximum Security, it's possible he could have obtained it from those that have visited him.

INTERVIEWER   How easy would it be for someone to take drugs in to the men?

WARDEN   Well, it's virtually impossible to prevent someone from hiding something as small as drugs on their person or in a cavity of the body.

INTERVIEWER   Aren't people searched, though, when they go in and see him?

WARDEN   Yes, the people are given a skin shakedown but that does not mean that you can explore every cavity of the body and ascertain that there is no medication.

INTERVIEWER   As the man responsible for Gilmore's well-being and safety, how do you feel about what happened today?

WARDEN   Of course I feel bad but I recognize realistically that if a person desires to kill themselves then it's pretty difficult to prevent over a prolonged period of time.

INTERVIEWER   Thank you, Sam.

The press was in a savage mood after this interview. One reporter remarked that with Sam Smith to listen to, you didn't need Seconal.

The joke among the press was that looking for a street address in any one of these Utah towns was like trying to locate artillery coordinates on a map. 2575 North 1100 West. "Yes, sir," wrote Barry Farrell in his notebook. "You have the right address. It's just that you're in the wrong town." Barry Farrell, there to do an article for *New West*, was at a point of frustration where his best pleasure was taking notes. He hated Salt Lake. "There is a Swissness to the place," he wrote, "a complacency that people from the Coast are likely to find infuriating.

Getting drunk here is like signing up for methadone maintenance."
Then he added, "After one o'clock, the only sound downtown is the
creaking of the neon signs."

It was hard to get near this story. Everything was shut off. Farrell couldn't remember too many occasions when the center of interest in a story had been so removed. He had not been a writer for
Life magazine over many a year without getting into a few places.
Often, he could obtain interviews others couldn't. There were, however, no interviews here. In his notebook, Farrell wrote, "One can only
imagine how suffocating Gilmore must have found it. . . . The claustrophobia that ensues when one finds himself without the opportunity to sin."

Earl Dorius was naturally concerned how the drugs had reached
Gilmore and he phoned the Warden for information. Sam Smith told
him the prime suspects were Nicole Barrett, Dennis Boaz, Vern Damico, Ida Damico, and Brenda Nicol. Dorius thanked him for the information.

When Gibbs heard the news, he thought back to a discussion
with Gary on how to smuggle drugs into Maximum. It was his advice, he remembered, to use balloons.

That night when Big Jake came on duty, he told Gibbs the prison
officials were stupid. Why, the Provo Police had informed the prison
that Nicole picked up two prescriptions of Seconal the day prior to
these suicide attempts. Yet they still didn't give her a real search. Big
Jake looked at Gibbs and added, "I'll bet you educated him on how to
get the stuff inside." Big Jake put on a big grin and walked off.

DESERET NEWS

Most Letters Urge Clemency

Nov. 16 — . . . A Minneapolis man asked why Gilmore
should be singled out for execution when other convicted killers live.

"Former Lt. William Calley, convicted of the 'premeditated murder of not less than 22 Oriental human
beings,' is now walking the streets," he wrote.

Ironically, George Latimer, chairman of the Board of Pardons which will decide Gilmore's fate, was Calley's chief civilian defense attorney.

DESERET NEWS

Nov. 16— The Daughters of Wisdom in Litchfield, Connecticut, speaking of Gilmore, said, "We believe he is meant to do something worthwhile for mankind. He needs time to find out what that something is."

DESERET NEWS

Nov. 16 — . . . Max Jensen's father, David Jensen, an Idaho farmer and stake president in the LDS Church, said, "His death made us feel sad, but it's something we are accepting. We sure wouldn't want to trade places with Gilmore's parents."

DESERET NEWS

Nov. 16 — Bushnell's widow, who is expecting another child shortly after the first of the year, has gone to California to live with her mother-in-law. Family members say she goes to pieces at a mention of her husband's name.

CHAPTER 7

Taste

1

On Monday evening, while Nicole was going over her Last Will and Testament, Larry Schiller drove out to the International Airport in L.A. to buy a copy of *Newsweek*'s cover story on Gary Gilmore. Schiller knew that airports received magazines a day earlier than the average outlet, and sometimes, working on a story, when he had to have a newsmagazine ahead of the competition, he'd even look up the local distributor.

Schiller spent part of Monday evening going over that cover story. It told him there were five people's rights he would have to buy. Gary's obviously, and Nicole's made two, but Monday night, for the first time, he heard of April Baker and decided he had better get her as well. Then he read Brenda Nicol's name in the article, and saw she was responsible for getting Gary out of jail. That could be a key link in the story. Brenda's rights had to be obtained. He didn't know she was Vern Damico's daughter, or even related to him, but Vern was the fifth name on his list.

First thing Tuesday morning, he called Lou Rudolph at ABC, and told him of his great interest in the story. There were a lot of different ways to do it, Schiller said, and quickly laid out a number of possibilities. He had learned a long time ago that in television you had to sell executives on the subject first. Had to establish it would still be bona fide television even if you did not obtain all the rights. If, for example, he got Gilmore's okay without Nicole's, a scenario could be worked up of a guy who comes out of prison and struggles with his old con habits, but finally kills a man, a real study of the pains of getting out of jail. That way they could do capital punishment and whether a man had a right to die, and never need to touch upon a love story.

On the other hand, said Schiller, if they got the girl, but couldn't succeed in signing up Gilmore, they might do an interesting struggle of two sisters both in love with the same criminal. They'd have to substitute a fictionalized criminal, but could still explore the triangle. Or they could focus completely on Nicole and turn the thing into a study of a young girl who has been married a few times, is saddled with children, then falls in love with a criminal. Play down the murders, but emphasize the romantic difficulties of trying to live with a man that society does not trust.

Schiller was not trying to impose judgment, he told Rudolph, on the relative merits of these separate scenarios. He was just saying you could bypass Gilmore, make it a woman's story, and still have something of value.

No sooner had he hung up, than the radio was informing him that Gilmore and Nicole had tried a joint suicide. Immediately he booked a plane ticket to Salt Lake. At the airport, he called Rudolph again to suggest another alternative. Still, assuming they couldn't get the rights to Gilmore, they could do a study of a girl who wanted to die and so entered into a suicide pact with a criminal, thereby looking for a starstruck way to solve an unendurable problem.

Schiller repeated that he was sure of the potentialities, and wanted ABC to finance him in a real way. Not hotel bills or airplane fares, Schiller said, because that, Lou, he could always handle with his credit cards; no, Schiller wanted backing to get in there and deal for Gilmore. He would call again from Salt Lake.

He might have known. The moment that suicide attempt hit the media, not only was Larry Schiller on the plane, but everybody was heading for Salt Lake, ready to check into the Hilton where each of the media monkeys could watch all the other monkeys. There were going to be a lot of monkeys in that zoo.

From stories that got back to him, Schiller knew he was well known in the media for his impatience and his funds of energy. He always gave his big friendly grin when he heard such stories. They protected his secret weapon: it was that he had patience. He didn't tell people. Cultivated the opposite image. But he didn't mind being in situations where he just had to sit and wait. Give him an airplane trip or a waiting room. If you counted the years from the age of fourteen when he began to make money as an expert on skid marks, he had, by his own estimate, been running like a maniac for close to twenty-five years. So he didn't mind sitting on occasion.

His father, who once managed the Davega store in Times Square, and knew enterprise when he saw it, bought him a Rolleicord when he was a kid, and a police band radio, and Schiller would hear accidents come in on the radio, get on his bike and ride to the place. If it was far away, and he only arrived after the vehicles had been removed, he could still photograph the skid marks. Then he would sell the prints to the insurance companies. It was his apprenticeship for getting to the scene.

2

Having broken into the media as one of *Life*'s youngest photographers, Schiller had covered Khrushchev at the United Nations, and Madame Nhu in a convent, was at the Vatican when the Pope died, and took a picture of Nixon crying as he lost to Kennedy, a famous picture. He knew how to travel without a suitcase. Syndicated the Fisher quintuplets' story and photographed the Alaska earthquakes, Dallas and Watts, the Olympics, covered the trial of Sirhan Sirhan. He reported income over six figures before he was twenty-four, and got awful tired of photographing different heads on the same body. He was conceivably the best one-eyed photographer in the world — lost the sight of the other in an accident when he was five years old — but he got weary of walking into people's lives, shaking their hands, photographing them, walking out. He left *Life* and went into producing books and movies and fast magazine syndications on stories that weren't small. Wanted to do people in depth. Instead, did

Jack Ruby on his deathbed, and Susan Atkins in the Manson trial. He got a terrible reputation. Schiller worked hard to change that image. He published a book, *Minamata,* about mercury poisoning in Japan, and created the still montages in *Butch Cassidy and the Sundance Kid* and *Lady Sings the Blues,* produced and directed *The American Dreamer* with Dennis Hopper, did the interviews for a book on Lenny Bruce by Albert Goldman. He won an Academy Award in Special Category for *The Man Who Skied down Everest.* It did not matter. He was the journalist who dealt in death.

Sitting on the airplane, resting from twenty-five years of galloping out of explosions into cover portraits, from riots to elections, sitting in one place with the fatigue of that twenty-five years embedded like skid marks in his limbs, sitting on this plane full of media monkeys heading for Salt Lake, Schiller thought it through. The Gilmore story would not help his reputation, yet he could not let it go. It irritated the nerve in him that never gave up

So far, after two quick trips to Salt Lake, he had come back with empty hands. He was not accustomed to such meager results. On instinct, he had gone to Salt Lake just ten days after Gilmore announced he would not appeal, but found nothing. Boaz was in control of the scene, and Boaz had little interest in him. Boaz was dealing with David Susskind.

Schiller read over the telegram he had sent two days ago to Gilmore.

NOVEMBER 14
GARY GILMORE
UTAH STATE PRISON, BOX 250
DRAPER UT 84020
ON BEHALF OF ABC MOVIES, THE NEW INGOT COMPANY, AND MY ASSOCIATES WE WISH TO PURCHASE THE MOTION PICTURE AND PUBLICATION RIGHTS TO YOUR TRUE LIFE STORY FROM YOU OR YOUR ELECTED REPRESENTATIVES STOP OUR OWN CREDITS ARE 14 YEARS OF MAJOR MOTION PICTURES AND 6 BEST SELLING BIOGRAPHIES STOP MORE RECENTLY WE PRODUCED THE HIGHLY RECEIVED FILM "HEY I'M ALIVE," THE TRUE LIFE STORY OF RALPH FLORES, A MORMON LAY PREACHER, AND A YOUNG GIRL WHO CRASHED IN A LIGHT PLANE IN THE YUKON

AND SURVIVED 49 DAYS WITHOUT FOOD STOP THIS FILM ABOUT FAITH
IN GOD AND CONVICTION WAS PRAISED BY THE MORMON CHURCH AND
VIEWED BY OVER 30 MILLION PEOPLE STOP AMONG OUR OTHER CRED-
ITS IS "SUNSHINE," THE TRUE STORY OF LYN HELTON A YOUNG
MOTHER IN DENVER COLO WHO GAVE HER LIFE AT A YOUNG AGE IN
RETURN FOR TIME WITH HER DAUGHTER STOP THIS STORY OF THE
RIGHT TO DIE ISSUE AND STRENGTH OF CONVICTION WAS VIEWED BY
OVER 70 MILLION PEOPLE AND THE BOOK IN HER WORDS READ BY OVER
8 MILLION PEOPLE STOP A COPY IS BEING SENT TO YOU UNDER SEPA-
RATE COVER STOP WE WISH TO PRESENT YOUR STORY AS TRUTH NOT
AS FICTION STOP I HAVE SEEN MR. BOAZ AND NOTED TO HIM THAT I
WOULD CORRESPOND WITH YOU STOP I LOOK FORWARD TO HEARING
FROM YOU OR YOUR REPRESENTATIVE STOP PLEASE CALL COLLECT AT
ANY TIME STOP SINCERELY YOURS
LAWRENCE SCHILLER

There had been no answer. His telegram might just as well have
gone into the dead-letter bin at the post office.

He went out to see Vern Damico at the shoe store in Provo and
Vern wasn't there. He bumped into a couple of local reporters in Salt
Lake and said, I'm not here to compete with you, just like you to tell
me who is what in this city, and how do you get in to see Gilmore?
They weren't getting in either. Schiller heard of Nicole, but also
heard she wouldn't talk to anyone. He kept missing her at the prison.

Those first and second trips to Salt Lake, Schiller was hitting
stone walls. Couldn't find the story. He got into his rented car and
drove from Provo to the airport in Salt Lake, and on the drive, staring
down the Interstate, said to himself, If I can't find the story, then nobody can find it. But if nobody can, then it has to be a good story. He
couldn't stop thinking about it.

The moment he heard news of the double suicide attempt,
Schiller said to himself, there is a story and it's real. Since it's real, it
has, in this case, to be fantastic.

At the Hilton, it looked like the crowd of press had expanded
from fifty to five hundred. The foreign press was beginning to come
in. The British in numbers. When the British arrived en masse, the
stamp was on the meat. The story would have the largest worldwide
appeal.

Schiller made a few phone calls. His luck seemed to have changed. Reached Vern Damico on the first ring, and had a good talk, asked Mr. Damico's opinion of where Nicole might be. Damico seemed to think she was at the hospital in Provo, and Schiller made an appointment afterward to talk with him. Schiller got into his rented car. The monkeys would stay at the Hilton and exchange theories on the crime, but he was on his way to the hospital in Provo.

The waiting room was small and had a lot of people. Schiller went up to the desk and asked for Nicole Barrett. They acted as if they had never heard of her. He went around the corner, and put a call in to the hospital administrator, and asked if any of Nicole Barrett's relatives could be located quickly. The woman said they were coming in and out all the time. The mother's been here, Schiller was informed, but she's not here right now. Schiller sat down in his heavy brown coat and prepared to wait. It was a hot waiting room, but he was comfortable. Gilmore was in the hospital, under guard. Gilmore was out of it and could not be reached. Back in Salt Lake, the monkeys would run back and forth, trading information, but there was nothing in the story that counted now except Gilmore and Nicole. Since he couldn't get to Gilmore, he would wait to make contact with Nicole. It was very simple to Schiller.

There was no anxiety about sitting there for hours. Other reporters would be on the phone, checking back to hear what was going down, but Schiller sat and relaxed and let the heat of the room pour over him and the fatigues of twenty-five years perspired slowly, a drop and another drop from the bottomless reservoirs of fatigue, and he sat there quietly thinking, and let his sins and errors wash over him, and reviewed them. He considered it obscene not to learn from experience.

3

His worst sin, his number-one error, he usually decided, was the Susan Atkins story. He had been in Yugoslavia when the Tate–LaBianca murders took place, but six months later, driving down the Santa Monica freeway, news came over the radio that a girl in prison named Susan Atkins had just given information on Tate–LaBianca to her cellmate. Next day, Schiller learned that one of her attorneys was Paul Caruso, who in 1963 had written the contract when Schiller sold a nude photograph of Marilyn Monroe to Hugh Hefner. It obtained the highest price ever paid for a single picture up to then, $25,000. Schiller now called Paul Caruso and said Susan Atkins's story could be sold around the world, and would help to pay for her defense.

So, Schiller was brought in to see Susan Atkins between her two Grand Jury appearances, and she confessed the murders in a series of three connected interviews. He did sell it all over the world. Then it was reprinted in America. Suddenly, Susan Atkins was no longer the State's star witness, because she now had a vested interest in her own story. Schiller had destroyed part of the State's case.

He was sick to the stomach over that, but it took a while to acknowledge the fact. It came upon him little by little. He was asked to dinner one night by a famous lawyer and couldn't understand why, until he saw that six eminent Judges were also present. They wanted to hear why a journalist would do what he had done. It was a very intelligent dinner, and he was delighted to sit with such fine and serious people, but unhappy to realize he'd been fucking them over.

Earlier, he sold the Susan Atkins story to New American Library for $15,000, a quick sale for a quick and rotten book, a way of liquidating his involvement, but it didn't liquidate so much as proliferate. *Newsweek* interviewed him about the book and he said, "Look, I published what Susan said. I don't know whether it's true or not." *Newsweek* ended their article with that quote: "I don't know whether it's true or not." It made the sweat break out on his forehead to think about it. He had learned one lesson he would never erase, and thought of it again on the night he dined with the Judges. The secret of people who had class was that they remained accurate to the facts. Schiller called it history. You recorded history right. If you did the work that way, you could end up a man of substance.

So when *Helter Skelter* came out, he said to himself, "Schiller, you really fucked up. With the profit you made on the original sale, you could have done a definitive study of the entire Manson family.

You threw away what should have been an important book." It was embarrassing to recollect. He even had to appear in Court to testify on how the Susan Atkins interviews took place. When the Judge said, "How would you characterize your occupation, Mr. Schiller?" he replied, "I believe I am a communicator." The courtroom laughed. They thought he was a hustler. The memory burned into the skin right under his beard. "I believe I am a communicator," and the courtroom laughed. He would do this Gilmore one differently. Lay a proper foundation for every corner of the story. And he sat in the room and waited in the heat in his heavy brown coat, and the hours went by.

There was a bearded guy at the other end of the room. Schiller with his black beard and the other guy with his bright brown beard eyed each other. After an hour or two, a girl came in who looked to be media and went over to the other beard and soon started bawling the shit out of the fellow. Schiller could pick up that his name was Jeff Newman and he was from the *National Enquirer,* and the girl was saying, "You knew she was going to attempt suicide and you sat on it. You and your fucking newspaper." It made Newman so upset, he got up and went out. Now, Schiller went over to the girl and said, "I'm Larry Schiller, representing ABC elevision." She turned on him like an eagle, claws out, said, "You, too!" Schiller didn't even know her name. She was a local stringer, but sure carrying on. The men didn't give a damn about the women, she was saying, and yet the women were killing themselves over the men. Schiller nodded and got away as quick as he could.

Then a very tall young fellow with dark black hair that came down to his shoulders, and a girl's name tattooed on his knuckles, came in, and looked so shook Schiller figured he had to be Nicole's brother, that is, if she had a brother and Schiller went up and introduced himself but it was apparent the fellow didn't want to communicate, so Schiller sat down again and waited, and another couple of hours went by before he saw a woman standing at the candy shop next to the waiting room. She was thin and small boned, had her hair in a bun, and looked like a very tough western woman who could have walked across the plains. By the expression on her face — such iron fatigue and held-in sorrow, he was sure it had to be Nicole's mother (although later he found out it was Nicole's grandmother, and Nicole's mother wasn't even forty yet) so he wrote a note to introduce himself as Lawrence Schiller and said he was here to discuss the events taking place in their lives in relation to the motion picture and book rights and would appreciate a meeting with her or her authorized representative, or an attorney (it was always better to say "authorized representative" before you said "attorney" so they knew you weren't suing). He finished by mentioning that he was prepared to pay Nicole a minimum of $25,000 for her rights, and put the note in an envelope that had Mrs. Baker written across it.

He handed that to the woman and said, "As you will see, I am Lawrence Schiller from ABC television. This is not the time and place, but when the occasion is right, I would appreciate it if you would open my envelope and read it." Then he turned around and walked out of the hospital. A contact had been made.

4

When the front-page story on Gilmore came out in the *New York Times,* November 8th, David Susskind was fascinated. For a front-page piece, it was well written, and gave a good description of the murders, the man's sentence, and his decision not to appeal. Put that together with Gilmore's previous criminality, and it all suggested a fascinating scenario.

Shortly after the article caught his eye, almost immediately in fact, Susskind's old friend and associate Stanley Greenberg called, and they had a good conversation. Stanley had written a TV story fifteen years ago about a man awaiting execution. The man had been so long on Death Row that he changed in character, and the question became, "Who was being executed?" *Metamorphosis* the play had been called, and Susskind always felt that it had had some effect on the end of capital punishment in New York State, and maybe even a little to do with the Supreme Court decision that saved a lot of men's lives on Death Row. "Of course," Stanley said now to David, "inviolate and forever simply means till the next generation. Then you have to do it all over again."

Greenberg was a man of some decorum, but Susskind could tell he was aroused. "What fascinates me about this Gilmore case," he was saying, "is that it's an open commentary on the utter failure of our prison system to rehabilitate anybody. Why, the guy's been in and out his whole damn life and he just keeps getting worse. It all escalated from car stealing up to armed robbery with a dangerous weapon. That's a devastating commentary," said Greenberg. "Secondly, it could offer a wonderful statement about capital punishment and how godawful it is, eye for an eye. I even think that reaching a large audience can probably save the guy's life. Gilmore says he wants to die, but he's obviously out of his head. I think our production could be a factor in the man's not being executed." That appealed to Susskind. "They can't execute this man," he said to Stanley, "he's deranged. He's insane. They should have understood that way back."

They talked a long time. Finally Susskind said to Greenberg, "Why don't you go to Utah? I think this story's got several layers of importance and interest and could make very exciting, dramatic material. If, on investigation, it holds up, and we can get the releases we need, we might have something here."

Greenberg couldn't go right away because of his contract at Universal, but each day they talked to each other, and Susskind began conversations with Boaz. He quickly decided Dennis was not your typical lawyer.

Boaz boasted, "I've got releases from everybody. Got them all." He kept talking about how he had locked up everything. Susskind called Stanley Greenberg and said, "This is a very odd attorney. However, he's got his eye on the money machine."

Dennis said, "Look, I can't cooperate if you don't put your evidence of good faith on the line. Money," said Dennis, "is not to be considered not of the essence," and giggled. "What do you want?" asked Susskind. "Well, now," said Dennis, "it's getting to be a worldwide case." "How can I," asked Susskind, "be sure you have all the releases you say you have?" "You," said Dennis, "have to start somewhere. You better start by trusting me. I have exactly what I told you I have. If you don't believe me, there are ten other people out here who want it. It's just that I like your reputation, Mr. Susskind. I'd like to give you first crack at it." He wanted a goodly sum, in the neighborhood of $50,000 for the rights of all the principals involved in the

case, and asked Susskind to put that into a telegram, which David
did, and sent it off.

Susskind also enclosed a legal package. It had a contract and
release forms. Boaz might have told him that he had it all, but when
Susskind asked him in what form were the releases, Dennis said,
"One- and two-sentence quitclaims."

"Oh, look," said Susskind, "that doesn't work at all, you're going
to have to use established legal forms, waiver of rights for the payment, all such. It has to conform to what we do in the motion picture
and television business."

Dennis said, "I don't understand why you have to have all that
folderol."

"It's not folderol," said Susskind, "it's of the essence. People can
change their minds. A one- or two-sentence release probably contains
language too loose to bear up under scrutiny. I'm sorry, I have to
send you release forms." He did. Susskind went to his lawyers and
they sent off the package.

5

By pure coincidence, Stanley Greenberg arrived at the Salt Lake Hilton on the 16th, the afternoon of the double suicide saga, and so precisely the busiest day of the month for the media. Stanley had telephoned the night before from Kensington in California, where he
lived just north of San Francisco, to confirm an appointment with
Boaz, but under the circumstances, in all the brouhaha at the Hilton
over the double suicide, he never expected the lawyer to keep his
date. To Greenberg's surprise, however, Dennis did show up, and
just late enough to have given Stanley Greenberg time to look carefully at the network news at six o'clock. Right after, to his astonishment, Boaz knocked at his hotel room door.

If not for this dramatic event today, they would almost certainly
have met, Greenberg thought, as adversaries, or at the least, he
would have felt obliged to deal with Boaz as a bizarre specimen of a
lawyer willing to kill off his client. Now, however, Boaz seemed to
have gone through a considerable shift of opinion in the greatest

hurry. So their conversation proved to be more productive than Stanley could have hoped.

As he explained to Boaz over the course of a drink, his hackles went up about a week ago when it became apparent there was a real danger of Gilmore being executed. Stanley explained that he found capital punishment personally repugnant. He simply couldn't sit around and let it happen. This might seem a romantic reaction, but he had felt obliged, nonetheless, to gather his forces and get together with David Susskind, who was the right producer in an endeavor like this.

Credentials established, Greenberg was now ready to discuss the case. He led off by saying he just didn't see where any criminal had the right to tell society what to do to him. By his lights, a criminal had no more right to demand capital punishment than to demand his immediate release. Society, after all, set the rules.

Dennis, who had been looking oddly subdued, given Stanley's preconceptions of him, now seemed fired up a bit. He replied that Gary wasn't demanding anything. He simply didn't want to appeal. Appeal law was based on the premise that nobody wanted to be executed, and so it offered all sorts of possibilities for relief, but Gary didn't want to pursue those possibilities.

It wasn't that simple, Greenberg argued back. The Supreme Court had said capital punishment could be resumed, but only if certain legal steps were taken. If you were going to execute people, it was important to kill them only under guarded and truly hedged-about circumstances.

At this point, Dennis again looked gloomy and said that he wasn't so sure he had done a very competent job. In any case, his feelings were undergoing a radical change. Up to now, he had supported Gilmore's plea because he felt the man had a right to determine his own life. Now, however, push had come to shove, and he had realized for the first time that Gary was actually going to die and that made him so upset he didn't know if he wanted to be a part of the process.

Greenberg had the impression Dennis was slightly stoned. Feelings of inadequacy certainly began to pour out. Greenberg even found himself liking Boaz more than he expected. On some levels he was quite attractive, sort of a free spirit. Of course, he was extremely and obviously disorganized, and not the sort of attorney Greenberg might want to entrust his fortune or future to. Still, he was likable, so likable. "Have you been in touch," Stanley asked, "with the local ACLU?"

Hosts of feelings poured forth. No, Boaz had not become involved with them. That was against his client's wishes. His client had this peculiar mélange of right-wing ideas and left-wing emotions. Gary hated blacks, for instance, but that, Boaz explained, was because they were a dangerous majority in a prison. All the white prisoners were in danger of being raped by blacks. Gary also hated the ACLU. That was because they preached freedom of the individual but wouldn't give Gilmore the liberty to choose his death. So, Boaz had not gotten in touch with them. But just an hour ago, talking to Geraldo Rivera, he had had a brilliant conception. Only he would need some help with it, in terms of paperwork. There were many motions that would have to be filed, for which he would need a Utah lawyer. So, now he wanted to get in touch with the ACLU. When Greenberg encouraged this, Boaz called up a representative named Judy Wolbach, and she agreed to come over to the room for a drink.

Before it was over, Greenberg decided it had to be one of the bizarre conversations of all time. An absolutely marvelous dramatic play. Simply couldn't have imagined it better. This thin, vibrant, intelligent woman, very high strung, very liberal, very suspicious of Boaz on the one hand, and on the other side, Dennis pouring out his soul at how he had been harassed by the legal community and was the number-one suspect at the prison for smuggling in Seconal.

There were tears in Boaz's eyes from time to time, and it was hard to know if he was more worried about himself — "I'll take a polygraph test," he said — or more worked up over poor Gilmore, dying, for all they knew, in Salt Lake right now, and Nicole somewhere else — was she also dying? Here, Greenberg thought, is this mad, churning young lawyer, and then this Judy Wolbach glaring at Dennis as if he were a *specimen*. She was *completely* distrustful of the auspices. Even the little bar in the corner of the room must have looked to her, under these circumstances, sinister.

Stanley could hardly blame her. Reading about Dennis in the newspapers, she must have seen him as some sort of hippie hustler. Now, there he was before her, agitated, smiling, arrogant, modest, first dejected, then haranguing her. Stanley couldn't imagine what he would be like at a time of less agitation.

Almost immediately, Dennis came up with this impossibly attractive and hopeless notion. He wanted to get Gary transferred to a Medium Security prison in some state where they allowed connubial visits.

Oh, it would work, he exclaimed. Nicole could get a job in the local town and bring up her children. On weekends they would have their married life, two nights a week. That could give Gary a motive for living. Why, if the court *really* understood what a fine person Gary was, they would do it. Gary could write and draw Cottage incarceration was what he was talking about.

Greenberg noticed that Boaz was now happy again. It was apparent: give him an original idea and some remote possibility of achieving it, and he couldn't be happier. It didn't matter if the conditions were unattainable — just give him a novel approach to the pursuit of happiness, and he was happiness itself.

Judy Wolbach didn't seem very impressed, however. Dennis had ended his presentation by saying that the ACLU should provide the services to accommodate this legal action. Judy Wolbach gave him a speech back. The ACLU in Utah, in case he didn't know, was very underfunded.

"Don't you want him to live?" asked Boaz.

Have you looked, she inquired, into the ways that his life might actually be saved? She began to talk about relevant law in Supreme Court cases, and civil rights procedures under Federal and State law. When Boaz admitted he had not read such cases, she shook her head, and asked if he was familiar with Gilmore's psychiatric file. In reply, Boaz became critical. Why was she not forthcoming? Why did she emphasize the legalistic rather than the humanistic? Greenberg couldn't believe his good fortune: what a play!

Boaz now said he viewed himself as a man of literature, rather than a lawyer lost in procedure. "In the Renaissance, man knew he could be a poet and a lawyer both."

"Well," said Judy Wolbach, "think about which hat you're going to wear, and stay in touch."

Showing Judy down the hall, Stanley Greenberg felt obliged to remark, "I really don't believe Boaz is the person to represent Gilmore."

Over breakfast, next day, he saw Dennis on "Good Morning America."

GERALDO RIVERA   Dennis Boaz . . . a man who up until now has supported his client's wish for the right to die. Dennis, welcome. You've argued in court, sometimes eloquently, that Gary Gilmore deserves the right to die. Do you still believe that?

DENNIS BOAZ   (long pause) I believe he has the right to determine his own fate. I can no longer support, uh, the execution by the State.

GERALDO RIVERA   Are you saying that you've changed your position, Dennis?

DENNIS BOAZ   Yes.

GERALDO RIVERA   Why?

DENNIS BOAZ   (long pause) Well, yesterday was a moment of truth for me, and I had a remarkable emotional experience which I reflected upon. And . . .

GERALDO RIVERA   Are you saying you came to the realization . . . what, tell me . . .

DENNIS BOAZ   Well, I see there's some possibility for . . . Nicole and Gary (his voice sounds shaky here) perhaps to be together, and as long as I can see that possibility, know it's there, I know Gary would want to live and Nicole also.

GERALDO RIVERA   After the discussion we had yesterday, and we talked for a long time, you don't even strike me as a man who believes in capital punishment. I want to know why you've gone through this dreadful charade?

DENNIS BOAZ   Well, I got into the case not because I was an advocate of capital punishment, but because . . . he needed support, and I did support his own wish to, in a sense, take more responsibility for his own life and death at that time. And he was attempting to take responsibility by accepting judgment.

GERALDO RIVERA   But now you think because of what's happened the situation has changed?

DENNIS BOAZ   Well, it certainly changed with me . . .

NEW VOICE   Mr. Boaz, David Hartman in New York. Mr. Boaz, you said you had an emotional experience yesterday. How exactly has your mind changed in the last 24 hours?

DENNIS BOAZ   Well, it's gotten in line with my heart.

DAVID HARTMAN   Be more specific, Dennis.

DENNIS BOAZ   I just can no longer be an effective advocate for this execution. I know we can't stop Gary from killing himself if he decides that's what he wants to do now. I can no longer be part of an official process that wants him to die.

GERALDO RIVERA   Will you withdraw from the case if necessary?

DENNIS BOAZ   I'll talk to Gary as soon as I can. We'll make a decision together.

GERALDO RIVERA   He'll probably attempt suicide again.

DENNIS BOAZ   I don't know.

DAVID HARTMAN   Geraldo, we have a little less than a minute left. What's the next step, and what do you see happening in the next 24 to 36 hours?

GERALDO RIVERA   Well, the Parole Board hearing has to happen presumably, once Gilmore is in sufficiently recovered physical condition for that to happen. He has to be conscious. They can't execute a man who is comatose, David. . . . I think that our story is going to be held in abeyance, at least while these two people recover.

DAVID HARTMAN   Thank you, Geraldo, very much, and thank you, Mr. Boaz, very much for being with us this morning.

Later that morning, Greenberg drove out to Provo with Dennis and visited Vern Damico whom he rather liked, he told Dennis later, rather a strong man, something of the self-made small entrepreneur about him, a man who could move in his own neighborhood, so to speak.

They ate in a glorified hamburger joint near the shoe shop, hamburgers, milkshakes — the absence of liquor made the whole thing difficult — but still they had a good conversation and Stanley got insights he thought helpful, especially in the choreography of the crimes. He got to see Vern's home in its physical relation to the motel and the service station down the street. Wonderful details for TV. Gilmore knocking on his uncle's door in the afternoon to say he's dirty and wants to take a shower and the uncle turning him away. Then getting his gun and that night walking right past the open window where the uncle is sitting by the television set — didn't take a Freudian genius to figure this one out.

As soon as he got back, Greenberg called Susskind and said, "It's fascinating, it's ugly, and it's complicated." Susskind asked if it was a good idea to go out to Utah himself. Stanley replied, "Things are so hectic I would not advise it at the moment. The principals are being bombarded on all sides, and at the moment, we can't see Gilmore, we can't see the fiancée, you can't get to any of the principals other than Damico."

Susskind agreed. The story, after all, rested on Gilmore's past deeds, and Stanley was there to get the foundations for that. No necessity to become acquainted with Damico and the others. Why, when he acquired the rights to Joe Lash's *Eleanor and Franklin,* he happened to know a few of the Roosevelts, Elliot, James, and Franklin Jr., in particular, but he hadn't tried to go around and meet any others, hadn't personally intervened and said, "I'm David Susskind. Let me tell you why I should get the rights." The thing to do, if necessary, was send a lawyer.

DESERET NEWS

Nov. 17, Salt Lake — Gary Gilmore's date with Utah State Board of Pardons passed today while the convicted murderer lay conscious and shackled in a hospital bed. . . .

Meanwhile, Nicole Barrett, Gilmore's girlfriend and apparent suicide pact partner, is in critical condition at Utah Valley Hospital.

When Gilmore returns to prison he will be moved to a tighter security cell, will have limited communications, and won't be allowed any physical contact with outside persons, Warden Sam Smith said. . . .

CHAPTER 8

Enterprise

1

That night, on the news, it was mentioned that Tamera Smith's story was being syndicated all over the world. Her phone began ringing, and she began hearing from people she hadn't thought about in years. Friends kept telling her that some of the biggest reporters in the country were here in Salt Lake, yet she had scooped them all. Next day, a fellow from the *New York Times* wanted to interview her, then a reporter from *Time* again, and *Newsweek*. It got pretty standard that if a new man came to town on the story, he rang up Tamera as soon as he checked into the Hilton. Dying for background on Nicole. She got a lot of free lunches that week.

It was kind of exciting, of course, but one little side of her wanted to escape. Milly from Philly left town to go hiking in the mountains, and that's where she wanted to be, just leave it all, let the world stay down in Salt Lake.

2

It was only after Gary had been at the hospital for 24 hours that the tube was taken out of his lungs. He had been awake for several hours, but they left it in until they were certain he could swallow. Then he was given oxygen by mask, and it was recorded that he was expectorating moderate amounts of phlegm. When they examined his throat, he said, "You're violating my privacy."

Next he wanted to know about his fiancée. Suddenly, he was alert, he was agitated, and he was refusing care. Told the nurse to get out. They had to put him in restraints. Then he refused to take a breath. Nearly turned blue before he had to open his mouth. He became extremely abusive. When the nurse tried to give him a needle, he spit in her face. Then he demanded to have the monitor recording his heartbeat removed from his chest. He demanded Fiorinal. When the nurses spoke to him, he refused to answer. On his chart they wrote, "Spiteful, revengeful, obscene." After the intern removed the trachial tube, Gilmore sat up, sputtered, and said, "I'll fucking well get you, motherfucker."

Most people who overdosed were not like Gilmore when they woke up. He was coming on exceptionally strong. It was dangerous to get within reach. "He looks," said one of the nurses, "like the demon that got into Linda Blair in *The Exorcist*." Other suicides were *depressed* when they came out of it. After all, that was why they had taken the overdose in the first place. Didn't want to live. With Gilmore, it was more like he wanted to die.

SALT LAKE TRIBUNE

Nicole's Mother Calls Slayer 'Manson Type'

Nov. 17 — Gary Mark Gilmore was described Wednesday as another "Charles Manson" by Mrs. Barrett's mother.

3

Given all those rides back and forth with Charles from Intensive Care to Pleasant Grove, Kathryne began to live in old memories. Neither she nor Charley was saying much, but she was feeling close to him. After all, they had lived all those years together. It was the kind of mood to let her think of the summer she met Charley and dated him when he was 16 and worked at the carnival and she was 14. Went together three months and never even kissed. But one day they decided to get married. Kathryne figured it meant going to the movies when you wanted to, and not taking orders from your folks anymore, so she talked her mother into driving them to Elko, Nevada. The Justice of the Peace there didn't believe Charley was 18 and said, "If I make a long distance call to your folks, son, how will they answer my question?" Charley started to stammer. "Well," the Justice of the Peace said, "you better say to your mom I'm going to phone." He was obviously advising them to tell her to lie.

Verna Baker, however, had started screaming, which made Charley finally speak up and say, "Knock it off, Ma. You tell him I'm 18." That was how Kathryne remembered it.

Same day, they drove back to Provo, and Kathryne's mother said, "Charley can sleep on the couch." He actually did that first night.

The following morning Charley came over with his friend George, and they went riding around all day in George's car, until Kathryne told Charley to have her home at 10 P.M., which he did. The following night, George and he came over again, but George finally drove them over to this motel called Back of the Pine-Trees and Charley got out to get a room. Kathryne started carrying on, at which point George said, "Get out. You're married to him." "I'm not," said Kathryne, "you take me home." "I'll tell you what, Nicky," George said — they used to call Kathryne "Nicky" after her middle name, Nicole — "you can go with me, or you can go with him." Kathryne had no choice. Nothing to do but go in and say hello to Charley. God, they were kids.

They'd fight and make up, fight and make up, and one time, in one of those fights, he enlisted in the Service. They didn't even find out she was pregnant until months later. She had missed periods so many times that she never noticed the real misses. When she started to feel a lump in her stomach, and it got larger, she thought, I bet I got a tumor, and went to the doctor by herself, really scared. When she found out it was a baby, she nearly died of embarrassment. The doctor said, "Are you married?" She didn't have her ring on. The one Charley had bought was too big, and they were waiting for her to grow into it. So when she said she sure was married, she could see the doctor didn't believe her. When he asked where her husband might be, she said he had just finished basic training, only then he asked where Charley was stationed, and she couldn't even remember the name of the fort, just said, "He's in the Army. Somewhere, you know." That doctor was so positive she wasn't married that when Charley came home a couple of weeks later, Kathryne hauled him down there with her for the second medical exam.

The way Charley looked at it, he and Kathryne had been married so long, one of them couldn't start thinking without the other. Two mules in traces. Brooding about how they got into marriage, Charley couldn't even tell himself now what interested him then. He still got mad remembering how Kathryne told him they had to get married because she was pregnant. Pretending she didn't want to marry, boo hoo, but her mother sat them down, and Charley had said, "Well, it don't matter to me." By the time he found out Kathryne wasn't pregnant, by God, she was.

Over the years, he must have dropped a total of $500 to different lawyers for starting a divorce. She'd start bawling and say, "What am I going to do? Can't raise the kids by myself." He'd back out every time, say "Forget about it, you know," and lose his down payment to the lawyer. They were the kind of thoughts to put Charley in a thorough state of gloom. His luck was typical of his life. By the time they reached the hospital, he couldn't even bear to sit down. Kept thinking about Nicole and how much he used to love her. Damn if he wouldn't see Uncle Lee getting drunk. Felt ready to kill Lee, that greedy child-molesting bastard.

They were no sooner in the door than Charley began to move around restlessly, and look at people as if he didn't know whether to glare, bust out, or bawl. Finally he had to leave, and Kathryne settled in for another vigil. Immediately, a fellow came up and said he was from the *National Enquirer,* associated with Jeff Newman, and the paper needed a better picture of Nicole. All the stills they'd seen so far were terrible, and they wanted something complimentary to do her justice. Kathryne remembered a picture taken at Midway when Sissy was pregnant with Sunny, and said, "You can put the head in, but that's all." Nicole was in a swimsuit and real pregnant. Her face was pretty, but her big pregnant bod was the last thing Kathryne wanted shown right now. An hour after the fellow took it, Jeff Newman came by and Kathryne found out the first fellow wasn't from the *Enquirer* at all. Some paper she'd never heard of. They got the picture for nothing.

4

In the afternoon, Earl Dorius received word to be down at Judge Ritter's Court by four. The message had been from Don Holbrook, one attorney Earl respected immensely. Holbrook said that the *Tribune* which he represented was filing a suit in Federal Court for the right to enter Utah State Prison and interview Gary Gilmore. Earl had an hour to get ready to argue before Willis Ritter, the toughest Federal Judge in the State of Utah. Conceivably the toughest in the nation. At seventy-nine, he was certainly the oldest, and a choleric personality if ever, one crusty, portly old man with a huge bay window and a full head of white hair. Earl's stomach felt stuck to his spine when he thought of going in to plead before Ritter without proper preparation. He didn't even have time to call the Warden.

Since Ritter's dislike for the Attorney General's office was about equal to his declared detestation of the Mormon Church, and since Ritter was bound to see Sam Smith as an agent of said Mormon Church and somebody therefore to give the shaft to, Earl did not have vast hopes for this coming encounter. People on the outside tended to see LDS church members as part of one huge well-organized Mormon conspiracy, when in fact it wasn't like that. But don't try to tell Judge Ritter. Earl just grabbed his law books and quickly reread old trusty *Pell v. Procunier,* trying to get himself psyched up to expect anything around Ritter. Kept reminding himself to present his argument quickly.

Judge Ritter did not allow you to expound your case at great length. It was wise to conclude a presentation in five minutes that you would normally do in thirty. "Don't get that mane of white hair bobbing," was the general wisdom of his legal colleagues.

In Court, Earl began with the simple statement that the case might be moot because Gilmore did not necessarily want an interview. Nobody knew. The *Salt Lake Tribune* had made no effort to find out. Not even by sending the convict a letter. Judge Ritter, to Earl's amazement, seemed to agree. Since Gilmore was unconscious in the medical center, he said he didn't see any urgency to issue a temporary restraining order against prison rules and regulations. He would deny the *Tribune*'s request for now. When the man recovered, they could take the case up again. Earl went back to his office feeling drained from all the adrenalin he had generated.

5

Larry Schiller's meeting with Vern took place in the Damico living room. Schiller had come prepared to make an offer. He knew Damico was not Gary's representative, but he still liked the idea. By delivering the offer, he would make Damico a representative, de facto. Gary would have to deal with him. A better approach than by way of Boaz.

So Schiller wanted to strike the right effect at this meeting. Under his dark brown winter overcoat, he was wearing a safari suit the color of a camel's hair coat, and a brown tie with a stripe in it. Ever since his days on *Life,* he always went out on a job with one set of colors, that is, all brown, or all blue, so he wouldn't have to worry about matchups. Today, brown was perfect. Blues would have been too cold, too much like Court. The brown was somber, warm, businesslike. The photographer in Schiller wanted himself placed in a field of colors reminiscent of family gatherings and cigars.

Soon as they got down to business, he told Vern he would offer a total of $75,000 for all the rights, and Nicole was worth a third of that, since without her, there was no story. In effect, he said, he was offering Gary $50,000. He added that he would not offer a penny more. This was a firm offer, he said, not a bargaining stance.

Schiller knew, of course, that this was way beyond the $40,000 ABC had given him to deal with. But, you couldn't come in with forty on this market. He would get around to telling ABC later.

Schiller proceeded to underline why the figure was $75,000. "It is," he said to Vern, "the economics of motion pictures that dictate this offer." He had brought ammunition with him: Xeroxes of Francis Gary Powers's contract, the Gus Grissom story contract, and Marina Oswald's. These were his samples and he spread them out in front of Vern and said, "Pick whichever one you want and take a good look at it. These contracts have been negotiated by the best lawyers in the country. Certainly," said Schiller, "Marina Oswald had the best lawyer available. So did Francis Gary Powers. This is not to put you down, Mr. Damico, but the lawyers writing these contracts for Grissom and Powers and Oswald were people who knew more about profit-sharing, more about percentages, and more about how much money can be made with a given film than people like yourself, or for that matter, Dennis Boaz. What I am trying to tell you is that no matter what anybody offers, you take a look at the figures in these contracts right here. These are the real prices available. Susskind may be telling you the property is worth fifteen million dollars eventually, but I say you will never see a piece of that. He is offering a small amount now and talking about the big piece down the road. The likelihood is that the big piece will never be seen. I, on the other hand, am willing to pay money right away. I am not offering it on the commencement of principal photography two or three or four years from now. I'm ready to gamble right this minute. I am taking the chance, not you." When he saw that Vern Damico had picked up one of the contracts and was studying it somberly in his big hands, Schiller added, "I've come today with three monumental things to offer. The first, as I have stated, is, my cash on the barrelhead. The second is that I will make you my promise to stay in this town, and work on the story from here. I am not going to buy the rights and then vanish to New York. I'm not wealthy yet. I'm not like David Susskind who has already got it made. No," said Larry Schiller, "I'm still climbing the ladder, so I'll be here to work and give you advice, and the day I don't deliver is the very day you have reason not to trust me."

"What is the third thing?" asked Vern.

"The third," said Larry Schiller, "is whether you are really going to allow 50 percent of this money to go to a stranger. Blood, I should think," he said, "is thicker than water. I don't know how Gary is thinking of providing for his mother, but if half of this money is to go to Boaz, then Gary's mother will be getting a percentage that is half the amount she's entitled to. Besides, I think there should be money to provide for the families of the victims."

All the while Schiller had been talking to Vern Damico, he had been changing his impression of Gary Gilmore. It was as if he had been given another look at the fellow. As Vern started reflecting on

Gary's days in the shoe shop and said wistfully, "He was a good hard worker, but I never knew how to get the best out of him," Schiller was cheered. It would make for a better story if Gilmore was not just some clever con who used and abused everyone. Then about the time he realized that Vern had his own sense of humor, Schiller got even happier. He had to obtain this story. That was fundamental. He wanted this story from his spinal cord out. But that he might even like it was a most agreeable bonus. Every minute he sat with Vern, he could feel Boaz losing the marbles. "If I were you," said Schiller in conclusion, "I'd get a lawyer. In fact," he said, "I don't want to make this offer in formal terms until you have a lawyer. Then I will lay it out with him. If you take my advice, you will pay the man by the hour. I've seen," said Schiller, "where lawyers get all the money in these things."

On the way out, Schiller left his number. He did not say that it was only a phone booth in Walgreen's Drugstore at the main inter- section of Provo, and that the girl behind the soda fountain was his local secretary pro tem. He had made an arrangement with her to take his messages. He could, of course, have used his number at the Hilton in Salt Lake, but such messages were left in your box and you never knew which of a hundred reporters might rip it off. He could have had people contact him through his secretary in Los Angeles, but that meant they'd have to tackle long distance. Using Walgreen's made it easy for local people to reach him with a local call. Some of these were simple folk who might hesitate to go through the compli- cations of area codes, operators and calling collect.

DESERET NEWS

Nov. 18 — Gary Mark Gilmore, having recovered from his suicide attempt, was returned to the Utah State Prison today to await the outcome of his plea for death. . . .

More than 3 dozen reporters and a dozen hospital workers were on hand to watch the handcuffed man with tousled hair get out of the wheel chair and into the brown prison car.

Gilmore, looking weak with an ashen face, scowled

at his audience as he got into the vehicle's back seat. He made an obscene gesture at the reporters.

A protective motorcade of 3 prison cars and 2 law enforcement vehicles escorted Gilmore back to the Utah State Prison in Draper.

There, the arrival was greeted with cheers and whistles from other inmates behind the prison walls. Gilmore was taken directly to the prison infirmary where he will be watched constantly.

Schiller was present when they moved Gary. After the motorcade drove away, reporters rushed to their cars and chased them down the highway to prison. Schiller didn't follow. There would be very little at the other end, and he had gotten what he wanted.

He had seen Gilmore face to face. Of course, at a distance of twenty feet, but close enough to increase his interest. Seen in news flashes on television, Gary did not look like a killer, but coming out of the hospital this morning, sunken and gaunt in his wheelchair, his face had been full of hate. It was the livid, vindictive look of a cripple who could kill you for sheer outrage at how life had ruined his chances. In fact, as Gilmore got into the car, he turned around, looked out the window and gave a wide thin-lipped grin at the press, a mean and merciless look, and raised his middle finger slowly in the air as if to implant it forever in each witness's ass. Schiller said to himself, That man could stick his knife in you and keep a smile while doing it.

6

Now that Gary was back in prison, Cline Campbell visited him in the infirmary and found him sitting on the floor, going through mail.

Said in greeting "Help me," and tossed over some letters. He was sitting cross-legged with his white prison clothes on, and as soon as he could, Campbell remarked, "In a way, I'm sorry it didn't work, because it would end this great trial for you. But I'm glad you're here." Gilmore said, "I'll do it sooner or later."

Campbell answered, "Yes, I know you're serious. Still, it's better not to kill yourself."

"Why?" asked Gilmore.

"Because," said Campbell, "you can test the law. If you kill yourself, nothing's been solved. Force them to the issue."

"The law means nothing to me, Preach."

"Well, then," said Campbell, "there's two families in Provo that are not taken care of, and if you do it right you're going to have enough money to make some contribution to the children."

Gilmore nodded. Campbell couldn't tell whether he agreed for Gary changed the subject. "Hey," he said, "if there is a God, and I believe there is, I'm going to have to face Him." He nodded again. "I know this creation we live in doesn't end up for nothing. There's got to be something over there." Then he added, "I'll come back on a higher plane."

Campbell said, "What if you come back as a prison guard?"

Gilmore said, "Oh, you dirty son of a bitch."

They began to laugh. In the middle of it, Campbell thought, "I laugh more with this guy than anybody."

The prison had been in touch with Earl constantly about who passed the drugs to Gary. Their present belief was it pretty much had to be Nicole Barrett. For that reason they were going to let the matter lie. Hard to prosecute a girl who had almost died herself and would probably be sent to a mental hospital. On the other hand, since the prison had no concrete information, there was no particular reason to terminate the inquiry. So long as they could keep it open, they could also keep the pressure on Boaz, and isolate Gilmore from visits with physical contact.

7

Nicole felt as if she were completely surrounded by beautiful soft darkness. Didn't even know she had a body. Everything was blackness. Then a hole came in, a little hole. She tried to close it, but the hole kept opening. It was whiter than white. Now she could see doctors' faces with the little mirrors they had over their foreheads. As if she were in a dream, she kept fighting to close that fucking hole.

Kathryne and Rikki had gone out to get something to eat, and Sue Baker was drowsing in the waiting room of Intensive Care, when she heard Nicole screaming, "I don't want to be here. I'm not supposed to be here."

The door swung open and an intern shouted down the hall. Nurses and doctors were going back and forth from Nicole's room for maybe an hour and Sue felt like she was listening outside a delivery room for a baby's first cry.

Then she could hear Nicole shout, "Fuck you, I want my cigarettes." It was a lot of babble. She heard the intern trying to talk to Nicole, but he finally came out, and said to Sue, "See if you can do something."

Nicole said to her, "I'm supposed to be dead, I'm not supposed to be here." Before Sue could even grab her hand the intern was back with help, and they were ushering Sue out.

By the time she got in again, they must have told Nicole that Gary was alive. She was in a different mood. Said to Sue, "Let's talk about happier things." "Right," said Sue. Now Nicole wanted to walk, and the intern agreed. So Sue paraded her up and down the halls. Nicole was wobbly and her legs acted so tired she could hardly make it, but she said, "Doesn't this remind you of the night I was drunk, Sue?" They thought back to that couple of nights when they were both drinking, and Sue felt beautiful that Nicole was up and talking and said, "Listen, lady, how could you do this? I need you too much, you know."

Nicole said, "I need you, too, but I wanted to be with Gary." Sue said, "Well, you're here now. You're not getting away again." Nicole sighed. "Aw, I'm not," she said. Then she walked a little and kind of winked, and said, "I'll try again if I have to."

By the time her mother got back to the hospital, Nicole was asleep once more. The next time she opened her eyes, however, Kathryne was there, and Nicole said, "I didn't give him enough. I knew I didn't give him enough." "He's just fine, Sissy," said Kathryne. Nicole started to pound the covers. "I knew it wasn't enough for such a big man. Why didn't I think?"

"Look, Sissy," said Kathryne, "if God wanted you, you'd be gone. You know, it just isn't your time. He doesn't want you yet." "I don't want to live," said Nicole. "Listen, baby," said Kathryne, "God has too much left for you to do before you can go." Nicole just laughed, and then she began to cry, and she said, "Oh, Mama."

8

Gibbs received a letter from the Salt Lake detective who was in charge of his case. When he opened the envelope, there was nothing inside but a newspaper cartoon of a man lying in a hospital bed. The nurse was saying, "Mr. Gilmore, wake up. It's time for your shot." At the foot of the hospital bed was a five-man firing squad.

Knowing Gary's sense of humor, Gibbs decided to send the cartoon. Just then, the radio announced: "Dr. L. Grant Christensen said Gilmore can leave the hospital and return to Death Row if he continues to improve."

Gibbs laughed so hard he almost emptied his works. It sure made him wish Gary was right there laughing with him.

9

In the prison infirmary, Vern and Gary talked through a telephone and sat on opposite sides of a plate-glass window. It was unusual speaking to a man that way, but with Vern's bad leg, it beat walking all the way out to Maximum Security.

Straight out, Gary said, "Vern, would you take care of things if I discharge Boaz?"

Vern said, "I'm a shoemaker. I don't know as I can do it. I'm not an attorney."

Gary said, "With your business ability and my brains" — he gave a big smile as he said this — "we can do it."

That was all they said about it. As Vern was getting ready to go, Gary said, "Know how to shake hands through the glass?" and put his open palm on the window. Vern touched the other side with his palm, and they wiggled fingers back and forth. A prison handshake.

Brenda was also there for that visit, and it was emotional for her. Gary was looking weak, she thought, like a lot of the fight was out. Brenda, however, decided to sail right in, so she said over the phone "Gary, you old shithead. Looks like you pulled through."

"You haven't changed any," he said.

Brenda asked, "Still mad at me?"

"Well, I don't like what you did," he said. Brenda replied, "I don't give a damn. I did what I had to do. I suppose you did what you had to do." She paused for breath, and said, "I love you and I'm glad you made it." Then she added, "Are you going to do something stupid like this again?"

"No," Gary said, "I don't think so. I have a hell of a headache."

There was a guard standing by, and he was having a conniption. After Brenda gave the phone back to her father, the guard walked up and said, "I wouldn't dare call him any of the names you did. He's mean. He'll kill you soon as look at you. I'd be scared to death to talk to him like that."

"God," Brenda said, "he can't hurt you. Look at him. Locked behind a door and in a weakened state. He couldn't hurt a pussycat."

The guard said, "Well, I wouldn't bet on it."

Back at the window, Brenda couldn't stop herself. The guard might just as well have egged her on. "Hey, Gary," she said, "how come you didn't take enough to do the job?"

"What makes you think I didn't?" said Gary.

"If you had," said Brenda, "you'd have been dead."

"What in the hell are you trying to do? You know I really meant to do it."

Brenda said, "You know more about drugs than that. I think you knew just what you were doing."

Gary started to tuck his lip in. Finally, he kind of snickered, and said, "Well, I might know one of my cousins would pick up on that."

Yet, in the way he said it, she was confused. He was perfectly capable of letting her think she was right when she was wrong. Gary liked to toy with her head.

It made Brenda mad. She said, "I think you're being a selfish lover. What about those two little kids?"

"Oh," said Gary, "somebody would have taken care of them."

"You're cold assed. You really are. You wanted to stay awake long enough to find out if she was really dead, then you wouldn't have to worry she'd take another lover."

Gary said, "I am jealous."

"Don't you know, there's a real possibility she'll be damaged in her brain?"

"Impossible. I don't even think of that," he said.

"Come on, Gary, isn't that what you wanted? If she has brain damage, nobody else is going to want her."

"You're cruel," said Gary.

"And you're an asshole," said Brenda. At that point, she knew she'd gone too far.

Gary said, "You have a vile and dirty mouth."

They started to stare at each other, and it got to be quite a contest. Even across the hallway, ten feet wide, through two panes of glass, Brenda could feel the heat coming out of his eyes, and she thought to herself, I'm not going to let him outstare me this time, not when he's half dead and there's all this protection between us. But, it went on so long, she finally remembered his favorite saying and quoted it to him on the phone: "An honest man will look you in the eye, but the soul of a man will try to convince you of his lie." At that point, Gary began to laugh, and said, "God, Brenda, you sure are a mess."

He gave her a wink before they said good-bye. On the way out, she put her hand on the glass, and said, "I love you," and he wiggled his hand from his side.

10

DESERET NEWS

Profile of a Wasted Life

Nov. 18 — . . . Through the study of psychodiagnostics, in which the writer has specialized, it is possible from a person's art efforts to draw some clues to the

state of his personality. . . . Some times such art will
indicate brain damage, psychosis, or at least anxiety.

In Gilmore's case, there is no such evidence. In picture after picture, we see remarkable coherent, organized, and disciplined work. In this writer's judgment,
these are not the product of a crazy or psychotic mind
. . . Gary Gilmore has an extremely keen mind.

SALT LAKE TRIBUNE

By Paul Rolly
Tribune Staff Writer
Provo, Nov. 18 — . . . Dean Christensen said members
of the Provo 5th Ward, where Benny Bushnell was a
home teacher, are "sick to their stomachs," about the
continued publicity Gilmore is receiving, and "at a loss
for an explanation."

The bishop said Benny's wife, Debbie, still writes to
him, asking for his advice.

"Of course, we cling to our religious belief that we
will meet again in an afterlife and I try to reassure her,
but she's taking it hard and it's difficult at times," he
said.

A police sergeant came out to Everson's house to interrogate
Dennis. He was a suspect at the prison certain enough. Dennis went
to Sam Smith's boss, the Head of the Board of Corrections, Ernie
Wright, a big man wearing a white Texas cowboy hat, and said,
"Look, Sam Smith is acting vindictive," and the Head of the Board of
Corrections looked back and said, "Frankly, Mr. Boaz, we don't trust
you." Stared at him like he had just squashed a fly. Then, he added,
"I don't care what the Warden's doing. He can continue doing it."

Not only was Dennis reduced to talking to Gary through a telephone across a hallway, but for all he knew, the phone was tapped.
And Gary was considerably less friendly. "Did you say on Rivera's show
that you can't work for my execution anymore? I don't appreciate
that." Dennis was feeling embarrassed over all that emotionality him-

self. "Well, I'm sorry," he said, "I still feel I can help you, you know."
He was damned if he was going to say, Go ahead and fire me, Gary.

Now, Gary started to query Dennis about expenses. He had
found out $500 had come in from the *London Daily Express*, and
$500 from a Swedish interview, and wanted to know why Dennis had
told him his half was $250, not $500. Dennis tried to explain. "You
said you were reckless about money, and I should be your financial
manager, so I held back $250 and only gave you $125 from the English interview. Then you asked me to give another $125 to Nicole.
That took care of your half."

Yes, but what about the other $500 from Sweden?

"Gary," said Dennis, "everything went to expenses. There are a
million things. I haven't cheated you." It wasn't good between Gary
and himself.

Outside the prison, Dennis had never felt more like talking to the
press. "I'm a character in this thing I'm writing," he said to them, "so
I don't plan out everything I do. I'm being acted upon by the real author of these events. Whoever or whatever that is. In fact, I almost
got fired today! Whew! It was close."

"What do you think of the suicide now?"

"Nonviolent," Dennis said. "Really mellow. Like Romeo and Juliet, they took a poison." Dennis thought the tragic aspects of this
relationship, if properly presented, could raise Gary and Nicole into a
kind of democratic Romeo and Juliet. Then every card he played
would have more value. He could get them connubial rights yet.

"Don't you think," said Barry Farrell, "that if Gilmore isn't executed, he'll slip right back in with four hundred and twenty-four other
condemned men and women? A lot of them may have more tragic
stories than Gilmore."

"Gary is the only one," said Boaz, "who has the courage to face
the consequences of his act."

"How," asked another reporter, "is Susskind going to do the
film?"

"Susskind," said Dennis, "has chosen a sensitive, dignified
screenwriter, Stanley Greenberg, to write it. Ask them."

"Is Schiller still in the bidding?" Farrell wanted to know.

"Schiller," said Boaz, "went around me and sent a telegram.

Now Gary feels I'm not telling him about all the offers. I don't have to wonder where some bad vibrations are coming from."

"Dennis," said another reporter, "you were fighting for Gary's right to be executed, and now you are trying to save his life. Square that realistically, will you?"

"The Declaration of Independence guarantees the right to life, but only if you haven't been brutalized by the system. Gary was, Gary wants to die. But only because he can't have Nicole. Gary would love it," said Boaz, "if he could be with her. Get him into a place where they could be together, right?"

"Name one American prison with connubial rights."

"Since their story has become international," said Dennis, "transfer them to Mexico. The real obstacle is to convince Gary to live. He's depressed right now. But if I can keep going on Geraldo Rivera and Tom Snyder and get people thinking in a new way, they might start demanding that Gary live. Legislators will have to listen."

"Will Gilmore listen?"

"If he knows that he's going to be with Nicole eventually, he'll do it. We're winning people's hearts with this case. When you get into their emotions, you've got them. Definitely, definitely. It's heavy."

"Are you saying that Gary will be living with Nicole in Minimum Security?"

"Or Medium Security," said Dennis. "A year at the outside. With the profits from the story, he'll be able to pay his own way, too. That will please the taxpayers. You see, it's not as preposterous as you think. Look at today's news. Patty Hearst's father has bought her a private prison on Nob Hill. Give Gary a little space, like that."

"You're tooting, Dennis," said Barry Farrell.

"You watch."

"I'll watch," said Farrell.

"What do you really think of Schiller?" Farrell now asked. It was a bad question for Dennis to answer — he had nothing to gain by the reply. He didn't like, however, to disappoint Barry Farrell. Boaz was impressed with him. Farrell was very Scotch in appearance for a man with an Irish name. Tall, good looking. Tall enough so Dennis could talk to him comfortably. Wore tweeds. Nearest thing to a British gentleman among the press corps. Well-trimmed pepper and salt beard, and those old *Life* credentials. Dennis vaguely remembered reading

Barry Farrell's column in *Life* on alternate weeks with Joan Didion. *Life* must have been trying to bring some literary class to the people.

He decided to use Farrell as a superpipeline. So he said, "Schiller is a scavenger, a snake."

11

Susskind had just gotten a phone call from Stanley Greenberg telling him that he had decided to leave Salt Lake City.

"It's getting to be a terrible mess," said Stanley.

Then Boaz called. "Listen," he said to David Susskind, "I'm being wooed by a lot of people, and I think I was too easy with you. Monetarily, I can do much better with somebody else. Do you wish to revise your bid?" Susskind said, "No, I don't, but who are you dealing with?" Boaz said, "A guy named Larry Schiller." "Well," said Susskind, "I know Mr. Schiller as an entrepreneur who put together a project that became a book about Marilyn Monroe, that's the only way I know him. I don't know him as a producer of films and television, but if he looks better than me, do it with him. I'm not raising the price." The story was getting to be, in Susskind's view, a very sensational, malodorous, exploitative mess.

Nonetheless, he called Schiller. Susskind was not in love with the idea of working with the man, but he called anyway and said, "You're throwing money and figures around, and that poor guy, Boaz, is dazzled. I don't understand it. Are you now in the film business?" "Yes," said Schiller, "I am."

"Look," said Susskind, "you're not a producer. Somebody, someday, is going to have to make this film. That's not your cup of tea."

"I am a producer," said Schiller. "I don't consider myself in your league, but I've produced some movies you don't even know about."

"Well, I think you're being unrealistic," said Susskind. "Of course, maybe you'll be lucky. Maybe you'll get the whole thing."

"I certainly hope so," said Schiller.

When Susskind spoke again to Greenberg, Stanley said, "I wouldn't feel too badly. It's not what we hoped it would be." Susskind agreed. "I don't think I'm going to bid anymore. Everybody's getting kind of crazy there. It's no longer a story about the breakdown of the criminal justice system, it's a farce, the girl's suicide, poison being slipped in." They agreed they didn't like the smell of it. Stanley said, "I think anybody who does the story now is jumping on a dead and putrefying body. It's bizarre and sick." They agreed. One of those to-hell-with-it conversations.

Still, they didn't really want to let go. Once some dust settled, the story might still have a lot to offer. They decided Stanley would try to keep himself available in case the right arrangements could yet be made.

CHAPTER 9

Negotiations

1

Next day, Gary brought it up again. "Are you ready, Vern, to take Boaz's place?" he asked.

"I don't know," said Vern. "Am I supposed to feel ready?"

"I'm going," Gary said, "to turn everything over." He nodded. "I just want a few thousand dollars to pay off a couple of people, and a couple I want to help."

"I don't know yet," said Vern, "who to make a deal with. A lot of people are ringing my phone these days."

"Vern, it's your decision."

"Well, if you think I can handle it," said Vern.

"Being a businessman in town," said Gary, "you know the way."

"This is a different type of business."

"Hell," said Gary, "I've seen you operate in your own store. You can do it better than Boaz."

In the afternoon, Vern got a call from Dennis. "Did you know Gary is talking of firing me?" he asked.

"Well, why did he do that?" asked Vern. "You mean he came right out and said it?"

"Between us," asked Dennis, "do you think you can take my place?"

Vern said softly, "I think I can do as well as you have."

After this conversation, Vern spent a couple of hours in thought. Then he called a few friends in Provo to ask advice about a lawyer.

That evening around ten, he phoned one fellow at home that they all recommended, a lawyer named Bob Moody. Vern could practically hear Moody think about the proposition. Then he answered, "I would be happy to take the case. I'll help you all I can. Do you want to get together tonight, or tomorrow morning, or Monday?"

"Monday's good enough," said Vern.

He felt as if he were moving an immense weight. Nothing was ever going to be the same again.

2

Nicole's cigarettes were becoming a problem. They had a lot of oxygen tanks around in Intensive Care, and wouldn't let her strike a match. She kept complaining, "I want a cigarette." They couldn't do much with her. "You had one a few hours ago," they would tell her. "Well, I want another."

Finally, they let Kathryne take her out to the utility room where, among the laundry sinks and old dirty cloth mops soaking in the bowl, Kathryne could sit with Nicole while she smoked. There they would relax. Once Nicole even said, "Maybe I'm glad I'm here. I don't know." Nicole never admitted it exactly, but Kathryne decided she hadn't really wanted to die, just had to prove to Gary she loved him enough. Finally, Nicole did say right out loud, "I thought it was wrong to take my life, and if God thought so also, then I'd stay alive. But if it wasn't a sin, I would die." Kathryne felt close to her then.

Naturally, next thing, this awful jumbled-up mess had to begin. The doctors wanted Kathryne to sign papers putting Nicole in Utah State Hospital. In the administrator's office, Kathryne tried to argue, but the man there said, "It isn't going to make any difference. There are already two physicians' signatures that she's incompetent and suicidal, and Nicole has also signed." Kathryne didn't know what to do. She didn't think Nicole was ready to come home. Come home to where? On the other hand, she was afraid that once they put Nicole in the nuthouse, she might never get out. Kathryne was afraid of state hospitals. Anyway, they pulled out the paper, and Kathryne wrote her name under Nicole's. She was shaking.

The moment Nicole had put her signature on the page, she knew it was an awful mistake. "Why didn't I just walk out of this motherfucker?" she asked herself. All the way to the ambulance she kept telling herself, "The reason you didn't, girl, is because you got nothing but hospital pajamas and a blanket." They had wrapped her good and she couldn't move her arms or legs. A bug all trussed up. As they drove, she couldn't see out of the ambulance, but there was something about the whine of the gears as the vehicle went up one long grade that sounded like the end of the trip. She was on the long approach road to Utah State Hospital. Oh God, the nuthouse they had had Gary in.

She was familiar enough with that. Same feeling. Even the same ward. It was shaped like a U, with the boys in one wing, the girls in the other, and a social room connecting them. The halls were long and narrow, with bedrooms and cells, and bright linoleum on the floor. Goddamned asshole paintings all over the place. Thoroughly stupid stuff like COMMUNITY IS US! painted in pastel watercolors that had caked and gone dead. Orange couches, yellow walls and plastic cafeteria chairs and tables. It depressed the hell out of her — like she was condemned to live in a visiting room forever. Everybody looked all tranked out. It would take you 150 years to die. Everything so goddamned cheerful and phony.

3

John Woods had had an upset stomach the night before, coughed up some blood, and thought, Jesus, now I'm getting an ulcer. He decided to stay home from the hospital, but a frantic call came in from the ward. They said, "Nicole Barrett's on the way to us."

"Like hell she is," said Woods.

He went over the Superintendent's office and first thing Kiger said was, "I sent her to your unit. That's where I want her."

Woods said, "Nicole oughtn't to be in Maximum Security. This is just another indication that the rest of the hospital can't carry their

634 / THE EXECUTIONER'S SONG

share. Thera-Mod should be able to take her." Kiger agreed. He
started to interrupt, but Woods was so mad, he said, "Let me finish."
He revered Kiger, thought he was the only man who had had a new
idea in treating psychopaths since they coined the word, and so it got
to him whenever he thought Kiger was doing something for less than
the noblest motive.

Of course, Woods's unit was the only one with enough security
to protect Nicole from the press. As Kiger said, "This is going to be
sticky, newswise." Every wire service, major newspaper and magazine was going to try every trick to interview Nicole. That meant
heavy pressure. The media would squeeze the politicians, and they in
turn would squeeze the hospital. If Nicole pulled off another attempt,
all their heads were on the block. It irritated the hell out of Woods
how much this was going to interfere with the therapy of everyone
else on the ward. His job had shifted. Now he was there to keep
Nicole alive.

Instead of working with the antisocial impulses of each patient
as it came into conflict with the group interest, instead of the group
being the anvil on which each patient's personality might get forged
into a little more social responsibility, the emphasis would now have
to be on surrounding Nicole, insulating her and cutting off the day-
to-day influence of Gary, so that he could not brainwash her with the
idea — oh, beautiful guru! — that their souls were scheduled to meet
on the other side. Woods would have to issue orders that no aide or
patient was to mention Gilmore's name. Not ever. If he was going to
keep Nicole alive, he had to neutralize that relationship. Woods could
recognize that if nobody would talk to Nicole about Gary, she was
nonetheless going to think about him all the time. Woods couldn't
stop that. He just didn't want Gilmore able to influence her thinking
anymore.

Yet, it killed him. It just wasn't Woods's idea of therapy. They'd
be junking a lot of their program just to keep a 24-hour watch on
Nicole.

The ideal way to run a hospital was to take your chances on
suicide. That was part of the risk in any innovative therapy. Here,
they had to cut the risk off. Kiger's ideas were so unconventional any-

way, that his program could receive an irreparable blow if they couldn't supervise Nicole. Nonetheless, it was the pits.

4

Nicole wanted to go to sleep like she never had before, but immediately a boss-looking chick, probably a patient, but domineering and awful sure of herself in a rotten limited way, was telling her, "No lying on beds in the daytime." "Take a shower!" "Take off your jewelry." They started to grab her, and she began to fight. That was when Nicole realized everything she did from here on out was going to be a fight. It came down on her like a disease. It would be a losing battle all the way. "I'm going to be suffocated by these fucking sheep," she said to herself. Yes, this was the place Gary had described where everybody ratted on everybody.

She tried to go to sleep, and they wouldn't let her. She lay on the floor and they woke her and she went right back to the floor and went to sleep again. Then Norton Willy's wife was shaking her. Mayvine her name was. The wife of Norton Willy who grew up right next door to her grandmother. Nicole couldn't believe that Norton had married this witch, a horrible huge ass-kisser who was now helping to run the place. They kept trying to get Nicole up and wouldn't let her sleep on the couches, but she felt three times as weak as in the other hospital. All she was interested in was being alone, and thinking about Gary.

5

Schiller went out to the airport. His girl friend, Stephanie, was coming in. Since she had once been his secretary, he knew she would not be surprised when he greeted her with the announcement that they had to go right away to Pleasant Grove near Orem, a good forty miles from the airport, to visit with Kathryne Baker.

Schiller expected there'd be press outside, but, in fact, the house was hard to find. Naming the streets by compass directions didn't work in Pleasant Grove. There were too many old country roads, paved cow pastures, and dry riverbeds. 400 North was likely to twist across 900 North and 200 East intersect with 60 West. It was not the kind of address that a reporter, fighting a five o'clock deadline, was going to lose a half a day looking for.

Schiller, however, had time for a long talk with Mrs. Baker. He thought it was a sloppy house, with old tires out in the front yard and metal skins rusting in the grass — you couldn't tell if the metal came from old jalopies or old washing machines. There were bits of jam on the table and dust and dirt and grease formed a pomade on many a surface in the kitchen. There were also an astonishing number of kids — he saw Rikki and Sue Baker's kids go through, plus some neighbors', and got them mixed up with Kathryne Baker's youngest child, Angel, who might have been six or seven and was astonishingly beautiful, looked like Brooke Shields. With all that noise it could have been confusing, but Schiller was counting on his ability to sell a proposition in a palace or a poolhall. He went right into a rap like the one he gave to Vern. "Whether I get the rights to your daughter's life or not, this, I think, is what you should do." And he set out to give her confidence in his understanding of the problems facing her. He told her she should change her phone and get the kids away with a relative. That way, the press wouldn't discover them. "You want to avoid having the children feel this is an indelible experience of horror." All the while, he knew what was impressing her most is that he did not sit there asking questions and writing her answers down, like he was stealing an interview, but was saying: Mrs. Baker, go get a lawyer. Kathryne said, "I don't know one." "Who do you work for?" asked Schiller. When she told him, Schiller said, "Call your boss and ask who his lawyer is." He could see it surprised her agreeably that he wanted her to obtain a representative to take care of her rights. He knew she was not used to talk like that.

Schiller had learned from the deal he made for *Sunshine* that if you wanted to get into big deals with movies and books, and play with producers and publishers, then you had to lay the right foundation, and draw up the right contracts from day one. Otherwise, you could end in a tree, swinging from limb to limb. With *Sunshine,* he had failed to get a separate contract from the dying woman's husband. Therefore Universal had to spend a lot of money later to buy his rights. That had been an item to haunt Schiller. So, he laid it out now for Mrs. Baker. "Get yourself a lawyer," he told her. "Get it before we even talk money."

On the drive away from the house, he had his first big fight with Stephanie. Her father was in the garment business. Way Schiller saw it, Stephanie's father had always been as deep in business as a sheep is thick in wool, but Stephanie was her dad's delight, and dad had done his best to protect her. Stephanie Wolf was one beautiful princess who hated to see business operating. She might have worked as a secretary, but it never rubbed off. She detested business.

Now, Stephanie was telling him that he'd acted like a manipulator with Kathryne Baker. "How dare you take advantage of that woman by talking business in the middle of all her grief? Her daughter was just committed yesterday." Larry tried to lay it out for her. "You don't mind," he said, "going to ABC's cocktail parties, but ABC couldn't care less whether they're going to have Larry Schiller at their party next week. I'm only as good as what I can do for ABC. Damn it," he said, "if you're interested in me, you've got to accept me as who I am. You've got to love the part you love, and if there's a part you don't like, you've still got to learn to deal with it. You can't bawl the shit out of me because of what I say in a living room, the very minute I walk out of that room." They really had a big fight. Stephanie, after all, was the girl for whom Schiller was ready to break up a marriage that had gone on for sixteen years, but he could see that their relation was going to be put to every strain during this Gilmore business. Part of his brain was beginning to work already on the possibility of sending Stephanie to Europe to take care of foreign rights. If she stayed around, he could lose the Gilmore story. The aggravations between him and her over this one episode had been close to apoplectic.

That night, unable to sleep, he got up at two in the morning and dictated a contract for the Gilmore rights to a legal service in Salt Lake City. Over the telephone, his words were recorded, and early in the morning some girl would type it up. However, he didn't like the idea that a stranger would hear the terms of the contract. It could easily be leaked to a newspaper. Schiller knew that if he was working for a local paper, he would try to have a pipeline into such places. You could get a story that way.

Still, he had to have something ready to show Vern's and Mrs. Baker's separate lawyers. So he pretended to be a buyer of sheep and cattle from California, and dictated how many lambs and cows were to be sold in return for conveying full rights to said stock. The humor of it appealed to him at two in the morning.

Tomorrow, he would change the sheep and cows into specific people. There were a lot of good businessmen in the world, and a lot of good journalists, thought Schiller, but maybe he was one of the few who could be both.

6

Over the weekend Barry Farrell interviewed Larry Schiller in Los Angeles. They had worked together on *Life* years ago, but Farrell had not been feeling friendly to Schiller lately. A little over a year before, Larry had been getting a book of photographs together on Muhammad Ali. He had called Barry to say he wanted him to do the text, and Farrell had gotten into conversations with his publisher about it. Then Schiller signed Wilfred Sheed. Farrell felt he had been merely another name to feed into the hopper, and was pissed off over that.

Every December, however, he liked to clean the slates, so he wrote Schiller a letter saying in effect, "I'm over my pique. We did some good things together in the past and maybe we will again." It cleared the air for Farrell. He thought he could talk without bias to Larry if something came up.

Nonetheless, soon as he heard that Schiller was in Utah trying to get the Gilmore story, Farrell was ready to travel with a sharp pencil. Larry would be exposing himself to the very thing he'd been criticized for in the past. It would be a great opportunity to observe how he would bid for Gilmore's corpse.

So Farrell arranged to do a piece for *New West,* and talked to the Warden of the prison, to Susskind, and finally got together with Schiller in Los Angeles on the weekend. By then, Farrell was hardly happy about Dennis Boaz. That fucking hippie, he told himself, persistently fails to understand the stakes. Here Farrell had started with a little animus against Schiller, but Susskind was talking future profits up to fifteen million dollars while offering peanuts. Farrell began to think somewhat gloomily — since Christmas resolution or no, he had looked forward to doing a couple of numbers on Schiller — that the man might be the only one with a realistic notion of what could happen when you died in public. Schiller had done it before, seen the relatives, held their hands. He was closer to the difficulty than Boaz, who was always presenting himself as more organic than thou.

God, Gilmore had need of protection. Nothing got covered on TV more than public death. Farrell listened to Dennis talking about Gary and Nicole in a prison cottage with a couple of pot plants in the backyard, and it disgusted Farrell. Gary's life was running out. There was no way they were not going to kill him in the State of Utah. Why, if Gilmore was not executed, a major wave of executions might be touched off. Every conservative in America would say: They couldn't even shoot this fellow who wanted to be shot. Who are we ever going to punish?

Schiller's rap, at least, was solid. Build foundations. Get those contracts up like walls. Let everybody know where they stand.

Farrell found himself being kind to Schiller in the piece he wrote for *New West*.

7

Schiller was on the radio a couple of times, and the nature of his phone calls was changing. He could feel the press coming nearer. He decided to get in contact with Ed Guthman of the *Los Angeles Times*. "Ed," he said, "I need an outlet. I'll give you two thousand words for your front page and an exclusive interview with Gilmore sometime before the execution date, if you'll give me one of your top criminal reporters now as a sounding board." Guthman had a good man named Dave Johnston, who was available for a day, and Schiller and Johnston tried to foresee the problems. If, for instance, you could get only one interview with Gilmore, what were the questions to ask?

In addition, Schiller needed a story in the next week or so about himself. Not a large story, but a quiet one on a Monday. He wanted to scale down the importance of his presence on the scene. No sudden focus of attention with everybody saying: Carrion bird is getting it. Instead, Johnston would write a piece about how the press had come into Salt Lake from all over the world, and Schiller would only be mentioned in the third or fourth paragraph.

Since this modest perspective would not benefit his standing with Vern Damico's and Kathryne Baker's new lawyers, Schiller took pains to tell them separately that the story coming out would give him the virtue of a low profile for the present. He went on to say that there would be times, handling the press, when he might make mistakes, but, "I have seen the heat come down, and I will do my best to protect your credibility. We will set it up like a team operation, and I will take the shots." Over and over he said, "There may be things I do that make you unhappy, we may have our disagreements, but I am still friends with all the people I have worked with. Look," he would say, "pick up the phone and call Shelly Dunn in Denver, Colorado. He was the lawyer on *Sunshine*. He will tell you how he and I are still friends now, and that, in general, I was right about the press, not right about everything, but often right." Then Schiller would mention Paul Caruso's number, and remind them that he was the lawyer on the Susan Atkins case. "We had a lot of trouble with that," Schiller said, "many disagreements, but feel free to call him." He named a couple of other lawyers as well.

In fact, Schiller did not have a clear or certain idea what all these attorneys might say about him, but, then, it had been his experience that very few people actually made such phone calls.

8

When Vern met his lawyer, Bob Moody, on Monday morning, he thought he was a quiet, confident, intelligent man. Moody was well built, and half bald, and his eyeglasses looked competent. His way of talking was very carefully spoken. Vern noticed that when Bob

Moody said something, he didn't have to repeat it. Assumed you understood. Vern saw him as in the category of upper class. Would
belong to the country club and have an expensive home in the foothills of Provo. "Mortgage Heights," Vern called it.

To Moody, Vern Damico seemed a concerned relative, sincerely
looking for good advice and the best deal he could shape up. He kept
saying that he wanted Gary's wishes to be carried out. He wanted
some kind of dignity retained for his nephew if possible.

Moody talked to him about the difficulty of trying to represent
Gary's criminal interests *and* his literary estate. Bob Moody didn't
think it would work to negotiate contracts for books or films while
trying to advise Gary on his legal situation. Suppose, at some point,
Gary wished to change his mind and appeal, why then the rights for
his life story would be considerably less. A potential conflict of interest existed right there. You just didn't want a situation where a lawyer might have to ask himself whether his client's death might be
more profitable to him. Vern nodded. A second lawyer would be necessary.

Bob now mentioned a fellow named Ron Stanger. A local man
with whom he had worked in the past. Worked with him, worked
against him. He felt he could recommend Ron.

In fact, Moody had already called Stanger over the weekend.
"How," Bob Moody had kidded, "would you like to take over from
Dennis Boaz?" They had agreed it would be fascinating. Lots of public appeal and great legal questions. In fact, a fellow like Gilmore,
capable of putting the State of Utah through hoops, ought to be interesting to meet.

Of course, they also wondered whether this would be another
crusade where you don't get paid. Moody had said good-bye to
Stanger with the mutual understanding that they would consider a
lot of things, and one was capital punishment. Of course, you could
assume it would not go that far. Probably, the convict was bluffing.
When it got to last push against last shove, he'd appeal.

Just about a week ago, Moody and Stanger had happened to be
leaving Court together, and saw Snyder and Esplin out on the court-

house lawn being interviewed by local TV. As they drove past, they catcalled. It was really funny seeing Craig and Mike under TV lights. Shortly thereafter, they ribbed Snyder in the coffee shop. How did it feel to carry out an appeal your client didn't want? "You really do good work," they told him with a grin. Snyder grinned back.

Even after the suicide attempt it was hard for Moody and Stanger to take the case with complete seriousness. By then, court-house talk was "Snyder, your work is going to blazes. Your man is carrying out the sentence himself." But, then, lawyers had to be like surgeons, joked while they washed their hands. So, on the phone that Saturday night, when Moody told Stanger there was a good pos-sibility he'd be called in, Stanger replied, "All we need is to be on TV and have Craig Snyder drive by."

Now, discussing it with Vern on Monday morning, Bob Moody said over the phone, "Ron, come over and meet Vern and see what he thinks of you." It was his way of telling Stanger he had the job.

Vern was struck with the difference. Ron was a real peppy fel-low. In fact, his physical appearance threw Vern. Stanger looked like a fresh kid out of law school. Vern wondered, "Can a man this young do what Gary wants?" He decided to hire him because of Moody's recommendation, but couldn't keep from saying to Stanger, "I guess you're kind of young."

"Not really," said Stanger, pointing to Moody, "this bald-headed guy and I are practically the same age." Vern didn't know if he liked him. Stanger's eyes were gleaming, like his hooves were flashing in the air. "Let's get it on," was his look. Maybe that was good for a law-yer. Vern was having to make a lot of decisions about people before he knew how much to trust them. That was not what he would call comfortable.

9

Exploring your feelings was an expensive procedure if you had to use unpaid office time to do it, but, from the outset, this job gave Moody more to think about than was customary. Most of his practice was domestic relations, personal injury work, local stores, stuff where he could deal with people. He liked to get out of the office. It was better to go on an investigative tour than get locked up in Probate and endless bookkeeping, so he usually enjoyed a criminal case if it came his way. Certainly, he had never found anything incompatible about being a criminal lawyer and a high member of the Mormon Church, and this case definitely gave him an agreeable tingle, but he could see that Gilmore was going to stretch many feelings. A lot of people would query the moral rights of what he was doing.

It was sometimes hard for religious-minded people to comprehend why a lawyer was there in the first place for certain defendants. They didn't understand that the basis of the adversary system was the right of a defendant to have his story told in Court as well as possible. So they could never comprehend that it was not unnatural for two lawyers to be at each other's throat in the courtroom, then sit down afterward to eat together.

A few years back, when Moody was Assistant County Attorney, he had been prosecuting a drug charge, and Ron Stanger had been defending. Ron's methods that day were downright insulting. Moody finally got so mad, the Judge called Stanger and him to the bench, and the Jury got a big kick out of that. Two lawyers fighting to the death. In the closing argument, Ron added the crowning blow of telling the Jury that if Mr. Moody had really been ready to prove his case, he would have taken this ten-dollar bill the prosecution said was paid over for drugs, and shown the fingerprints on it. It was a closing argument, with no opportunity for rebuttal, so Bob couldn't reply that a ten-dollar bill has no less than ten thousand fingerprints on it. He was plenty upset. Part of the game was to win your case — you loved to win — but Ron's tactics had gone further than a friendly jab or two.

While waiting for the Jury to decide, feeling emotionally uptight, they nonetheless had lunch together. The Jury, passing by the coffee shop, saw them eating and laughing, and actually sent a couple of representatives to the Judge to say the lawyers were not sincere. So Bob could see what was coming up. That episode wouldn't be a whiff to the fumes which would arise in this case.

10

Vern took a couple of letterheads from Moody's office and Stanger's, and brought them to Gary next day. "These lawyers are local people," he told Gary. "My truthful opinion is I don't think you can go wrong. They'll fight for your rights."

Gary asked, "Do they believe in capital punishment?"

Vern didn't know exactly — it occurred to him he hadn't even asked Moody — but he said, "They'll defend your rights regardless of how they feel."

Moody and Stanger came over to the prison a little later. Gary wanted to look them over. So, they met. On opposite sides of the glass. Spoke by telephone, and it was a cold meeting. "Do you want us to represent you?" they asked, and Gary answered, "Let me talk to my uncle."

A long conversation went on between Gilmore and Vern. Moody heard words on Vern's side, like, "I feel confident," but Gilmore seemed squirrelly. He certainly wasn't talking freely. He looked gaunt and his color was poor. Kept talking about his headache. He was obviously suffering the aftereffects of the sleeping pills. Then they learned that he was on a hunger strike as well. He was not going to eat, he said, until they allowed him a telephone call to Nicole. He said that and then was silent. He stared at them.

Now, Gary brought up capital punishment. Moody got ready to say he didn't believe in it, but was still mulling over such a speech, when Ron said through the other phone that he, personally, was opposed to it.

"Will you carry out my directions, however?" Gary asked.

"Yes," Ron said, "I'll represent you."

Now Bob said to Gary that lawyers were accustomed to working against the grain. There weren't many people you could defend, if you carried your beliefs into everything.

Still, it never got good with Gilmore this day. He kept answering questions with the remark, "I won't know until I see it in writing." He was suspicious of mankind in general, and lawyers in particular.

"Nothing personal against you guys," Gilmore said, "I just don't like lawyers." Then he'd burp. The sound of an empty stomach was in the earpiece of the phone.

Given the bleakness of these circumstances, Moody decided he might as well make certain of their ground. So he mentioned Dennis Boaz. "Is his relationship with you officially severed?" he asked.

Gary replied, "Dennis was the only man that really wanted to help for a while, so I owe him something. But it's over. This afternoon, I'm going to fire him."

He yawned. Moody had heard how the first few days of a fast were the worst, and if true, that was just as well, for he felt a profound stubbornness in Gilmore that spoke of a hunger strike that could continue for quite a while.

11

Dennis said, "I spoke to Vern, and he indicated you want to fire me."

"Uh, right," said Gilmore.

"I think that's a good idea," Dennis said.

It blew Gary out of the saddle. Right through the glass, Dennis could see him shifting his feet like he had been set to go in one direction, and now was looking for new footing.

"I didn't appreciate you talking on TV with Geraldo Rivera," said Gary. "I also didn't appreciate you calling the Warden ignorant. You've made things more difficult for me." He yawned fiercely.

"Gary," Dennis said, "I feel like there's a complete cutoff of communications between you and me."

Gilmore said, "It doesn't matter." Then he nodded, as if to himself, "Dennis," he said, "you're entitled to something. How much do you want?"

Dennis said, "All I want is to write about it." He was thinking that he might have to call his character Harry Kilmore, not Gary Gilmore. He could balance out his book by having one theme on the murders and the other on his own work with the bus drivers: two legal cases, one a litigation to increase people's safety, the other a search for death. Might make a good novel.

He could feel how impressed Gilmore was that he didn't care about the money.

"We have a little difference of opinion," said Gilmore. "But, I'll tell you, Dennis, I'm going to invite you to my execution."

Dennis was pissed. Suddenly, he was damned mad at the way he had been let out of all this. "I don't want to see your execution," he said. That would bother Gary. He would want friends there. But Gilmore only nodded again, and they said good-bye, each of them kind of muttering, "All right, see you, take care." Dennis couldn't help it. At the last, he said, "Look, if you want me there, I'll come."

After he left the prison, however, he got mad all over again. Called up Barry Farrell, and said, "I want to take back what I told you about Schiller being a snake. He's a grade above. Call him an eel. My middle name is Lee, which is eel spelled backwards, so I understand eels. Schiller has ascended from snake to eel." Farrell was laughing. "You guys will probably work out some kind of deal," he said. "I'm not even thinking," said Dennis, "about that anymore. But I'll tell you what really gets me."

"What, Dennis?"

"How your life can turn into something new so fast."

Farrell called Schiller for his version. "I had nothing to do with it," said Larry Schiller. "This news comes as a shock to me."

"It looks like you're going to get it," said Barry.

"Nothing is settled," said Schiller in a gloomy voice. "There are a lot of obstacles ahead."

"But you still have enthusiasm for the story?"

"Between us," said Schiller, "I have a big problem. Where are the sympathetic characters?"

"You have a love story," said Barry.

"I'm not so sure," Schiller told him, "I haven't met Nicole. I don't have your question 100 percent answered."

Farrell went out into the cold November sun. In the valley across the desert, the smoke from Geneva Steel in Orem was pouring forth a storm of poison so fierce that Farrell's eyes, even if long adapted to Los Angeles smog, were still smarting. He felt like one of the carrion birds. In town with all the others to see whether Gary Gilmore would die. Driving up and down the Interstate, going from one newly built town to another, heading south down a smoke-filled valley, only to turn north again. Farewell Dennis. Barry Farrell couldn't decide whether he liked him or thought he was an absolute outrage to the sort of exquisitely civilized behavior Gilmore was, under it all, demanding.

CHAPTER 10

Contract

1

Schiller decided to get out of Salt Lake and move down to the Trave-Lodge in Provo. From his room he could look out across University Avenue to the mountains, and each morning they showed more snow on the peaks, and the letter Y set out in white stone on one mountain began to be covered over.

Right away, he made appointments with Phil Christensen, Mrs. Baker's attorney, and with Robert Moody. Christensen was at three, Moody at four. He supposed the first meeting would take a half hour and then he would walk over to the other's office. They figured to be in the same area. Having scouted out the legal scene in Provo, he knew the law offices were clustered around the courthouse. Schiller didn't even bother to look up Moody's address. Bound to be around the corner. So when he walked into Christensen's building, he had a surprise. The sign downstairs read: "Christensen, Taylor, and Moody." Same fucking firm. Schiller was beaming.

This office had a small-town look. Even the veneer paneling and the yellow-orange carpet and small dark brown leather chairs, all fit. The kind of stuff you'd find in a prefurnished little vacation home. Perfect. When you had two partners in the same firm representing separate clients in the same case, these lawyers would take pains that they didn't have to drop out for conflict of interest. Having already proposed that Gary get $50,000 and Nicole $25,000, these two lawyers were not likely to fight the suggestion and lose the kind of fees they could collect.

Phil Christensen turned out to be a distinguished senior party with white hair, but before five minutes were gone, Schiller felt as if he had begun to reach Christensen with his knowledge of law. Right off, he said, "I don't want the legal expenses to be deducted from the money I'm offering Nicole Barrett, so I'll ask you what would be appropriate." Christensen told him a thousand dollars might be right, and Schiller said, "Let's make it $26,000 to Nicole Barrett, but I want Mrs. Baker to pay your retainer out of that." It was Schiller's way of establishing that Christensen would be the lawyer for Nicole's mother, not for Schiller. That really impressed Christensen. Then, Schiller said, "Of course, it's understood that all this has to be approved by the Court." He didn't want to move ahead until Christensen got a legally appointed guardian. Schiller said he thought Nicole's mother ought to be appointed as guardian of the estate and the Court, of course, be guardian of the person. Christensen looked at him. "How'd you learn about that?" he asked. It was one more way to increase Christensen's respect.

A little later, when Kathryne Baker came into the meeting, Christensen even said, "We haven't settled all the financial questions, but I can tell you I feel very comfortable with Mr. Schiller." In fact, Christensen did ask for more money. He wanted $5,000 for April's medical bills, and Schiller agreed to pay that in several installments. Schiller also stipulated that he would want the rights to April's story and the grandmother's, Mrs. Strong. So it went, comfortable, professional. When it was time for Schiller's appointment across the hall with Bob Moody, Christensen came into the meeting. Ron Stanger also popped over, and Schiller began to lay it out. He found himself talking a good bit to Stanger who was full of patter and quick enough on his feet to be the host on a television talk show.

Schiller started pulling out contracts and talking money. He did not tell them he had been on the phone with ABC saying $40,000 wasn't enough. It had to be fifty. All the while, the final figure he knew was going to be a lot more, but he had calculated that for now sixty thousand in cash would get him by. Gary would have to be paid his fifty up front, but Nicole being in a mental home, he could structure her contract to give ten now, ten when ready to be interviewed, and five when the film was produced. Just give him ABC's fifty, and he could always find another ten.

Next day, to get things advanced a little further, Larry said to Vern, "Look, I said to you that my signing of a contract is not contingent on you getting any releases, and it isn't, but let's avoid future hang-ups. Will you go over and get Brenda to sign and her husband Johnny? I also need your signature, and Ida's. Tell everybody I'm not going to ask for an exclusive contract where they can't speak to anyone else, just a simple release." Vern was agreeable, got in his truck, and went around picking them up. The total would add to another $4,000.

Vern told him that Gary would not agree to any contract until he met the man. Schiller nodded. Right. That's the way it should be. Vern said, "But, no way are you going to be able to meet Gary."

"Look," Schiller said, "tell me about the daily routine at the prison. I've been told before that I could not get into places and I got in." Larry said, "Draw me a map. Tell me, do they search you? Does the time of day change things? Do they allow you to go day or night? What type of guards are there at different hours?" Schiller was thinking: Gary will have help on the inside. He hasn't been a prisoner in this place for long, but, on the other hand, he has status among convicts and guards. "Vern," said Schiller, "let Gary tell us how. He'll know when the moment comes."

2

Susskind got a call from Moody and Stanger. They told him that Dennis Boaz had been dismissed. To Susskind, these new lawyers seemed straight and very sound. Very small townish in a good sense. Virtuous men, he decided.

The thing had been handled very badly indeed, they said. They didn't think they could get any cooperation from Boaz so they would like to learn firsthand of Susskind's offer. David wasn't about to raise his bid, but he did get into discussions about the money that might be realized, and pointed out how they could gross $150,000. Susskind felt interested again. The question was whether momentum could be gotten together this late.

Then the November 29th issue of *Newsweek* appeared on Tuesday morning, November 23, with Gary Gilmore on the cover. DEATH WISH was printed in large letters across his chest. Moody felt it gave a big push to the bidding.

A couple of conversations followed with Susskind, who wanted to know if Bob had ever heard of Louis Nizer, and then mentioned a couple of other hotshot lawyers like Edward Bennett Williams. Hell, the next thing Moody knew, a voice was on the phone.

"Mr. Moody, this is Louis Nizer. My friend David Susskind asked me to call to let you know that he's exactly who he says he is, and I think you'll enjoy dealing with him. I know. I've dealt with him."

Bob replied, "It's nice to talk with you, Mr. Nizer, but, in fact, you hardly need sell me Mr. Susskind. We've seen his work and I'm aware he's a very talented, able person." It wasn't going to cut the mustard with Bob Moody. He didn't enjoy being treated as a hick.

Moody had had considerable dealings with San Francisco and Los Angeles lawyers and rarely were they patronizing. They lived near enough to Salt Lake to assume a few reasonably important things might be going on in Utah, but, dealing with lawyers from New York or Washington, D.C., you could feel them cultivating good old Provo.

So Moody told Susskind that maybe he ought to think about coming out. Schiller was making a better and better impression with Vern Damico, Moody explained, and it was Vern who had the input to Gary.

Susskind got real critical of Larry Schiller then. "Gentlemen," he said, "I don't want to brag, but the difference between Susskind and Schiller, producer to producer, is like the gap between the Dallas Cowboys and a high-school football team." Moody repeated that to Schiller, who smiled inside his black beard, a grin so big you could make it out through all that hair, and he said, "Susskind's right. He is the Dallas Cowboys, and I'm just a high-school football team. But here I am, all suited up, and ready to play. Where are the Dallas Cowboys? They're not even in the stadium."

Moreover, Moody was finding Susskind all too firm on one point. Nobody would get any money from him until they'd sewn up the rights to Nicole, Bessie, and a number of other people. Susskind wanted the lawyers to deliver the package. Take on the headaches. He was making them, in essence, a Larry Schiller. Since Larry virtually had Nicole signed up, and Phil was handling that, Moody didn't look forward to a situation where he and his old partner might have to represent different people with highly conflicting interests.

In the middle of these calls, Schiller invited Ron and Phil and Bob to a suite at the Hotel Utah. They had a quiet party, no drinks, but lots of Mormon-type whipped-cream-and-pastry desserts, and were introduced to Stephanie. Most impressed with her. She was so beautiful. She was slim and had finely chiseled features and a look of being absolutely sensitive to what she felt, but ready to offer the resistance of stone to what she did not care to feel. "Lord Almighty," said Stanger afterward, "that girl's as fetching as Nefertiti." He began to kid Larry. "What's a beautiful girl like Stephanie doing in the company of a fat guy with a beard?" and added, "Say, Schiller, any guy who has a girl like that can't be all bad." Still, you had to be impressed. A real dog-and-pony show, thought Stanger.

Then Universal Pictures appeared on the scene. The same attorneys who were representing Melvin Dumar in the Howard Hughes will contestation, came down to Provo and chatted in Bob's office for a couple of hours. One of them was even a tax attorney who had been in law school with Bob. He offered his considerable expertise in working out powerfully advantageous contracts for Gilmore and Vern. Moody was tempted. Along with everything else, these fellows were good Mormons. It looked all right. At the end of the day, however, they said, "We're embarrassed to tell you this, but the contract is only effective if the execution is carried out."

When Moody and Stanger told Gary, he laughed from his side of the window, and said through the phone, "You guys don't think that's a good contract, huh?" He took a sip of coffee — allowed himself coffee with sugar on his fast — and said, "Goddammit, the execution is going to take place." Moody replied, "Well, Gary, maybe that's beyond your control." At this point, Gary blew up, "Those sons of bitches, those sons of bitches," he kept saying. He looked awfully bleak.

Meanwhile, Larry Schiller was on the phone telling Stanley Greenberg that he had tied up Damico, and Nicole's mother, and the only element missing was the writer that Schiller wanted: Stanley Greenberg.

Then David Susskind called Stanley, and said, Schiller doesn't have it tied up. There are new Mormon lawyers in his place. Stanley got this picture of fourteen fire engines racing around Salt Lake and Provo. It looked like everybody was trying to make a buck off poor Gary Gilmore. Very distasteful. Stanley wasn't about to get into a competition for picking the bones. He wanted to do something about the effect of capital punishment on the public at large, rather than this scenario on ambulance chasing.

Schiller called back and Stanley Greenberg said no. Nothing against Mr. Schiller personally, but no, he had reached the point in a life's career where he wouldn't take a job with a producer he didn't know. He wouldn't. Stanley thought it was just too damned dangerous.

3

If Greenberg had agreed to do the script, Schiller could have hit ABC for more money. Now, they were bound to ask for a piece of the book rights. That was one thing he did not want to give up. He would have to figure out another way. Maybe sell Gary's letters to Nicole. The samples he had seen in Tamera Smith's story looked good. But for such a transaction he would need a cover. So, he called Scott Meredith in New York about being the agent.

To his horror, Meredith said, "Larry, are you sure you're getting the rights? Susskind was in here today saying he had them."

"No deal has been signed yet," said Schiller. "Not by me, not by Susskind. Scott, you have to decide who you're going to believe. I am telling you nobody has signed." "Well," Meredith said, "whose money are you using?" "I'm representing ABC," said Schiller, "but I own the magazine and book rights." Meredith sounded unhappy. "Susskind was just in here telling me he represents ABC."

"WHAT?"

"Yes," Meredith said, "he assures me he represents ABC."

Schiller called Lou Rudolph in L.A. "What are you doing," he shouted, "it's not fair." "Larry," said Rudolph, "I swear Susskind's not working for ABC." There was a pause and then Rudolph said, "Hold it. I'll call New York." Word came back fast. In fact, Susskind did have a deal with the New York office. New York never told L.A. L.A. never told New York. Oh, boy.

Schiller was unwell. Susskind had just produced *Eleanor and Franklin*. Nobody could look prettier to ABC at this moment.

He said to Lou Rudolph, "When did Susskind make the deal? What's the date? I want the date. Whoever made the deal with you first is the one who's got ABC's backing."

They came back with the dates. Susskind had not made contact with any studio guns until the 9th of November, the day after Gilmore's story first appeared on the front page of the *New York Times*. Schiller's input to the studio was on the 4th.

"I applied first," said Schiller, "I want the backing." The studio refused. There were phone calls between New York, Los Angeles and Provo. Finally, a decision. ABC would withdraw its backing equally. Neither Susskind nor Schiller could now say it was an ABC project. On the other hand, whichever one of them brought the Gilmore contract in first would get the money. Schiller was near apoplexy. ABC had done nothing but protect itself. They simply didn't want to let it get out that they were consummate fuck-ups.

Now Susskind was calling him again. Schiller stood in the phone booth of Walgreen's Drugstore and listened to Susskind make an offer.

"What are we fighting each other for? Why are we getting this price up?" Susskind asked. "You're in the field. I'm out here in New York. Let's become partners." Schiller sure listened. "I will be," Susskind said, "opening a production company in L.A. Let's use this project to see how our relationship goes. Afterwards, maybe you'll make films for us." "I would love to make films with you," said Schiller, "but that's a separate issue, David."

Schiller was so tempted he could feel his nostrils tingling. It was like the expectation of sex when you were young. But it would also mean that Susskind would do the TV show. Schiller might land the project, but it would never be his. Schiller stalled.

After he hung up, it came clear. If Susskind wanted to join forces, then Susskind could not get the rights without him. That meant it was his. He could have it, if he was ready to take on the worries. Well, he wanted the rights to Gary Gilmore like he had never wanted anything in the economic and creative sphere before. Didn't know why. Just knew.

That meant he would be worrying about money every minute from now on.

Schiller prepared to go back to the Coast with Stephanie for Thanksgiving weekend. He hadn't seen his kids in a while, and was going to take them to La Costa in San Diego. This would be the first Thanksgiving with his children where his wife, Judy, was not there, the first such. While the kids were now in the process, he felt, of getting to like Stephanie a lot — taking into account their loyalty to their mother — this would still be a Thanksgiving with ghosts. Ghosts plus his goddamned problems.

So he went to La Costa with square-edged economic concerns banging around like bricks in his head and wasn't there a day before on Friday, the 26th, in the evening, he got a phone call from Moody. "We think we can get you in to see Gary tomorrow afternoon," said the lawyer. "If there's ever going to be a chance, now's the time."

4

Geebs, you wouldn't believe the volume of mail I'm getting. 30 to 40 letters a day. A lot of young chicks, fifteen, sixteen, but of course I always was a handsome little devil. And you wouldn't believe how many Christians and religious fanatics there are in this world. I received so many bibles I could open a church — need a bible? One man wrote and said, if he could trade places with me he'd do it. I think I'll write him back and say, "Brother, they will be there to pick you up bright and early Monday morning." I'll bet they'd have a hard time finding his ass.

Hey, I'm allowed to invite five witnesses to my execution. Would like to invite you so I can tell you goodbye in person. Let me know. . . .

Gibbs thought: That has got to be a first. I have been invited to Weddings, Birthdays, and Graduations, but I never heard of being invited to an execution.

He wrote back: "If you want me there, I'll be there."

5

Moody and Stanger were preparing the way for Schiller. To the authorities at the prison, they explained that they were dealing in technical matters out of their own ball field. Tax planning had to be done on Gary's potential earnings from his life story, and incorporated into a will, which made for many complicated factors in the contract. They were bringing a man named Schiller from California to discuss this with Gary. "He's going in as your consultant?" Moody and Stanger were asked. "Yes," they said, "our consultant." They were telling the truth. Just couching it carefully.

Schiller flew to Salt Lake and drove out to Point of the Mountain early Saturday afternoon. He was full of adrenalin, and scared of blowing it.

The guard picked up a phone and was on it for ten minutes before he let Larry in. To his astonishment, Schiller did no more than pass through two sets of sliding barred doors and there on the other side, not twenty feet down the hallway, in a locked room on the right, was Gilmore looking out a small window. Across the hall, on the other side, in a room with an open door, were Vern and Moody and

Stanger, all grinning at him. Now, he could see that Gilmore was smiling, too. They had brought it off.

Vern made the introductions, and Larry sat down with his overcoat on, in the chair Vern had been using, and let the door stay open. He looked across the ten-foot width of the hall to the room where Gary stood behind a small window, and their eyes locked. Schiller recognized immediately that this man loved to stare into your head. You had to talk as if he were the only force that existed.

Schiller didn't mind such contests. He always felt a subtle advantage. He had vision only in one eye. The other person would stare into a flatness of expression in the other eye and wear himself out.

Gilmore, however, had positioned himself behind the small window in such a way that if Schiller leaned to the left, he, in his turn, could also lean to the left and thereby keep the window frame in the same relation to both of them. It was as if he were looking through a pair of sights. Being farther away from the glass, Schiller began to have the feeling that he was in the prison, while Gilmore was outside and free and peering in.

Anyway, Schiller started his rap. He said, in a formal tone, "You obviously know the reason I'm here," indicating by a slight shift of his eye that for all they both knew, the phones were tapped. "Bob and Vern have no doubt told you I am here to *consult,*" he said with a little smile, getting all the benefit out of the word, "here to broach matters concerning your estate and assets and things like that, you know." Now they each gave a little smile. About that time, a guard came and sat on a bench in the hallway not far away, and Gary said, "No need to worry about him," just as the guard picked up a magazine and started reading. "He," said Gilmore, "is one of the two guys who are with me all the time whether I'm in my cell or outside. Pretty good guys." He said it like the leader of a team who knew the other players are proud to be associated with him. Schiller was surprised to see how ordinary he looked. It was more than a week since he had seen him leave the hospital, and he certainly had a different appearance today. Vern had told Schiller that Gary was on a hunger strike, but there was no way of seeing it. He looked a lot healthier than the last time. And kind of calm.

From what Vern and Moody and Stanger and Boaz had said, Larry was expecting a man replete with intelligence and wit. Instead, here was this fellow who looked like he wouldn't be comfortable in a restaurant with a tablecloth.

Schiller guessed he had fifteen or twenty minutes to get the message across so he talked in a fast, hard rap, never taking his eyes off Gilmore, and not a question was asked that first fifteen minutes, until finally Schiller had to say, "If you want to interrupt me, please do," but Gilmore said, "No, no, I'm listening." Then Schiller branched off into the speech he had given Kathryne Baker and Vern, except he used the word "shit" a lot, and "fuck-up" and "con me," and occasionally, would say, "I had a line run on me." All the while, he watched Gilmore and was wondering. Where's this guy with the high I.Q.? Schiller had gone completely through the fifteen prepared minutes and had been traveling on improvisation for quite a while before Gilmore finally took his first real cut at the ball and said, "Who's going to play me in the movie?"

Half an hour in. "Who's going to play me in the movie?" To Schiller, it meant: Your wits against mine. "You see," Gary drawled, "there's an actor I like. I can't remember his name, but he was in this movie called *Bring Me the Head of Alfredo Garcia* and he also did another flick with Sam Peckinpah." "I think," said Schiller, "it's Warren Oates you're talking about."

"Well," said Gilmore, "I really like that guy. I want him to play me." He nodded, still looking right at Schiller and said, "I want, as part of our agreement, that this actor do me in the movie."

Schiller took time to reconnoiter. "Gary," he said, "you've been listening to me, but I don't know much yet about you. There may not be a story here. Let's get a good screenplay before we talk about anything else."

"I think," said Gilmore, "that I would like Warren Oates to play me and I want that as part of the agreement."

"I can't," said Schiller, "make that a part of the agreement. I can't get us involved in a condition that could put us in a straitjacket. Warren Oates might not be available. I might not want Warren Oates. There might be more suitable actors around. Or it might be that a big block of money could be obtained only if we were to take another actor. You are getting into my part of the business now. I have to say 'no' to the idea that Warren Oates is a condition of our agreement!"

Gilmore gave a smile. "Larry, I hate Warren Oates," he said.

"All right," said Schiller, with a big grin. "Who do you really want?"

"Gary Cooper," said Gary Gilmore, "I was named after him."

That cracked the freeze. Gilmore looked ready to speak about himself now.

"When you were a kid," asked Schiller, "what did you want to be?"

"A gangster," Gilmore said, "one of the mob." He started talking about how he'd been a little hood as a kid, lifting things here, breaking in there. He and a friend had been in a wild car chase. Took the cops half an hour to catch them. His face lit up as he spoke. He was like a fellow telling you about attractive chicks he'd made it with.

After they had been going about forty-five minutes, Schiller said, "I've told you about myself, and you've told me something about yourself, and I guess we'll have a chance to talk again and make a decision as to whether I can be of service to you."

Gilmore said, "You have a place to go?"

"No," said Schiller," but they won't let me sit here forever."

"Why not?" asked Gilmore. "Stay all night."

"Really?"

"Oh, yeah, Vern and I talk six hours long if we want."

Now, Schiller began to feel how much Gilmore was in control. From time to time, he would turn to the guard and say, Where's my pills? or, Get me my coffee, and do it in a tone that had no question he was going to get what he wanted. Bring me my coffee, like, Bring me the head of Alfredo Garcia.

When more time went by, however, and the coffee had not arrived, Gilmore abruptly, screamed out: "WHERE'S THE COFFEE?" Schiller had been able to see a little irritation building, but this really came without warning, a shrill and screeching sound, that showed,

so far as Schiller could see, Gilmore's absolute insensitivity to any
ugly impression he might leave with Vern or the lawyers. It was like
talking to a woman who suddenly starts caterwauling at her kids.

Finally, an attendant in a white uniform brought in some pills,
and Gary really cussed the guy out. "You've been keeping me waiting
an hour and fifteen minutes," he said. "Don't you know that when I
ask for medicine, I am supposed to have it? It's a rule. You people
make the rules, then you don't fulfill them." He was so rude, in fact,
that Schiller was surprised they did not manhandle him back to his
cell. It was amazing how far Gilmore was willing to push it.

His coffee soon followed in a cardboard cup, and he began to
rave that he was not supposed to eat out of paper utensils. The regulations called for real crockery. Then, he said to Schiller, "These guys
expect me to live by the rules, serve my time by the rules, go to bed
by the rules, get executed by the rules, but they bend them all over
the place. They break them whenever they want." He went on for a
ten-minute tirade, and suddenly, Schiller knew who Gilmore reminded him of: it was Muhammad Ali off on a rant, that same hard,
implacable, inhuman voice that Muhammad could turn on and off.
Once Schiller had been in Ali's room in the Hilton Hotel in Manila
and had had to sit there for an hour and listen to Muhammad Ali in a
temper, and Gilmore had the same tone. Didn't care what you
thought of him. So Schiller said: "You really did kill those two guys,
didn't you?" "Of course I did," said Gilmore, almost looking hurt,
"you know that." And then Schiller said, "You *killed* them," as if to
say there was a difference between killing somebody in a rage, and
being a cold-blooded killer who only had to throw a little switch in
himself. Gilmore was in the second category. He could kill you because you gave him coffee in a paper cup.

That took a lot of warmth out of the conversation. Schiller knew
it was time to back off, so he said, "Vern, anything you want to say?"
and Vern got on the phone for a couple of minutes. When Schiller
figured it was cool again, he said, "Look, Gary, it's dinnertime. Want
me to come back afterwards?" And Gilmore said, "Yeah, oh yeah.
We'll sit here all night and talk." He had gotten over his chill. Schiller
went out thinking, Boy, what I'll be able to do with this guy. He's a
great subject for an interview.

6

As the interview went on and on, Moody and Stanger began to worry over being discovered and professionally embarrassed. They weren't above a little prodding to get Schiller out, but Gary wanted to keep talking. Obviously was enjoying himself. Since the lawyers could only hear Schiller's end of it, they had no real idea what Gary was saying.

Then they began to worry that he might be spilling his guts and giving Schiller the story without a contract or anything. Gary had certainly lit up. It was the first time Moody had ever seen him enthused about anything. It confirmed his feeling that Schiller was a good choice, but they were also wide open for an end run. If Schiller was getting tons of material, he might want to double-cross them.

In the restaurant, Schiller kept asking if this is the way Gary acted all the time. Everybody started saying, "Man, he's never talked to anybody the way he talked to you." Schiller didn't know if they were saying that to stroke him, but Vern said quietly, "I think he really likes you." So, Schiller's confidence was building. When they went back he started talking to Gary about a number of subjects, only the conversation hadn't gone fifteen minutes when there was an interruption on the phone, and a long conversation between Moody and somebody at the other end. The Warden or the Assistant Warden. Schiller was terminated.

Gary was very upset. Kept asking, "Who said that? Who gave the order? He's on my lawyer's team. He's allowed to be here." Schiller said, "Don't worry about it, Gary, we'll have plenty of time." Then Moody got up and said, "Here, Gary, is the contract we've discussed." They held up this long piece of paper and started reading the money figures over the telephone, and Gary said, "Yes, have the thing typed up. I'll look it over again and sign it."

After the lawyers and Schiller had left, Gary asked Vern, "In your opinion, is he the right fellow?" Vern said, "I don't know just exactly yet, but I think he is."

"What about Susskind?" asked Gary, and answered himself. "I feel like Mr. Schiller is the one. I like his way of doing business."

That Saturday night and Sunday morning, Schiller worked with Moody and Stanger doing the contracts, making the changes, bringing in secretaries, working the goddamn computer typewriters. The lawyers didn't go to church, and there was a lot of kidding about that. But by Sunday afternoon, the contracts were drawn, and Schiller went back in his motel to wait for the signing.

About then, Boaz called Susskind collect. He always called collect. Susskind said, "Don't you even have a phone?" Dennis giggled. "No, look," said Susskind, "you've gone too far. I don't know what you've done, but you're out and other men are in. You have no more rights in this matter." "Oh, yes," said Boaz, "it can't be done without me."

"Oh," said Susskind, "it can, and it will. But it isn't going to be done by me." "Listen," said Dennis, "maybe I'm no longer the lawyer in the case, but I have a few documents and I got . . ." Susskind decided he was raving. "You are a poseur," he said, "and a liar and a flaky man. I think you're a very nasty person. Don't ever call me again, collect or otherwise." Things had certainly ended up on an extremely sour note, rancid.

7

Moody and Stanger got a little rest, and then went up to the prison late Sunday afternoon. Talking on the telephone across the hall, they went through the terms of the contract. Gary didn't want many changes and it was only when they discussed access to his letters that he became angry. He scratched out the clause with his pen and wrote on the contract that no such access was granted until he had spoken to Nicole. The attorneys tried to argue. "You don't have anything to say about it," Moody told him, "they're Nicole's letters now."

"Well, goddammit," said Gary, "they are not going to be read until I give my consent."

All the while, Schiller was waiting in his room. He sat in that motel until 3 A.M. Monday morning, waiting for them to call. Even phoned the prison to discover they were not there. So, he called

Moody's home and woke him up. They'd been back for hours. Back, in fact, since eight-thirty in the evening. It just never occurred to them that he was waiting. All the while he'd been going through desperate scenarios in his head.

8

Big Jake came back to the tank with a large jar of instant coffee, a large jar of Tang, and a carton of Gibbs's brand of cigarettes, Viceroy Super Longs. He told Gibbs that Gary had asked Vern Damico to drop them off at the jail. Also a message: *Geebs, all of a sudden, I've become rather rich — if you need anything, you just have to ask.* Gibbs figured Gary had sold his life story to somebody. He sat down and made a cup of Tang.

Boaz called Susskind one last time. It wasn't collect. "I told you," said Susskind, "I don't want to talk to you." Boaz said, "I got a whole new angle. I want to do *my* story." "Boaz," said Susskind, "you're crazy." "No," said Dennis, "the real great story is my own. It's a great story," Dennis repeated. "I've kept notes." "Please, *please*," said Susskind, "go see Mr. Schiller. I'm sure he'd love to do it."

Next day, Gibbs received an index card in an envelope.
On it, Gary had written an invitation:

BANG!   BANG!
A real live Shoot'em up!
Mrs. Bessie Gilmore of Milwaukie, Ore cordially invites you to
the execution of her son: Gary Mark Gilmore, 36
Place: Utah State Prison. Draper, Utah
Time: Sunrise
EARPLUGS AND BULLETS WILL BE FURNISHED

With the card, came a letter.

I'm going to be giving away a lot of money shortly. Would like to give you about (2000) two thousand. Please don't say no. Accept it in the manner I give it to you, as a friend. I might as well give some of my money to you, cause if I don't, I'll just give it to someone else.

PART THREE

The Hunger Strike

CHAPTER II

The Pardon

1

Earl Dorius was into an awfully tricky matter. The prison wanted to know whether they could break Gilmore's hunger strike and make him eat. These days, force-feeding was considered equal, legally, to forced medication, and there had been a Supreme Court decision in 1973 that said you had to have the consent of the prisoner.

There were, however, recognized exceptions. Earl wrote a letter to Warden Smith which emphasized that prisons had to preserve order and could not be a part of any suicide attempt. "It would be a serious abuse of discretion to allow an inmate to starve to death." Earl concluded that the prison physician had "legal authority to order the force-feeding."

Earl contacted the press and some of the local news stations to tell them he was issuing the opinion. Fully expected it would be the big Gilmore story of the day and was frankly looking forward to it. His letter to Sam Smith had involved considerable research which he felt had good reasoning attached, but it all got swallowed. Holbrook, from the *Salt Lake Tribune,* called on this same afternoon to give an hour's notice: the *Trib* was going back to Judge Ritter to try again for a temporary restraining order against the no-interview rule for Gilmore.

Earl was frustrated. He had fully intended to find fresher material than good old *Pell v. Procunier.* However, the force-feeding issue had taken up his working hours. Whereas, the *Trib* came in well prepared. Judge Ritter granted the temporary restraining order. The *Tribune* would be able to send a journalist out to talk to Gilmore this very day.

2

Schiller was at the prison when the reporter got there, and it all came as a surprise. He was in the middle of interviewing Gary, and had just started to talk about the cover story in *Newsweek*. By that route, Schiller figured he could learn whether Gilmore had a real interest in publicity. So he mentioned a couple of verses *Newsweek* had quoted Gary as writing, and remarked that the poetry was pretty good. Gary laughed. "It's a poem by Shelley called 'The Sensitive Plant,' " he said. "Dammit, Schiller, that's real stupidity on the part of *Newsweek*. Anyone who recognizes the poem is going to think I was pretending to write it myself."

Later, Schiller thought he must have sensed he would not be able to talk to Gary much longer, because he brought up a touchy subject even though it was his principle to save hardnosed matters for last. No use cutting off an interview by an impertinent question. Schiller's temper, however, was not always to be controlled and so he found himself saying, "Why did you stipulate in the contract that I can't have your letters to Nicole? She's in the hospital. You know I can't reach her."

"Schiller," said Gary, "that goddamned Dr. Woods is keeping me from calling her. Won't even let me write a letter. I've gone on a hunger strike to dramatize that I am being kept away from the one person in the world who I truly care about. So I put that clause into our contract." He looked right at Schiller. "I can see you're a go-getter. You are going to get Woods to allow me to communicate with Nicole. I don't care if you bribe him, but, man, until I talk to her, you get no letters, okay? Let's say I'm putting the hook into you."

It wasn't altogether surprising to Schiller. He had thought from the beginning that Gilmore's hunger strike was not begun in despair, but as a way to make Gilmore the dealer. He had been adept, Schiller had heard, at getting convicts to riot over at Oregon

State Penitentiary, and did it on more than one occasion. Of course, he had been in that joint for twelve years, more than long enough to belong to one or another convict clique. Whereas here he might be a celebrity, but the question was whether he could extend his strike from himself to ten men or fifty. Gary could be a killer, and even considered crazy, but who would fear him on Death Row when he had no contacts or loyal friends in the place? Schiller wondered if money and publicity were spoiling Gary's judgment. So far, nobody had joined the strike.

Just then the guards came in with the news. Gus Sorensen of the *Salt Lake Tribune* was outside, holding Judge Ritter's order. The prison had to let him in. Sorensen could interview Gary Gilmore.

A rocket went off in Schiller's head but he never blinked. "All right," he said to Moody and Stanger, "let Gary talk. Maybe it can help our public posture. Our stance is that we are not here to watch a man die, but to come to understand him." He walked down the hall and met Sorensen as soon as the man emerged from the gate, introduced himself, said, "Mr. Sorensen, I can tell Gilmore not to talk to you, but that's not my interest." It certainly wasn't. Schiller was not looking to alienate the *Salt Lake Tribune*. A pipeline into the biggest local paper could enable him to affect the output on the AP and UP stories. Besides, Sorensen was considered the leading crime reporter in the State of Utah. He could be useful for background on the prison.

Still, Schiller wanted to avoid certain hazards. How could he know what Gilmore would choose to give away? If the fellow decided to commit suicide, any casual interview could end up being Gary Gilmore's last words. So it was a matter of setting up some ground rules.

He could hear Sorensen on the phone saying, "The guy bought Gilmore's rights. He's not letting me talk unless he's there." All the while, Schiller was sweating. That morning he had delivered a check for $52,000 to Vern. If Gary felt like double-crossing him this afternoon and telling all to Sorensen, there would not be much he could do. Schiller was gambling that Gilmore would not throw over the situation for the sheer pleasure of it. Meanwhile, he could hear Sorensen saying, "Well, I don't know. Heard good things and bad about Schiller." Larry got on the phone and said to Sorensen's editor, "Look, I'm not interested in stopping the press. I have no objection to Mr. Sorensen speaking to Gary. I just want, since we hold the rights, to make sure your copyright to Mr. Sorensen's interview reverts back to us." That meant the editor had to call the *Tribune*'s lawyer. While that was going on, Schiller spoke to Gary, and said, "This can work to our advantage. When you talk to Sorensen, don't get into the murder. Talk about the prison the way it is now, day to day, or the reasons for your hunger strike. If I think you're giving away something of great value to you, I'll rub my chin. So long as I don't, it's okay to answer the question. Mainly, don't give a lot about your personal life. That's what the world is interested in, Gary."

Schiller sat next to Sorensen during the interview, but there was only one phone. He couldn't hear what Gilmore was saying. After Sorensen asked his first few questions, however, Schiller decided the man was a classic newspaper reporter. Not looking for insight about Gary's inner life. Just a few paragraphs that the headline writer in the newsroom could clap intriguing words on. Besides, you could probably trust Gary. The fellow was looking for his cues.

After Sorensen finished, he and Schiller went out through the barred gates from Medium Security to the administration foyer, and there, in the small cramped dirty lobby, under the fluorescent lights, it seemed as if every fucking journalist in Salt Lake had crammed into the place. They were all screaming at once. Sorensen, they knew; Sorensen had just interviewed Gilmore. But Schiller was giving them a hard-on. "Who are you, who are you?" they kept asking, and Gus Sorensen — Schiller could bless him — didn't say a word, payment of loyalty right on the spot. Schiller understood, however, that he was in real trouble. There had to be people in the crowd who knew him. He could feel whispers circulating. Finally, one reporter said, "Come on, Larry, you bought Gilmore's story, didn't you?" Schiller was trying to figure the angles. If he kept denying it, by tomorrow, he would be nailed. Don't get journalists cocked like hunting dogs. In twenty-four hours, they would have the story, and never forgive him. It looked like a toe dance of pure evasion was called for.

Dumbo the elephant, high on his toes, said Schiller to himself, and side-stepped to the left, side-stepped to the right. "What are you here for?" they asked, and he said, "I'm a consultant for estate affairs." Journalists who knew him hooted.

He'd have to give some version of the truth, Schiller decided. Something vague and dull, not eminently printable. "Oh," he said finally, "I've acquired the rights for a potential four-wall motion picture production." Maybe that was far enough over the horizon so they wouldn't see him as the man getting exclusive stories from Gilmore. But the voice in his head remarked, "Should have told them 'No comment.' " The computer back of his eyes was ringing every alarm bell.

Moody and Stanger were aghast. "Well," whispered Moody, "Schiller just blew us out of the saddle." "Estate Consultant" next to "Hollywood producer" was going to baste their goose right here at the prison. Stanger said, "That son of a bitch double-crossed us. He wants to get his own story across."

Deseret News

Carnival Atmosphere Surrounds Gilmore
Movie Deal Weighed

Nov. 29 — In a circus-like atmosphere at the Utah State Prison, Monday, night, the news media, lawyers, literary agents and movie producers milled about discussing interviews, and movie and story deals.

3

When he saw Schiller on the TV news that night, Dorius was outraged. He called Utah State and gave one of the Deputy Wardens hell. "I've been working my fanny off to keep the *Tribune* out. Here," he said, "you let a Hollywood producer in."

Earl saw nothing but endless cases ahead. One newspaper after another, TV stations, radio stations all bringing lawsuits. Ritter would probably open the prison to everybody. Even if Dorius appealed each of his decisions to the Tenth Circuit in Denver, it was time-consuming to get litigation up to the next tier. Could take as long as a year. All the while, reporters would be running rife through the prison. There was no telling what Gilmore would say once he found himself able to talk to the press.

Dorius started asking through the office if anybody had experience in overturning Ritter in a hurry. Petition for Writ of Mandamus, he was told. That would call for an immediate review by the Tenth Circuit. Dorius wasn't the type to gulp, but filing a Writ of Mandamus against Judge Ritter was where push certainly came to shove. It would be equal to saying that Ritter, who doubtless prided himself on being the finest jurist in the State of Utah, Ritter, who had served on the bench with Judge Learned Hand, had in this case proved so ignorant of well-established principles of law that the only redress was exceptional: a suit brought by Dorius against the Judge. That was one slam-bang of a drastic move — a young lawyer like himself suing a Federal Judge. Ritter might not forgive in a hurry.

4

DESERET NEWS

Point of the Mountain, Utah, Nov. 28 — Condemned killer Gary Gilmore in a letter to the Utah Board of Pardons said, "Let's do it, you cowards. . . ."

Gilmore asked for immediate execution before a firing squad. "I do not seek or desire your clemency," he wrote, underscoring "not" three times.

During the Board of Pardons Hearing, Schiller wondered who the neat well-built little fellow with the trim mustache might be. Looked like a young prep-school instructor, a respectable package tied with the right string. Who might he actually be? The fellow kept glaring at him.

He was the kind of young establishment lawyer, or young Utah bureaucrat, who didn't glare often. But when he did, watch it, liquid fire came out. Schiller shrugged. He was used to people blasting him with their thoughts. At times like that, fat felt comfortable — one more layer of asbestos against the flames.

Still the fellow disliked him so intensely, Schiller had to ask about him. It took several newsmen before one could say, "That's Earl Dorius. Attorney General's office." Later, Schiller saw him talking to Sam Smith, and that was another sight. Sam Smith was ten inches taller.

Schiller was finding the prison difficult to understand. They kept saying they wanted no publicity, but were holding the Board of Pardons Hearing in a conference room off the main hallway of the Administration Building. The press had been invited. That was like throwing a little meat to a lot of lions. There were TV cameras, microphones, still cameramen, flashbulbs, lights on tripods, overhead lights on stands. The perfect definition of a circus. The hottest room he had been in for a long time.

Everybody was standing on chairs to get a better look as they brought Gilmore through the door in leg shackles. It was like a movie Schiller saw once about the Middle Ages where a fellow in a white smock trudged in to be burned at the stake. Here, it was loose white pants and a long white shirt, but the effect was similar. Made the prisoner look like an actor playing a saint.

Schiller was changing his mind about Gilmore's looks again. It was as if he could take off one mask, hang it on the wall, pick up another. Today Gary did not look like a janitor, a door-to-door salesman, or an ice-cold killer. The hunger strike was ten days old and it had left him pale. The pits in his face showed, and the scars. He appeared good looking, but frail. Eaten away at. Didn't look like Bob Mitchum or Gary Cooper, but Robert DeNiro. Same deadness coming off. Same strength in back of the deadness.

All around, CBS and NBC crews were talking, and Schiller was not comfortable with how much they despised Gilmore. They spoke as if he were some low jailhouse lawyer who had enough tricks to get this far. One fellow from the local press muttered: "Can you believe the attention this cheap punk is getting?"

Schiller remembered that the Head of the Pardons Board, George Latimer, was once the defense attorney when Lieutenant Calley went to trial for machine-gunning Vietnamese villagers at My Lai. To

Schiller, Latimer was one more red-faced Mormon with a big bulldog head and eyeglasses. A pompous self-satisfied look. Fever and bilious emotions. What a room. The only pleasant face he could see was Stanger. Schiller didn't know if they were going to get along, for Ron Stanger impressed him as too lippy on one side, and too casual about important details on the other, but right now Ron's boyish middle-aged fraternity man's face was loaded with expression. He was acting very solicitous toward Gary.

Stanger was, in fact, enjoying it. Up to that point, Gary had always been highly suspicious of him. That was fine with Stanger. He didn't believe in the death penalty, and wasn't convinced Gilmore was serious either. The action interested Stanger more than the merits of Gilmore's position. The action was beautiful. Something new every day. That was fun. Since Gilmore could — although Stanger didn't believe it — end up dead one day, he didn't want to get too close to his client.

All the same, it was natural to work on improving your relations with any human being you had to see all the time. When Stanger, therefore, made a promise to Gilmore over some small thing, he tried to carry it out. If he said he would bring pencils, he brought them; if drawing paper, drawing paper. Today in Court, however, was the first time Ron felt proud of working for the man. He hadn't known until now how Gilmore would prove under pressure. From Stanger's point of view, however, he was terrific this day, just as intelligent as hell.

Behind the dais was a blue flag and four men at a long conference table who all looked to be Mormons to Schiller, all wearing glasses and blue suits. Schiller was taking in as many details as he could remember, it was history he kept saying to himself, but he was bored until the chairman told Gilmore he had the floor. That was when Gary Gilmore began to impress Larry Schiller, too. If it weren't for the white uniform of Maximum Security, Gilmore could have been a graduate student going for his orals before a faculty of whom he was slightly contemptuous.

"I am wondering," he began by saying. "Your Board dispenses privilege, and I have always thought that privileges were sought, desired, earned and deserved, and I seek nothing from you, don't desire anything from you, haven't earned anything and I don't deserve anything either."

Everybody in that crowded, steaming, incandescent room fixed on him. He drew all eyes, all lenses. Schiller was now twice impressed with Gilmore as an actor. He did not rise to this occasion like a great ham actor, but chose to be oblivious to it. Merely there to express his idea. Gilmore spoke in the absolute confidence of the idea, spoke in the same quiet tone he might have employed if talking to only one man. So it became the kind of acting that makes you forget you are in a theatre.

What a screen star this fellow would have made, thought Schiller, and was filled with elation at the thought that he had the rights to his life, and in the next instant swallowed the misery that the right to talk personally to Gary had been cut off. From now on, he might always have to ask his questions through intermediaries.

5

GILMORE   I had come to the conclusion that because of Utah's Governor Rampton, I was here, because he bowed to whatever pressures were on him.

I had personally decided he was a moral coward for doing it. I simply accepted the sentence that was given to me. I have accepted sentences all my life. I didn't know I had a choice in the matter.

When I did accept it, everybody jumped up and wanted to argue with me. It seems that the people, especially the people of Utah, want the death penalty but they don't want executions and when it became a reality they might have to carry one out, well, they started backing off on it.

Well, I took them literal and serious when they sentenced me to death just as if they had sentenced me to ten years or thirty days in the county jail or something. I thought you were supposed to take them serious. I didn't know it was a joke.

Ms. Shirley Pedler of the ACLU wants to get in on the act but they always want to get in on the act, the ACLU. I don't think they have really ever done anything effective in their lives. I would like them all, including that group of reverends and rabbis from Salt Lake City to just butt out — this is my life and my death. It's by Courts that I die and I accept that. . . .

CHAIRMAN Now, in spite of what you may think about us, you can rest assured that we are not cowards, and you can rest assured that we are going to decide this case on the statutes of the State of Utah and not on your desires. . . . Is Richard Giauque out there?

We are going ahead with people who have asked to speak.

Richard, we have received from you a brief, and by the way, I commend you for it, it's a nicely written brief. I may disagree with some of your concepts but anyway, it was nice the way it was presented.

At this point, Schiller watched a slim, blond man with a prominent nose, rather small chin, and a look of considerable elegance, stand up. Schiller assumed the man had to be a lawyer for the ACLU or some such group, and made a mental note to interview him when the time came, for he looked interesting. Giauque carried himself with the superiority of knowing he was probably more intelligent than nearly anyone he talked to. Perhaps, for this reason, he never once looked at Gilmore. Gary, in turn, stared at him with considerable intensity, and Schiller could feel the basis of Gilmore's rancor — a man from the other side of the tracks was talking about him.

GIAUQUE Mr. Chairman, I would like to make a very brief comment here that goes to the power of the Board. We are asking that the Board continue the present Stay of Execution, until such time as the questions that we do not believe you can decide, have been decided by a Court.

Society has an interest in this wholly apart from Mr. Gilmore's wishes. I do think that there are some facts here that ought to be looked into. One of them is whether or not he has voluntarily waived his legal rights, or whether or not he is asking the State merely to become an accomplice. . . . It is not Mr. Gilmore's desire that is paramount here and I would merely ask, Mr. Chairman, . . . that the decision to utilize the death sentence not be made by Mr. Gilmore and not be made by this Board, but . . . be resolved by the Courts.

CHAIRMAN Well, I am going to answer you. . . . We are not going to continue this case to wait for somebody else to decide what the law may and may not be. . . . We are here to see that the case does not continue forever, and back up everybody, and the State of Utah, on the capital punishment laws. From my personal standpoint, I would not favor a continuance.

A little while later came the first break in the hearing. Gilmore was led out, and the members of the Board of Pardons quit the room. Few among the media gave up their positions. In fact, they looked to better them.

By now, Earl Dorius was close to rage, as close as he ever got. He still hadn't prepared his Writ of Mandamus to the Tenth Circuit Court, yet here he was losing an entire morning at this hearing that was being conducted in the worst possible fashion. He couldn't understand how Sam Smith had ever allowed it. What did he see in the intermission — you had to call it an "intermission" rather than a recess, they were creating such TV theatre — but this fellow Schiller sitting in one of the chairs that belonged to the Attorney General's staff. Like a director's chair, it had been carefully marked with Bill Evans's name on masking tape. Dorius kept whispering to Evans, "Just pull that chair out from under him," which was about as uncharacteristic for Earl as anything he could remember. He didn't usually go around suggesting people lay their physical hands on other people, but the state of this place, the disregard of the media for the premises, was truly disgusting.

Dorius was amazed at the lack of security. There were no electric scanners at the door, and nobody had been patted down by hand search. One strange cameraman after another came in with huge equipment bags. My God! Anybody could bring in a Magnum and blast a hole through Gary. The Warden should have had the ultimate authority to tell the press to stay out, but somebody higher than him didn't seem to mind the publicity. Dorius was disgusted with his own client. If they had to televise it, why didn't the prison, for heaven's sake, ask for a pool arrangement, one camera, one member of the radio medium, one writer? It was crazy the way everybody had jammed in. Still, Earl was impressed with one thing. It was actually possible this fellow Gilmore was not for show.

6

At the County Jail, they let Gibbs out to the front office to watch the hearing with some cops and jailers. They were all glued to the TV set. Gibbs thought it was one hell of a soap opera. When Gary told the Court they were cowards, Gibbs started laughing so loud the cops gave him a funny look.

Gary won by a vote of 3–2. On TV they said the likelihood was that his execution would be set for December 6th, in order to come in under the sixty-day rule from his sentencing on October 7th. Gibbs thought, Gary Gilmore may only be on earth another week.

DESERET NEWS

Salt Lake, Nov. 30 — The National Coalition Against the Death Penalty, an association of more than 40 national, religious, legal, minority, political and professional organizations, issued a strong statement late Tuesday over the action of the Utah Pardon Board.

"This makes possible the first court-sanctioned homicide in the U.S. in 10 years" the statement noted. . . .

Organizations participating in the coalition include the ACLU, the American Ethical Union, The American Friends Service Committee, The American Ortho-Psychiatric Association, The Central Conference of American Rabbis, and others.

CHAPTER 12

The Government Servant

1

Earl knew he wouldn't call it admiration, but during the Board of Pardons Hearing, he did get to feel good about the way Gilmore was conducting himself. The man was on a hunger strike, yet his intellect was keen. Dorius was glad to feel something positive. He had lost a great deal of respect when Gilmore tried to commit suicide. All that big dramatic talk about justice, and then the chicken way out. In Dorius's eyes, Gilmore was redeeming himself.

Earl realized how ironic it was. The only thing he and Gilmore had in common was looking to expedite the execution, each for his own reasons. Hardly what you would call a bond. Still, there he was rooting for the man at this hearing as if they were members of the same team. But then, you had to applaud the other guy when he made a really fine play. Of course, Earl supposed his feeling had self-interest. The Gilmore business would probably be the only thing he'd worked on that they might still write about fifty years from now. After Gilmore, sob, sob, my life will be downhill. Truly, it was doubtful he would ever again be so active on a case of national and international concern. People he had met years ago in England on his LDS mission were even beginning to correspond with him again, people he had actually brought into the Church seven and eight years ago. So it had to please Earl that he was the first man in the office to recognize the importance of it all.

He supposed the reason he now took pride in Gilmore was that the convict also respected the situation. It would be disagreeable to work on something this momentous and feel the individual at the very center was nothing but a con artist with shoddy motives. Gilmore's desire, if genuine, was in line with a few of Earl's own objectives.

In recent years, some of the Justices of the U.S. Supreme Court had been saying that the most poorly represented client in the country was state and local government. That teed Earl off personally. He wanted to improve the image of people who worked in government offices. If he had an ambition, it was not to get into politics, or see his name in lights, but to become known as the best advocate before the Utah Supreme Court. Be an authority on prison law. He wanted to establish a reputation for thorough research and high competence. In fact, if there was a constructive criticism he would make of his work, it was that he tended to research an assignment to death. It killed him to turn in sloppy work. For as long as Gary Gilmore was occupying his working life, therefore, Earl knew he would be putting in fourteen- and fifteen-hour days. Even his kids understood it had to cut into family life. Now, if the children picked up the phone, they could expect half the time to hear a stranger asking for their father.

When he and his wife went to a party, everybody wanted to know the ins and outs. For that matter, Earl didn't mind telling. After all the hard work, it was kind of a fun payment to fill people in on what he was doing. Still, he also tried to get the idea across, as reasonably as possible, that they weren't a gang of boobs over at the A.G.'s. Were actually trying to do a job they could be proud of.

Earl knew better than to announce to the world that he was in the job he wanted, and his work gave him the roots he had always craved. During those years in law school when, to keep his young family afloat, he had had to put in killing hours working as a law clerk afternoons and nights, there had been one driving force to carry him through, one dream to take him through missionary work, college, marriage and law school, the idea that finally he would be able to settle down somewhere and get a few things established. Now he had a home instead of an apartment, and was the father of a growing family, liked his job, was proud of his wife, and spent a lot of time with his children. It could be seen, he knew full well, as a reaction to the continuous moving around of his youth.

Earl's father — and he didn't say this to be critical, but simply accurate — had been somewhat of a loner. His dad's idea of entertainment had been to take his easel and canvas and go off on his own, then come back at the end of the day with a beautiful landscape. All through Earl's childhood, living around Virginia, Los Angeles and Salt Lake, his father had been an attorney with the Pentagon, and they kept him moving. Since Earl had no brothers, and his only sister was married by the time he was thirteen, he was practically an only child, and had an oddball inner life. He became, for instance, the best cartoonist of his school in the fifth grade, and wrote letters to Walt Disney asking if they would hire his talent despite his youth.

In high school in Virginia, however, he did get to be popular. He played in a dance band and was pretty good at high-school sports, got heavily involved in basketball and track until he broke his leg giving a gymnastic demonstration. It wiped out his athletic career, but got him elected junior class president and he was about to run for student body president, was even dating the head cheerleader, when boom! family had to move to Los Angeles. His dad was being relocated, and Earl, once more, was being dislocated.

He was a nobody going to University High School in West Los Angeles. Huge student body. He ate lunch alone, didn't know a soul. It was the one time in his life when he felt like being disobedient. He wanted to return to Virginia and live with his uncle and see his girl again.

His father was saddened by this unhappiness. Maybe that was enough recognition. Earl said, "I'm sorry, I'll stay," and did, but his senior year in high school was not the happiest.

Then his dad had a transfer to Utah. That was not as bad. His folks, being LDS, had always kept a little place in Salt Lake where they would go for summers. Since the cheerleader back east was no longer a viable alternative, Earl began to date the sister of his best friend in Salt Lake. They never stopped dating until they were married.

He figured life had left him more stable than the average man his age, but only because he knew his faults. Knew he had a temper. These days, he contented himself by screaming at the TV set. "Look at that imbecile," Earl would shout at the tube. But only in the privacy of the family. When he was younger, his father would take him aside, counsel him, and refine that temper, to the point where now, conducting an oral argument in front of a Court, he never shouted at his opponent. It was all right to be forceful, but Earl tried to keep contention out of the presentation. That was why he took such pride in Gilmore at the Pardons Hearing. It was as if, within his mind, he kept telling Gilmore to hold his anger.

2

Earl knew what he could do well and what he couldn't, and cross-examining witnesses had never been his strongest point. One reason he liked the Gilmore business was that he was drawn to cases which required analysis of new legal facets but didn't ask you to get bogged down by resistant testimony. Earl knew he was weak at framing questions in such a way that he could use the witness's answers against him ten questions later. He wanted to get right to the heart of the issue. Maybe he had been interrupted a couple too many times in his young life, but he knew that, as lawyers went, he had no large ability to set up pertinent questions and then lead an adversary down the primrose path. He thought it was corollary to how he kept his acquaintances limited. Even now, the circle of his family and friends didn't go beyond his wife, his brother-in-law, their immediate friends, a few neighbors, and office acquaintances. Most of his closest friendships were made through work.

His alliance with Sam Smith was a good example. He could almost describe the Warden as a dear friend, yet they never saw each other socially. It was more that the two of them had practically learned their prison law together. Sam had been made a Warden just about the time Earl first came to work in the Attorney General's office. Getting to know Sam, Earl had also learned a great deal about prison problems, and thought the Warden was more liberal than people gave him credit for. For one thing, he allowed contact visits in Maximum.

That was exactly what had made Gilmore's suicide attempt possible. If they had kept Gilmore away from people, the drugs might never have passed through. Earl had spoken about that, but Smith said, "Oh, well, it hurts those boys in their rehabilitation if they can't have any physical contact with the outside world." From Earl's point of view, the Warden, if anything, erred on the side of benevolent administration and that was what got him into situations where people would call him incompetent.

In Earl's belief, the bottom line of Warden Smith's secret story was that he was all heart. Far from being strict or stern, Earl wondered how many Wardens got up early to go over and have breakfast in Medium Security with their inmates rather than take it with their own family. It was one reason Earl felt he had to protect Sam from all those newspaper suits to gain access to Gilmore.

The problem, which you could not explain to a newspaper man too easily or to a Judge either — not if it was Judge Ritter — was that tension in the prison often resulted from attention being focused on one inmate. He could get to be like a baseball star who wouldn't obey his manager. The risk of media exposure went deeper than Gilmore being able to shoot off his mouth — the risk was in the reaction of other inmates. Any time a convict became bigger than the prison, it had to create disciplinary episodes all over the place.

3

On December 1st, Earl sent off his petition for a Writ of Mandamus to the Tenth Circuit Court in Denver. Earl pointed out that Judge Ritter had made extensive findings of fact in the *Tribune* case when no evidence had been taken. Same morning he received a phone call from Leroy Axland, representing ABC News. Axland was going to file a suit in State Court tomorrow for a temporary restraining order like the *Tribune*'s, so ABC could also interview Gilmore.

Next morning, the *Deseret News* joined ABC in the action and Robert Moody appeared for Gary Gilmore. Even Larry Schiller was present. Plenty of legal power against Earl that day. He wasn't happy with his performance.

Earl's largest weakness, in his own eyes, stood out again. He started to cross-examine Lawrence Schiller, but got so mad that he could not keep composed. Schiller, right on the heels of having sneaked into the prison as a phony consultant, now had the gall to say on the stand that he had interviewed many inmates in many prisons and had always complied with the rules and regulations of the place. Earl knew he should walk the witness through a calm cross-examination, but became so angry he began to lead his own argument. With a little skill, he might have led Schiller to admit to stretching the rules at Utah State but got so angry, at thinking of how on the prison's side, there was all this sincerity and on his opponent's side blatant cynicism for the rights of others, that he started to harangue the man, and the Judge, Marcellus Snow, cut him off.

Earl was not surprised, therefore, when Judge Snow granted the restraining order. A TV interview with Gilmore would be conducted that evening.

MOODY   Okay. We've been in Court all day with Schiller, ABC-TV, and numerous attorneys. Judge Snow is signing an order permitting the press to interview tonight. Larry took the stand as a witness, and I think he's the one that convinced the Judge to let him go ahead.

GILMORE   Well, I imagine that the guy would do a pretty good job anywhere. He knows how to talk to anybody. . . . What time we do it?

MOODY   Beginning at nine.

GILMORE   I hope it ain't any later than that. Man, I get tired and like I wake up at five in the morning. . . . When you talk to some syndicate like ABC you got to be at your best. . . . Does Larry sit in a position that he can give me signals? If he doesn't want me to answer the question, just rub his chin, that's cool.

4

As soon as Earl got back from Judge Snow's court, he started writing another Mandamus. To his pleasure, when he looked up the State law, procedures were the same as for Federal. All he had to do was paper-doll the documents he'd written for Denver and put in new names. He had his secretary type it through lunch hour, and was ready to file appeal by early afternoon.

He went upstairs to the Utah Supreme Court Clerk, and told Chief Jusice Henriod that Judge Snow's order might not be ready until late afternoon and so if the Court didn't stay open past five, there would be no way to stop reporters from getting interviews with Gilmore tonight. It was not normal procedure, but Judge Henriod indicated he'd keep things going. Dorius said, "I'll run from Judge Snow's Court as fast as I can."

He did. But first he was obliged to go over a few other hurdles. Judge Snow's proposed order had been drafted by the news media lawyers and while Earl was arguing over a couple of their points, the Court Clerk handed him a note. Darn if the Tenth Circuit wasn't going to hear the Writ of Mandamus against Ritter tomorrow afternoon. Earl would have to make an appearance in Denver just when everything would be argued here.

On top of that, comes 4 P.M. Judge Snow decided to move the proceedings over to a big media room where he could broadcast his decision. That began to use up the clock. Finally, Dorius said to himself, "The Judge has signed the order, whether he had handed it out or not." He told an assistant to grab a signed copy as soon as he could, and Earl sprinted up the Hill to Utah Supreme Court.

Three Justices were sitting and they read his document, and granted a temporary Stay for this evening. The Mandamus, they said, could be argued tomorrow. That would stop TV from interviewing Gilmore tonight.

The corridors of the floor of the State Capitol Building were beginning to look like a political convention. Nothing but microphones, marble walls, TV lights. Earl gave a couple of interviews, then rushed downstairs to the Attorney General's office to start educating a couple of his fellow attorneys into what had to be done in Utah Supreme Court tomorrow. He had been handling all this material up to now.

5

That evening, at home, Dorius reminded himself that Gilmore's execution was probably only four days off. The sixth of December. If they could just keep the press out another four more days, the prison would be able to make its point. Reporters didn't go barging into a bank president's office to say, "Tell us what you know." But they couldn't comprehend that a Warden might h..ve the same interest in decorum.

Sam Smith called right on these thoughts to say that he appreciated the work Earl had done with force-feeding, but was going to wait awhile. Gilmore, at the moment, seemed in no danger of dying. In fact, fasting made him more feisty. He was throwing back his food trays at the guards. It was reassuring, therefore, Sam Smith said, to know they could force-feed if and when they had to. Wasn't a pleasant prospect to execute a man who hadn't had a meal in two weeks.

Earl went to sleep thinking that he would have to argue tomorrow against Donald Holbrook. The lawyer was a close friend of Earl's family, and had even bought his parents' house. He supposed that if there was any individual he idolized in his profession, it was Holbrook, who had a tremendous reputation in Salt Lake. Earl hoped he'd be worthy of the confrontation.

Next morning Earl got a phone call from his office. The largest kind of news. The United States Supreme Court had just put a Stay on Gary's execution. It seemed Gilmore's mother had filed a petition through Richard Giauque, and they were asking the Court to grant Certiorari. Mulling it over on the airplane, Earl didn't know if he was ready for this large a new development. The burden of working twelve and fourteen hours a day had certainly caught up. It annoyed him, for instance, that Holbrook was sitting in first class, and had plenty of room to spread out his legal documents, while Earl, a government servant, was jammed back in economy in these narrow seats. All the while he was trying to get his mind off the U.S. Supreme Court and onto today's work in Denver.

For that matter, the atmosphere in Tenth Circuit Court was awesome enough, but after a while Earl calmed down. He could see that no conclusion would be reached in Denver this day, since the *Tribune* was claiming favoritism had been shown to Schiller and Boaz by the prison. Earl thought that was a big mistake for the other side. It called for fact-finding which meant delay. Besides, Schiller had gotten in by misrepresenting himself to the guards, so the affidavits when gathered would weaken the newspaper's case. Earl flew back to Salt Lake feeling fairly good, but wondering how well he could take on the prodigious work to be done this weekend for the U.S. Supreme Court pleas. He would have to rally some very tired energies.

When he got in, he found out, however, that Bill Barrett had been assigned. Earl should just take a rest, he was told. He had earned it. Well, Dorius knew he needed the time off. What with the eighty-hour weeks he had been putting in, he was not in shape to tackle a brief of this dimension. All the same, he felt like he'd been left on a siding. The real momentous Supreme Court stuff would go roaring by.

6

STANGER   Gary, have you seen the petition for the Stay of Execution that has been filed by your mother?

GILMORE   I heard about it on the radio.

STANGER   The attorney is Richard Giauque. Remember that blond-haired guy from the ACLU who represented all the ministers and rabbis? Do you have any idea how he got to your mother?

GILMORE   I don't know. I'd like to talk to my mother. . . . Anything further on me getting to talk with Nicole?

STANGER   Yes. The hospital director, Kiger, called back about two hours ago. You've got his back up so tight, he won't move at all. What do you think about bringing some public pressure on him?

GILMORE   I think it's a damn good idea. That's why I haven't been eating. I was hoping that the hospital would be besieged with public pressure.

STANGER Yes.

GILMORE I'd like to shoot Kiger.

STANGER He's kind of weird.

GILMORE Well, all them doctors are weird. You ever met a psychiatrist who had all his marbles?

STANGER God, he's crazier than those he treats.

GILMORE You know I spent $160 today on canned foods and all kinds of different snacks and stuff like that and I have them locked in the cell next to me and as soon as I get my phone call to Nicole I'm going to have them open that cell. I've got a can opener and I'm going to have at it. Now, I'm a pretty hungry son of a gun and if you can do anything to facilitate that phone call . . . I'll accept whatever restrictions they want to put on it. But it's got to be a conversation, not a tape recording, and, uh, then I can go eat my food.

CHAPTER 13

Birthday

1

Two nights earlier, Schiller had arranged to meet Dave Johnston at the Salt Lake Airport. He wanted somebody besides himself to work on questions for Gilmore. Since Dave had been of help earlier in November, and then had done an agreeable piece for the *L.A. Times,* Schiller felt he might be the one available top-notch professional who was sympathetic to his purposes. Tonight, Johnston was coming in from San Francisco for the hearing next day where Schiller would appear, but for now he greeted Schiller with a big grin, and a list of the new questions in his hand.

Talking on the cab ride to the Hilton, it was obvious Johnston knew a lot about Salt Lake, so much in fact that Schiller was curious where Dave, who came from Michigan, and was now writing for a Los Angeles paper, got all this knowledge about Latter-Day Saints. But Johnston just gave a tough genial smile and said, "I'm a Mormon myself." It didn't surprise Schiller completely. He had already taken a peek at the questions, and one of them certainly stood out. "Do you fear what a reincarnated Benny Bushnell may do to you?" That might be a heavy Mormon concept. It stimulated Schiller to write the subsidiary question, "What do you believe will happen to you after death?"

Later that night, alone in his room, Schiller began to think of criticism he had run into a few years ago after making his film with Dennis Hopper, *The American Dreamer*. That had been a study of

Hopper's life, and the underground papers plus the *Village Voice* and *Rolling Stone* were all at the press showing. *Rolling Stone* even gave four full pages to the article. Their critic said the film was very good, but added that producer-director Schiller didn't understand an important side of Hopper. "Schiller went absolutely blank on Dennis Hopper's more mystical ideas."

What Larry called the Dennis Hopper light now went on in his head. Schiller didn't believe in heaven or hell, didn't think about it particularly. If you died, your soul, so to speak, ceased to function. He had an occasional moment when he thought about death, but didn't see himself going any place afterward. So, as he reread Johnston's questions, he kept saying, "There is a whole side of Gary Gilmore involving life after death. The guy really believes in it." Schiller shook his head. A whole other side of the coin. For the first time it hit him that Gilmore might want to go all the way. Up to then he had assumed Gilmore would accept his execution because he was a proud con trapped in a role. Now he understood that Gary might expect to find something on the other side. Not only willing to gamble on it, but gamble everything. It must be, Schiller thought, the way he sometimes felt shooting craps when he knew he was coming up with a seven. Yes, Schiller decided, that was close to feeling like Gilmore. Sometimes, just before rolling, he could see the seven on the cloth. But this kind of thinking left Schiller disturbed. He preferred not to deal with ideas too far out of his own domain. It might be that he would need help. The thought came to him of hiring Barry Farrell, and he put it off for further reflection. Time enough to decide when he saw how Barry had written about him in *New West*.

Next day, after Court, Schiller heard the first tape Moody and Stanger had done with Gary. He was not encouraged. Moody and Stanger looked like they were developing a rapport with their client, but it might have nothing to do with journalism. Just legal discussions, and man-to-man jokes. Not in a rush to touch charged subjects. So Schiller decided not to insert Dave Johnston's ten questions and his own twenty or more into the lawyers' next interview with Gary, but instead would ask for handwritten replies. On the basis of those few letters to Nicole printed in the *Deseret News*, Schiller thought Gilmore took pains in his writing.

2

WHY DID YOU KILL JENSEN AND BUSHNELL?

There is so much similarity between Jenkins and Bushnell: both mid 20's in age, both family men, both Mormon missionaries. Perhaps the murders of these men were meant to occur.

To answer your question:

I killed Jenkins and Bushnell because I did not want to kill Nicole.

WAS BUSHNELL A COWARD? WHAT DID HE SAY?

No, I wouldn't say Mr. Bushnell was a coward. He did <u>not</u> seem a coward. I remember he was anxious to comply. But I don't remember anything he said except he asked me to be quiet and not alert his wife who was in the next room.

He was calm, even brave.

DO YOU WISH YOU HAD NOT KILLED BUSHNELL?

Yes.

Wish I hadn't killed Jenkins, too.

DID JENSEN RESIST AND DID JENSEN SHOW FEAR?

Jenkins did not resist.

He did not show undue fear.

I was struck by his friendly, smiling, kind face.

DID JENSEN AND BUSHNELL DIE LIKE MEN? LIKE YOU WANT TO DO?

They showed no more fear than you'd expect from a man being robbed.

I'm almost certain they didn't know they were going to die until it was done.

DO YOU RECALL ANY FILMS OR NEWS REELS IN WHICH YOU'VE SEEN MEN DIE BEFORE A FIRING SQUAD?

Private Slovak —

Sure said a lot of Hail Marys, didn't he?

IF YOU HAD A CHOICE, WOULD YOUR EXECUTION BE ON TELEVISION?

No.

Too macabre.

Would you like your death televised?

At the same time, I really don't give a shit.

WHAT DO YOU BELIEVE WILL HAPPEN TO YOU AFTER DEATH?

I could speculate, but I don't know — if the knowledge of death is within me, as I believe it is, I can't consciously bring it to the surface.

I just think it will be familiar . . . I must keep my mind singular and strong — In death you can choose in a way that you can't choose in life. The biggest mistake you could make when you die is to be afraid.

DO YOU FEAR WHAT A REINCARNATED BENNY BUSHNELL MAY DO TO YOU?

I have pondered that — But I don't fear it. Fuck fear. I may meet Bushnell — if I do, I will never avoid him. I recognize his rights.

WHY DID YOU KILL, AND COULD YOU HAVE STOPPED YOURSELF FROM KILLING IF YOU WANTED?

I never felt so terrible as I did in that week before I was arrested. I had lost Nicole. It hurt so fucking bad that it was becoming physical — I mean I couldn't hardly walk, I couldn't sleep I didn't hardly eat. I couldn't drown it. Booze didn't even dull it. A heavy hurt and loss. It got worse every day. I could feel it in my heart . . . I could feel the ache in my bones. I had to go on automatic to get thru the day.

And it grew into a calm rage.

And I opened the gate and let it out.

But it wasn't enough.

It would have gone on and on.

More Jenkins, more Bushnells.

Lord . . .

It didn't make any sense —

Gary said over the phone to Vern, "Some of this is getting too damned personal."

Vern replied, "If you don't want to answer, just tell him. He's not going to twist your arm."

"Yeah, I know," Gary said, "but I still don't like the questions."

"Say," said Stanger, reading the replies. "It's Jensen, not Jenkins."

"Did I say Jenkins? Dammit," said Gary, "I hate getting his name wrong."

"That's fantastic stuff," said Stanger when he brought the answers to Schiller. "Don't you think?"

"I'm not so sure," said Schiller. "He's still giving it off the top."

The last answer had been interesting, but many of the others were flat.

HOW DID YOU FEEL WHEN YOU GOT YOUR SENTENCE? WAS IT FAIR?
I probably felt less than anyone in the courtroom.

HOW WOULD YOU DESCRIBE YOUR PERSONALITY?
Slightly less than bland.

YOUR GREATEST ACCOMPLISHMENT?

He had not answered that one. Blank space was there to look back at Schiller. Gilmore was still selling himself as a tough con, heartless, no weakness. Shooting down targets. Schiller wanted to get beyond these cold con answers. It wasn't much warmth to find in a man on his birthday.

3

DESERET NEWS

Utah Slayer, Now 36, Still Wants to Die

Point of the Mountain, Dec. 4 — Condemned killer, Gary Mark Gilmore, still professing his wish to die, observed his 36th birthday in the Utah State Prison today.

Gibbs got Big Jake to buy him a card, and sent it to Gary. It read, "I hope you have many more happy birthdays." He knew that would hit Gary's funny bone.

Brenda and Johnny had a birthday visit on the phone. "Hey, cousin," she said, "did you know that you are the most notorious convict in the United States? That's what they said about you last night." He answered in a strained little voice, "I would much rather be acclaimed on my art ability and my intelligence." It was his hungry stomach speaking. He sounded like an empty eggshell. "I don't appreciate this kind of publicity," he complained.

Brenda said to herself, "Maybe Gary don't like the publicity, but he's sure enjoying it."

Gary had given Vern a list of names and the amount of money he wanted each person to receive. Brenda was to get $5,000, and Toni $3,000. Gary also gave $5,000 to Sterling and Ruth Ann. Wanted to give $3,000 to the baby-sitter Laurel and her family, but Vern gave an argument about that.

Then Gary talked about a couple of girls in Hawaii who had been writing him love letters. He wanted to send them a few hundred dollars. Vern agreed, but never withdrew the money. Figured about the time Gary had given it all away, he'd be happy to discover a few hundred left. Of course the way Gary handed it out, was enough to make you sick.

There was a convict out in the midwest named Ed Barney. Gary got a letter from him one day and told Vern he'd known the guy at Oregon State. They'd put a lot of time in Segregation together. "Ed Barney is a great guy," said Gary. "One of my very best and dearest friends. I want you to give him a thousand dollars." Vern thought Gary was talking like his mother. When Vern first knew her, Bessie could never describe a good-looking man or woman without getting carried away by the power of the description. At the end she would always say, "That was the best-looking man I ever saw." Or, best-looking woman. Must have described a hundred people that way. Gary was the same about friends. Today, Sterling was the best friend he ever had. Yesterday, LeRoy Earp, or Vince Capitano, or Steve Kessler, or John Mills or many another prison buddy Vern couldn't even keep in mind. Tomorrow you knew another fellow would be nominated. Gibbs, probably. So, Vern decided to hold on to the award to Ed Barney. With the way they kept delaying his execution, Gary would be broke before he knew it. A few thousand dollars could buy him a lot of comfort in prison.

Vern did, however, have to give $2,000 to Gibbs. Gary was insistent. Then, there was another fellow named Fungoo. Gary said he'd hurt the man's feelings something awful with a tattoo he had drawn once. He wanted to give him a sum. Vern had a hell of an argument. Finally talked him out of that.

Then there was the mystery recipient. A particular fellow was to receive a total of $5,000 in two equal installments. Vern was to meet him on the street corner and hand over $2,500. Gary said he wanted the job done *without argument*. Vern had a pretty good idea what was up. He finally had a meeting with the fellow, and gave over the money in a restaurant, hated the idea. A wanton waste. Was glad when Gary never paid the second installment.

Now, on his birthday, Gary wanted to give $500 to Margie Quinn. "Margie Quinn?" asked Vern. "You know," said Gary, "that nice little girl Ida introduced me to." "Well, why do you want to give her $500?" asked Vern. "Well," said Gary, mimicking the way Vern said "well," which was always very soft as if he wanted to draw you close, "well, I happened to break the windshield on her car."

Vern wasn't too surprised. "I thought you did, you dirty bugger," he said. He remembered how Margie Quinn's mother had asked him months ago if Gary had done it, and Vern replied, "I don't know. He may have." That was $500 Vern didn't mind paying.

From time to time, Gary would say, "See that my mother is taken care of," yet he didn't talk of real money. It seemed to Vern that Gary wanted to believe his mother did love him a great deal and worked with the evidence pro and con. Yet he must have kept turning on that evidence, for he sure was acting stingy toward her. Vern actually had to say, "You can't give $3,000 to your baby-sitter when your mother is living without money." "All right," Gary answered, "cut it down. Take a thousand off. Give that to my ma." Then he would hesitate. "But don't mail it," he would say, "you and Aunt Ida fly down and give it to her in person." Vern couldn't understand. If Gary was afraid somebody might rip it off, he could have a bank in Portland deliver the thousand by special messenger. Good Lord, it would practically cost half that much for Ida and him to fly there and back. Brenda got into the act. "Just a thousand, Gary?" she asked. "Yep," said Gary. Brenda gave her father a look to say, "No sense going further."

Vern thought Gary might be provoked at his mother because of the Supreme Court Stay, but then he recollected that even before Gary heard of Bessie's legal actions, he had never included her in the money to be given out.

4

On Sunday, Bob Moody and Ron Stanger were interviewed by TV people from Holland, England, and a couple of other countries. Then they went to the country club for lunch. Then out to the prison.

GILMORE Hey, uh, maybe the *Tribune* would print an open letter to my mother.

STANGER I don't see any doubt about that.

GILMORE I'll make it brief, if you want to take it down.

STANGER Go ahead.

GILMORE Dear Mom. I love you deeply and I always have and I always will. (pause) But please disassociate yourself from the Uncle Tom NAACP. Please accept the fact that I wish to be dead. That I accept it. That I accept it.

MOODY Do you want to put "That I accept it" more than once?

GILMORE Please accept the fact that I want, that I accept death. What's a better way of saying that? Please accept this.

MOODY Maybe, please accept the fact that I accept that which has been imposed upon me by law, is that what you're trying to say?

GILMORE Yeah. That would be all right. I don't want it to look like a death wish by saying I wish for death.

MOODY I just accept what the law is.

STANGER Carry out the law.

GILMORE Uh, I would like to talk to you. I'd like to see you. But I can't, so I'm sending you this letter through the newspaper. (long pause) We all die, it ain't no big deal.

MOODY Is this in the letter?

GILMORE Yeah. (long pause) Sometimes it's right and proper. (pause) Please, disassociate yourself from that Uncle Tom NAACP. I'm a white man. The NAACP disgusts me that they even dare associate theirself with me or that they dare even, or that they dare anything. Well, read that to me and I'll think of what I want to say. . . . Uh, I could have made a few disparaging remarks about niggers but I do have a few black friends you know, and, uh, very few. But, the NAACP ain't among them. I mean they're so goddamned phony. Do you know anything about the NAACP?

STANGER Oh yes.

GILMORE Every spook I know hates them.

MOODY Is that right?

GILMORE Yeah, just like they hate Martin Luther King because he was such a pacifist, you know. The NAACP, they're nonmilitant, they're passive. They're very wealthy people that run it.

MOODY What do you think the average black man would like?

GILMORE Just some watermelon and some wine.

The prison had moved Gary back to the hospital and today they could not see him, only hear his voice over the telephone. It sounded acidulous. "Black people," he said, "learn by rote more than anything else. You show them how to do something, and they can do it." He paused as if imparting valuable information. "On the whole continent of Africa, they never found the wheel or anything more deadly than a spear. That's what I think of black people. It ain't a hatred, just fact. I don't care if one guy did something with some peanuts a long time ago."

Ron could feel the growling in Gary's empty gut and the hatred coming through the telephone wires. A dark side of Gilmore was running like a current into his ear. Man, he had an evil nature when he felt like it. Stanger was very happy at this moment that he had never belonged to the NAACP or the ACLU.

5

On her visits, Kathryne would tell Nicole that Gary had intended for her to die, not him. Nicole would think that it could be true. Gary didn't ever want her with another man. Still, it couldn't change her feelings. It wasn't like he had been trying to do it cynically. He would certainly have followed in the near future. So Kathryne's accusations never bothered Nicole. She just wanted to see Gary.

It was making her crazy not to be able to have a phone call or a letter. Sometimes she'd think of getting ahold of a gun. She would tell them if they didn't let her talk to Gary, she would blow her head off.

Ken Sundberg, who had been retained by Kathryne at Phil Christensen's advice, brought Nicole a letter. It was the first word from Gary since she had taken the pills. He just told her not to let the place get to her. Didn't talk about death or dying. Only wrote about how much he loved her. Later, Nicole found out that Sundberg, who was a nice fellow but an uptight Mormon, had agreed to bring in the envelope provided Gary made no reference to suicide at all.

After Nicole finished reading, she wrote a couple of lines at the bottom, and sent it back. Then, she got an idea. Everybody was accustomed to see her writing poems in her notebook, so for Gary's birthday she wrote a letter instead, tore it out when no one was looking, put it in her shoe and slipped it to Ken.

At the top she had written December second, but put a question mark after it. She was uncertain of the date. Beneath it, therefore, she wrote, *Wednesday nite*. Later she found out it was Thursday night.

Gary
   i love you. More than life.
   i think about you constantly. You never leave my mind.
   Before i got your letter i felt as if i was only half alive not knowing how you were. They won't tell me nothin here. When i awoke in U.V. hospital i was only told that you had also awaken. i tryed callen you then — Next thing i knew i was being escorted here. And here is like being buried alive. Cut off from life. You. Oh, Baby, i miss you —
   i've read your letter every chance i get. Your words touch my soul.
   i love you

As you said in your letter, you do not need my life for yourself.
i am yours through all things and time. All Things and Times. i
was thinking of the best nite we had . . . that was a nite of ecstacy
and Love more tender than mere words can speak on. I call it Sweet
Apprehension.

I despise this place. This place despises me. it is all you said it to
be. Sheep, rats.
Darlin lites are out. i can jest barely see these lines.
Touch my soul with your truth . . .

Forevermore
NICOLE

CHAPTER 14

The Next Friend and the Foe

1

Mikal had not spoken to his brother since that moment in Court four
years ago when Gary was sentenced to nine more years in jail, but he
heard his name often enough these days. Ever since November 1, the
syllables of Ga-Ry Gil-More came in over the radio with increasingly
hypnotic interest in the voice of the announcer, and the leads on top
of news stories leaped out from the paper until they were front-page
headlines. It wasn't far into November before Mikal made a phone
call to Utah State Prison.

On the line, Gary was perfunctory. He spoke tersely. Mikal was
informed that Gary had just hired a lawyer named Dennis Boaz and
would appear with him at the Utah Supreme Court next morning. At
that time he would ask for the execution to be carried out.

"Are you serious?" Mikal asked.

"What do you think?"

"I don't know."

"You never knew me," said Gary.

Mikal could only request Gary to ask Dennis Boaz to give a ring.
That night the lawyer called and brought Mikal up to date on a few
details, but it was not much of a conversation. As soon as the Utah
Supreme Court made its decision, Mikal asked, would Boaz phone
again?

"Is it okay if I call collect?" said Dennis, "I'm a poor man."

Boaz never did call. Mikal learned the outcome by watching TV. When Mikal phoned Boaz to complain, the lawyer said he'd been swarmed with calls. When Mikal wanted to know where Boaz had practiced in California, Dennis said he found Mikal's attitude "belligerent." After that call, Mikal had to recognize that Gary had cut the family off. He decided to wait.

A few days later, a lawyer named Anthony Amsterdam phoned Bessie to express his interest in the case, and said he would soon be talking to her son. Mikal was ready, therefore, when the call came.

2

He had already looked into Amsterdam's credentials. They certainly seemed prestigious. The man was a professor of law at Stanford University and an expert on capital punishment. A friend of Mikal's who was going to law school said Amsterdam had won a famous Supreme Court case called *Furman v. Georgia* which showed that black prisoners on Death Row were being executed in numbers far out of proportion to white prisoners with the same sentences. The case had produced a landmark decision by the Supreme Court that ruled out capital punishment for a while.

Over the phone, Tony Amsterdam now explained to Mikal that he was associated with an organization called the Legal Defense Fund and they had contacts with a nationwide network of lawyers willing to cooperate on death cases. When one of these situations took off, Amsterdam usually heard about it from several sources. In the last couple of weeks, he had certainly heard quite a bit from Utah. There had been an early call from Craig Snyder to "inform" him of the problem, and another from a prominent Salt Lake attorney named Richard Giauque. In the last few days, half a dozen lawyers he respected had gotten in touch to say the case was shocking. So Amsterdam thought it might be time to get in touch with Bessie Gilmore.

He had been, he said, considerably affected by that conversation. Bessie Gilmore had impressed him as a person of great strength who was in great pain. One had to respect the spiritual and psychic stress of this ungodly situation. He told Mikal that he believed his mother would welcome a little help, but was not yet certain she wanted to assert herself in Gary's case. So she had asked him to discuss it with her youngest son.

Mikal knew this exposition was accurate, since Bessie had told him much the same, although with some suspiciousness of strangers calling. In turn, Mikal spoke to Amsterdam of his concern that people interested in abolishing capital punishment might not care about Gary so much as they were looking for an ideological ax to grind.

Amsterdam answered that he was not about to subordinate Gary's interest to the service of ideology. He was not a man to sacrifice the individual for abstract issues. However, he said, there was a limit to how much you could or even wanted to convince somebody over the phone. If Mikal was willing to talk further, Amsterdam would like to meet him.

Mikal was not unimpressed, but said he wanted to discuss the matter with his mother and sleep on it. In the meantime, he was curious how much the fees might come to. Amsterdam explained that his practice was exclusively pro bono. He accepted no fees. In fact, he would write into the retainer that all services were to be rendered free of cost of any sort.

They agreed to speak again two days later.

Over the period, Bessie came to think it would be a good idea to retain Amsterdam. She liked, she said, the voice of this man very much. She could feel confidence in it. Next morning she heard of Gary and Nicole's suicide attempt.

Mikal phoned the prison a few days later and Gary was in a terrible temper. He had just fired Boaz. Hoping this might prove an opening, Mikal said that the affair had become a circus. It was taking away any claim Gary could have to dignity. It was also wreaking its toll on the family. The last remark was a mistake. "What do I owe you?" Gary snapped. "I don't even think of you as a brother."

"You're running," said Mikal, "over a lot of people's lives."

Gary hung up. Mikal brooded about it. After a day or two, he

decided to authorize Anthony Amsterdam to take action on Bessie
Gilmore's behalf.

3

Amsterdam laid out to Mikal the moves he proposed to make. He was
going to ask them to consider a Next Friend petition. They were
going to claim that Mikal's mother was acting on behalf of an individual who was not able to protect his own interest. That gave them a
right to sue the State of Utah. Next Friend was just a legal term to
indicate closeness to the person on whose behalf they were suing. It
did not have to be next of kin, but as a practical matter, that was
good, since a Court would be more sympathetic to the idea if the
Next Friend wasn't a crank or meddler, but, in fact, a close relative.

Discussing the brief he would file, Tony Amsterdam said he
must touch upon a delicate point. In his opinion, Gary was a sick
man and not acting in a competent manner. The fact that he'd been
certified as sane came to no more than three form reports turned in
by three form shrinks writing three form conclusions. It didn't tell
you a goddamned thing. Even then, the doctors couldn't ignore the
fact that Gary was suicidal. Having talked to Craig Snyder, Amsterdam would judge that discharging a competent lawyer, when you are
under a death sentence, is a form of suicide in itself. Gary had raised
questions about free will and self-determination, but wasn't the situation analogous to watching a distraught woman getting ready to
jump off the San Francisco Bay Bridge? These were strong words to
use, and he certainly would not speak in this fashion to Bessie Gilmore, but he wanted to underline that the question of whether Gary
was mentally competent had not been satisfactorily settled.

Such incompetence, however, was not going to be the foundation of the suit. There were two other very important elements. Gary,
in these recent dramatic days, had been receiving his legal advice
from Dennis Boaz who was writing about this damn thing. If Gilmore
became the first man to be executed in ten years, Boaz had a great
deal to gain. That would also be true of the lawyers now retained by
the uncle, Vern Damico. For that matter, the uncle was in the same

position. Gary had not been and was still not being advised adequately. Even if he was mentally sound, he was still a layman making a legal decision to kill himself without the benefit of unbiased legal advice.

Then there was a third point. When Gary appeared before the Utah Supreme Court, the proceedings had failed to satisfy what the United States Supreme Court had said, over and over again, was a necessary procedure for a defendant to follow if he wanted to waive any important rights.

Amsterdam said he was offering this advisedly. It was not a matter of his bias or his opinion, but *advisedly*. These Utah Supreme Court Judges were not trial Judges. They were not accustomed to warning people and making proper trial records. They were an Appellate Court and, in this case, they did it all wrong. The proceeding failed by a country mile to measure up to U.S. Supreme Court standards.

Following this conversation, events moved quickly. Amsterdam needed a lawyer in Utah to file the Next Friend petition in the Supreme Court and chose Richard Giauque. Next thing Mikal knew, the Supreme Court had granted the Stay. It all seemed to happen overnight.

4

By Monday, December 6, Earl was feeling the benefit of a weekend without work, and went to the prison and took affidavits from the guards who let Schiller in, and flew them to Denver. Next day, the Tenth Circuit Court granted the Writ of Mandamus against Ritter, and the media was again barred from contact with Gary. Even though Bill Barrett had just sent off the Attorney General's brief to the Supreme Court, and office talk was all about that, Earl still felt the day was a high point for him. He had won a case against Holbrook.

It was now Bill Barrett's turn to be exhausted. The answer to the Supreme Court had had to be filed by 5 P.M. Tuesday, December 7. There had only been four days and two hours to get the job done.

That Friday evening, four days ago, Barrett had called all available law clerks into his office, sat them down, and said, "Let's divide this thing up." He broke the issues down, assigned them out, and everybody proceeded to work his tail off. It was a little tricky in the beginning because they hadn't seen Giauque's papers yet, but they did read the brief Giauque had submitted to George Latimer at the Board of Pardons and it looked like mental incompetency would be the brunt of the attack. "*Allowing a defendant to waive judicial review of a death sentence,*" Giauque had said in that brief,

. . . is tantamount to committing suicide. The Talmud, Aristotle, Augustine, and Aquinas all characterize suicide as a grievous private and public wrong. At common law, suicide was held as a felony, and was attended by forfeiture of property and burial on the highway. . . . A criminal defendant such as Gilmore, who declines to pursue legal proceedings which could save his life is, in fact, choosing to commit suicide, and the overwhelming majority of psychiatric opinion regards the impulse to suicide as a form of mental illness.

Barrett never computed how many hours were expended that weekend. He was afraid to. All through Saturday and Sunday, law clerks came in while others went home, and Monday, three of them stayed up all night to prepare the final draft. Next morning they distributed the typing among four secretaries. It got so close to the deadline, they had to contact Michael Rodak, the Supreme Court Clerk, to tell him they couldn't get it to D.C. in time by air.

Arrangements were made instead with Senator Garn's office. Law clerks started shuttling pages down to his office five blocks away, and using his telecopier to get it to Washington. Into the brief, they had thrown everything, including — Barrett was sure he could find it — the kitchen sink, but the main emphasis was that Bessie Gilmore did not have the authority to act on behalf of her son. It was his case, not hers.

Whereas, the other side, sure enough, was arguing that Gary was mentally incompetent, and that gave Mrs. Gilmore the right to step in. It was one heavy issue. It worried Bill Barrett. Since the attempted suicide on November 16, no psychiatrist had assessed Gilmore. So there was, at present, no solid base for the condemned man's sanity or lack of it. Between the 7th of December, when they handed it in, and Monday, the 13th, when the Supreme Court was likely to come back with an answer, there would be lots of time for worry.

Still, through these days of waiting, Barrett reread the four-day brief, and felt pretty good about certain sections:

All suicides aren't pathological or an indication of incompetence. The U.S. Supreme Court in the recent case of Drope vs. Missouri, 420 U.S. 162 (1975) noted:

". . . the empirical relationship between mental illness and suicide is uncertain and a suicide attempt need not always signal 'an inability to perceive reality accurately.'" 420 U.S. at 181.

Mr. Gilmore had sufficient experience of prison life to estimate . . . what it would be like for him to languish in prison. Historical, religious, and existential treatises suggest that for some persons at some times, it is rational not to avoid physical death at all costs. Indeed the spark of humanity can maximize its essence by choosing an alternative that preserves the greatest dignity and some tranquility of mind.

CHAPTER 15

Family Lawyers

1

Schiller had been going over finances to see what he would require for releases, motel and hotel bills, stenographers, and office equipment, and decided he was going to need another $60,000 above ABC's contribution. There was only one way to raise that. Acquire Gary's letters to Nicole and sell them.

The ethics, however, as far as Schiller was concerned, were a trade-off. After all, he had trusted Gilmore. He had turned over a $52,000 check in one shot, a dramatic way of showing that he would not dole out the money. Schiller had his reasons. He didn't want everybody to keep thinking of David Susskind. Once Gary's lawyers could call the bank and know the check was good, they would be ready to see Larry Schiller as a big businessman, not a small one. This was his sensible motive. He also had what he called his romantic motive. Romanticism, after all, turned him on, songs like "The Impossible Dream," and the lyrics of *Oklahoma* and *Carousel,* "The Sound of Music" with the Alps in the background. So he wanted to show that he wasn't trying to out-con a con, but instead was delivering his best thing, was saying, "I'm smart enough not to try to feed you a hundred dollars a week. I don't want to put your mind onto thinking how to outfox me. I want to deal with you, the man. The money is only *mechanics.* Here it is, up front. You can rip me off now, but you won't because I trust you. A nice businessman in an office will cheat me faster than you."

That was Schiller's unvoiced address to Gary Gilmore. He said it in his head several times a day. He knew it was a logic Gilmore could recognize.

On his side, Gilmore was certainly being unreasonable about the letters. They were intrinsic to the transaction, and as far as Schiller was concerned, part of his capital. So he felt no compunction about acquiring them however he could. At the end of the first week in December, he went over to see Moody and Stanger, and explained what he wanted.

They replied that they did not know how to obtain them.

Now, Larry lost his temper with the lawyers for the first time. "Don't give me that," he yelled. "You're Gary Gilmore's attorneys. You just ask Noall Wootton to turn them over. Do you mean to say this state has no laws of discovery? You're allowed a copy of everything the prosecution is holding against your client."

It was getting to Schiller that Stanger, in particular, had not done anything. Not only had he not picked up the letters, but he had done nothing about getting a transcript of Gary's trial. Gary didn't want a transcript, Stanger replied.

This had nothing to do with Gary's defense, Schiller explained. It concerned the book and the movie. How could you do the trial without a transcript? Besides, Schiller pointed out, they had a legal duty to perform. What if Gary changed his mind and wanted to appeal? If they had no transcript, and were not familiar with Snyder and Esplin's notes, they could lose a crucial week. A man's life might be lost. He got hysterical in his indignation. "I want you guys to get on the goddamned phone," he said, "and start pulling things together." He could see they didn't like it one bit, but they also knew that any additional money further down the road was going to come from him.

Schiller couldn't get over the way these lawyers worked. Wootton had never bothered to transcribe the trial. What if the Supreme Court of the United States needed the record? A little later, Moody's secretary called back to say that the legal stenographer thought the job would cost $600. "I'll pay for it," said Schiller, "don't worry." What was more important was that Wootton agreed to turn over the originals of the letters if they would provide him with a set of Xeroxes. So Stephanie went over as Moody's messenger and picked the lot up.

After Larry looked them over, he estimated that Gary must have written through August, September, October, and November, up to the suicide attempt, an average of ten pages a day. Quite a few letters actually went on for twenty of those big, yellow office-pad pages. The total had to be well over a thousand pages. He just skimmed. He could see Gilmore was writing about everything. One place he'd give Nicole a college education with essays on Michelangelo and Van Gogh, in another, pages of fuck talk. Must be tons of meat and potatoes in those envelopes. Schiller figured that he would need at least six complete copies, one for Wootton, one for himself, one for the future writer of the book, and at least three others for sale in different places. He called the main office of Xerox in Denver and asked about the fastest machine they had, and who might have it. He was prepared to fly Stephie to Denver, Dallas, San Francisco, wherever, when damn if they didn't tell him that right in Provo, the Press Publishing Company had just such a machine. Right in fucking Provo. A Christmas card company. Schiller shook his head. Sometimes these things happen.

Obviously he was not going to tell a Christmas card company that Gary Gilmore was what he intended to use their machine for. He merely asked to rent the machine from eleven at night until three in the morning, and used Moody and Stanger as references. Stephie and he went in with a man from the plant and it ended up taking six and a half hours.

There was magnitude to the job. Gary's letters were so carefully folded, it was unbelievable. One small white prison envelope might hold a dozen legal-sized pages. Gary had not only folded the sheets that closely, but Nicole maintained the folds. Schiller began to feel the relationship of Gary and Nicole in the way those letters had been opened and put back, opened and put back.

Later, when he had a chance to read more, Schiller began to feel a little security. Even if the Supreme Court took back their stay and Gary was executed in a week or so, these letters still offered the love story. He not only had the man's reason for dying but Romeo and Juliet, and life after death. It might even be enough for a screenwriter.

The next problem was where to sell some of them. The *National Enquirer* had made a firm offer for sixty grand to Scott Meredith, but Schiller was debating whether he should offer a package to *Time* instead. He could probably get no more than a third as much, but at that price, Schiller liked *Time*. It was not only the prestige. In essence, *Time* magazine was a sales letter printed everywhere in the world. Gilmore's importance would be amplified internationally. That alone could pick up the $40,000 difference.

All the while, he was playing with the *Enquirer* on the side. Their offer had gone from sixty to sixty-five. Schiller needed more money the way a farmer without a tractor needs a tractor, but he hated how the *Enquirer* would cheapen the property. In the interval, *Time* looked like they might even go to $25,000.

Then he got the idea to sell an in-depth Gary Gilmore interview to *Playboy*. That ought to be worth another twenty. Splicing the rope with *Time* and *Playboy*, plus the ABC money already spent, plus whatever he could pick up in Europe by selling the letters ought to come to more than a hundred thousand total. That should be enough to take care of all expenses, past and pending.

2

The lawyers, however, were having their difficulties. Schiller's admission to the press that he was a Hollywood producer had turned everything around at the prison. Sam Smith said he was going to see that nobody profited from the execution of Gary Gilmore. "Not while I'm Warden." He began to put a lot of restrictions on the visits.

When they talked to Gary these days, there was always a guard present. The lawyers would put down the phone and refuse to talk until the guard got the hell out of there. Sometimes the fellow would go to the opposite end of the room, but then, you had to be paranoid that the phones were bugged. It was hell talking around a corner to a client whose face you couldn't see. One day, Moody even went to the mat with Sam Smith over his right to tape-record visits with Gary. "For executing his Will," complained Bob, "I have to record his re-

marks in case he changes his mind." He knew the argument was a
waste of time, but he did it to keep pressure off the unauthorized tape
recordings he was already making. They were difficult enough at
best. You had to sneak the machine into the prison under your coat,
and then there was the apprehension that a guard could notice the
little rubber recording cap that had been slipped onto the earpiece of
the phone. Discovery would leave them professionally embarrassed.
Of course, the Bar Association hadn't done anything with Boaz and
probably wouldn't start up with them, but all the same, if you valued
your reputation this became one more uncertainty to carry around.
Other times, the guards would try to inspect their attaché cases as
they walked in. Then they would have to put on a real show. They
were Gilmore's laywers, and their briefcases were not to be touched!
It meant they had to psych themselves up every time they came to
the prison gate.

One occasion, Ron got into a hell of a fight with Sam Smith. "I'm
going to interview my client the way I want," Ron told him, "and
you're not going to tell me how to do it." "Look," said Smith, "this is
my prison." Ron said, "Piss on that." He started yelling. Smith tried
to calm him down. "Now, Ron," he said, "now Ron," said Sam, and
Ron answered, "Bullshit, you're not going to tell me how to conduct
an interview. I've got to have a record. If my man gets executed, and
somebody sues, I want these talks on record. I'm going to handle my
client the way I want." "Well," said Sam Smith, "you're going to have
to go to Federal Court to find out if you have that right." Ron said,
"Buddy, if I have to, I'm going."

It was a hell of a yelling match, and got them nowhere. The
Warden would never tell you what you could or couldn't do. He
would just say, when asked, that it was against policy. Ron even had
a go with Ernie Wright, the Director of Corrections. Ron was one of
the five members of the State Building Board, and that was real leverage. Any time the prison needed a new facility or, hell, even a new
shed, they had, like any other State institution, to get permission
from the State Building Board. So, Ron had had a day-to-day acquaintance with Sam and Ernie for some time. On this one, however,
he ran into a wall. Ernie Wright finally said, "No movie producer is
going to make one dime out of Gilmore. It's not fair. We're the ones
who take the criticism, and nobody is going to make any money out
of this." It got as emotional as that.

"Where is it against policy?" Bob would ask. "In which book?"

"Oh, it isn't written," Ernie Wright said just like Sam, "it's just prison policy."

Moody and Stanger discovered they could get a lot more done by working with Assistant Wardens and Lieutenants. The two prison Chaplains were also useful. Campbell, the Mormon, was fighting the prison half the time, so you could expect him to become frustrated and walk around in a pout with a tight steely face. But, the other Chaplain, the Catholic, Father Meersman, was an old boy, and he would tell the lawyers, "Butter 'em up. Don't ask whether you can or can't. Just go as far as you can. When they cut you off, try some other time." Father Meersman had worked in the prison for years and en- joyed a smooth relationship, a pleasant-faced man, gray-haired man, not tall, not short, not heavy, not slim, moderate in every one of his physical details. "Just say, 'whatever is fair, Warden, whatever's fair.' "

Of course, Gary could get caustic about Father Meersman. "The padre," he said to Moody and Stanger one day, "gave me a cross to die with. Specially made. Fits in the palm of your hand. That papist prick ought to be a used-car salesman."

Moody also got a little pressure in Mormon circles. He was a member of the High Council, one of twelve Elders to advise the Pres- ident of his Stake in Provo, but now and then words would come back that some people thought he should be kicked off the High Council for accepting blood money. On the other hand, Church members in good standing would say, "You're doing a fine job. We admire you for that." Half and half.

Moody brushed it off. It was like the flak he took when he de- fended one man for killing another while driving under the influence of alcohol. "How could you do that?" he was asked, "You're a Mor- mon. You don't drink." Some Church people didn't understand the system or his role in it.

Still, it wasn't all bad. By this time, Ron Stanger could hardly wait to get home and catch himself on the tube. He frankly enjoyed the publicity more than Moody. Bob wasn't so much in love with his bald head that he wanted to rush over to see his image, but the kids liked it. "There's Daddy," they'd scream. Fun to see them having pleasure. And, of course, at the courthouse and on the street, everybody was asking how they were doing, everybody said they saw them on TV. It was a good feeling for Moody to run into attorneys he had gone to school with, who were now, perhaps, making more money than him, and be able to chat about the case. On the whole, he felt relaxed. Gilmore hurt his practice, and helped it. Changed it. Moody liked to think of himself as a man who wasn't paralyzed by the idea of change.

3

GILMORE   You tell Larry Schiller I want that phone call to Nicole. I'm sure that Schiller can put pressure on people if he wants to.

STANGER   Larry's quite a mover, all right.

GILMORE   You guys have made some moves, but it hasn't been enough, I haven't gotten the phone call.

STANGER   It hasn't been successful.

GILMORE   Man, I've gone sixteen days without eating, and I'll go forever. I'll do whatever I have to do to get that phone call. If it takes a bribe, pay it. I don't give a shit what it takes . . . I want to talk to Nicole and I don't know if I'll be cooperative with anybody until I do. I guess that sounds like an ultimatum. I don't know if I have the right to ask you to arrange a phone call in order to get answers to these questions, but I guess that's what I'm doing.

STANGER   You've got a right to ask what you want, Gary.

GILMORE   I want to talk to Nicole.

As soon as the lawyers returned to Provo with a tape, Schiller, if he was in town, would come over to their office to make a copy immediately. That gave him an opportunity to listen in the lawyers' presence. When Gary now said, "Arrange a phone call," Schiller turned to Moody and remarked, "Come on, does he think I'm going to give somebody twenty-five dollars?" Moody said, "Gary thinks five thousand should do it." "To whom? Who gets it?" Schiller asked. Moody replied, "Gary says, 'Look for a doctor.' " Schiller said, "I don't think we should get involved in that, Bob. We're going for the long haul."

He had the feeling Gary was testing how far he would go. In effect, they were all asking: How much money does Schiller have in his pocket? Has he another five thousand to hand out? Larry considered it a good way to establish his integrity with Moody if he didn't go along. "I don't think we should get involved," he repeated. "I'll send Gary a telegram."

DEC. 5, 1:30 P.M.
GARY GILMORE
UTAH STATE PRISON BOX 250
DRAPER UT 84020
IN REFERENCE TO YOUR REQUEST TO COMMUNICATE WITH A THIRD PARTY, THIS IS NOT THE MOMENT OR THE TIME, AND THE MEANS YOU HAVE SUGGESTED ARE REJECTED BY ME. I AM HERE TO RECORD HISTORY, NOT TO GET INVOLVED IN IT. REGARDS.
LARRY.

"Actually," said Schiller to himself, "I have become part of it. All around me, I'm becoming part of the story."

Now that Gilmore wouldn't answer his questions, Schiller decided he'd better pick up a couple of collateral interviews. Vern had told him that his daughter'd be well worth talking to, so with Stephie he went to visit Brenda and Johnny. It wasn't a great interview but he was delighted with Brenda. She was out front, wisecracking and offered a real image for a TV show. Almost good looking enough to be a Charlie's Angel-type girl. Her husband Johnny also impressed Schiller, but in another way. He felt a little uneasy of him physically. A strong man, reluctant to talk.

All the while, he loved having brought Stephie. Taking her to the interview warmed Brenda up. Stephie gave these awkward interview situations a little — he didn't want to say class — a little bit of culture, the little bit of softness needed. She was an asset. That is, until they left the place. "You sat there and ate all those hors d'oeuvres," she said, "all that ham and pineapple." Had to be said, Schiller told himself. She was an asset going in, and a liability going out. Her criticisms were so rough, he was fucked for the rest of the day.

So he was half relieved to interview Sterling Baker and Ruth Ann later in the week when Stephie was not along. He couldn't get over what a gentle fellow Sterling was. So shy, in fact, that he had to take him out to a restaurant. The man just could not sit and be interviewed without something like food to distract the atmosphere. All the same, Sterling showed another side of Gary. Here was this fellow, real gentle, and Gary had been drawn to him.

4

Moody and Stanger were trying to devise a way for Gary to telephone Nicole. Many a scheme was discussed.

In the meantime, to keep Gary happy, they were getting a few letters ferried to and from Nicole. Naturally, Gary wanted to know how good looking Ken Sundberg was, and Moody had to assure him Sundberg was a serious young Mormon who would not drive a wedge between Nicole and himself.

GILMORE   Can I ask you guys a personal question? Sometimes when things become a reality, people don't think about them exactly like they might. You guys aren't going to have any second thoughts?

MOODY   Let us say this, Gary, I think Ron and I both have come to look upon you and feel and treat and consider you to be a good friend and I don't like the thought of your being executed, but damnit, we're here to do what you want. We'll continue to work at that even though it is not a pleasurable thing to even think about.

STANGER   It certainly is not.

GILMORE   You know I'm not asking that you like me. I'm not a likable person, right.

STANGER   Whether you like it or not, we've grown to like you very much.

GILMORE   The only thing I ask is just respect my own thoughts about death.

Stanger didn't really believe Gilmore was ever going to get it. There were too many Judges secretly hostile to the idea of capital punishment. On the other hand, Stanger didn't see why he couldn't give his utmost. He liked to respect the role he had assumed. In a manner of speaking, he had been an actor all his life. Of course there were all kinds of ironies in this case anyway. Here he was supposed to be interviewing Gilmore on his past, yet Gary got off more on getting Ron to talk about his own life.

Having been born in Butte, Ron could get a quick laugh by saying, "Leave out the 'e' and you got it spelled." His two older brothers, he told Gary, used to sell newspapers over his near-dead body. Ron would start hawking on the best corner, and quick enough, a couple of bigger newsboys would jump him. As they did, his brothers would jump them, and get the corner for a while.

Back in the '40s, feeling cold and dirty in the winter, he'd be tired from carrying papers around. He'd go to bars and those old gals drinking would buy all he had left out of sympathy. Greatest practice for the law was learning to make those faces that draw sympathy.

Then the family moved to Oregon and there were hardly any Mormons in the town. The church was above a laundry one time. He met people who believed Mormons had horns because they kept more than one wife. Stanger was just a kid but he would say, "I'm all for it." In fact, his grandfather had been a polygamist. When Stanger first came to BYU, they asked in assembly how many of the kids had polygamous ancestors. Near everybody stood up. Of course, those polygamist families were not particularly happy, thought Ron. "You gave so and so a baby," one wife would yell, "and you ain't given me one." If you came from a second family, like his dad did, you knew the difference between first and second. Hell, it was hard enough to keep one wife happy.

Gary asked him to go on. Thought all this was fascinating.

Ron said he was the first member of his family ever to go to college, and hardly knew why he picked BYU unless it was to be in a place where Mormons were the accustomed thing. He hadn't been to school more than a few days when this gal who was blond and cute said something about Ernie Wilkinson. Ron opened his big mouth and said, "Who is that?" Thought Ernie was her boy friend. How was he supposed to know Wilkinson was the President of the University. The gal got so sarcastic Ron walked away. "There," he said to his friends, "is one girl I could never go out with." Now they'd been married twenty-two years, and had quite a family. Five kids, all in adolescence at once, all adopted.

When Ron and Viva couldn't have children, they waited five years, then put in an application through the Church, and had to wait another two years to get their first adoption. It took so long they already had a bunch of other applications out, and within a year three more children were in the house. Four kids under four years of age. They were going to hold out for a girl on the fifth, but heard about an infant they could get immediately from a sister agency in Oregon. Ron and Viva took all four and jumped on a plane to Portland to pick up the new little one.

Once aboard, they distributed children to everybody. Said to strangers, "Here, we got too many, would you take one?" On the way back, they had a tyke in the lead, then the twins, barely walking, Ron next, holding the next-to-littlest one, and Viva coming up behind with one more baby. Two old ladies came over and said, "We need to ask a question. Are you Mormons?" When they nodded, the old ladies said, "We could tell. It's such a big family." Later, on the plane, Viva remarked, "Wouldn't it have been funny if you told them we were both sterile?"

He and Gary laughed a long time over that one.

CHAPTER 16

A Bridge to the Nuthouse

1

Schiller got an advance copy of Barry Farrell's article in *New West*. It was called "Merchandising Gary Gilmore's Dance of Death" which sounded bad, and the piece covered Gilmore's negotiations with Boaz, Susskind, and Schiller. To Schiller's satisfaction, the parts on himself, while plus and minus, were generally okay.

> Uncle Vern seemed less attracted to Susskind than to Larry Schiller, who made a point of getting around to meet the family. Schiller's advice to one and all was to hire a lawyer, and when the lawyers were hired they found in Schiller someone who could talk their language, who knew all about court-appointed guardians and trusts, who carried with him a briefcase full of elaborate contracts for the rights to stories even more spectacular than Gilmore's.

That was good. Farrell was treating him with some seriousness. All the more unhappy did it make Larry then that the next line said:

> The man was something of a carrion bird: Already he'd done business with Susan Atkins, Marina Oswald, Jack Ruby, Madame Nhu, and Lenny Bruce's widow.

Once Schiller got over the impact, it didn't bother him too much. A magazine writer had to put in zingers, and after being screwed on the Muhammad Ali book, Farrell owed him a shot anyway. Besides, the rest of the piece was brilliant. A very good article. "Carrion bird" was going to get picked up, but on balance he was ahead. He began to think again of inviting Farrell to work on the questions.

Schiller was suffering with Moody and Stanger's interviews. He just could not accept how little the lawyers were bringing back. Gary had said he would not answer any more questions, but he meant written ones. Talking to him for hours, they should have been able to elicit more. On top of that, they made technical errors.

In the beginning, the lawyers didn't really know how to use a tape recorder. Once, Stanger did an interview with a dead battery. Schiller had to buy fresh ones. He couldn't comprehend how Stanger could keep laughing it off. Once the cassette was not turned over. The lawyers had recorded twice on the same side. Must have sat there, and rewound the tape, then recorded on top of themselves. Ron's attitude seemed to be: If we make a mistake, we get it tomorrow. One time Schiller had met Ron and Bob in a little coffee shop just a couple of miles down the road from the prison. Right away they wanted to listen to a tape just smuggled out. Played it in the coffee shop. Schiller said, "Let's go back to the office for that." But they had to hear what they had done. There, in the fucking restaurant. People nearby could have overheard it all. They couldn't seem to comprehend it wasn't wise, that tomorrow it could all be cut off. Why, they acted as if it was their prison. Schiller, trying to hold on to his temper, sometimes had to tell himself, maybe it is. It was practically their hometown, after all.

"Forget Larry Schiller the businessman," he told them. "That's a side of me, but we're forgetting it. We have history here. We have to get that." When they continued to show resistance, he said finally, "I'm going to give these interviews over to Vern." He was halfway serious. It couldn't be any worse and Gary might open up. What was making Schiller paranoid is that the lawyers didn't bring back a tape every time they went out. He began to wonder what they did discuss when they wouldn't tape. Kept saying to them, "Take down everything and anything, even your legal discussions. Talk about the will. It's all part of history. You never know when it's going to be important." Sometimes he would give them a message for Gary and not be certain it had gotten through. Certainly didn't hear it on the tapes. "Vern may not have your education," he would then threaten, "but he'll listen to me." It all consumed one horrendous week. He didn't have the hours to deal with ABC, movie rights, planning the story, getting ready for the execution, or time to study the letters.

Finally he told them to instruct Gary to call each of them Larry when doing an interview. It was better for Gilmore, he explained, to be thinking constantly of the man to whom he was telling the story of his life. Maybe that way, Schiller thought, they would find it easier to ask a tough question or two. Schiller was trying everything.

More and more he was thinking of an approach to Barry Farrell. There were a lot of memories he kept of Barry from *Life* magazine, so Schiller continued to feel pretty damn pleased with the overall respect Farrell had shown in *New West*. In the old *Life* days, Schiller had never been able to get rid of a feeling that Barry Farrell had a subtle contempt for him, and was made out of more exceptional stuff than himself. Not more exceptional, maybe, but certainly special. The first time he worked with Barry was after a period of six months Schiller had spent on and off with Timothy Leary, then Laura Huxley. *Life* was doing a big piece on LSD and Schiller had done fifty hours of taped interviews and taken thousands of photographs of adolescents and junkies, and college kids, and middle-aged people who took the tour with gurus and had profound experiences. Schiller had begun to think how much he'd like to be a writer, and realized he didn't know how. When he got back to New York, *Life* had assigned Barry Farrell to write the text, and the man just sat in his fucking office and worked. Schiller really got upset. How could you write a major piece on the use of this drug, he asked Barry, without going out in the field? So he developed an antagonism for Farrell, even a hatred. Yet when the piece came out, the guy had done it all. Really shaped it. That was the year, 1966, when Larry Schiller went from one side to the other on Barry Farrell, and developed a great regard for him as a craftsman and a writer. He did not see why Farrell could not do the same stuff with the Gilmore interviews.

Of course, this was only part of his feeling for Farrell. Barry was not only a craftsman, but a great ladies' man. The type to get away with three-hour lunches. He wore the right suits and right ties, and

Schiller was frankly envious of anybody who could go out that long, come back a little tipsy, and still do a hell of a job. Schiller wasn't that good looking then, no beard, pointed nose, small chin, a hungry look. He was just a working photographer, a kind of maniacal smile on his face because he was trying to do ten pictures at once while toting a big load of equipment on his back. Knew he looked bizarre, but tried to be part of the woodwork. The less a photographer was noticed as a human being, the better the pictures. Your camera could be dynamite when people paid you no more attention than a fly on the wall. Whereas Farrell, the ladies' man, had a bit of magic about him. Schiller remembered how Barry began to go around with this black girl who was a researcher at *Life*. A beautiful black girl, oh, God, Schiller remembered, in the '60s to be black and beautiful was to be a star. She was sweet, she had this nice honey voice, she was intellectual and not street-wise. There was a whole fineness to her, beauty to her, black, beautiful and intelligent. Now she and Barry were married and had a child together. Schiller decided the hell with it, he was just going to see if he could hire Barry Farrell. It would be like getting a prize.

He called Barry and asked if he'd be interested. Right from the start, he said it would be no pie in the sky. Nothing like the Muhammad Ali project. No great returns promised. No book involved. But definite work for definite good pay. Five thousand dollars for editing the *Playboy* interview. That was all right with Farrell. He had his own book to get back to, he said, and they sparred a little, then discussed it back and forth. To Schiller's surprise, he had the feeling there was less of a selling job here than he had psyched himself up for. They ended with Barry agreeing to take a look at the letters and interviews done so far. In a week or so, he ought to be able to decide.

"I'm running a bold move," Schiller told Stephie.

She didn't understand the interplays, didn't see how Farrell could write something like "carrion bird" and still respect you. Stephie was furious at the term. Besides, she didn't want Larry to give the interview over to anybody. He obviously wanted to do it himself, she said. Schiller only won the discussion by telling her about *The American Dreamer*. " 'Schiller went absolutely blank on Dennis Hopper's more mystical ideas' — you want to hear that again?" he asked her. "Don't you see, there's a side of Gary I can miss completely. I don't know from shinola about karma." That convinced her. When he could talk Stephie into something, he could convince anyone in the world. She was beautifully sales-resistant.

Barry Golson now flew out to L.A. to discuss *Playboy* doing the Gilmore interview, and Schiller could see that the editor was arriving in town with a $20,000 face, just what Schiller thought it was worth, plus expenses. It was also obvious that he and Golson were going to be abrasive on each other. Golson looked at him as a businessman, pure and simple.

"We're going to need," said Schiller, "a really good writer to edit these interviews." He mentioned Barry Farrell. Golson didn't indicate he knew who Farrell was. "He wrote a book on the actress, Pat Neal," Schiller said. He also gave Golson Farrell's *Life* credentials. Golson didn't seem to care. Maybe he wanted his own man in. There might be trouble later, Schiller thought, but he tied the deal for $22,000.

Schiller couldn't resist telling Farrell that Barry Golson of *Playboy* didn't seem to know him. "It's perfectly understandable that I never heard of Golson," said Farrell in reply, "but I consider it a shocking bit of illiteracy that Golson doesn't react to my name." Schiller laughed. It would be a couple of weeks before he'd come to realize that Farrell had not said it altogether in jest, and was even annoyed that Golson, being the *Playboy* Interview Editor, might not be aware that Farrell had done one bang-up job for them years ago with Buckminster Fuller. Barry had come to the place in his life where he was counting his achievements in preference to scoffing at them.

One reason for accepting Schiller's offer was that Barry Farrell didn't mind getting out of L.A. He was feeling some unaccustomed doubts about himself as a professional. Lately, he had been having trouble on deadlines, his wife was not well, and he was being sued in a major way by a publisher for nondelivery of manuscript. Being a man who had always taken his good reputation for granted, his life in Los Angeles of late produced the feeling that he was spinning his wheels. He actually felt grateful to Schiller. Somebody who trusted him to do a job.

Barry had been doing a book about the Mustang Ranch in Nevada when the most extraordinary thing happened. This group of heavies and whores he had been writing about suddenly turned on each other. A killing took place. The dead man was the Argentine heavyweight Oscar Bonavena. A good friend of Barry's, just about the main character in his book, Ross Brymer, was arrested for the deed.

That really knocked the wind out of Farrell's book. He couldn't go on with it. Felt the meaning of the word for the first time — crushed. Then Farrar, Straus & Giroux filed suit in Federal Court. The offer from Schiller felt like pure escape. To be able to labor long hours far away from his own concerns would be like an expense-paid vacation in Tahiti for him.

2

Tamera was now living in Salt Lake with her brother, Cardell. Out of nowhere, Larry Schiller called one night and said he would like to talk to her. Maybe she would be able to work with him. Just wanted to discuss the possibilities. Could they meet?

Tamera suggested he come to her brother's home. Cardell was an insurance salesman, and fourteen years older, and she followed his judgment greatly. Schiller had a pretty questionable reputation around the journalists she knew.

After all, a lot of newspaper people were having to get their Gilmore stories however they could, and Schiller had just flown in with his checkbook and tied the whole thing up. Everybody was mad at that. Still, she agreed to see him. She thought she was an open person. Even if she had a bias, she wouldn't be content to live with that.

Once Schiller began to talk, Tamera couldn't hold on to her dislike. Cardell, who was a shrewd businessman, was also swayed. Schiller just sat there and told them quietly, "I think you ought to know who I am." His career, as he recounted it, sounded pretty good. She could see Cardell liked the thorough way Schiller had handled the contracts so that there would be something substantial for Nicole's children, and the heirs of the victims. It didn't seem like he was just out to get the money.

Once he finished talking about himself, he said to Tamera, "I'm not going to mislead you and suggest you're going to have a key part in writing a book or movie or anything like that." Still, there was a lot she could do for him, and a great deal he could offer her. If they could set up a working cooperation, he would let Tamera sit in as an assistant on many a meeting. She would meet a number of important people in journalism and television on a different basis from all her lunches and dinners with them heretofore. Those occasions might have been fun for her, but what he offered would be more substantial. She could be present when important decisions were hammered out in confrontation. She would get a dramatic inside view of how a big story is put together, and know a great deal more when she was done.

Schiller liked her, although that hardly mattered. She was not exactly pretty, but she was attractive. Her features were a little too irregular to make her a beauty, but she was tall and had nice ash-blond hair and was full of energy, real clean-cut country pep. *Wham! Pow!* Stick her tongue in her cheek to show her confusion, or — *Sock!* — skew her lower jaw to the side to register embarrassment. With such a girl, Schiller knew his offer was better than catnip. It was these clean, slightly straitlaced young ladies with a wild ambitious career streak who could never resist opportunity.

He needed, he said, a newspaper to be his source 24 hours a day. His eyes and ears in a strange city. He could tell Tamera that he had lived and worked in many a new town for a week or month, and before he was done, he sometimes knew more about what was going on in that region, be it Provo, or Tangiers, than the natives. Nobody could figure out how he did it, but he would tell her it was simple. He always tried to get a pipeline into a local newspaper. Would she be his pipeline to the *Deseret News*?

He wanted, he assured her, a relationship that the newspaper would understand and profit from. He would supply them with pieces of information about Gilmore. In turn, she would feed him the local Salt Lake news plus what came in from Orem and Provo. Let him know what was — he used the local expression — coming down, what the Governor was up to, and the Attorney General's office. He wanted to have his finger on it.

When she began to look worried, as if he were proposing a little too much, he went back to his main theme. "Tamera," he said, "even if you don't drink yourself, you're going to see big reporters drinking, and going after a story, and working on their interviews. It's all there to learn."

What he did not mention was his private motive. He had to worry about Nicole. There would come a day when she would walk out of the hospital, and Schiller would go up to her. If, for any reason, she saw him as a Hollywood type waving a contract, then good relations with Tamera might be indispensable.

Cardell left the room for a moment, and Larry nailed the relationship. He was proud of it afterward. Just a hunch, just a gamble on his instinct, but he knew there had to be some inside reason Tamera had gotten so close to Nicole. Something the two girls had in parallel. When they were alone, Schiller said, "I bet you made it with a con, and then he fucked you over."

Tamera couldn't believe it. She stammered, "It wasn't that kind of relation. Wasn't sexual. But I was in love, and Nicole let me read Gary's letters because I told her about the wonderful letters I used to get from my friend."

Schiller went back to L.A. on the night plane. He had a professional link with Sorensen on the *Trib,* and what might prove a real connection on the *Deseret News.* Barry Farrell, whom he called from the airport, said, yes, definitely, he would work with him. The pieces were coming together. Schiller enjoyed an airplane trip at such times.

3

The first few weeks Nicole was in the ward, they couldn't get her to do a thing. She really told them off. It was absolutely against the rules to have people locked up, but there they were running this surveillance on her all the time. She let them know they were breaking their own rules. She was a bitch, verbally.

Doctor Woods disgusted her. She would ask him innocent things, like, "Do I have to eat all you give me, every meal?" and he would look at her like you could lose your ass giving a solid reply. She thought he was a great pussy. This big, good-looking guy who would never commit himself.

She was so angry at herself for failing in that suicide. Now she had really lost control of her life. They took care of her actions. Told her when she could go to the bathroom, watched her when she ate, just about gave her permission to close her eyes. In the daytime, they didn't allow you to rest your head on a chair. You couldn't go to sleep before eight at night. Here were all these patients, fuck-ups and con-victs, kids in for some bump or hassle with the law, yet letting that be done to them. Even acted like they liked this business of living by their own rules.

Every day the patients would sit down at a committee meeting — one came right after another — and discuss their rules. Rewrite them. Then they'd get into new hang-ups carrying out the new rules. It took Nicole a long time to realize that that was the way the place was supposed to work. A lot of them got to like writing and rewriting the rules. You could discuss the shit out of the changes, and play a lot of games with people. Fuck them over and get points for it. Go back to the world knowing the ropes. It was a comedy. A real shift in the power trip, thought Nicole.

She wasn't interested. Every time she would look out their sec-ond-story window, she would think of jumping through one day, making it to the road, making it out of town. But she knew she couldn't get free that way. They would really lock her in. Her best chance would be in her next Court appearance. She would have to convince them she wasn't suicidal.

Nicole didn't try to decide where she was on that. If they let her out, maybe she would play it straight. Or, she might decide to start running down the Interstate until some big semi clapped her in the ass. She just wanted to get away. The place was too full of shit. Everybody squealing on everybody. "You broke the rules!" they were always screaming. Then, they would argue it up and down. Nicole tried not to get involved, but after a while, she couldn't help it. Those rules were so fucking stupid. You had to try to improve them.

Then, she dug that there was one rule they were telling other patients but not her. Nobody was to mention Gary Gilmore's name. And no newspapers in the ward. If Nicole brought up Gary, nobody answered. People looked at her like she was kidding. Ha ha. Finally, they told her she was not allowed to say his name. She didn't care. It offended her to speak into the ears of these sheep.

One time, Stein, her grandfather, came to visit, and to say something about Gary. Right away, the posse asked him to leave. She threw a fit. They put her on silent treatment. Nobody swore or got mad, just dead-ass posse staring at her. She would call them names until she could see them cringe, call them sheep and rats, say they were pussy-whipped. She told them she wouldn't go to committee meeting. They carried her over bodily. After a while, she went by herself. She didn't want to be subjected to physical embarrassment. One night they had a dance, and when she refused to join, they lifted her up again and carried her part of the way down the hall. She had to tell them to put her down. She would walk. Then, they started playing the song "King of the Road." She liked that so much, she even danced.

The stuff going on in the meetings was incredible. She was no great brain, but compared to these asses, all totally involved in their own bullshit, she couldn't help opening her mouth to show them a better way. She had to laugh at how they were all working to become the number-one sheep. Of course, number-one sheep got to be the sheepherder.

God, they could draw maps on how to be an asshole. If you left a pack of cigarettes sitting around and somebody stole a couple, that started tension. Who did it? Can I trust you? So they would vote that you couldn't carry your own cigarettes any more. Somebody else had to dish them out. Like you could only get one on the hour, every hour.

Nicole developed this ability to sit through a meeting and not hear a word. She had to. When she took a bath, three girls stayed in the room to watch her. Must have been afraid she'd go down the drain. When she talked to Woods, she tried to run a line on him about all the nice things she was going to do when she got out. Some of it was real, some was made-up, but she would talk about getting away from Utah or going to school. She wanted, she told him, to take real care of Sunny and Jeremy. She put on such a good act, that after a while, it wasn't that she wanted to live exactly, it was that she wasn't so sure she wanted to die. You couldn't keep being enthusiastic about all these groovy things you were going to do when you got out, and not begin to wonder a little. Way inside, the enthusiasm didn't always feel completely phony.

She tried to make Woods believe she was ready to live without Gary. She never once said it without also saying to herself, "I'm putting the man on." Yet, she could also hear herself saying, "Keep it up. You'll believe it, too."

They had this rule you couldn't sleep without a nightgown. She hated that. Always liked to sleep with nothing on. One night, she slipped her nightgown off under the covers. Damn if three girls didn't come down on her to put it back. All through the night, there'd be a girl taking her turn in a chair to keep a watch on Nicole.

She felt as if slowly, real slow, but real sure, they were smothering her soul. Sometimes it would come over her right in a meeting. She would be sitting in a line of girls, listening to them bitch and holler and would put her head on her knees and never even look up, not once, never react to anything going on. Just sit through a whole meeting with her head on her knees crying away. Nobody paid any attention. There was always one girl or another off like that. Goddamnedest government she ever saw, half the kids crying, and the others half passing laws or standing up to make speeches full of bullshit. A lot of them wouldn't even remember what they started to say. They'd argue about how you got the floor in the first place, when, in fact, they were sitting on the floor already. And they'd rat on each other. One girl would say, "You were having eye language with Billy," and the other would say, "I wasn't." "Fuck you, you were."

Nicole wanted to say, "You goddamned idiots, I don't care what any of you do. You're all so dumb you think I'm sick. It doesn't matter. Even if you think I'm crazy, this is the way I want to be. I don't want to change." Then, she would realize she was never going to hear Gary's voice again.

CHAPTER 17

I Am the Land Lord Here

1

Gibbs wrote to Gary and said he was coming up for trial around the twentieth of December. He figured he'd be released, and wanted to know if there was anything Gary wanted done before he left the state, because he wouldn't be hanging around. He was going, he wrote, to show Utah what Mae West had showed Tennessee. Her ass, as she was leaving.

On December 11th, Big Jake brought Gibbs out to the front desk where an older fellow with a mustache was waiting. He walked with a cane and carried a briefcase. This gentleman introduced himself as Gary's uncle, Vern Damico, and said Gary had asked him to deliver a token of his friendship. Then he opened his briefcase and handed over a check made out by a local law firm for two thousand bucks.

Gibbs asked if Gary's mother was financially taken care of, and when Mr. Damico said she was, they shook hands. Gibbs introduced Mr. Damico to Big Jake, and said here was the only jailer Gary had any respect for. Mr. Damico replied, "Yes, Gary has spoken well of you, Big Jake." Damico then said he had some other appointments to keep, wished him good luck and left. Big Jake said, "We should have asked him if Gary would invite me to the execution."

A couple of guards had been standing in the doorway and they were gawking with envy. Gibbs laughed and made a call to Salt Lake, and had a friend come down for the check and put it in the bank.

That evening, Gibbs wrote to Gary again, thanked him for the money, and mentioned how Maximum was filled now, six prisoners altogether, including Powers. Gary answered, *"If I were there, we'd keep all of them lying on their bunks like little church mice and we'd put Powers in charge of licking out the Open Pit Sulphur Mine with his tongue."* In the letter he also said he was still on the hunger strike and wasn't going to eat *"until they let me talk to my sweet lady Nicole."*

"I've been trying," Gary wrote, *"to keep my thoughts and my mood pretty constant, but lately I've been growing increasingly irritated and angry. I don't like the idea they got Nicole down there brainwashing her."*

"Just as a matter of my personal curiosity," Moody said, "is there any way you will stop this hunger strike other than the phone call to Nicole?"

"Nothing," said Gary, "that's it." He paused to indicate that he knew the price of the remark. "I'm awful goddamned hungry, man," he whispered over the phone.

"I admire you for your courage," said Moody.

"It," said Gilmore, "is just goddamned stubbornness."

"Not very many guys," Moody told him, "have the strength of their convictions like you do."

"I spent eighteen straight months in the hole one time," said Gilmore. "I don't think this even compares."

Ron felt that Gary was putting on a show of strength. Each day, he made a point of going through his exercises, and he would do a head-stand on a chair to show he wasn't suffering. He was, however, not only losing a considerable amount of weight, but it seemed lately to have an effect on his thinking. He would stumble on words. His cheeks started to sink in. For the first time, Ron became conscious of Gary's false teeth. His loss of weight seemed to change their placement on his gums, and he said everything slowly and deliberately, as if working around a marble in his mouth, sort of a tongue-tied orator.

2

At this point, Gary told Vern he definitely wanted Ida and him to go visit his mother. Bring her the thousand dollars. Vern talked to Schiller, who latched on immediately. Bessie, once she got talking to Vern, might allow an interview.

So Moody drew up the papers. Schiller said, "I'll pay for the airplane fare, the phone calls, and put a thousand dollars on the top for her release. If you need more, just call." Vern said, "I think I'll need more. Come on, Schiller, you know you can give it to Gary's mother." And Larry knew he would, but a thousand might be right for starters.

So Vern and Ida took the plane from Salt Lake to Portland, rented a little Pinto hatchback, found the trailer park on McLaughlin Boulevard, and knocked on Bessie's door.

At first, it looked like they wouldn't get in. They stood on a little half porch for the longest time with no answer. It was cold, and Vern's leg was aching again from the operation. Bessie's first words were, "Go away. I can't let you in. I'm not presentable."

They had to talk pretty loud to be heard through the door. Finally they identified themselves. Said they'd come clear from Provo. Had things to talk over. Things Gary wanted to tell. Finally Bessie let them in.

They hadn't seen her since the funeral of Grandpa Brown almost eighteen years ago. She had certainly changed. She was no longer beautiful. She had the washed-out, unhealthy look of someone who was in a great deal of pain and rarely saw fresh air. Ida couldn't get over it. Bessie's green eyes had been bright as gems. Now there seemed to be a dull gray film on them.

Ida knew why she hadn't wanted to let them in. With her arthritis she could hardly clean up the litter. When Bessie had lived in Provo, waiting for Frank Sr. to get out of prison, her little house had been immaculate. Ida thought of tidying up a little, but could tell by the expression on Bessie's face that she better not do a thing.

Vern, however, did look in the cupboards and refrigerator, and Bessie was certainly short of food. So he drove down to a grocery store, and brought back about fifty dollars' worth of stuff. After the groceries were laid away, he told Bessie he had some legal papers, and explained there was also a thousand dollars he would leave as a gift from Gary. When she started to thank him, Vern said, "I'm just the mailman. I deliver, that's all." He added there was another thousand she could have by signing papers Larry Schiller had sent up.

Bessie looked at the release, thought about it, said, "I don't think I'll do it right now."

Vern had promised Larry he would try hard. When they came back next day, he brought up the subject again. He could feel how wary she was in business affairs. Like a deer downwind. Didn't matter if you were approaching with a rifle in your hands, or a carrot, there wasn't much talking to the deer. "At this time, Vern," she said, "I'll just hold off." He didn't press her too hard. He said, "My opinion is, you *should* sign. To help out matters, let's all stick together. See if we can't make something out of the whole thing. I believe Schiller's a good, reputable man."

Bessie just said, "No, I want to wait and see." Vern let it go. No way you could drag something out of Bessie against her will. Just as soon try it with Gary.

As they got up to leave, Vern took out a thousand dollars in cash and laid it on the table. It was the closest Gary came to being there. Bessie broke down and wept. She and Ida embraced, and Bessie said, "Well, I can certainly use that." They also left a red hand-knit shawl with her, and fluffy house slippers to keep her feet warm. Somehow, they had never got around to talking of Bessie's case in the Supreme Court. It wasn't until they got back to Provo on December 13th, that Vern heard of the decision in Washington, D.C.

3

Ten days after the stay, Stanger got a call from the Clerk of the U.S. Supreme Court, who said, "I just want to let you know we're going to have a decision today. They're in hand-twisting right now," and Ron got a picture of nine Supreme Court Justices wringing their mitts. The thought that the Supreme Court was breathing the same legal air on this day as everybody in Utah was exciting.

At the Attorney General's office, word arrived from the Clerk that the vote was being taken, and all the staff got around a large table and listened on a conference call, tallying feverishly as the Clerk read the decision of each Justice. They were so excited they had to add it up a second time to discover they had won 5–4. Bill Evans, Bill Barrett, Mike Deamer, and Earl Dorius were ecstatic. The Stay of Execution had been lifted. It was GO again.

DESERET NEWS

No More Delays Gilmore Says

Salt Lake, Dec. 13th — In an order Monday, the U.S. Supreme Court ruled that Gary Mark Gilmore had made a knowing and intelligent waiver of his rights.

On hearing the decision, Gilmore ended a 25 day hunger strike.

Coming into the prison, Moody and Stanger noticed that the guards in the front lobby looked happy. The mood permeated right out to the gate. There was a lot of pressure lifted now that Gary was done with his strike.

When Bob and Ron saw him, they just said, "We understand you came off," and he gave a nod of his head, said, "It was my decision." It was as if he had been the one controlling the situation. They were careful not to mention that he never did get his telephone call to Nicole. Since they had failed to get it through, they were in no hurry to tease him. Besides, he was in an awful good mood about the Supreme Court.

Actually, it was a relief to the attorneys as well.

4

Talking about the end of the hunger strike, Stanger said to Schiller, "Gary proved his point." Schiller couldn't resist saying, "What point?" "Everybody knows he was serious now," said Stanger. It all struck Schiller as a little fuzzy. The truth, obviously, was that nothing was working. Gilmore had expected a lot of results from his hunger strike, got none, and had enough sense of public relations to go back to eating on a day when there was a bigger story to interest the public.

What made Schiller's day, however, was that Gary informed Stanger he would answer the second batch of written questions and was willing to look at a new set that Larry had prepared.

The second set of answers proved, however, disappointing. It was as if the longer the hunger strike had gone on, the more Gary had had to play the con. So many questions were left blank. Invariably, the best ones.

WHY DID YOU TAKE THINGS WITHOUT PAYING FOR THEM — BEER — GUNS — GRAND CENTRAL, ETC.?
Didn't always have time to stand in those long checkout counter lines.

DO YOU WANT TO KNOW WHAT YOUR SUBCONSCIOUS MIND WAS DOING WHEN YOU KILLED?
I probably wouldn't mind knowing if I could know the truth, exactly.
I don't want it explained to me by some idiot headshrinker who's full of bullshit conjecture.

WHAT DID YOU AND NICOLE FIGHT ABOUT? GIVE ME DIFFERENT KINDS OF FIGHTS.
Ask her.

WHY AND WHAT TOOK PLACE ON JULY 13, 1976, THAT CAUSED NICOLE TO LEAVE YOU? PLEASE ELABORATE.
Ask her.

BEFORE THE PROVO KILLINGS HAVE YOU EVER ATTEMPTED TO TAKE
YOUR LIFE? IF YES ARE YOU UPSET THAT YOU FAILED AND WHY?

   . . .

PLEASE TELL ME EVERYTHING THAT TOOK PLACE AT THE MOTEL FOR
THE TIME YOU WERE THERE WITH APRIL.

   . . .

WHY DID YOU STOP AT THE GAS STATION AND WHAT TOOK PLACE?
WHAT WERE YOU AND APRIL TALKING ABOUT BEFORE THE GAS
STATION?

   . . .

WHY DID YOU ROB BEFORE YOU KILLED — WHY NOT JUST KILL OR
JUST ROB?

   Habit, I guess.

   My lifestyle.

   We're all creatures of habit.

   Somebody else from a different background might do it different.

   *That's a good question. A valid question. I may as well have just
killed — but I'm a thief. An ex-con, a robber. I was reverting to
habit — perhaps so that it made some sense to me.*

   Hope I've answered this one.

   *Now Larry, I have a question for you and I'd appreciate a
prompt honest answer.*

   Have you read the letters I wrote to Nicole?

   Tell me.

It threw a scare into Schiller. He would have to move quickly on
getting Vern and the lawyers to agree to sell the letters overseas. If he
waited much longer, Gary might begin to make a large issue of
these letters.

Schiller put the problem out of mind and went on to the next
batch of answers. Gary had done those on the day he began to eat
again and thankfully, there was more to his replies.

DID YOU REALLY WANT TO "START OVER" WHEN YOU CAME OUT ON
PAROLE THIS TIME? DO YOU THINK THINGS JUST STARTED SNOWBALL-
ING AND YOU GAVE UP TRYING? YOU WERE FUCKING UP ANYWAY SO
WHAT THE HELL . . .

Yeah, what the hell! Wish I could talk to you, Schiller. I don't like to write. Just ain't the same as talking. You'd get more spontaneity in verbal exchange and, hence, better answers. I'm very concerned that you understand me correctly.

I can tell by your questions that you really don't know what I want to tell you. You're about 35 degrees off the mark. This is a piss poor way to communicate.

WHAT DO YOU THINK ABOUT BEING IN JAIL?
  — You could easily do away with a lot of jails.
  They're shit. They breed, they don't deter, crime.
  Right now, I'm a prisoner of my body —
  I'm trapped in myself —
  Worse than jail!

DID YOU EVER THINK ABOUT DEATH BEFORE YOU WERE FACED WITH THE DEATH SENTENCE?
  A lot.
  In depth.
  A very lot.
  Oh, yes.

HOW DID YOU FIRST MEET NICOLE? HOW DID YOUR RELATIONSHIP START?
  It was, to each of us, like finding a part of us that had been lost and missing for a while. I can't prove it, but I know.

  Want to know something else! I've been famous before — not infamous like now, but famous and rich too. Maybe that's why this don't mean a whole lot to me right now. This is all happening as it was meant to. Inward — in that quiet place that counsels — I always knew. It's no surprise. Nothing to get choked up about.

IT MAY SEEM LUDICROUS, TERRIBLY PSYCHOANALYTICAL, INANE, WHATEVER, BUT WHAT DO YOU THINK OF YOUR MOTHER AND HER ROLE IN YOUR EARLY LIFE?
  I love my mother. She's a beautiful strong woman. Has always been consistent in her love for me. My mother and I have always had a good relationship. Besides being mother and son we're also friends. She's a good mother of pioneer Mormon stock. A good woman. What do you think of your mother?

DO YOU GENERALLY CARE WHAT PEOPLE THINK ABOUT YOU?
Yes.
Everybody does.

Yes, he did care, thought Schiller. It gave one more reason the letters should be sold and printed. The public would be less completely hostile to Gilmore.

As a sign of friendship, or was it an indication of Gilmore's own interest in presenting some better picture of himself, he had also sent along a poem he had written several years back. Schiller wasn't sure what to make of it, but thought he could pull some lines to give *Time* or *Newsweek* when they got desperate for copy.

> *The Land Lord*
> *an introspection by Gary Gilmore*
> *Feeling a backoning wind blow thru*
> *The chambers of my soul I knew*
> *It was time I entered in*
> *I climbed within and stared about —*
> *I was home indeed my very seed*
> *A mirror of me reflecting myself*
> *From every curve and line and shelf*
> *Every surface there   Every texture bare*
> *Every color tone and value   Each sound*
> *Pride   Hate   Vanity*
> *Sloth   Waste   Insanity   Lust Envy Want*
> *Ignorance black and green*
> *I felt myself at every turning*
> *Set my very mind to burning*
> *Face to face no way to dodge*
> *Headlong I tumbled thru this lodge*
> *I felt and met alone myself*
> *A red scream rushed forth   But I caught*
> *it back and checked its force*
> *It crescendoed into a hopeless heavy weight*
> *in the blood and fell . . .*
> *A beat of wing I felt and heard*
> *Not at all like any bird*

Overhead I saw myself   contorted black
and brown and twisted mean — borne aloft
by a gray bat wing — growing from
my shoulders there . . .
One thing was peculiar clear
There was no scorn to menace here
This is just the way it is
Laid bare to the bone
And I built this house   I alone
I am the Land Lord here

PART FOUR

The Holiday
Season

CHAPTER 18

Penitential Days

1

One of the jurors from Gary's trial wrote a letter to the *Provo Herald*. The Utah Supreme Court hadn't found any error, he said, so why had Gilmore's case gone to the U.S. Supreme Court?

Judge Bullock started to think about the juror. From the tenor of his letter, Bullock got the impression that some Jury members were wondering if they had done their job properly. There had been so many appeals. The Judge thought: "I'm going to ask that Jury to come back in. Maybe I'm sticking my neck out, but I want to explain the legal procedures."

He had his clerk make each contact. Didn't want the jurors to feel there was pressure from Judge J. Robert Bullock himself, so the clerk merely announced that the Judge, strictly unofficially, would be willing to meet with them and go over any legal questions they might have. Every juror accepted. They all came in.

He met them in Court when nobody was around one evening, and put them in the Jury box. He sat down in front, and explained the right of appeal, and how this case was likely to go on for several more years. In fact, it would be unusual if it was brought to conclusion in less time. He pointed out that people had a right to go to Court to fight for legal principles in which they believed, and said the law on capital punishment had not been settled. People hadn't been executed since 1967, so it was highly appropriate that delays take place. But he wanted the Jury to understand that they had not done their part of the job incorrectly.

There was the sore spot. Judge Bullock told them that their verdict could not be impeached under any circumstances. "I," he said, "could have made errors in telling you what the law is, but you have not made errors. You have done your job." He could feel these words helped them. They now felt better about it all.

He also repeated it might take a few years, and said, "That's the way it is, let's not fight the system." To his surprise, shortly after this meeting the Supreme Court lifted their Stay. In consequence, Gilmore was now scheduled to be brought back to his Court for resentencing on December 15. Judge Bullock had to start agonizing again.

He knew Judges who were ready to take their own lives before they would pronounce the death sentence. Judge Bullock didn't see himself as a conscientious objector, but he still didn't like capital punishment.

Before Gilmore, he had never even had a capital case. He had tried all kinds of second degree, five years to life, but never Murder One. It proved harder than he expected. The Jury had found Gilmore guilty, so he had only had to express the sentence. Yet, on that October day, he shook within, he agonized. Outwardly, Judge Bullock hoped he maintained composure and dignity. Inside, he felt more emotion than he would ever have expected.

Now, he'd have to sentence him once more. It would be the same sentence, but a different date. He would nonetheless have to utter the words. That tearing and churning at the pit of the stomach, that long emotional drain over a few words, would begin again. And all the public clamor. If the guy wants to die, give it to him right now.

No, said Bullock to himself, I will not rush it. The processes have to be followed. Those who will want to appeal are entitled to have the time to go to Court properly.

When he heard therefore that Moody and Stanger, on Gilmore's instructions, would move for an early date, he did not feel disposed toward the idea.

2

Coming down the courthouse corridor, Gilmore looked like a man coming in with hope. To Schiller's eye, Gary didn't seem nearly so frail as during the hunger strike. He might be just two days off his fast, but he was carrying himself well. Had a little cadence to his walk, as if even with the shackles, he could take small, prancing steps that were a little faster, a little more stylish, than the plodding pace of the guards next to him. Something nice about the way he moved, as if hearing an inner beat.

Of course, Schiller knew the reason. This morning, Gary was expecting to talk to Nicole. Bob Moody had filled Larry in on what he hoped to pull off in the courthouse today. He and Stanger intended to get their client back to Bullock's empty chambers, and from there ring up the hospital on the Judge's phone, and ask to speak to Sundberg. Ken would then pass the phone on to Nicole.

Bringing off the phone call had become a commitment for Bob Moody. The first time he ever laid eyes on Gilmore had happened to be outside this same courtroom when the Bushnell case was being tried. On that day, Bob had seen Nicole rush up to embrace Gary, and some special intensity in the demonstration of affection had stirred Moody to say to himself, "There's one girl immensely in love."

It wasn't uncommon in Moody's experience that when a young criminal was taken out of Court — especially if he was good looking and had one of these macho mustaches — that a young woman would come running up to kiss him. In fact, such embraces usually went on for quite a while. This one, however, between Gilmore and his girl, must have been the longest and most passionate Bob ever saw. It went over the edge of decorum. He had to wonder a little about people who felt that strongly.

Moody might be fairly high in the Church, but saw himself as something of a liberal. From time to time, he liked, for instance, to contemplate such problems as why it was that good-looking girls like this always seemed to go for criminals. He knew his own experience wouldn't provide the answer. He placed himself as one of those steadfast fellows whose biggest problem in life had been whether to become a dentist, a businessman, or a lawyer. Now, he and his wife had five children, which made for a different relation than you were going to see in a courthouse corridor.

Still, the memory of that first time he laid eyes on Gilmore always gave flavor to what Gary said about Nicole. It provided Moody with a bit of sympathy for what others might have seen as an outlandish desire to reach the girl at all costs. So Moody had been going to some ends to bring it off.

3

When they got down the hall today, however, they were put in a room without a phone. Their plan was simply wiped out. Gary had to step into Court on a full head of frustration. Schiller could see that even his body was starting to tighten. He had begun to flick his eyes back and forth, and was almost reptilian. Looked like he was planning where to strike.

Gary whispered, "The Judge looks like Phil Silvers."
"Who?" Moody whispered back.
"Sergeant Bilko."
Something to it. Same horn-rimmed eyeglasses, bald top, somewhat pendulous nose, same halfway pleasant expression. If Gary was getting contemptuous of the Judge, however, it meant Gary thought he was licked.

Then Wootton took over. The 30/60 statute, he argued, could now be measured from today, December 15, which would place the earliest date of execution at January 15. It was not healthy, legally speaking, he said, to ram through an execution. Bullock kept nodding.

Schiller could see Gary give a look like everyone around him was scum. Damned if he didn't use his turn to say that nobody here had guts enough to let him die. All they were doing was jacking him around. The way he said "jacking" was obscene. It sent a ripple through the room.

Bullock ignored the remark. How could you sentence a man to Contempt when he was already bound over to execution?

"Unless this is a joke," said Gilmore, "I expect . . ." and he went on to say that he expected his sentence to take place in the next few days. "I'm serious about wanting to end my life," said Gilmore. "The least justice can do is to recognize that."

Bullock set the date for January 17. "We're not here," said the Judge, "to accommodate you."

After Court, Gilmore happened to pass Wootton in the corridor. He took the opportunity to say, "Why don't you suck my cock, you motherfucker?" Wootton didn't reply.

4

Now that they had a full month before the execution, Schiller had a time-line long enough to sell the letters. So, after Court, he invited Vern and Bob and Ron out to lunch. Even asked them to pick a good restaurant. Since there was nothing around Orem or Provo that qualified, they ended up in some big Bavarian place in the foothills of Salt Lake City, and had to wait for a quiet corner table while a lot of businessmen were talking away at the top of their lungs. Schiller, however, wanted the right situation for this talk.

Since he figured he would have to sell Moody on the proposal more than Stanger, he put Ron to his right and Moody across. Thereby he could look directly into Bob's eyes while making his pitch. Over food, he got into it all, really laid it on the line. He told them that he wanted to sell some of the letters in Europe for publication shortly before the execution, but could conceal the transactions in such a way that nobody would ever know who made the sale. The letters, after all, had been printed already in the *Deseret News*. There had to be at least one set of Xeroxes floating around.

He couldn't pretend, he said, not to be concerned by Gary's reaction. The shit, Schiller assured them, would certainly hit the fan if Gary found out. Still, it wasn't going to hurt the man. Gary was more sympathetic in his letters than any other presentation he gave of himself. Moreover, his privacy had already been breached. The lines Tamera had quoted in the *Deseret News* had been syndicated across half of the world. Schiller said he would repeat what he had told them at the beginning: there were going to be a lot of things they might not like, but he would always lay it out. He would not work behind their backs.

A lot of discussion went on. Schiller felt the lawyers were surprised he was this open. As he'd expected, Moody was relatively against the project, and discussed with Stanger what the public effect might be if it all came out. They certainly didn't want to be tagged with Boaz's posture. Schiller kept repeating that if the letters they held weren't published, foreign papers would buy from other sources. Somebody was going to make money on Gary Gilmore.

Schiller could see that Vern was being torn right down the middle. Subconsciously, he estimated, Vern wanted the money, but never did say, "I have to discuss this with Gary." It was ripping him up, however. He didn't talk, and went deep into himself. It wasn't that he was unfriendly so much as troubled. Still, Schiller decided, Vern was going to go for the money.

Finally Larry convinced them by saying "I could make a sale in Germany or Japan, and you'd never know a thing. Nobody could ever point to me as the man who sold them." It was the subtlest kind of threat. After all, they knew he had six Xeroxes. How could they be certain he had not made seven? They never gave any hard fully acknowledged consent, but from that moment he had the go-ahead.

After lunch, when Ron Stanger saw Gary again at the prison, it was like talking to steel. Worse than the pits of the hunger strike. Gary was as cold and hard and icy fevered as Ron had ever seen him. It burned your eyes to look into his rage. Man, Gary was triggered. Call it possessed.

On the drive back, Ron tried to make a joke of it. "Christ," he announced to Moody, "it was like a horror film. I could almost see his teeth getting longer."

5

<hr>

DESERET NEWS

Gilmore Attempts Suicide Again

Salt Lake, December 16 — Convicted murderer Gary
Mark Gilmore was in a coma at the University Medical
Center today after another suicide attempt.

Gilmore, frustrated in his efforts for a quick execution, was in critical condition.

He entered the hospital at 10:20 A.M., after being
found unconscious in his prison cell at 8:15 A.M. . . .

The second time, Gilmore really tried to do it. That was Dr.
Christensen's opinion. Gilmore had taken phenobarbital at a 16.2
milligrams per cent level. Any phenobarb greater than 10 milligrams
per cent proved fatal for more than half the people who tried it. Gilmore had been well into the lethal range.

This time, when he came out of it, he wasn't obscene. One of the
nurses even commented, "Gee, he seems a little nice." In fact, he
acted subdued. There was a difference. There really was.

Stanger got to the hospital as soon as he heard the news, and ran
into a bizarre episode. An old friend who had shared an office with
Ron in Spanish Fork years ago, an optometrist named Ken Dutson,
was now dying in the same emergency room where they were working on Gary. Stanger practically bumped into Dutson's wife and family. They were really upset. As soon as Gary was brought in, the hospital gave their main attention to him. Stanger was sure poor Dutson
had reached the point where he couldn't be kept alive, but you could
hardly expect his family to be happy that a killer was rushed in, and
all of a sudden, personnel were swarming around that case.

Gilmore's recovery seemed crazy, it was so fast. He had been at
the honest brink of death, Stanger learned from the doctors, but his
system seemed to have learned how to get rid of the poisons quickly.
It was a joke the way they kept him only one day at the hospital
before rushing the man back to Maximum Security as if afraid Gil-

more would get loose and prowl the streets. Of course, he did look terrible. When Stanger went to see him back at the prison, Gary was still so intoxicated from the phenobarbital that he couldn't even sit on the stool. He'd just start tilting. And slurred his words slow as molasses running uphill. Even while talking, he slowly keeled over until he fell right to the floor.

"Did you hurt yourself?" asked Vern.

"I'm all right."

"You sure?"

"I'm all right even when I'm not all right," said Gary.

Schiller sent a couple of urgent questions:

WHEN YOU ATTEMPTED SUICIDE, DID YOU SEE ANYTHING OF WHAT IT IS LIKE ON THE OTHER SIDE?

I can't tell you exactly whether it was light like daybreak or sunshine, or like a break in the darkness, but it was light. I felt I was talking to people, meeting people. That's the memory I came back with.

WHAT IS GOING TO HAPPEN WHEN YOU MEET BUSHNELL AND JENSEN ON THE OTHER SIDE?

Who knows that I will? It could be that with death you pay all your debts. But they have their rights, just like I do, and they have privileges, like I guess I have privileges too. I wonder — do they have any more right to do something than I do now? It's an interesting question.

6

The second suicide attempt bothered Bob Hansen. It also got Earl worried about Gilmore's sanity. The State certainly didn't want a situation where the public would think they were executing a madman. So, Hansen and Sam Smith and Earl Dorius had a number of talks over who the psychiatrist should be. There was the idea for a while of getting Dr. Jerry West who was well known because of his testimony in the Patty Hearst case. West was very opposed to capital punishment; Hansen thought that if they could get him to say Gary was sane, it would settle the question for the public beyond any doubt. Earl, however, thought that was risky, and definitely going in for overkill. He set it as his goal to change Hansen's mind. Let the prison psychiatrist, Van Austen, give the evaluation, he said. It would satisfy the statute. No matter what you did, it was possible that public opinion was never going to be satisfied.

So they went with Van Austen. His evaluation declared Gary sane. Things could quiet down for a couple of weeks at least. Dorius hoped to enjoy his Christmas season.

7

Schiller's reaction to the second suicide attempt was that Gary had to be a very impatient man. Didn't want to die because of reincarnation, just out of spite. Had attempted to kill himself to show the world Gary Gilmore was in control. So Schiller lost respect. It was idiotic to kill yourself just to fuck the Judge. A streak of childish vengefulness. Maybe that was what kept Gary from doing anything with his life.

Schiller began to think more and more of April. He kept having the feeling that the night Gilmore had spent with April might be the key to a lot. Gary had certainly refused to say anything about her. The empty pages in those questionnaires intrigued Larry. He had been trying to talk Kathryne Baker into letting him meet her daughter, but now he tried harder. When he spoke to Phil Christensen, he went so far as to say it was imperative to meet the young lady.

Kathryne was afraid that April might freak out if she knew she was talking to a reporter. April seemed to believe that media people had all kinds of crazy powers. So, it took a bit of convincing, but Kathryne finally agreed when Phil offered to take April out of the hospital for Christmas shopping. They even brought one of Christensen's secretaries along who would go into the women's stores with April.

Larry waited in the car while Phil came out of the hospital with this nice little adolescent. Schiller opened the door for her, and she got in the back seat, and he slid in next. It was a good, bright, sunny day, not at all cold, and she was wearing a skirt and blouse and little jacket, and her hair was neatly tied back in a ponytail. Schiller immediately noticed that she gave no eye contact. After he introduced himself as Larry — he and Christensen having agreed she might have heard the name Schiller on television — she said, "I'm April," and he cracked a joke. "I know a girl by the name of Tuesday," he said. "Tuesday Weld." Very little response. She just sat there looking prettier than he'd expected, a little plump, teenaged girl. Didn't give the impression of somebody who was kept in a mental home. Maybe on a sedative, but certainly not a heavy one.

When they discussed shopping at the University Mall, April said, "I'm going to buy Sissy a present." Something in the way she said it, told Schiller that Sissy had to be the family nickname for Nicole. Quite a nickname for a girl who got into suicide pacts.

When Christensen gave April $100 to buy gifts for everybody, she said that was the most money she'd ever had to spend. After a while she said she was going to get Sissy a Timex.

It didn't take long before Schiller had had enough of winter sunshine, mountain air, shopping centers, and jingle bells. He was dropped off, smiled at April, and said, "I hope to see you again. Get some nice presents." At that point, she did look in his eye and gave a nice, big smile. He came away fairly confident he'd be able to interview her. Schiller was excited. Other than Vern and Brenda and Sterling, this had been his first contact with somebody who knew Gilmore intimately before the murders.

8

Brenda went up to see Gary, but they wouldn't let her past the gate. A couple of days later, the prison finally agreed to some arrangement where she could see him through the glass. He was holding a phone on either side of his head so he could talk to Vern and her at the same time. Brenda just sailed in. "Gary, you dumb turd," she said, "you screw everything up. If you're not going to do it right, for hell's sake, quit trying." He said, "Brenda, I tried. Honestly, I tried. They just keep finding me too soon." She said, "You shithead, why don't you use a gun?" Then she made a face, and said, "Never mind, don't use a gun. You don't know where the trigger is."

He said, "God, I know. My hand still hurts."

They said good-bye the way they had the other time, touching fingers and palms on opposite sides of the glass.

Sunday morning, a girl from *People* magazine showed up at Brenda's house with a photographer. Her little son, Tony, let them in. Brenda was in the shower and came out with nothing but a negligee on. Since it had a low neckline, she used a washrag to hide the cleavage as best she could. In the mirror, she saw herself. Might as well be a cockatoo in heat. All the while, this girl reporter, Sheryl McCall, was talking about how she wanted to do an article on Cristie. Sheryl had found out that Cristie was going to be the recipient of Gary's pituitary.

Brenda said "Get out. Don't use anything here, or I'll sue your ass." The photographer, whose name turned out to be John Telford, was shifting his weight and arranging the cameras hanging off his neck. Brenda thought he did it so they wouldn't bang together, but found out later he was taking pictures. Caught every angle of that awful negligee. Later *People* printed her picture. She was one of "Eight Tortured Women in Gary's Life." A real tacky and trashy article. Brenda was described as a barmaid. When she learned that Tony had left the storm door shut, and McCall and Telford had opened it and walked in, she contacted an attorney, and began suing *People* magazine.

Brenda also had a bad physical condition. It was getting to the point where she just couldn't bear the pain. She was having such attacks, she had to miss work pretty frequently. It was simply too difficult to wait on tables. So she went for a checkup and they made tests and fluoroscoped her.

Then the doctors explained. It seemed the inner lining of a woman's uterus was shed every month, but in her case, that lining built up on the outside of the uterine wall. At present, it was attaching to her intestines, where it would rupture and bleed. Like cancer, except it wasn't cancerous. But, most definitely it had attached itself to the bowel. When this menstrual tissue broke, the doctors explained, it took the lining off. Very painful. They weren't sure they could get it under control without surgery. Meanwhile, she was hemorrhaging quite a bit. They gave her pain pills, but she still felt as if she were tearing inside. A couple of times when she went out to the prison, the sitting and waiting made the pain unendurable. Finally, when they showed no signs of letting her in, she stopped going. Then, walking got painful. Sometimes it would pull on her merely to stand up. There Vern was, just getting over his operation, and here she was, feeling stuck together and twisted inside.

9

It was Sundberg who told Nicole about Gary's second attempt. That was upsetting. She didn't understand how he could try to step out on her. It was like Gary was saying, "I've got to look out for myself." All the same, she was embarrassed that he had failed again. Should have gotten it done right.

She was flabbergasted when they nominated her for vice-president of the women's side. Just trying to get another government together. Nicole couldn't believe a couple of the idiots they picked with her. Of course, they didn't have a whole lot to choose from, just fifteen girls on the ward, and five were so loony, April would sound logical next to them. She was probably one of the few people in the ward who could add, say, five and eight. But it wasn't like she'd worked for the nomination. Most of the time, she still wouldn't talk to anybody, just ignored the meetings all day long. When they would turn to her for an opinion, she would say, "Humph." Just "Humph." Maybe she was saying it in a way that really got their attention, like she was smelling the finest and most peculiar shit.

CHAPTER 19

Advent

1

It was not the kind of news you could anticipate. In fact, it was unbelievable. Bob Moody received a phone call from Gary's friend, Gibbs, who said he was a police informer and was going to testify at a trial in the next couple of days. Having been Gary's cellmate in County Jail, he had quite a story to tell, he told Moody, and wanted ten thousand bucks and a chance to get on the Johnny Carson show. Moody informed Vern immediately of the conversation, and a couple of hours later, visiting the prison, Vern passed it on to Gary. When there was no reply, Vern explained again what Gibbs had said to Moody.

Gary puckered his lips so tight, it looked as if he had taken out his plates.

"I'm sorry, Gary," said Vern. "As you know, I already paid him the $2,000."

"You know that guy," Gary said. "I *trusted* him. You don't trust too many people in the world."

"I'd like to run into him," said Vern. "I'd change his head."

"Well," Gary said, "don't worry, Vern. You can't do anything about it, but I can." He nodded. "I can take care of it right from here." He was certainly serious, thought Vern. "Yes," said Vern to himself, "if Gibbs doesn't leave town, he's going to get taken care of."

Schiller and Barry Farrell were working together that morning in Los Angeles when Moody called with the news. Gibbs, he said, was eager to talk to Schiller about a deal. Larry had been mentioned in the pages of *Helter Skelter,* and so he thought Schiller might want to buy inside stories on Gary, stuff no one else had. Schiller was plainly worried, and got on the phone and put in a call to Gibbs, and heard him repeat everything he had said to Moody. Then Gibbs asked that Schiller not divulge any of this private information to Gary. Schiller, hanging up, said to Farrell, "It's ridiculous. Does he think Moody is going to keep it from his client?" Farrell, fresh from reading Gilmore's letters full of encomiums to his cellmate, said, "Gibbs has got to be the lowest of all creatures."

Schiller had already decided to find out whether Gibbs really knew enough to do any damage to his exclusive, and, if so, sign him up at the lowest possible price. Since he and Barry were about to take off for Provo that afternoon, and were ready to prime Moody and Stanger with new questions, it would be relatively simple to interview Gibbs as well. Indeed, it would be the first job they would do in Utah together. Might be a way of christening their relationship. "Behooves us," said Farrell, "to wring Gibbs out like a washrag."

On the airplane, en route to Salt Lake, they went over the interrogatories Barry had prepared. In the last week, Farrell had read everything available, the letters, tapes, and every sheet of yellow paper on which Gilmore had written answers, and then had come up with a new and thorough set of questions. Schiller now read this work with attention and discussed each query and they changed a number of them.

At Salt Lake, they rented a car, drove to Provo, and put up at the TraveLodge. Then he brought Barry over to meet Moody and Stanger. It took a while to convince the lawyers not to inform Gilmore about Farrell. "If Gary knows another man has been brought in, he's going to have to learn to trust the new man," Schiller said. In fact, after Gibbs, who would he accept?

Then Schiller tried, in the politest way, to lay out some of his criticisms of the lawyers' interviews, and convince them why the approach from now on had to be mapped by Farrell and himself. "Here," he showed them, "is our first full-dress interview." He went through the questions, and emphasized the possible follow-throughs.

Did his best to psych them up. It seemed encouraging. They obviously accepted Farrell as a working journalist — as always Barry made a good impression — and Schiller could feel the special attention they offered today. Quite likely, he thought, they were also worrying over Gibbs. God, if they didn't start to produce, Gibbs's story might look better and better.

That afternoon, Moody and Stanger went out to the prison, and did a tape with Gary. It went on for hours, and they didn't get back until midnight. Next day, when he heard it, Schiller was excited. Gary had talked at length about his childhood and reform school and prison and the murders. Since this was only four days after his second suicide attempt, the responses were impressive. It was as if Gilmore was also concerned about Gibbs and had decided to tell his story. In fact, Schiller was ecstatic. After Farrell edited it, they would have, at the least, a good beginning for *Playboy*.

2

The meeting with Gibbs had been arranged by Moody through a detective named Halterman, who turned out to be a big, blond fellow with glasses, wearing a brown leather coat, a smiling teddy-bear type, Schiller thought, except he was obviously one tough teddy bear. Halterman had set it up for the interview room at the Orem Police Station, a cubbyhole with a desk and a couple of chairs.

Gibbs was in there, chain-smoking. Schiller's first impression was of a small, slimy, ratty, jailhouse guy. Red squinty eyes. He had a receding hairline, a Fu Manchu goatee, a little dingbat mustache. Bad teeth. Pale as a ghost. A guy who would stick a shiv under your armpit. Farrell liked him even less. He looked like a poor old weasel sitting there. The total stamp of jail was on the man.

First thing after making introductions, Schiller took out a pack of Viceroy Super Longs and handed them over. It made Gibbs uneasy. Yesterday, on the phone, Schiller acted like he had hardly heard of him. Now, he seemed up on his habits. Gary had obviously, Gibbs thought, informed Schiller of his personal preferences. Besides, there was something about the man, and his associate, this Farrell, that made Gibbs uncomfortable. They didn't look like rich writers or producers from Los Angeles. They were wearing old parkas and dungarees, and looked like they had been brought in for vagrancy. Gibbs could feel the big money disappearing. Worse. He also felt a lot of warnings, so, even as he said hello, he asked if Schiller had disclosed their conversation to Gary. "I have to tell you," Schiller said, "I believe I made a mistake. I didn't understand that I wasn't supposed to tell him, and I did."

"You gave me your word," Gibbs said.

"I'm sorry," said Schiller, "I got it all mixed up."

"What did Gary say?" asked Gibbs.

The other fellow, Farrell, shook his head, and said, "Oh, Dick, Gary was so disappointed." On top of everything else, Gibbs hated to be called Dick. The name was Richard. He looked over at Halterman, and Ken was almost puking. He gave a signal to Gibbs, and they stepped out of the room. "That's the oldest con game in the world," said Halterman. "Oh, Dick," said the detective, mimicking Farrell, "Gary was so disappointed." Then Halterman cussed. "You should have said, 'What do I care? He's just a cold-blooded killer.' " Still, he didn't disagree that it might be worth talking to these Los Angeles characters about a deal.

Gibbs was as upset as a man could be. First of all, he was in a state of confusion, and that was not his accustomed place. Then, this fellow Schiller started to run a line on him. "Look," Schiller was saying confidentially, "Gary has gone *crazy* with anger, but I think I can get him calmed down. You see, I might be able to explain to the man that you're ready to work with us."

Gibbs didn't believe a word, but then he didn't dare not to believe him either. So when Schiller took out a Sony tape recorder from his pocket, Gibbs agreed to be interviewed. It was hard, however, to figure where Schiller was coming from. That guy Farrell just kept glaring at him.

When Schiller asked if he would sign a contract for his story, Gibbs asked, "How much?" He knew already there was nothing like ten grand in it, but he still wanted to get on Carson. Have all of America see his face, then use the proceeds to get a face-lift, ha ha. Still, he did think Johnny Carson had quick wits. They'd make a good fit. There'd be a fast understanding back and forth.

Schiller, however, just looked to be in pain at the idea of laying out money. "You are trying," he said, "to sell your information after Gary has already given you a check for $2,000 which is the fourth-largest amount given out to anyone, including his mother."

"Gary gave me that money out of friendship."

Schiller looked him right in the eye and said, "When I told Gary of our conversation, he wanted to stop payment on your check."

"I don't believe you," said Gibbs. "Anyway, it's cashed."

Gibbs had received a letter two days ago from Gary that said Powers was telling people that he, Gibbs, was an informer. Gary wrote that Powers was a no-good son of a bitch for trying to start such rumors. Now, this. Schiller certainly had to be the most insensitive individual in the world. He actually had the gall to say, "Gary is talking bad about you. I would worry about being seen in Salt Lake."

Stuff like that came out of a turkey's asshole. Gibbs knew better than anybody that Gary didn't have connections in Salt Lake. Still Gibbs felt full of weak sentiments. He didn't know if it was fear, or just feeling horrible that Gary knew, but it couldn't have been worse.

"How long have you worked for the police?" asked Schiller.

"I've been twelve years undercover," said Gibbs. "This is the first time I've had to come up."

"It must scare you," said Schiller.

"Not that much," said Gibbs, "I know my job. Yesterday in court, I was up against what is probably the heaviest criminal element in the State of Utah." Gibbs puffed on the Viceroy Super Long. "When I got on that stand yesterday, they didn't say, is this guy an informer or a paid fink, they asked, is he a reliable counterintelligence agent? If they wanted, I could have given them names of FBI agents I worked for, showed plane tickets they gave me, vouchers. Halterman can tell you. I've got a photographic memory. I could sit on this tape recorder for a day, and tell you everything about Gary."

"Did they place you next to Gary for any reason?" Schiller asked.

"No," Gibbs said, "he didn't know anything they needed to know.

It was just for my own protection. I didn't like the idea of being in the main tank. Some of the people I was going to testify against could have had friends passing through."

"Did you feed Halterman any stuff on Gary?" asked Barry Farrell.

"The only thing I told Halterman is, 'Watch. If they give Gilmore the death penalty, they're going to have to execute him.' "

"What if they had asked you to spy on him?" Farrell went on.

"I don't think I would have," said Gibbs. "I liked the guy."

Without a pause, Farrell asked, "Is Gary well hung?"

"I don't know," Gibbs said, "I never paid no attention."

"I'm just curious," said Farrell, looking carefully at him.

"I never paid no attention to it," said Gibbs.

"Did Gary have sex with April?" Schiller asked.

"Gary ain't no raper," Gibbs said. "If he did it, he fooled me better than I fooled him."

3

What with the fact that Gary now knew his occupation, Gibbs was feeling so nervous and out of tune, that to get himself humming right again, he ended by giving Schiller and Farrell a list of the outfits with whom he had been associated over the last ten years. What the hell, they could get it anyway from the court transcript.

Gibbs had worked, he said, for the Salt Lake City Police Department; Salt Lake County Sheriff's Office; FBI; Treasury Department; Bureau of Alcohol, Tobacco and Firearms; Regent Eight Task Force; and the University of Utah Police Department, Narcotics Division. "I've been a crook and I've worked for law enforcement," said Gibbs, "and either one by itself is not enough."

"What are you going to do now?" asked Schiller.

"Well," said Gibbs, "Halterman is going down to the Board of Pardons tomorrow, and get me released. They'll give me new papers, a new name, and let me carry a pistol. The fact of the matter is I've got to make a run for my life. I have a target on my back." The hand holding the Viceroy Super Long didn't shake that much, but he said, "Okay, I'll tell you. In twelve years of working under, I've never had the fear like I got it right now. Yesterday, Halterman had to clear the courthouse for me, that's how worried he was."

"Halterman a good friend?" Farrell asked.

"I would say," said Gibbs, "he is nobody to fool with." He giggled. "Ken likes to tell how he's a bad shot, because one time he tried to hit a friend of mine in the heart, but missed and hit between the eyes. Now he wants to be on the firing squad for Gilmore." He giggled again.

"What are we wasting our time with this snitch for?" Farrell asked Schiller. "I don't even like to be in the same room." He got up abruptly and walked out. They were really trying to reduce the price, Gibbs thought.

Halterman happened to be in the corridor. Farrell buttonholed him. "I heard that story how you hit the fellow between the eyes," he said.

It caught Halterman by surprise. "Well," he said, "ha, ha," trying to get started.

"Have you put in your application for Gilmore's firing squad?" Barry asked.

"I'd be proud to get on it. Gilmore is a homicidal maniac."

"Well," said Barry, "when it comes to Gary, you must not miss! Gilmore's eyes, his kidneys, his liver, and some other valuable organs are going to people who need them. If you shoot, get the heart." Halterman looked back at him like he didn't know if Farrell was a lunatic or a Judge.

"You get it straight," said Halterman. "I'm not a bad shot, I'm a good shot. I aimed to hit Gibbs's friend in the eye and I hit him in the eye. You have to know you can take a human life before you ever put on a police uniform."

Gibbs knew he had been talking to Schiller too freely. Supposedly, it was just samples, but he was really giving it away. Yet, divulging the information seemed to cool his fear a bit.

Trying to up the ante, he said, "Gilmore has told me things he hasn't told anyone else alive."

"Gary has already given us everything you said," Schiller replied.

More turkey product, thought Gibbs. But he had blown it, he knew. The offer, when it came, was for two hundred, no more. A release, not an exclusive.

Schiller was feeling good. Gibbs had corroborated every story they picked up in Gary's letters. He had talked about Luis the wetback jailer, and Powers, and the dixie cup with the string that burned, and Gibbs's generosity with money. There was the mending of the false teeth, the haircuts, painting on the walls, painting each other's faces — all of it had been told again by Gibbs. Moreover, he was no threat. He really didn't know much about Nicole. Just a sidebar to the main tale.

So Schiller had gained a lot. That phrase of Gary's: "Larry, have you read the letters I wrote to Nicole? — Tell me" was still vibrating in his head. He had needed a way to ask Gary questions that originated from the letters, but he had also needed a means of concealing how he acquired such information. Gibbs's stories would take care of that.

4

Maybe it had gone too well. Even as Schiller reached into his pocket for the release, and said, "Two pages. One for you to keep, one copy for me," Gibbs looked back with a real sleazo grin. "You just dropped some money on the floor, you got so much," he said.

Schiller looked down. There were green bills all over. "Ah, shit," said Schiller, "am I that rich?" A key from the TraveLodge was also on the floor.

"You and Barry," asked Gibbs, "staying at the TraveLodge?" At this point, Farrell nodded, and Schiller shook his head in the negative. Gibbs commented. "He shakes his head yes, you say no." Schiller said, "You didn't ask me if I was registered at the TraveLodge, you asked me if I was staying there." He laughed loudly. "Well, I'll advise you of your rights." Gibbs gave him a look, and changed the subject.

By the time they got back to the motel, Farrell realized that Schiller was taking Gibbs seriously. Of course, Gibbs had done some talking about his connections with the heaviest gang in Salt Lake City, but Farrell expected such connections were about as good as his own to the Johnny Carson show. However, as soon as they parked their car at the TraveLodge, Larry went to see the woman at the desk, and said, "Give me two blank registration cards, and two rooms that are empty, okay?" While the woman stood by stupefied, Schiller make up cards for empty rooms, backdated them to yesterday when he and Farrell had moved in, and tore up the current registration cards for Barry and himself. "Bet they didn't teach you this at the TraveLodge Training School," Farrell said to her. He was feeling entertained by all this registrationmanship, but also thinking, "Maybe I'm really underestimating what went on."

The way Schiller looked at it, Gibbs was capable of hating him. No reason why he shouldn't. So Gibbs might want to finger him. Walking out of that police station in Orem, it had hit Schiller. He was not only dealing with some dangerous people, but living pretty exposed. He might need a little protection. There was a bodyguard he hired in Los Angeles from time to time, Harve Roddetz, who worked for one of the Cadillac limousine companies as a driver, but farmed out on special occasions. Harve had protected him in the Watts riots, and right after Schiller's house had been bombed in the aftermath of the Susan Atkins story. So Schiller felt like having Harve around now. After all, he was situated in this motel room on the ground floor. Anybody could walk up to his door, blow a Magnum through the window, and take off in a car. But he reasoned the problem through. The thing to do for tonight was not change rooms. At this hour it would attract attention, and anybody watching would see him move luggage. It was simpler to switch the registration cards. That way, if Gibbs talked a cop into making a call here to find out the room numbers, the registration would provide incorrect information.

Meanwhile, Schiller could see that Barry was enjoying it. Maybe he just has a more cavalier attitude toward certain types of danger than I do, thought Larry. All the same, he decided, provisionally, to do without Harve Roddetz. It was paramount that mutual respect between Farrell and himself be maintained.

5

In the morning, they visited Gibbs and paid over the $200 for a release. Gibbs, getting out that day, seemed less nervous, but Schiller was not in a good mood. On the way back to the motel, going over his problems, his revenues, and his potential outlets, Larry began to feel a cumulative fatigue. He also felt hungry for a little time alone with Stephie. She was still pissed at the way they never did have a real Thanksgiving. It gave him an idea. What if he went with her to Hawaii for Christmas week? They could visit his brother. While he was gone, Barry could take up the slack.

When he told Moody and Stanger that he wanted a rest before the big push in January, Stanger said, "If you're going to Hawaii, maybe it's time for us to grab a vacation as well. Where are *our* airplane tickets?" He was kidding, but it was as close to the line as you could get. Schiller blew. "This is no expense-account scam. I'm going to Hawaii on my own. If you want to go, pay for it."

Then the first phone call next morning was from *Time*. They were still willing to give proper space for Gilmore, but were definitely having second thoughts about paying the $25,000. They would give four pages plus the cover, and no money. A policy decision had been made in the last week to stop checkbook journalism. It was all fashion, Schiller thought unhappily. In another two months they would reverse themselves and buy things again, but for now it certainly forced his hand with the *Enquirer*, and that meant less revenue from the foreign sales. Still, right after the vacation, he would send Stephie, his mother, and her mother over to Europe to sell the letters. For something like this, they were the only people he could trust.

In the last day before he left, Schiller got together a force of typists in Los Angeles to transcribe Gilmore's letters to Nicole, a huge job. Fifteen hundred pages of manuscript. Still there was no other way to sell the stuff overseas. Foreign editors couldn't even read typed English without lighting a cigarette. They certainly wouldn't go through hundreds of pages in longhand.

He also wanted to give something to Gary before he left, but in fact didn't know whether to send a Christmas present. Since he was going away, and this was resented, okay, it was the wrong time to try to impress him with an expensive gift. He decided to send a telegram. Fifteen years ago, covering the Hemingway suicide in Ketchum, Idaho, for *Paris Match,* Schiller had written a line to go out under his photographs. It said Hemingway had not wanted to evade the greatest adventure of his life, which was death. That became *Paris Match*'s headline for their picture essay on the funeral. Now, Schiller thought he would use it, or something like it, for Gilmore. Make the man think of him while he was gone. A touch of the mystical.

DEAR GARY
EACH MINUTE BRINGS US CLOSER TOGETHER AND I KNOW THAT WE WERE RIGHT TO EMBARK ON THIS CHALLENGE STOP I AM THOROUGHLY CONVINCED THAT AS I GO DEEPER THE MEANING OF YOUR LIFE BECOMES MORE CLEAR STOP IT IS AN ADVENTURE FOR ME AND THAT ADVENTURE CAN NEVER BE REPAID UNTIL I COME UPON THE GREATEST ADVENTURE STOP I WISH YOU A MERRY HOLIDAY AND I LOOK FORWARD TO SEEING YOU.
LARRY

Not an hour before plane time, there was a call from Bill Moyers. He was starting a TV show called "CBS Reports." First show would be on Gilmore. When he heard Schiller was on his way to Hawaii, Moyers even said, "We'll visit you there." Schiller said, "Come on, Mr. Moyers, I am not going to be photographed lying on the beach, doing checkbook journalism with my bare belly out to the sun. That's neither the way I see myself, nor the way I intend to present myself." Moyers began to chuckle. "You're sharp, aren't you?" he said.

Schiller found out that the show was tentatively scheduled to air just before Gary's execution. He told Moyers he would be happy to get together with him in Provo after New Year's and might cooperate provided certain things were understood. It was his way of telling Moyers that he knew the name of the game. Off to Hawaii!

CHAPTER 20

Christmas

1

On the morning of Wednesday, December 22nd, Ken Halterman appeared before the Board of Pardons. He testified that Richard Gibbs had been a witness for the State of Utah in two felony trials, the first in Provo against Jim Ross, the other in Richfield, Utah, against Ted Burr, and his testimony had helped to convict one of the largest theft rings ever uncovered in the State of Utah. It had been a million-dollar-a-year operation, stated Halterman, that dealt in stolen recreational vehicles, boats, camper trailers, horse-trailers, and trucks.

Gibbs got out of Orem Jail around eleven, and was driven to the University of Utah Police Department where he acquired an ID in the name of Lance LeBaron, after which he picked up $400 that the Salt Lake Police was paying him, and went from there to the bank, where he withdrew the balance of Gary's $2,000.

Next morning, Gibbs got license plates for the big 98 he had just bought, a blue and white 1970 Olds, and then went to a barber shop and got his hair cut and his mustache and goatee removed, after which he took off for Helena, Montana. He had the idea he might even push on to Canada.

2

It was about noon when Gibbs left, and he stopped at Pocatello around four, filled up with gas, and went on to Idaho Falls where he stopped at the Ponderosa Motel. Downtown, he picked up a girl in a bar and got laid. No big deal. On the other hand, it didn't cost nothing.

In the morning, he went over to see his grandmother and aunt who lived in Idaho Falls, and were 89 and 65 respectively. His grandma was going to turn 90 on January 17, Gary's new execution date, and that made him think of "psychic powers, Geebs," a bad thought.

He spent a couple of hours with these ladies, and left a fifty-dollar bill for their Christmas, then stopped and ate, drove for a few more hours, got the car greased, the oil changed, antifreeze checked, bought a new filter and had the tires rotated. It took an hour. While he was waiting, he had a few drinks. Then he headed out, hoping to get to Helena that same night.

About fifteen miles north of Butte, he was heading up a mountain road in the dark when a logging truck came down fast around a turn and barreled over onto his side of the road. Huge headlights. Gibbs had a quick choice: hit the truck or ditch. He went to the right and smacked into something in the gully.

When he came to, his head was bleeding and his false teeth were broken. The side of his face was screaming with pain. He managed to get the car door open, but when he went to step out, he fell face down in the snow. No way could he put any pressure on his left leg, he had to crawl to the edge of the highway. The first car that went by saw him lying on the side of the road but just kept going. A few minutes later, a pickup stopped. Two men helped him in, and took him along the road to a cafe called the Elk Pack. There, they phoned the Highway Patrol. The bartender gave him a wet towel to wipe the blood off his head, and Gibbs sat on a barstool so his leg could hang down without pressure while he drank three straight shots of whiskey.

The ambulance came and put an air bag around his leg, inflated it, laid him on a stretcher, and started down the road. Then they had to stop because a wrecker was blocking the highway in order to lift Gibbs's car out of the gully. He raised his head long enough to ask if they could get the luggage from his trunk, and the officer said he would. With it all, Gibbs noticed that his headlights were still on.

At the hospital, the doctor stitched up his scalp, and split his pants to x-ray the knee, leg, ankle and foot. Turned out his leg was shattered and his jaw fractured. The doctor also said that the tendons were torn so bad in the calf and ankle his leg would probably have to be amputated. It was certainly swollen twice its size. His foot was completely black. The rest of the limb was purple. Immediately, Gibbs said, "My leg ain't going to be taken off. Just give me a shot for pain, and I'll leave."

Before he could get out of there he had to show the highway patrolman his identification. The cop proceeded to write two tickets, one for traveling too fast under existing conditions, one for no driver's license in his possession. They hadn't had the fake one ready in Salt Lake by the time he left. So the cop said it would be $20 bail for the first, $15 on the other. Cash. Gibbs signed the tickets, paid over the $35, and asked to be taken to one of the nicer motels. The cop got him out to the patrol car in a wheelchair, and dropped him off at the Mile High. It was about midnight. They had to wake the lady who ran the place, then help him inside to register, next wheel him to Room 3 with his luggage. The shot that doctor had given was beginning to take effect, and his pain eased, and Gibbs went off to sleep. When he awoke next morning, Christmas Day, his leg was killing him.

He called the Owl Cab Company in Butte and asked the lady dispatcher if a cab could pick him up a bag of ice, a six-pack of Coke, a fifth of Canadian Club and some cigarettes. Once the booze arrived, Gibbs managed to get out of bed by holding onto the back of a chair, hopped to the bathroom, looked in the mirror at the stitches and his black eye, then got back into bed and fixed a good stiff drink. It did nothing for the pain, so he fixed several more. Helped a little, but not much. It wasn't like taking whiskey for a toothache.

That evening, he could stand it no longer, and called the motel lady and asked if her husband would take him to the hospital. She wasn't married, but she had two friends who had eaten Christmas dinner with her, and these gentlemen brought him to the St. James

Catholic Hospital, after Gibbs asked for the best doctor in town. There it was. The fellow's name was Best. Dr. Robert Best. One of Evel Kneivel's own personal doctors.

Well, Best wanted to admit him to the hospital, but Gibbs again said no. Instead, he left with a pain prescription for codeine, and one for Oral Varidase to break up the blood clots. Plus a cast. "You better hope," said Dr. Best, "that phlebitis doesn't set in." This was Gibbs's Christmas Day.

3

After the second suicide attempt, Campbell said to Gilmore, "Look, if you want to talk about the firing squad, I'll be your sounding board." Gilmore said, "Aw, hell, we don't want to talk about that. We're just going to shoot this old half-drunk thief, you know." They would joke about it.

Once in a while, Gilmore would ask him what the other prisoners were thinking, but Cline did not tell him that more than a few were fed up with Gary Gilmore. It was because everything he did affected the affairs of other prisoners in Maximum. What with needing three guards for him, it even hurt the classroom schedule. Chow got delayed not once, but several times. When it was anything very big, like a suicide attempt, the place got locked up. The convicts were tired of all those hassles.

On the other hand, they never said Gary was crazy. He'd been in prison eighteen years. Everybody empathized with that.

Of course with Gary on deathwatch, that is not only on Death Row, but with a date to be executed, he had a whole three-cell section to himself. A suite. His own cell, the middle one, had solid walls on three sides and regular cell bars on the door. They let it stay open, however, and allowed him access to the short corridor facing the three cells. Of course, there was always a guard present. Gary could even walk up to the cell-block gate and look out on the main corridor and talk to any officer or prisoner walking by. Sometimes, in the late hours of the night, Father Meersman would visit, and Gilmore would bring a stool or sometimes just sit on the floor, his back against the bars, while Meersman would camp on a chair out in the main corridor. They would converse through the bars. Everything around them was painted in a light, pastel green.

Whereas when Gary would be brought out to the visiting room to meet his lawyer or uncle, they would take him down the long main corridor of Maximum from which shorter corridors led off at right angles to the one-story cell blocks. At such times, as a precaution against escape, no other inmate would be in the main corridor. While Gary walked along, passing the barred gate to each cell block, the prisoners would see him coming, and call out, "Hey, Gary," or "Hang in there."

"Stay with it," they would yell.

Toward Christmas, Moody and Stanger went out to the prison every morning and then again every afternoon or evening. It got to the point where they had to assign the rest of their cases to other people in the office. They didn't mind that much. Their feeling for Gary was definitely getting warmer. In fact, he soon had them on another mission.

There was a murderer named Belcher in the cell block next to Gary in Death Row, and he'd been described to Moody and Stanger often enough to have a clear picture. Belcher was a heavyset fellow, maybe six feet tall, barrel chested, short-cropped hair, dark complected, and he had a protruding forehead, an overhanging brow, big features, big arms, very muscular. Gary described how his head was always swiveling around, always suspicious. Often he wouldn't talk. Stanger heard from the guards that Belcher was an obsessive-compulsive and kept things in his cell like cans of soup, or any kind of trinket they let him retain, really one of those crazy recluses whose apartments were like junk shops. He was certainly property conscious. Would throw fits if you tried to take his things away. A very territorial man. From what Ron could gather, he lived like a bear, as if his cell was a cave. Yet he and Gary, of all people, got along well. From what Moody heard, Belcher also liked kids.

A few days before Christmas, at Gary's suggestion, Bob got one of his law clerks to take a picture of a large group of children, holding up a big sign that said, "HI, BELCHER!" It tickled the daylights out of Gary to pass the photograph over on Christmas Day. "Here," he said to Belcher, "here's a shot of some kids rooting for you."

4

Dec. 23

Oh Gary i love You So
    i miss you! God how i miss you. More than the sky and the earth. More than my freedom and more than my children. . . .
    The lawyers gave me a letter from you today. But these scuzzy sheep herdin Aids took it before i got to read it. The Punks shake me down even when i visit with my mother an Kids. Fuckin Looneys. Oh Baby i wanted so bad to read your lovin' words.
    Babe, what is to become of us? God, what is happening? i need to see you. How could they let you die so alone, my love? i want so bad just to look into your eyes once again.
    God ain't it crazy? Aint it so fuckin crazy.
    i'm furious with the ways an wiles of Love Life and the Ultimate Wisdom, furious with God. And furious with myself for not being patient and doing things right the first time with jack an jill.
    Love to have that pretty white bird sitting here on my night stand. You remember that i spoke or wrote to you once of my childhood daydream of being through with this senseless life and being born once again but if the choice be mine it was to be born into the wings of a small white bird. And still would i choose the same if i could.

Christmas Eve
Dec. 24

Long days waiting
For your Love again
Long nights restless
Scattered thots
Wondering whats become
Of all our chances.
        Nicole

Dec. 25

it is not really a fear jest such a great sadness to think of the uncertainity of days ahead.

Nicole

DESERET NEWS

No Move for Nicole

Provo, Christmas Day — Nicole Barrett has been ordered committed indefinitely to the Utah State Hospital in Provo.

Fourth District Judge David Sam ruled that the mother of two young children should stay in the mental hospital. . . .

Meanwhile, a turkey dinner with all the trimmings was the highlight of Christmas Day at Utah State Prison where Gilmore is in isolation for disciplinary reasons.

Gilmore was not allowed to receive any presents and today was a non-visiting day, so he had no visitors a prison spokesman said.

Sterling Baker's wife, Ruth Ann, wrote a letter.

Dear Gary,

I was thinking about you and how you are going to be alone on Xmas. I wish I could be up there with you. I really love you a lot. I hope in the next world we can meat, and be able to know each other well. But please don't try to hurry it. I don't want you to die.

Usually the Damico family would have a big Christmas party. One year they would get together at Brenda's house, next year at Toni's, then Ida's. This season, being no joy for it, they met at Toni's to exchange gifts, said a prayer for Gary, had a cup of coffee, went back to their separate places.

Mikal came over to the trailer on Christmas Day but Bessie's mind was on other times. She remembered one Christmas when

Gary was not in Reform School and was watching his baby brother unwrap the gifts. She had tended to spoil Mikal in those days. It had taken her half the night to wrap his presents, but in the morning Mikal kept saying, "This is an awful day. I've got so many things I don't want." Gary kept laughing.

Gaylen, on the other hand, came home one afternoon that year just before the holidays and said one of the Sisters told them how there was no Santa Claus. He was very upset. Bessie said, "Gaylen, there's only the spirit of giving. That exists. You've had the good heart to believe in Santa Claus longer than anybody else."

Then her thoughts came back to the trailer. These days all thoughts returned to the trailer. Her heart turned over, as if a great wheel had revolved. She felt a tear drop, pure as sorrow itself.

GILMORE   What is Christmas? These holidays in jail are a bummer. You don't get any mail. The routine is disrupted, the day just seems slower. They act like they're really doing something by giving you a big meal, but it ain't like the menu in the paper. You don't get it good, you know. I don't like weekends in jail, but holidays I hate.

5

Shirley Pedler, Executive Director of the ACLU in Utah, had gotten her job right after college. She applied for the post, and there she was, Executive Director, with a general membership of a few hundred people. The funds to keep the office going came from membership dues, and a modest grant from the national office. Five or six Salt Lake attorneys volunteered their time on a regular basis, and as many as twenty might help once a year. It was small stuff and, right now, beleaguered. In Utah, belonging to the ACLU was like being a Bolshevik.

Once the ACLU got into the Gilmore case, Shirley Pedler began to receive a lot of hate mail and crank calls. For more than a month they called her at work and at home, all day, all night. She knew it would continue until Gilmore was dead. She was living by herself, and sometimes after a long day, she would dread going home to hear the phone ringing. "Something bad's going to happen to you," a voice would intone. "I hope you get shot with Gilmore," the next caller would say. Sometimes the men were obscene. One remarked that since she was good looking and single, he was ready to do this and that to her.

They usually hung up quickly. By now, these days, she was tending to flare up. Didn't hesitate to tell her callers off. Her nerves had never been well insulated, but with the loss of sleep and the loss of weight, she had nightmares about Mr. Gilmore. A man would kick a platform out from under him. As he hung in the air, they would release gas pellets. Some of the dreams were bloody.

Raised to be active in the Church, she was no longer a practicing Mormon. All the same, these callers were like people she had grown up with. She didn't feel betrayed so much as unable to believe what was going on. "The injustice in this case is so apparent," she would say to herself. At the Board of Pardons Hearing, she thought Chairman Latimer was totally inconsistent. "Why is there no public outcry?" she wanted to know. It had been a travesty, and in the middle was Gilmore, a terribly pale and quite attractive young man, Shirley Pedler thought. His fasting made him look ghastly, but unforgettable. He was so pale.

Afterward, she became personally self-conscious about the fact that this man's life, due to the maneuverings going on, was in very uncertain circumstances. He did not know his fate from day to day, and yet she was part of those maneuverings.

So she wrote a letter to Gilmore. She told him that she regretted the discomfort that the ACLU was causing him and the terrible uncertainty. She wished she had the opportunity to talk to him directly, and explain what they were doing. She knew his life was being made more difficult by her. She wanted to tell him why she thought it had to be done. She wished they could cooperate, instead of finding themselves on different sides.

She thought that if she could speak to Gary Gilmore, she would say that she was not personally out of sympathy with his wish to commit suicide. She could see how confronting life at Utah State Prison might warrant taking one's own life, and he had a right to decide whether he was going to live or die. But she did feel the State had no business participating. Capital punishment was not only wrong, but his execution would touch off others, for it would demystify the taking of life by the State. The real horror was people lining up to blow somebody away with a lack of passion, a methodical, calculated turning of the machinery of the State against the individual. Why come to terms with it? That was what she wanted to say.

As lawyers, Moody and Stanger were able to beat the no-visitor law, and they went to see Gary late on Christmas afternoon.

GILMORE   Shirley Pedler wrote me a personal letter. . . . What does she look like anyway?

STANGER   She's a slight, young woman, about thirty, not bad looking. I've never seen her in person. I've only seen her on TV. She wears a suit with pants.

GILMORE   I don't know what we can do to make the ACLU butt out. The Supreme Court said they're not gonna rehear it. What else can they do? Go to the United Nations? . . .

Shirley Pedler had Christmas dinner at her parents' house. They were pretty conservative people, and her father worked for the State, but never, until this meal, had they had a knock-down drag-out about capital punishment. Today, however, her brother started to attack her on the ACLU position, and Shirley had to defend it. Her brother kept saying, "What about the victims and the families?"

It escalated. Shirley had been going in a different direction from her family anyway, but the discussion did ruin the dinner and she felt bad about that. None of them was able to get really comfortable after that.

GILMORE   Would you like to hear a poem?

STANGER   Sure.

GILMORE   I'll give you a little preamble to it. You know prisons are noisy places. And I talked about that guard blowing his nose for five minutes. And this morning he carried on a two-hour conversation, and I finally asked him to shut up. This poem is in the book that I wrote for Nicole. This is the preamble: *I get irritable at the noise I have to listen to, toilets flushing, water pipes jarring, stupid conversations, screened conversation — Now here's the poem:*

Dark thots of mayhem on a cold steel nite,
when the little noises won't let you sleep.
Dark thots of mayhem, murder and gore.
A bore. Too few dark debts are ever paid.
A fool down the way laughs at the loss of day,
another sighs and another cries
at the lies of their lives.
Dark thots of mayhem murder and gore,
too few dark debts are ever paid
More owed.

I wrote that poem in '74 listening to noise I didn't want to hear. I like it quiet. I would love an absence of sound so profound I could hear my blood. I guess that's one of the things I've always hated worst about prison, the noise, listening to motherfuckers barf and cough, and listening to frustration. On the seventeenth of January I hope to hear my last harsh noise.

STANGER   Hum, it's a good poem.

CHAPTER 21

The Octave of Christmas

1

Julie Jacoby had a good opinion of Shirley Pedler and thought her very attractive with that long thin build and her beautiful long hands. The strain of the Gilmore situation, however, was really making Shirley lose too much weight. She had been a pretty intense woman to begin with, but after these last weeks, she was beginning to resemble a cigarette.

Although Shirley was twenty-four years younger, Julie Jacoby thought they were a lot alike. They would both rather be reclusive, yet were always in the middle of political activity. So Julie was not surprised when Shirley, during Christmas week, asked her to aid in the formation of the Utah Coalition Against the Death Penalty.

Of course Julie had not been doing a great deal in the year since she and her husband moved from Chicago to Utah. It was nothing like the Days of Rage in Chicago in the summer of 1968 when people were beaten by the police. That was when, in her own mind, she moved on from being little more than just another society lady from the North Shore who came down to United Charities twice a week to spend an afternoon sympathizing with the mothers of black children who came into the office in various states of coma from eating lead paint that had peeled off the walls. Some of those society ladies used to appear for work wearing diamond rings, and Julie had spent time trying to get the idea across that these ladies ought not to carry more wealth on their finger than the person in need across the desk could make in a year.

Her husband was an executive and Julie would say that he seemed never to have recovered from a shock in the womb that left him a deep-dyed forever Republican. Julie, Phi Beta in medieval history from the University of Michigan, had gone to Chicago to seek her fortune, and found it in the good German fellow she married, for he rose in the ranks of his corporation while Julie brought up their children and became — her first clue to future shifts — a lapsed Episcopalian. She might have done no more than join the League of Women Voters, read the *National Observer,* the *New York Review of Books* and *I. F. Stone,* but the Days of Rage on Michigan Boulevard shook her to the roots. She felt radicalized. After Attica traumatized. She thought Rockefeller was shooting the fish in the barrel that day. She worked with the Alliance to End Repression.

Then the company moved her husband to Utah. Out in Salt Lake, the ACLU was the only game in town. Julie wanted to start another Alliance to End Repression, but the energy was no longer there. Utah depressed her. She felt that she and her husband were living in a deteriorated relationship, and her young son, ripped from his native soil at the age of twelve, was not happy. It just about took Julie down. She became so occupied with her son's problems that she felt defanged on social issues.

She thought she was in an extremely right-wing place. The Church and State were deeply entangled. Julie went to visit the opening of the Legislature and here was this trio of sour-faced *old* men sitting up front. They did the opening prayer. She was there that day to testify against capital punishment, and the chairman of the committee, a Mormon, said that as long as he had to listen to the Episcopalian point of view, he would like to read something to close the meeting, and opened a red-bound book and quoted Brigham Young. Those who shed blood must pay in blood. It chilled her. The Church *was* the State. She would have liked to tell that chairman, "We live in a world of fallible people where prosecutors decide whether the charge is second- or first-degree murder and nobody knows who or what is influencing the prosecutor. They don't have the right to take an individual's life under the protective coloration of the law."

She might have a problem with her child, and her marriage was dead, and she loved the pleasures of seclusion, and the nourishments of reading, God, she loved to read the way others would insist on three meals a day, but when the call came from Shirley Pedler to help in organizing the Utah Coalition Against the Death Penalty, she knew she would go out in the world again with her freaky blond hair, blond to everyone's disbelief — at the age of fifty-four, go out in her denims and chin-length-hanging-down-straight vanilla hair to that Salt Lake world where nobody would ever make the mistake of thinking she was a native Utah lady inasmuch as Utah was the Beehive State. The girls went big for vertical hair-dos, pure monuments to shellac.

So she went to the meeting for a Coalition Against the Death Penalty and twenty people showed up to see what they could do about convincing Gary Gilmore that he was 100 percent wrong in wanting the State to shuffle him off this mortal coil. The Coalition would seek to get the idea across that the State should not be able to kill anybody. Gilmore was a sensitive artist, but he was also, thought Julie Jacoby, acting like a very selfish man.

Shirley Pedler had been intending to organize the meeting herself, but came down with a terrific case of semi-pneumonia, so Julie discovered a fellow named Bill Hoyle from the Socialist Workers' Party had been handed the bill. He was there, he said, to do the legwork. There was a pastor from the United Church of Christ, the Reverend Donald Proctor, and the Reverend John P. Adams from the United Methodist Church who was on the Board of the National Coalition Against Capital Punishment. They discussed what sort of action they should take.

Don Proctor had ideas that Julie thought were something Alinsky-esque. He wanted a highly visible rally, a get-together, say, in the center of a busy shopping mall on a Saturday.

No one was comfortable with that. For one thing, you had to get permission to go on private property. They finally decided to have a mass meeting in a hall prior to January 17, and then a vigil on the prison grounds all through the night before the execution. More ministers might turn out then. Right now was Christmas week, a time of heavy business for reverends.

In the meantime, they had $100 in working funds contributed by the Society of Friends. Bill Hoyle said he'd get some flyers printed and they could count on buttons from the Fellowship of Reconciliation in Nyack, New York. The buttons would say, *"Why do we kill people who kill people to show that killing people is wrong?"*

2

Back in the motel, Gibbs was eating codeine like candy, but he was careful to take Oral Varidase only as prescribed. Day after Christmas, he called his mother and she told him to keep his leg elevated and put a heating pad on it. She'd been a registered nurse for thirty-five years. She also told him to be careful shaving. If he was even to nick himself, he might not, because of the Oral Varidase, be able to get the bleeding to stop.

Gibbs also called Halterman. Ken's first words were, "If it wasn't you, Gibbs, I wouldn't believe it." Then he said, "Know anybody can get in more jams?" That's all Gibbs needed to cheer himself up.

He phoned Owl Taxi for cigarettes, whiskey, Cokes, ice and some canned tomato and mushroom soup, which he figured to use on the little courtesy coffeepot heater in the room. Until he got his upper plate fixed, he would have to live on soup. Then he called the Highway Patrol to see who had brought his car in, and asked the kid who'd done the job to look in the front seat for the other half of his teeth. An hour or so later, the fellow came to the room with the missing piece. Since the car was totaled, he wondered if Gibbs would consider selling the engine. Could pay around $25 a month. The boy had just gotten married and didn't have much money. Gibbs said, "Take it from me as a late wedding present."

After a couple days of tomato and mushroom soup, Gibbs asked the lady who ran the motel if she knew of a restaurant that offered take-home food. Right offhand, she didn't, but asked what he would like. When he said soft-boiled eggs, toast and milk, she brought it to his room and he paid her $5. She told him two would be sufficient, but he insisted on five. She was one of the most agreeable people he ever met in his thirty-one years of life.

The following day he called a florist shop in Butte and asked the saleswoman to have flowers delivered. Then he asked her to write on the card, "To the nicest lady in the world" and please sign it Lance LeBaron. He explained he did not know her name, but sure did know how well she had treated him. The woman at the florist shop not only agreed she was nice but said the name was Irene Snell, and the flowers were delivered an hour or so later.

From then on, every night, Mrs. Snell brought his meals. After he got his teeth fixed, she would tell him what she herself was having for dinner. He ended up eating everything from spaghetti to steaks and always had to argue with her on the price. In the meantime, the doctor came by to check his leg, refill his prescription and remove the stitches from his forehead.

Slowly, his cash was going down, but Gibbs didn't think about it. He had never been able to manage money anyway. Between $25 and $60 a day was being spent in long-distance phone calls, and he made a point to pay the motel bill each morning. It was hard not to feel sorry for himself. Each night he'd get drunk, and then he'd want to cry on someone's shoulder. That was hell at long distance. One old girl friend he almost asked to fly up to stay with him, but decided he wouldn't. Then he called another old girl friend. Almost did the same thing. But he couldn't think of a girl who might not disclose to the wrong people where he was and, worse, what condition he was in. He made a point to tell everybody he called that he was lying in bed with a nine millimeter Browning Automatic right next to him, and thirteen good reasons in the clip why nobody, unless invited, better come through his door. When he mentioned this to Halterman, Ken said, "For somebody who's trying to hide, you sure talk your butt off." Even the operators in Butte started using his name. As soon as he'd ask for Salt Lake, they would answer, "How are you, Mr. LeBaron? It's room three at the Mile High, is it not?" He had left Utah with $1,370 and was now down to $500.

Lying in bed, he would sometimes go out of his head a little and imagine what it would be like when he went to the execution. Would he get to go up and talk in person? If they let him, he would say, "Gilmore, remember how you once told me you never misjudged a person who has done time? Well, let me tell you what I do for a living." Then he would ponder whether he really would say it, assuming in his mind, somehow, that Schiller had never told anybody, which, of course, he had. "Gary," Gibbs would say, looking him in the eye, "you have met your match. Your sixth sense about good convicts has served you wrong in regards to me. I am the one person who has been able to fool, deceive and turn the tables on you, Gary Gilmore." Then it would all come down on him again, his pain, his situation, his fucking life, and he would say to himself, "Gary, that ain't the speech I'd make. I would say, 'Goddamn you, you got more guts than any son of a bitch I ever knew. I just wish I had as many balls as you. Hell, fellow, A man knows a man whenever they meet,' " and he would blink back his sadness, for it was a sentence Gary had written to him in a recent letter that could just as well have been received years ago.

3

Half the value of Schiller's vacation was quickly blown. He had brought Stephie out to meet his brother and sister-in-law and it was a social thing, and she was spending all her time with them, and where was he? On the phone. What headaches.

The lawyers for Max Jensen's insurance company had filed a Wrongful Death suit for recovery of $40,000 from Gary Gilmore's estate, and as a courtesy to Colleen Jensen, had hooked on a million-dollar suit for her. Now, while Schiller was trying to go belly-up to the sun, damn if the insurance lawyers didn't get a Court order that Gary had to give a deposition. When Schiller found out about it, he hit the fucking ceiling. He was stuck to the phone. Said to Moody, "Did you agree? You didn't fight it? What do you mean you didn't?" He did not enjoy shrieking at Moody because it was highly nonproductive. Moody was too stubborn for that. Just sat behind his glasses. A real poker player. Yet Schiller couldn't help himself. He was climbing the walls and bouncing.

"What are you upset about?" asked Bob Moody. "What's the big thing about a deposition?"

Schiller almost said, "Are you out of your mind?" He did say, "Don't you understand? The *Enquirer* can make a goddamned deal with those lawyers, go in for three hours, and pick up Gary's whole life story. Even if they can't get any of their own reporters in, they can coach one of the attorneys to pump Gary." It was awful. They had a right to start the deposition with where-were-you-born, then go into Gilmore's criminal record. "The whole story," shrieked Schiller, "can be pulled out in one session."

Moody said, "We can't stop it."

"Bullshit," said Schiller. "I want you to go right into Court. If you can't block the deposition, at least file a motion that it's got to be put in bond." He smacked his fist against the night table, feeling a whole kinship with the notion of bond. "The tapes from that meeting," he said, "have got to be sealed right in the jail, and the Court has to give an order that they're not to be transcribed for so many months, blah blah, you understand what I mean, et cetera." Stephie was ready to kill him. Here it was supposed to be a vacation, and he was living on the phone. "Is this what it's going to be like when we get married?" she cried out. Was she just another woman? Was she a business deal? Schiller waved her off. Over the wire, he was practically writing out the motion. What a relief when he learned a couple of days later that the Judge agreed to seal the stuff in wax, literally, until March.

There, in the balmy air of Hawaii, Schiller began to breathe. The *Enquirer* could still try to get those insurance lawyers to take notes, but he didn't worry about that. Now that there was a Court order invoking secrecy, a lawyer could be disbarred for making such a deal. Besides, no local Mormon would fight a Judge's order. It had been close. A possible catastrophe averted.

Yet when the lawyers went to the prison next day to take the deposition, they had to wait six hours, and Gary never showed. It seemed his food had come on a paper plate, and he threw a tantrum, and refused to leave his cell. Double insurance.

From Hawaii, Schiller was making phone calls all over the world to set up the sale of the letters so they couldn't be traced to him. This all involved dealing with the right editor. It was only every few years when he had a particularly big offering, that he would contact the major foreign magazines. He knew, therefore, they wouldn't cross him. He wasn't obliged to be on the phone with them tomorrow making still another deal. He was not an agent who had ten projects moving at once with the same people, and so could say, "All right, I'll give you this concession, if you give me that." Under such conditions, each side could afford to double-cross the other occasionally. Ten mild double-crosses, say, in a hundred deals. But doing custom work, as he did, custom jobs, editors were hardly going to trick him. They'd never have another opportunity to bid on his work.

In Hawaii, he hired secretaries to type the sales contracts. That way, anyone on his traveling team, either his mother, Stephie, or Stephie's mother, Liz, would only have to fill in the amount and the name of the publisher. Since he was doing this preparatory work on the phone, the letters could be presented in lots. Package #1 would offer the magazine a sample contract and five Gilmore letters. The editor would only be allowed to look at them while one of Schiller's women was in the room. That was to make sure no juicy quotes were copied out. If the editor liked what he saw, he could then open Package #2. That contained the complete set of letters, a large package. He would then be given so many hours to make a decision. Except for the solitary editor in on the secret, nobody on any of those magazines would have the remotest idea who those three women might be.

That much to the good. On the other hand, he did not feel comfortable with the way Barry was now handling the Utah operation. On the flush of their terrific interview on December 20, Farrell had planned to keep the work going while he was gone, keep it moving like clockwork. The intention was for Barry to call the lawyers each morning from Los Angeles with a new set of questions. Moody and Stanger would then carry them out to the prison, interview Gary, and put the tape on a plane that night. Farrell would pick up the package at the airport, listen to the new tapes, and compose a new set of questions, call them in by the next morning — it would all be very productive. A strong arrangement, but it was falling through completely. In one week, things could travel a long distance down the wrong tube.

An unconscionable amount of time was being lost, Farrell explained, dictating the questions to the secretaries. They kept garbling them, and then the lawyers weren't working much. It was like they weren't about to do Schiller's business while he was out of town.

"When you get back," Barry said, "we'll go down together." Before he knew it, Schiller was agreeing. But he was infuriated. If Barry was getting such shitty returns, why didn't he travel to Utah on his own and come to grips with the situation instead of limping along with the telephone? But Schiller didn't dare have it out at long distance. That, of course, kept the pressure up everywhere in his system. What a vacation!

4

Sometimes Brenda would feel as if cords were hooked into her flesh and pulling on her organs. Sometimes the pain would hit her when she was seated and she couldn't stand up. Sometimes, standing, it would grab her so suddenly, she'd have to sit down. Long after she stopped going to the prison, she kept trying to call Gary, but it was awfully tricky to get through. Once, she ended up with Sam Smith. "I didn't think," Brenda said, "phone calls were that much of an inconvenience." Smith told her they had to bring Gary out of a cell each time. "Why don't you put a phone in his room?" asked Brenda, "Good God, he *is* on Death Row." "Well," Sam said, "he could hang himself with the cord." She hadn't thought of that. "Or take the parts out and use them to cut his wrists." She hadn't thought of that either. "We are," Sam said to her softly, "giving him more privileges than the average prisoner." "I think you've got a tough job," Brenda said.

Between Christmas and New Year's, two different days in that same cold week, she tried twice, at Gary's request, her gut pulling and aching and horrifying her, to go down to Utah State Hospital and leave a rose for Nicole. Finally she gave up. The hospital wasn't going to receive it. She sent word back through Vern, and Gary was angry at her again. He had to be the most determined man in the world about working a gripe back into shape. If gripes had feathers, he'd fluff them up.

5

To Those Who Oppose

Gilmore Issues an Open Letter

Provo, Dec. 29 — "An open letter from Gary Gilmore to all and any who still seek to oppose by whatever means my death by legal execution. Particularly: ACLU, NAACP.

"I invite you to finally butt out of my life. Butt out of my death.

"It does not concern you.

"Shirley Pedler, Gees, baby, lay off. I wouldn't dare to be so presumptuous as to presume I could impose any unwanted thing on your life. . . . Get out of my life Shirley.

"NAACP, I'm a white man. Don't want no uncle tom blacks buttin (sic) in. Your contention is that if I am executed then a whole bunch of black dudes will be executed. Well that's so apparently stupid I won't even argue with that kind of silly illogic.

"But you know as well as I do that they'll kill a white man these days a lot quicker than they'll kill a black man.

"Y'all ain't really disadvantaged lak (sic) ya used to be.

"As for those of you who would question my sanity, well, I question yours.

> "from my heart
> Gary Gilmore"

A couple of days after Christmas, Sundberg brought Nicole the book Gary had written. It was the kind of notebook you could buy in a drugstore with a nice hard cover. Maybe fifty empty pages. Sundberg was in a hurry and she sort of leafed through while he was there, and he promised to bring it back the next day. On that occasion, she was able to steep herself a little more. Just a simple book but she loved every word because it was a real book with covers, and Gary had put a little writing on every page.

This fuckin guard sittin out here just got done blowin his nose.
Took him 5 minutes. Musta really had something lodged up there.
A harsh grating ungodly sound.
When he finally got done I told him: "Well, your horn works.
Now try your lites." He gave me a bleery-eyed red-nosed look.
Now the guard is pacing. Clopping back and forth in about a
size 13EEE shoe that looks too tite. The boorish fucker is bored stiff.

I got a couple books in the mail about Jesus and I looked 'em over
and they were too Christian.
I mean I wouldn't mind reading a book about Christ the man,
Christ the Jew, Christ the Messiah, but not Christ the Christian.

In OUI magazine in the Openers section they always got some
tomatoe who sent in four flicks of herself in the foto-booth with her
boobies out. I always check 'em out when I read OUI. I thot about
sending them your flicks — I mean I thot about it, I'm not going to
do it.
I know, tho, that they would print them.
Even if you weren't famous they would print those flicks cause
you're so sexy and pretty and the look on your face with your tongue
stickin out a little and your elf boobies just look so fuckin good.

Baby, before I die I'm going to destroy your letters. The reason is
that they are simply not for publication. Not for the public.
I was going to try to return them to you, but I know if I did,
that they would end up in the hands of Larry Schiller, movie pro-
ducer.

Then Gary pasted a news clipping in the book:

SALT LAKE TRIBUNE

Gilmore Answers Query of Eastern Girl

December 4, 1976 — Lisa LaRochelle, Holyoke, Mass., as part of a religion course, sent letters to a number of well-known persons asking:

"What will be the first question you ask God when you see Him?" . . .

"Dear Lisa," Gilmore wrote in red ink on a legal sized sheet, "I'm not a 'prominent' person. I've just gained some unwanted notoriety. But in answer to your question . . . I don't feel that any questions will be necessary when we eventually meet God."

"Sincerely, Gary Gilmore."

Miss LaRochelle wrote the same letter to Walter Cronkite, football stars O.J. Simpson and Roger Staubach and others.

These guards can sneak down the catwalk outside my cell and watch me without me knowing it. They can see me but I can't see them. Probably a few of them are hoping to catch me jackin off so they can stand there and watch.

6

Dec. 31
Friday

Love

Last nite i flew in my dream
like a white bird through the window
came through the night and the cool wind with a few
bright stars in the darkness
And got lost. And Woke up.

Got to go for now
Love you every minet
Nicole

Dec. 31
Fri.?

Oh Darlin

i am in a place i dislike beyond words. My situation calls for me to convince a lot of intelligent important people of my desire to live and my capabilities to exist as a competent mother and human being.

*im givin it all i got rite now. Sometimes i almost have to con-
vince myself of some things before i can attempt to convince anyone
else.*

Strange Lady, Me.
LOVES YOU

New Years Eve

Oh Baby Nicole
 Myself, my wife
 *. . . a card from a lady in Holland that was very beauti-
ful — she said: "Trust Everybody. Love All the People."*
 God I'd like to be that strong.
 In My last letter I told you that they are gonna shoot me Jan. 17
. . . those 4 .30 *caliber slugs will release me.*
 And I will come to you — little white Bird.
 I have 17 *days.*
 I think of you all the time.
 I think only of you.
 *Baby, I always knew you were a white bird, you're the little
white bird that perched on my shoulder before we were both born again
into this life and we made certain vows to each other then.*

Jan. 1, 1977

Mornin My Love
 *Hey, How bout that, Gary, it's the new year! Happy New Year
Love. Here is a little poem i wrote.*

For lost is my mind
Silent by dawn
Loves away stolen
And hurting is Long

So ask me no questions
Sing me no songs
Follow me nowhere
im already gone

 *if ever i find a quiet moment i think there is a soft tune i would
hear in my mind to go with it*

Darlin. They just flipped my light. i Love you God how i Love You Gary.

Dream of me . . . . i will be dreaming you into my dreams.

Your Everlovin
Baby Nicole

7

Father Meersman always felt that he'd come to offer his services to Gary Gilmore very, very honestly, not even having a consideration whether the condemned man was Catholic or not. It was just that Gilmore had said he wished to die with dignity and that impressed Father Meersman. He had gone over to visit him one night in early November and said he understood such a desire and would be willing to help him with it, if that accorded with Gilmore's own desire. Father Meersman had assisted at other executions, and knew something of the routine of it and the pitfalls, and as a result of this conversation, as Meersman saw it, they became good friends.

Gilmore didn't do too much sleeping at night and enjoyed a visit. The Chaplain would come in the evening after all visitors were gone and the prison had quieted down. Meersman was free to see the inmates at any time, but the place had to be run along the prison standards, and at Maximum Security, for instance, when it was time to eat, you wouldn't want to visit. The prison had to be occupied with one thing at a time. That was the way it ran. Since you certainly never wanted to interfere with the custody system, Meersman would drop in on Gary late.

They would talk about little things. One night, for example, Father Meersman, as was customary for him, was standing on one side of the bars out in the main corridor and Gilmore, on the other side, was leaning against the bars, when Father Meersman took out his Meerschaum pipe. Gary asked him what it was, and Father Meersman went into it and explained how as you smoked such a pipe, it gradually mellowed. Then, another night he brought a bunch of foreign coins along and Gary was very curious to look at them. He liked to learn things. He was very interested in the specifics. Since

Father Meersman, after the Second World War, had studied at the North American College in Rome, he would ask the priest a lot about Europe.

They would talk about history and the rise and fall of different people, whether it be Julius Caesar or Napoleon, and Father Meersman could see that he liked people who rose to heights and became famous, like Muhammad Ali. They would also discuss what Gilmore had read in the newspapers and magazines that Father Meersman brought him. He would say, "Hey, Padre, what do you think of Jimmy Carter?" or, "Padre, what do you think of serving food on paper plates?" To each of these questions, Meersman would reply, "Oh, Gary, whatever's fair." If he said that once he said it a thousand times, and Gilmore would answer, "Padre, there's nothing fair." Then they would both laugh. He always called him Padre.

Gilmore also stayed very aware of the aura of his public image, and thanked Father Meersman each night for the newspaper. It was certain Gary liked to talk about his case. He was fascinated the night Father Meersman brought a copy of *Time* magazine dated right after the first of the year, first issue of 1977 (although it came out a couple of days before the new year). In it were a couple of pages facing each other that said "Images '76," and there you could see photographs of President-elect Carter and his mother and wife, of Betty Ford, and Isabelle Peron from Argentina, and a photograph of the body of Mao Tse-tung lying in state, together with a picture of the leg support of *Viking I* that had landed on Mars, and Secretary of State Henry Kissinger holding an African sword in one hand and a shield in the other while out in Kenya, and a photograph of the young gymnast Nadia Comaneci, and yet, on the same two pages, was also a picture of Gary Gilmore in his Maximum Security prison whites. There he was grinning at the camera just after he'd received the date of his death sentence at the Board of Pardons Hearing. It didn't fail Gilmore's attention that in the yearly roundup of 1976, he was in elevated company.

PART FIVE

Pressures

CHAPTER 22

A Hole in the Carpet

1

Farrell felt in no hurry to go back to Utah and deal with Moody and Stanger, for he was enjoying the work on what he had already. While Schiller was in Hawaii, Barry had begun to lay out the *Playboy* interview. To make it more readable, he trimmed the dialogue, moved paragraphs around, and added relevant material from some of Gary's written answers to the earlier interrogatories. Usually, he rewrote Moody and Stanger's questions to smooth the flow, and offer something like the flavor of a *Playboy* interview. He did decide, however, for his own ground rules, that he would not take anything from the letters. The interview would be built out of responses, verbal or written, to their questions.

That interview of December 20 was what he depended on most, however. Trying to get Gilmore on record over a broad range of topics, Farrell left a certain naiveté to the questions. He had been hoping for answers from which to dig out deeper questions, but figured these simple inquiries would allow Gilmore to feel superior. The results were astonishing. Gary came back in surprising volume. It looked to Farrell as if Gilmore was now setting out to present the particular view of himself he wanted people to keep. In that sense, he was being his own writer. It was fascinating to Barry. He was being given the Gilmore canon, good self-respecting convict canon. In fact, it was good enough for Farrell to begin to wonder whether the interview itself would ever get out of that tone.

INTERVIEWER   As far as we can tell from your prison record, you've been locked up almost continuously since you entered reform school, and that was twenty-two years ago. It's as if you never saw any choice but to live out a criminal destiny.

GILMORE   Yea, that's kind of a way of putting it. In fact, that's very nicely put.

INTERVIEWER   What got you started thinking like a criminal?

GILMORE   Probably going to reform school.

INTERVIEWER   But you must have done things to get yourself sent there.

GILMORE   Yea, I was about fourteen when I went to reform school and, ah, thirteen when I started getting locked up.

INTERVIEWER   What had you done to get locked up at thirteen?

GILMORE   Well, I started out stealing cars . . . but, ah, I guess my first felonies were probably burglaries, house burglaries. I used to burglarize houses on my paper route.

INTERVIEWER   Why? What were you after?

GILMORE   Why? Well, I wanted guns, mainly. A lot of people keep guns in their homes and, well . . . that's what I was primarily looking for.

INTERVIEWER   How old were you then? Eleven? Twelve? Why did you want guns?

GILMORE   Well, see, in Portland, at that time, there was a gang. I don't know if you ever heard of it — probably not. But, man, I figured that, well, I would like to be in the Broadway gang. And I figured the best way to get in was to go down and hang around Broadway and sell 'em guns. I knew they wanted guns. I mean, I — I don't even know if the gang existed . . . it may have been a myth. But I heard about 'em, you know? So I thought, I wanted to be a part of an outfit like that . . . the Broadway boys.

INTERVIEWER   But instead you got caught and sent to reform school?

GILMORE   Yeah, the MacLaren School for Boys, in Woodburn, Oregon.

INTERVIEWER   Was that the point at which you just told yourself, From here on, I'm in for trouble?

GILMORE   (laughs) I always felt like I was in for trouble. I seemed to have a talent, or rather a knack, for making adults look at me a little different, different from the way they looked at other kids, like maybe bewildered, or maybe repelled.

INTERVIEWER Repelled?

GILMORE Just a different look, like adults aren't supposed to look at kids.

INTERVIEWER With hate in their eyes?

GILMORE Beyond hate. Loathing, I'd say. I can remember one lady in Flagstaff, Arizona, a neighbor of my folks when I was three or four. She became so frustrated with rage at whatever shit I was doing that she attacked me physically with full intent of hurting me. My dad had to jump up and restrain her.

INTERVIEWER What could you have been doing to get her so mad?

GILMORE Just the way I was talking to her and the way I was acting. I was never quite . . . a boy. One evening in Portland, when I was about eight, we all went over to these people's house, and there were two or three adults there. I don't remember just what I did, giving everybody a lot of lip, fucking with everything in the house — I don't remember what all — but anyhow, this one lady finally flipped completely out. Screamed. Ranted. Raved. Threw me out of the house. And the other adults there supported her and all felt the feelings she felt. Apparently, shit like that didn't have much effect on me. I can remember just walking home, about three miles, whistling and singing to myself.

INTERVIEWER It sounds as thought you were on the course you've always followed well before you went to reform school.

GILMORE Well, I always knew the law was silly as hell. But as far as courses go, you react in a certain way because your life is influenced by all the varieties of your experience. Does that make any sense?

INTERVIEWER It's hard to say. Give us an example.

GILMORE Well, this is kind of a personal thing. It'll sound like a strange incident to you, but it had a lasting effect on me. I was about eleven years old and I was coming home from school, and I thought I'd take a short cut. I climbed down this hill, a drop of about fifty feet, and I got tangled in these briar bushes, and blackberry, and thornberry. Some of these bushes were fifty feet high, I guess, down in this wild, overgrown area in southeast Portland. I thought it would be a short cut, but there was no pass through there. Nobody had gone through there before. At one point, I could have turned around and gone back, but I chose to just go on, and it took me about three hours to pick my way. All during that time, I never stopped for a rest and just kept going. I knew if I just kept going I'd get out, but I was also aware that I could get hopelessly stuck in there. I was a block or so from any houses, and if I screamed . . . well, I could have died in there. My screams would have gone unheard. So I just kept going. It was kind of a personal thing. I finally got home about three hours late and my mom said, well, you're late, and I said, yeah, I took a short cut. (laughs) It made me feel a little different about a lot of things.

INTERVIEWER   What things?

GILMORE   Just being aware that I never did get afraid. I knew that if I just kept going, I'd get out. It left me with a distinct feeling, like a kind of overcoming of myself.

INTERVIEWER   Well, why then did you say it was going to reform school that got you started?

GILMORE   Look, reform schools disseminate certain esoteric knowledge. They sophisticate. A kid comes out of reform school and he's learned a few things he would otherwise have missed. And he identifies, usually, with the people who share that same esoteric knowledge, the criminal element, or whatever you want to call it. So going to Woodburn was not a small thing in my life.

INTERVIEWER   Was it bad at Woodburn? How did you fit in there?

GILMORE   Man, that place made me think that was the only way to live. The guys in there I looked up to, they were tough, they were hipsters — this was the Fifties — and they seemed to run everything there. The staff were local beer-drinking guys that put in their hours, and they didn't care if you did this or did that. They had a few psych doctors there, too. Psychoanalysis was a big thing then. They would come in and they would show you their ink-blot tests and they would ask you all kinds of questions, mostly related to sex. And look at ya funny and . . . things like that.

INTERVIEWER   How long were you there?

GILMORE   Fifteen months. I escaped four times, and after that, I finally got hip that the way to really get out of that place was to show 'em that I was rehabilitated. And after four months of not getting into any trouble, they released me. That taught me that people like that are easily fooled.

INTERVIEWER   Did other inmates ever try to make you their punk?

GILMORE   No . . . nobody ever . . . I've never had any trouble like that. No, never once. If it had happened I would have handled it in a decisive violent manner. I would have killed somebody — or beat them with something, you know, if they were too big. I would've took some weapon to 'em. But that never did happen to me.

INTERVIEWER   How did you feel when you were released from Woodburn?

GILMORE   I came out looking for trouble. Thought that's what you're supposed to do. I felt slightly superior to everybody else 'cause I'd been in reform school. I had a tough-guy complex, that sort of smart-aleck juvenile-delinquent attitude. *Juvenile delinquent* — remember that phrase? Sure dates me, don't it? Nobody could tell me anything. I had a ducktail haircut, I smoked, drank, shot heroin, smoked weed, took speed, got into fights, chased and caught pretty little broads. The Fifties were a hell of a time to be a juvenile delinquent. I stole and robbed and gambled and went to Fats Domino and Gene Vincent dances at the local halls.

INTERVIEWER   What did you want to make of your life at that point?

GILMORE   I wanted to be a mobster.

INTERVIEWER   Didn't you think you had any other talents?

GILMORE   Well, yeah, I had talents. I've always been good at drawing. I've drawn since I was a child, and I remember a teacher in about the second grade telling my mom, "Your son's an artist," in a way that showed she really meant it.

INTERVIEWER   Did you ever have a time when you had second thoughts about that criminal destiny, where you thought you might change?

GILMORE   Well, I figured if I could get something going as an artist — but it's so damned hard, you know. I wanted to be successful on a large scale — a fine artist — not a commercial artist. After a while I figured I'd probably just spend the rest of my life in jail or commit suicide, or be killed uh, by the police or something like that. A violent death of some sort, but there was a time as a kid when I thought seriously about it, you know, being a painter.

INTERVIEWER   How long was it before you were locked up again?

GILMORE   Four months.

INTERVIEWER   Four months! We thought you said that reform

schools educate. Couldn't you have used your esoteric knowledge to stay out of jail?

GILMORE   It was just the pattern of my life. Some guys are lucky all their lives. No matter what kind of trouble they get into, pretty soon they're back on the bricks. But some guys are unlucky. They fuck up once on the outside and it's the pattern of their lives to be drawn back to do a lot of time.

INTERVIEWER   And you're one of the unlucky ones?

GILMORE   Yeah, "the eternal recidivist." We're creatures of habit, man.

INTERVIEWER   What's the longest stretch of time you've been free since you first went to reform school?

GILMORE   Eight months was about the longest.

INTERVIEWER   Your I.Q.'s supposedly about 130, and yet you've spent almost nineteen of the past twenty-two years behind bars. Why were you never able to get away with anything?

GILMORE   I got away with a couple of things. I ain't a great thief. I'm impulsive. Don't plan, don't think. You don't have to be a superintelligent to get away with shit, you just have to think. But I don't. I'm impatient. Not greedy enough. I could have gotten away with lots of things that I got caught for. I don't, ah, really understand it. Maybe I quit caring a long time ago.

   All that was fine. Farrell was not for buying any of this without further examination, but the man was at least trying to give a presentation of himself. Clearly, it was the way he wanted the world to think of him, remember him. A mighty different man from the letters!

2

Farrell and Schiller agreed that the trick was to get Gary to talk truly about the murders. Something always happened then. Gilmore's readiness to comment on himself disappeared. His account fell into the same narrative style every hustler and psychopath would give you of the most boring, or of the most extraordinary evening — we did this and then, man, like we did that. Episodic and unstressed. Resolute refusal, thought Farrell, to attach value to any detail. Life is a department store. Lift what you can.

GILMORE   April got in the truck and, man, she turned the radio on real loud and moved right over beside me and told me she didn't want to go home, and I told her, Well, look, I'll keep you out all night, if you want. So I drove down to the place where I'd bought my truck and I talked to those guys about the financial arrangements. I give 'em my Mustang as the down payment and we drank some booze and just kind of made a loose arrangement about the truck, they were more or less just holding my guns for me, and, uh, I kept one pistol with me, the loaded one, and I signed the papers and took ownership of the truck and left my Mustang there, and then I was driving around with April and we got out into Orem and I pulled around the corner to this service station and it looked fairly deserted. That's what I guess drew my attention to it. I just drove around the corner and parked and told April to stay in the truck. I'd be back in a moment. And I went over to the gas station and told Jensen to give me the money, and he did, and I told him, well, come on in the bathroom and get down on the floor, and it was pretty quick. I didn't let him know it was coming or anything. It was just a .22, so I shot him twice in rapid succession, to make sure that he was not in any pain or that he wasn't left half alive or anything. And, and, I left there and I drove to, uh, I don't know just where that Sinclair station was, but I drove back to the main drag. State Street, I guess it is, and I went into Albertson's and bought some potato chips and different things to take to a movie and half a case of beer and some things that April wanted to eat.

Finally, one of the lawyers asked a question. Farrell couldn't help but note that it produced better results. It was obvious Gilmore had to be pushed out of the psychopathic flats.

INTERVIEWER   Now, one thing. When you stopped at the gas station, did you have any intention of either robbing Jensen or killing him?

GILMORE   I had the intention of killing him.

INTERVIEWER   When did that concept form in your mind? To kill somebody —

GILMORE   I can't say. It had been building all week. That night I knew I had to open a valve and let something out and I didn't know exactly what it would be and I wasn't thinking I'll do this or I'll do that, or that'll make me feel better. I just knew something was happening in me and that I'd let some of the steam off and, uh, I guess all this sounds pretty vicious.

INTERVIEWER No. No. Did Jensen say anything to annoy you?

GILMORE No, not at all.

INTERVIEWER What prompted you to leave the truck and go into the office where Jensen was?

GILMORE I don't really know.

INTERVIEWER What do you mean by that?

GILMORE I mean, I don't really know. I said the place looked deserted. It just seemed appropriate.

INTERVIEWER Apparently, killing Jensen didn't do anything to take the pressure off. Why did you go out the next night and kill Bushnell?

GILMORE I don't know, man. I'm impulsive. I don't think.

INTERVIEWER You killed him the same way you'd killed Jensen the night before — ordering him to lie down on the floor, then firing point-blank into his head. Did you think killing Bushnell would give you some kind of relief you didn't get with Jensen?

GILMORE I told you, I wasn't thinking. What I do remember is an absence of thought. Just movements, actions. I shot Bushnell, and then the gun jammed — them fucking Automatics! And I thought, man, this guy's not dead. I wanted to shoot him a second time, because I didn't want him to lie there half dead. I didn't want him in pain. I tried to jack the mechanism and get the gun working again, and shoot him again, but it was jammed, and I had to get my ass out of there. I jacked the gun into shape again but too late to do anything for Mr. Bushnell. I'm afraid he didn't die immediately. When I ordered him to lie down, I wanted it to be quick for him. There was no .chance, no choice for him. That sounds cold. But you asked.

INTERVIEWER Was there any difference in the way you approached the two killings?

GILMORE No, not really. You could say it was a little more certain that Mr. Bushnell was going to die.

INTERVIEWER Why?

GILMORE Because it was already a fact that Mr. Jensen had died, and so the next one was more certain.

INTERVIEWER Was the second killing easier than the first?

GILMORE Neither one of 'em were hard or easy.

INTERVIEWER Had you ever had any dealings of any kind with either of those men?

GILMORE No.

INTERVIEWER Well, what led you to the City Center Motel, where Bushnell worked? We're just trying to understand the quality of this rage you speak of. It wasn't a rage that might have been vented in sex?

GILMORE I don't want to mess with questions that pertain to sex. I think they're cheap.

INTERVIEWER But if, on the night you killed Bushnell, you had wound up with a friendly girl who could offer you beer and company and a relaxing time, wouldn't that have helped you feel better?

GILMORE I don't want to answer that question.

INTERVIEWER You seem to find it easier talking about murder than sex.

GILMORE That's your judgment.

Good stuff, thought Farrell. A good beginning.

3

All through Christmas week, however, there was a pall. No more interviews of merit. Farrell began to wonder if he had scared Gilmore off. Or was Gary disabled from the holidays? Looking over his bitter responses about Christmas in prison, it was not hard to read between the lines: my last New Year's on earth.

Barry also began to worry that the lawyers might be the cause. Day after day, in that last week of the year, they went out and bantered with Gary, skipped around key points, ignored any reasonable follow-up to good responses, and read Farrell's more elaborate questions as if they were too literary for real men to get their mouth around.

Barry would call up Stanger's office and, with great difficulty, dictate new questions. A day or two later, the tape would come back so empty of content that Farrell would wonder whether the lawyers wanted to show they could not only produce, but hold back. He figured they must still be mad over Schiller's trip to Hawaii. Maybe there was something unholy in interrogating a man on the way to his death, but virtually nothing came back.

STANGER Have you ever been any good as a prison politician?

GILMORE In the last period when I was in Oregon I got off into a revolutionary bag a little bit, and then I just seen them revolutionaries ain't gonna revolution shit, so I fell out of that. (laughing)

STANGER Okay. You spent more than four years in the hole. Is this because you choose to do it the hard way? Or, because your acts are beyond your control?

GILMORE (laughing) . . . I gotta pick A, or B now, huh? (laughing)

STANGER Multiple choice . . . (laughing)

GILMORE Man, I'm just a fuck-up.

About the way it went. Certain exchanges drove Farrell up the wall. In the interview on December 20, there had been a clue in the back-and-forth:

INTERVIEWER Your sense of the inevitability and the rightness of your fate suggests that the killings were a long time coming. Had you fantasized yourself in the killer's role long before it became a reality? (pause) It's a good heady question, isn't it? (laughter)

GILMORE Yeah, it is. I wonder if I could go take a hit 'n' miss? (laughter) That's rhyme in Cockney for "piss."

INTERVIEWER Sounds good. Let's do it.

GILMORE And come back and answer that one. I'll give that some thought.

INTERVIEWER Okay.

GILMORE It's rather religious.

Then Gary had come back with his long and half-satisfactory account of killing Jensen. That was last week. It proved what Farrell had expected. Secretly, Gilmore did like literary questions and highly formulated approaches. It dignified his situation. Here, despite the lawyer's mockery of the question, he had still worked to find some kind of answer. But such willingness to reply would not bear up if the lawyers kept responding with nothing but jokes. It was like people making quips around the bed of a man dying of cancer.

4

Moody and Stanger might not have been overworking the mine, but they were sure curious about sales. As soon as Schiller came back from Hawaii they began to question him about the overseas sales. Schiller had to give them details on deals before they were even discussed. His remark at lunch that he could sell the letters, and they would never know, had come home to him. They paid a lot of attention to the prospect of money coming in. He hoped it might fire them up to do better interviews, but it only made them feel that they were doing the work for everybody else. They even started to claim that the interviews were not part of their original arrangement, and they should get additional compensation. He could tell it would be an ongoing discussion.

The problem, Schiller decided, was that vis-à-vis Gary, the lawyers were feeling stronger all the time. They had made a point of letting him know that while he was sunning in Hawaii, they had been out at the jail on Christmas Day. They had also been out New Year's Day. And every day in between. That Gary had sure been lonely. The lawyers informed Schiller as if he had been absent for years. There was no question Gary looked forward to the visits they would make. It enabled him to leave his cell and go to the booth just off the visitors' room. Even after a couple of hours of conversation, they had no more than to hang up the phone and start to leave, when they would hear a tap on the window. Gilmore was pulling them back. He wanted to inquire about their children. He would give advice. When they do something wrong, punish them. But keep telling them you love them.

Those daily sessions had given the lawyers such concern for Gary's daily situation, Schiller decided, that they were not seeing the big job. It had become natural for them to downgrade it.

5

Schiller's most worrisome problem on returning, however, was with Gary. First, he had to tell him about the *National Enquirer*. That piece would be out in a few days. From Hawaii, he instructed the lawyers to explain to Gilmore that he had sold a few rights to the *Enquirer* because they were going to do a story on Gilmore anyway, and he thought they should pick up some money. That worked. Gilmore agreed. But then, in another telegram, Schiller made the mistake of using a code name for Nicole. Not wanting the prison to know what he was talking about, he sent in some questions referring to her as Freckles.

Too late, he realized that Gary sometimes called her that in his letters. What a prize goof! He must have wanted to confess to Gary that he had read the letters. If Gilmore would only agree that reading those letters was no crime, it might encourage more intimacy in the questioning. No chance. While Schiller was still in Hawaii, Moody read him a note from Gary.

Dear Larry,
  Freckles?
  Her name is Nicole.
  Dig?
  You've read the letters — I don't like that.
  I've got about a hundred letters right here in my cell that Nicole wrote to me.
  You aint reading them.

"I will before it's over," thought Schiller.

  I don't question your motives. I know you need to know all you can.
  But some of your methods . . .
  Its a matter of how you approach me Larry —
  You can offend me.
  I would rather you didnt
  May I suggest — that you be utterly straightforward with me. Because I'm a literal man.
  When I asked you not to read those letters you didnt argue with me or try to persuade me.
  The next time you offend me it will be forever Larry.
  But, for the nonce, this one time, I will let it ride.
  Now you know.

                                                    Sincerely,
                                                    Gary

DEC. 30, 3:43 P.M.
GARY GILMORE UTAH STATE PRISON
PO BOX 250
DRAPER UT 84020
I UNDERSTAND YOUR POINT AND IT WAS WELL MADE STOP I WAS NOT
TRYING TO HIDE THE FACT STOP REGARDS
LARRY

When there was no answer, Schiller sent another telegram.

JAN 2, 1:42 P.M.
GARY GILMORE
UTAH STATE PRISON BOX 250
DRAPER UT 84020
NICOLE'S PRIDE IN YOUR LETTERS ALLOWED HER TO SHARE THEM
WITH SEVERAL PEOPLE INCLUDING MYSELF STOP SIDE BY SIDE BOTH
SETS OF LETTERS COULD ONLY LEAVE A TRUER AND MORE COMPLETE
RECORD OF YOUR LOVE THAN EITHER OF THEM ALONE STOP I WANT TO
DEFEAT THE IDEA THAT YOU HAVE A POWER OVER HER STOP THAT IS
THE EFFECT THAT IS BEING DRAWN WHEN ONE READS ONLY YOUR
SIDE STOP HER LETTERS IN MY OPINION WOULD BE THE STRONGEST
WAY OF GIVING THE TRUE PICTURE OF YOUR RELATIONSHIP STOP THIS
IS NO WAY TO COMMUNICATE BUT IT'S THE BEST THAT WE GOT.
LARRY

The answer came back on tape via Moody and Stanger:

GILMORE I got a mailgram from Larry and he asked if he could have
the letters Nicole has written to me. Just tell him that I destroyed
'em, I won't elaborate. He uses a little abstract psychology and that
doesn't work with me. He sort of suggested . . . it was kind of an
innuendo, too, that you know, a lot of people think I've got some kind
of hold over Nicole and maybe if we could see this correspondence,
we could clear that all up. I don't like that kind of suggestion. There's
no way he can see her letters, they're printed in my heart. That's
where they're at, and they're gone, so, this'll save me from writing
him a letter. . . . (laughs)

6

Next, it looked like the blip was going to hit the fan altogether. The *National Enquirer* came out with their piece, a disaster. It wasn't so much the letters Scott Meredith had sold to them, as that they analyzed a tape of Gary speaking, and put his psyche all over the page.

NATIONAL ENQUIRER

Murderer Gary Gilmore is Lying —
He Does NOT Want to Die!

By John Blosser

That's the conclusion of Charles R. McQuiston, a former top U.S. intelligence officer, who used a PSE (Psychological Stress Evaluator) to analyze a 20-minute tape of a telephone conversation with Gilmore at the Utah State Prison. . . . (The PSE is a device that is used by law enforcement agencies to determine when a person is lying, by charting stress patterns in the voice.)

"I am totally convinced that Gilmore does not wish to die. He is very emotionally involved with this process of meeting his Maker, and he is very scared," the intelligence officer said.

"He wants clemency for his crimes," McQueen told The Enquirer.

Here are some excerpts of Charles McQuiston's PSE analysis:

GILMORE "The law has sentenced me to die. I feel that is proper."

MCQUISTON'S ANALYSIS

"There is extremely heavy stress on the words 'to die.' This means there is no way he wants to die."

GILMORE "I'll simply go out there and sit down and be shot."

MCQUISTON'S ANALYSIS

"His cyclic rate goes wild on this statement. He may

be forced to do this (face the firing squad) but it's not simple — and he certainly doesn't want it to happen."

GILMORE "I guess you could say I do believe in a life hereafter, and that makes it a little easier for me (to face death)."

MCQUISTON'S ANALYSIS

"The stress patterns show that he does believe in a life in the hereafter.

"That is a true statement. However, it doesn't make it easier for him.

"It makes it much more difficult. He believes.

"But he feels that he is going there (to the hereafter) without the proper credentials — and he is scared."

JAN 5 4:31 P.M.
GARY GILMORE
UTAH STATE PRISON
PO BOX 250
DRAPER UT 84020
IT HAS TAKEN ME 24 HOURS TO CALM DOWN AFTER SEEING THE EN-
QUIRER OTHERWISE WESTERN UNION COULDN'T TAKE MY WORDS.
THEY BOUGHT MATERIAL AND OBVIOUSLY USED ONLY A SMALL PART
OF IT. I GUESS I SHOULD HAVE EXPECTED IT BUT IN SOME WAYS I'M
STILL NAIVE. I'M JUST ASHAMED THAT THIS IS THE FIRST THAT YOU
SEE BUT YOU KNOW THE REASONS WE WENT THIS WAY. THAT MARKET
IS NOW SATISFIED AND WE CAN GO FOR WHAT WE WANT.
LARRY

Jan 5

Dear Larry,

Just read with unengrossed interest the National Enquirer. Very distasteful . . .

I guess people can print and read and think what they like. But I am curious . . .

I mean, I would assume a man in your position — and your experience and first-hand knowledge of yellow journalistic papers like the Enquirer — would be able to exert more control over what is released, what is printed . . .

Or did you exert all the control you cared to?

I'm distantly curious —
Not greatly interested . . .
You see, I know the truth of the matter. And so does Nicole. And I don't have to account to anybody but myself and Nicole.
Im not a nice guy or a hero. But I'm not the guy the Enquirer says I am, either.
Larry, you can think, print, and produce according to the conclusions you, yourself, reach. I believe you are a man of some sensibility and interested in the truth.
My sole re-but to the Enquirer is this:
Everybody knows that the National Enquirer is not exactly what you would call an "unimpeachable source."

GARY

Moody and Stanger told him Gary had no larger reaction than that. Schiller had to feel confused. This piece in the *National Enquirer* had impugned Gilmore's honor in death, and yet this reply was all it brought forth. Call Nicole Freckles, however, and Gary almost wouldn't speak. It nearly brought Schiller to a halt. He had to ask himself whether he was qualified, at bottom, to know Gary Gilmore?

7

Hey Darlin Companion — i Love you!
i am often lost here and i will be that way often wherever i am — till i feel your soul wrap around me.
i am alone with myself most of the daylight hours.
But at night . . . oh, the nights i love so. i can go anywhere, do anything, feel anything and all things good. . . .
Hold you close and warm with your ruff wiskery face in my hands. . . . Take you to places i loved as a child, a dark little glen in the forest of pines. it was my "room" So tightly knit around with tall pine trees and forever bearing blackberry bushes, that finding the tunnel leading into it was sometimes a challenge. i used to lay in the middle of it on the soft springy carpet of warm damp sweet smelling pine needles — gazing straight up from the walls of the trees — up to a crystal blue sky and watch the cotton clouds sneak by. Listen to my enchanted forest talking softly in its thousand tongues.

God, how i loved that place so long ago.

i remember talking to my aunt Kathy there. she loved it. Dug a little hole in the carpet for her ashtray. And kept herself quiet and listened with me.

i went there again with you only a night or so back.

Oh crazy me.

SALT LAKE TRIBUNE

Salt Lake, Jan. 6 — KUTV yesterday filed suit in U.S. District Court for Utah seeking the right to witness and report the scheduled execution on Jan. 17 of convicted murderer Gary Mark Gilmore. . . .

CHAPTER 23

Out Where the TV Is Made

1

SALT LAKE TRIBUNE

Cover Execution? Not Barbara

Salt Lake, Jan. 7 — Barbara Walters would be horrified if she were asked to cover the execution of Gary Gilmore next week. She would probably turn down the assignment.

    Her co-anchor person Harry Reasoner, on the other hand, might move his job to Salt Lake City for the day.

    In fact he believes this case should be given national attention by being televised live. "But only this one," he said. . . .

Early in January, on the night Schiller met Bill Moyers at the Utah Hotel in Salt Lake to discuss going on "CBS Reports," he asked Tamera Smith to come along. She would, Schiller thought, jump at the occasion. This was the first payoff on all he had promised at her brother's house. Moreover, he wanted to see how far he could get Moyers to commit himself in front of a stranger.

    When they got to the table, Larry introduced her by name, and Moyers was cordial, but he didn't make the connection to the *Deseret News*. Knew all about Vern Damico, and Kathryne Baker, but certainly wasn't holding the names of the little players.

They had a table with this incredible view. There they were on top of the Hotel Utah fifteenth-story level, looking at the towers of the Mormon Temple across the street at the same height, most important Mormon temple in all the world. Those towers had floodlights on them that made the temple look like a castle — a very dramatic sight. Still, Schiller wasn't altogether impressed. Chartres, when he saw it, had been a delight for his photographer's eye, and there was always something beautiful about Notre Dame. But this Mormon Temple was the same from every angle. Just a massing upward, with lots of all-out pious feeling. High ambition. It did, however, have another kind of mystery. Schiller had heard you couldn't visit the Mormon Temple the way a tourist might enter a famous cathedral. To get in, you had to be LDS in good standing with a key, which meant a Recommend by your local Bishop. It underlined how secret a society the Mormons really were.

Maybe it was the idea of this church you couldn't enter, being right across the street, but Schiller got carried away and decided to gamble. As soon as the preliminaries were over, and Moyers said straight out that he wanted to interview Larry concerning the financial side of the execution of Gary Gilmore, he smiled nicely in reply, and said, "I don't want you tearing me apart on your show." Of course, as if he were a catcher, he could see the throw coming in slow motion from the outfield to home plate. "I have something," he began, "which you want and I'll give it to you. I'm going to let you read the transcripts of the Gilmore tapes, and pick three minutes for your show. But first, you have to understand my terms. I want you to take twenty minutes right now and listen while I tell you who I am, and what I am, and where my head is at. Then you can decide whether I'm a bona fide journalist or an exploiter."

It wasn't the easiest twenty-minute version of his life story to give. Next to a man like Moyers, Schiller considered himself naive in many ways. Still, he always looked at the positive side of things. So he gave Moyers his best shot. Emphasized the face of Larry Schiller that people did not know much about, the work he'd done on artificial kidneys, and on mercury pollution in Japan with the eminent photographer Eugene Smith. Told how his emotional involvement with such worthwhile subjects had changed his life more than others could recognize. There might have been years when he ran fast to come in first, but he was motivated now by the quality of his work. That had to be understood about him. When he felt he had reached Moyers to this degree, Schiller said, "I'm going to let you read the transcripts of Gary Gilmore's interviews tonight, and you can select three" — he expanded that — "to five minutes' worth of tape, only there are the following conditions: You can only use Gilmore's voice, not the interviewer's. Nor can you say on the show who is asking the questions." Moyers nodded. "Then," said Schiller, "I have the right to kill anything you pick. I'll be reasonable, but I must have such control. I cannot give you carte blanche." Moyers said, "What do you want in return?"

Schiller could see that Moyers was going to jump at it. He had to. There was not much TV in Salt Lake without Gilmore's presence. "One," said Schiller, "I want a journalistic background when you interview me. I want to be photographed in, let's say, a newspaper office, at a typewriter, or on the phone. I need," said Schiller, "such background to give me credibility. I have no control over how you're going to editorialize about me. I may have a little control over what you film, because I know a lot about cutting, so I can see what you'll be up to, but I have no control over what you, personally, say about me. Therefore, I need a visual background. The second thing is talk of money matters. That can only be discussed if I'm on the move." "What," asked Moyers, "do you mean by that?" "I have to be moving as I talk," said Schiller, "either walking or driving. I will not discuss money matters sitting down."

"Why not?"

"Because," said Schiller, "no matter how you shoot it, I'm overweight. If you take me with a normal lens sitting behind a desk, I look like a money man. Shoot with a wide-angle lens and I'm King Farouk." Moyers chuckled, then laughed. Schiller said, "If you're willing to make such a deal, and, remember, I'm leaving myself wide open — because you can still say anything you want about me — then I will give you the transcripts. Read them tonight and pick what you want."

Moyers could, of course, run off and Xerox the stuff. Moyers could do a lot of things, but Schiller trusted him. Besides, there was more than trust. Schiller was confident he could present himself well enough at the news level that Moyers would have bigger things to do with his show than expose him as a character.

Moreover, he had respect for Moyers's integrity. He thought Moyers had made a pretty strong editor at *Newsday*. On the basis of being able to give that compliment, Schiller could also say to the man that he wasn't necessarily going to make a very good "CBS Reports" personality. "You got to learn some acting, Bill." Moyers said he was aware of the problem. He had even, he confessed, tried looking in the mirror when he spoke, which wasn't his normal way of doing things.

They began to relax. Moyers mentioned, that in November, when he had first proposed Gary Gilmore to CBS, the word had been, "Do Fidel Castro. We want credibility for your new show." Then, as Moyers got it from in-house gossip, somebody very big at CBS said to Frank Stanton, "Why not Gilmore? Everybody is talking about him." Stanton kept saying no until he went to a meeting with Paley who declared, "That's phenomenal. That's what we want for Moyers, ratings."

So Bill had moved his entire team to Provo, film editors and all, and planned to air "CBS Reports" the night of the execution. He figured they would get the top rating that night. Schiller was thinking: I have to sell myself as not being exploitative, but CBS, holier than thou, is going for the good old ratings.

2

Tamera found the dinner really special. When Larry told her they were having dinner with Bill Moyers she didn't even know who the man was. When she found out, therefore, it was exciting. Not every day did you get to go to dinner with the man who managed press relations for President Johnson.

Up till then, she had been very relaxed. Actually, kind of bored. The men were talking business and she hadn't felt included. She had had to fascinate herself by trying things on the menu of a sort she'd never eaten before. They all shared a Caesar Salad, for instance. Then, she had a soup something like cold borscht but awful, Gazpacho, she hated that, and, for entree, frogs' legs. Dessert, she tried the Crêpes Suzettes. She really did try.

The frogs' legs were pretty good, although actually the whole meal didn't hit that well. Later, about four in the morning, she went out to Sambo's and had a good old hamburger.

3

Next morning, Moyers came by to have breakfast, and said, "This is phenomenal. I want to do the entire show with your tapes."

"No way," said Schiller, but decided he had to throw Moyers a bone. "I have photographs of Gilmore in Maximum," he said. "You can't mention who took the pictures, but if you want to run a montage of stills, well, I won't give you the prints, but I will shoot a movie film of the stills, provided you pay the lab costs. However, I must design it."

Moyers's producer hit the fucking ceiling. "This is news," he declared, "not entertainment." Moyers, however, went along with Schiller. After all, the man was giving up his own pictures.

Schiller figured he could design the montage to make Gilmore human, rather than a cold-blooded killer. There was a vulnerability he might be able to communicate. He wanted to get Gilmore before the public looking half-ass acceptable, anyway.

The problem was not that Gilmore was a killer. The problem was not even that he was challenging all the straight people out there. The real difficulty was that he was making fools of them. The public could live with a killer who was crazy, mixed-up, insane. But for a murderer to start controlling the issue — that was developing a lot of active hatred for Gilmore. People felt as if the world was being tipped on edge.

If Schiller was going to have a successful book and a successful film, he had to defuse the public animosity, and get across that there was a whole human quality about his man Gilmore. Every time he saw the reporters at the Hilton going monkey see, monkey do, and thought of the interviews he would have gone out to get if he had been on the job, he couldn't believe it. They just didn't do their work. Didn't try to get an insight into Gary by interviewing the people who might be accessible. Instead, they sat around, drank, swapped stories, worked up a consensus, and therby put a common evaluation on the story the way an open market arrived at a price. They all used the same few stories in common. Yet if he, Larry Schiller, were to offer examples of interesting human qualities in Gilmore, no one would accept them. They would say he was painting that nice picture for his own financial benefit. Therefore, he had to have the portrait painted by somebody else. Right now, that was going to be Bill Moyers.

4

Jan. 8 Sat.

Hello my Love

My Mother in Law Marie Barrett brought Sunny up to see me yesterday.

She's gettin so damn pretty an sassy. An happy as a lark. Peabody too. Got himself some little levis an boots. Looks like a tuff little shit Kicker, but hes sweet as pie. . . .

Guess i Kinda lost touch with my Love for them a little while before all this came about. . . .

Would you believe — i get strip shook after visiting with them.

i got a bit of infection, an the doc ordered me a supository. But they insist on watchin me insert it so i said to hell with it — ill rot first. forgive my vulgarity Love. . . .

its a crazy life these days. i wonder what destiny we are waiting for. Entering.

if you are shot Jan 17 . . .

What will be in me? will i be nothing — if you go away. . . . Will i be more? Will i be lost or be found? i don't want to be without you. i dont think i would continue to exist if i should be ever a day without Your Love in my soul.

Jesus, Gary. Be with me.

i love you so very much.

Larry asked Tamera if they could use a desk at the *Deseret News* for the interview, and what with the shooting being done on a Saturday night, she didn't have too hard a time getting permission. Hardly any of the staff was there.

This setup was just what Schiller wanted. He had a big city newsroom behind him all the while he spoke. There he was sitting at a desk, then a shot of him listening to a tape of Gary, then going to work on the typewriter. Moyers's crew filmed away full blast.

Schiller was sitting in front of the news desk when Tamera came up during a break, and said, "You got to look at something." Took him to a corner of the room and handed a tear of paper just come off the wire. ABC had pulled out. Fucking *pulled out!*

There it was, right on a wire service teletype. The President of ABC, Frank Pierce, was not producing any entertainment stories on Gary Gilmore. Incredible. It meant that ABC was 1) writing off seventy grand already spent, and 2) they were leaving Schiller up in the tree.

Now, the game was to finish the interview before Moyers saw that news story. The moment he did, the questions would come.

Schiller remembered a press conference in the Americana Hotel on the day he released the interview he had done with Jack Ruby. Right in the middle, a reporter had stood up and said, "Mr. Schiller, Jack Ruby just died. What do you have to say now?" He had had to give an extemporaneous answer in a hideously delicate situation. Awful. Now, he could practically hear Moyers: "Mr. Schiller, even though we both agree you are not an exploiter, ABC obviously thinks you are." This was being done on CBS. They could slap ABC right along with him.

The moment there was a real break and they started moving the setup for a new angle, Schiller called a couple of ABC people in L.A. Nobody knew anything. "It's right from the top," said Schiller. "You guys better get prepared. Tomorrow morning they may be interviewing you." He laid it in how they hadn't been protecting his flanks.

Moyers never brought it up. He interviewed Schiller twice after that, but didn't say a word. Schiller really respected him for that.

By morning, Schiller decided he might be in a good position. At least he wouldn't have to deal with a TV show that would milk the real merits of the story. He still had the rights, and could do the book and the movie. All the same, he had to learn how it happened. It was too incredible. During the day, he found out that a top ABC executive's wife was attending Columbia School of Journalism and came back one night indignant that the network was doing the Gary Gilmore story. She said to her husband, "How can you get into this? Exploiting history." The top executive — they wouldn't tell Schiller his name — never spoke to anybody on the West Coast, just told the New York office, "We're not doing Gilmore as entertainment." Of course, he was probably worried the FCC would go all over ABC's ass. "Circus" was no word to face the government with.

5

Holed up in the motel room, ready to go crazy with the pain, Gibbs was still trying to get his story connected with a paper. Trouble was everyone he called spoke to Schiller.

Finally, he came to an agreement with the *New York Post*. For $7,500. Gibbs told them that he had a handwritten invitation from Gilmore to go to the execution, and lots of letters. The *Post* had a reporter out in Aspen covering the Claudine Longet trial, and wanted Gibbs to go there, but he was afraid of being recognized by Salt Lake reporters, so talked them into letting him stay at the Royal Inn in Boulder, Colorado. Said he would check in under the name Luciano.

CHAPTER 24

Waiting for the Day

1

Brenda had had some worrisome hemorrhages. Going in for a checkup, she said to her doctor, "God, give me something for this pain. I don't know if I can keep going." Waitressing at La Cosa there were nights when she was ready to cry out. The doctor had been giving her pills, but on this day he said, "Brenda, it's not getting any better. You've got to come into the hospital and get it taken care of."

"Not now," said Brenda.

He shook his head. "I have one opening. Then I'll be jammed for three months. You can't wait that long. We'll have to bring you out on an emergency basis, and it's no good that way. Too high a risk."

"Oh," said Brenda, "shit on you. I'll call you back."

In the meantime, Johnny talked to the doctor and made arrangements. Brenda couldn't fight it. She was so tense from withstanding her twinges that she seemed to be tearing more. She said to herself, "Am I trying to get out of going to the execution?" Then thought, "No, I want to be there." She had been talking to Gary on the phone, and feelings had improved. Their last conversation she had said, "Gary, I'm just hoping you're as intelligent as you keep telling me you are, and so you will, at least, try to look at my point of view." God, he was single-minded, but she had the feeling he was softening.

In fact, when Gary got word that Brenda was going to the hospital, he asked Cline Campbell to see the Warden about letting her in for a last visit, but Sam Smith said, "He's had a disciplinary write-up for throwing a tray at a guard, and I will not bend the rules."

"Hell, Warden," said Campbell, "the man's going to die."

Sam Smith shook his head. "I can't do it without permission from Ernie Wright," he said.

Gary was drinking a cup of coffee when he heard the news. In one motion the cup and coffee went flying past Campbell's head and smashed on the wall. It was not right next to his head, but not that far away either. Campbell didn't jump. It had shocked and surprised him, but he didn't want to show fear. Gilmore now cursed, turned around, said, "I'm sorry," and walked away. In thirty seconds, he came back and said to the guard, "Where ya been? I want to clean this mess up." It was gone, like that.

After Brenda checked in, they put a white mini around her that stayed open in the back, and she felt safe in bed. She began to think about Gary a lot. He had been born in December and would be killed in January and she thought back to the night he came over with April and made a joke of calling her January, and then, Brenda began to count how long it was since Gary was out, nine months to the day from April 9th until this day on January 9th that she was entering the hospital. If they did execute him on the 17th, his death would come nine months and nine days from the time he first came out of prison. By God, she thought, that is just about the term of pregnancy. Hardly knew what caused it, but she began to cry.

2

GILMORE Have you ever heard of a guy named Zeke, Jinks or Pinkney, or some goddamn Dabney?

STANGER Yea, he's the ACLU lawyer.

GILMORE Listen to this shit. Mr. Dabney said that there's still a chance that Gilmore may flip-flop and change his mind about wanting to be executed. You know that term "flip-flop," man, has a certain jailhouse connotation. You guys don't know what it means, but I do. I'm pretty sure Dabney does. It means a guy who will fuck somebody in the ass and get fucked in the ass. Flip-flop. You can see what the term means. I'll read it to you, and I'd like you to release it Monday. V. Jinks Dabney of ACLU, what a phony-sounding name. You said in the *Salt Lake Tribune* there is still a chance that Gilmore may flip-flop and change his mind about wanting to be executed. No chance, V. Jinks Dabney, no way, never. You and ACLU are the flip-flops. You take one stand on abortion, which is actually execution. You are all for that. And then you take another stand on capital punishment. You're against that. Where are your convictions, V. Jinks Dabney? Do you and ACLU know where you really stand on anything? You have simply let this thing about me develop into a personal matter. You can't take losing. Well you've lost this one, V. Jinks Dabney. NAACP, look boy, I am a white man. Get that through your Brillo Pad heads, boy. I know a lot of black dudes, and I don't know any who respect the dumb niggers of NAACP. Giauque, Amsterdam, all you other nosy publicity-hunting lawyers, butt out, you punks.

3

SALT LAKE TRIBUNE

Salt Lake, Jan. 10 — Officers guarding Gilmore indicate he is starting to get nervous as the date for execution draws near.

Nicole, some guards said in the newspaper that I'm nervous. I've never been nervous in my life and I ain't now.
They are.
I'm just pissed off because I hate being watched —

Sam Smith called Earl Dorius to discuss the execution one more time. There was still the question of whether to carry out the death sentence on the prison grounds. That could have an adverse effect upon the convicts. On the other hand, if they took it outside, there would be problems of security and demonstrators. They would also have to locate some suitable facility on State land. Dorius and Smith both came back to the conclusion it was better to face the unpleasant consequences of having it take place within the prison.

Sam returned to another crucial question. In November, in December, and now again there had been popular talk. of employing volunteers from the general public as executioners. A few people had even sent letters. From the beginning, however, it had been Dorius's flat-out recommendation to use peace officers. The statute was silent on the matter, but Earl thought any system set up for screening possible kooks among the volunteers would be expensive, and the legalities a tangle. Like it or not, Earl didn't see it as a viable choice. It came down, as it always had, to using peace officers. Earl thought it was important, however, not to use anyone from the prison. Sam agreed it could only get a guard labeled a convict-killer, and thereby make him a future risk if he wanted to continue working inside. He would be an affront to the inmate population. So, they agreed: peace officers. From either the Salt Lake County Sheriff's Office or the Utah County Sheriff's Office. Sam would keep the names secret.

It was Earl Dorius's view that the ACLU would have to file some action by Wednesday, January 12. Otherwise, should they lose in the lower Courts, they would not have allowed themselves time to appeal. Bob Hansen, however, made Earl a bet. The ACLU would save Judge Ritter, their ace in the hole, for the very end so there might not be time to obtain an override from a higher Court. "They'll wait until Friday the fourteenth, just before closing."

Hansen was ready to tell you his opinion of Ritter. "The law can be bent," he would say, "we all twist the law, a little. But Ritter tortures it." And he would go on to speak of the Judge's habits.

One of Ritter's most unendurable characteristics, according to Hansen, was that he might have a list of forty trials and, on one day, call in *all* the attorneys in *all* forty cases. Then he would go down the list asking, "Are you ready? Are *you* ready?" He'd let them know, "All right, you're number two, you're number three," so forth, but when the first trial would end, he would call everybody back in, and say, "I've decided on number twenty next instead of number two." It sounded like a bad joke, but that was the way he ran things. Number twenty had to start a trial in five minutes. It was crazy. You never

knew when you were going to be on. You'd have to have your witnesses ready four or five trials ahead. If they came from out of town,
you had to put them up in motels. It was a disaster.

Of course, as a practical matter, give Ritter forty trials, and
thirty-eight got settled out of Court. Nobody could stand the goddamned suspense. That might be all right for some, but if you were
working for the government, and didn't have a budget to keep your
witnesses indefinitely available, and so they weren't there, Ritter simply dismissed the case. It could be a major felony, or a securities
fraud, even an indictment the government had been working on for
twenty years, Ritter would dismiss. You had to go up on appeal to get
a reverse. That would usually be won, but then the government had
to rearrest the parties all over again. A horrible waste of time. He just
tortured the law.

4

By January 10, one week to go, there were press people in and
out of the ACLU office all day. Cameras and microphones were
always cocked. One didn't have to get prepared for them, they were
there. Shirley Pedler felt as if she was always on. It had her up the
wall that her hair needed to be constantly combed. She never knew
when someone was going to be pointing another lens. And her
clothes had become a problem. She could no longer come to work in
dungarees and a T-shirt. Shirley decided to keep the Levi's, but wear
a good shirt and a nice blazer. Since you were photographed from the
waist up, it worked.

At least she began to lose that awful awareness of "Hey, you're
on TV. A lot of people are going to see this!" It was a relief. She'd
been going for a long time with the feeling they were going to lose, so
it gave her a heavy sense of responsibility when she didn't do things
right with the media. She was so wound up that even when she
managed to leave the office at seven or eight at night, she would just
pace at home and smoke. She'd always been a smoker, but now she
never quit. On a chain from morning to night.

That morning, January 10, Shirley and some of the attorneys were discussing final legal operations and when she stepped out of the conference room into the hall, she was almost knocked down by press people. Didn't even have a statement. The conference had been called to determine which group could do what, but the lawyers hadn't come to any conclusions. Shirley started to say, "I have nothing to say," and dropped her papers. The haste with which she stooped to pick them up got some of the press laughing, as if she was trying to conceal dark deeds. Shirley couldn't get over how the media thought the ACLU was the center of a lot of legal action coming up. In fact, they had about decided there were good reasons for the ACLU to stay out. In the Utah community they were seen as such a radical group, that they hurt a cause by coming in.

So, it was one glum conference. They felt they had no real standing. Their best hope was with Richard Giauque who had informed them that Mikal Gilmore was arriving in Salt Lake tomorrow. If Giauque could bring in a suit by the brother, or Gil Athay come in with one for the hi-fi killers, then the ACLU could enter as Friends of the Court. But the only real shot they could fire on their own was a taxpayers' suit. That was on the shakiest ground. They had such slim pickings that the best idea proposed this morning was for somebody to go out to the hospital and try to see Nicole. Maybe she could get Gary to change his mind about dying. Dabney said he would give Stanger a ring.

STANGER Jinks said, "How much influence does Nicole have over Gary?" I said, "Why, what are you talking about?" He said, "Well, we were thinking that possibly we could get her to try to talk Gary into fighting."

GILMORE They're clutching at straws, aren't they?

5

Schiller decided it was time to set up an office in Utah for the big push. Told his secretary in L.A. to call some agencies and hire a couple of hard workers to type the transcripts. Single girls who could make the move to Provo and be able to work twenty hours a day, if necessary. Keep their mouths shut. Under the circumstances, Schiller wasn't about to look for local Provo talent. He arranged to have phones put in at the Orem TraveLodge and began making as many as two trips a day between Salt Lake and Los Angeles. With better than a week to go, the new hired girls, Debbie and Lucinda, came to Utah, and set up his office in the motel. First thing he told Debbie was, "I want the night phone numbers of two Xerox repairmen." When she said, "Can't we always get a repairman?" he told her, "Debbie, I may need a guy at three in the morning. Get that number. Give him a twenty-dollar bill. If he goes out to dinner, I want to know. I want him to call us. That's the way it has to operate." Wanted to break her in right.

In the meantime, he was making plans to sneak a tape recorder into the execution. It had to be small enough to fit inside a package of cigarettes. He didn't know whether he'd use it or not, but had to have the tool. Psychologically, he told himself, he would spend thousands for things he might never use, just to feel secure.

Of course, he wasn't really spending thousands. Schiller had made a deal with a private investigator in Las Vegas who would sell him this minuscule tape recorder for $1,500 and buy it back for $1,300. Schiller would have to advance the entire amount up front and there'd be the cost of airfare to Vegas and back. Even so, he'd have an extra implement that might prove crucial for no more than a few hundred dollars.

All the same, he was getting in deep, but deep. The last week was shaping up, no question about it, as an $11,000 week. Off-duty policemen had to be hired as guards. He wanted Vern's home protected for the last three or four days, and talked Kathryne Baker into moving out of her house with her kids. Then he set up his office in the motel practically like a fortress. Was obliged to. Now that ABC had pulled out, NBC would have their hounds running. They had staked him out as if he was Mrs. Onassis. Frantic. NBC knew Schiller had given Moyers material for CBS. Another guy might have double-crossed the first commitment and given a couple of minutes on Gilmore to NBC to get them off his back. Otherwise, they would, he knew, begin to harass him. In fact, one night, staying over in Salt Lake at the Hilton, he actually had to call the police at 4:30 A.M. in order to have a couple of NBC reporters removed from the hall outside the room he was occupying. Afterward, Gordon Manning, NBC Executive Producer for Special Broadcasts, kept describing him to media people as a lizard. That was television. When you didn't cooperate, they did their best to squash your nuts.

All the while he was trying to stay on top of his options. What if Gary did change his mind? What if the story became "Gilmore Takes His Appeal"? He and Barry discussed it. They were not sitting there hoping Gary would be executed. They were prepared to go either way. With Gilmore alive, the story would not be as obviously dramatic, but it could be good. You could show the slow subsidence of a man's hour in the great light of publicity. Gary's return to the shadows. The thing was not to panic, and never to try to influence history, never force the results. He would realize the story potential whatever it was. They might call him a carrion bird, but he knew from deep inside that he could live with Gilmore's life. He did not have to profit from his death.

6

All the same, temptations were commencing for Schiller. No sooner had he set up the office than some crazy offers started to come in. Before they were even settled at the TraveLodge in Orem, Sterling Lord, acting as Jimmy Breslin's literary agent, was on the phone. He had heard that Schiller might be one of Gilmore's five guests to the execution, and Lord wanted to see about switching that invitation to Jimmy. It wasn't clear whether the *Daily News* or the column's syndicate was going to pick up the check, but the offer started at $5,000.

Schiller said, "It's not for me to sell. I can't even swear to you, Sterling, that I'm going to be there." Lord called back and said, "I might be able to get as much as thirty-five or even fifty thousand." "It's not for sale," said Schiller. Breslin called. "I'll give you a carbon of my story," he growled. That meant Breslin would own it on Headline Day, and Schiller could have it for the rest of time.

Schiller decided Jimmy Breslin did not understand where Larry Schiller was really at. Of course, he had a lot of old friends these days. All of a sudden, Sterling Lord was his old friend. Jimmy Breslin was his old friend. "Where should I stay?" Breslin asked Schiller, and Larry answered, "Well, you can be a monkey and go to the Hilton, or come out here and slum with me." Breslin took a room right next to them in the motel. He had great instincts that way.

Barry got upset. "Why Breslin?" he asked. "I'm sorry," said Schiller to Farrell, "I can't do it all alone."

"While we're at it," said Farrell, "why did you invite Johnston here from the *L.A. Times?*"

"Don't you realize," said Schiller, "I want to give these fellows a little piece of the story, so at least I won't have the *L.A. Times* and the *New York Daily News* against me. I got to get some people on our side, you know." Couldn't Barry understand how alone he was now that ABC had pulled out? The umbilical cord had certainly been cut.

"Yes," thought Farrell, "he does everything with a motive. He's always got a good reason. It's never that he's drunk or horny."

Schiller, decided Barry, was getting awful close to giving the goods away. He simply did not understand that each piece, no matter how small, still belonged to one potentially beautiful structure now being put together, and so were not separate chunks of wampum to be traded off at forest clearings to propitiate media dragons.

Farrell told himself that he should have been prepared. All the precautions had been going too well. From the time they moved into the seven rooms Larry had taken at the Orem TraveLodge, complete with their own rented typewriters, tables, two secretaries, guards, office room, writing room for Barry, archive room, Barry's bedroom, Schiller's bedroom, each girl's room, plus direct telephone lines so they only had to use the switchboard for standard incoming calls, and no motel employee could listen in on them, Larry had been dodging the media. Dodging them well. In the middle of all that heat, with everybody trying to get to him, Schiller had been careful to leak only the right stories through Gus Sorensen and Tamera, thereby coloring Salt Lake news, and so indirectly shaping the wire service output. Still, after all that hard-achieved control, Barry had only to walk into the main office to Xerox a page, and there was Jimmy Breslin, notebook in hand, twenty days late on the story, nicely driven down, thank you, in a hired Lincoln with a chauffeur. There was Schiller telling Jimmy Breslin about the eyes. The eyes.

Well, Farrell liked Jimmy. Breslin had done some nice things for him over the years. When Farrell was doing his column for *Life* back in '69 and '70 and got into a large dispute one time with his editors, a make-or-break conflict, Breslin did him the favor of talking it over for an evening. Farrell came to the conclusion that Breslin was very smart. "You know, Barry," Jimmy had said, "your column is your real estate," a phrase to stick in Farrell's mind. "Never give up your real estate," Breslin said, "fight and fuck around, patch it up, spackle it, make compromises, but don't give up the real estate." Farrell had followed his advice and thought it was right, so he had a soft spot for Jimmy Breslin.

The soft spot vanished, however, in one hot minute when he walked into the room and there was Schiller with this idiotic blissful smile on his face, rapping away to Breslin about the eyes. He could have been selling a new kind of floor polish on TV. And there was Breslin sitting on the couch, fat as a wild boar, taking notes three weeks late. One monument of bulk accepting tribute from another.

For weeks, trying to push these interviews uphill, Farrell had felt like he was searching in a dark room for a somber object. So when the story about the eyes came through, Farrell felt as if, finally, a little light was being generated. Living with Gilmore's rap sheet, going through his long prison record and petty busts, Farrell had about decided that Gary's life, by the measurement of its criminal accomplishment, would not rank high on any self-respecting convict's scale. He would be looked upon not as a heavy, but a ding. Sufficiently unpredictable for other convicts to give him a wide berth, but not a convict with real clout on the inside. In fact, close to a total loner. The kind of guy police terminology referred to as a germ. On human scale, a weed. Yet, just yesterday, coming toward the day of his death, talking about his eyes, Gilmore had said something fine as far as Farrell was concerned.

GILMORE I told you that this ninety-year-old man wrote and asked me for my eyes . . . ah, eh, he's too old. I mean I don't want to sound harsh about it, but this other guy is only twenty, and I think it might be better. Would you like to call this doctor and, ah, just tell him simply: . . . you got 'em! Gary Gilmore. And to draw up the papers through you guys.

MOODY We'll bring it up with the Warden.

GILMORE In his letter here, he says something about the young guy's life is just dwindling. Like the guy is really living a hopeless life. I'd rather the eyes be his than just give 'em to the Eyebank. I'd kinda like to know where they went. All right . . . call him collect. (laughing) . . . Ask him if he'll accept a collect call from Gary Gilmore.

The fact that Gilmore could come up with that kind of thinking moved Farrell right down to the gut. The interview had come in the day before, and after he and Schiller had listened to it, Farrell played it again when alone in his room. It was late at night. He had been working for a long time that day. Gilmore's voice got to him. Barry was crying and laughing and felt half triumphant that the man could talk with such clarity. Farrell's own eyes were good, and he always thought of them as precious cargo. While he would sign a card giving any part of his body to anybody, willingly, cock included, it would be after he died his normal death. Here was a fellow who had an execution date — imagine that, Barry said to himself after twenty hours of work, alone in a room at three in the morning — an execution date, and everybody wants a piece of him. Everybody is writing to ask for this part of his body or that, yet, he could think clearly about it. Sure there were people who carried cards in their wallets that said, "If you find me dead, you can have my kidney," but that was not the same as knowing you were going to be gone on the 17th of January, and applicants were coming around now, one week before, asking for your liver, your spleen, your left nut. Why a small-minded man could see it all as cannibalism, and cry out, "For Christ's sakes, leave me in peace. I want my eyes."

By God, was Gary like Harry Truman, mediocrity enlarged by history? Christ, he had even become the owner of a cottage industry: the precise remains of Gary Gilmore. That, to Farrell, was more impressive than any ability to steer a firm course toward execution. Farrell had not been much impressed by that bravery. Gilmore, he thought, had a total contempt for life, his life, your life, anyone's life. Waived his own away because it was a boss thing to do, showdown shit, pure pathology that came out of long years of playing chicken with prison authorities. Yet, now, overnight new celebrity, movie star without portfolio, Gilmore was responding humanely to all the attention, actually functioning like a decent man. Those eyes redeemed the scene. Farrell was feeling very protective about this story.

So when he saw Schiller and Breslin on the couch, he went into a tantrum. Barry liked to keep his cool, but twenty-hour work sessions had certainly heated him up. "You have a cop," he said to Schiller, "sitting up all night across the corridor to make sure nobody breaks into this office, but you ought to have that cop sitting on your upper lip." He was mad enough to smash a table. "Schiller, you're not handing this over to Breslin."

Before the fight could even develop, however, Jimmy took out his pad, pulled the page he had been writing on, tore it in little pieces, and threw them up in the air. Beautiful, thought Farrell. He was very pleased with Breslin.

CHAPTER 25

Getting to Know You

1

Farrell had to be glad the eyes had been kept for him. He needed something nourishing in the marrow, for he had been discovering an awful lot about Gilmore that was not so good. Rereading the interviews and letters, Farrell began to mark the transcripts with different-colored inks to underline each separate motif in Gilmore's replies, and before he was done, he got twenty-seven poses. Barry had begun to spot racist Gary and Country-and-Western Gary, poetic Gary, artist manqué Gary, macho Gary, self-destructive Gary, Karma County Gary, Texas Gary, and Gary the killer Irishman. Awfully prevalent lately was Gilmore the movie star, awfully shit-kicking large-minded aw-shucks.

GILMORE   Here is that other girl who writes to me: "How's my wild pony with those wild eyes. . . . I wish I could kiss you just once. I don't know, Gary, how to say good-bye to you. Gary, I'm cryin' right now on your letter, I love you, I hate the fucking system, I hate that they won't even let you call Nicole, the fuckers. Execution. What is this? Wild, wild West? My love is with you, Gary. I love you." (laughing) I think she's got a case for me, eh? I got three letters from her today. A good thing for me I'm not in California. Christ, oh, ah, man, she'd wear me out.

STANGER   Is she fifteen? Holy mackerel.

GILMORE   Pretty hard to keep up with.

Then there was the old con full of jail-house wisdom:

GILMORE After you get known as a troublemaker, it's so easy to keep getting in trouble, 'cause all them guards, man, like they put your picture on the hot list in the fucking guards' lounge. You know, watch this guy, suspected of doing this and that. Some guards take a personal dislike to you, man, and antagonize you in little ways that'll make you blow up, you know, in a situation where you're always wrong — and never right — because you're the prisoner. They got the hammer, you know?

The subtlety of the self-pity was cloying. Still, Farrell was loving the job even more than expected. One twenty-hour day after another, sure enough, but what absorption! What delight to be altogether out of himself. By God, Barry thought, I have all the passions of an archivist. I'm proprietary about the material.

Once in a while, he even laughed. One night when he and Larry were so tense from overwork that they could hardly look at one another, a tape came in from Gilmore that got them laughing so hard they almost slid off their chairs. It had to be the tension. Yet for one glorious minute, Gilmore was as funny to Farrell as Bob Hope on a good night, same maniacal see-through X-ray eye, same hatred of horseshit. God, sometimes he saw into the bottom of the pot, thought Farrell.

GILMORE Oh, hey, man, I got something that'll make a mint. Get aholda John Cameron Swazey right now, and get a Timex wristwatch here. And have John Cameron Swazey out there after I fall over, he can be wearing a stethoscope, he can put it on my heart and say, "Well, that stopped," and then he can put the stethoscope on the Timex and say, "She's still running, folks."

2

Nonetheless, it offended Farrell to be so hooked. He often thought that if less attention had been paid to Gilmore he might have changed his mind and looked to avoid his execution. Now Gary was trapped in fame, and it gave him a crazy strength. Of course, one

Barry Farrell had become an integral part of this machine that was making it impossible for Gilmore to take an appeal. Hardly a flattering light on yourself. You could try to say, "I'm not the locomotive, only one of the cars, and in my car, the best, most sensitive, thinking is being done about the situation. Therefore, my moral responsibility is to stay with it. If I leave," Farrell told himself, "Gilmore is abandoned to the likes of 'Good Morning America.'"

Nonetheless, in the quiet of 2 A.M., Barry would recall how his *New West* piece described Larry Schiller as a carrion bird. Now he had to wonder if Barry Farrell was not the blackest wing in journalism. Somebody was always dying in his stories. Oscar Bonavena getting killed, Bobby Hall, young blond girls getting offed on highways in California. One cult slaying or another. He even had the reputation of being good at it. His telephone number leaped to the mind of various editors. Barry Farrell, crime reporter, with an inner life exasperatingly Catholic. Led his life out of his financial and emotional exigencies, took the jobs his bills and his battered psyche required him to take, but somehow his assignments always led him into some new great moral complexity. Got into his writing like a haze.

Yet there was one aspect of the interviews he did not question. There was something marvelous about the energy Gilmore had to give. Cline Campbell stopped by at the motel to say hello, and remarked to Farrell, "Your work .is a godsend. This is Gary's one chance to express himself." Looking at the daily bits and pieces of produce, Farrell would think, Yes, you could see Gilmore's attempt to form a coherent philosophy in relation to some incredibly tangled ethical matters.

MOODY   What are some of the things you could never do?

GILMORE   Oh, I couldn't snitch on anybody. I couldn't rat on anybody. I don't think I could torture anybody.

MOODY   Isn't forcing somebody to lie down on the floor and shooting him in the back of the head torture?

GILMORE   I'd say it was a very short torture.

MOODY   But how could any crime be worse than taking a person's life?

GILMORE   Well, you could alter somebody's life so that the quality of it wouldn't be what it could've been. I mean, you could torture 'em, you could blind 'em, you could maim 'em, you could cripple 'em, you could fuck 'em up so badly that their life would be a misery for the rest of it. And for me, that's worse than killing somebody. Like, if you kill somebody, it's over for them. I — I believe in karma and reincarnation and stuff like that, and if you kill somebody, it could be that you just assume their karmic debts, t-t-thrr-thereby you might be relieving them of a debt. But I think to make somebody go on living in a lessened state of existence, I think that could be worse than killing 'em.

STANGER Then there are crimes that you consider worse than murder?

GILMORE Well, Jesus, I don't know, there's all kinds of crimes, you know . . . what some governments do to their people, you know? Forms of brainwash in some countries. . . . I think some forms of behavior modification, like, ah, you know, the irreversible forms, like lobotomies, and ah, you know, Prolixin — I won't say they're worse than murder, but man, you gotta give it some thought. . . . You don't interfere with somebody's life. You let people meet their own fate.

STANGER Didn't you interfere with Jensen's and, ah, Bushnell's lives?

GILMORE Yes.

STANGER You think you had any right to do that?

GILMORE No. (sighs)

MOODY If you really believe that your soul is full of evil, and if you really wish to atone, why haven't you attempted . . . some expression of remorse?

GILMORE I don't believe my soul is that full of evil.

MOODY Do you think it's filled with any?

GILMORE More evil than yours, or Ron's, or, uh, a lot of people's. I think I'm further from God than you are, and I would like to come closer.

MOODY Do you think expressing remorse is mushy?

GILMORE I'm afraid the newspapers would interpret it in a mushy light.

Campbell might be right. With all his poses, Gary was still rising to the interview so well it was frustrating on occasion not to be able to conduct the interviews oneself.

Yet Farrell was just as glad it couldn't happen. He was saved thereby from having to muster that twinkle of the eye at which he had become so reassuring. Or that firm handshake which said, "I'm here to listen to you, man to man, buddy to buddy." All those things interviewers did, those up-front sympathies, those gut-grinder empathies. This way, there was no quickly-arrived-at brotherhood to betray. He could sit at the typewriter and compose his questions, Moody and Stanger would truck them out, Debbie and Lucinda would type the tapes, and he could study it long enough to write new questions. He and Gary were immunized from one another. No need to twist his face full of instant humanity in order to keep Gilmore talking.

Even more important, he would not have to run the risk of getting too friendly with Gary and so forgetting that some basic pieces might be missing in Gilmore, that he, Barry Farrell, as a brother of Max Jensen, ought not to forgive for too little. Yes, it was better this way.

3

Still, the tapes were endlessly irritating. Barry was developing quite a dislike for the lawyers. It was too cruel a demand on his nervous system not to know whether a serious question was going to be presented properly, or if Moody, or particularly Stanger, would giggle his ass off. To Farrell, straining to listen at the end of a tape, the lawyers seemed too cautious when they were not too flighty. Some of those Sisters at the Catholic school in Portland, Gilmore would confide to the lawyers, gave us real whippings. "They used to go insane with frustration," Gary said, "trying to make me conform. I got beat by nuns more than once. It wasn't like when they disciplined other children there. My father finally took me out of the school." Farrell was up on tiptoe for the development of this theme. The key to every violent criminal could be found in the file of his childhood beatings, but Gilmore claimed his mother never touched him, and his father never bothered to. So here, at last, might be the beginning of some nitty-gritty. Stanger, however, chose to say, "Oh, gee, those nuns always seemed so nice in the movies." Gilmore answered, "Yeah. In the movies." Stanger cackled.

To Farrell's ears at that moment, it went: Cackle, cackle, cackle. He went wild listening to those tapes late at night in Orem, in the ice-cold middle of winter.

Sometimes he and Schiller would sit down with the lawyers and go over the questions. Moody and Stanger would seem to know what they were doing as they left for the prison. Then they would come back saying great, great, and leave the tape. Schiller would play it — oh, God. The lawyers were hopeless as journalists. All that stuff they didn't get around to.

GILMORE This kid come to me and asked if he could talk, and wanted to come out in the yard with me and asked if he could walk around with me. I asked him, "What's wrong?" and he said this, uh, nigger was trying to fuck him. He was going to turn himself in, you know, into the hole, to be locked up to get away from it. He didn't know how to handle it. I told him, "Well, listen, man, what do you want me to do?" and he says, "I'll be your kid if you'll protect me," you know. I says, "Well, I don't want a kid, I don't like punks, ya know, and I don't want you to be a punk anyway." I asked him if he was one. He said, "No," and he didn't want to be one. So I just went and got another guy and told him about it you know, and he said, Let's kill the motherfucker. As it turned out, we didn't kill him. Gibbs will say that we did, but we didn't. We just caught this guy coming up the stairs and we both had pieces of pipe in our hand, you know, and we beat him half to death and drug him down to another nigger's cell, and put him on the bunk. He was unconsicous. We hit him so fast and so hard . . . he was a boxer, we didn't give him no chance, slammed the door, and left. He knew who did it, you know, and, uh, he never tried to do anything about it. He accepted it and, uh, that's the way it was.

That's the way it was. They never asked Gilmore another question. He could have shouted in frustration. He would not have let Gilmore get away with that story. Farrell would have liked to learn if Gilmore had ever been turned out by some black guy. Maybe as far back as Reform School, maybe later. But there was something in the story that left Farrell suspicious. This big, black brute who aroused Gilmore sufficiently to defend a sweet white boy — it was like a girl calling you on the phone to say, "I have a friend who's pregnant. Do you know a doctor?" Gary was walking tall in the tale, but what if that little white kid had been Gary?

So there would be hours when Farrell would be seized with depression at how few were the answers they had located in the inner works of Gary Mark Gilmore, and the size of the questions that remained. How could they begin to explain things so basic, for example, as the way he had led Nicole into suicide? That was clammy. Could you call such depths of lover's perfidy a product of environment? Might you dare to explain it by saying that only an urban cowboy could pass through psychological machines that would stamp you out that badly? Could you say that you had to eat the wrong foods, sleep in the wrong places, take the wrong drugs, drive the wrong cars, make the wrong turns, do all that for an awful long time before you turned into a force who did horrible things to people who loved you?

Or did you put the blame on heredity, and say Gary Gilmore grew out of the evil seed of mystery in things itself? Why, there were thousands of people who could stick up a motel and shoot the motel owner. Afterward they would utter the same kind of half-stoned things Gilmore had testified to. Didn't quite know, didn't quite remember, it was like a movie, man, no reason. A veil of water over the mind, you know. But planning for Nicole's suicide — that, to Farrell, had evil genius. "Little elf, how can you do this to me?" Gilmore would implore. Then, at the top of the next page, as if Gilmore had just swallowed a lightning bolt of rage, why, FUCK, SHIT, and PISS would be written in letters two inches high.

Farrell got formidably suspicious of those letters. The mood, he noticed, often changed at the beginning of a new page. In effect, each sheet was being worked on as a separate composition. Gilmore — good old Renaissance man — wasn't about to sully the calligraphy of a pretty page with obscenities, not if he was planning to finish the pretty page with a drawing of an elf.

GILMORE   If I talk to Nicole before I'm executed, I'm not going to ask her to do any particular thing, and I may encourage her to go on living and to raise her kids. Uh, I don't want anybody else to be able to have her, though.

MOODY You're really on the horns of a dilemma.

GILMORE Yeah, you might say it's giving me a little pause.

MOODY She has a pretty heavy responsibility to those kids.

GILMORE Aw, no more responsibility than anybody has for their kids. Listen, your kids come through you but they're not really of you. I mean . . . everybody is an individual little soul. Those kids come through her but they are not a part of her.

MOODY Do you think they could get along as well without her as with her?

GILMORE I guess this sounds like a cold-blooded thing, but I'm not really overconcerned about them kids. They're not going to starve to death. (pause) I'm concerned about Nicole and myself.

MOODY Might it be kinder and more loving to instruct her to forget you, get over you, and find a man for herself and her children who would give them a chance for a better life than they've had?

GILMORE Kinder and more loving to who?

MOODY To her and the children.

GILMORE I'm not going to answer that.

Well, a coherent philosophy came no more easily to him than to anyone else.

4

All this while Schiller was having his own reaction to Farrell. He didn't like the way Barry tended to shape his questions upon conclusions he'd already made. In a way, very Catholic, thought Schiller. Catholics were supposed to know what they thought. Sometimes the habit carried over from church to a lot of other things. Start with preformed conclusions, and your investigation would move on tracks. In his own classy way, Barry could be as narrow-minded as an FBI man. He certainly wasn't exploring karma enough. Nor was Schiller certain that Barry had a good sense of Gilmore.

The real friction, however, was that Farrell didn't like to listen to tapes when they came in. For Schiller, that was the creative experience of the day. He'd have an immediate reaction. At such times, he felt he understood Gilmore at a moment-by-moment level. But Barry didn't like to listen. He waited for the tapes to be typed up. That left him a full day behind. Still, Farrell argued, he couldn't work until they were on paper. Then he could underline them and analyze them. Schiller would say, "Don't you hear his voice? Gary is ready to answer questions on this subject now." Barry would reply, "Well, I want to look at the transcript." Of course, their relations never got uncivil, except for that blowout over Jimmy Breslin.

CHAPTER 26

Nothing Left

1

In December, after the Supreme Court turned them down, Anthony Amsterdam called Mikal. The decision, he explained, had not said the State of Utah was right and they were wrong. Only that the request to have the case heard immediately was being refused. That was merely a setback. Bessie or Mikal could still file the same argument in a lower Federal Court. The case would go up again.

Mikal, however, replied that Gary had called his mother and asked her not to take any further steps.

Bessie's decision to stay out looked final. Any new action, therefore, would have to be brought, Mikal said, by himself. He also told Amsterdam that he did not know what conclusion he would come to. Mikal thought he might have to go to Utah to decide. He confessed to Amsterdam that he hated the thought of such a trip.

Mikal ought to recognize, Amsterdam said, that the Damicos wouldn't necessarily want him to visit his brother. Amsterdam said he did not pretend to know Vern Damico, but the uncle and his attorneys could have a financial interest in Gary's death. They would hardly be unaware of the possibility that Mikal could change Gary's mind. They could believe themselves full of human decency and family love, yet still offer a lack of cooperation.

Mikal got ready to go.

2

On January 11, Richard Giauque met Mikal at the airport in Salt Lake, and drove him out to Point of the Mountain. Since Giauque's own car was being repaired, he showed up in his partner's limousine, a silver Rolls-Royce, and apologized for its gaudiness. Mikal, full of the tension of walking into an interview with a brother who might be hostile to him, was hardly observing in which car he traveled. In fact, once they passed the prison gate, and were escorted down the lane between the two high wire fences that led to Maximum, a long, one-story warehouse of a building, he was most surprised he was not searched. By way of Ron Stanger, Giauque had made arrangements for the visit, and been told that it would be a ninety-minute "one time only, no physical contact" affair. The Warden must have changed his mind, however, for Mikal was quickly passed through two sliding metal gates and brought into a chamber about 20 feet by 30, the visiting room for Maximum Security. In this room, everything was painted beige, a drab beige, old and grungy. There were cigarette butts on the floor, and, more than ten days after New Year's, a Christmas tree shedding its needles in the corner — an ill-kept dirty room.

Gary came strolling in through another sliding gate. He was wearing red, white and blue sneakers, and white coveralls. Like a juggler, he was wigwagging a comb through his fingers. He had a big smile. "Well," he said to Mikal, "you're as damn skinny as ever."

As soon as they began to speak, however, of the purpose of Mikal's visit, Gary said, "I don't want the family interfering." He stared into Mikal's eyes. "Amsterdam is out of this, I hope." Before he could reply, Vern and Ida came through the door. Mikal couldn't believe it. He had been promised a private visit.

Vern had brought along a large green T-shirt with a computerized photo of Gary on it. Below was printed: GILMORE — DEATH WISH. Mikal couldn't tell if they were serious, but they kept talking about Gary wearing one of these T-shirts on Execution Day so they could auction it off, bullet holes and all. "Take it to Sotheby's," said Gary, laughing. Such talk consumed a lot of time. Vern and Gary were like veterans talking over old capers in front of a rookie.

After the Damicos left, Mikal had a moment alone with Gary. He was promptly offered a shirt.

"It wouldn't be much use to me."

"Well," said Gary, "it is too big. Maybe you can grow into it."

Mikal couldn't keep from saying, "Are you really planning to sell it?"

"Do you think," said Gary, "that I have no more class than that?"

3

Back in Salt Lake, Mikal settled in for a long talk with Richard Giauque. Like Amsterdam, this lawyer was confident, and seemed very concerned about the issues.

As Giauque presented it, Gary was being used by many people. To help get elected, the new Attorney General, Bob Hansen, had gone all out for capital punishment. He, and a great many other conservatives obviously wanted to use Gary's willingness to die for their own political ends. While, eventually, Giauque allowed, this so-called right to die, this right to commit suicide, might have to be supported by people like himself — at least if one believed that self-determination applied as much to individuals as to nations — nonetheless, given the circumstances prevailing here, Gary had been taken over by many people. In Giauque's opinion, this outweighed his other rights. Personal freedom couldn't extend so far that it injured the very fabric of society. Right now, to recognize one man's right to die could have a deadly effect on four to five hundred lives in death row. In Utah, public opinion was running 85 to 90 percent in favor of capital punishment already, and "Here is your brother expressing his own *personal* desire to die. He's walking right into the hands of every gang that's looking to join a posse."

Mikal spoke of his dilemma. He was worried that saving Gary's life by legal methods would only guarantee his suicide. On the other hand, he certainly detested capital punishment.

Giauque nodded. It was always dangerous to assume the authorities had enough righteousness on their side to take a life. In the practice of law, Giauque said, you got a little suspicious about absolutes, particularly the power of the State. Too many smug people sat in powerful seats.

Nonetheless, the real question to Mikal was whether both sides did not wish to use Gary. Giauque had not said it; maybe — to do the man justice — he had not even thought it, but one logical conclusion you could take from his remarks was that people opposed to capital punishment would work to stop the execution, even if it brought on Gary's suicide. That way, at least, the State would be deprived of its body. Mikal did not know how to think this through. He recognized that he would have to stay a little longer in Salt Lake, and try to visit Gary again.

Later, he called Vern to find out if Moody and Stanger were available and learned that they could not meet him that night. Schiller, however, was flying in from Los Angeles and willing to talk, wanted to.

4

Larry didn't get to the hotel until midnight. There, in the lobby of the Hilton, a young fellow, somewhat taller than average, came over and introduced himself. Schiller was surprised. This young brother had long hair and was somewhat delicate and looked like an intellectual. He was wearing slacks and a sweater and had a small pliable plastic briefcase under his arm. Was ready to talk right there in the middle of the lobby. After they sat down, one of the first things Mikal said was, "I have a lot of questions I want to ask," and he started taking notes even as Schiller embarked on the ten-minute version of the speech. Before it was over, something in the note-taking made Larry uneasy, and he joked, "With all the stuff you're taking down, you might have a book." Only weeks later did Schiller find out that Mikal was indeed writing an article for *Rolling Stone*.

There was a family resemblance, but Schiller found it hard to believe that Mikal was related to Gary. He had a very soft voice, a very calm young man with thin hands, very pleasant manner, considering the intensity of the situation, and he sat most properly in his place, not leaning back or putting his feet up, but forever taking papers out of his briefcase, consulting his notes, then replacing them. He seemed academic to Schiller. If not for the long hair he would have looked like a thin scholarly Mormon, one of the more prissy BYU kids.

It was only when Mikal began to talk about himself that Schiller got it. Having to decide whether to go ahead with Amsterdam and Giauque was heavy shit. The boy wasn't in tears, but it was obvious he was feeling shaky.

Then, out of the blue, no preparation, *zap!* like Gary Gilmore, Mikal asked: Would Schiller rather see Gary dead, or alive? There it lay, the key question. Schiller looked Mikal in the eye and said, "I'm here to record history, not to make it." Mikal took down this answer, and asked more questions. He was not a very sharp or persistent questioner, Larry decided, just accepted Schiller's answers, did not persist, did not pursue, did not challenge. Just wrote it down, then looked at the page as if studying his own handwriting. It was late at night and Schiller was awfully tired. He had flown to L.A. that day and come back, and now he was wondering why Mikal wanted to see him rather than Vern or Ida or anyone else. "Do you intend to speak to the Damicos?" he asked. "I'm here," Mikal said, "to talk to Gary, and make the decision." There was, Schiller decided, no feeling of warmth in the man, or rapport. It was a cold meeting. "Why are you taking notes?" Schiller asked at last.

Mikal replied, "So I can analyze what you're saying."

Nevertheless, they agreed to contact one another again, and to keep secret their conversations. After Schiller dropped Mikal at his hotel, he went down the Interstate to Orem with the feeling that the evening had been a breakthrough. Mikal might have been distrustful, but Schiller felt their next meeting would take a turn for the good. Through Mikal, he could get a glimpse of Gilmore's family, and intimate childhood things about him that were nice and not so nice. Since Mikal was so different from Gary, it opened hope for an independent view. Schiller felt so good about it, he told Vern of the meeting. That would soon prove, from Schiller's point of view, a mistake.

DESERET NEWS

Salt Lake, Jan. 12 — Utah Atty. Gen. Robert B. Hansen today received a letter from Salt Lake City attorney Judith Wolbach saying she had talked with well-known lawyer Melvin Belli who estimates Gilmore's relatives could file claims for a wrongful death action. The family could ask $1 million in general damages and $1.5 million in punitive damages, against state officers . . . if Gilmore is executed and the U.S. Supreme Court later rules unconstitutional the State's death penalty statute. . . .

5

Barry Golson from *Playboy* came in. Schiller had already received a first payment of close to $12,000. After two days of talking and haggling like crazy over the last details of the contract, they were getting on each other's nerves. Breslin's presence disturbed Golson. Was Schiller giving away *Playboy* material?

"You can get the hell out of the office," Schiller said. "Try being a little more courteous," said Golson, "and I will." What an ego contest!

Then Moody and Stanger started again. They came to the motel and told him they wanted a bonus. Otherwise, they wouldn't interview Gary anymore.

Schiller did his best. "I have to tell Gary what you're trying to pull," he said. Wondered if he was right. "I'm just going to send," said Schiller, "a telegram." When he saw they weren't the least bit frightened, he took another line.

"Look," he said, "you're falling prey to what every attorney falls prey to. You're holier than thou, until it comes to money." Finally, Schiller refused a bonus unless Vern agreed. "If he comes to me," Schiller said, "I'll give you what he OK's." It was a peculiar fight, because actually, it wasn't money out of Schiller's share, but Vern's, and so more a clash of personalities. They were definitely feeling frayed.

After dinner, Ian Calder of the *National Enquirer* called from Miami, to say that he had an idea that might be worth *six figures*. "Get Gary," said Calder, "to agree to submit two small personal objects that are at present in his possession, and have him write twenty-five words, whatever they are. We'll send a bonded messenger to pick up the sealed envelope and put it in a vault. Before Gary dies, we will tell our worldwide network of seers and clairvoyants to key in on the exact moment of his execution. Then we'll see how close they come to guessing what those two objects are, or what the words in Gary's message might be." Schiller said into the phone, "Ian, how deep into six figures are we talking?"

"If it works, Larry," said Calder, "I mean, it's a hundred thousand idea. That's what I'm talking about. A hundred thousand dollars if it comes off."

Larry said, "What if nobody's guess comes close?"

Ian said, "Well, of course, then it would be worth much less."

Schiller said, "Good night," and hung up.

6

In the left-hand corner of the visiting room was a booth with three seats, three phones, and three small windows. Next day, when Mikal went to visit Gary, he could see Moody and Stanger talking to his brother through the glass. There was Gary with two phones to his ear, the voice of Moody in one receiver, Stanger in the other. None of them was aware, however, that Mikal was also there behind them, and could have gone over to pick up the last phone. Instead, he sat in a corner, unobserved, and listened to Moody say, "Schiller met with him last night. He thinks Mikal is going to stop the execution." Then Moody added, "Did you know Giauque brought him out in a Rolls-Royce?"

As he got up to leave, Moody must have taken a good look, for he seemed startled. Then Mikal heard him asking one of the guards who the visitor might be.

Gary came into the visitors' room wearing a black sleeveless sweat shirt. He was twirling a Scotsman's cap on his finger.

"Gary, I don't want to play games," Mikal said. "What your lawyer said is true. I may seek a Stay."

Gary's face took on the expression of his newspaper photos. All jaw. Flared nostrils. "Is it also true," he asked, "that Giauque brought you out here in a Rolls?"

Mikal saw how it looked to Gary. Wealthy liberals who never gave a damn about him in other years, were now gathering their wealth and power to frustrate him. "It's not important," Mikal tried to say.

They fought over Amsterdam and Giauque. "Who do you think they are," asked Gary, "holy men? They're trying to use you."

"Just recognize," said Mikal, "that I can take action without them. I can still go in and get a commutation of your sentence. They wouldn't be doing it, I would."

"Could you really?" asked Gary.

"I believe I could."

Gary paced around. "Look," he said, "I've spent too much time in jail. I don't have anything left in me."

A guard's voice came into the room. "Time's up."

"Come back," said Gary. "Talk to me tomorrow."

Even as Mikal was passing through the door, Gary called out. "Where were you, years ago, when I needed you?"

All the way back to Salt Lake, Mikal heard, "Where were you when I needed you?" He had been ready to sign the paper for Giauque, but now he did not know if it was his choice or Gary's. His brother's voice kept saying, "I don't have anything left in me." Mikal wanted to disappear into a place where choices did not exist. After a bad night, he decided to write a letter to Gary.

In it, he said that when he was face to face with his older brother's anger, he could never remember what he wanted to tell him. He wrote to Gary that he had always been frightened of him. Only in their last two meetings had he come to realize that, in fact, he loved him. Whatever choice he made would come from love. If

Gary chose to live, he hoped they could take down the barriers be-tween them. He ended by speaking of his belief: one's best chance for redemption was found through choosing life over death. In life was where one found redemption, not death.

That afternoon at the prison, a guard read Mikal's letter and de-livered it to Gary on the other side of the glass.

Gary looked it over quietly and began to cry. Just a tear or two. Then he wiped an eye with his finger and smiled. "Well put," he said over the phone. He asked Mikal, "Are you familiar with Nietzsche? He wrote that a time comes when a man should rise to meet the oc-casion. That's what I'm trying to do, Mikal."

They sat there. Gary nodded, "Look, kid, I was thinking of what I said yesterday. That was unfair. I wasn't around when you were young. So get it straight. I don't hate you. I know you're my brother and I know what that means."

Gary's hand might just as well have been laid on Mikal's heart. Mikal could feel himself being manipulated here, softened there. He obliged himself to say, "What would you do if I tried to stop this?"

"Oh, you could have my sentence commuted," Gary said, "but you wouldn't have to live in prison. Do you know how strong you have to be, year after year, to keep yourself together in this place?" Gary asked.

Mikal would have been ready to concede then. Yet on his first day in Salt Lake, he had met Bill Moyers. He had spent hours with him ever since. Moyers, he felt, had to be one of the wisest and most compassionate men he had ever met, and Moyers had said, "If we are confronted with a choice between life and death, and choose any-thing short of life, we're choosing short of humanity." Gary might lis-ten to such an idea. It was so clear cut. Gary liked ideas that were logical propositions. Mikal did not really think it would make a dif-ference. Yet before he left, he asked Gary to talk to Bill Moyers. "Not for an interview. Just for a meeting."

"I'll do it," said Gary, "but it's got to be off the record. We can't forget my deal with Larry Schiller."

CHAPTER 27

Cutting the String

1

janvier 13
jeudi
Bon maten mon Soul Mate
je Love vous. Oh! Je Love vous!
et avoir besoin de vous tant!
This morn i have only a few minutes to write as my lawyer should be here soon.

i have been having fun with an old french book. It is a beautiful language. i would like to learn it maybe even live in France one day.

Away from here — oh well . . .

Sundberg informed me that all of the doctors involved in this mess i am in are planning already to recommend that i be released on January 22 (1977 hopefully)

These long days are truly drawing nearer to your execution date. i find that reality hard to grasp onto.

Not so much that soon you will die but that i cannot be with you now while it is so near to that time. Why should it be so? There must be logic behind my destiny but i cannot see even a partical of it. . . .

There are no longer words that can express the Love that is in my soul and my heart for you mon Soul Mate

You have all my love. i believe that you know

And i know i have yours

if you die . . . so soon . . . i will know and feel your soul! wrap around my thots and this soul who loves you so deeply.

Goodbye now my love
Till then and forever
No matter where i walk
ill walk alone
Till again im by your side

I Love you
Ever Yours
NICOLE

2

Larry talked it over with Farrell and they agreed. When it came to talking about himself, Gilmore, no matter how frank he might seem in the interviews, still lived behind a psychic wall. If they were going to learn more, they would have to make a breach. The questions must turn critical of Gary's poses, cut through the sham. So Farrell worked on a special set to give to Moody and Stanger. Schiller also instructed them that Gilmore was to read each question aloud, then answer it. They did not want either lawyer's voice affecting his reaction.

Over the phone in Maximum, Ron Stanger said, "Our friend is thinking he would like to have some *serious answers.* Quote, unquote."

"I've been playing serious all along," said Gilmore. "As serious as I've been playing anything."

"Okay," said Moody.

Gilmore began to read: "It seems to me now that in your situation with your sense of fate and destiny and karma, this conversation we're struggling to have is really an important event in your life as well as mine."

"Thanks, Larry," said Gilmore to the introduction.

"I think," Gary continued, "we both owe it to the importance of the situation to try hard to replace superficial speculative interpretations with deeper harder ones."

"Right," he said, answering his own reading voice.

"Sometimes you sound like you're telling a story you've told many times before," went the next question. "My reaction is — oh, Gary, do you tell that to all the girls, or all the shrinks, or all the people who see something of interest in you and want to know you better? A number of stories told in the course of these interviews are stories that you also told Nicole in your letters oft accompanied by, let us say, sweetheart touches, little indications that you wanted to charm the reader, the lover, the observer in a very practiced, calculating way. That's my honest reaction. Tell me where I might be wrong."

"You're wrong, Larry," said Gary.

Then Gilmore laughed. "Shit, ain't nothing calculating about that. I get lonely. I like language, but I tell the truth. In jail you rap a lot, you know, to pass the time. Damn near every convict has his little collection of reminiscences, anecdotes, stories, and a person can get sorta practiced at recollecting. You probably got a few yarns you spin on occasion yourself. You know, you gotta go to dinners and different things and, ah, talk to different people, Larry, so you've probably got your favorite little stories yourself. The fact that you tell something more than once to more than one person doesn't make that thing a lie." Gilmore paused. "Larry, I do emphasize things . . . I've spent a lot of time in the hole, and in the hole you can't see the guy you're talking to, 'cause he's in the cell next door or down the line from you. So, it just becomes necessary to . . . make yourself clear and heard because there might be other conversations going on and a lot of other noise, guards rattling keys and doors. Think about that, you know."

"I am not so sure," said the question, "that you remember the truth of your early childhood."

In a different voice Gilmore answered, "Do you remember the truth of *your* early childhood, Larry?"

"You've said," continued the question, "that your mother's love was always strong, constant, and consistent, strange adjectives, by the way, to describe a mother's love."

"I don't think," said Gilmore, "they're strange. I don't respect your question."

"I don't think," the question came back, "that I've ever heard 'strong, constant, and consistent' employed in such usage before."

"You probably haven't," answered Gilmore, "but have you ever asked anybody about their mother before?"

"My impression, Gary, based on talking to others in your family, and based on listening to your voice on these tapes — is that you may have been treated rather cruelly when you were a small child. There are people in the family who say that efforts were made by your grandparents to assume custody of you. That you came at an awkward moment in your mother's life and that she seemed to resent you, when you were small. Is there any truth to any of this?"

"Not that I know of, Larry," Gilmore replied.

"What kind of son is it, after all," continued the question, "who does these things you do, and in so doing takes a very beautiful revenge against all those who have failed to love him enough. Maybe that's psychoanalytical bullshit, and if so, I stand accused, but I am yearning to understand how this well-loved young boy grew up to reward his mama with the life you've lived. I think, Gary, that you have been exacting revenge against something that happened to you when you were too small to fight it off. Another reason I am tempted to believe this, is that when the conversation turns to any question where emotion is involved, a trace of a stutter appears in your voice."

"Dat, dat, dat, dat," Gilmore snickered.

"You begin," the question continued, "talking like a reformed stutterer. I don't think you're a man without feelings. I think you're a man who somehow can't bear to admit what his feelings are."

There was quite a pause before Gilmore replied. "Larry, I swear to God that I cannot recall, and I have a terrific memory, my mom ever hitting me. I don't think she ever even so much as spanked me. She always loved and believed in me. Fuck what everybody in the family says. I have a beautiful mother. Fuck what everybody in the family says. I have a beautiful mother. I repeated that because of the background noise. I don't know if you can hear it on the tape, but I can."

Gary stopped reading for a moment. "Some feelings are personal," he said to Moody. "Christ, the guy wants to x-ray me publicly. Shit."

Moody said, "I think he's just trying to find out the facts."

"Dammit," said Gilmore, "Larry's probably trying to bring me a bit of anger here, so I might answer a little more spontaneously."

He went on with the interview, he read the rest of the questions, but nothing further developed. Gilmore did not get excited again.

Barry felt as if he had thrown his best punch and the man had taken it. Maybe the mother was not the sore spot. He gave up hope of a breakthrough. The *Playboy* interview would have to be constructed out of materials at hand plus whatever more came in on the Moody-Stanger local.

3

After the interview, Sam Smith had a conversation with the lawyers about a last-minute appeal. The Warden was worried that if Gary changed his mind at the very end, there would be no mechanism to stop the execution. Smith thought the lawyers ought to inform Gilmore of that.

Gary did not even care to discuss it. "There are no precautions to take," he told Moody and Stanger. Wouldn't even authorize them to have another conversation about it. The lawyers decided it was highly unlikely Gary was going to change his mind and, if he did, they still didn't see how the Warden could avoid contacting the Governor, no matter what he said now.

Sam Smith also consulted Earl Dorius. Should Gilmore be hooded? The man wanted, he said, to be able to stand up and face his executioners. However, Smith remarked, he had to think of what was best for the firing squad. The hood was for their benefit just as much. Who wanted to stare down his sights at a man staring back? Besides, Smith said, What if the fellow lost his nerve at the last minute and started dodging bullets?

By his reading of the statute, Dorius said, the details of execution were up to the discretion of the Warden. If Sam wished, Gilmore could be strapped in a chair with a hood over his head.

GILMORE   Warden didn't come right out and say it, but I believe he is concerned that my standing and looking at the firing squad will unnerve them. I asked him for a good reason why I had to wear the hood, and he couldn't give me one, but he seemed to be thinking about something. Listen, he did say right in front of Fagan, he said, usually they come to your cell, put the hood on you there, and you wear the hood from the time you leave your cell till you're dead. He said he would not do that to me, he said he wouldn't put the hood on me until after I'm in the chair. Now I want the son of a bitch to keep his word on *that* at least.

Gilmore was certainly showing them how cool he could be. The only newspaper story that irritated him lately was the one that described him as nervous. If Gary was anything, he was not that. Moody would query him all the time. "Aren't you scared?" he would ask. "No," Gilmore would say. Never once did he admit fear. Never once was there anything to suggest he wanted to change his mind. His lack of wavering became unbelievable to Moody. Gilmore seemed to be backing his intentions with every cell in his body. Not only was his emotional strength increasing, but his physical. "How do you feel?" Bob Moody would ask. "Did you sleep?" "I slept good last night." "How's exercise?" "I'm building myself."

To demonstrate, Gilmore would do a headstand on top of a stool. His muscle tone was certainly excellent. These convicts in Maximum seemed to live for nothing but their muscle tone, yet Gary still looked good compared to the super muscle tone of prisoners around him. Moody never thought of himself as being easy to shake, but Gilmore was beginning to impress him.

4

When Gibbs handed over Gilmore's letters, the *New York Post* gave him $5,000, holding up the last $2,500. The next thing Gibbs heard from the *Post* was that they'd checked the list of people invited to the execution and his name was not on it. Still, after checking out his credentials from Treasury and the FBI, the *Post* people did an interview in a bar, and took about thirty pictures of him.

Once the reporter and photographer left, Gibbs just kept drinking. But it didn't mix with the Oral Varidase, and he got sick to his stomach. The bartender had to help him to the rest room. Gibbs had sent off a thousand of the five thousand right away to his mother, but had been flashing money like a fiend. In the restroom, first thing he knew, a broad was standing there with her dude right behind her. She lunged at Gibbs, figuring that with his bad leg she could push him down easy but he dropped her with a fist, then nailed her boy friend. This was how he told the story later. When he went back to the bar, two cops happened to be in the restaurant and arrested Gibbs. The Lance LeBaron didn't seem to work — and he was in the slammer with $100,000 bail.

5

With the execution scheduled for Monday, Schiller had begun to feel the final pressure by Thursday. Rupert Murdoch started calling from New York to offer sums for an exclusive on the execution. All Schiller had to do was walk out to the press after the firing squad did their job, make a short public statement, then go into a room with one of Murdoch's reporters. Schiller realized he couldn't just say no, or Murdoch might try to get into the execution chamber some other way, bribe a guard, whatever. Rupert Murdoch hadn't bought control of the *New York Post* and the *Village Voice* and made a fortune in Australian newspapers for nothing. So, Schiller planned to string Murdoch along. For that matter, he was keeping *Time* and *Newsweek* and a couple of others on the string.

Then an Englishman called Schiller. "We want you to walk the Last Mile." Larry replied, "I am not Edward G. Robinson." "You mean to say," said this British journalist, "that somebody's not going to walk the Last Mile with your man?"

"I'm not walking any Last Mile," Schiller screamed. "I don't even know if I want the fucking guy to be executed."

Then, an interview was brought in by Moody that covered Gary's feelings about the hood. It could be fleshed out to 1,500 words for the newspapers, yet not give away the vitals of the story. Schiller decided to release it to a few chosen reporters. That would be Breslin, Dave Johnston, and Tamera Smith.

Barry and he almost came to fists. "Don't you fucking tell me how to run this," he said to Farrell, "I'm really using my head."

These last couple of days, the world press had been coming in, by God, flocking over Salt Lake as if it were the scene of a heavyweight championship. Now, he didn't have to worry about twenty local reporters who hated his guts. He had three hundred guys to deal with and each wanted a lock of Gary's hair or a fingernail cutting. Plus, the execution itself. He had better get ready for that.

Schiller called Gus Sorensen and brought Barry Farrell down on himself again. Schiller said, "I have to deliver a message to the Warden. I want to make sure Sam Smith realizes I ain't going to screw him if I get invited to the execution. The Warden is the only one who can stop me, okay? The law says he can't, but he can. So I got to deliver a message that if I'm invited, I'll conduct myself his way."

Gus Sorensen came over Thursday afternoon, and Larry gave the interview. It was designed to show that he saw his responsibilities and would abide by the rules of the prison.

6

Stephanie's team only made three or four sales in Europe. While Stephanie had enjoyed being in Paris at the Georges Cinq, she hated being a businesswoman. A couple of the foreign magazines agreed to buy, then backed out. In France, where Schiller had been counting on a big sale, some local murder took headlines away from Gilmore. So after Larry paid off the cost of the trip, which for the three women came to ten grand, he had netted no more than another ten. No bonanza. To make it worse, Stephie had decided to stop in New York. She would most definitely not come out to Utah. The whole thing, Gilmore, the press, the execution, was repulsive to her.

It was near midnight, while Larry was digesting Stephie's news, that Moyers phoned to say he was going to get in to see Gilmore. Wanted Schiller to know that. "No," said Schiller, "no way."

"Well, Larry," said Moyers, "Gilmore's willing to see me."

"That's a lie, Bill. I would have heard."

But would he? Moyers wasn't the type to call, unless he was pretty sure. Schiller was trying to figure out how the man could get in. It had to be through Mikal. So now he asked, "Have you seen Gary's brother?"

"Yeah," said Moyers, "he's in my room. He's been in my room for days."

There went the ball game. Schiller felt wiped out. God knows what kind of good, incredibly valuable information Moyers had been pumping out of Mikal. Lost was an organic form of communication.

After he hung up, he knew pure ego jealousy. They wouldn't let him in to see Gilmore. He had tried every goddamned trick and still had no more relationship with the guy than a fucking tape recorder. He called Bob Moody and said, "Bill Moyers claims he's getting in. Get to Gary and tell him how it will blow everything we've built up here and worked hard for."

Larry called Moyers back, and started calmly. But when they got to the place where Moyers still said he would see Gary Gilmore on his own, Schiller blew. "Bill," he said, "you're double-crossing me. I've been helping you on the assumption you're playing ball with me, and you're trying to get in through Mikal. That's not the guy I had dinner with." Schiller was putting all his strength into the mouthpiece of the phone. "I wouldn't use a brother to get in," he said to Moyers. "The guy has come here to save his brother's life. He has to make that decision, and you're befriending him just to see Gary Gilmore." Right over the phone, Moyers came roaring back. "You have no idea," said he, "what I'm going through. I've been trying to encourage Mikal to think the thing out. I've sat with him. He was in my room all last night, for God's sakes," said Moyers. "Don't tell me I've been using somebody," and Schiller thought he sounded ready to cry. So, Schiller took the phone, which had a long cord, and walked with it into the bathroom in order that the two secretaries couldn't hear. To Moyers, he said, "I don't want the fucking guy to die." Moyers said, "I don't want him to die either." It came over them that everybody was walking around with death in his belly. At a given moment a man they knew was going to be killed. On signal, everybody was going to leap across an abyss.

After he hung up, Schiller went to his bedroom and began to study the view from the window. It was snowing. Suddenly Schiller hated snow. He couldn't have said why. Felt like a blanket was slowing his efforts. It seemed dreamlike and this situation was crazy enough that he didn't want to be in a dream.

Now, somewhere around midnight, a big call came in from Murdoch. He was ready to make his top offer. One hundred and twenty-five thousand dollars. But for the execution. A firsthand exclusive account from Lawrence Schiller.

Years ago, Larry had gotten $25,000 for a single photograph of Marilyn Monroe nude. Now he was being offered a hundred and twenty-five grand to describe the shooting of a man. It would be pure gravy. He wouldn't have to give up the book, or the *Playboy* interviews, not the movie, nothing. Murdoch wouldn't even know if he got the whole execution or not. Schiller could save the best parts for himself. Give Murdoch one-half: he would probably be just as happy. The publisher was interested in the exclusive — in raising circulation. He could never even print the whole thing. It really was tempting. It really was.

Schiller walked to the window again. The snow was coming down hard by now and he was tired. His hand ached from squeezing the phone. He started crying. He could not explain what it was about, or why he was crying, but it went through him uncontrollably.

He said to himself, "I don't know any longer whether what I'm doing is morally right," and that made him cry even more. He had been saying to himself for weeks that he was not part of the circus, that he had instincts which raised him above, a desire to record history, true history, not journalistic crap, but now he felt as if he was finally part of the circus and might even be the biggest part of it, and in the middle of crying, he went into the bathroom and took the longest fucking shit of his life. It was all diarrhea. His system, after days of running nonstop and nights with crummy sleep, was by now totally screwed up. The horrors were loose. The diarrhea went through him as if to squeeze every last rotten thing out, and still it came. When he thought he might be done, he looked out the window at the snow and made the decision that in no way was he ever going to sell Gary Gilmore's execution. No. No way could anybody convince him. He would not make that fucking mistake for greed or security. No. He didn't care if he never saw a penny at the end. He had to stay by what his gut told him. He started crying again and said to himself, "I can't even spell decently. I can't write the way I feel and want to express myself." It got real heavy and he heard again the disgust in Stephanie's voice over the phone when she refused to come from New York, and thought of what was going to happen when he told Murdoch and *Time* and *Newsweek* and the *Enquirer* and all the others he had kept on the string that he wasn't going to give them any big private story on the last minute in the life of Gary Gilmore. They would really be after him then. He understood some of the fear at the center of his diarrhea. He was not only turning down the easiest money he had ever been offered, but was going to take a beating, and he thought back to the time when he was a kid in San Diego, and Chicanos would waste his brother and him coming home from school, do it every day, and knew something of the same child's fear now, and found himself crying once more, all alone in his bedroom, all alone and the night turning into a lighter blue, and the dawn coming up, exhausted beyond belief, fucking wondering why he was there and trying to decide that he had a responsibility above all business shenanigans and everything else to report as best he could. "I owe that to whatever I am," he said, "whether a journalist or an entrepreneur, whatever I am. I may never wind up being anything, but I owe it to myself to build my integrity," and he had an inspiration then that all the people who were respected in all the worlds he had gone through, respected for their integrity, had maybe not all been born with it, not every last one, but built it, job by job and night by separate night, until he got up, at last, and dressed and went out to the corner of University and Center Street in Orem and stood there with a pad and a pencil in his hand, looking at the heavy early traffic going by at the biggest intersection in town in the early morning, all the factory workers' cars going to Geneva Steel, out there slipping and sliding on the snow-slick, wide, wide streets and he would look down to his notebook and check whether the writing had been legible. He realized that if he was going to take accurate notes at the execution, he might not have a second to remove his glance from the scene, and so he had to learn to separate his hand from his eye, and do it without ever referring to the pad, and to himself he said, "For the first time, Schiller, you can't fictionalize, you can't make it up, you can't *embroider*."

Then he went back to the motel and spent the first part of the morning calling up Murdoch and the *Enquirer* and NBC and told everybody the word was no. He would not deal, he would not sell. Instead, he would give it away. After the execution, he would release his private eyewitness account to all the media at once. Nobody in the bidding liked it. The *Enquirer* griped and groaned, and NBC made it clear what they would do. He could hear the sound of the hunting horn. Only Murdoch was a gentleman. "Appreciate your calling," he said.

CHAPTER 28

T. G. I. F.

1

As Mikal came into the visiting room on Friday morning, Gary said, "Schiller doesn't want me to see your friend. It jeopardizes his exclusivity. I ought to fire him, and I would, but it's too late to find somebody else." When Mikal did not reply, Gary said, "What I could do is revoke his invitation to the execution."

Mikal was planning to leave Salt Lake that evening to spend Saturday and Sunday with Bessie. Gary, however, asked him to stay another day. "I haven't told this to anybody," he now told Mikal, "but I'm not so sure how Monday morning is going to be." He looked through the glass at Mikal. "Maybe that's why I need Schiller. He'll be there recording it for history, so I'll keep cool." He shook his head. "I didn't mean for it to become such a big thing. I thought maybe there would be a few articles." Put his hand up, and Mikal pressed his on the other side, and they touched but for the quarter inch of glass between.

Back in Salt Lake, Mikal met with Richard Giauque for the last time and told him he had decided not to intervene. After he said good-bye, Giauque made a phone call to Amsterdam who said he was aware of what it must have cost Mikal to come to that point, and hung up. There was not much doubt in Amsterdam's mind that the decision was final. Giauque had astute judgment. He would not have passed on such a message if there had been any chance of Mikal's changing his mind.

2

By Friday morning, with the execution not seventy-two hours away, Earl Dorius knew a number of legal actions were going to be filed. Law was always, to some degree, a game, and that was one good reason, Earl had long ago decided, to keep its processes slow and orderly. It helped to tone down the sporting and competitive aspects. Now, however, they had all gotten to the point where they were calculating the hours needed to file each action and counteraction. The side of law that was closest to a game had become predominant.

Earl telephoned the Tenth Circuit Court of Appeals in Denver — Utah being one of the six states in the Tenth Circuit — to speak to the Clerk, Howard Phillips, and tell him the Utah Attorney General's office was fearful some last-minute and, legally speaking, curious efforts might be made to prevent the execution. He wanted, therefore, to be able to contact the Court over the weekend, particularly on Sunday, in case the A.G. needed to make a countermove at the eleventh hour.

Dorius had his secretary check airline schedules, and learned that the last flight from Salt Lake to Denver was at 9:20 on Saturday and Sunday nights which information he passed on to Mike Deamer, Hansen's Deputy Attorney General. It meant that if they had to get to the Tenth Circuit Sunday night after 9:20, special transportation would be necessary.

Earl's next call was to Michael Rodak, the Clerk of the United States Supreme Court. Rodak and he discussed the mechanics of last-minute appeals to Washington, D.C. They also agreed on a special code Rodak could use if the Supreme Court had to reach Dorius. That was very important. They did not want some crank or overmotivated party to be able to call Utah State Prison at the last moment and claim they were the Supreme Court and announce a Stay of Execution. The prison had to know it was the Clerk, and only the Clerk, of the U.S. Supreme Court speaking. So Michael Rodak now told Dorius that his nickname was Mickey, and he had been raised in Wheeling, West Virginia. The code would be "Mickey from Wheeling, West Virginia, is calling."

Friday afternoon, two cases landed on Earl. The first was from Gil Athay representing his Death Row client, Dale Pierre, one of the hi-fi killers convicted for pouring Drano down customers' throats in a stereo and hi-fi store. Athay was arguing the execution of Gary Gilmore would create a public atmosphere that would injure his client's chances for appeal.

Just as Dorius was walking over to Hansen's office to discuss this development, another call came. The ACLU was bringing a tax-payers' suit before Judge Conder in State District Court. Two cases and one afternoon to do them in.

It was decided Bill Evans and Earl Dorius would oppose Gil Athay, and Bill Barrett and Michael Deamer would argue the other.

A couple of hours later they came back with victories in both cases. It was mainly, Earl thought, because the plaintiffs couldn't show any rights denied by the execution. Gilmore's immediate family might be able to claim standing, but there it ended. You simply couldn't have everybody going to Court. Thank God for *standing,* thought Earl. That afternoon, he had argued the public would be harmed by any further delay of execution, and he meant it. The nightmare of public circuses was that the longer they went on, the more they could make everything worthwhile look ridiculous.

3

Friday afternoon after Court, Phil Hansen found himself thinking again about Nicole and Gary Gilmore. After a couple of meetings with Nicole had failed to come off, he had kept thinking about Gilmore and assumed his girl friend would get in touch with him for the appeal. Hansen was so busy with his own practice that it was hard to sit down on any given day and take positive steps about some-thing not even in his office. Before he knew it, therefore, Gilmore was refusing to appeal. At that point, Phil began to wonder how he could possibly step in. Could you save a man who didn't want it? Still, the idea of Gilmore being executed was personally offen-sive. Phil hadn't spent his years saving a few lives nobody else could — it was in fact the pride of his career — without deciding

that the death sentence was an obscenity. If you were a devout
Catholic, and a great football coach, it would be obscene if you were
coaching Notre Dame and they lost 79–0. This particular week,
the execution had been hanging over every puff of cigar smoke in the
corridors of every Court in Salt Lake. Hansen came to the end of
Friday afternoon with the realization he had had three cases back to
back before Judge Ritter, and, in fact, two of the Juries had even been
out while the third case was being tried. So, by Friday afternoon,
Hansen said to Ritter at the bench, "You worked my ass off all week
long. You owe me a drink." Ritter laughed and invited him back to
his chambers where he poured quite a few for Phil — Ritter not
drinking much anymore — and they talked about Gilmore and waited
for a call from Dick Giauque, and tried to find Giauque's partner,
Daniel Berman, who was doing legal work for Judge Ritter, and then
tried to call Matheson, the new Governor, and all the while, such
calls failing to reach anybody, Hansen was brooding over the idiocy of
the oncoming execution. "Yes," he said, "Sam Smith will never die of
a brain tumor." And chuckled through his cigar smoke, and said, "If
all else fails, I'm going to bring a suit that I believe is a novelty."
When he used to be Attorney General — one of the small irritations
of Phil Hansen's life these days is that people still kept mixing him
up with Bob Hansen — he used to bring in suits as the Attorney General, even called it an Attorney General's suit, on matters affecting
the public good. Thinking on it now, his impression was that it might
be feasible to start a suit as a citizen of the United States who happened to live in the State of Utah. "Why," he said to Ritter, "do I have
to have a title to bring it in? Why can't a citizen just stop the execution?" They talked about it awhile, and Hansen finally decided that
what with the ACLU sending in a new plea tomorrow after losing
this afternoon, he would save his bid for a last resort.

4

LOS ANGELES TIMES

Crochety or Creative?
Utah Judge Is a Caution

Salt Lake City — Somewhere between the charge
by his enemies that he is a mean-tempered old man

and the claim by his friends that he is a creative legal scholar, probably lies the truth about U.S. District Judge Willis W. Ritter.

For 28 years the controversial Ritter has been a dominant force in Utah legal affairs, despite the fact he is a liberal, anti-Mormon Democrat in a state ruled principally by conservatives and strongly influenced by the Church of Jesus Christ of Latter-day Saints.

"He has been lord of the manor and Utah has been his fiefdom," former U.S. Atty. Ramon Child said.

Now, however, the judge, 78, is facing an unprecedented challenge to his authority by federal and state officials.

State Atty. Gen. Robert B. Hansen has filed petitions with the 10th Circuit Court of Appeals in Denver asking that Ritter be disqualified from hearing any cases to which the United States or the state of Utah is a party.

The petitions accuse Ritter of repeated misconduct on the bench, a strong prejudice against the state and federal governments, and, generally, behaving erratically.

Utah Sen. Jake Garn, a Republican who has called Ritter a "disgrace to the federal judiciary," is leading efforts in Congress to dilute the judge's authority.

But in a letter last October to Rep. Peter W. Rodino Jr. (D.N.J.), chairman of the House Judiciary Committee, Ritter outlined how he sees his problems.

"Malice, Mormonism, McCarthy-Nixon dirty tricks are written all over it by extreme rightist elements in the Republican Party," Ritter wrote.

"The Mormon church has taken over practically every other public office in the State of Utah. They have been trying for a long time to take over the federal court for the district of Utah."

Ritter was a law professor at the University of Utah when he was appointed a federal judge in 1949 by President Harry S. Truman, but the appointment was hotly contested by Morman forces. Ritter was accused of personal immorality and public corruption.

When Congress mandated age 70 as the retirement age for federal judges in 1958, it exempted 32 sitting chief judges. Ritter is now the lone survivor of that action.

Bob Hansen was just as annoyed when people mistook him for Phil Hansen. There was no doubt what he thought about Ritter. The Judge, he would say, had real malice of the heart. Of course, Hansen would not argue that Ritter was not brilliant. Maybe he was even a genius. It was possible that if you took guys with brains, Ritter was in the upper one-tenth of one percent among them, but he was also a perpetual fury machine. In fact, Ritter was so violently anti-Mormon that the Church had become, in Hansen's opinion, oversensitive to the idea that when it came to Ritter, they had to lean over backward. Hansen considered that a policy of appeasement. He wasn't about to let Ritter take over the Gilmore business if he could find a way to outmaneuver him.

CHAPTER 29

Saturday

1

On their last visit, Gary gave Mikal a drawing of an old prison shoe. "My self portrait," he said. They were still on the phone when Warden Smith came into Gary's booth and began to discuss the exact moment when the hood would have to be put on Gary's head. After Mikal could listen to that no longer, he rapped on the glass and said he would have to leave soon. He had to catch his plane. Would the Warden allow a final handshake?

At first, Smith refused. Then he said yes, but on condition Mikal agree to a skin search.

When that was over, two guards brought Gary in. They told Mikal to roll up his sleeve before they shook hands. It could not be, the guards warned, anything more than a handshake. So soon as Gary grasped his palm, however, he squeezed it close to crushing, and a light came into his eyes, and he said, "I guess this is it." He leaned over and kissed Mikal on the mouth. "See you in the darkness," he said.

Mikal knew he couldn't stop crying and turned away. He didn't want Gary to see it. The guard handed over *The Man in Black,* a book by Johnny Cash, that Gary wished to give to Bessie, and then a drawing of Nicole. Mikal could feel Gary's eyes following him toward the double gate. "Give my love to Mom," Gary called, "and put on some weight. You're still too skinny."

This same Saturday morning Schiller had been listening to the tape of the lawyers talking to Gary on Friday afternoon. There had been quite a bit about Melvin Belli's rhinestone cowboy boots.

"He buys his clothes," Gary said, "at Nudi's in Hollywood."

"What is," asked Stanger, "the biggest item you ever smuggled into a cell?"

"A 340-pound Norwegian woman wrestler."

They all laughed.

Schiller listened to talk about good guards and bad guards and what made the Warden tick. Schiller heard conversation about legal moves, and personally inscribed Bibles that came to Gary in the mail.

Then Stanger dropped by the TraveLodge and asked what Larry thought of the interview.

"Stanger," Schiller shouted, "why don't you get off your ass?"

"You, Schiller," Stanger replied, "can stick it up *your* ass." He stormed out.

"I'm never going to speak to Schiller again," said Stanger on the drive out to the prison. He was seething. Stanger considered himself a darn good cross-examiner. So was Bob Moody. Either one of them could rip through Gilmore, cut him left and right, exactly how Larry wanted. But there were a couple of things in the way. One was the questions Schiller and Farrell were so proud of. They seemed stupid to Stanger. Bore very little relation, from his point of view, to what Gilmore was all about.

Schiller had this huge operation going, and might end up with too little, and Ron could see the point of Schiller's worries, but his job was to build up, not break down Gilmore's confidence. Gilmore was his client, and he was there to fill his wants. Larry looked for questions that would make Gilmore react. Stanger didn't feel like going out to prison to get the guy angry. It was okay to seek information, but not all right to probe Gary like a lab rat and keep poking wires into him. Gary was already caged up all day long.

"I'm not going to interview him today," said Stanger to Moody.

"Goddammit," said Moody, "if we're going to do a job, we're going to do it."

That was probably as large a difference between them as they ever shared on any trip to Maximum.

2

Moody also thought they were doing a hell of a job, under the circumstances, even if Schiller and Farrell didn't agree. All the same, Schiller was right. There were only two days left and all kinds of valuable material to get. Moody sighed.

GILMORE Look . . . is this on the recorder?

MOODY Yes, uh huh.

GILMORE The Warden told me I could invite five people. I named 'em and he said, "Don't you want any clergymen there?"

MOODY The statute's very clear that you're entitled to two clergymen and in addition, five people.

GILMORE I don't want the clergymen to get barred. They've been looking forward to this all along.

MOODY Come on, as if anybody looks forward to it. I think ah . . . it would make them feel they were fulfilling their duties.

GILMORE I don't care what their motives are. They both want to come.

MOODY It's just gonna be a damn painful forty-eight hours for everybody.

GILMORE Man, I'm not in pain.

MOODY I know you're not, but others are. Your Uncle Vern, your Aunt Ida are going through hell. (pause) Others are physically ill.

GILMORE Who?

MOODY Well, I am, Ron Stanger is, Father Meersman.

GILMORE It's no big deal.

MOODY We know it's no big deal, but it's empathy for you.

GILMORE I'd like to see Nicole. The sucker won't give me an answer.

MOODY I think that's your answer, you're just not going to face reality.

GILMORE   I didn't hear.

MOODY   I think that's the Warden's answer. He's not going to answer you. Period. That's no reason to shut out everything else. You still have forty-eight hours to live. Well, live it.

GILMORE   Shit. Up until the last hours I only had one guard, and if I didn't talk to him, he didn't have nobody to talk to. So it was quiet.

MOODY   Yeah . . .

GILMORE   Now they've put two of them fools out there. All they do is talk to each other and play cards.

MOODY   Well, they tell us that's part of an execution.

GILMORE   Man, ah . . .

MOODY   When you get an execution, you get a deathwatch. That's what you're undergoing right now.

GILMORE   Well, I don't like to listen to the cocksuckers right in front of me.

MOODY   You may not, but it's part of your sentence.

GILMORE   Well, okay then.

MOODY   If you're gonna get shot, you're gonna have a deathwatch too. That's part of it.

GILMORE   Yeah. . . . (pause) Okay, man.

MOODY   Do you want me to send these questions in?

GILMORE   I'm not really all that choked up about answering any more.

MOODY   Okay.

GILMORE   It, man, is so noisy. If I could have some quiet during these last fucking hours.

MOODY   You doing your exercises or anything like that to pass the time?

GILMORE   Yeah . . . I do all that.

MOODY   You reading any?

GILMORE   No, ah . . . I don't read anymore. . . . I've real all I'm gonna read.

MOODY   Draw anymore?

GILMORE   No.

MOODY   You going to draw that self-portrait?

GILMORE Don't have a mirror.

MOODY Well, I guess you don't have much of anything, do you?

GILMORE I've got myself. (long pause) I don't want to ah, fuck around with writing the answers to these questions. I guess he deserves answers, but *God damn it* I don't like the way Schiller does some things.

MOODY Well, there are lots of times we don't like the way he does things, but his is a style, and he's in a tough racket and you develop a style like his.

GILMORE Is everybody just supposed to accept that?

MOODY No, I don't think so. But he's got a damn difficult job. He's trying to do it. That's all. He's working his ass off.

GILMORE I asked him not to read those letters and he did.

MOODY Okay. (long pause) Don't you feel that you owe Larry something?

GILMORE Go ahead and read the questions. I'll answer 'em. I want Larry to understand that he don't have the right to say who the fuck I can or can't speak to. My brother asked me to talk to a friend of his, and I told him yeah. I know who Moyers is. I wouldn't have answered anything that you wouldn't have wanted me to say.

MOODY You're really splitting hairs over nothing. 'Cause there's no way in hell Moyers is going to get in to talk.

GILMORE I know that. I was pissed off because Mike was unhappy.

MOODY Okay.

GILMORE All right.

MOODY The next question has been asked a number of times. Have you ever killed anyone before Bushnell and Jensen? . . . How about this guy that you beat with the pipe?

GILMORE He lived. (sigh) Kind of altered his life, though.

MOODY Don't you find shooting pretty damn grotesque?

GILMORE What's grotesque is the fact that you have to be strapped in the chair with the hood, and all that horseshit.

MOODY Doesn't the blood and guts of a shooting appeal to you?

GILMORE (laughs) Fuck you, Larry . . . the blood and guts. . . . Yeah, man, that really appeals to me. I'm gonna take a spoon.

The questions went on. No breakthrough.

From the two executions Father Meersman had previously attended, he had learned things could go badly wrong. The person to be executed might become so upset he would lose his own particular kind of calmness. Father Meersman always tried to keep a man in such a state ahead of the execution, tried to let him know what was going to be done. He figured if the man more or less knew you went to this place, point A, and from point A you were moved to point B, and then, at a certain time, you would go to point C, and so forth, he wouldn't have to say, "Where are we going now?" and maybe get upset over it. Some little thing like that could bother a man much too much.

Whereas, if they knew ahead, so they could go through it sort of smoothly, and if everybody leading them was calm, then that could prove a contributing factor to their own calmness, just knowing more or less how the mechanics were going to be. You didn't want anything of a surprise to happen. Everybody was very tense when an execution was taking place, and you didn't want anything to get out of step or make the man balk.

Meersman always felt he was the one who succeeded in explaining to Gary why they put the hood on. It wasn't personal, he told him, just that you wanted to be very still, so the target didn't move the slightest bit. Any slight movement could throw the bullets off. If Gary wanted to die with dignity, then he had to respect that very, very simple thing about the hood. It was there for practicality to allow the thing to run very dignified, and no movement. Gary listened in silence.

3

On Saturday afternoon, Gil Athay came out of Judge Lewis's chambers in the Federal Building and faced the press in the corridor. The reporters were frantic. Judge Lewis's regular courtroom was in the Tenth Circuit Court, Denver, and his chambers here, while commodious, had simply not been large enough. Many had not been able to jam in for the proceedings.

So now there was chaos, and cameras flashing, and the call letters of microphones from foreign and domestic radio stations in his eyes. Athay felt as if he were marching into one of the rings of the circus.

If was hard not to resent such an atmosphere. For days he had been fighting his way down corridors made narrow by the bodies of reporters. It had gotten out of hand. He was a dapper man with eyeglasses and a brush mustache, and he was not tall enough to avoid getting swarmed over in crowds. So at this point he said, "I'll be happy to make a statement, but it has to be downstairs." There remained a complete pandemonium. In his ears, he could still hear Judge Lewis saying, "You make it very difficult for me, Mr. Athay, to place it all on my shoulders, you know. If you'd given us time, there could have been three Judges to hear this." But Athay by then had been sufficiently keyed up to answer, "Well, I think, Your Honor, that's true, but we have to make the decision, and can't hide behind the committee." Had he really said that? The case of Dale Pierre must have tightened his temper.

He had come to believe that his client, Dale Pierre on Death Row, was innocent. That was an extraordinary belief to most. The public was convinced Dale Pierre was one of the hi-fi killers who had poured Drano down people's throats and stuck ball-point pens in their ears. The wife of a prominent gynecologist had been killed in that record store, and her son's brain had been permanently damaged. Stove-in by the killers. A horror of a case, but Athay had come slowly to the conclusion that Dale Pierre was innocent and had been convicted by the Jury because he was black, a condition to avoid in the State of Utah. In Utah a black man couldn't become a priest in the Mormon Church.

So Athay had embarked on a crusade. In fact it had cost the full price of a crusade. When he ran for Attorney General in the last election, Bob Hansen, his opponent, had made Dale Pierre one of his most powerful talking points and won by a good margin. Would-you-want-this-man-who-defends-clients-who-stick-ball-point-pens-in-middle-aged-women's-ears-to-be-your-next-Attorney-General had been the whispered theme of the campaign. Nothing Athay could do. You couldn't tell every voter that he had been made Pierre's lawyer by Court appointment, nor that in the beginning, in fact, he had seen it as an unpleasant duty, and only later had become convinced of Pierre's innocence. You couldn't tell the voters that Dale Pierre was a complex man, a difficult man, but now, to Gil Athay, rather a beautiful black man, and besides, Athay had always hated capital punishment.

He was ready to argue there was no rational way you could justify the death penalty, except to admit it was absolute revenge. If that, he would say, was the foundation of the criminal justice system, then we had a pretty sick system.

So he had worked with the ACLU on this Gilmore business, and today had entered an appeal which had been audacious in the extreme. After standard opening remarks that the lack of mandatory appeal in the Utah statute was unconstitutional, Athay had introduced his legal novelty. Let one execution be carried out under a defective law, he argued, and it would be hard in the future to find a higher Court ready to declare that same statute unconstitutional. No Judge would want to say to a fellow Judge, "You know, you executed that man in error." Gary Gilmore's death threatened, therefore, the life of Dale Pierre. An interesting argument, but difficult. To get the Court's attention, you had to make your language virtually insulting.

In the meeting on January 10, the ACLU therefore put Athay's venture next to last on their list. But by Friday afternoon, with the sad word coming from Giauque that Mikal Gilmore was not signing any papers, Gil Athay went to Judge Anderson's Court. Anderson was a rigid Mormon, but he was also the only Judge available at that hour. While there was hardly any realistic hope, Athay got caught up, nonetheless, in his own reasoning, and came to feel he had a good shot. Judge Anderson had listened carefully. The basic problem, however, remained. Nobody wanted to face the sinister merits of the argument. Judge Anderson turned him down.

Having failed there, Athay had gone to Judge Lewis on Saturday afternoon, but by now, the legal weakness of his case was apparent. He had no statistics to offer. He couldn't show that 50 percent of the state population, say, had once thought Dale Pierre should be executed, but now because of the emotionalism of the Gilmore case, the figure had gone up to 90 percent. Nothing to muster but logic.

So Athay lost again in Judge Lewis's Court, and knew as he fought his way past the press in the corridor, that one way or another, he would try to get to the U.S. Supreme Court tomorrow.

4

The Utah Coalition Against the Death Penalty held its meeting in the State Office Building auditorium on Saturday afternoon and Julie Jacoby thought it was all rather decorous. The only outsider who got up to speak was Henry Schwarzschild, and he didn't go on for long. It was best if locals did the talking. Professor Wilford Smith, a bona fide Morman from BYU, was a true catch, and there was Frances Farley, who was not only a Utah State Senator but a woman, and Professor Jefferson Fordham from the University of Utah Law School, then James Doobye, President of the Salt Lake City chapter of the NAACP. Buttons were available at the door — WHY DO WE KILL PEOPLE WHO KILL PEOPLE TO SHOW THAT KILLING PEOPLE IS WRONG? — and the program said, "Your donations are greatly appreciated."

Hoyle counted the house at 175, a decent turnout. There were men and women present that Julie didn't know, plus all the ACLU folk she could recognize. It was what you could call the liberal community in Salt Lake.

Once again, the committed were preaching to the converted. In Julie's mind it was futile. Everyone knew the mouse was fighting the elephant.

Nonetheless, they wanted to do something. The idea, as Julie saw it, was not to let those unthinking bloodthirsties swallow the day without some resistance. The world was watching Utah, and so they wanted the world to know some people in Utah did not agree with the prevailing forces.

In fact, they got some publicity. The *Salt Lake Tribune* gave them the front page of the second section and ran a marvelous picture of Dean Andersen of St. Mark's Episcopal Cathedral in front of a beautiful banner a couple of students had made. It was navy blue with white letters and said, "No EXECUTION."

SALT LAKE TRIBUNE

"Official Blood Bath"
Protestors Say of Utah Death Penalty

Salt Lake, Jan. 16 — The execution of Gary Mark Gilmore has turned into a "super bowl of violence," an Episcopal priest charged Saturday.

"It is complete with a Barnum and Bailey circus atmosphere and movie rights, reserved seats, T-shirts and love letters. We could all laugh about it, but in two days a team of volunteers will kill Gary Mark Gilmore without appeal," the Very Rev. Robert Andersen said.

DESERET NEWS

Salt Lake, Jan 15 — About 15 or 20 bishops from the National Council of Churches are expected to arrive Sunday afternoon to participate in a Sunday-Monday vigil at Utah State Prison.

Henry Schwarzschild, coordinator of the National Coalition against the Death Penalty, called the execution "a brutalizing horror," a "dangerous precedent," and "judicial homicide."

5

That same afternoon, the Warden held a press conference and Tamera brought back a firsthand account of how they were going to move Gary from Maximum Security over to the cannery, where he would face the firing squad. Sam Smith had also given out regulations for the media. The outer gates to the prison were going to be closed to the press on Sunday night at 6 P.M. They would not open again till 6 A.M. of the 17th. That meant any of the press who wanted

to be on the grounds at any time during the hours preceding the execution would have to spend the night in the prison parking lot.

Schiller now had a problem. If he went in at six in the evening
he would not be able to receive any last-minute phone calls Gary
might be able to make to the motel. On the other hand, Gary was
going to be allowed to spend his last night with Moody, Stanger, and
members of his family. There was even a small chance the Warden
would let Larry join that group. In that event, it was better to be right
on the prison grounds. A dilemma.

While he was pondering this, Tamera said, "Larry, I'd like you to
come to BYU this afternoon and give a speech about Gary Gilmore to
the Social Sciences class." "Tamera," said Schiller, "what is this?"
"Look," she said, "my Bishop asked me."
Schiller thought, Maybe she hopes to improve her standing with
the Church. Probably thinks of herself as inactive, lately. So he said,
"All right, it's an excuse to get out of this madhouse."

He carted himself to the university on the afternoon of the 15th
and went into this hall at BYU with something like four hundred
fucking college students, all Mormons, and this teacher who was a
Bishop got up and blah blah blah. He introduced Tamera Smith, said
she was once a student here and now works for the *Deseret News,*
and Tammy got up and made a ten-minute speech, very pious, ideal
Mormon girl striving for her Recommend. Then the Bishop introduced Schiller who stood there and made his indictment-of-
journalism speech. Couldn't remember a word afterward, but it was a
standard thing he kept in the back of his mind. Any day he couldn't
talk for fifteen minutes would be a very bad day.

After a while, he asked for questions, and thirty hands flew up,
and he pointed to a student who said, "Mr. Schiller, can you please
tell me why you're wearing a Gary Gilmore belt?"

Larry looked down and, by God, he had a Gucci on. Interlocking
G's on the buckle. So, he explained the initials to those four hundred
Mormons, and then said to the fellow who asked the question, "You
are a journalist, because you have turned one thing into another, and
that is journalism." The rest of it was simple, very simple and very

placid. He wouldn't call the students bright or intelligent, so much as in their own world. They were hostile to Gilmore, of course, but hostility in a Mormon was so reserved, you didn't even see it. It just showed in the questions. "Why," they would ask, "don't you do the story about Ben Bushnell rather than Gary Gilmore?" and Schiller would answer that at this point in the realm of the United States, Gary Gilmore was making history. Fair or not, Benny Bushnell and his death never would. The kids didn't like it, but he was very straight on. Told them he was not there to please them, but to show the other side of the coin. "I'm not going to hide what I am," had been one of his first remarks. So it went. They asked. He answered. Two hours out of his life.

Back at the motel, Schiller had an interesting conversation with one of the police officers, Jerry Scott, that he had hired on Moody's recommendation. Scott was a great big fellow with dark hair, reassuring in appearance, and had taken a leave of absence from his cop job to work for Schiller. He obviously knew the name of the game. Since he could only protect one entrance of the motel building at a time, he generally parked his police car on the back side to scare off anybody coming from that direction. On the near side, there was Scott waiting.

This afternoon, right after BYU, Larry discovered Scott was the same policeman who had driven Gary Gilmore from Utah County Jail to Utah State Prison on the day his trial ended. What a bonus. It gave Schiller the idea that Jerry Scott was bringing good luck. Just as well. Scott was getting paid about five hundred bucks a week.

By Saturday evening, Schiller decided that he ought to have a 16mm movie camera in action. So he made arrangements with CBS for one of their crews and explained he would need long shots of the prison with snow on the ground, and all the atmosphere they could find. It would cost another three thousand bucks, but he had hopes. Later, when he saw the film, it was lousy. The crew didn't know how to shoot anything but newsreel footage. Blew all the opportunities for mood building.

He also made one last attempt to get Stephie to come in from New York. Again she refused. First, he asked her, then he begged.

She would not come. It was a long and heated argument, and he didn't often lose such discussions, but she was adamant. He was really mad.

"You're always criticizing me," he said.

"Don't you see," she cried out, "I criticize you because I love you, and I want to help you."

In certain ways, he felt as close to breaking up with her as he ever had. Yet he knew he wouldn't. That could be the reason in a funny way it was going to work. Maybe, he told himself, he had come to understand that Stephie did not see herself as a total go-down-the-road-with-him gambler — which is what he'd always demanded of his first wife. Rather, Stephie had a nervous system, and it was delicate, and she wished to protect it. She had been in a terrible car accident just a few years before and scarred by it. Her beauty was delicate, it was vulnerable beyond his understanding, and at that moment, maybe it was the weight of every emotion he had been carrying, but he felt a great tenderness toward her, even if she wouldn't join him.

6

Shirley Pedler had been called down to a studio by ABC News and ran smack into Dennis Boaz. "You're going to get what you want," she said to Dennis, "I hope you're happy." Boaz looked at her, and said, "Gee, Shirley, can't we be friends?" "I don't want," she told him, "to be your fucking friend." He stood there a little taken aback, and finally turned to the people with him. "Oh, she says she doesn't want to be my *fucking* friend," he said, and tried to laugh it off. Away he went, away she went, and she was furious. That was one man who had come in to gratify prestige needs. All he wanted, she thought, was to be involved in an event of national import.

Of the two girls in the office, Debbie was a former Playboy Bunny, a small good-looking redhead who gave you a lift with her personality and did her work well. The other, Lucinda Smith, was an absolute beauty, Barry decided, dark hair, fabulous eyes, the sweetest voice, one of those intimate, purring, matter-of-fact California voices. Barry liked having her there. She was emotional and cried easily, and there was so much to cry about in the last week that he thought she was indispensable to the office. A chorus, nay, a brook of clear feeling to bring a breath of tenderness to the plasticoid abyss of their motel. God, she wasn't that many years out of Corvallis run by the Religious of the Sacred Heart of Mary. Lucinda had been the only Presbyterian there. Her father, Barry learned, used to be head writer and director for Groucho Marx, and she had grown up in Studio City, just as secluded as you could get in the San Fernando Valley, had had an honest-to-God coming-out party, and gone to UCLA. Perfect Southern California pedigree. Now she was listening to Gary Gilmore say fuck, piss, shit.

She had gotten her job through an exclusive employment agency run by two girls. Lucinda had been an English major, and when Schiller called, the agent thought of her immediately, told her it would be an interesting experience. While Lucinda hadn't met Mr. Schiller before the job began, she did have a talk with his secretary in Los Angeles, and was told that if she didn't cut the mustard, she'd be sent home immediately. It gave her the feeling of a boss who laid down the law before they even met. That was stimulating. They would treat her on her merits, rather than her social standing.

Since the other girl had gone in a day ahead of her, she took the plane from Los Angeles by herself. When she got to the Orem Trave-Lodge, Mr. Schiller was very polite, and said, "Do you want to rest for a while?" She said, "No, I'll get started." Hardly put her bags down before she began to transcribe tapes, one after another. That tempo would increase. Lucinda started at twelve hours a day, and was close to working around the clock by the weekend. She didn't really want to sleep. There was kind of an eerie feeling over the whole thing. She felt better being with Larry and Barry and Debbie. Alone in her room, it would start to come over her what was going on.

On Saturday night, she did take a break and turned on the TV. There was "Saturday Night Live." They had a parody of Gary Gilmore. The cast was putting makeup on an actor playing the convict and the director kept saying, "A little more light over here, a little more eye shadow." They were getting him ready to be shot for the camera. Very sarcastic. Kept putting on the makeup. She never thought television would be this weird. She had always thought "existential" was an odd word, but it now was so bleak and cold outside, just a little bit of eternal snow on the ground, and she felt as if no one had ever gone out of this motel with these Xerox machines, and the typewriters.

7

Barry Farrell was studying Gary's old letters to Nicole. Reading one of them, he nearly groaned. It was too late in the day to question Gilmore about this, not too late, that is, to ask the question — God, they had asked him everything — but it was certainly too late to get an answer that would reveal anything. They should have prepared the ground over many weeks.

"*I was in the State Hospital in Oregon,*" Gary had written, "*trying to beat an armed-robbery beef and this 13-year-old boy came in 'cause he couldn't get along at home. He was really pretty, like a girl, but I never gave him much thought until it became apparent that he really liked me. I was 23 then. I'd be sitting down and he would come up and sit beside me and put his arm around me. It was just natural to him, a show of friendship. One time he came up in the locker room and asked if he could read this Playboy I had. I said sure, for a kiss. Man, he was dumbfounded! His eyes got big as silver dollars and his mouth dropped wide open. He said 'No!' and it was really pretty, and I fell in love on the spot. He thought it over then and decided he wanted to read that magazine pretty bad, 'cause he gave me, or rather let me take, a very tender little kiss on the lips. I used to watch him down at the swimming pool. He was one of the most beautiful people I've ever seen, and I don't think I've ever seen a prettier butt. Anyhow, I used to kiss him now and then, and we got to be pretty good friends. I was just struck by his youth, beauty, and naivete. Then one of us was sent elsewhere.*"

Barry valued it greatly, that kiss. Gilmore was confessing. It struck him as the most moral moment in the letters. Finally Gilmore was admitting to something that had been on his mind all along, something which had gone right through all his evasions with sex — all that transparent discomfort with sexual material. Yet here, in this little confession, it was lifted. He could say it. What a sweet kiss. A nice moment.

Farrell didn't think it was a matter of homosexuality as such. He took it for granted that Gilmore, like the majority of men, Farrell knew, who lived their lives in prison, had been one sort or another of situational homosexual. The choices, after all, were homosexuality, onanism, or abstinence. Farrell thought almost nobody chose abstinence, and those that did were probably none the better. It was just that Gilmore had a skewed and miserable relation to sex. Like many another prisoner, his natural sexual fantasies must have been burned out long ago by masturbation. No woman could do it as well as one could do it oneself. So his confession wasn't to homosexuality. It was Gilmore admitting to Nicole how difficult, and pretty, and far-off, and kooky, was sex for him.

Farrell decided to break his own rules and insert the letter as part of the bona fide interview. A cheat. So be it. As Schiller had said, "Get down in the gutter with us sinners."

Then he came across something else. From way back in December. It had been under his nose all the while:

GILMORE   All right. (pause) There's a book I would like, but I don't think you can get it in Provo. You might be able to get it in Salt Lake. It's called *Show Me*. A book of photographs of kids. You think you can get it? It's probably about a $15 book.

INTERVIEWER   Yeah, I think we can.

GILMORE   I tried to buy it in Provo. It was advertised years and years ago. It may be banned in places like Salt Lake.

INTERVIEWER   What is it about?

GILMORE   About the photographs of children.

INTERVIEWER   Why would it be banned?

GILMORE   Because it's a sexual book. I read about it off and on for years and I got real curious. They banned it in some parts of Canada and the United States. But they got it in Salt Lake. . . .

INTERVIEWER   This is an educational book?

GILMORE   Well, it's a high line, a real classic. It was made in Germany and all German children and they're really artistic, tasteful, tactful photographs. It's not a piece of smut, but I wanted to see it.

Farrell passed it by and then came back. That little elucidative light one depended upon was flickering again. Yes. Could it be said that Gilmore's love for Nicole oft depended on how childlike she could seem? That elf with knee-length socks, so conveniently shorn — by Gilmore — of her pubic locks. Those hints in the letters of hanky panky with Rosebeth, the rumble with Pete Galovan. Barry nodded. You could about say it added up. There was nobody in or out of prison whom hardcore convicts despised more than child molesters. The very bottom of the pecking order. What if Gilmore, so soon as he was deprived of Nicole, so soon as he had to live a week without her, began to feel impulses that were wholly unacceptable? What if his unendurable tension (of which he had given testimony to every psychiatrist who would listen) had had something to do with little urges? Nothing might have been more intolerable to Gilmore's idea of himself. Why, the man would have done anything, even murder, before he'd commit that other kind of transgression. God, it would even account for the awful air of warped nobility he seemed to extract from his homicides. Barry felt the woe of late discovery. He could not say a word about this now. It was too insubstantial. In fact, it was sheer speculation. If Gilmore was willing to execute himself for such a vice, assuming it was his vice — beware of understanding the man too quickly! — then let him at least die with the dignity of his choice. In fact, how much could a word like dignity conceal?

8

On Saturday evening, near midnight, Father Meersman set up the Maximum kitchen as a chapel and said a Mass for Gary, using one of the portable metal serving tables as an altar. In order to be able to see everything, Gary sat up on one of the fixed kitchen tables with his feet on the bench. A guard who had once been an altar boy served Mass.

Father Meersman laid out the portable altar stone, which in these circumstances, coming from his Mass kit, was a cloth, and then he laid on miniature altar linens, put out the corporal, the chalice, and the paten, the candles in their holders, set the crucifix, and gave a missalette to Gary so he could participate. Father Meersman wore a complete set of vestments, white alb, cincture, stole, maniple, and chasuble. Across from him, Gary was wearing a white shirt and pants.

Father Meersman recited the Confiteor, ". . . I have sinned through my own fault in my thoughts and in my words, in what I have done, and in what I have failed to do," and heard the echo of the old Confiteor. "Through my fault, through my fault, through my most grievous fault."

Then the priest read from Gary's favorite Psalm. From experience Meersman knew it was most familiar to him over the first few lines.

> Bless the Lord, O my soul: and let all that is within me bless His holy name.
> Bless the Lord, O my soul, and never forget all He hath done for thee.
> Who forgiveth all thy iniquities: who healeth all thy diseases.
> Who redeemeth thy life from destruction: who crowneth thee with mercy and compassion.
> Who satisfieth thy desire with good things: thy youth shall be renewed like the eagle's.

Father Meersman read next from the Gospel, Mark 2: 1–12, and again he gave only the first part. "Son, thy sins are forgiven thee." Strictly speaking, thought Meersman, he wasn't supposed to deviate from the Gospel of the Day, but in a case of this sort, he didn't think anybody would fault him for it.

"This is My Body . . . this is My Blood," said Father Meersman, consecrating the bread and wine, and held up the host and the chalice, and the guard who was serving as an altar boy rang the bell thrice — so would Father Meersman describe it — rang the bell thrice.

"Lord, I am not worthy that You should come under my roof. Speak only the word and my soul shall be healed."

Father Meersman took communion. After he had drunk the

wine, and the altar boy had gone to communion, and the other guards at the head table behind Gary, being Mormon, merely watched, Gary took the wafer on his tongue in the old style, mouth open, way back, in the way, observed Father Meersman, he had received as a child, and then he drank from the chalice. Father Meersman stood beside him while Gary consumed the bottom of the cup.

Father Meersman thought it was a beautiful night and very good. Gary had blessed himself at the beginning of the Mass, and then had listened in a subdued way. Now that it was all over, he kidded Father Meersman. "Padre," he said, "I don't think the wine was as strong as it could have been."

Sunday, 2:00 A.M.

Hi Elf

When you are released go to Vern's. I have given him a lot of things to give you.

They will be in a black duffel bag, taped shut —

There will be my photo album, some jewelry, a lot of books, Gary Gilmore T-shirts, a few letters, mostly from foreign countries.

A Sony radio.

I been tryin to get a sacred eye ring from the Aladdin House Jewelry Company in New York. If I can get it today, I'll put it in with the stuff.

Oh Baby Baby Baby I miss you!

I love you with all I am.

They play our song a lot. "Walking in the footsteps of your mind" I don't know if you get to listen to the radio. KSOP in Salt Lake really likes us. They play "Valley of Tears" for us.

In about 30 hrs. I will be dead.

Thats what they call it — death. Its just a release — a change of form.

I hope I've done it all right.

God Nicole. I feel such power in our love. I don't think we're s'posed to know right now what this is about. We're just supposed to do it right. It's inside of us; the knowledge. But we can't consciously know it till later.

Angel its a quarter to 3 in the mornin. I'm gonna get some shut-eye. Write you some more in a little . . .

9

The Mormon boy whom the Church sent to look after Bessie was a young married man named Doug Hiblar, and he felt he had come a little closer to Bessie in the last month. Sometimes, she still would not let him in, and he would just tell her through the door that he loved her, and leave, but there were days when she was receptive, and encouraged by that, he once made the mistake of telling her he understood how she felt. That was an error. Bessie said, "You *don't* know." He thought about it and recognized he didn't, and would never know, and did not use such words with her again. Perhaps it made a difference. She seemed to talk to him more after that.

Saturday night, he went to visit her, even as he had been visiting all week, and she seemed calm. It was as if she expected the Courts would postpone things. She had been talking the week before of going to Utah, but he got the idea Gary convinced her not to. Doug figured it would take from her son's strength if he saw her.

Bessie may have looked calm, but she couldn't sleep. All week she had been afraid of a night when she would go to bed and come awake with Gary dead. So, each night, she spent most of the hours sitting up. After Mikal's call came in each evening from Salt Lake, she might drowse, but then she would stir again, and there would be no more sleep. Just the long storm of insomnia to travel through. In her mind, like telegrams she could not bear to open, would appear the words, "How can I reach Gary? How can I tell him what it will do?" For she felt as if a sword would sever one half of herself from the other when the moment came.

She would think of Y Mountain in Provo and of the day she went back to Utah when her father was dying. Mikal was with her, and the boy had said, "Will you show me your mountain?" It was night and she answered, "I'll show you in the morning." The dawn, however, came in with fog, and Mikal remarked, "I don't see a mountain." He was eight years old.

"It's there," Bessie said. "The mountain is telling me that my dad is not going to live." Indeed he died, a few days later.

One of those nights in Provo, waiting for her father to pass away, there had been a rally for a football game, and BYU students went filing up the mountain with torches. Mikal said, "Mother, come out and look. You have never seen anything like this."

"Oh, Mikal, I have seen it before," she told him. "Remember, this is my mountain."

All her nieces and nephews looked at her as if to say, "Who do you think you are? You don't even live around here." She would smile at them. They did not understand. When people asked her, "Don't you get homesick to come back?" she would reply, "No, but I get homesick for my mountain. Because I own that." She knew they thought she was uppity.

On this recollection, she said good-bye to Saturday night and greeted the dawn.

CHAPTER 30

Sunday Morning,
Sunday Afternoon

1

It's 10 A.M. Sun Morn. I got up and showered and shaved — well first I did my exercise, 10 minutes running. These fucking guards think I'm nuts when I run up and down the tier. Almost all these guards are fat lazy fuckers.

Hey you're an elf, ain't ya?!

They asked me who I invite to watch me get shot. I said

Number One: *Nicole*

      Two: *Vern Damico*

    Three: *Ron Stanger, lawyer*

     Four: *Bob Moody, lawyer*

     Five: *Lawrence Schiller, big Wheeler dealer from Hollywood.*

I knew they wouldn't let you come, so I said to just reserve a place in your honor.

The New York Post said I was auctioning off seats —

Lot of people write a lot of shit in the paper.

Baby you said if I am shot . . . what will be in you?

I will.

I will come to and hold you my darling companion.

Do not doubt.

I'll show you.

Baby I've been avoiding something but I'll come to it right now.

If you choose to join me or if you choose to wait — it is your choice.

Whenever you come I will be there.

I swear on all that is holy.

I do not want anybody else to ever have you if you choose to wait.

You are mine.

My soul mate.

Indeed, my very soul.

Do not fear nothingness my Angel. You will never experience it.

Sunday morning, Lucinda was typing the transcript of yesterday's interview when all of a sudden, she couldn't help it and made a sound. Schiller turned around. She was crying her head off, right there on Sunday morning.

Vern was on the phone to Larry. Offers were coming in from wax museums to buy Gary's clothes. The sums were up to several thousand dollars. While there was no question of selling, it had now become a matter of safeguarding the last things Gary wore. Then they decided they had better protect his remains as well. While the prison would deliver Gary's body to the Salt Lake hospital where his eyes and organs would be removed, Schiller decided to post his own guard. He had truly lucked into Jerry Scott. Just the man to keep watch when they moved Gary from the hospital to the crematorium.

GILMORE   Fagan said, "There's still a chance you'll get your phone call from Nicole." I told him, "You foul, sleazy cocksucker, fuck you in the ass." He said, "Oh, ah ah ah ah." He says, "My hands are tied." I said, "Well, how does it feel to walk around with your hands tied? Have you ever thought about feeling like a man, you piece of shit?" I don't even know if I'll come in to the visiting room tonight. Fagan will say, "Well, we really treated him great on his last night. We gave him unlimited visits. We let him see his uncle and his lawyers." (laugh)

Moody began his last list of questions.

MOODY   If on your passage you meet a new soul coming to take your place, what advice would you have for him?

GILMORE   Nothing. I don't expect someone to take my place. Hi, I'm your replacement . . . where's the key to the locker . . . where do you keep the towels?

MOODY   I don't know, wouldn't you have something to tell him about the life that ah . . . awaits him?

GILMORE   Shit. . . . That's a serious question.

MOODY   I think he wants you to be very serious about it.

GILMORE   I've talked to people who know more than I do, and people who know less, and I listen, and I decided the only fucking thing I know about death, the only real feeling I have about it, it'll be familiar; I don't think it'll be a harsh, unkind thing. Things that're harsh and unkind, are here on earth, and they're temporary. They don't last. This all passes. That is my summation of my ideas, and I might be all wet.

MOODY   Do you know what Joe Hill's last message to the Wobblies was?

GILMORE   Joe?

MOODY   Joe Hill. He's a man who was killed in Utah a number of years ago.

GILMORE   His name was Joe Hillstrom. What did he tell the Wobblies?

MOODY   "Don't mourn, boys, organize."

GILMORE   Don't warn?

MOODY   "Don't mourn, boys, organize."

GILMORE   Well, I got something like that I kinda like: "Never fear, never breathe." That's a Muslim saying. I don't know where they got it, but you can apply it to anything, it makes pretty good sense. "Don't mourn, boys, organize."

MOODY   You know the old line in the war movies, "Any man who said he ain't scared is either a liar or a fool"?

GILMORE   What about it?

MOODY   Doesn't that apply at least a little to your situation?

GILMORE   I didn't say I wasn't scared, did I?

MOODY   No. But your message to the world has the connotation of don't fear.

GILMORE   Well, why fear? It's negative. You know you could damn near call it a sin if you let fear run your life.

MOODY   You're certainly determined to defeat fear.

GILMORE   I don't feel any fear right now. I don't think I will tomorrow morning. I haven't felt any yet.

MOODY   How are you able to overcome fear from coming into your soul?

GILMORE   I guess I'm lucky. It hasn't come in. You know a truly brave man is somebody who feels fear and goes out and does what he's supposed to do in spite of it. You couldn't really say I'm that fucking brave because I ain't fighting against fear and overcoming it. I don't know about tomorrow morning . . . I don't know if I'll feel any different tomorrow morning than I do right now, or than I felt on the first of November when I waived the fucking appeal.

MOODY   Well, you're remarkably composed.

GILMORE   Thank you, Bob.

MOODY   I don't know what to say, I just really . . .

GILMORE   Look, man, I'm being kind of rude. You guys are a little upset about all of this, aren't ya?

MOODY   It's hard, Gary. I'm physically ill.

At this point, Bob Moody began to cry. A little later, when he got control of himself, he and Gilmore and Stanger talked a bit more. Then, they said good-bye. They would return in the late afternoon to visit through the night. As they went out, Gilmore said, "Don't forget the vest." "The what?" asked Bob. "The bullet-proof vest," said Gilmore. "I'll wear it in myself," said Moody. "You guys take care," Gilmore said.

Sunday morning, Vern went to Maximum Security and talked to Gary on the telephone, looking through the glass. For once they spoke about his mother's sisters in Provo. Gary was curious why none of his aunts, except for Ida, had been to see him. "What do you think?" he asked directly.

"Oh, Gary," Vern said, "I'm sure they wanted to, but I can't answer for them." In Vern's head, he was still hearing one of Ida's sisters say, "I just can't make myself go up and talk to him."

Gary said, "Mom is too sick, or she would be here."

There was such a long, grim silence that Gary began to sing a Johnny Cash song. Rolled his eyes back and tried to let her out.

When Gary saw Vern laughing, he said, "Well, I satisfy myself." Vern roared. "I'll sing you a little ditty," he told him.

Gary groaned. "Not 'Old Shep.'" Vern was famous for singing

"Old Shep." Every year when the Archery Club had their dinner, Vern would sing it.

"Yes, 'Old Shep,' " said Vern.

> When I was a lad, and Old Shep was a pup,
> Over hills and meadows we'd roam.
> Just a boy and his dog, we were both full of fun
> And we grew up together that way.
>
> As the years went along, Old Shep, he grew old
> And his eyesight was fast growing dim
> Then one day the doctor looked up at me and said,
> "I can't do no more for him, Jim."
>
> With a hand that was trembling, I picked up my gun
> And aimed it at Shep's faithful head
> But I just couldn't do it, oh, I wanted to run,
> And wished they would shoot me instead.
>
> Now, Old Shep, he knew he would go,
> He looked and licked at my hand,
> He stared up at me, just as much as to say,
> "We're parting, but you'll understand."
>
> Now Old Shep, he has gone where the good doggies go,
> And no more with Old Shep will I roam,
> But if dogs have a heaven, there's one thing I know,
> Old Shep has a wonderful home.

"Yuck," said Gary.

"That's all for today," said Vern. "That's as good as you deserve."

2

The Legal Defense Fund of the NAACP made available a lawyer in Washington named John Shattuck. He was going to present a petition for Athay to the United States Supreme Court. After the loss, therefore, in Judge Lewis's Court on Saturday afternoon, Athay's office dictated a brief over the telephone. On Sunday it was hand-carried by Shattuck to the Supreme Court, and filed.

At 6:25 in the evening, D.C. time, which was 4:25 P.M. in Utah, a phone call came in to Athay from the Clerk of the Court, Michael Rodak. Justice White had endorsed the following quotation: *"The application for stay is denied. I am authorized to say that a majority of my colleagues concur in this action. Bryron R. White, Associate Justice."*

Since the decision was not unanimous, Shattuck tried to approach other Justices. If one could find the right man on the minority side, he might grant a Stay. That would give an opportunity to offer one's arguments.

Justice Blackmun responded. *"The application for stay having been presented to me, after its denial by Justice White, is denied. Harry A. Blackmun, Associate Justice, January 16, 1977."*

Justice Brennan had not been contacted. The advice came from Washington that if Athay were to call and express the urgency of the situation, it might have impact. Justice Brennan had shown inclinations favorable to cases like this. So Athay, provided with an unlisted phone number, phoned person-to-person, and a voice came on and said, "This is Justice Brennan speaking." Athay had no more than introduced himself and said, "I'm involved in the Gary Gilmore case," when "Oh, my," he heard on the other end, and a click. He placed the call again. He could swear the same voice came on to say, "I'm sorry, he's out of town." He felt aghast. He knew, yet how could he ever know for certain whether he'd reached Justice Brennan or not?

Athay had now exhausted everything he could do for Dale Pierre.

3

Waiting through Sunday morning and Sunday afternoon was murder. Schiller had a list of questions pinned to the wall next to the telephone. If Gilmore called again, and he wasn't there, Barry could take the call, or if Barry was also out, one of the girls would talk. The questions were ready. You didn't have to hem and haw, or conceal identities. Gary understood they were in a countdown.

All the same, Schiller was depressed. The high ambitions he had had for this interview were by now pretty thoroughly defeated. Mikal had left Utah, and with him had gone Schiller's best chance to get a few last-minute insights to Gary. He felt as if he had lost contact. Who could believe Gary would have gotten so angry about Moyers? When Mikal threatened to be a major obstacle to the execution, Gary must have set out to neutralize him. Became the big brother Mikal had never seen. The role had gotten too good. Gary was carrying on as if Schiller had really violated him. After all, belief in your own role was crucial to a hustle. But Schiller felt it was a steep price to pay.

Moody telephoned from the prison. "You're going to get a call from the Warden," he told Schiller. "You *are* going to see the execution." Though the news had been in the papers, Larry had not yet received official word. So he was worried. If Sam Smith refused him at the gate, there would have to be last-minute legal maneuvers. The statutes might be all on his side, but such a situation would still be horrendous with tension.

In five minutes, the phone rang again. Deputy Warden Hatch was saying, "Warden Smith has asked me to advise you to appear tomorrow morning at six A.M. at the prison gate with no cameras and no recording devices, if you wish to witness the execution of Gary Mark Gilmore." Schiller said, "Thank you. Will you please deliver this message to the Warden. The statement I made to Gus Sorensen is correct. I do not intend to violate any rules and regulations that he has set up. Please assure him that I will conduct myself in the manner in which he would want me to conduct myself."

In that last phone call with Moody, he had been told that Gary wanted liquor brought in, and they had discussed how to do it.

Schiller told Debbie to go to the pharmacy and buy a couple of curved bottles. "If the pharmacy doesn't have them for sale," he told her, "just buy cough syrup, and pour it out."

Debbie wanted to know why the bottles had to be curved. He had to explain they were like a hip flask, and made less of a bulge under your coat. Then he decided the amount would be insufficient, so he sent Tamera over to Western Airlines to purchase, if she could, some 1½-ounce bottles of the sort they served on airplanes. In Utah, however, Western wouldn't go near liquor on Sunday. He called the Hilton and found out they didn't sell or serve until late that day. Finally, he heard of one Salt Lake bar where individual-drink bottles were sold, so he had Tamera call the *Deseret News* to send somebody over. Schiller figured they'd call a high-level meeting about it.

Meanwhile, Tamera had come to feel sentimental about getting this liquor to Gary. Of course, by now, everybody was liking him. Even the people that didn't like him, liked him.

Schiller could smell it in the air. Everybody was starting to think, What are we killing Gilmore for? What's the death going to accomplish?

Breslin was walking around the office, cursing up a streak, "How dare they shoot the fucking guy, these fucking people?" Breslin was even furious at Gilmore for wanting to be offed.

Larry decided to relax at the Xerox machine. It was agreeable to work at some mechanical activity. Then, Tamera came up to say her newspaper wouldn't go for the liquor. "I don't care who does it," said Schiller, "get somebody." Tamera called Cardell, who had to be one of the most active Mormons in Salt Lake, and would you believe it, he agreed to go over and get it as a Christian act? Thought a dying man ought to be able to have his last request. That was something. Tamera's brother was straight arrow like you wouldn't believe.

Schiller called Stanger, and asked, "Will the Warden let me see Gary before the execution?" When Stanger said he didn't know, Larry called the prison. The Warden still wouldn't talk to him. Schiller told himself, "If they do change their mind, I want to be right at the front door."

Now, he studied the prison plan for the media, and decided it was very professional. "I don't believe the Warden made this out," he said aloud. It was just too sensible. Through the night, public announcements would be made every thirty minutes on the speaker, and a prison representative would come out frequently to talk to the reporters. A few minutes after the execution, the Warden would make a statement. Ten minutes after that, the press would be allowed to visit the site. It showed a knowledge of how to handle the media that had not been evident before. The very layout of the language intrigued Schiller. He said to himself, "I now have a match for my intelligence," and had one of his Dream-the-Impossible-Dream ideas. Maybe he would yet meet the author of this plan tonight and be able to explain why they should let him in to talk to Gary. "Yes," he said to himself, "I'm going to enter now as a member of the press."

Of course, he had made plans for such a contingency. John Durniak, the picture editor at *Time,* had told him he could use *Time* credentials if he wished. Lawrence Schiller, Witness to the Execution, who would not be allowed into the prison until 6:30 A.M., was now ready to enter at 6 P.M., better than twelve hours earlier, with his new press pass as Lawrence Schiller, accredited to *Time* magazine.

At least an hour before six, Schiller didn't feel like waiting around Orem any longer, and he put the liquor-filled cough-syrup bottles in his pocket, and told Tamera to have Cardell meet them at the gate of the prison. Then they took off from the TraveLodge. When he got to the gate, a lot of press was already going in. If they had been calling it a circus before, it looked now like a gypsy caravan. A great many television vans were lined up on the access road outside, plus all the vans for the movie-reel people and second crews and remotes, in addition to several hundred members of the press who were jammed into every conceivable kind of vehicle, all going one by one through the main gate. What hit Schiller was that everybody was drinking.

4

The prison press release had not stated whether the press could bring liquor or beer, but, of course, this omission was no flaw in the master plan. Who had ever heard of the world press staking out a place for twelve hours without liquor? Besides, it was so bitter cold that without booze, they would all freeze. Schiller flashed to six in the morning and three hundred newsmen stiff on the prison grounds. What a shot! Not a stringer alive to send out word. Yes, this was truly a master plan. Any demonstrations that took place would be off on the access road, well outside the prison. The objectors would be shouting their opposition from 1,500 feet away. If not for this plan, some of the best men in the media might have been looking right now for interviews with the demonstrators, even encouraging them to come up with scorching remarks. By morning, there would have been numerous stories of what was said by spokesmen hostile to the execution. So this was brilliant. The press might be livid, but the plan had a beautiful concept: lock up the press.

Of course, next day, the stories would be vindictive, but then the press had been rough on the State of Utah all the way. At least, the execution would take place without a mob scene in the dawn and everybody trying to get into the prison grounds at once. Now the mob scene would take place at six o'clock the night before, and the antagonism of the press might even wear out by morning. Drinking all night, they would be stupefied at dawn. By the time Gilmore was transferred from Maximum to the cannery, these reporters would be so happy to come in from the cold, they would probably wait without grumbling in whichever room they were penned. This plan, Schiller believed, had to come from Washington. Somebody in the FBI or Department of Justice, at least.

When Schiller went through the outside gate, they only asked, "Who are you?" "Larry Schiller." "Who with?" "*Time* magazine." They gave him the go-ahead. He started down the hill to the parking area but the guard standing there was Lieutenant Bernhardt, who had let Schiller in that first time close to two months ago when he had said he was an estate consultant. Now, Schiller drove by, looking straight ahead, but out of his rear-view mirror, he could see Bernhardt getting into a vehicle to chase after. So, Schiller stopped and got out. Bernhardt came up saying, "Get the hell out of here. You're not supposed to be in until six-thirty in the morning." Bernhardt even started screaming, which called attention to Schiller, last thing he wanted.

Bernhardt got on the radio and called someone. Then he said, "All right, you're in. But you're staying until six the fuck in the morning. Just remember that. You're not getting to see Gilmore." He shouted it all out in front of any number of the press. Whatever small cover Schiller might have had, was blown. He was going to be waylaid for the next few hours by microphones.

Later, Tamera slipped him the minibottles she had picked up at the gate from Cardell. Reporters milled around, talking and stamping their feet. Soon, everybody was back in their vans. Six o'clock came, and that was it. They were locked in. The long winter night came down off Point of the Mountain, passed over the parking lot and the prison, and chased the last of the evening pale across the desert.

PART SIX

Into the Light

CHAPTER 31

An Evening of Dancing
and Light Refreshment

1

Julie Jacoby went out early to the vigil, and with her in the first car
was Reverend John Adams who was an old hand at demonstrations
and wanted to speak to the Salt Lake County Sheriff about protection
for the vigilants.

Only trouble is they were not let inside the grounds. The State
Police steered them over to an access road. After a while, they
learned that very few reporters were available to cover them.

It got dark, it got cold, but they conducted a religious service.
Forty or fifty people had turned out, and they read a litany by the illumination provided by a television crew who were kind enough to tilt
their lights until the group making the responses could see the print.

At John Adams's suggestion, Julie had scoured her house for
heavy clothing and brought it along for people who might show without enough protection. Then the minister borrowed her Subaru and
kept ferrying new vigilants out from the Howard Johnson Motel in
Salt Lake, a rendezvous point. Through the night he brought people
back and forth.

2

At five in the afternoon when Toni went in to visit with Gary, the
press already collected in the parking lot, crowded around her at the

gate leading to Maximum. It would be a lot worse when she came out. More press. Walking down that corridor between the wire fences over the snow with the wind coming in off the mountain, Toni was thinking of the first time she'd gone to see Gary at the prison, two days before his birthday. She hadn't known then whether she was ready to forgive him or never would but after seeing how tickled he was at her visit, she asked what she could send, and he wanted two dark sweat shirts with the sleeves cut off, extra large with the shoulders reinforced so that they would peak without sleeves. She had gone to visit him again after that. He would always greet her by saying "God, you're beautiful," which had her blushing.

This Sunday, however, was different. It was, of all coincidences, her own birthday, and Howard's family was coming for supper. So all the while that Toni had been planning her visit to the prison on this last evening, she also had been cooking the meal for the evening party, and worrying how she could visit Gary early enough so that she could get back by seven for Howard's folks.

It was ten of six before they even let her into the visiting room, and then she had to wait twenty minutes with the other guests. When they opened the door for Gary, he saw her first and put his arms around her and gave a hug as if he were cracking all the ice of winter with one squeeze, held her so hard and long, she didn't think he would ever let go. Her mother was right with her, and said, "Now, it's my turn." So Gary released Toni with one arm, and hugged Ida, but he never let go completely. In fact as soon as Ida stepped back, he lifted Toni till her feet came off the floor, and gave her a great big kiss on the lips. He was still holding her fifteen minutes later when she absolutely had to leave.

Gary said then, "You are coming back, aren't you?" That was the first Toni considered it. It was the look in his eyes. "Go home," he said, "and take care of your family, then come back." But it was going to be complicated. Not to mention her in-laws, this was also the solitary day Toni would have with Howard all week. He was working on a construction job in southern Utah and only got home on Sundays.

Before she could say yes or no, Gary gave her another big birthday kiss. Then Moody and Stanger took her mother and herself out along the corridor through the wire fences and the crowd which was now massive. Toni knew why they called them the press. They almost squeezed her to death. But that was no more weird than leaving this prison to go back to her birthday party.

3

Sunday had started for Bob Moody at six in the morning with a High Council meeting. That lasted until eight. At nine-thirty, he went to Priesthood meeting, came back to take his family to church, went out to the prison, and came back to pick up his family when Sunday School concluded at 1 P.M. Then, all of the Moody family went home to dinner. By 4 P.M. Ron Stanger and he were ready to drive to the prison.

In the parking lot were Vern and Ida, then Toni, and two middle-aged cousins of Gary's named Evelyn and Dick Gray. All of them, together with Father Meersman, were taken over to Maximum Security, and Lieutenant Fagan was cordial on this night and showed the facilities. The prisoners had been fed early, and the gates between the visiting room and the main dining room for Maximum Security were open so that they could pass back and forth between the two rooms during the evening. A considerable space altogether. Perhaps so much as a hundred feet of movement in the longest direction, half of that the other way, plus a couple of smaller extra rooms adjacent for more private conversations. Lieutenant Fagan's office was open, and the kitchen, and the booth with the glass window where formerly they talked with Gary.

All this was at the front of Maximum Security just back of the two sliding gates that separated them from the exterior. At the rear of the visiting room, also barred by a gate, was the long hallway through Maximum off which were set the various cell rows. Moody had never been back there, and was not familiar with the area, so much as respectful of it. It was like the hallway that led to the cellar stairs in a large oppressive old house. Just as you imagined you could hear groans in those old cellars, so from the cell blocks came cries and shouts and moans and slamming sounds clear up to the visiting room, but muted, as if under the rock.

Since they planned to be there through the night and wanted to save their good clothes for morning, Moody and Stanger had come with a change. They had also brought crackers and soft drinks which proved unnecessary, for the prison offered light refreshments all evening. Tang and Kool-Aid and cookies and coffee. Then, Father Meersman procured a TV set and plugged it in. Somebody had managed to bring a portable stereo with a few records, and what with the three or four guards circulating through the kitchen and dining room and visiting room, and, at various times, Father Meersman and Cline Campbell and the two lawyers and the cousins and Vern and Toni and Ida, it was almost enough people for a party. Not to mention the guard on duty all through the night in the bullet-proof glass-enclosed booth that overlooked the visiting room.

Every couple of hours somebody would come from the pharmacy with medication. As the evening went on, Bob Moody came to recognize they were giving Gary some kind of speed. Doubtless, the pharmacists saw it as a blessing and kept it coming, and in the early hours of the evening, Gary did keep getting happier and happier. In the beginning, he was so delighted to see Toni, and held her for so long, and kissed her with such cousinly gusto, that Bob and Ron and Vern and the others just sat back and waited, didn't want to interrupt when Gary was so obviously delighting in her visit. Besides, there were chores to accomplish. The guards had brought in a couple of cots with mattresses, and provisions were being laid out for the evening, and then Toni was hardly there very long before Ron and Bob had to take her down between the barbed-wire fences into the swarm of press. It was practically an operation. Until they got her into the truck, it felt like their eyes were being seared with strobe lights and their souls with the general mania. For they were magical to the press tonight. They had seen the man and could report on him.

They kept saying "No comment," and looked for Schiller, and talked enough to keep the media close up with their microphones and tape recorders. That gave Vern time to slip around and have a talk with Larry.

Moody and Stanger might have been temporarily satisfying the majority of these reporters, but there was a great deal of press, and

Larry and Vern also became the center of a swarm. In the squeeze, Vern could only whisper, "Have you got the liquor?" and Schiller said, "Yeah." "How," whispered Vern, "am I going to get it in?" "Put the little bottles under your armpits," said Larry, "and keep your elbows close." "Fine," said Vern, "but how do I get it under my coat?" The press was surrounding them as tightly as a crowd packed around two players of the winning team caught on the field after the game.

Schiller turned and shouted, "Can't you let this man have a little privacy? You're hounding him. Get back." Physically he pushed on the press a little, not laying on rough hands so much as using the mixture of pressure and slight hysteria that worked best with reporters. "Give him a little privacy," he repeated. They retreated two feet, maybe three, room enough for Vern to do something with the liquor. By the time Larry turned around, Vern was ready to go back to the glare of the lights in the visiting room with the record player going and the TV set, and Gilmore beginning to spend his last night on earth.

4

The little bottles went fast. Gary would dip into a back room and take a nip, then come out with a wink. Moody thought it was appropriate. If that was what the man wanted, then he ought to be able to enjoy a drink. It had been years since Moody had tasted alcohol, but this was a social event. If some corner of Moody's mind could hear the criticism that Gilmore was going to meet his maker in the morning, and that might be wiser on a sober head, still Moody thought, this is more like a last meal. If he wants to go out drunk, he has a right. He thought of how Gary had deliberately not requested his six-pack of Coors at the end because he did not want the world to think he would be unable to face it without something to help him. But now, the speed was coming in, and the booze.

Yet, at the sight of Gary's pleasure, and the way he enjoyed the feeling of slight intoxication, for he didn't get very drunk, it began as a nice evening. Gary even took one of the guards into one of the back offices and gave him liquor from the curved medicine bottles Schiller had also sent in.

Bob, himself, loved the idea that he was able to go up to Gary, shake hands with him, hold him, look at him for a second, face to face — it was unexpected how great a need had developed to do something as simple as that after all these weeks. In fact, this was the first face-to-face meeting without urgent business to discuss. So, it was a pleasure to see Gary become loose and grow to enjoy the night.

It was easy and it was relaxed. During the course of the hours, Ron or he would get up and walk out and get a soft drink in the kitchen, and Evelyn and Dick Gray would go back and forth, and Vern. There was not any terrible feeling of a clock or any sense that outside the prison, lawyers might be preparing to seek a Stay.

5

Early that evening when they first came into the room and Gary was there without a pane of glass between, actually able to go up and touch, Stanger greeted him warmly, shook hands, put his arm around his shoulder in kind of a semihug, a masculine hit on the shoulder. It was kind of a victory, if you will, thought Stanger, that they were together. He stayed in that sense of glow.

A little later, while the evening was still pleasant, Ron started talking about his boxing experience on the team at BYU, and Gary mentioned that he knew a little about it. They got up, and started sparring. Ron had assumed it would be a matter of throwing a mock punch or two, but Gary wanted to make it more of a contest. While he couldn't really box, he was a street fighter, and threw a lot of punches. Ron kept stepping aside to avoid getting hit, but, of course, that wasn't the purpose of the whole thing. Only Gilmore kind of got this glint. The harder he hit, the more there was to enjoy. Gary sure had his little mean streak. Hit with fists closed, Ron had to catch it on his shoulders and hands. At one point, like it was still in fun, Gary analyzed his own style, said, "I don't lead, I'm a counterpuncher," and threw a lead. Ron slipped it, turned his shoulder into Gary to tie him up, then bailed out and walked away. Gary kept pursuing. It wasn't like normal sparring where you go in, tap a man, then with-draw to show how you could have hit the guy hard. Gary was throw-ing one real bomb after another. A couple almost clobbered Ron good. Of course, for the first twenty or thirty seconds, Ron was still feeling beautiful. He was faster than Gary. It was just that after a minute, he began to count his age with every breath, and Gary was a couple of inches taller, and had longer reach. Soon, there was the same flavor Stanger would find whenever he walked into Maximum. All these cons worked out with weights, knowing they had bodies. Their pres-ence leaned on you psychologically. It was as if their bodies said, "I got more right to be free than you, boy." So, Ron was glad when he found an opportunity to clinch with Gary, hug him, grin, and indicate it was over.

After the boxing, Gary began to make some phone calls. Ron could hear him on the line with the station that played Country-and-Western, and he kidded them about how bad they were and thanked them for playing "Walking in the Footsteps of Your Mind." Next, he went into Fagan's office to make a call to his mother. Of course, Ron didn't try to listen, but Gary came out all excited because he also was able to get a call in to Johnny Cash. Then he began to move around restlessly as if it bothered him that the record player was going, and there was nobody to dance with. Yet, things were still in a good mood. The boxing had set up a kind of intimacy between Gary and Ron. While ups and downs were beginning to appear in the evening, still, it was okay, and the mood was all right. Like any long night, there had to be peaks and valleys. During one of the lulls, Gary now came over to Ron and said he wanted to tell him something, wanted to be alone with him. They took a bench in a corner of the visiting room, away from the others.

Gary said he had $50,000, and looked Ron right in the eye. His pale gray-blue eyes looked as deep as the sky on one of those odd mornings when you cannot tell by the light of dawn whether good or foul weather lies ahead. "Yes, Ron," he said, "I've got $50,000, or to be exact about it, access to $50,000, and I'll give it to you. All I want is that the next time you go outside, leave me the keys to your extra clothes." Those other clothes were in a locker back in one of the little rooms. "There's so much hubbub around here," Gilmore said, "that the guards won't know. Just leave your key."

"What do you have in mind?" Ron asked. Ron couldn't believe how stupid he was acting. "Well, what, really, Gary, do you have in mind?" he asked again, and then it hit him, and he felt doubly stupid. "Ron," said Gary, "if I can get through that double gate in your clothes, I'm out. There's nothing past there but the outside door, and that's always open. I'll just skin up the barbed wire and flip over the rolls at the top. That wire'll put a few holes in me, but it's nothing." "Then, you drop?" asked Ron. "Yeah," said Gilmore. "Then you drop, and start running. If I get out there, I'm gone. You leave those clothes, all right?"

Now Ron realized what had been going into those arduous calisthenics Gary had done every day. He forced himself to look back into Gary's eye, Ron would say that much for himself, and he answered, "Gary, when we started, part of our bargain was no hanky-panky." Then he made himself say, "I've grown very close to you. I'd do anything I could for you. But I'm not going to put my children and my family in jeopardy." Gary nodded. Acknowledged it all with that nod. Didn't seem discouraged so much as confirmed.

Ron was remembering that as Toni and Ida left, Gary had gone into a playful little scene where he put on Toni's hat and Ida's coat and pretended to get into the double door with them. All very funny at the time. Everybody was laughing, including the novice guard on the gate, a young kid Ron had never seen before, but all that guard would have had to do was, by mistake, open both doors at once. Gary would have been gone. Wow! It came over him. This guy meant what he said. If he had to stay in prison, he wanted to die. But if he could get outside, that was another game.

6

Sitting on a bench, trying to keep his thoughts above the pain in his knee, taking it all in with sorrow and fatigue and considerable churning at the core of his stomach, Vern was feeling pretty emotional. He knew his face was set like stone but it was getting hard to hold up. He almost busted out once — didn't know if it was to cry or laugh — when Gary said over the phone, "Is this the real Johnny Cash?" That was as crazy as you would want.

Now, Gary was going around in the hat Vern had bought for him at Albertson's food store, a Robin Hood type of archer's hat, way too big. It had been the last one left. Vern had looked at Ida and said, "He wears funny things anyway, so I'll buy it." How could you love a guy because he wanted to wear a crazy hat? Ah, Gary was so full of love this night. Vern had never seen him this rich. The only thing in the world he could still get mad about was the prison, and he even had a funny attitude there. "My last night," he kept saying with his grin, "so they can't punish me anymore," and Vern came near again to that feeling he was going to cry. He remembered that day so many visits ago that Gary had said, "Vern, there's no use talking about the situation. I killed those men, and they're dead. I can't bring them back, or I would."

7

A little later, Stanger was feeling restless. Talking of escape with Gary hadn't exactly calmed him down, so he said, "Hey, let's get some pizza," and asked Lieutenant Fagan, "Can we get cleared?" Everybody liked the idea. Stanger only had six bucks on him, so Father Meersman kicked in a little and Fagan was good for two, and some of the guards pitched in. Then Vern came up out of a reverie and said, "Nobody contributes. I'm buying the pizzas. You just take care of getting them."

Fagan volunteered a car with a man to drive them, and then Ron and Bob and the guard went out and stopped in the parking lot long enough for Stanger to slip out of the car, walk around, find Larry, and tell him, "Gary wants to call you around one-thirty in the morning." Schiller said, "Okay, I'll go with you."

By now, the press wasn't on Schiller's ear and elbow anymore. The cold had gotten to everybody. People stayed in their vans drinking, and Schiller was able to stroll around the perimeter and get to the police car unobserved. The guard in the front seat said, "Who are you?" but Schiller only replied, "I'm supposed to be going out with you," and got in, and lay down in the back. Stanger, in the meanwhile, had gotten waylaid by a reporter. It took five minutes before he and Moody could return. Then they went up the road, and the outer gate swung open and they were out of the prison grounds. Schiller got off the floor and everybody started laughing.

If they drove Larry all the way back to Orem, the prison would wonder why the car had been gone so long. It was better they head north to the near outskirts of Salt Lake. From there, Schiller called his driver. With it all, he still got back to the motel before midnight, there to wait for Gary's call.

The Pizza Hut was the only place open, and they were the last customers, and ordered the stuff with ham, salami and pepperoni, Bob Moody thinking he'd hit everybody with the selection, and they picked up some beer in a grocery. Back at the prison, their car was searched, and the beer confiscated. It made them mad, but the guard examining them was a stiff, and said alcohol would not be tolerated on prison grounds. The irony was that he didn't even look at the pizza boxes. They could have hidden five pistols in there. Then they proceeded from the outer gate down the entrance road to the front of Administration and the guard at the top of the tower spoke down to them like God's voice coming out of a dark cloud to say there had been a ruling against the pizza. Not acceptable.

While they were still disputing that, new word came. They could walk in with the pizzas after all. It was just that Gary wouldn't be able to have any. He had not put it on the list for his last supper.

Moody could conceive of the scene in the Warden's office. One big heavy meeting. What? Food brought in from outside? Stop it! By the time they arrived at the door to Maximum, Bob and Ron were so angry they stood out there to eat their pizza in the cold, and by the time they went in, Lieutenant Fagan was very embarrassed over the situation, very. He was a small man, with white hair, a mustache, and a lean build, usually a crisp and pleasant man, but hangdog now over the way his superiors had reacted. After a while a guard came up and said Gary could have a piece, too. Of course, Gary wouldn't go near the stuff by then. Gave a look to blister paint, and said, "I hope everybody's enjoying my last meal."

Meanwhile, Father Meersman kept entering and going out again. He kept them posted with what was going on in the Administration Building and, presumably, thought Bob, kept the administration posted on what was going on with them.

After this episode, there was a feeling of humiliation all over. Last night, Gary could have requested any of a hundred dishes. The Warden would have initialed the form and he could have had it tonight. Now, it was too late. A couple of pharmacists, however, came to give him more pills. He couldn't eat pizza, but they would feed him speed. Stanger decided the best word for the prison administration was "beautiful."

They also heard that Sterling and Ruth Ann Baker were not being let in to visit. The prison had run a check on Sterling and he had a record. Two traffic citations. A real big criminal record. Grotesque, Moody was muttering to himself. Stupid. Idiotic. Asinine.

8

At Toni's birthday party, there were dozens of phone calls from friends, so Toni didn't have to think about Gary. All the same, she kept saying to her mother, "I want to go back up," and Ida would reply, "Oh, hon, all those reporters know who you are now." Toni thought, "All right, I'll get up at five."

Her in-laws left early, and she and Howard just sat there talking. She knew he could feel how she wanted to be with Gary again. Of course, she also didn't want to leave Howard. Besides, that press! The lights in your eyes were frightening, and you could hear reporters' nerves snapping on every question. It was the first time she had ever felt like an animal in a cage with other animals.

Howard must have been reading her thoughts because he said, "Come on, honey, I'll get you through the reporters." So, they left a note for Ida, and took off. It was close to ten by the time they reached the prison and they must have used up forty-five minutes getting through the gate. Security was tight by then. They were accustomed to her face, but Howard was new, and they wouldn't clear him. She had to go and talk to the Warden, and that did mean pushing through the reporters outside Administration by herself.

Sam Smith wouldn't let Howard in. Toni had the feeling the Warden would relent if she kept pushing, but Howard didn't want to. He just kept saying, "How can you sit and talk to someone who is going to die in a few hours?"

When they opened the double gate, there was Daddy and Gary sitting together on a cot. Vern was sleepy, and Gary was uptight, but they must have been used to people going in and out, because the first gate slammed behind her and they didn't even look up when the second gate opened. She was actually in the room before Gary saw her and jumped to his feet and held her in the air. He said, "I knew you'd come back. Thank God you came back."

He whirled her around and hugged her and gave her another big kiss. Vern said, "What are you doing back here? It's a long way from morning," but he left them alone.

They sat down and started to talk, and Gary just held on to her hands. He said, "I wish we had more time together." "I'm sorry too," said Toni.

"Well," he said, "maybe it's for a reason. Maybe if we'd developed a relationship earlier, tonight wouldn't mean so much." Then he asked if she wanted to see some pictures of Nicole, and got out a carton he had taped, and carefully unwrapped it, and showed Nicole as a child. "These," he added, "you don't have to look at, if you don't want to," but pulled out a couple of beautiful drawings of Nicole nude. Then a whole series of pictures taken on photo machines where you would get four shots for half a dollar. Nicole was showing her breasts. It was obvious these pictures meant a lot to Gary, and Toni thought they weren't foul. Really kind of meaningful. All the while, Gary kept bringing up more snapshots of Nicole when she was five, and eight, and ten, saying what a beautiful child she was.

Toni said, "She's a beautiful woman now." What was all this carrying on about how she looked as a child?

"I wish," said Gary, "I could have seen her one more time."

Then he taped up the carton again, and opened another box full of photographs of prison friends, and told her which institution they'd been in. Some officials came in with medication, and handed him the cup and said, "Take them *now*," and Gary said, "You sure don't trust me, do you?" When they left, Toni was still alone with Gary. He took the plaque that Annette had given him that long time ago, and said, "I want this given to Nicole." That was when Toni decided Gary must truly have been innocent. Otherwise, he would hardly leave it to Nicole.

The record player was going and Gary said, "Come on, I haven't danced in years." So, they got up. She had heard him sing once and he was a terrible singer, but she could see he was going to be even worse as a dancer. Yet, she enjoyed it. Sitting on the floor, looking through his things, she had felt so close. Like Brenda, Toni had been married four times, twice for only a few months. Her fourth marriage had been with Howard and that had lasted nine years. In less trouble now than ever, it was a good marriage, but Toni had never exactly felt the kind of special feeling she had now. It was like she'd known Gary for a lifetime in these couple of hours.

The music was fast. Gary put his funny hat on Toni, fluffed her hair, and they danced. She did her best to follow. When they finished, Gary said, "I never really was very good, but I haven't had much chance to go to dances," and they laughed, and he told her that he had talked to Johnny Cash on the phone but it was a bad connection. Still he had asked, "Are you the real Johnny Cash?" and right after the answer, hollered back, "Well, this is the real Gary Gilmore."

They sat down again, Gary said, "I have found something with you tonight that I knew with Brenda through all these years, and I wish I'd made things more equal between you and your sister." When Toni looked puzzled, he said, "I gave three thousand dollars for you and Howard, and five thousand to Brenda and Johnny. I'm sorry I did not make it equal. I never really knew you." She told him the money didn't mean anything.

He said, "You're so many people to me tonight. You're Nicole, and you're Brenda, and in a way, you're like my mother in the way I remember when she was young." Toni didn't know if she was reading his mind, but she thought he was feeling a strong urge to put his arms once more around his mother, and Toni thought of Brenda who had wanted to be with him so bad tonight and was now in the hospital, and Toni felt as odd as if she were both Brenda and herself, both of them there, dancing and holding his arms.

Every now and then a couple of guards would come in to shake hands with Gary, and he would say, "Do you want my autograph?" "Sure, Gary," they would tell him. So, he would borrow a pen and sign the pocket of their shirt or their cuffs and Toni thought they all acted like they really liked him. When the pharmacist came back, Gary said, "Here's this old boy who takes care of me," and the pharmacist grunted and said, "Yeah, you keep me pretty busy with all your shenanigans."

All the while, Toni was reminding herself that Howard was out there shivering in the parking lot. Finally, she told Gary, "Look, I'll bring Mother back by five," and Gary said, "I want you here in the morning with me," and put his arms around her to give another big hug and said, "Thank you, for tonight." He held her one more time, and said, "A cool, peaceful summer evening, a love-filled room. You just brightened my whole night, Toni, and filled it with love," and he cuddled her face in his hands, putting one hand on each cheek, and gave her a kiss on the forehead. "You brought my Nicole back to me tonight," he said. Then he gave her a big hug, and Toni said, "I'm going to have to go."

Gary walked her toward the gate. "I'll see you in the morning," he said. "Go home and take care of Ida." Then he added, "Tell Howard hello. It's so great that Howard came to try to see me." Toni went out letting him think that the only reason Howard had not been there was that the Warden would not let him. When the first gate closed behind her, Gary held the bars to watch until they opened the other gate and when that closed behind her, she put her coat on, and left. She never got to see him again.

9

Up till then, despite the pizza, it had really been a party and everybody was feeling good, and there were no problems, except one so large it removed all sense of the others. But, now, after Toni was gone, Gary started to get mad about the pizza all over again. He became very solemn, very upset. Ron remembered how Gary always said, "I don't want a last meal, because they'll play games with me." Ron knew he didn't want to talk to Gary now.

Nor did Moody. A sense of death had come into the visitors' room. It had been there before, but it gave everyone strength. Now it was as if it came creeping like smoke beneath the door. It was getting late. Things had quieted. The record player was not going, and Vern had gone to sleep. Dick and Evelyn Gray were snoozing. Ron went to the kitchen to talk to the guards. It was then that Gary came over to Bob.

"You wouldn't change clothes with me, would you?" he said, and Bob answered, "No, I wouldn't." Gary began to describe how he could get out, if Bob would just give him the clothes. The guards were paying no attention. He could walk through those twin gates as Bob Moody, be out the door of Maximum and over that barbed-wire fence faster than you could ever believe. He would just climb up the wire, then do a forward roll over the roll of barbed wire at the top, pick up a hole or two in his skin, nothing, and be running, man. They would not find him. It was a somber moment. "I know," said Gary, "that I can get out of here if you will do it." Bob just had to get his clothing from the locker and put it over in the corner. If Bob wanted, it would also help if he took Gary's crazy Robin Hood hat and wore it for a while. That would be about all a sleepy guard would look for in the way of Gary Gilmore. "No," said Bob Moody, "I can't do it, Gary, and I won't do it."

Cline Campbell had been in and out all night so he saw the change in mood. For the first couple of hours you would have thought it was Christmas morning. But Campbell had to leave by 7:30 that evening to give a lecture in Salt Lake, and didn't get back until close to midnight. By then it had all changed. Earlier, a guard had been sitting at the head of a cot, Gilmore in the middle, and Campbell at the foot. In the middle of talking away about nothing at all, Gilmore reached under the pillow and came up with a sample bottle of whiskey. "Oops," said Campbell and looked away. "I see no evil, hear no evil, speak no evil. But have at it, partner, just have at it." Gilmore laughed. That was earlier.

After the speaking engagement, Campbell rushed back to the prison without stopping to eat, and discovered everybody had gone through the pizza. There was none left. He and Gilmore were the only two with empty bellies. When they were alone, Campbell said, "It looks like this time will be it."

"It'll go through," said Gary. "They can't stop it now."

"You know," said Campbell, "we're to meet again. It will be the same for you and me, no matter what's on the other side." They were in Lieutenant Fagan's office and Gary was still wearing the hat with a feather that looked like it belonged to Chico Marx. "It doesn't matter," said Campbell, "whether what you feel, religiously, is right, or what I feel, either way, we're going to see each other again. In whatever form, Gary, I want you to know I think you're a good guy." It was awful, thought Campbell, the more time he spent with Gilmore the less he was able to remind himself that Gary was a man capable of murder. In fact, by now, most of the time, Gilmore looked not at all capable of that, at least not compared to most of the faces Cline Campbell saw every day in uniform and out.

Father Meersman said to Moody and Stanger that he had this advantage over almost everybody else that he'd been through two other executions. He explained to them how he succeeded in convincing the Warden and his staff that it was necessary to walk through the procedure on this night for every step ought to be taken equal to those steps which would be taken in the morning when the real execution took place, and they had done that. Some of the prison officials had agreed to a dry run and taken the steps so that it would be calm and dignified when they all participated. They had gone through the whole thing and somebody had a stopwatch and timed it, and that was a normal thing to do for such an important procedure. It was important to have a run-through of the whole mechanics of the execution.

CHAPTER 32

The Angels and the Demons
Meet the Devils and the Saints

1

More than twelve hours earlier, before noon that Sunday, Earl Dorius had received a phone call from Michael Rodak that Gil Athay was seeking a Stay. A little more than an hour later, Rodak called again. Justice White had denied Athay's application. When no further word came from Washington, Earl felt confident Athay had used up his legal actions, and therefore went with his wife and children to her parents' house, and relaxed for the first time that day. Returning home, however, early in the evening, there was a phone call from Bob Hansen to say that Jinks Dabney wanted a hearing that night on a taxpayers' lawsuit. It would be in Ritter's Court.

Nonetheless, Earl's initial reaction was not one of great alarm. Dabney couldn't show that any Federal tax monies at all were being spent on the execution. The whole thing had the dank smell of a last-ditch attempt.

When Dorius and Bill Barrett walked into the lobby of the Newhouse Hotel Jinks Dabney was already there with his co-counsel, Judith Wolbach. Bob Hansen was present, and Bill Evans, and Dave Schwendiman, plus the bellcap. That was it. They sat around in the nineteenth-century decor of the Newhouse's lobby, real elegant Wild West. Halfway between a palace and a brothel. There was overstuffed furniture in bright red velvet, and red rugs and a double white stairway that fanned out in two half circles before coming together at the mezzanine level, a large and formal room, a little shabby now, but the hotel was famous for being the lair of Judge Ritter. After a couple of hours, however, it was no great place to wait.

Ritter was up in his room and he must have known the ACLU and the Attorney General were downstairs, but no further word was coming. Bob Hansen, thinking what to do if Ritter gave the Stay, called Judge Lewis. As a member of the Tenth Circuit Court, he would be a tier above Ritter, and could override him. Hansen asked if the Judge would convene a special hearing later that evening in Salt Lake.

Judge Lewis, however, said he would not hold such a hearing by himself. It was too great a responsibility for one Federal Judge to overrule another, especially when you were sending a man to death by such a decision.

By nine o'clock, Dabney got up his nerve, and told the desk clerk to inform Judge Ritter once more that they were there, and he was sending his legal documents upstairs. In less time than Dabney expected, Judge Ritter telephoned down that everyone was to go across the street to the courtroom. A security guard would let them in.

There was nothing rousing in the way Dabney gave Hansen this news. Originally from Virginia, his name was V. (for Virginius) Jinks Dabney, a bland-looking fellow with horn-rimmed glasses, who wore seersuckers in summer and tweed jackets in winter. He had a perky, remote way of speaking as if he might know you for ten years but that was no reason to raise his voice. It was obvious he downplayed drama. Did it so well, he could make his lack of it dramatic. All the same, when Earl heard the news, he had a dramatic reaction — a sure feeling the case was lost. He had honestly supposed Judge Ritter wouldn't even consider it. The legal arguments were so thin, and the thing had been submitted so late. Then his gloom increased with the knowledge that Bob Hansen wouldn't even be with them. Thought it would literally hurt their chances if his face was seen in Court. So, Bob left. He was going to get some sleep. That depressed Earl further. Bob sounded like he expected to be needing that sleep later.

It was spooky going down the halls of the courthouse in the dark, with just a few maintenance lights on, but by the time the lawyers had settled at their tables, a number of crime and court reporters started filtering in. Everybody was beginning to feel more serious by the moment. Then began a long wait for Ritter.

At the table for the Assistant Attorney Generals, which in this case was the defendant's table, Earl sat watching Jinks Dabney and Judith Wolbach on the plaintiff's side. Earl was trying to quiet his temper, and reminded himself of the time he had failed to cross-examine Schiller properly. No matter, he was furious. It was outright unfair of the ACLU, he felt, to wait until now to go to Court. He didn't mind that their case was weak. It was ethical to bring in anything that was remotely plausible. You could try, even if 99 percent of the facts and the law were against you, but it was unfair to wait till the night before an execution. What if Earl's office had not devoted good working hours to troubleshooting these issues? Without such foresight, the ACLU would have caught them unprepared. That would have been unfair to the State of Utah.

2

Over at the plaintiff's table, Judy Wolbach was also feeling pretty mad. Jinks Dabney was a good courtroom attorney, but she herself had little experience in cases of this sort, and she was pissed off at her own ACLU. Why, in a major case like this, could they only come up with herself, unqualified, and with Jinks, only partially willing? He was an awfully good lawyer, but not exactly an enthusiastic adherent of the ACLU. Jinks had a promising career ahead in Salt Lake, and it didn't help a rising young legal talent to be known among all these gung-ho Mormons as a civil liberties advocate. Where were all the big ACLU boys from the big firms in the East who were supposed to contribute their massive liberal expertise? She couldn't comprehend it. A case as big and interesting as this, being left to the local talent.

Judy had tried every trick she knew, including the release she gave to the newspapers of her conversation with Melvin Belli to throw a scare into Bob Hansen. It could be disastrous for the Attorney General if Utah lost a few million bucks because of him. All she had gotten for her pains, however, was a truly weird and pompous response. Hansen said there was no question as to the constitutionality of Utah's death penalty statutes. No question? Why, only an idiot Legislature could pass a statute that didn't insist on an appeal for the death penalty. The whole idea, even among conservatives, was to be cautious about capital punishment. Nobody wanted bloodbaths anymore. Even from a conservative point of view, the best way to obtain your capital punishment was by emphasizing every safeguard against killing a man for too little. Yet, Utah — good old Utah — had neglected to make the appeal mandatory. What could be more defective, an idiot child?

All the same, this taxpayers' action was awfully hokey for a suit, Judith thought. The only good thing about it was the letters she'd been able to send to the Governor, the Lieutenant Governor, the Attorney General, and the Warden! All accused of wrongful acts and unlawful expenditures. She wished she could have seen their faces. Those letters had been delivered by her own daughter, who, bless her heart, maybe because of the Jewish blood of her father, was a very politically conscious young lady, and had been upset when she discovered her mother was practicing law to make money. Thought that was wrong. One should not worry about money. One should just go ahead and file political suits. Bless her heart, Judy Wolbach thought. Thank God she feels that way. Still, the measure of how picayune were ACLU resources was that Judy might not have gotten those letters out to any defendants this Sunday without her daughter to serve as runner.

3

While he was waiting, Jinks Dabney began to think of stories he had heard about Judge Ritter. According to the gossip that came back to him from people who knew the Judge well, Ritter regarded himself as an outpost of good sense in a desert of craziness. The accusation that he was carrying on a vendetta against the Latter-Day Saints wasn't true, he would say. He didn't regard Mormons as worthy of a vendetta. While born a Catholic, and now a subscriber to no religion but the U.S. Constitution, the Judge had no patience with any desire to sway people's minds through religious doctrine. Still, he actively disliked the manner in which the Mormon Church owned the land, ran the banks, and controlled the politicians. That offended him more than their religious doctrine. That he merely considered silly. All those Joseph Smith miracles. On the other hand, he would never decide against them just because they were Mormons. Liked to think he had too profound a respect for the facts in a case.

Ritter's attitude toward incompetence among lawyers, however, was enough to put fear into the stomach of many a good member of the bar, Mormon or not. One time he became disgusted with the job a lawyer was doing and asked how much he had charged his client. When Ritter heard it was $500, he said, "That will be the fine." To the client, he said, "You have already paid your fine. Don't give your counsel another penny." The poor lawyer wanted to crawl under the desk. Another advocate kept speaking in so low a voice that Ritter asked him, "Why are you whispering?" The fellow answered, "Because I'm scared." A veteran trial lawyer would go into Judge Ritter's courtroom the way common mortals went to the dentist, but then Ritter had a mind that could see where arguments were leading faster than a dentist could locate decay. He gave hell to people who wasted his time. You not only had to do a good job, but do it quickly.

That impatience, even Ritter's defenders would say, got the old Judge in a lot of trouble. Once a legal matter became clear, he was going to make his judgment. Just would not plod through the production of a long careful opinion with fifty or one hundred citations. Then the Tenth Circuit would complain that the record was not complete, and reverse him. Later, the Supreme Court would affirm him. His affirmance rate with the U.S. Supreme Court was exactly the opposite of his reversal rate with the Circuit Court. "They're just too stupid to see I'm right," he would say of the Tenth Circuit.

Of course, this contempt for Judges he considered unintelligent closed Ritter off from recognizing that the party for whom he had found was the one hurt the most by the reversal. By the time the Supreme Court affirmed Ritter two or three years later, it was often too late to do the original fellow any good.

Some of these stories were legend in Salt Lake law courts. But Dabney also had talked to people who knew Ritter well enough to tell you about the Judge's personal life, where the legends were not true. Ritter, actually, led a lonely life. Most days, he only crossed the street from his rooms at the Newhouse Hotel to his chambers at the Court. He had the reputation of being a drinker and a womanizer, and maybe he had been some of that in the old days when he taught at the law school, but nobody had seen him in recent years with a woman, and he rarely drank. It had been said for years that the best bar in town was Judge Ritter's chambers, and it was true that Willis Ritter had some nice things located under his desk, and there were times when he might invite a lawyer to have a glass with him, but he was hardly an alcoholic. It had been years since the doctors had told him he couldn't drink much, and he didn't. In fact, nobody, when you got down to it, had seen him drunk in years. Once on a trip to San Francisco, Craig Smay, his law clerk, had gone to some pains to find a bottle of Ritter's favorite Scotch, Glen Livet, but the bottle sat under the desk for six months, and Ritter finally gave it back to Smay unopened. Couldn't drink it. His health forbade. He would get heart attacks, or have to go into surgery every three or four months, yet for all that he'd be back on the bench two weeks later looking like an old Olympic athlete, white hair, ruddy face. You couldn't believe the man's capacity to recuperate.

Yet always a lonely man. He had for friends only a few lawyers he'd known for years, and a few old reporters. Ever since the Mormons had raised those accusations against him back in Harry Truman's administration, Ritter had stayed away from everyone. The only time anyone had ever seen him with a number of people was one year on Christmas Eve when Ritter insisted Craig Smay and his wife come to dinner. When they got to the hotel, a room had been rented, and inside were twenty-five people around a big table, older people with their sons and daughers and grandchildren. Everybody was calling him Bill. They were friends from the time he'd been a boy. Up to that moment, Craig Smay never thought of the Judge as one of those human beings who naturally have a first name.

Given the length of this wait, it was better to remember only those tales about Ritter that could warm you. So Dabney was trying to savor the story about Ritter and the wild mustangs. Some Indians had sued the Federal government for rounding up a few hundred mustangs on their reservation and sending them off to the stockyards. Ritter had given the Indians $200 a horse. The government appealed and Ritter was overturned, but the case came back to him. In the next trial, one of the tribal chieftains testified that the horses were *ceremonial* ponies. On that basis, the Judge decided they were each worth $400.

Ritter later confided to a few friends that the evidence which caused him to think the government ought to pay, and pay well, was that the horses had been packed into a truck with open boards, and one mustang's leg was sticking through the slats. The people who were doing the job could have opened a door to extricate the horse, but that would have been a lot of work, so somebody just took a chain saw and cut the horse's leg off. Those animals were going for dog food anyway. Ritter said, "This shows the cavalier attitude of the government toward our horses."

What Ritter gave you, Dabney told himself now, was excitement. After leaving his courtroom, you could say to yourself, "There isn't another Bench like this in the whole country." Whether you won or lost didn't have to be so important as that you had a hell of an experience. Why, Judge Learned Hand had written that Willis Ritter possessed one of the finest minds he had ever known on the Bench. That was what you had to count on.

4

Considering it was well after ten o'clock on Sunday night, Earl thought Judge Ritter looked surprisingly spry when he finally showed up in Court. Judy Wolbach was impressed with his God-like voice. Ritter said no more than "The papers appear to be in order. I'll hear you," but she fell in love. A slow, deep voice with a lot of resonance. Such a plump, nice, stern-looking man. He would make a good Lord for the flood, if God was close to eighty.

Gil Athay happened to be in Court, Judy noticed, and some of the top liberal lawyers in town like Richard Giauque and Danny Berman, his partner, about as Salt Lake Establishment as you could get, if you were also a liberal. Jinks, with them for an audience, would be off to a good start. He loved trial work, and under this kind of pressure, didn't falter a bit. Began with a dry, perfect presentation, exactly the reason he was a successful attorney. If she had been up there, Judy thought, she would have wasted time carrying on about how Attorney General Hansen didn't even have the nerve to appear, which probably would have been a mistake. Instead, Jinks went right into his argument.

Dabney had tried two jury trials in front of Ritter and been in his Court twenty-five or thirty times. Maybe it was the legends, but you never got over the anxiety that you might run into one of Ritter's sore spots. He could rule against you right then. Given the Judge's love of dispatch, Dabney knew he was taking a chance in talking a lot tonight, but in variety lay the strength of his frail case.

"Your Honor," Dabney began, "we have attempted to obtain justice in virtually every Court in this country, and this is the final effort to stop what we consider to be a clear unconstitutional exercise by the State of Utah to execute a man before the death penalty statute has been examined by either the Utah Supreme Court or the Supreme Court of the United States. . . ."

Dabney did not have his argument written out. What he had to say was placed in five piles of paper. Once he got going, he could reach for a group of notes, and explore their points, but first he had to summarize the complaint. Since it was a taxpayers' lawsuit, his argument had to be that public funds were being spent "unlawfully." So now he said that if the Utah statute was found unconstitutional, the State could yet be found liable.

Having completed his introduction, Dabney decided to add a ghost claim, not present in his brief. "It has recently," he said, "come to our knowledge that Mr. Gilmore might consider fighting for his life, if Nicole Barrett were to indicate to him that he ought to do so." Since the only way this knowledge had *come* was through discussion with a few other ACLU attorneys, plus a quick unprofitable talk with Stanger, Dabney added quickly, "We are not positive that we really have a basis upon which we can ask for this relief, but if Mr. Gilmore is of that particular state of mind, we ought to allow him to have some kind of access to Miss Barrett in the presence of her attorney, or court-appointed psychiatrist, to determine whether he would change his position. It seems to me that's a very small request considering that we're confronted with the execution of a man."

Dabney threw it in because it sounded good. It could have the effect of moving the Judge's stomach over a little nearer to ruling in the ACLU's favor. Often, to win a case like this, you not only had to give a Judge good legal reasons to satisfy his mind, but also something that appealed to his gut. Dabney would soon give his argument why Utah's death statute was not valid, and Ritter might decide the ACLU was right, yet still say, "Gary Gilmore wants to die, so what the hell?" If, however, you could suggest that Gilmore could change his mind about dying, and all it would take was one meeting with Nicole! — well, Dabney thought that might appeal to Ritter.

Now, the lawyer went into the legal merits. The Utah statute, he said, had no mandatory review. That removed a vital precaution. You had to appeal a death sentence, regardless of a defendant's wishes. How else could you protect other defendants in later cases? The original Judge might have made some serious legal error that could be repeated.

Dabney next brought in the Constitution. Everyone knew that Judge Ritter had been keeping a tattered copy in his desk since law school days fifty years ago. So Jinks remarked that the Eighth and Fourteenth amendments were going to be violated by this case. They had a requirement that the death penalty not be "capricious or arbitrary."

Earl Dorius was certainly going to quote the majority opinion of the Supreme Court in the Bessie Gilmore case. Dabney, therefore, did it himself: "Gary Gilmore, knowingly and intelligently, with full knowledge of his right to seek an appeal in the Utah Supreme Court, has waived that right," Dabney read aloud. These words, he said, meant that Gilmore had a right to appeal and chose not to use it. But one had to keep in mind that the question of mandatory review had not been brought before the Court. Indeed, Justice White had even said that Gilmore was not able "to waive the right to state appellate review." Burger had then added: "The question is simply not before us." So the Supreme Court, Dabney argued, had not decided the issue in the Bessie Gilmore case. To the contrary. On the basis of their decisions in *Gregg v. Georgia, Proffitt v. Florida,* and *Jurek v.*

Texas, the Supreme Court had upheld statutes that called precisely for mandatory appellate review, and, in addition, *Collins v. Arkansas* and *Neal v. Arkansas* had been sent back by the Supreme Court for just such lack of mandatory review.

"Your Honor," Dabney said, "this Court is the last chance for justice to prevail." He had concluded his opening statement.

5

Dorius began his reply. They were here in Court because "Federal monies are being expended unlawfully . . . for the purpose of executing Gary Mark Gilmore." However, Earl stated, "We know of no Federal money that has been appropriated specifically for the execution."

The argument had come to the place where it could be decided at a stroke. Judge Ritter spoke for the first time. "What," he asked, "do you say to that, Mr. Dabney?"

"If it please the Court, our information is that the Division of Corrections' budget for the fiscal year 1976–1977 contains a Federal grant in the amount of $501,000."

Dorius replied that this was a general appropriation. "The plaintiffs," he said, "are unable to show that any of these particular monies have been designed for the carrying-out of this execution."

Dabney was ready to say, "Half a million dollars in Federal funds was given to the Utah Bureau of Prisons. I assume the Utah Bureau of Prisons has *something* to do with the proposed execution of Gary Gilmore," but when Ritter made no comment, and seemed ready to let them remain in Court, Dabney let it go.

Earl Dorius would certainly attack the point again, and in reserve, Dabney had an elegant Supreme Court decision to introduce. It could dignify standing in the most dubious taxpayers' suit. Dabney, however, did not want to put it out too early. The decision was more than ten years old, and later Supreme Court decisions had weakened it. Better to save it for the end, so as not to give the other side too much room to chip away.

Dorius's next argument was that "These issues that are being raised tonight, under the guise of an eleventh-hour appeal, are issues known to these plaintiffs at least two months." There had been a tremendous delay in filing the action. In *Gomports v. Chase,* a 1971 Supreme Court decision in a school desegregation case, Justice Marshall stated that "under normal circumstances, the injunction would issue," but the case had come in too late. So, Justice Marshall denied it. The ACLU, in submitting this action "just nine hours prior to the execution, is very analogous to the *Gomports* case. The plaintiffs have sat on their rights too long," said Dorius.

For the Attorney General's office, it was Bill Evans's turn next. The Supreme Court, he argued, had only insisted on two conditions for death-penalty cases. One was the need for a separate trial and Mitigation Hearing. Utah had that. The other requirement was that whoever determined the sentence must be provided with standards for guidance. That element was also in the Utah system. Besides, the Supreme Court had never said that mandatory appeal was the only system to satisfy them.

Bill Barrett was next. "With this taxpayers' suit, the plaintiff is attempting to stop an execution, not stop the wrongful expenditure of tax dollars. They have not established that they have a good-faith pocketbook action." It was a short point and a strong one. Dabney felt the time had come to produce his special argument.

"If I may, Your Honor," said Dabney, "Mr. Barrett left out a very significant case when discussing the standing question. That is *Flast v. Cohen,* a decision of the United States Supreme Court in 1968. In that case, Your Honor, which was a taxpayers' case to prevent the expenditure of certain funds by Congress and the Senate, Mr. Chief Justice Warren wrote that the only basis upon which this particular action was brought was that the plaintiffs were taxpayers of the United States government. Nonetheless, Chief Justice Warren found that there was, in fact, adequate standing." Judge Ritter looked up. "Tell me that again," he said.

Here was the crux, Dabney felt. He would emerge with or without standing. The basis upon which Chief Justice Warren found for the taxpayers, he explained, was "a balancing concept between the amounts of money on the one hand, with the type of legal interest on the other." If you had a taxpayers' suit where the danger to public rights was not important, but a lot of money was involved, that was a legitimate suit with good standing. "On the other hand, if the legal interest is of extreme importance, then the Court does not have to become so concerned with the financial interest." If low on one side, you had to be high on the other. Since the death penalty was the ultimate sentence, it seemed to Dabney that you did not need very much taxpayers' money to have standing. The right was so important that the sum of money could be small.

6

After that, Dabney felt stronger. Ritter did not reply, but Dabney felt standing grow underneath his toes. Now he could attack other aspects of the case.

"They say that Mr. Gilmore had a hearing before the Utah Supreme Court," said Dabney. "The only hearing had there, Your Honor, was questions to Mr. Gilmore: 'Do you want to appeal or not appeal?' And he said, 'I don't want to appeal.' They said, 'Do you know what you're doing?' He said, 'Yes, I do.' And they said, 'All right, we'll dismiss your appeal.' Now that's the hearing they had up there. The fact that Mr. Gilmore doesn't want to take an appeal does not dismiss the Utah Supreme Court from taking it. There must be mandatory, meaningful appellate review, and a twenty-minute hearing before the Utah Supreme Court cannot in any way be so construed. Regardless of what Gilmore wanted, the Utah Supreme Court had to take that case. When they didn't, we couldn't know whether the sentencing of Mr. Gilmore to death was in contravention to the Eighth and Fourteenth amendments of the United States Constitution, as interpreted by the United States Supreme Court. The only way to know if it's capricious or arbitrary is to compare Gilmore's case with every other case on appeal involving the death penalty. The Gilmore case has not been compared with anything. I'm at a loss to

understand why the Utah Supreme Court didn't even have a transcript of the trial or the sentencing."

Evans stood up. "Your Honor, we submit that it is patently illogical for the U.S. Supreme Court to rule that Mr. Gilmore has intelligently and voluntarily waived his right to appeal if, in fact, the Court is
of the opinion that he *must* have an appeal. That is patently illogical.
One completely eliminates the other in our opinion."

Dabney replied: "I think the State of Utah does not really have
an appreciation for the question we have raised. We're not concerned
with Gary Gilmore's waiver of appeal. The question is whether the
State can execute an individual in violation of the Eighth and Fourteenth amendments. Can they do it capriciously or arbitrarily? The
only way you examine that question is by comparing all death-
penalty cases at the appellate level," but at this point Judge Ritter interrupted. "I think," he said, with the first touch of acerbity in his
voice, "I think I understand it." Dabney nodded. He had been given
his warning. "With that, Your Honor, I will conclude my arguments
and simply indicate that we believe we've established what we think
is a good lawsuit. We would simply indicate that this is the last
chance we have. We respectfully request the Court to sign an appropriate Temporary Restraining Order staying the execution of Mr. Gilmore. Thank you."

The State had nothing further and Judge Ritter declared a recess
at 11:39 P.M.

7

At first Judith thought they had won. It had been such a good case,
and both sides had had a full hearing. No attempt to rush anyone,
and no innuendos from the Bench. Judge Ritter had hardly said a
word, then he had gone out. The only trouble was that now he stayed
out. When he didn't come back in twenty minutes, Judy Wolbach
began to worry.

When he didn't return in an hour, she couldn't understand what
was going on. If Ritter was taking this long, he must be ruling

against them. After Dabney's fine work, it would be very difficult for Ritter, ethically and morally, she thought, to go along with Gilmore's execution. If the Judge was taking this long, he must be ashamed to come out. Judy began to feel all over again how very weak their case had to be.

On the other side of the courtroom, Earl Dorius had come to the opposite conclusion. Precisely because the Judge was taking so long. Usually, Ritter didn't write out his opinions. He released them from the Bench. Sometimes, it was a split second after the attorneys had finished. The fact that he was writing an opinion suggested he was trying to put out a paper sufficiently well reasoned to hold up on appeal. Mike Deamer agreed with Earl. He went out to phone Bob Hansen with the prediction they would lose. If so, Hansen told Deamer, they should all go over to the State Capitol Building after the verdict was read.

It got to be a very long recess. The lawyers mingled with the news reporters. Everyone seemed uneasy. It was sinking in on Earl how extremely fatigued he felt from the last few days. One suit after another, faster than birds flying overhead.

About this time, fifty miles away, Noall Wootton went to bed. But he could not sleep. In the quiet night of Provo, he lay awake after midnight. Wootton was waiting for 6 A.M. to come and his investigator to pick him up and drive him out to the State Prison to witness the execution.

CHAPTER 33

Gilmore's Last Tape

1

About one o'clock in the morning, with everybody half asleep, Gary moved into Lieutenant Fagan's office and got a call out to Larry Schiller at the TraveLodge Motel. Schiller, who had been waiting by the phone, seized it with all the questions of the last month in his throat. "How are you, champ?" were his first words.

"All right," said Gilmore, "What do you want to ask me. What do you want to know?"

"I'd like to go over a couple of things."

"May I tell you something personally?"

"Yeah, I'd like you to tell me something personally."

"You offended my brother," said Gary, "and I don't like it."

"Yeah, I heard that on the tape," Schiller told him.

"Well, I wanted to tell you personally. I didn't like that."

Schiller thought, "He doesn't sound that mad. He's really saying, 'Let's get on with it.'"

Larry cleared his throat. "Okay, I can take it from there, okay?"

"Go ahead."

He got to the subject fast. "At this point, Gary, at one in the morning . . ."

"Pardon," said Gilmore.

"At one in the morning," Larry continued, reading off a card, "do you think you still have to hide anything about your life?"

"Like what?"

"I'm not asking you to tell me what it is, you see? I'm just asking if there's the feeling that you want to hold back something."

Gilmore sighed. "Do you have anything specific?" he asked.

"Well, let's say," said Schiller, "did you ever kill anybody besides Jensen and Bushnell?"

Maybe it was more of his romanticism, but he had the idea that if a man was about to die, he would be ready to reveal himself, and Schiller really wanted to know if Gilmore had ever killed anyone before.

"Did you?" repeated Schiller.

"No," said Gilmore.

"No," repeated Schiller. One more frustration. There was a silence. No way to continue. He had to try another line of inquiry.

"Is there anything about your relationship with your mother or father," he asked, "that is so personal to you, that even at the moment of death you'd rather not talk?" What kind of relationship could a mother have, he was thinking, that she would not come to see her son? Even if she had to arrive by stretcher! Schiller couldn't comprehend it. There had to be some buried animosity — something Gary had done to her, or she to him. If he could only get a clue to that. But nobody got to Bessie Gilmore. Dave Johnston had gone up to Portland on his own for the *L.A. Times* and couldn't speak to her. When Dave Johnston failed, you had a woman not ready to talk.

"Goddammit," said Gilmore over the phone, "I'm getting pissed off at that kind of question. I don't give a damn what anybody else has said. I've told you the fucking truth. Man, my mother's a hell of a woman. She has suffered with rheumatoid arthritis for about four years and she's never bitched about it at all. Now, does that tell you anything?"

"That tells me a fucking lot, right now," said Schiller hoarsely.

"My dad got thrown a lot in jail, when we was kids," said Gilmore. "He was a rounder. My mother would say, 'Well, he walked out,' and she let it go at that. She did the very goddamned best she could, and man, she was always there, we always had something to eat, we always had somebody to tuck us in."

"Okay," said Schiller, "I believe you."

"What about *your* mother?" asked Gilmore.

"My mother," said Schiller, "was a rough, hard woman. She worked every day. She used to put me in the movies with my brother. We'd watch movies every day while she scrubbed floors for my dad." Much of human motivation, he had decided for himself in later years, came from the idea of behavior that movie plots laid into your head. When you could make remarks that brought back those movie plots, people acted on them. So the story he told Gilmore was something of a film scene. In actuality, his family had been in financial straits for only a few years, and in that period, his mother had to scrub floors at times, but the idea of a life spent on one's knees certainly mollified Gilmore.

"My mother," said Gary, "worked as a buswoman. She didn't have any money, and she was trying to hold on to a beautiful house that we had with a nice swing-around driveway where you drive up and it makes a circle. She wanted that. She wanted some things. She lost it. When she did, she moved into a trailer. She never bitched about it."

"You really love her, man, don't you?" said Schiller.

"Goddammit, yes," said Gary. "I don't want to hear any fucking bullshit that she was mean to me. She never hit me."

At that moment there was an interruption on the phone. "Hello," said a voice. "Hello," said Gary. "Is this Mr. Fagan?" said the voice.

"Who's this?" asked Gary.

"This is the Warden."

"This is Mr. Gilmore," said Gary modestly, "I'm making a phone call that Mr. Fagan approved."

"Okay, thank you," said Sam Smith, "pardon me," and he hung up. There was something in the Warden's voice that sounded like he was just about holding on to himself. It gave Schiller the feeling he had better hurry.

Next to Schiller, lying on the floor under the table, was Barry Farrell listening to the conversation through an earpiece attached by a short wire to the tape recorder. Schiller wanted to see Barry's face and get his reactions, but all he could manage from the angle at which he sat was the occasional sight of Barry's hand writing on a 3 × 5 card.

Schiller took his last crack at the question they could not get Gilmore to respond to. "I believe you had rough breaks," said Schiller. "You got into trouble, and had a temper and were impatient, but you weren't a killer. Something happened. Something turned you into a man who could kill Jensen and Bushnell, some feeling, or emotion, or event."

"I was always capable of murder," said Gilmore. "There's a side of me that I don't like. I can become totally devoid of feelings for others, unemotional. I know I'm doing something grossly fucking wrong. I can still go ahead and do it."

It wasn't exactly the answer Schiller was hoping to hear. He wanted an episode. "I still," he said, "don't understand what goes on in a person's mind who decides to kill."

"Hey, look," said Gilmore, "listen. One time I was driving down the street in Portland. I was just fucking around, about half high, and I seen two guys walk out of a bar. I was just a youngster, man, 19, 20, something like that, and one of these dudes is a young Chicano about my age and the other's about 40, an older dude. So I said, Hey, you guys want to see some girls? Get in. And they got in the back. I had a '49 Chevrolet, two door, you know, fastback? And they got in. And I drove out to Clackamas County, a very dark . . . now I'm telling you the truth, I ain't making this up, I'm not dramatizing, I'm going to be blasted out of my fucking boots, and I swear to Jesus Christ on everything that's holy that I'm telling you the truth ver-fucking-batim. This is a strange story."

"Okay."

"They got back there," said Gary, "and I got to telling them about these broads, I was just embroidering how they had big tits and liked to fuck and had a party going and how I left the party to get some guys bring out there because they were short on dudes, and these two were about half drunk, and I drove 'em down this pitch-black fucking road, it had gravel on it, you know, not a rough road, black, smooth, flat, chipped fucking concrete, that's how I remember it, and I reached down under the seat — I always kept a baseball bat or a pipe, you know — and I reached down under the seat . . . just a minute."

Schiller was not following the story. He knew they were getting it on tape, and so he leaned over the table to see if Barry had a question for Gilmore, and as he did, he was listening to something about a pipe, a baseball bat, or whatever it was, and then he heard Gary say, "Jesus fucking Christ."

Schiller could feel a shift in the silence.

"Lieutenant Fagan just told me that Ritter issued a Stay," said Gary. "Son of a bitch. Goddamn foul motherfucker."

"Okay," said Schiller, "let's just hold this shit together. You can hold it. You've held it together before, man." Now, he wanted to hear the story.

Instead, he had to listen to Gary talking to Fagan. "Ritter definitely issued a Stay," Gary said to Larry finally. "Says it's illegal to use taxpayers' money to shoot me."

"Yeah," said Schiller softly. There was a long pause and then he declared, "You couldn't define what the roughest torture is. What Ritter just did, is." "Yeah," said Gilmore, "Ritter's a bumbling, fumbling fool. Yeah, yeah," he said, "yeah, yeah, yeah, yeah, yeah, yeah. Foul cocksuckers. A taxpayers' suit. I'll pay for it myself. I'll buy the bullets, rifles, pay the riflemen. Jesus-fucking-goddamned-Christ, man, I want it to be over." He sounded like he was close to crying.

"You have a right for it to be over," said Schiller, "an inalienable right."

"Get ahold of Hansen," said Gilmore.

"Get on the fucking phones, girls," shouted Schiller to Lucinda and Debbie. "Get an attorney in Salt Lake City named Hansen."

Gilmore said, "He's the fucking Attorney General of the State of Utah."

"Attorney General of the State of Utah, okay?" Schiller repeated to the girls.

"Tell him to go to the next highest Judge, and get Ritter's bullshit thrown out."

"Maybe," Schiller thought, "I've seen too many movies myself." He could hear his voice exhorting Gary to live. It was the kind of pep talk he had heard in many a flick.

"Gary," Schiller was saying, "maybe you're not meant to die. Maybe there's something so phenomenal, so deep, in the depths of your story, that maybe you're not meant to die right now. Maybe there are things left to do. We may not know what they are. Maybe by not dying you may be doing a hell of a lot for the whole fucking world. Maybe the suffering that you're doing now is the way you're giving back those two lives. Maybe you're laying a foundation for the way society and our civilization should proceed in the future. Maybe the punishment you're going through now is a greater punishment than death, and maybe a lot of fucking good's gonna come from it." Abruptly, he realized he was affecting himself a good deal more than he was moving Gilmore. "Oh, am I going to sound like a schmuck in the transcript," thought Schiller, and aloud he said, "You're not listening to me, are you?"

"What?" said Gary. "Yeah," he said, "I'm listening."

"Let's look at the other side of it," said Schiller, "Let's get through the next hour together. You know they're making you suffer like nobody's suffered."

Gary's voice sounded like it was close to snapping. "Do me a favor," he said. "I got to get off this fucking phone. Because Mr. Fagan wants to use it. Get ahold of your girls."

"Right."

"Give 'em each a kiss for me. Tell 'em to get ahold of Mr. Hansen. Find out what the fuck can be done to overcome that guy immediately. That fool Ritter. He'll do any given thing on any fucking given day. And call me back."

"You gotta call me," said Schiller. "I can't call you."

"I'll call you back in a half hour."

"In one-half hour. Keep your shit together."

"Yeah."

"It's shit," said Larry, "but keep it together."

"Jesus Christ," Gary replied. "Shit. Piss. Gawd!"

2

It had taken until 1 A.M. for Judge Ritter to come back to the Bench. "The Utah death penalty statute," he read aloud to everyone in the courtroom, "has not been held constitutional by any courts. . . . Until doubts are resolved . . . there can be no lawful executions. Consent of the defendant gives no power to the State to execute." It went on, and Judith Wolbach began to breathe again, and happiness went through her. The terror she liked to keep away went back to its far-off place. She could have embraced Judge Ritter. In his resonant old voice, he concluded, "There is too much uncertainty in the law and too much haste to execute the man." God, that voice sounded as good to her as old newsreels of Franklin Delano Roosevelt! Then the Judge signed the Temporary Restraining Order for Dabney and Wolbach, and set January 27th, ten days later, at 10 A.M., for a hearing on these questions.

It was a dejected gang that went back to the Attorney General's office, although Bill Barrett, Bill Evans, and Mike Deamer were trying to decide on the next step. They had all about concluded the best approach was to file a Writ of Mandamus in the morning and rush it to Denver. If they could obtain a delay from Judge Bullock, the execution could still take place tomorrow, although twelve or fourteen hours late.

3

Judge Bullock had been in Salt Lake to a social affair. On his return, before he went to sleep, he turned on the radio and heard about the Stay. To himself, he thought, "That's it." There was an unmarked Sheriff's car parked outside, and Judge Bullock went out to the street and told the fellow, "No need to hang around now. Might as well go home."

The Sheriff's office had called earlier that night to inform Judge Bullock there might be demonstrations by people opposed to the execution. They wanted to watch his house. The Judge thought, "Well, I don't have fear for my own safety, but who knows, maybe these groups might burn a cross on my lawn or something." He did not anticipate real violence, but just to protect the property, he thought he would accept the Sheriff's offer. A little surveillance might protect his wife and children from being disturbed.

Judge Bullock wasn't worried about local people. But when somebody got executed, hundreds of thousands of persons all over the country became incensed, and some might have come to town. They'd be pacifists, and not disposed to real violence, but they did have an interest in demonstrating. The Judge thought: There could be a cross on the lawn.

Now that Judge Ritter issued the Stay, however, there was no question of trouble. Bullock went to sleep thinking there would be an appeal to the United States Tenth Circuit Court, then it would go on to the Supreme Court. They would eventually debate different issues from the ones being decided now. Through his drowsiness, he told himself, "It is in the stream, and I may not live that long to have to worry about the end." Some cases went for twenty-five years. Judge Bullock fell asleep.

4

Julie Jacoby had gone home from the vigil to get a little rest before returning to the prison for the rest of the night, but she turned on the TV for a few minutes, and learned of the delay. Her husband called her right then from where he was staying at Sanibel in Florida. Said he'd seen her on television earlier. She had been filmed in the vigil. Then she got a call from an ACLU member who was planning to go out with her to the prison early next morning. This woman said, "Did you hear the news? I guess we won't be getting up so early." Julie's understanding was that Judge Ritter's ruling could not be tampered with. She, too, went to sleep.

5

In the visiting room, Stanger heard a great groan come up from the inmates in Maximum Security. It rolled down the long corridor which went from cell row to row. Stanger had completely forgotten there were all those men back in Maximum listening to the radio on their earphones. All of a sudden, you could hear the sound. He couldn't tell if they were clapping or cheering, or moaning. Some deep confused sound, like earth shifting. He could hear, "There's a Stay!" being yelled through the cell rows, and he turned on the television. At that moment, Gary came back from making a phone call and almost charged into the set. Stanger thought he was going to put his fist through it.

Cline Campbell had seen Gary get angry once or twice before. He took on wrath in a different way than most people. Gilmore's anger, Campbell had long ago decided, came from very far inside. Other men might slam a wall or grab a book and throw it down, but Gilmore would only grit his teeth and give a low growl. Then he would hold his hands and press them together as if to crush the anger. This night, when the news came through about Ritter, it looked like Gary was going to break his hands. Campbell had never seen him as angry as this.

Bob Moody had what he considered an inappropriate leap of the heart. There could have been nothing more impermissible for him to say to his client at the moment than, "Wait a second, excuse me, Gary, they don't have to kill!" But, then Bob saw the look on his face. Gary had prepared himself to receive the sentence. By what method, Moody did not know, whether by whipping his will into line, or pulling off his fears, like leaves. No matter how he had done it, the Judge had just consigned him to hell. Something began to collapse in Gary. He was more sullen, more threatening, and he had less stature. Went around saying, "I'll hang myself before eight in the morning. I'll be dead. Those shoelaces will be used." Moody had heard of the shoelaces. Stanger told him of an occasion when he and Gary had been alone in Fagan's office for twenty seconds. Fagan had had to go out for a moment. Call it less than twenty seconds, ten seconds. In that time, Gary stole a pair of shoelaces out of Fagan's desk drawer. They kept him under such guard it was not easy to steal anything nor keep it, but he had held the shoelaces these last two weeks. Now he was talking of using them.

Moody and Stanger couldn't take it anymore. They went out of Maximum Detention and over to the parking lot where they mingled with the press. Suddenly, a roar went up. A lot of TV lights started to shine on a particular car that was leaving the prison grounds. Just then, Stanger and Moody heard from a reporter that Judge Ritter had driven up to the prison with a Federal Marshal to make certain the Stay would be delivered in person to the Warden. It seemed Ritter, large and old as he was, had gotten down on the floor of the car when it passed the parking lot in order not to be visible to the press. That was typical of the Judge. Deliver the paper himself. Probably expected the Writ to slip between the floorboards if he didn't.

Now that he had just driven out of the gate, Moody and Stanger could hear the press grumbling. Furious to have been cheated of the interview of the night. Yet they were roaring at the possibilities for headlines. "Ritter Delivers the Writ," said one. "Writ Rides with Ritter," came back another. There was a funny bad taste in the back of everyone's mouth. They had been waking up in the cold to start the motors of their vans, then drinking some more, and falling asleep again. The Stay of Execution, if it held, would make this add up to one long night of suffering.

Back in the visitors' room, Moody could see that the prison, in effect, had decided, Okay, Gary, no more speed. You couldn't give it out to a man who was an ordinary resident on Death Row again. He might be around for thirty more days. So there was Gary full of anger and speed, obliged to start coming down from his high.

After a while, he went off by himself. Father Meersman had brought a recorder, and Gary had been planning all night to make a tape for Nicole to be given to her after his execution. Stanger couldn't imagine what would be on it, but didn't have long to wonder. Not a half hour later, Gary sat down close to Ron, and said, "I'll let you listen to it."

<h1 style="text-align:center">6</h1>

"Baby, I love you," the tape began. "You're a part of me, and a long time ago, we made in the month of May, vows to each other, to teachers, masters and loved ones of Nicole and Gary, because we've known each other for so long."

"This may be awfully personal," Stanger said to him.

"Just listen to it," said Gary.

He told Stanger, "You know Nicole and I talked about more personal things together than you could think of. I've discussed every personal thought I've ever had with her." He nodded. "I'd like you to have an idea of what it's like when we speak to one another."

So Stanger started listening. But the tape really got personal and sexy. About the time Gary started to talk about kissing her private parts, it entered the area of the very personal and very crude. Stanger began to protest again. "Gary, you know, it is very personal." "Well, what do you think?" Gary said. Stanger said, "I think, Gary, it's very, *very* personal."

The voice in this recording was unlike anything Ron had heard coming out of Gary before, a funny voice, fancy and phony and slurred. Every now and then it would be highly enunciated. It was as if each of his personalities took a turn, and Ron thought it was like an actor putting on one mask, taking it off, putting on another for a new voice. Sometimes Gary would sound pompous, sometimes weak and close to crying. All in all, Stanger wished he did not have to listen. Whenever Gary walked away, Ron kept turning the Fast Forward so he would not have to hear it all. Yet, it surprised him. The speech was more eloquent than you'd expect. Stanger did not know if he could ever address anyone he loved in such words.

7

"In the early morning when your mind is clear, that's the best time to know, but you're in a place like I am, you don't want to be part of ringing bells and hollering get up, get up, or we'll come in and take your bedding. I have to listen to the clanging and banging of steel and concrete and it's bullshit and I wake up and I can't, you know, think pure thoughts, these need quiet and relaxation. Hey, Elf, I love you," he said, "I want to suck your little cunt. God-fucking-damn, I was ready to die. Ohhh, the fuckers. Just remember that I love you, and like any foolish man, my head stays sort of funky and all the girls write to me, girls from Honolulu wrote to me, they're fourteen, their names are Stacy and Rory and they was just talking about fucking, smoking dope, but you know they come from good families, and one of 'em wrote, Man, tell me about Nicole. I want to know about her, and I told her, Man, she's the most beautiful, sexy girl in the world and I kept her naked most of the time 'cause she's such an elf, and a cute little elf, the elf, the elf, my elf." His voice trailed off, and then he seemed to collect himself, and told Nicole, "She wrote back and she says, Well, I got red hair and freckles, too. It was just before Christmas and I sent 'em each a hundred dollars, a Christmas gift from Gary and Nicole, they didn't ask for it, they weren't looking for nothing — it's just I like to do things like that," and he stammered a little and said, "I sent 'em each a Gary Gilmore T-shirt, and I asked 'em to wear it, or whatever, I told 'em they could wear it with nothing on underneath. A lot of girls write to me and they say different things, and love, they don't know me, if they knew me, they wouldn't love me. They're in love with the motherfucker that's got his name in the paper every day. You know, I flirt with them a little bit, but I always tell them, Ah, look, I got a girl, I didn't mean to fucking mislead your ass, but I got the most terrific girl in the world, she's part of me, nobody but you, Nicole, never, ever, ever. . . . I love you with all that I am, I give you my heart and my soul." He sighed. "I read things in the paper . . . they say this evil son of a bitch with his hypnotic, charismatic, fucking personality talked this girl into suicide . . . whew, whew . . . I'm not going to tell you what to think. Like you said, you're on that fucking forensic ward, you're watched by the posse, I think most posses, man, are shooting on you. You got some money. Baby, I took sixty fucking phenobarbital. I laid there for twelve hours. I have this pretty strong body, you know, I haven't ruined it with too much drink and smoking 'cause I've been in this ole prison so long. If they do stay my execution, I'm going to hang myself, fuck 'em in their goddamn rosy red asses." He took a breath and began to sing. He had one of the worst singing voices Stanger had ever heard, never on pitch, and Gary had no idea when he was off. When he thought to croon, he groaned. The groans strangled. When he came near a note, he was sour. Still, he began to sing "Rock of Ages." "While I draw this fleeting breath, when my eyelids close in bed . . . when I soar to worlds unknown, see Thee on my judgment time, rock of ages, let me hide myself in Thee." He stopped singing. "Oh, man, I told you I talked to Johnny Cash, god-damn." Gilmore laughed. "Johnny Cash knows I'm alive, he knows you're alive, he likes us. . . . Oh, Nicole . . . I'm not a Charlie Man-son type, I'm not swaying you to do this . . . if you want to go on liv-ing and raise your children, you're a famous girl, you've got a lot of money and I want to see you get a lot more, too, go ahead, baby, but don't let nobody fuck you." Now, he whispered, "Don't let nobody have you. Baby, don't, you're mine. Discipline, restraint — maybe a girl, I don't know, shit. . . . I was supposed to be executed at seven forty-nine. . . . I got this hymnal in front of me, you're pretty, sexy and you got something about you, baby, that just sticks right *out*. Well, I know them guys got designs, they're designing motherfuckers, take advantage of opportunities. They see you, see how pretty you are, think I'm going to be dead, they want your money, they want you, there's something about you that anybody would want, I hope, God I hope, oh my God, I just fucking hope . . . man, I want you, baby." He started to cry right there. "Oh, fuck," he whispered, "I feel so bad right now. I thought I was going to be dead in a few hours . . . free to join you . . . I don't care if you want to go on living . . . you got children, I'm not telling you . . . to come out and commit suicide, I have such a hard thing to do. . . ." Now, he whispered, "I just don't want anybody to fuck you, I want you to be mine, only, only . . . only, mine. Oh, baby, I want to be fucking free of this planet. . . . I gave all my money away, a hundred thousand dollars. . . . I didn't want to tell you about that, I didn't want to seem like I was bragging, you got more money than I do, I just want to be honest with you, I thought they was going to kill me, the chickenshit sorry cocksuckers . . . fucking sleazy motherfuckers . . ." The words wore down. He was droning into the tape recorder, "Nicole, I don't know what's happening. Maybe we're supposed to live a little longer, listen, I took everything you gave me . . . twenty-five Seconals, ten Dalmane at midnight. I don't have to but I know so many hymns. It's a Catholic hymnal . . . the priest come out last night and said a Mass, God, nothing more boring than Mass. . . . Nicole . . . you're mine, God, I feel such power in our love . . . baby, I asked you to love me with all that you are. I miss you so fucking bad, I want only you, and I swear to God, I'll have you. I ain't going to the planet Uranus. I don't care what I have to go through, the demons I have to fight, no matter whatever I have to overcome, I'm going to make myself plain to you. I don't give a shit what I have to do, torture, suffer, how many lives, you can know if I love you tenderly and softly, wildly and rowdy, naked, wrapped around me. . . ."

8

Vern had been watching Gary carefully. After everybody else began to sleep, Gary turned on the radio so loud it was practically offensive. Then he lay down and pretended to sleep himself, but it was obvious he couldn't. A little while later, he got up, shut the radio off, milled around, glowered, looked like he might throw a punch at the wall, then tried once more to sleep.

Evelyn Gray, who was a nice lady, a slender, middle-aged lady with eyeglasses and short curled red hair like she went to the beauty parlor regularly, went up to Gary now and tried to console him. "Gary," she said, "is there anything I can possibly do for you?" Gary looked up at her and said, "All I ever wanted was a little love." Evelyn Gray came away so touched, she had moved over into tears. "There you go," said Vern to himself. "All I ever wanted was a little love."

Earlier in the evening, when the guards brought Gary out from his cell to meet the company, they also, since he would not go back to Death Row, carried in his belongings. Those filled several cartons, and a number of plastic bags contained his mail. Now, after trying to rest for a little while, he got up and said to Vern, "I want to show you some stuff."

They sat there, side by side, while Gary went through trinkets and foreign coins. Then he asked Vern to help him in taping up a package for Nicole. They started to pick out letters and special items. When done, Gary rearranged the cartons. He looked up at one point and said, "Vern, if they don't do it, I'm committing suicide." Said it so quietly and evenly that Vern finally decided it would be that day and Gary wasn't going to wait too long after the hour was passed. "One way or another," Vern put it to himself, "dead before noon." They went through the papers a last time, and Gary took off the Robin Hood hat that Vern had bought him and put it in the box for Nicole. Then he taped her carton. "I want you to swear that this will all go to her," said Gary, and Vern said, "You know I'll do what you want."

CHAPTER 34

Over the Mountainous Abode

1

Earl, Bill Barrett, Mike Deamer, and the others had hardly gotten back to the office when Bob Hansen phoned. Judge Lewis, he said, had agreed to hear an appeal in the next few hours, but stipulated that that serious a decision would have to be made by a three-man Court in Denver. Therefore, Hansen was letting the boys know that all legal documents had to be finished in time for departure from Salt Lake by 4 A.M. Given the speed of a small plane, it would be a two-hour flight over the mountains, and they would get in before dawn at 6 A.M. Not much time to draft a paper of quality to submit to the Tenth Circuit Court.

All Earl could feel was fatigue. They would have to do it right there in the middle of the night, no secretaries present. Ironically, that was the worst part. They had already researched the law. By divvying up the assignments, they could certainly write the papers in the time they had. Earl, for example, could save three hours on his Writ of Mandamus because he had already drafted one back when Judge Ritter granted the *Tribune* those exclusive interviews with Gilmore in November. Now he only had to plug in the facts of the current case to procedural steps already learned. It was the simple absence of secretaries, however, that could hold you up. Schwendiman and Dorius began to type, awfully slow going. Earl had to suffer at the idea of turning in a document so filled with typographical errors to a Court as high as the Tenth Circuit Court of Appeals in Denver. While he had been told to just get any kind of paper done, still it was hellish to hand over such a sloppy piece of typewriting. He was relieved when the Salt Lake Sheriff's dispatcher sent over two girls to help.

Other problems came up. A phone call from Gary Gilmore. Of course, they didn't take it. Everybody in the office had the same reaction: Don't talk to him. All they needed was for the State to confer with the condemned man. Just the same, Earl was impressed. He had still been expecting Gilmore to say at the last second, "I want to appeal." Having conned society one way, he would turn them around at the end. But now in the bottom of the night, Earl began to believe that maybe Gilmore really wanted his sentence carried out.

A new anxiety began to weigh on the Assistant Attorney Generals. Bob Hansen planned to get them in to Denver by 6 A.M., but the execution was scheduled for today's time of sunrise, 7:49. In the hour and fifty minutes after landing, how could they drive to Court, conduct the case, and have the Judges come back with a decision? They had a law clerk named Gordon Richards spending the night out at the prison as a stand-in for Earl, and Dorius called him now. Richards said that unless Sam Smith got word by 7:15, he could not, repeat, definitely could not, bring the execution off by 7:49. Also, Gordon would need a code message like "Mickey from West Virginia," to make certain any phone calls he received from Denver were legitimate. Dorius knew that Howard Phillips, the Clerk of the Tenth Circuit, lived on Eudora Street in a suburb called Park Hill, so he gave Richards: "Eudora from Park Hill."

Now, Dorius began to research whether it was imperative that Judge Bullock's order be in fact carried out at 7:49. He looked up the appropriate statutes in the Utah code. Sure enough, the two relevant ones were in conflict. Section 77-36-6 said the Court would declare a *day* on which the execution was to take place. Another, 77-36-15, said the Warden was to execute the judgment at the specified *time*. Earl had a legal chestnut. Day versus Time.

Odds were Judge Bullock had set the execution at sunrise merely to put a little frontier flavor into the judgment. Essentially, it was gratuitous language. In this particular instance, Earl felt it could be ignored, especially since the second statute said that if the execution was not carried out on the day set, then there had to be a new time declared. That certainly seemed to indicate "time" was being used as a synonym for day. It didn't make any sense to assume that if you set a date for execution and it wasn't carried out, then the next execution had to be more specific, that is, done at a given minute. Such a practice could lead to chaos. What if you had the Warden with his hand up and he was one second late? Unworkable! Earl decided that the intent of these statutes had to signify day, not time. Judge Bullock's "at sunrise" could legally, therefore, be declared gratuitous language. That was his thinking on the problem.

He talked about it quickly with Mike Deamer. As Deputy Attorney General, Deamer would be holding the fort in Salt Lake, while Bob Hansen and Schwendiman and Barrett and Evans and himself flew to Denver. But it was a hurried conversation. They were, after all, caught in the pressure of getting out their papers. Already, they were running late. Bob Hansen's takeoff at 4 A.M. would have to be delayed. That hand moved around the clock like anxiety circulating in one's chest.

2

In Washington, Al Bronstein, an ACLU lawyer, was phoned at 5 A.M., Eastern Standard Time. That, of course, was three in the morning in Utah. The call came from Henry Schwarzschild, head of the National Coalition Against the Death Penalty, and he now told Bronstein of Bob Hansen's intention to fly to Denver. Schwarzschild had just learned the news himself and hadn't seen any papers, but he thought the Attorney General would have to apply for a Writ of Mandamus against Judge Ritter, and he wanted Bronstein to go to the Supreme Court and be available there in the event the Tenth Circuit did overturn the Judge. So, Bronstein spent the last of this night trying to prepare legal papers without knowing the name of the case, nor the caption on it. Completely without the starting point of Who versus Whom. He called the Supreme Court which, by law, technically, was open 24 hours a day, but there was no answer.

Somewhere after four in the morning, Phil Hansen got out of bed and put the radio on, and God, all of a sudden, he could hear this thing on KSL that the Attorney General, and every other principal were going to fly over to Denver. Of course, he phoned Ritter and the Judge said he should have second-guessed it, should have known in his dreams they would pull that. At any rate, the more they discussed the situation, the less risky it seemed. As they calculated the time, there wasn't any means by which the Tenth Circuit would be able to get through every step before 7:49. It was hardly more than three hours away now. Not possible to execute him on time. The Tenth Circuit, at worst, would resentence him for the future. Tomorrow, thought Phil Hansen, there would be time to put his wheels in motion for the citizens' suit.

3

Judith Wolbach and Jinks Dabney had not been prepared for Denver. They had gone out into the street from Judge Ritter's Court arm in arm, but when they got to the plaza, it was jammed with newsmen. They had to run to Jinks's office to get away. Judith liked press people, but Jinks didn't, had a distaste of getting bogged down in something like that, so they fled to the library. The press was already in his outer office. Then a call came from Jinks Dabney's wife to say that Bob Hansen wanted to notify him about the new move.

Judith stayed in the library trying to check out procedures in the Tenth Circuit Court while Jinks called the airlines. He came back to say there were no commercial flights. Therefore, he couldn't go. Bob Hansen had procured a plane, but it was uninsured. He would not fly in it. Judy said, "Jinks, you're the one with Circuit experience. Far better for you to handle this case." Dabney told her nothing was worth it. He wouldn't take that kind of personal risk.

She was quite surprised. Of course, there was quite a count of people you heard about through the years, who got smashed to bits flying light aircraft over the Rockies. You could even take the view there were spooks in the mountains. It was a phobia she had run across before, and normally she could almost sympathize, but right now, her problem was that she didn't know enough law. She would have to stand up and and argue all by herself in Tenth Circuit Court. Never been to Tenth Circuit before, or any other Circuit. God, it was like leaving her alone on an expert trail. Hey, she felt like yelling, I'm just an ex–anthropology student. This law is too rarefied for me.

She hardly knew the man, but it was crystal clear Jinks was not going to fly in that little plane. "Nothing is worth it," he repeated quietly.

Before she left, Judy Wolbach grabbed a copy of the Tenth Circuit rules and a couple of volumes from *American Jurisprudence*. That was sort of a ground-level legal encyclopedia. She and Jinks did get through on the phone to some ACLU lawyers in Denver who had considerable experience with the Tenth, and they promised to meet her at the Federal Courthouse. They would argue the technical aspects, they said. Judy was impressed with the ACLU people in Denver. What a gift to have such good lawyers ready to pitch in on short notice.

Getting to the plane, however, turned out to be gross. Hansen called to say he would pick her up and they would drive together to Judge Lewis's house, then all go out to the airport. Judy had no desire to fly with the Attorney General's people, but there was no choice. So Hansen came by, picked her up, and she began to do a slow boil. Instead of traveling west toward the airport, they had to cut back all the way across Salt Lake to the East Bench for Judge Lewis. This was time Judith could have used doing research instead of pooting around these Ivy League streets, Harvard Avenue and Yale Crest, with these big homes patterned after New England townhouses. All Judy was seeing were a lot of empty elm tree branches waving in the middle of the night. Thought it was petty of Hansen to pull a trick like this, and almost told him so except Hansen would probably say he wanted a witness to the fact he had no prior conversation with the Judge.

Well, in the time it took him to walk up to the Judge's door, which was set back quite far on the lawn, and then chat with the man in the vestibule before they finally came out to the car, he had time to say anything he wanted. Talk of influencing the man, Hansen and Judge Lewis were into fishing, and how things were going in each other's office, and Judy was thinking, Boy, I'd really like to get a word in edgewise and tell the Judge what's going on, but no, Hansen was speaking of Judge Lewis's wooden golf clubs. Judy heard them go back and forth about drivers and niblicks, and how wood was coming into its own again. The man's world! She ought to ask the Judge about some tournaments he'd been in, and say, By the way, I've got this client I'd just as soon you didn't shoot.

She had heard Lewis was a Utah Republican appointed to the Tenth Circuit by President Eisenhower. He was sure conservatively dressed, a modest, keen-looking, clean-shaven face, a silver fox. Had the kind of gray demeanor that would make him perfectly happy in a boardroom some place. Right now, he and Bob Hansen were talking like sixty about everything but the case. All very nice and fair, but she had a recollection of Judge Lewis's being quoted in the papers about Judge Ritter. Something uncomplimentary.

At the Salt Lake Airport, they drove around the main terminal out to one of the small light plane depots. When they arrived, it was only to discover that Hansen's deputies were not yet there. Judge Lewis looked somewhat concerned about the time.

4

Dorius, Barrett, Evans, and Schwendiman had all been waiting for the last pages to be Xeroxed. At 4 A.M., Schwendiman put the documents in a cardboard box, and they raced through the halls to the exit. Newsmen surrounded them outside, and the glare of camera lights. A Highway Patrol car was waiting by the south door. They were off. Turning on his flasher, the trooper took a route to the airport through back streets Earl had never seen before. They must have traveled 60 miles an hour past those sleeping homes.

On arrival, they were caught up in a roaring of questions from newspapermen, and shouts, noise, and blue-white lights so intense neither Dorius or Schwendiman could see where they were going as they followed the others out of the hangar, across the tarmac and into the plane, a twin-engine King-Air which they boarded about 4:20 A.M. amid another flurry of newsmen and lights. Bob Hansen, Bill Barrett, Bill Evans, Dave Schwendiman, Jack Ford who was a newsman with KSL, Judge Lewis, Judy Wolbach and Earl took off almost immediately. By now they were running ten minutes late.

Soon as they were airborne, Bob Hansen began this conversation with the copilot. Wanted to know the speed of the plane, the velocity of the tailwinds, and the anticipated arrival time. Then, he asked the pilot to check on his radio to see if taxis would be there to meet them. Did the drivers know exactly which part of the airport to go to? Were they up on the best route to the courthouse? He wasn't leaving anything to chance.

What made it all the more annoying to Judy was the way they were seated. Judge Lewis, in order to avoid getting into, or even hearing, conversations with either side, had selected the most uncomfortable spot on the plane, a little jump seat at the back that was terribly cramped. Then there was a reporter in front of him. Then a long curving seat like a bench running from fore to aft so you sat sideways. Judy had been placed there between Hansen and Schwendiman, which couldn't help but give her a little claustrophobia. If there was one lawyer she was not mad about in the State of Utah, it was Bob Hansen. He had such a strong, righteous groundwave, a good-looking man with a stiff, numb face, dark horn-rimmed glasses, black hair, business suit, all saying, "I am a total bureaucrat, total executive, total politician." That was Judy's kindly view of him.

Schwendiman on the other side was all right, she thought, a sweet man, really, whom she had known in law school, but she didn't want to embarrass him now by admitting to any friendship. Across the aisle was that eager beaver, Dorius, just as neat as a terrier with a mustache, all perky and ready to go, and Bill Evans, another lamb in the mold of gung ho. Then Bill Barrett, a tall skinny fellow with glasses and a mustache. God, she was surrounded by Attorney Generals and Assistant Attorney Generals, and were they dumb!

Right in front of her, Hansen was asking Dorius if he had done any research on delay of execution, and there again, right in front of her, Dorius replied that the relevant cases seemed to indicate an execution was legal even if it took place after the exact hour and minute. Hansen said this information ought to be communicated to Warden Smith. Judith then said, did Hansen really think it fair to place that heavy a burden with the Warden, "on such dubious grounds"?

It had been tense enough in the cockpit before this. Adversary lawyers should never be thrust so close together before an important hearing, especially in a pukey little plane, but after "dubious grounds," the atmosphere was heavy. Hansen did not respond to her directly, yet a little later, he instructed Schwendiman to get to a phone as soon as possible after landing to telephone the Warden and Judge Bullock and County Attorney Wootton so that they could arrange for the order of execution to be amended. Then he dictated the language to be used: "At such time later on this date, when the legal impediment shall be removed, or as soon as possible thereafter." Judith took out a pad and pencil to write his words down. She expected Hansen to react when she stated that she was recording his instructions verbatim, but he didn't make a move. Merely told Schwendiman to be sure that Ron Stanger was also asked to stipulate to this amendment.

Hansen was worrying again about the scheduling of the execution. "As soon as we get there," he repeated to Schwendiman, "I want you on the phone." Judith was thinking: The Utah law says you must go before the Court, but it's all being done by telephone. This is spooky.

She decided to be as nasty as she could. Kept turning to them with a smile to ask, "What did you say again?" Hansen would reply, "I said to call this person," gave the name. She wrote it all down. She was feeling awfully hostile. When he asked the pilot if the motor was in good enough shape to keep up its present air speed, she thought: It ought to be, brother. It's half Mormon-owned, just like half of downtown.

Mormonism, thought Judy, plain old primitive Christianity. So literal. She thought of devout Mormons, like her grandparents, still wearing undergarments they never took off, not even when they went to bed or copulated. Once a week, maybe, they dared to expose their skin to the contaminating air. Might just as well be Pharisees. Always the letter of the law.

She hated blood atonement. A perfect belief for a desert people, she thought, desperate for survival, like those old Mormons way back. They had believed in a cruel and jealous Lord. Vengeful. Of course, they grabbed onto blood atonement. She could hear Brigham Young saying, "There are sins that can be atoned for by an offering on an altar . . . and there are sins that the blood of a lamb, or a calf, or of a turtle dove, cannot remit. They must be atoned for by the blood of a man."

Yessir, satisfy your blood lust, and tell yourself you were good to the victim because blood atonement remitted the sin. You gave the fellow a chance to get to the hereafter, after all. This business of living for eternity certainly contributed to capital punishment, brutality, and war. Why, Brigham Young with his countless wives pining on the vine had the gall to state that if you discovered one of your women in adultery, it would behoove you as a good and Christian act to hold her on your lap and run a knife through her breast. That way she'd have her whack at the hereafter. Wouldn't be relegated to the outer darkness. Judy made a noise of disgust. Primitive Christianity! She was glad she'd gone to Berkeley.

5

After Ms. Wolbach stopped asking questions, Earl went over portions of his oral argument, then tried to get a little sleep. But it was a dark night and a bumpy flight. A very strong tailwind kept slamming them through more and more turbulence. With the engines now souped up to full thrust, a full load of sound vibrated through the cabin. Dorius began to worry that the craft might be getting unmanageable. It certainly was flying in heavy, erratic fashion. Fifteen or twenty minutes from Denver, they hit exceptionally powerful turbulence, and dropped several hundred feet in one big jolt. Dorius happened to be looking to the rear when it happened, and saw Judge Lewis fly up in the air, bang his head against the low ceiling, and immediately throw the documents he was reading onto the floor so he could hold onto the roof of the fuselage and keep from banging his head again.

Earl was terrified. The sound was the most violent caterwauling of wind and motor, and the turbulence had to be the worst he had ever flown through. The thought passed through his head, Boy, if I go down and Gilmore lives — wouldn't that be something!

Earl didn't see God as rewarding people for righteousness or punishing them for misconduct. In fact, it might even be the reverse. Religion didn't make you safer, not that way. The current leader of the Mormon Church, Spencer Kimball, had had, for instance, a life of one tragedy after another. His mother died when he was twelve, and he came down, in later years, with throat cancer, and half his throat was removed. Yet, he continued to be an orator. Then, he had open-heart surgery. A man of impeccable virtue, but he had passed through one catastrophe after another. It could be that the more righteous you were in your life, the greater the challenge you posed for the Adversary. The Adversary worked harder to get at righteous people. So this turbulence, while Earl wouldn't dignify it as a force any greater or more sinister than natural elements, was still cause for some private thoughts. This was the worst plane trip ever.

On the jump seat, sitting literally on a padded cushion over the john, Judge Lewis was having his own rough trip, and after he banged his head, decided to bum a cigarette. In his job, traveling the six-state Circuit, he had flown a million miles, but hadn't been in a prop plane for a long time. Whether it was the noise, or the way neither he nor Mrs. Lewis had gotten any sleep since Saturday afternoon, the phone going constantly after that Athay hearing, calls ringing in at ungodly hours — newspapers had a right to know what was going on in a Federal Court — he found himself looking for the solace of a cigarette. Hadn't wanted one this bad in a year.

Then, he had had to wake Breitenstein in Denver at 2 A.M. this night to tell him they must be in Court at dawn, and listen to Breitenstein use a few words you couldn't call judicial. It was no news with which to wake a colleague. Still, something had to be done about Gilmore. These Stays were beginning to come under the head of cruel and unusual punishment.

Judge Lewis broke down. Maybe the bump on the head did it. That roller-coastering through typhoon gulch. He called forward for a cigarette, and the pilot replied that he had a whole carton, why not take a pack? The Judge did, lit his first cigarette in a year, and knew before he lit his second that he was smoking again, and would be for quite a while. Lighting that cigarette was like going home.

Judge Lewis's father had been a Judge and his older brother a lawyer, and he had grown up with never a question in his mind that he, too, would be a lawyer, and possibly a Judge. In his family, the law was equal to a feeling for one's own land. It gave roots. So Lewis always felt he understood Ritter to some degree. Lewis had even studied under Ritter at the University of Utah Law School. He could comprehend Ritter's ruling tonight. You wouldn't find Lewis highly critical of a Judge who thought any execution was outrageous. Why, working against the clock in a capital case had to be the most traumatic thing a Judge could get into. You always needed time to feel free and clear of any sentiment that the examination had not been sufficiently thorough.

This morning, however, they would have to come to grips with the other possibility. Maybe it was cruel to put Gilmore through his execution again and again. Lewis lit his third cigarette. That shifted his thoughts.

Now he was worrying whether an execution today, the first in many, many years, would be an encouragement to return to the old bloodbath. Would this start a new bang, bang, bang and get rid of a lot of men on Death Row in a hurry? That could hardly aid any world image of the United States. Lewis was glad two of his brothers would be sitting in Denver with him for this one.

6

The plane arrived just ten minutes late, and Judy decided the only way to hold up proceedings now was to fall down while disembarking and break her leg. Then they'd have to stop. Of course, they might not. Anyway, she was too big a coward. Before she'd break her own leg, she'd have to be her own client.

They taxied to a halt at the Beechcraft-Texaco Small Plane Airport. At the parking area, some extremely bright spotlights were on, and as they stopped, more lights came up, and the atmosphere, Dave

Schwendiman noted, became surrealistic. They had departed out of such a scene in Salt Lake, and now they were back in the same scene. Had crossed through a dark sky in a terrible storm only to return to incandescence on the ground. The door to the plane came open, bright as the lights in a dream of spotlights. Media-men everywhere. Blinded, the lawyers headed toward taxicabs waiting with their motors running.

At the courthouse, other media-men swarmed over the plaza with movie cameras and microphones. An anchorman from Salt Lake City, Sandy Gilmour of Channel 2, had taken his own plane and flown to Denver ahead of them. Now, he kidded them. What took so long? Good God! Other comedies ensued. Judge Lewis had difficulty obtaining entrance to the building. The security guard on duty only worked nights and he had never seen the Chief Justice of the Tenth Circuit before. So the guard wasn't in a rush to let anybody in at this hour.

Finally, the doors were opened and the Judge told them to take the elevators to the fourth floor. They literally had a footrace with the media to the courtroom.

7

About this time, close to 9 A.M. in Washington, Al Bronstein arrived at the office of the Clerk of the Supreme Court, Michael Rodak, with a handwritten application addressed to Justice White. Bronstein had captioned his paper, "The Honorable Willis W. Ritter vs. The State of Utah," and told Mr. Rodak that they had a peculiar procedural posture here. To his knowledge, the Court of Appeals in Denver had not yet acted, but time was running short, and he wanted to be here with the paper in case there was need for it. Rodak said, "Fine, we'll wait together," and set up a little temporary office for Bronstein.

CHAPTER 35

Dawn

1

Toni had gotten home from the prison early enough to have a little time with Howard before he had to be up at 4:30 to start for south Utah and Monday morning's work. Under these circumstances, however, they hardly had any sleep before they were out of bed again.

Then back at the prison this third visit, they told her it was too late to see Gary again. His visitors, she was told, would soon be leaving Maximum so they couldn't bring her in. That was ridiculous. They kept her waiting a long time in Minimum Security before Dick Gray was brought in and said, "Toni, don't try to get back. Remember him like you did last night." She shook her head. "I got to say goodbye." "No," Dick Gray told her, "that could just make it harder for Gary to go to his execution. If you break down, maybe he would too." At that moment, Toni had the feeling Gary was real scared, and didn't want to die.

When Schiller got to the gate at 5:45, the guards couldn't believe it. "I never went in last night," Schiller said. "Oh," they said, "yes, you did."

"Well," Schiller agreed, "yeah, I went in at five-thirty, but I came out five minutes before six." That was his answer. They shrugged. They knew he was lying, but what could they do? An officer came to guide him to the holding area. Schiller parked his car and they began to walk all the way down to Minimum Security in the ice-cold night with the sun just starting to stir somewhere beyond the ridge. It was dark still, but the sky was turning pale way to the east.

In these mountains, it might be only half an hour to the dawn, but two hours to the rise of the sun, and Schiller kept walking. The guard was really nice. He seemed to sense that Schiller hadn't slept for a long time, and said, "If you want to stop and rest, you can."

Schiller didn't know whether they were all getting near some kind of release, but this guard had a nice personality. "You want some coffee?" he asked. Just a guard walking him down, but Schiller was feeling a calm and a serenity he had never experienced in a prison before. It was five minutes to six, and when he turned around, the sky had come up another shade of blue from dark to light. There was a clear light on the eastern horizon and the buildings of the prison around him began to feel like a monastery.

They led him to the visitors' room in Minimum Security, where he was one of the first to enter. As he sat and thought of the notes he was going to have to take on the execution, he reached inside his pocket to get his pad, the very pad he'd taken out with him two days before when he decided to write without looking at the paper, but all he had with him was his checkbook. He would have to take notes on the backs of checks. At that recognition, his bowels flared up like a calf bawling. Of all the fat-ass things to do. There were tears in his eyes from the effort of holding his gut through the spasm. If a reporter ever saw him now with checks in hand.

There was a bathroom near the visitors' room, and his condition had him going back and forth every five minutes. In addition, he had a near to overwhelming desire to urinate, but nothing was coming out. Nothing. All his insides were fucked up. He had never felt like this in his life. Everything was going crazy.

2

Mike Deamer, who had stayed behind in Salt Lake, was holed up in his office with whatever library he could get together to research the question of how late past sunrise you could still have a lawful execution. He was getting more and more discouraged to discover he could find nothing. If Deamer was the man to sweat, now was the time, there alone with such an important argument to make, and no materials to base it on. At 6:30 however, a call came from Schwendiman in Denver with Hansen's message. They would not have to rely on a legal opinion if Noall Wootton could get Judge Bullock to rewrite his order.

Wootton had lain in his bed through the night, hating the thought of morning. Felt like there was no reason for him to witness the shooting. Didn't want to. Days ago, he had conferred with Judge Bullock, who interpreted the word "invite" in the statute as an offer that could not be refused. Wootton went to another Judge who said. "You've got a moral obligation. You started it." Still another Judge remarked, "Tell them to go to hell." So, Noall spoke to Warden Smith and said, "I respectfully decline the invitation." Sam Smith replied, "I'd appreciate it very much if you'd be here. The Attorney General says it should be you." That was it.

The hours went by. He didn't sleep, but then he didn't turn on television or radio either. It was only when Brent Bullock, his investigator, arrived in the morning to accompany him to the prison that he heard of Ritter's Stay and decided to go out anyway and see what was happening.

When he popped into Administration he learned that Bob Hansen had gone to Denver. Just as the Warden asked what to do in the event they weren't ready to proceed by 7:49, a call came from Deamer in Salt Lake. They wanted Noall to get the language changed in the Death Warrant.

Judge Bullock, however, had to be brought up to date. He was startled. Had not expected anybody to take an airplane in the middle of the night. Didn't think you could get Judges out of bed for things like that (nor out of a bar, for that matter) but didn't even voice the thought to himself. Now Noall was asking if he were ready to change his order of execution because of the sunrise problem. Judge Bullock didn't have time to ponder it, but felt the old agonizing begin to come back. You don't have to sentence him again, he told himself,

that decision has already been made. The only question now is the
hour. So he said yes to Wootton — he would change the order, and
even remembered how back in October he had set the time for eight
in the morning, but by December when they ran past the sixty days,
the Warden said, "If we ever do this again, can you make it sunrise?
Eight o'clock interferes with breakfast and cleaning up in the prison.
It sure would help from the standpoint of administration to have it
real early." Judge Bullock had said, "Sure, any time, early or late.
Have it at midnight, it's all right with me." Sunrise was just a military thing; there wasn't a good hour to execute anybody. You didn't
have to be the devoutest Mormon in the world to feel a little uneasy
at consigning a man to death when you might have to meet him on
the other side.

3

About ten of seven, some guards came into the visiting room at Maximum Detention and told everybody they would have to say good-bye
to Gary. The Warden had sent word to proceed as though the execution was on. So they began to get him ready. Of course, until word
came from Denver, nobody would know for sure. It was a funny
leave-taking, therefore. Kind of scattered. Evelyn and Dick Gray had
already left, and now Ron and Vern went out through the double gate
and into a waiting car. Cline Campbell and Bob Moody remained,
while Gary shook hands with his regular guards. Even put his arm
around one. "You've been great, you know," he said, and to another
he grinned, and stated, "You're sort of a black bastard, but I like you
anyway." The black guard took it with good humor. Here were these
tough, rough young fellows and they were almost crying. Then this
other damned gang of officers had to come in. They stood there with
shackles in their hands, dressed in maroon jackets, real big fellows,
and Gilmore turned to them, and said, "Okay, start."

He was calm. He put out his hands and Campbell left to go
to the waiting car. After Cline passed through the gates, however,
he turned around and could see a scuffle going on. Over the leg
shackles.

Moody saw it clearly. "Look," said Gary to the guards, "I'll walk out. You don't really need those things." The guards were saying, "This is prison procedure. We're following orders." It was a mistake. Gary was all the way down from the speed by now. Just about crashing. It was the wrong time to push.

Before it was over, it looked like a gang rape. It was like he had to have one final fight to show the guards he was not going to take it ever again. Moody wanted to cry out, "Couldn't you just come in and say, 'Okay, Gary, it's time,' and see if he'll walk out like a man? If he doesn't, then go to the shackles? Dumb dumb gorillas." They kept grabbing ahold of Gary, and Gary kept saying, "I'm not ready to go yet." He was looking to pick up some last object, whatever it was. Then they seized him and took him through another door. Other guards were requesting Moody to exit, and he passed outside and into the vehicle that would carry him to the appointed place.

Mickey from Wheeling, and Eudora from Park Hill

1

As soon as the Attorney General's people were in the courtroom, the panel of three Judges came out from their chambers. With Lewis were Judges William E. Doyle and Gene S. Breitenstein. Earl glanced at his watch. It was ten to seven.

Bob Hansen stood up, introduced his assistants, and began to present the basic background. One of the Judges interrupted. Would he get immediately to the merits? Bob nodded, and asked Earl to present the first portion of the case.

Earl started to make his opening comment. At that point, Judge Lewis looked down from the high bench and remarked that no one was present for the ACLU. It was bewildering. Their counsel table was empty. No one knew where they were. That left Earl up on the podium by himself.

He was furious. Everybody had to recognize the urgency. The ACLU must be deliberately attempting to delay the hearing. Earl stood there, three minutes, five minutes, six, then seven minutes ticking away. The longer he waited, the angrier he became. Finally, Judy entered the courtroom with the other ACLU attorneys, and he glared at her. In fact, he got into a staring contest with her. She stared back in equal fury.

2

Coming into the building, the first thought in Judy's head had been, Where do I meet my people? Everything was up in the air. The separate parts of the case had been assigned on the telephone. Now, soon as she got into the lobby, a charming young lady whose name she never caught whisked Judy down the hall to four ACLU lawyers who were waiting for her in the attorneys' lounge. They had just barely sat down when Schwendiman came rushing in with the Clerk and said, "They've started. You're wanted in Court." Oh, my God, thought Judy, what a way to start out, Contempt of Court already.

Then she tried to walk in without being too obtrusive about it, but the atmosphere was pompous. The Judges were wearing robes and sitting way up on a bench higher than any she'd ever seen before. Must have been six feet above the floor. Looking up to address them, you felt as if you were on your knees.

Then Dorius began to glare at her. At seven o'clock in the morning! Judy could always put on a perpetual glare at that hour. She just said to herself, "I hate and despise him," and glared back as good as she got.

Earl proceeded through his opening statement. "Members of the Court," he said, "we have a severe time problem. Mr. Gilmore is scheduled to be executed at seven-forty A.M." It was now 7 A.M.

Judge Lewis informed him he would have fifteen minutes to offer argument, but Earl didn't take ten. The pressure, he felt, was intensifying his argument. He said plaintiffs had commenced their action at 9 P.M. the evening before, and that was a little late to be concerned about a dramatic abuse of the rights of taxpayers. He felt full of the truth of this remark. "The ACLU," he continued, "is using the device of a taxpayers' action for the purpose of delaying a lawful exercise of State power." He felt attuned to his indignation. No standing, no standing whatsoever!

Judge Ritter, he argued, had grossly abused judicial discretion. Nobody had been able to demonstrate that any specific Federal monies were being spent on this execution. Moreover, Judge Ritter had assumed that the Utah statute was unconstitutional. Yet the constitutionality of this statute had, in effect, been before the United States Supreme Court already. The Court would hardly have ruled that Gary Gilmore could waive his right to appeal if they thought the statute defective.

Bill Barrett was supposed to speak next and show why the ACLU had no standing. The Court, however, said they wanted to hear from the ACLU first. So, Steve Pevar, one of the ACLU lawyers, tried to plead that this case was not properly before the Court. He had been back and forth on the phone with Jinks Dabney from three in the morning until dawn, and they had come to the opinion that the State of Utah couldn't ask for a Writ of Mandamus because Ritter had not acted beyond his authority. If the Governor of the State of Utah had been ordered to move the Capitol Building three blocks south because some little law was being broken, that would fit Mandamus. But this, at least on the face of it, was a bona fide lawsuit. A motion had been made and granted. Why, the Attorney General's office wouldn't have even dared to bring in a Writ of Mandamus if it wasn't Willis Ritter. So the more Dabney and Pevar discussed it, the more they felt in good shape.

When Pevar tried to bring out these arguments, however, Judge Breitenstein grew incensed. Ooh, Judith couldn't believe the man's face. "I know what the law is here," he told Pevar. "What do you think we've been reading since five-thirty this morning?" Classic. A young lawyer being keelhauled by an old Judge. "We don't need you to instruct us on the law, blah, blah, we've heard enough from you, blah, blah. Please get on with the merits of the case." That was how Judith heard it. One testy Judge. Pevar kept trying to get back to the point that you couldn't slap Writs of Mandamus on Judges for too little, but the Court did not accept it. Another few minutes, and the ACLU was warned that they were prolonging the case. One of their attorneys stood up then, and said Ms. Wolbach would proceed.

Judith gave her case. It was just a rush and a repeat of what Jinks had presented, and she glared at Earl Dorius as she presented her points. He irritated her profoundly this night, but not because of anything he had done. It was because he thought he was right.

When Judith sat down, another member of the ACLU team spoke against the death penalty in general. The Justices cut him short. Now the case started rushing faster and faster. Bill Barrett tried again to discuss the issue of standing, but the Court said they were familiar with that. Would the Attorney General's office move ahead? Bill Evans began to defend the constitutionality of Utah's statute. The Judges stopped him. That issue was not, they said, relevant to the case before them. It was getting more and more abrupt. When one of the ACLU lawyers tried to discuss capital punishment, the Panel cut him off, and declared a recess. The Judges would now write their opinion.

Just before he left the Bench, Judge Lewis spoke. "Among other people who have rights," he said, "Mr. Gilmore has his own. If an error is being made in having the execution go forward, he has brought it upon himself." Then they went out.

Now, Earl Dorius turned to Dave Schwendiman and told him to get Gordon Richards on any phone he could find. He would first have to identify himself with the code words "Eudora from Park Hill," and then tell Gordon to wait on the line. Schwendiman went out immediately to the Clerk's office, trying all the while to walk rather than run. No one but a secretary was there, so he sat down at an unoccupied desk and placed a collect call to Richards at Utah State Prison. After he gave the password, he said it looked like they were going to prevail. Keeping the line open, they chatted and Richards told him how cold the night had been, and that the van which would carry Gilmore and the automobile that would transport the witnesses were both ready, respectively, outside Maximum and Minimum Security. Their motors were on.

Waiting in the courtroom for a verdict, Earl was certain his side had won. He even felt calm for the first time in the last several days, and turned to Bob Hansen and started thanking him for pushing them all to do the job, and getting to Denver. As he spoke, he had so much more emotion than expected that he had a momentary panic he might look tearful. He was certainly thankful to have an Attorney General who was willing to get this involved in a case and wasn't hesitant to push his staff to their utmost limits.

The Judges were back in three minutes. They did not read their verdict. The Clerk of the Court, Howard Phillips, did it for them in a dry offhand voice. As he spoke, Judy thought that of all the things they did not do, they didn't have a Court Reporter. There would be no transcript. Awful. Zap! The Judges had moved out. Zap! They had moved back. She sat there, listening to the Clerk.

"It is ordered: One, the Writ of Mandamus is granted. The Temporary Restraining Order entered at about 1:05 this morning by the Honorable Willis W. Ritter, Judge of the District Court of the State of Utah, is vacated, set aside, and held for nought. The Honorable Willis W. Ritter is ordered to take no further action in any manner, of any kind, involving Gary Gilmore unless such matter is presented by the duly accredited attorney for Gilmore, or by Gilmore himself. Done at 7:35 A.M., January 17th, 1977."

Earl raced out of the courtroom, banged into a couple of newsmen, screamed at them to get out of his way.

Dave Schwendiman heard a rush in the hallway, and Earl came tearing in, seized the phone, and said to Gordon Richards that the Writ had been granted. The prison should commence all activity necessary to carry out the execution.

On the other end of the line, Richards sounded extremely tense. He kept asking whether this was final and whether the other side was going to appeal to the Supreme Court. Earl kept repeating in greater detail precisely what had happened, and told Richards to order the execution to commence. Gordon said it would take at least half an hour. Was it essential that it be carried out by sunrise? Cause they couldn't make it by then. Dorius said the conclusion reached was that the only thing essential was the day, not the time of day. Richards still seemed unsure. Said he would speak to Deamer. Dorius agreed. Check it with Deamer.

Richards, however, still sounded tense. Could the ACLU, he asked, obtain a Stay in the next half hour from the U.S. Supreme Court?

They could. Unlikely, but possible. Such a message, said Dorius, if it came, would arrive from the Supreme Court itself. "'Mickey from Wheeling, West Virginia" would be calling. Richards repeated that he would call Deamer.

Then the ACLU attorneys came running in. They wanted to call the Supreme Court. Howard Phillips, who had arrived with them, said, however, that it was not permitted to use his phone. Immediately, the ACLU guys laid a finger on Earl. He had been using it, they said, why couldn't they? Phillips replied that he had not known, and asked Earl to get off. He did, promptly. By that time, Phillips was so unhappy he told the ACLU people he had a pocket full of quarters. They were welcome to use them for a coin phone.

After they were gone, Dorius went out to the hall and looked out one of the windows in the corridor of the fourth floor. He could see reporters down in the plaza below interviewing Bob Hansen. The sun was coming up in Denver, and Dorius felt a real warm sense of gratification that the argument just presented was the best they could have made under the circumstances. By his reflection in the window, he noticed he had a growth of whiskers, and his eyes were bloodshot. He needed a bath, but he felt good.

Judge Lewis was thinking it had been very unpleasant. Probably the most traumatic and emotional few moments he had ever had on the Bench. Then he said to himself, "Well, the Supreme Court never got into it. They had every opportunity, but they didn't." There was a reasonable certitude that he and his two brothers of the Bench were right.

CHAPTER 37

Going Down the Road

1

Gordon Richards called Mike Deamer at 7:35 A.M. and said Denver had lifted Ritter's Stay. Could they now go ahead with the execution? Deamer had a complete sense of surprise. He shouted into the phone, "They did?!" He was totally shocked.

Deamer had never expected it to happen that fast. He half thought it would be pushed off another thirty days, or if it did take place it would be much later in the morning. Near noon, say, there might be clear word. Now, however, he recovered quickly and told Richards the Warden could move. Richards, however, was troubled. He said the American Civil Liberties Union was trying an appeal to the Supreme Court. Should they wait on that? Deamer replied that the only lawful order in effect at present was Judge Bullock's revised time of execution. He did not see any legal impediment to going ahead. They were not required by law to anticipate a Stay from any Court, including the Supreme Court. Deamer knew it was going to take at least half an hour to move Gilmore from Maximum Security over to the cannery. Since Denver had spoken, he saw no reason not to get started.

As soon as he and Richards were finished speaking, however, he did call the Tenth Circuit and spoke directly to Howard Phillips, asked him to verify the Court Order. Phillips read it aloud to him over the phone. Right after, a UPI reporter who had Deamer's private office number rang up for an interview. Deamer said he would call back, but the reporter kept asking questions, not rude but persistent enough that, finally, to get off the phone, Deamer had to say, Yes, we're going to execute him. Didn't want to refuse the reporter entirely.

Around 7:55, Gordon Richards called again. Gilmore had now been moved to the execution area, and Sam Smith was ready to proceed. What did Deamer advise? Again, Mike was surprised at how fast everything was moving. He confirmed to Richards that he had heard nothing about any other Stays, and told Richards to go ahead. Call him as soon as it was over.

Deamer felt it was important that he take the responsibility. Gordon Richards was just a third-year law student. If he gave legal counsel to the prison, in something as big as this, it could prove a deterrent on his later ability to practice law. The State Bar Commission would never forgive a student for rendering advice. So Deamer was making it clear that he, Deamer, was the one saying, Execute Gilmore. If the ACLU later filed a Wrongful Death action, he would be the man who had taken the responsibility. Deamer could, of course, have tried to get in touch with Bob Hansen, but Bob and he thought very much alike on nearly all topics, and he was certain Bob would not say anything different than he had. So, he thought, let them sue us. They know where to find us.

Now, he could also have called Governor Matheson to ask if there was any change of mind in that quarter, but he had had a couple of conversations with the man already, and the Governor's position was that he didn't want to get involved. So why give him the opportunity now? For all he knew, Matheson was home in bed asleep. Deamer didn't want to wake the Governor and have him sit there early in the morning and possibly get disturbed, and suddenly decide, Yeah, I'd better do something, and call the prison. He thought he'd just as soon keep the Governor out of it entirely.

All the while, Deamer was hoping that they would get it done close to 7:49. Bringing it in near to sunrise would make the problem cleaner. While Deamer was familiar with Earl Dorius's argument that *time* meant day, he also thought there was a counterargument which would claim that there had to be some degree of specificity to an order. If the other side ever raised the issue that Judge Bullock's new order had been obtained improperly because they never had a hearing on this point, Deamer didn't see any reason to beef up their argument. The closer to sunrise that Gilmore was executed, the better. The law didn't like to make too much out of too little. There would be less exposure to counterargument if they missed execution by a few minutes rather than a few hours.

After he told Gordon Richards to go ahead, however, he realized he was sitting at the desk with Gary Gilmore's heart beating in his hands. It was a moment of truth, really. Deamer had been in the Army Reserve six years, with six months of active duty in artillery, but he had never been in combat. So he wondered now if his present feeling might be equal to the kind of emotion you might have if you were about to kill somebody right in your sights. He certainly had more of a mixed reaction than he expected. It was difficult, for instance, to stay in his seat after he hung up. Too quiet and lonely in the office. He'd worked all through the night, he told himself, was dead tired and felt awful grubby. He had a considerable growth of stubble and smelly socks. Not only tired but near used up. Sundays were a big demand. He was number-two man in Bob Hansen's office and also second counselor to his Bishop. Church activities took twenty-five to forty hours a week except when legal duties like Gilmore consumed sixty to seventy. Even so, he had spent the whole of yesterday in church, and now all this last night working into Monday dawn. It came over him that even if he was in favor of capital punishment, he had been going through a long emotional drain. Somehow he had always expected to be the one to carry out the sentence. After all, he believed in it.

2

Deamer felt we were here on earth to be tested on whether we could live righteously. Repentance was the key. An individual had to make restitution in his lifetime for what he'd done wrong, except for those few crimes for which you could not obtain forgiveness in this life. One was murder. You could obtain forgiveness for murder, but not in this life. It had to come in the next. To repent, you had to allow your life to be taken. Deamer didn't feel, therefore, that by giving the go-ahead, he was rendering null and void the existence of Gary Gilmore. Rather, he was enabling Gilmore to pass on to a spiritual sphere where at some point down the road of eternity, the man would obtain forgiveness for these murders.

Sitting in his office all alone, contemplating the scruffiness of his big body, Deamer might be bone tired, but in line with his goals and ambitions, he also felt that an individual occupying his position had to be able to make a decision and stand by it. So, while he waited following that last call from Gordon Richards, he said to himself, "Maybe I've been given this job for a reason. Maybe I'm the one who is able to handle it." That was the kind of thought which occurred to him about everything he did. He liked to think he had been sent to earth as a person with a mission to do some good for the betterment of society. It was his hope he had been foreordained to be part of a larger plan.

Whenever Bob Hansen chose, therefore, not to run for Attorney General, Deamer was going to be ready. He had been active in Republican politics for years and he had his ambitions. Eventually, they would include being Governor. While the Church had a belief in free will, it did instruct that God has plans which are foreordained, and will happen, unless individuals fail to carry them out. If he, Deamer, ever became a government leader, then it was likely he had been foreordained to do so, and was truly carrying out the plan. It could even be part of his mission to take the weight of executing this individual today, a preparation for what might be a large weight of responsibility in the future.

3

In Washington, at the Supreme Court, Al Bronstein's papers went in to Justice White about 9:40, which was 7:40 in Denver. In ten minutes the papers came back. Justice White had denied the application for a Stay. Bronstein was prepared. In a case involving a Circuit Court, you first had to appeal to the Supreme Court Justice directly over that Court, in this case, White. Now, he resubmitted the same application to Justice Marshall. It was sent back in a few minutes signed, "Application denied."

Now, Bronstein asked it be given to Justice Brennan for submission to the entire Court. Michael Rodak went out with it, and a minute later, Francis Lorsen, the Deputy Chief Clerk, came back to tell Bronstein that the Supreme Court had been in the robing room, ready to start a regular session, but that they had turned back in order to consider Bronstein's application. That was highly unusual. Five minutes later, Rodak handed Bronstein a short letter. It said that the full Supreme Court, through Chief Justice Burger, had denied the Stay at 10:03. It was now three minutes after eight in Utah, and every last legal resource had been used. Nothing could prevent the execution of Gary Gilmore.

CHAPTER 38

The Turkey Shoot

1

In the Minimum Security room to which Schiller had been escorted by the guards were a lot of people he didn't recognize. One by one, they would pass in, try not to look confused, take a folding chair and sit down. Nobody was talking to anyone else. It did not have the atmosphere of a funeral, but there was an utter and polite calm.

Then Toni Gurney walked in. For the first time, Larry saw somebody he could say hello to and chatted with her. It was not so much that he was the man who broke the ice, but at least one conversation had begun, and soon a lot of people began to converse.

After a while, Vern came over and pointed out a fellow Schiller had noticed, a rather icy-looking man, wearing an obvious toupee, accompanied by two severe-looking women. Schiller assumed the fellow was a mortician, but Vern said, "That's the doctor who's going to take Gary's eyes out."

Then Stanger came into the room and he was furious. Judge Bullock had delayed the order. Now, Gary could be executed at any time during the day. "Would you believe that, Larry?" Schiller could see that Stanger didn't want Gary to be executed, and, in fact, when Moody came up, Ron still maintained that this would be another dry run. The execution was simply not going to come down. Schiller heard someone in the corner say, "They may keep us here three hours."

Just then a guard came running in from the back door and yelled some words over his shoulder. "Overturned," he cried out. "It's on." At that moment, Stanger, for the first time, understood that Gary Gilmore was going to be shot. It went through him like he had been kicked in the chest. Then he felt chilled. It was an appalling sensation. The strangeness of the reaction went all through him. For the first time in his life, Ron could feel the ends of his nerves. His heart could have been caked in ice. He looked over at Schiller taking notes on the back of some paper and thought, "I'm sure glad he's recording all this, because I can't even move. I don't know if I can walk."

Then they started to transfer the guests. As they led him to the car, Stanger knew he must look ready to throw up. He felt as close to death as breathing, and wondered if he were going mad, because he would have bet a million Gary Gilmore would never be executed. It had made his job easy. He had never felt any moral dilemma in carrying out Gary's desires. In fact, he couldn't have represented him if he really believed the State would go through with it all. It had been a play. He had seen himself as no more important than one more person on the stage.

2

Out in the parking lot, the reporters were being awakened. There was a lot of banging on the doors of vans. "The firing squad is coming," someone shouted.

Robert Sam Anson, covering it for *New Times*, was taking notes: "*Once again, everyone is running. A hundred yards away, in Maximum, a police car, followed by a van, has pulled close to the gate. Now Sam Smith strides toward the building, erect, determined, coatless, oblivious to the cold. At 7:47, a small party of people emerges from the Maximum door; even at this distance, Gilmore can be seen quite distinctly. He is wearing white pants and a black T-shirt. . . . 'It all looks pretty good,' one of the guards comments. 'All that's left now is the paper work,' his partner answers.*

"*With the appearance of Gilmore, the reporters become a mob, a herd spooked into stampede. Camera lights tilt crazily up into the air as their bearers struggle to shift them into position. Producers are shouting orders. Directly in front of the prison building, Geraldo Rivera, attired in black leather jacket and jeans and looking cool, the way only Geraldo Rivera can look cool, is shouting into his mike. 'Kill the Rona segment. Get rid of it. Give me air. You'll be able to hear the shots. I promise. You'll be able to hear the shots.' "*

When Gary came out of Maximum Detention, he was escorted to the van and seated behind the driver. Meersman sat next to him and then Warden Smith came in, and three new guards. The van drove slowly with the seven men, the only car moving in all that quarter mile of prison streets from Maximum Detention to the cannery.

As soon as they started, Gary reached in with both manacled hands to a pocket of his pants and took out a folded piece of paper and put it on his knee so that he could look at it. It was a picture of Nicole clipped from a magazine, and he stared at it.

When the driver of the van turned the key for the motor, the radio, having been on before, now went on again. The tension in the van was sufficient that everyone jumped. Then the words of a song were heard. The driver immediately reached down to turn the radio off, but Gary looked up and said, "Please leave it on." So they began to drive and there was music coming from the radio. The words of the song told of the flight of a white bird. "Una paloma blanca," went the refrain, "I'm just a bird in the sky. Una paloma blanca, over the mountains I fly."

The driver said again, "Would you like me to leave the radio on?" Again Gary said, "Yes."

"It's a new day, it's a new way," said the words, "and I fly up to the sun."

As they drove along slowly, and the song played, Father Meersman noticed that Gary no longer looked at the picture. It was as if the words had become more important.

> *Once I had my share of losing,*
> *Once they locked me on a chain,*
> *Yes, they tried to break my power,*
> *Oh, I still can feel the pain.*

No one spoke any longer and the song played through.

> *No one can take my freedom away,*
> *Yes, no one can take my freedom away.*

When it was done, they drove in silence and got out at the cannery, one by one, disembarking in the way they had practiced in the early hours of the morning when these same prison guards had walked through the scene with a model standing in for Gary. Now, they brought him into the cannery, very, very smoothly. Meersman felt that the practice had paid big dividends.

> *Last nite I flew in my dream*
> *like a white bird through the window . . .*
> *Tonite i will tell my soul to fly me to you.*

3

All through the trip from Maximum to the cannery, all the while "La Paloma Blanca" was playing, Father Meersman did not have any particular feelings as such. Like anything else, one had to proceed to each particular stage in order that it all run smoothly. That was the uppermost thing in his mind, to be thinking ahead to the next step, so that even getting into the van, there wouldn't be any stumbling.

It had been beautifully planned, Father Meersman thought. Even to the care with which they had arranged that as the vehicle with Gary Gilmore in it moved from Maximum to the cannery, all the traffic in the prison compound would stop with no vehicles moving while this one vehicle made its way, so that for the purposes of security, everything was protected. The authorities had timed this transfer with a stopwatch whereby they knew as far as you can humanly know how long it would take for the van to go to this corner and then to that corner, and Father Meersman had occupied himself so intensely in the logic of these steps that he did not have a feeling he could really reflect on other than his paramount concern that Gary

Gilmore not be upset in any way through this whole thing. It was Gary Gilmore's calm frame of mind he wanted to carry through the procedure smoothly and have finished smoothly, and on the flow of such quiet thoughts, his black wintertime coat wrapped around him, Father Meersman arrived with the others at the cannery.

Now, it was important to make sure that the van be as close to the steps as possible. Gary would be wearing shackles, and uppermost in Father Meersman's mind was that he should not have a long, slow, painful walk. In fact, Father Meersman did not take his mind away from the mechanics of these activities until the entire procedure had come to its conclusion and they had mounted the nine or ten wooden steps that would take them into the room of execution, and Gilmore was set in that chair. Then Father Meersman felt they were home, and everything would go smoothly.

Noall Wootton left the Warden's office to walk over to the cannery. He was taking his time. With luck, it might all be over before he got there, but the Utah County Sheriff made a point of stopping to pick him up, and they drove to a door in a warehouse where the Assistant Warden, Leon Hatch, waved Wootton in. It was a big room with gray cement-block walls. That was all he could see, for he went immediately to the rear. Noall was struck with how many people were there. A lot of huge guys were in front of him. Wootton couldn't see a thing. That was fine. He didn't want to get in anybody's way. He just stayed in the back with the empty paint cans, the old tires, and the discarded machinery.

4

Out in Denver, Earl Dorius was wandering down the corridor when he noticed Jack Ford of KSL on the telephone. As soon as Jack came out of the booth, Earl inquired what was going on at the prison, and heard that they were proceeding, and the car carrying Gilmore had just reached the cannery.

This was the first time, during what Earl thought of as the entire ordeal, that it became real a man was about to be killed. Now he felt in his own nerves the tension that Gordon Richards had felt when Earl first gave him the message, and these feelings also gave Earl a clue to the sentiments of the prison personnel. He passed through a very heavy feeling of anguish for the Warden. It would not be easy for his friend, Sam Smith, to order the execution of a man.

Earl decided that he, however, really did not feel any pity for Gilmore. The impact this man had had on the families of his victims, even the vastly lesser impact on Earl's own life these last few months when he hardly saw his children, was not conducive to feeling much compassion. Only sorrow for the Warden.

After Judith Wolbach left the courtroom, she looked down from a high window in the corridor at the gray dawn coming in, and became aware of an emotional void in herself. The thing most disturbing to Judith at this moment was that she felt so dirty. She hadn't even had a chance to go home that night or change her shirt. Just felt sweaty and tired and really disgusted. It shocked her that she had no other reaction. She thought the Bench had exhibited despicable behavior, and she felt nasty about Dorius, and that was it.

5

Outside Minimum Security, cars were waiting for the people who would witness the execution, and at the end of a short drive, Schiller saw a camper back up against the cement-brick building they called the cannery and he said to himself, "That's the executioners." Then he heard a noise above and was startled. The press release put out by the prison had stated that the air space above the prison up to 1,500 feet was going to be off limits. But there was a copter directly overhead. Later, Schiller found out that a newspaper had been able to get away with it and take pictures of Gilmore being transferred, because the release had specified airplanes, not helicopters.

Just in back of the cannery, Schiller saw a black canvas structure that had been built out on the loading platform like an extra room, and he realized the executioners must be waiting in there. Then his car went around another corner of the building, and he saw

Vern, Moody, and Stanger get out of the automobile ahead and go up the entrance steps. When it was his turn to walk through the door, Schiller could see from the corner of his eye that Gary was to his right and strapped in a chair. What hit him before he even took a true look, was that Gary's end of the room was lit, not brightly like a movie set, but lights were on him, and the rest of the room was dark. He was up on a little platform. It was like a stage. With the chair so prominent, it felt more as if an electrocution was going to take place than a shooting.

As Schiller walked forward, the rear view of Gary's head changed to a profile, and then he was able to see a little of his face. At that point, Gilmore acknowledged his presence, and Schiller nodded back. The next thing he noticed was that Gilmore was not strapped tightly into the chair. It was the first detail that really hit him. Everything was loose.

There were straps around his arms and legs, but they all had a good inch of slack. He could have pulled his hands right out of their restraints. Then, as Schiller continued to move forward, he saw a painted line before him on the floor, and an official said, "Stand behind that," so he wheeled and faced the chair. Now, with Gilmore again on his right, Schiller could see to his left a black blind with slots in it, and he estimated the distance at twenty-five feet from himself and about the same distance from Gilmore. Then, he took a good look.

It was the first time Schiller had seen Gary in person since December. At this moment, he looked tired, depleted, thin, older than Schiller had ever seen him, and a little glassy-eyed. A tired old bird with very bright eyes.

The next thing to impress Schiller was that Gary was still in control. He was carrying on conversations, not loud enough to hear, but saying something to the guards strapping him, to the Warden, and to the priest. Maybe there were eight people around him in maroon jackets. Schiller was about to put down in his notes that they were prison officials, but that was exactly what he wished to guard against. No journalistic assumptions. So he would not suppose they were prison officials. Just people in red coats. Then, as his photographer's

eye grew accustomed to the scene, he could not quite believe what
he next observed. For the seat of execution was no more than a little
old office chair, and behind it was an old filthy mattress backed up by
sandbags and the stone wall of the cannery. They had rammed that
mattress between the chair and the sandbags, a last-minute expedi-
ent, no doubt, as if, sometime during the night, they had decided that
the sandbags weren't enough and bullets might go through, hit the
wall, and ricochet. But the dirty mattress repelled Schiller. He said to
himself, My God, they stitched the black canvas neatly around the
rifle slots for the assassins. Then he realized the word he was using.

Still, you could not ignore the contrast between the meticulous
preparation of the blind, and Gary's chair with its filthy ramshackle
backdrop. Even the bindings around his arms looked to be made out
of cheap webbing.

6

Ron Stanger's first impression was how many people were in the
room. God, the number of spectators. Executions must be a spectator
sport. It really hit him even before his first look at Gary, and then he
was thankful the hood was not on yet. That was a relief. Gilmore was
still a human being, not a hooded, grotesque thing, and Ron realized
how he had been preparing himself for the shock of seeing Gary with
his face concealed in a black bag. But, no, there was Gary staring at
the crowd with an odd humor in his face. Stanger knew what he was
thinking. "Anybody who knows somebody is going to get an invite to
the turkey shoot."

Stanger hadn't thought there would be anybody here to speak of,
but there must have been fifty people behind the white line. Any cop
or bureaucrat who had a little pull had gotten in. Stanger could hear
Bob Moody's words about Sam Smith, so often repeated. "He's a very
sincere man. It's just that he's incompetent. Totally incompetent."
Here were all these Sheriffs and County Troopers Stanger had never
seen before, come right out of the woodwork — how could you be
respected in your profession if you weren't here?

Moody also felt anger at all the people who had been invited. Sam Smith had given them such fuss whether it would be five or seven guests. Now there were all these needless people pressed behind the line, and the executioners back of the screen talking. You couldn't hear what they were saying, but you could hear them, and it incensed Bob that Ernie Wright, Director of Corrections, was dancing around greeting people, practically gallivanting with his big white cowboy hat, looking like a Texas bureaucrat.

Moody had the feeling that the riflemen behind the blind were purposely not looking at Gary, but keeping their backs to him, chatting away in a group, and would only turn around at the last minute when given the order. Ron Stanger, situated next to Bob Moody, wanted to get up and say to all, "Here, bless your heart, you wouldn't give this man a piece of pizza before you blow his guts out." That's what he wanted to say, but he didn't dare. It would have been too hysterical. Couldn't let the man, he would have shouted, have his pizza and a six-pack of beer. Rather have it wind up in a correctional belly, wouldn't you?

Cline Campbell's first thought when he walked into the room was, my goodness, do they sell tickets to this? All the same, Campbell could feel how everybody was scared to death. It hung over the execution. The good old bureaucratic fear that somebody in an official place was going to forget something. Then there'd be all political or legal hell to pay. Campbell just contented himself with saying to Gary, "How are you doing?" and then he stood to one side of the chair and Father Meersman to the other, and Father Meersman got a cup of water and Gilmore took a sip of it as the priest held it to his mouth.

An official came up to Vern and said Gary wanted to speak to him. Vern walked over into the light that was on Gary, and his nephew looked up at him with those baby-blue eyes of his, and Vern felt he'd like to pull him out of that chair, just pull him out of that chair and make him free again. Vern was feeling a great deal of emotion. He didn't want him in that chair, really.

Gary said, "Look, take this watch. I don't want anybody to have it but Nicole." He had broken it and taped it with the hands set at 7:49. Now, he handed it to Vern. Must have been holding it all this while.

Then Gary said, "I want you to promise you'll see to it that Nicole is taken care of." How in the world Gary figured he could take care of her, Vern didn't know, but Gary had to ask somebody. They shook hands and Gary started to squeeze his hand, right there in the chair as if he could crush Vern's knuckles. He said to Vern, "Come on, I'll give you a go," and Vern said, "Gary, I could pull you right out of that chair if I wanted to."

Gary said, "Would you?"

Vern went back to his place behind the line and thought of the conversation he'd had weeks before when Gary asked him and Ida to be witnesses, and Vern had said, "I don't want Ida to see it," and Gary said, "but I want *you* there, Vern."

"I don't know whether I can take it or not," Vern had said, "I don't think I can." Gary had said, "Well, I want you there."

"Why?" Vern asked. "Why do you want me?"

"Well, Vern," Gary said, "I want to show you. I've already shown you how I live" — he gave his most mocking smile — "and I'd like to show you how I can die." Vern thought all this now must be part of what he had said then because, back behind the line, feeling Gary's hand still on his, Vern wanted to tell him, "That was so good, Gary, what you just did."

Bob Moody came next, and he shook hands. Gary had a smaller hand than Bob had expected, but neither cold nor feverishly warm, just a shock, for it was a warm, living hand like any other. Gary looked at him and said, "Well, Moody, I'm going to leave you my hair. You need it worse than I do."

Schiller was next. As he walked up, he kept worrying about the right thing to say. But when he got there, he was dazed by the immensity of it all. It was as if he was saying good-bye to a man who was going to step into a cannon and be fired to the moon, or dropped in an iron chamber to the bottom of the sea, a veritable Houdini. He grasped both of Gilmore's hands and it didn't matter if the man was a murderer, he could just as well have been a saint, for either at this moment seemed equally beyond Schiller's way of measure — and he said, he heard it come out of him, "I don't know what I'm here for."

Gilmore replied, "You're going to help me escape." Schiller looked at him sitting in the chair and said, "I'll do it the best way that's humanly possible," and was thinking by that, he would treat it all in the most honest way, and Gilmore smiled back at him with that funny tight grin of his, just a little expression in the upper lip, as if he alone knew the meaning of what had just been said, and then the grin broadened into that thin-lipped smile he showed on occasion, evil as a jackal, subtly jeering, the last facial expression Schiller would have to remember of Gilmore. They shook hands, Gilmore's grip kind of weak, and Schiller walked away not knowing whether he had handled the moment the way he should. Didn't even know if it was a moment to be handled. He felt like he had no real relationship to Gilmore.

Vern had gone first because he was the patriarch, then Bob Moody, but Schiller had tried to be last. Stanger had thought, "You've got to be kidding, you're even doing it now," and won the maneuvering. Larry went ahead. When it came Stanger's turn, he couldn't think of anything to say. Just murmured, "Hang in there. Stick with it." Gary didn't look very tough. Wan, in fact. His eye showed the effect of all those drugs wearing off. He was trying to be brave, but just said, "Cool," like it wasn't that easy anymore to get the words out, and they shook hands. Gary squeezed real hard, and Stanger put his arm around his shoulder, and Gary moved the hand that was loose in the straps to touch Ron's arm. Stanger kept thinking that Gilmore's hands were skinnier than you'd think they'd be. And they looked in each other's eyes, kind of a final embrace.

As soon as Ron returned to his position behind the line, a prison official came up to ask if he wanted cotton for his ears. Then Ron noticed that everybody was taking cotton, so he stuffed some into his head, and watched Sam Smith walk over to the back of the room where a red telephone was on a chair. Then Sam Smith made a phone call, and walked back and came up to Gary and started to read a declaration.

Schiller, trying to listen, decided it was some official document. Not the sort, by the sound of it, that he would listen to normally but, through the cotton he could hear Sam Smith going blah, blah, blah. All the while, Gary was not looking at the Warden, but rather, leaning in his chair from side to side in order to stare around the large body of Sam Smith, practically tipping that chair over trying to see the faces behind the executioner's blind, catch a glint of their expression.

Then the Warden said, "Do you have anything you'd like to say?" and Gary looked up at the ceiling and hesitated, then said, "Let's do it." That was it. The most pronounced amount of courage, Vern decided, he'd ever seen, no quaver, no throatiness, right down the line. Gary had looked at Vern as he spoke.

The way Stanger heard it, it came out like Gary wanted to say something good and dignified and clever, but couldn't think of anything profound. The drugs had left him too dead. Rather than say nothing, he did his best to say it very clear, "Let's do it."

That was about what you'd expect of a man who'd been up for more than twenty-four hours and had taken everything and now was hung over, and coming down, and looking older than Ron had ever seen him. Ah, he was drained out. Ron could see deep lines in his face for the first time. Gilmore looked as white as the day the lawyers first met him after the suicide attempt.

Father Meersman walked up to give the last rites, and Noall Wootton braced himself and took a peep between the shoulders of some of the big men in front of him, and remembered Gary when he had come to the Board of Pardons Hearing, very confident that day, like he was holding all the cards, the ace and everything else you might need. Now, in Wootton's opinion, he didn't have it.

And Schiller, looking at the same man, thought he was resigned in his appearance, but with presence, and what you could call a certain authority.

Father Meersman finished giving Gary Gilmore the last rites. As they came forward with the hood, Gilmore said to him, "Dominus vobiscum." Father Meersman didn't know how to describe his emotion. Gary couldn't have said anything that brought back more of an automatic response. This was the greeting Father Meersman had given to the people again and again over the ten years and twenty and thirty since he had become a priest. "Dominus vobiscum," he would say at Mass and the response would come back, "Et cum spiritu tuo."

So now, when Gilmore said Dominus vobiscum, Father Meersman answered like an altar boy, "Et cum spiritu tuo," and as the words came out of his mouth, Gary kind of grinned and said, "There'll always be a Meersman."

"He wants to say," said Father Meersman to himself, "that there will always be a priest present at a time like this."

Three or four men in red coats came up and put the hood on Gilmore's head. Nothing was said after that.

Absolutely nothing said. They put a waist strap on Gilmore, and a head strap, and Father Meersman began to think of how when they were first strapping him in the chair, Gilmore had wanted water and Father Meersman had given him water for the throat that was too dry. Then he had wanted another drink.

Now, the doctor was beside him, pinning a white circle on Gilmore's black shirt, and the doctor stepped back. Father Meersman traced the big sign of the cross, the last act he had to perform. Then, he, too, stepped over the line, and turned around, and looked back at the hooded figure in the chair. The phone began to ring.

Noall Wootton's first reaction was, God, it's just like in the movies, it isn't going to happen. Schiller was taking notes on the checks he'd been careful to remove from the checkbook holder, and he noted that the hood came down loosely like a square carton over Gary's head. Not form fitting in any way. You could not have a sense of his features beneath the sack.

Stanger, listening to the phone, thought, "It is a final confirmation of some kind." Then Sam Smith hung up, and walked back to his place behind the line, and it happened to be next to Schiller. He handed Larry more cotton and they looked into each other's eyes. Then, Schiller didn't know if Sam Smith made a movement with his arm, or didn't, but he felt as if he saw something in the Warden's shoulder move, and Ron and Bob Moody and Cline Campbell heard a countdown begin, and Noall Wootton put his fingers in his ears on top of the cotton, and Gary's body looked calm to Campbell. Cline could not believe the calm he saw in that man. Gilmore was so strong in his desire to die right, that he didn't clench his fist as the count began.

Stanger said to himself, "I hope I don't fall down." He had his hand up to protect his head somehow. Right through the cotton, he heard the sound of heavy breathing and saw the barrels of the rifles projecting from the slits of the blind. He was shocked at how close those muzzles were to the victim. They sure didn't want to miss. Then it all got so quiet your attention was called to it. Right through the cotton, Ron heard these whispers, "One," and "Two," and they never got to say, "Three" before the guns went, "Bam. Bam. Bam." So loud it was terrifying. A muscle contracted from Ron's shoulder down to his lower back. Some entire school of muscles in a spasm.

Schiller heard three shots, expecting four. Gary's body did not jerk nor the chair move, and Schiller waited for the fourth shot and found out later that two must have come out simultaneously. Noall Wootton tried to look at Gary at that point, but couldn't see anything from the rear of the crowd and went out the door before anyone else, and straight to his car which was up by Minimum Security, got in it, drove out. There were reporters interviewing people and photographers, but he didn't stop. He didn't want to talk to anybody.

7

Vern just heard a great big WHAM! When it happened, Gary never raised a finger. Didn't quiver at all. His left hand never moved, and then, after he was shot, his head went forward, but the strap held his head up, and then the right hand slowly rose in the air and slowly went down as if to say, "That did it, gentlemen." Schiller thought the movement was as delicate as the fingers of a pianist raising his hand before he puts it down on the keys. The blood started to flow through the black shirt and came out onto the white pants and started to drop on the floor between Gary's legs, and the smell of gunpowder was everywhere. Then, the lights went down, and Schiller listened to the blood drip. He was not certain he could hear it drip, but he felt it, and with that blood, the life in Gilmore's body seemed to lift off him like smoke. Ron Stanger, feeling dizzy, said to himself, "You're the only one that's going to pass out, and it will be embarrassing to end on the ground with all these people here," and he staggered backward from the force of the contraction in his back, put his arms out, grabbed hold of somebody to steady himself, and turned back to get another look at the body. That was when he saw Gilmore's right hand lift.

Ron closed his eyes and when he opened them again, the blood was a pool in Gary's lap, running to his feet and covering his tennis shoes, those crazy red, white and blue tennis shoes he always wore in Maximum. The shoelaces were now blooded over.

A doctor came along with a stethoscope and shook his head. Gilmore wasn't dead yet.

Ron thought of the day when Gary was in Fagan's office for a moment, and in that ten seconds Gary was all over his desk like a butterfly. He opened the desk drawer and took out a spoon, and shoelaces, went through everything like a guy leading an orchestra. It was beautiful. Gilmore was a *talented* thief, after all, and finished just as Fagan said, "Yeah, okay, Joe." By the time the Lieutenant turned around, old Gary was sitting there calm as a nodding owl, and Stanger on the other side of the glass had his eyes wide open.

Gary made jokes about the shoelaces after that. They were good enough to hang himself by, he would tell Ron, and now the hand that had done the stealing moved up in the air and came down. It could have been pointing at the blood on the shoelaces.

They waited about twenty seconds. Then the doctor went up again, and Father Meersman came up, and Sam Smith, and the doctor put the stethoscope to Gary's arm once more, turned to Sam, and nodded. Sam Smith unloosened the waist strap, slid Gilmore out from underneath the head strap, and looked behind the body at the shot pattern where the holes came through.

Stanger was furious. The moment Gilmore was shot, everybody should have been walked out, and not served for a party to all this. Even as Sam was examining the body, Gary fell over into Meersman's hands. The padre had to hold the head while Sam went fishing all over Gilmore's back to locate the exit wounds. Blood started coming onto Meersman's hands, and dripped through his fingers, and Vern began to weep. Then Father Meersman wept. An officer finally came around and said to the people standing behind the line, "Time for you to leave." Schiller walked out saying to himself, "What have we accomplished? There aren't going to be less murders."

All the while Father Meersman and Cline Campbell were unbuckling Gilmore's arms and legs. Campbell kept thinking of the importance of the eyes. He said to himself, "Why doesn't somebody move? We've got to save the eyes."

8

Over at the Warden's office, just a few minutes earlier, Gordon Richards had received a phone call from an Assistant Clerk in the U.S. Supreme Court, who was saying that the full Court — with Justice Brennan not participating — had just acted on the application for a Stay from the ACLU and had denied it. Richards got a little upset. This Clerk who was named Peter Beck had been told nothing about "Mickey from Wheeling, West Virginia." Well, did Mr. Beck know, Richards asked, where Mr. Rodak was born and what his nickname was? "Is it Mike?" said Beck. Richards then asked if Mr. Rodak could call him. Before he knew it, he got put on hold. "Hurry, please," Richards called out to Beck, "it's crucial." There he was sitting with unconfirmed information from the Supreme Court. So he called out to the prison officials there with him in the Warden's office, "Tell them to hold at the cannery." The officials shook their heads, however. The execution had just been carried out.

Three minutes later, Rodak came on the line. Richards asked for his nickname and his birthplace. The nickname was Mickey, he said, but he had been born in Smock, Pennsylvania.

"What about West Virginia?" asked Richards. "I was born in Smock," said Rodak, "but I went to West Virginia. I'm a member of the West Virginia Bar."

Had he offered this information to Earl Dorius? asked Richards. Didn't think so, said Rodak. Finally, he remembered. "Oh, yes, the fellow wanted to make sure that he didn't get any false telephone calls." Right. "Is," asked Rodak, "the execution over yet?"

"Wouldn't it have been horrible," said Richards to one of the officials, as he hung up, "if that had been simultaneous calls?"

9

Vern, Bob Moody, Ron Stanger, and Larry Schiller got into a car and drove over to the Administration Building. During that minute, they discussed whether or not to issue a press statement ahead of the Warden.

Stanger said, "I think we ought to. What do you say, Larry?" Schiller replied, "We have no obligation. The first person who gets there is the first person the press will talk to," and Stanger said, "Let's beat the Warden to the punch."

Vern said, "Can you answer questions about the execution, Larry? I don't want to talk about that."

The press conference was being held on the second floor of the Administration Building in a large conference chamber that looked like a courtroom. It was already as crowded as the Board of Pardons Hearing, same bedlam of media, cameras and crazy white light, people pushing to get in, close to 100 degrees inside. No room to breathe.

Trying to get upstairs, they were buffeted every way. Some TV guy was working with a couple of electric cables in front of Bob Moody, and got so rude about letting Moody pass that Bob just grabbed a male-female connection crossing his path and yanked it apart. The TV man cried out, "My God, I've lost power, lost power," as Moody went by.

When they reached the stage, Schiller said to Vern, "Why don't you talk first?" and Vern sat on a chair to rest his aching leg.

He did not speak long. "It was very upsetting to me," Vern said, "but he got his wish, he did die . . . and he died in dignity. That's all I have to say."

Bob Moody told them: "I think it's a very brutal, cruel kind of a thing, that I would only hope that we could take a good and better look at ourselves, our society and our systems. Thank you."

Ron said, "He was always trying to keep the spirit light because he made the statement he had received a gift, and that gift was he knew he was going to die, and he could make the arrangements and, therefore, he was indeed fortunate. He always said that he looked forward to the time when he could have quiet, when he could meditate, and today, Gary Gilmore has quiet, and he has quiet through eternity."

Schiller said, "I'm not here to express any of my personal feelings, but after Vern has left, I'll be more than glad to relate any of the facts anybody here would like to know. I don't think it would be proper to relay them in Vern's presence, but I will answer your questions then." He threw a look around the room and the only smile that came back was from David Johnston of the *L.A. Times* and the Orem TraveLodge. Then Gus Sorensen gave a wink.

ANNOUNCER FOR THE TV POOL Leaving the platform now are Ron Stanger and Robert Moody, two attorneys who have helped Gary Gilmore in the last couple of months to get the wish that he said he wanted at that time, that he wanted to die, these men helped to see that he got there. Also leaving, Vern Damico, Gilmore's uncle from Provo, Utah, the man who took Gilmore in after he was paroled from a prison. And now, Lawrence Schiller, a literary agent/filmmaker who's been involved in this case for some time.

Dave Johnston, watching Schiller, decided to give points to the guy's cool. Here, at this press conference with everybody hating his guts for tieing up the story, Schiller was still doing a real reporter's job. His adrenalin had to be high enough to make his frame shake, thought Johnston, yet not a quiver was showing.

Schiller spoke of the yellow line and the black hood and the black T-shirt Gary was wearing and the white pants, and the shots. ". . . Slowly, red blood emerged from under the black T-shirt and onto the white slacks. It seemed to me that his body still had a movement, for approximately fifteen to twenty seconds, it is not for me to determine whether it was an after-death or prior-to-death movement. The minister and the doctor proceeded towards Gary," Schiller said, and kept on speaking in slow, clear sentences, trying to make the note-taking easy for tired reporters.

Then it was Sam Smith's turn.

SAM SMITH I have no formal statement. I think Mr. Schiller pretty well covered the detail. I will respond to questions.

QUESTION What was the official time, Warden?

SAM SMITH The official time was 8:07.

QUESTION How did you give the signal?

SAM SMITH I didn't really give the signal. I indicated all was in readiness.

QUESTION How did you do that?

SAM SMITH Just by a motion.

QUESTION Was there a squad leader?

SAM SMITH Yes, there was.

QUESTION Did the squad leader give the signal?

SAM SMITH What happened inside of there, I have no knowledge.

QUESTION Who were the forty people present?

SAM SMITH Well, I didn't count the same as Mr. Schiller.

QUESTION But you disagree with his figure of forty, though, Warden?

SAM SMITH Yes, I would definitely disagree with that figure.

QUESTION How many were there?

SAM SMITH Less.

QUESTION Thirty? Twenty?

SAM SMITH I wouldn't give you an exact number.

QUESTION Warden, can we inspect the site now?

SAM SMITH As soon as we find out that everything is clear and that we can handle the traffic.

When Sam Smith stepped off, Johnston went up to Schiller and said, "You amaze me. You really are a journalist."

Schiller got a glint in his eye. Johnston could see the compliment go all the way in. "Yes, it was swell," said Johnston, "but why did you give it all away?" Larry cocked his head, and got a sly grin like a big German shepherd who is lolling its tongue. He said, "I didn't give away anything that mattered."

But he couldn't keep it in. "Gilmore's last words," Schiller confessed, "were not what I said they were."

Johnston laughed. He had a feeling there was more to the story. "Larry, there are some," he said, "who might look on that as a lie."

"No," said Schiller, " 'Let's do it' was the last thing everybody heard."

Johnston said to himself, "This is one secret he'll have to tell. He's like a kid who'll have to tell one person anyway."

"Well," said Larry, and swore him to secrecy, "Gary spoke in Latin to the priest."

"He did? What were his words?"

"If I knew them, I couldn't pronounce them," said Schiller, and gave his sly grin again. "But I'll find out."

They drove over together to the execution site. When they got inside the cannery, Schiller couldn't believe what he now saw. His description of the events had been accurate in every way but one. He had gotten the colors wrong. The black cloth of the blind was not black but blue, the line on the floor was not yellow but white, and the chair was not black, but dark green. He realized that during the execution something had altered in his perception of color.

He left the place of execution a second time with a memory of reporters swarming over the chair, the sandbags and the holes in the mattress, creatures of an identical species feeding, all feeding, in the same place. As he went out the door, one man was explaining to another that steel-jacketed bullets had been used so they would make no larger hole in the rear than in the front, which would avoid, thereby, the worst of the mess, and the body jumping from the impact.

PART SEVEN

The Fading
of the Heart

CHAPTER 39

Television

1

While Earl stood in the corridor, one of the newsmen came running by and said, "Gary Gilmore is dead." Again, Earl looked out the window and saw other newsmen down in the plaza, and the sun shining in Denver, and people going to work. When he came downstairs to the main lobby, Sandy Gilmour of Channel 2 television in Salt Lake asked to interview him, and Earl said, "Yes," and Gilmour asked him how he felt to be the one to inform the prison that the execution could proceed, and Earl explained his only responsibility was to let them know the Tenth Circuit had overruled Judge Ritter. That was all, he said. He did not feel like discussing the intricacies of his emotion.

Then, Earl, Bob Hansen, and the rest of the staff moved out in a taxicab. Judy Wolbach, they heard, would be traveling home on another plane.

2

Toni was waiting in Minimum Security with Ida, Dick Gray, Evelyn Gray, and all the people who had not been invited to the cannery. A guard in a maroon jacket walked into the room, and said, "Anybody come to tell you?" Toni said, "No." The man was pale, and trembling terribly. He said, "It's over with. Gary's dead."

Ida started to cry. She had held up real well, but now it over-flowed. The guards were wonderful then. Several came over to ask if there was anything they could do about transportation, and Toni told them she was waiting for her daddy to come back. In a while, one of them said her father was waiting by the tower where their trucks were parked. The prison officials were wonderful to her on the way out, and that reminded her how just before the execution, they had been very attentive, wanted to see if there was anything her mother needed, or did they want coffee? It was almost like being in a funeral home, and these were the attendants.

When they got to her truck, Vern wasn't there yet, and the parking area seemed massive with cars and people. Reporters clustered around like flies, interviewing her mother through one window, herself through the other, until Toni finally got foulmouthed. By then, she had really had it. She was smoking with the window open, and one of them came over and kept asking for an interview even though Toni was shaking her head. This TV man had no respect for her feeling that she didn't want to talk and he set his microphone in the window and said, "Can I put this here?" That was when she told him where he could put it. His hands flew all over. Later, a girl friend told her that on "Good Morning America" you could catch where they cut a few words.

Then she could see Vern, cane in hand, trying to walk up to them. His face was distraught. He was obviously in pain, and she had the feeling his knee was going to go on him. So, she jumped out of the truck to run over, and three reporters grabbed her arm. So help her, three. "Please give us a few words." She grabbed one of the microphones as if to say something, then threw it to the ground where it broke into a dozen little pieces, and shouted to Vern, "Get your truck out later. It's stuck behind the others now." Then she led him to her truck, and drove to her home in Lehi, gave him coffee, got him settled down, then took him for breakfast to the Spic and Span Cafe in Provo. About two hours later, he went out to the prison with her and recovered his vehicle.

3

All through the night before Gary was executed, Pete Galovan had been working at the city swimming pool. He was very tired when he got home early that morning, and he knelt down and prayed. Asked the Lord to forgive him for some of the harsh feelings he had had toward Gary. He didn't want to hate him in any way. He felt concerned about that. In fact, Pete got so concerned he began to cry. Then he felt Gary come into the room.

Pete was there praying on his knees, and Gary came into the room accompanied by two other men. Gary was wearing a white shirt and white pants, and the two men with him were dressed in white suits and wore ties. They might be relatives of some sort from the past or the future. Pete didn't know.

Gary now said to Pete that he did not hold anything against him. He explained that right after his execution, his relatives had been there to receive his spirit. The Lord had sent them. It was very very clear to Pete that this was exactly what Gary was saying.

Gary was in a good mood and said he was experiencing all kinds of new sensations. They were really funny. He told Pete he was walking through walls, and it was an experience. He felt like a kid in an amusement park. He would now be able to visit every prison in the world, he said, and he planned to go all over as soon as his ashes were cast from the plane. Then he would come back to Provo from time to time.

Gary now revealed that because he had been full of valiant feeling at the end, the Lord was planning to use him as an example for people who had problems similar to his. At the end of a thousand years of peace, his spirit would come forth. He told Pete he had a very good chance of becoming one of the higher people. He had been told he was a dynamic spiritual person who had made a very deep choice in this life, and that could counteract a lot of bad decisions earlier. If he faced up to things now, the Lord was really going to use him.

Right after Gary left, Pete called Elizabeth, and told her about it, and said he would slip Gary's name onto the prayer rolls, so that Gary

M. Gilmore would be in every Mormon temple in the world, and every day countless people would be praying for him.

4

From a memo by Earl Dorius on the events of January 17:

The taxi driver heard us talking and toward the end of the ride, he asked whether we had anything to do with the Gilmore case, and we all smiled and filled him in on what had happened.

When we arrived at the airport, I remember that in the waiting area there was a group of people watching the news on television. They told us they had just heard that Gary Gilmore had been shot and is dead. I remember Jack Ford asking them in disbelief how they knew this, and acted like he did not know anything about it. I turned to Jack and told him he was cruel in leading on the people when in fact we were the ones that had argued the case, but we joked and then boarded the plane and flew back to Utah. The plane trip back was much more relaxing. We talked about subjects other than Gilmore but it seemingly took longer to return home than it took to get to Denver.

When we arrived back in Utah, there was not a single member of the news media at the airport. Salt Lake City seemed extremely quiet. We deplaned and walked to our car alone with no news reporters asking us any questions. It seemed fitting that with the death of Gary Gilmore the publicity also ended.

But on the last leg from the airport, not a block from his home, Earl saw an empty billboard on which somebody had painted, "Robert Hansen, Hitlerite." He didn't know if it had been put up because Bill Barrett and he lived out there, and somebody in the community wanted to let them know what they thought, or if it was just a coincidence.

5

Brenda had gone into the hospital on the tenth of January and surgery was the eleventh. Six days later, the execution came right in the middle of feeling surgically cut up. The day before, she couldn't believe how many people kept calling. She was being given prayers on the telephone and hearing them again on the radio station. People in the hospital told her they were praying. Then, Geraldo Rivera called and wanted to do a live TV interview in her hospital room. Brenda thought, How atrocious. Got to be kidding.

She couldn't handle it. The night of Toni's birthday, she had one phone call with Gary and knew it was the last time she was ever going to hear his voice. To add to it, she couldn't sleep. They brought her a Seconal capsule. It didn't do a lot of good. Two hours later, the nurse was in with a flashlight to see if Brenda was asleep. "How can you sleep with that light in your eyes," Brenda grumbled, so the doctor ordered another.

Every two hours, they gave her Seconal, but she couldn't fall asleep until four in the morning when they came in with a shot. Then, she woke up at seven-thirty, half-crocked from the drugs, but had to find out if they were going to kill him or not. Switched on the TV and drove everybody in her room crazy until she heard he had been granted a Stay, first news she picked up that morning, and Brenda went completely bananas, so hysterical she didn't know if she was happy or sad. Then, in a few minutes, reversed. By then, she didn't know if it was her adrenalin or her heart that was flaming up and down. In just a few more seconds it flashed across the screen: GARY GILMORE IS DEAD! The surgeon came to see her a minute or two after this, and stood patiently waiting for an end to her hysterics, said, "How do you feel today?" She thought, "Oh, you simple son of a bitch, get away from me."

She didn't want anybody near. The doctor asked again how she felt and the nurse explained what had just happened. The doctor said, "Oh, that's really too bad, but they should have wasted him a long time ago." Brenda said, "You can give me my release papers. I want a prescription for pain, and get your ass out of my room." She picked up her pillow and threw it at him. He said, "If you want to get hard about it, I'll suggest you not be released today." She said, "What in the hell do you care for? I don't like you anyway. If I had known you were cutting me, I wouldn't have come in." That was one man she could say she detested by now.

After he signed the release, she called Johnny. By eleven o'clock she was out. They had to sneak her the back way, so she could get home without a lot of reporters bugging her. Brenda didn't remember a whole lot from that event until three days later.

6

At the hour of Gilmore's execution, Colleen Jensen was at home in Clearfield getting ready for school. She was now a substitute teacher, and had begun the job just two weeks before. Today, she was having her first class with a new group of students, and while she got dressed that morning thinking the execution was stayed, for that was what she heard on the first news, by the time she reached school, it was over. Kids in the class were talking about it as she came through the door. She could hear their whispers about her involvement in it. So, she gave a little speech to the class.

She did not tell them that in the evenings when she sat downstairs, nursing Monica, and rocking her to sleep, she would show the baby pictures of her daddy, and tell Monica who he was. At such times, Colleen would try to speak to Monica out of the stillness of herself, and thereby tell the one-year-old that Max was dead, her daddy was dead. For now, talking to the class, she merely said that for those who did not know, she would tell them who she was, and what her part in it all had been. She added that it was not something they would need to discuss again. She also said she was ready, if they were, to get on with the teaching and the class.

7

Phil Hansen woke up and watched in bed that morning, just shaking his head and uppercutting himself. As he looked at the TV, he thought, "If I'd had one inkling they were going to bring off that midnight ride, I would have prepared papers and had Ritter sign another Stay."

8

On Monday morning, at seven o'clock, Lucinda was typing Gary's last tape with Larry. She could hear Gilmore's voice coming in over the earphones, and it was pathetic the way he kept telling Larry how badly he wanted to die, and she felt so sorry for him.

The television was on in the office. There was Geraldo Rivera saying, "Well, we're here in front of the prison." All of a sudden it hit her that the whole world was watching, and the voice of the condemned man was in her ear, this little voice coming out.

She and Barry and Debbie had stayed up all night and were really drained. Now they were switching the channels. Game shows like "Jeopardy" kept coming in — at seven in the morning, in Orem, they were getting "Jeopardy." Then one game show after another. They couldn't get the news. The most chaotic jumble trying to find out if he'd been shot or not. Barry was freaking out. He began to curse the TV screen. Incredibly literary and obscene language. The TV was just so awful, Lucinda thought, a blast of awful things, and here they were waiting to find out. All those images flashing, just mumbo jumbo, then a voice saying "Gary Mark Gilmore is dead." Squawk!

9

It was a beautiful sunny day, and Julie Jacoby had been up early, watering the plants, feeling good about the Stay, thinking, Thank God. She was just loving the winter sunlight. Then a call came from a man with the Catholic News Service in Washington. "It's happened," he said. She didn't know what to do with herself and went around in circles. Only later did she feel a little relieved that she had not given herself totally to this thing, which she had always known would not change the world.

Further along that morning, she saw a news clipping in the *Salt Lake Tribune* that got her name wrong. She had been one of the four people whose names had been on the taxpayers' suit in Judge Ritter's Court, but the *Salt Lake Tribune* had printed it as "Mulie Jacobs" rather than Julie Jacoby, and she laughed when she saw it, for she knew that her twelve-year-old son would never fail from now on to call her Mulie when it would be of use to him. She would also be spared the hate mail and telephone calls full of compressed murder that were rendering Shirley Pedler so thin.

10

Shirley was alone in the office when the word came over the radio, and it hit her as if she felt the shot. Her head went down on the desk and she started to sob.

Later that morning, she made several statements. It was incredible — it was really an affront — the press had all of a sudden vanished. Shirley found that the most horrifying aspect of the whole thing. It was as if these reporters were saying, "He's blown away, so there's no news anymore." God, press from all over the country had dominated every good restaurant in Salt Lake, and now they were gone. She sat in her office the day of the execution and was not hounded at all.

11

Gibbs had been sitting in jail all day every day in the week leading up to Gary's execution, and was in a pretty drugged state because of his leg the night before the execution. In the morning, when he heard the news on the radio he just felt dumb and groggy.

12

Dennis Boaz had been out in Iowa for a couple of days in December and got into a symposium on a TV program where he heard that President Ford might commute Gary's sentence before retiring from office. So, he sent a telegram saying that if capital punishment was going to be applied, it should be applied equally. No executions until there was one law for everyone. Never heard from Ford.

On the day of the execution, he felt a kind of silent sadness and tears came to his eyes. Gary died on January 17, a day whose number came to 6, which was the motherhood of brothers, and, of course, that made him think of Cain and Abel. In the period Dennis was working with Gilmore, he had sprouted a red mark above his right brow, not a pimple, but a mark signifying death. First discovered it toward the end of November. It was round and it was red, but not a pimple. It was there nearly two months, and then faded away after Gary died. Interesting, at any rate. He noticed things like that.

13

Nicole had found out that Gary was going to be executed today, but she had no idea of the time. In the morning, walking back from the ward dining room, she suddenly felt a great need to lie down on her bed. They started making a big thing of it, but she just walked toward her room. Nobody said anything more. Then she lay there, and tried to think about Gary. For days she had been dreaming of the moment he was shot and falling back. She always saw Gary standing up when he got it. Now, in her mind, she saw nothing but those red blocks they gave the patients to put together into a cube.

They were in her head, and she was trying to push them away, when suddenly Gary's face came to her out of the darkness, came in fast with a look of pain and horror. He didn't fall back, but right up toward her. Her body flipped around on the bed, her eyes opened, and that was all. She kept trying to feel him again that day, but couldn't. He wasn't near her at all for a few days.

14

After Gaylen was dead, Bessie thought she would never get over it. But this was going to be worse. When she called the prison and said good-bye to Gary on this last night, he had said, "Don't cry."

"I'm not going to cry, Gary," she had told him, but she had wanted so much to say, "Don't die, Gary, don't. Please, please, don't." Only it would hurt what he was building up — whatever it might take of him to go out there. So she had to be careful. It was a nightmare.

Listening to the clock through the hours Bessie could not keep from thinking, "His nightmare will be over, but mine will never be."

When Mikal got the paper early that morning, it said the execution had been stayed. They turned on "Good Morning America." A little earlier, Bessie had said, "Don't put it on." She didn't want to hear it. If it happened, she didn't want to know about it for hours. She certainly didn't want to hear about it on TV. Yet after Mikal brought in the paper, somebody — was it Frank Jr., or Mikal, or his girl friend: she could never remember for fear she would not forgive — one of them said, "It is safe now. There's a Stay. We can turn on 'Good Morning America.'" They did. A voice stated, "Gary Mark Gilmore is dead." It sounded like it came from above. Bessie cried into the sore flesh of her heart.

Maybe half an hour later, Johnny Cash called and gave Mikal his condolences.

By the time Doug Hiblar came by, Bessie had turned bitter. She had the look on her face of a woman who had just had her home bombed. "Get out," Bessie said, "you people have killed my son."

"What do you mean, Bessie," stammered Doug, "I didn't even know him."

"You people in Utah killed my son."

He did not say, "I'm from Oregon."

"Mountain, you can go to hell," said Bessie to herself. "You're not mine anymore."

Outside, around the court, photographers were gathered with their cameras at the door of Bessie's trailer.

CHAPTER 40

The Remains

1

On the drive home, Stanger asked, "What are you going to do now?"

"I don't know," said Moody. "I can't go to the office."

Stanger laughed. "Need a default judgment to occupy your afternoon?"

"No," said Moody devoutly, "I couldn't stand it."

They had to talk to somebody who had been a part of it. Even though they were going to go on a week's vacation with their wives in a couple of days and so now had to run around like hell to leave their affairs in some kind of order, they couldn't go back to the office now. Instead, they said, "Let's go to Larry's place," but when they got to the Orem TraveLodge, Schiller hadn't come back yet, so they talked to Barry Farrell. It was important to keep talking.

While driving, they had been getting flashes. Stanger had seen Gary's hand rising and falling, and the blood on his pants. Stanger couldn't keep that out of his head. He wanted to extirpate such thoughts. Put his hand right inside his mind, grab the thought and flip it out.

They were happy to talk, therefore, to Barry Farrell. While they had never gotten along that well before, Ron could see how under all his professionalism, Barry was having a strong reaction, so he felt good about the conversation. So did Moody.

And Farrell, who had ranted through many a night at how these guys, Moody and Stanger, had such a paucity of humanity that they could not pursue a question profitably, did not indeed have even the curiosity of a lawyer, felt a reason now to temper his outrage. For they were so moved at Gary's death. They really did understand that somebody has gotten killed, thought Farrell.

Besides, he was eager to hear every detail and wanted to communicate to them how appreciative he was feeling toward Gilmore for approaching his death with this much integrity, my God, absolutely as much as his intellect could muster. Barry couldn't imagine what Gilmore might have done better. That helped to relieve him of his own doubts about his own involvement in these last days, this whole obscene, niggling business of translating the best thoughts of one's soul and conscience into one more rotten question, one more probe into the private parts of a man as protected from self-revelation as a clamshell from the knowledge of a caress.

When Schiller came in, they babbled, and recounted, and asked each other questions, and sputtered it out of them, until they ran down and then Moody and Stanger went home. Ron was thinking that the only event which had ever come close to having this kind of continuing reaction on him was the day President Kennedy was killed. Now, arriving at his house, he felt exhausted and immediately went to bed, but couldn't sleep. When he closed his eyes, he would see all the sights again and his skin hurt to the touch.

2

When they were alone, Farrell said to Schiller, "Have you had breakfast?"

"No," said Schiller.

"Any interest?" asked Farrell.

"I'm all diarrhea," said Schiller and thought he might go to sleep.

At that point, Barry looked up and said, "Oh, yes, listen, your mother called."

Schiller hadn't spoken to her in two weeks. He picked up the phone and learned she had seen the press conference on television after the execution, and wanted to make sure he was all right. She didn't like the way he looked. A little worn out, she thought.

Schiller assured her that he was still among the living. When the call was done, he went upstairs and actually fell asleep, and was awakened a few hours later by a girl from the *New York Times* to whom he'd promised to give an interview, but now, he said, he wouldn't do it. *Time* was calling. *Newsweek* was calling. The phone was ringing. They wanted to know if he had pictures of the execution. Wanted to come over and interview him. Schiller had to go into his speech about how he would not be a punching bag. "Your editors are asking for pictures," he said to *Newsweek* and to *Time,* "so, if you want to talk to me, we will have to discuss what you're going to say. You are not going to call me an entrepreneur. I want to make sure you're going to call me a journalist." Really started to lay down the law. "Two weeks ago, you called me an entrepreneur, called me a promoter. Now, you want pictures. Want me to give you more about the execution. Well, I'm taking offense," he said. "We got to lay out a few ground rules. If you want to say that I hustled interviews from Lenny Bruce's widow, then I also want you to write about Minamata which is a book I'm proud of. If you want a picture of Marilyn Monroe, then also put in a picture from the story I published on mercury poisoning." He said, "If you're going to slant the story one way, balance it the other," and he banged it back, and he banged it forth, and could feel his blood flowing through his veins again, instead of all that shit.

3

DESERET NEWS

Silent Majority No Longer Silent

By Ray Boren
Deseret News staff writer
Jan. 17 — According to a nationwide Louis Harris survey last week, Americans favored by a margin of 71–29 percent Gilmore's death before a firing squad.

DESERET NEWS

Emotions High Before Sunrise

By Tamera Smith
Deseret News staff writer
Utah State Prison, Jan. 17 — Anticipation, resignation, anger, disappointment, frustration and confusion were emotions that followed close upon each others' heels during the early morning hours today in Gary Mark Gilmore's prison quarters.

At 4:07 P.M., Gilmore's last meal was brought to him in his cell. It consisted of steak, potatoes, bread, butter, peas, cherry pie, coffee and milk. He had only coffee and milk.

Between 8 and 9 P.M., he asked prison staff members to call Radio Station KSOP and request two of his favorite songs — "Valley of Tears" and "Walking in the Footsteps of Your Mind."

Two switchboard operators spent the night taking calls from all over the world.

From Munich, Germany, one woman called 17 times.

"My husband died in a concentration camp," she said. "The same thing is happening there. America's no better than that," was her repeated contention.

Another woman caller cried, saying she had a dream three weeks ago that Gary should not die.

4

Schiller had reassigned Jerry Scott from watching over the office to meeting up with Gary's body in Salt Lake. Jerry was to make certain no kooks tried something while the autopsy took place.

On the drive from Orem to the hospital, Jerry Scott was mulling over how he had been the one to take Gary to Utah State Prison from the County Jail right after his trial, and now, he'd probably be the last

one to view the remains. That was a large enough coincidence to occupy your mind.

The autopsy room on the fifth floor at the University of Utah
Hospital was good sized with two slabs and Jerry, by way of his police
work, was familiar with it. Postmortems for the State were held there.
This morning, they had just brought in the body of a woman who
had drowned in a river north of Salt Lake, and they had her beside
Gary, the two tables about ten feet apart.

At first, it was hard to tell who were the doctors what with three
males and three females all around the tables, and a couple of them
busy removing Gilmore's eyes, and then another team on the organs
for the transplants. They all seemed to be working in a great rush,
and obviously had to get everything out pretty quickly. All the same,
another doctor, watching, kept saying, "Can you hurry? I have a lot
of work to do," and just a little later, "Aren't you done with him yet?"
Finally, the last of the special doctors said, "Yes, he's yours," and the
regular autopsy crew took over.

Jerry Scott stood only three or four feet away. He was curious to
see what was going on, and the medical examiner told him he could
be a witness to the postmortem, and took his name, plus the name of
Cordell Jones, a Deputy Sheriff whom Jerry Scott was glad to see
there, because Jerry expected trouble later with the people outside
when Gary's body would be transported from the hospital to the crematorium. In fact, he asked Cordell Jones to help on crowd control.
Jerry had counted at least twenty people down below at the hospital
door of which only a couple were bona fide newsmen, and, more than
a good dozen, oddballs and thrill-seekers. So, at the least, Jerry was
expecting problems and a confrontation, possibly with agitators.

The doctor who had been getting the transplants had left Gary
open from above the pubic hair to his breastbone. Now, the autopsy
crew washed him down and the examiner took a scalpel, and continued the incision up the breastbone to the neck, and continued the
cut on out to the shoulder on each side. Then, he started pulling up.

He skinned Gilmore right up over his shoulders like taking a
shirt half off, and with a saw cut right up the breastbone to the

throat, and removed the breastplate and set it in a big, open sink with running water. Then, he took out what was left of Gilmore's heart. Jerry Scott couldn't believe what he saw. The thing was pulverized. Not even half left. Jerry didn't recognize it as the heart. Had to ask the doctor. "Excuse me," he said, "is that it?" The doctor said, "Yup."

"Well, he didn't feel anything, did he?" asked Jerry Scott. The doctor said, "No." Jerry had been looking at the bullet pattern earlier, and there had been four neat little holes you could have covered with a water glass, all within a half inch of each other. The doctors had been careful to take quite a few pictures. They numbered every hole with a Magic Marker, and turned Gary over to photograph where each bullet exited from his back. Looking at those marks, Jerry could see the guys on the firing squad hadn't been shaky at all. You could tell they'd all squeezed off a good shot.

Of course, Jerry was always thinking about getting shot himself. It could happen any time on duty. He had to keep wondering what it would be like. Now, looking at the heart, he repeated, "He didn't feel anything, did he?" The doctor said, "No, nothing." Jerry said, "Well, did he move around after he was shot?" The doctor said, "Yes, about two minutes." "Was that just nerves?" Jerry asked. The fellow said, "Yes," and added, "He was dead, but we had to officially wait until he quit moving. That was about two minutes later."

After this, it got really gruesome. Jerry had to admit it. They started removing different parts of Gilmore's body. Took his plumbing out, stomach, entrails and everything, then cut little pieces out of each organ. One guy was up at the head just working away. Next thing you knew, he had Gilmore's tongue in his hand. "Why take that?" asked Jerry Scott. He didn't know whether his questions bothered the doctors or not, but since he had to witness, he thought he might as well find out what was going on. The dissectionist answered, "We're going to take a sample of it." Put the tongue down on the slab, cut it in half and sliced out a piece. Put it in a bottle of solution.

Jerry Scott had seen a lot of bodies, and gone to a lot of plane wrecks, and he knew what a person dismembered could look like, but just sitting there, watching them cut away, got to him. These fellows were really good at it, and kept talking back and forth, but they couldn't have been less excited if they were in a meat stall doing a job on a quarter of beef. Once in a while they'd call across to some other medics working on that woman who had drowned. She was so fat, that when they cut her open, her stomach hung over her thigh. Kept working like it was nothing.

Now, the fellow who was at the head of Jerry's table made an incision from behind Gary's left ear all the way up across the top of his head and then down below to the other ear, after which he grabbed the scalp on both sides of the cut, and pulled it right open, just pulled the whole face down below his chin until it was inside out like the back of a rubber mask. Then he took a saw and cut around the skull. Picked up something like a putty knife, and pried the bone open, popped the top of the head off. Then, he stuck his hand inside the cavity and pulled the brain out, weighed it. Pound and a half, it looked like to Jerry Scott. Then they removed the pituitary, put it aside, and sliced the brain like meat loaf. "Why are you doing that?" asked Jerry Scott. "Well," said one of the doctors, "we're looking for tumors." They started explaining to him about the different areas of the brain, and how they were looking to see if there were any problems in Gary Gilmore's motor system. Everything, however, looked to be just fine.

Then they took pictures of his tattoos. "Mom" had been written on his left shoulder, and "Nicole" on his left forearm. They took his fingerprints, and then they took all the organs they did not need for dissection and put them back into the body and head cavities, and drew his face up, pulled it right back taut over the bones and muscles, like putting on the mask again, fit the sawed-off bone-cap back on the skull, and sewed the scalp, and body cavity. When they were all finished, it looked like Gary Gilmore again.

During all of this, Jerry Scott noticed that Gilmore only had two teeth on his bottom gums and none on the top. Then they put his false teeth back. Looking at him now, reconstituted, Jerry Scott was amazed to see he had quite a layer of body fat for a fellow as skinny as he was. Still, he looked in pretty good shape, practically the build of an athlete, but for that belly fat.

Jerry looked at his watch then. It was one-thirty in the afternoon. He had been there four hours. Then the fellow from Walker Mortuary came over, and they put Gilmore on a rollaway-type bed with sheets covering him and a nice blanket over the top, and scooted him out to the street and loaded him in a hearse where they took him over to the Shriner Crematorium in Salt Lake. Maybe because of the four hours it took, there was no crowd waiting outside the hospital, and although they had two other police to meet them when they arrived, no crowd was at the crematorium either.

Since the coffin would be incinerated with the body, they had only a welfare-type casket waiting. It was made of plywood, although covered in maroon velvet, and it had silver rails on the side, and nice white satin on the inside, plus a real nice satin pillow. It was better than just a plain wood box, although nowhere near one of the fancy metal jobs.

Among Jerry Scott's orders this day was to make sure the right guy was being burned. So, just before they put the casket into the furnace, he lifted the sheet to verify Gary's face. Then they lifted the big oven door they had slammed down earlier to protect against the four-foot flame that shot out during the preheating, and inserted the box and body. Once it was in the kiln, and burning for a few minutes, they opened the door another time for Jerry, and the guy who ran the place took a long poker and knocked off the head of the casket. Then they stared through a furnace hole about fourteen inches by fourteen through which Jerry Scott could see Gary's head. Already the scalp was burning and the skin was falling off to the side.

Scott could see Gary's face going, and the top flesh blacken and disappear. Then the muscle began to burn, and Gilmore's arms which had been folded on his chest came up from the tightening, and lifted until the fingers of both hands were pointing at the sky. That was the very last recognition Jerry Scott had of him. He kept this picture in his head all the while the body was burning, and that was plenty of time, for he had gone to the furnace at two-thirty, and the work wasn't done until five when there was nothing left but a bit of ash and the char of the bones.

5

A couple of waitresses, friends of Toni Gurney, who worked at The Stirrup, came over to the place before the evening shift to sit at the bar. It was a large, dark cocktail lounge with a dance floor and, of course, being Utah, you had to buy a membership in the club to get your drink, but that was not too difficult. The Stirrup was lively in the evenings, and one of the few nice places between Provo and Salt Lake where you could drink and dance. Now, however, being afternoon, it was quiet, and only a couple of people were there in the half dark.

One of these friends, named Willa Brant, asked Alice Anders, the hostess, who the three guys were sitting in the lounge, for they were certainly new. Alice replied they were some of Gary's executioners. "How do you know?" asked Willa. The hostess replied, "Well, I signed them in. They're members of the Pronghorn Club in Salt Lake, and we honor that membership." Willa went to get a pack of cigarettes, and made a point of passing their table. One of the men said, "Why don't you sit down and talk to us?"

They were sitting there drinking and playing liar's poker with dollar bills. After Willa took a seat they played only a little while before one of the men said, "I bet you think we are bloodthirsty bastards, don't you?"

"Well," said Willa, "it had to be done. That was what Gary wanted." She left it at that. Didn't say she knew Toni Gurney and the rest of the family. Then the executioner said, "Want to see something sadistic?" He showed her a strap of webbing, and the slug of a bullet, and he said, "This is one of the bullets that killed Gary, and this is one of the nylon straps that was holding his arm." Asked if she wanted to touch them, Willa said, "No," but couldn't help herself. She did it with a slight smirk on her face. Then he put them back in his pocket.

Another one at the table now said he had the hood out in the car. He didn't talk much about it. Merely said he had it. They were certainly drinking.

One of these men was short and stocky and in his mid-thirties, bald on top, and another was also in his mid-thirties with light brown hair, around six feet tall, average weight, only he had a real potbelly and wore glasses. Those were the two talking the most. The third one who didn't talk had dark hair and an average build, but he had a real full beard and a mustache that was graying and he had tears in his eyes. Finally, he said if he had known what he was getting in for, he would never have done it. Then, a young married woman named Rene Wales, whom Willa knew slightly, sat down with them, and they all played a lot more liar's poker.

After a while, the executioners began to talk about their CBs. All three were equipped, but one began to brag about the distance he could get on his. Before you knew it, Rene Wales left with him to go check out the CB in his pickup. Before she got back, forty-five minutes had passed. Rene came in with the fellow, and both had a look on their faces like they'd been sopping up some of the gravy.

CHAPTER 41

Burial

1

Next morning, Tuesday, January 18, Schiller had a meeting with Debbie, Lucinda and Barry Farrell about cleaning up the office and returning the rented equipment. Right in the middle of such housekeeping, a phone call came from Stanger. There was going to be a memorial service in Spanish Fork that afternoon for Gary. Everybody wanted Larry and Barry to be there.

When Schiller told the girls, they wanted to go, too. Debbie even began to cry. So, of course, that took care of it. They were also invited. Then the service had to be moved a couple of times to elude the press and was finally held not in a church, but at a mortuary in Spanish Fork.

Tamera walked in the office about that time, and Schiller made a decision not to tell her. Felt he couldn't trust her not to write about it. From what the girls were saying, however, she picked up quickly what was happening and confronted Larry. She was livid. Just out of her mind. "I've been with you," she was saying, "I'm part of the team. Why can't I go?" Schiller had to say, "Well, it isn't that I don't trust you, Tamera, I can't take the chance. It isn't my story to give out." Tamera got mad, and then madder. She was terribly jealous of the fact that Lucinda and Debbie were going. It was the nearest she ever came to looking ugly. In fact, Tamera looked so mad, it was like she was on fire. A pure reporter.

The mortuary was on the main street, a one-story, pale stucco with a horizontal band of colored-glass window that ran around the front. It was supposed to look like stained glass, Schiller assumed, but it came out looking more like a mosaic on a coffee table. No great building, that was certain.

There were, to Schiller's surprise, forty people there. He was introduced to many of Bessie's sisters and didn't even try to remember their names, but one by one, they came up and started thanking him. Schiller didn't understand what for. Then, the organ music began.

CAMPBELL   Our Eternal Heavenly Father, with deep humility we pause at the beginning of this special memorial service, on behalf of one of our departed, Gary Mark Gilmore, with deep sense of respect and awe for the great character which he was and is and shall forever be. Father, a great tragedy has taken place many years ago in the juvenile justice system to throw a young man, a great person, a child of Thee, into the Courts, and into confinement in this country. We knew him as a great, lovable person, we shall always retain and keep that memory. Be with us now, we pray, in the name of Thy Son, Jesus Christ, Amen. (pause) We have, this afternoon, a message to be delivered by Toni Gurney from Gary's mother.

TONI   Aunt Bessie has asked me to give her message to everyone. She says, "I have many wonderful memories of my son, Gary. Beautiful things he has given me, the oil paintings that he painted, and the hand-tooled leather purse he had ordered for me, but the most priceless things Gary has given me, was his love and kindness." . . . I also want to say on behalf of myself and my sister, Brenda . . . (breaks down)

VERN   (reading Toni's message) Ah, I also want to say on behalf of my sister, Brenda, we will all miss Gary. We watched him in time of happiness, and in time of suffering, and we all know he is in peace now.

CAMPBELL   Thank you so much. Mrs. Evelyn Gray wrote some special poems to Gary, that she gave him personally, one of which she would like to read today. Evelyn is a cousin.

EVELYN   To my dear Gary:

> *Can death then end such spirit lives,*
> *as from life's stormy sea it drives,*

> *the frail soul drifting o'er the tide,*
> *no, they through dark portals guide,*
> *to sail upon a broader sea*
> *until another port they see*
> *when home they sail through the calm*
> *held in the hollow of His loving palm.*
> *They sail a beautiful sea, so broad,*
> *its bounds are known, only to God.*

Thank you.

CAMPBELL Another person who came to know Gary very well, through many visits, a man who came into his life, through the legal system, Attorney Robert Moody.

MOODY My dear friends, I think it's appropriate that we take this time to remember Gary. When we talked about it, he said, Yes, yes, I would like to be remembered, I would like a service held in my memory, and I would like Uncle Vern to say something there, to those who see fit to come. As we met with Gary for so many hours over these past several months, we came to know a human being, a creative individual, an individual who thought deeply. Gary didn't have the opportunity that any of us here have had, he was self-taught, and self-taught he was. He'd read widely, and had come to know about many, many things. Gary developed his own philosophy, and he developed his own sensitivity with God, and he did so through the limitations of the incarceration that was inflicted upon him. And this self-education taught something to each of us who conversed with him. . . . I think the one thing we will always remember, is that Gary, who looked so long, and so hard for love, only realized in these last few weeks and months that love was in the world, that love was for him, love that he'd never been able to find. As we remember Gary today, let us remember that indeed, love is for all, and no matter what others may say about Gary, his love was there, and I'm assured that Gary's in peace . . . that Gary found God. Thank you.

CAMPBELL Thank you, Bob. Brother Dick Gray would now like to present a special message.

DICK GRAY I feel a great loss. I will read these messages that were sent from his brothers. "There are many stories circulating about Gary Gilmore now, and some are good and some are bad, some are true and some are not, but the Gary Gilmore that I knew, was both good and bad, like everyone else. That is what I remember most about Gary Gilmore, that he was exactly like everyone else, when he was young before the law reformed Gary Gilmore, yes, before the law reformed Gary Gilmore, he was like everyone else. To make a long story short, we are gathered here today, because the law reformed Gary Gilmore." His brother Frank. The next is from his brother Mikal. "Gary, I pray you have found a better and more merciful world, I pray that your legacy will be one that will remind us of the value of life, not the glorification or the marketing of death in any form. I pray for our families as I pray for the families of those who have already suffered, and I pray . . . that no man, who claims to represent our interest, forgets the debt to those families. I wish, Gary, that we could have had more time. My love and remorse, Mikal."

CAMPBELL Thank you, Dick. Thomas R. Meersman, Father at the Utah State Prison, would like at this time, to share with you, Gary, from inside.

Now, nearly everyone present listened with great interest, for most of them, being Mormons, had never heard a real address from a Catholic priest before.

MEERSMAN So you know my name is Father Meersman, and I'm the Catholic Chaplain at the Utah State Prison, ah, my relationship with Gary Gilmore was perhaps different than any of yours. I came into his life because of a very unusual statement I heard a man make when he was condemned to death. I told him that when I met him the first time. I said it's quite an unusual statement and if you mean it, why I will offer you all that I can to bring it about. And the statement that he made is one I imagine that you've all heard: I wish to die with dignity. And so, we began our relationship, we would meet, especially at night, 'cause during the day he was very busy about many things. People coming to see him and to visit him ah . . . his name became more and more famous and he gained world and international recognition at least of his name and of what he was doing and things like that. . . . We kept it going like this, and when it looked like the end was, of course, very near, well, you have to get serious. There's a time and a place for all things, and so, the night before his deathwatch, we gathered together and it was just about midnight, and the church was in the kitchen, and one of the guards happened to be a Catholic, and he's the one, in our terminology, who served the Mass, and assisted the priest, who happened to be myself, and during two parts of the Mass, we used Bible readings, and when the question was asked,

"What Gospel should we read?" in his own inimitable way, he said, "My name is Gary Mark. Read something from Saint Mark." Afterwards, well, the guards were moved to a certain extent, and they noticed, of course, that he was extremely reflective, especially afterwards he didn't move, he just sat there on the table. And ah, we said to him very simply, We came into your life when you said I want to die with dignity. And we'll stay into your life, we'll stay within your life till that's accomplished. But we want you to know this, that every day of my life as a Catholic priest, when I stand at an altar, wherever it may be, in the Utah State Prison, in a hospital, at Saint Peter's in Rome, that every day of my life you will be prayed for. And so, I don't know, these are some of my thoughts. There probably are many more, but I didn't have too much time to jot too much down but I hope that they will help you who loved him so much. And will miss him, of course. That will help you to know him, perhaps, that we said these words, at this time. And I can say nothing better to you than his last words . . . Dominus vobiscum. May the Lord be with you all. Thank you.

CAMPBELL   Thank you, Father. I'm deeply moved as all of you are, as we begin to expose the real Gary Mark Gilmore. Another person who has come to respect him, Ron Stanger.

STANGER   I think Bob and I were a part of his adopted family. I think with the exception of maybe three or four days, we were with him every day, and if you don't believe us, ask our wives. Ah, they knew that very well. There I was on Christmas Day, and the family was together, and all the merriment that you always have on Christmas, and guess where Moody and Stanger went? But indeed, it seemed to me to be very appropriate that for the first and maybe the only time in my lifetime that I consider myself to be a good and true Christian, because I did what the Savior said, and that is to go into prisons and to try and help those people in need.

May I challenge all of us, however, to do the thing that I also learned from Gary as he would talk with me about family and we all know that he loved children. He would ask us how we were getting along with our children and he'd always say, Ron, raise your family, be close to them, be strict with them, let them know that if they make little mistakes they'll grow into bigger ones. He said one time, when he had that smile he would get on his face, he said, "They might, if they keep doing things wrong, they might end up being another Gary Gilmore."

CAMPBELL Thank you, Ron. Gary has done for me a great favor. He pushed me over the hump. I'm going to quit the prison in six months. Gary has convinced me that an ounce of prevention is worth a pound of cure, that the two words juvenile and justice don't go together. My plans are to move into southern Utah where I have some property and build a boys' ranch and take those up to the age of fourteen who find themselves in difficulty with the law and love them. You've gathered from those that have spoken, that the thing that Gary wanted to leave was love. He probably had more capacity to love than anybody at that place. He gave to me a deep love and I want you to know that I have in me a portion of Gary Mark Gilmore that will never leave.

He asked that a special song be sung at his memorial, and as he told me about it, he said this is me as I leave this earth. The song is a great Christian hymn, called "Amazing Grace," to be delivered today by Mrs. Robert Moody.

MRS. ROBERT MOODY (sings)

> *Amazing Grace, how sweet the sound*
> *That saved a wretch like me*
> *I once was lost but now I'm found,*
> *Was blind, and now I see.*
>
> *Through many dangers, toils, and snares*
> *I have already come*
> *Tis Grace has brought me safe thus far*
> *And Grace will lead me home.*

CAMPBELL Thank you very much. That was beautiful. I know it's true that Gary loved all of you. But one, in particular, where I know love came from both sides in tremendous and great abundance, was his Uncle Vern. . . . And Vern will now deliver the final message.

VERN Brothers and sisters, friends, on this day, the eighteenth day of January 1977, I stand before you because Gary asked me to. And this is all very strange to me, I've never done this before. . . . But I promised him and I would try to say a few words for him. Not to excuse him for what he did, but to try to explain why he did it. Which I'm sure this is going to be difficult for me. The best way that I can explain is that Gary was deeply in love with a girl that was deeply in love with him. And the problems that they had themselves was probably the same problems that some of us have. But Gary just couldn't handle them. He had to strike out at something, somebody, and unfortunately, he did. Gary has gone to his death hoping that this will atone for what he has done. He's done this thing to two fine families, but he tells me he has only one life to give, and he wished he had more. And he would give more. He has given special parts of his body to people and to science, hoping that it will help some unfortunate person to be healthy again. I've learned to know Gary . . . the last few months, more than I ever had since I'd known him, I've seen the inner side of Gary, and he is human, tender, and yes, understanding, very capable of love. Gary is on his way to a new life with God, and so, as Gary would say, "You people be cool." In the name of Jesus Christ, Amen.

2

After the service, Stanger asked Larry Schiller into the side room where the urn was standing. There Larry learned that Gary had requested that his ashes be spread over Spanish Fork because that was where his loving memories were. Vern felt Gary didn't want to be in an enclosed place again. He had been enclosed all his life. Now he wanted to be on top of the earth and free to roam as the wind blew.

They were going to do it from an airplane and Ron told Larry that Gary desired him on the flight. It was his request. Schiller said he didn't want to go. Didn't feel that that was the place for him. They said Vern had been asked, Father Meersman and Cline Campbell, and then there would be Ron Stanger and himself. Finally, he had to agree. But, he still felt it was wrong. All through the memorial service, he had not felt near to Gilmore nor close to all the emotions the guests had obviously been feeling. The airplane ride would be more of that. Still, it was arranged that next morning, they would all go up in the plane. Schiller spent the rest of the day packing.

On Wednesday, the 19th, there he was out at Provo Airport and they all got into this six-seater, the pilot and Stanger in the front two seats, Vern and Campbell behind, Meersman and himself in the rear.

It all proved very simple. They had this cardboard container the size of a shoebox, and once they were in the air, Stanger opened it. Gary's ashes had been put into a plastic bag of the sort you sell bread in, a cellophane bag with the printing from the bread company clearly on it. That freaked Schiller out. Here, Stanger was holding this bag up next to the window, and it had colored printing all over it, not festive, but cheap, a 59¢ loaf of bread. Schiller imagined that the ashes would be black and somber and kind of dignified, but they were gray and white and had bits of bone in them, a seedy, used-up color.

Gary had specified how he wanted those ashes deposited. He had picked a number of places in Spanish Fork and Springville and Provo, and so Stanger had to strew the ashes in four or five takes. He never even put his hand out the window, however, just tucked the opening of the bag next to where he cracked the vent. The pilot would bank to put Stanger on the down side, and the air would suck out the ashes. A slow business, not very dramatic. In the back seat Meersman started to talk to Schiller about the memorial service. It was obvious to Schiller that Meersman wanted to suggest that Gary had returned to the Catholic Church on his dying day, but it didn't ring right to Schiller. Gary had hated the name Mark, even crossed it out in his contracts. Of course, he could have been AC-DC about his middle name, but Schiller was only buying Meersman's story with a bag of salt.

After they spread the ashes and came down, Barry Farrell was waiting at the airport. With him was a girl from the *New York Times* whom Schiller certainly did not want to be interviewed by. He had, however, neglected to inform Farrell of that little fact. So, right after disembarking, he had to face the *Times* girl. By the look on her face, it was obvious Barry had told her what they were all doing in the plane. Schiller was pinned against the wall, and did a horrible interview. The story got out. No longer a secret where Gilmore's ashes ended.

Later that day, he also did an interview for *Time,* and one for *Newsweek,* and took a jet to L.A. Both magazines had agreed to his conditions, but then, he had a grip on both. In November, *Newsweek* had been in collaboration with Schiller for a day or two, so he told them now that if they didn't mention that little fact in their article, he would inform *Time*. In turn, he told *Time* that if they didn't agree to the idea of a balanced portrait, he would inform *Newsweek* how *Time* had slipped him a Minox to give to an associate on execution night for taking photographs of Gary. Thereby, he had magazines giving him fair and decent treatment. Not preferred treatment, just fair and decent — that was all he ever asked for.

CHAPTER 42

In the Ebb of the News

1

TIME

What the warden called "the event" took just 18 minutes. Hearing the fusillade, prisoners in three nearby cellblocks screamed obscenities.

SALT LAKE TRIBUNE

ACLU Calls Hansen Murder Accomplice

January 18, 1977 — Henry Schwarzschild, New York Coordinator of the National Coalition Against the Death Penalty and director of the Capital Punishment Project of the American Civil Liberties Union, had only harsh words about the execution and Utah officials.

"This was not a suicide of Mr. Gilmore but a judicial homicide with Mr. Hansen as an accomplice," Mr. Schwarzschild said at a Salt Lake Hilton Hotel press conference.

The speed with which "the state attorney general raced to the 10th Circuit bespeaks nothing but bloodlust," Mr. Schwarzschild added.

"I am appalled at such a performance in this society which calls itself civilized," the capital punishment opponent said.

"I could not gauge the depth of callousness and human depravity that brought about this spectacle."

Mr. Schwarzschild said his words were harsh, but added the situation called for a strident tone. "Let Mr. Hansen make of them what he will."

SALT LAKE TRIBUNE

Justice Has Been Served, Hansen Says of Execution

By Dave Jonsson
Tribune Staff Writer
January 17, 1977 — Utah Atty. Gen. Robert B. Hansen, who personally argued in court against stays of execution of Gary Mark Gilmore, said Monday after the convict's death, "Justice has been served."

"Capital punishment is symbolic of society's determination to enforce all of its laws. If we don't enforce the severest of our laws, the criminal mind might conclude (punishments of) other laws won't be imposed against them," Mr. Hansen said.

"No death can be elevating, and there is much sadness when anyone dies," added Mr. Hansen, his face drawn after 30 hours without sleep, "but I am infinitely more sorrowful about the two victims' families than the fact Mr. Gilmore is no longer alive."

Hansen's story was printed right next to a big photograph of him in the *Salt Lake Tribune*. Next to that story, however, was the adjoining headline on the Schwarzschild story, and it said: "Judicial Homicide."

Bob Hansen was used to seeing pretty savage things written about himself, but "Judicial Homicide" offended him. He debated for a long time whether to sue the ACLU guy. Since he was a public figure, he knew he would have to show a lot of malice. While Schwarzschild's statement, from Hansen's point of view, was reeking with malice, the difficulty was that Schwarzschild could hardly be responsible for the headline. Which was the most blatant part of the story. It was a problem, and Hansen was very much offended.

2

One day, shortly after the execution, Judy Wolbach went over to the State Capitol Building to tell Earl Dorius what she thought of him. It was not a very well advised thing to do, but she sat down in his office and asked him what he thought of himself. Earl said, "Judy, you've got to understand that while you may think everything we did was terrible, we believed in our turn, that everything you did was completely unfair. We'll have to work together on other cases in the future, so I'd be happy if you could stay in some control of your feelings." He may not have used exactly that language, but she heard him making a speech on that order. She could hardly listen. "Earl," she answered, "tell me. You have little children. Doesn't it disturb you when they find out that you were, as it were, a helpmate to this execution?" He nodded. It did disturb him, he told her. One of the children had heard some comment that he and Attorney General Hansen had been involved in a cold-blooded murder. He had to explain it all to them.

From his side of the desk, Earl felt Judy was entitled to come up and confront him. In fact, he was glad she had done it. After an emotional case such as this, attorneys went their separate ways. He didn't like it when they ran into each other later on the street and could only glare back and forth. In fact, he thought it was big of Judith to have the courage to come up, and get it off her chest. Better than going on over the years with a feud.

After she left the office, it occurred to Judy that she had been waiting to feel a lot of pain from the execution, but it hadn't come. Only the wrath that consumes. She must have been reacting deeply or she would not have gone to see Earl Dorius, but there simply had not been any emotional reaction to Gilmore's death itself. She wondered if it had to do with the awful feeling she'd had from time to time that she *was* colliding with Gilmore's rights.

Salt Lake Tribune

Utah Execution: We Came Killing

By Bob Greene
Field Newspaper Syndicate
January 20, 1977 — We didn't tell you how we crawled around the sandbags in front of the dead man's chair, the sandbags still fresh with his blood. We didn't tell you how we hurried into the firing squad's canvas booth, and how we squinted out of the vertical slits where the rifles had been, squinted out at the chair and made ourselves a gift of the same view the executioners had viewed.

We didn't tell you how we touched everything, touched every possible surface in the death shed. We didn't tell you of the looks on the faces of the prison guards, who watched in amazement as we went about our doings with such eagerness, such lust. We didn't tell you what we did to the death chair itself — the chair with the bullet holes in its leather back. We didn't tell you that, did we? Didn't tell you how we inserted our fingers into the holes, and rubbed our fingers around, feeling for ourselves, how deep and wide those death holes were. Feeling it all.

3

Brenda was completely exhausted. Back in her own home, afloat in her own bed, people came to see her, but she could hardly remember who they were. She talked, but couldn't remember what she said. Three days got to be like one. Then she caught fever, and started vomiting pretty heavy. Only thing she could think was, "I've got to get cleaned up and go to that funeral." Made it as far as the bathroom. She didn't know that the funeral had taken place two days ago. She really was shattered to find out. She wouldn't be with Gary at his last service. That was letting him down.

4

A few nights after the execution, Nicole got into a fight. As evening
came on, she felt again a powerful desire to go to bed. It wasn't time
yet, but she stretched out, and four or five patients came to drag her
off. When they touched her, Nicole started swinging.

She almost busted somebody's nose, and at one point came
near to laying out all five girls. It probably lasted over three minutes.
That was a long time to fight five girls. Finally they got her stretched
out flat on her back but she kept getting her feet loose and kicking
them, so they turned her over on her stomach and lay on top of her
for, she could swear, twenty fucking minutes on that cold floor, each
of them sitting on an arm or leg. All of a sudden, she realized how
funny it was, and started laughing. Laughed as if her heart would
burst.

The people holding her weren't seeing it as funny, of course. Yet,
she felt she was not laughing alone. Somebody was there with her.
Then she knew it was Gary. He was just about saying in her ear,
Hey, cunt, now you know what it's like.

Afterward, they locked her up for a few days. During that time,
she'd often bust out laughing. Felt like she still wasn't laughing
alone.

All this time, she never cried about Gary. It wasn't necessary. He
was not pitying himself. She kept hoping he would feel close to her
when she got out of the nuthouse, and thought maybe she would still
take her life, but did not really know. It was hard to tell.

5

Stanger and Moody were booked on a Gulf of Mexico cruise that left
on Saturday, but they didn't want to wait for the weekend, so took off
for New Orleans with their wives by Thursday afternoon. They had
dinner at six, and were so physically exhausted they went back to
their motels and didn't wake until twelve hours later.

The following night, sitting in a restaurant, the gal at the next table got a touch obstreperous. Her husband said with a grin, "Just leave her alone, and she'll go home." He was joking, but she drew herself up and said, "I want you to know that I am a *law* student, and I have been doing *re*search on an important case, the Gary *Gil*more case. Have you ever heard about *that?*"

Bob's wife, Katherine, couldn't hold it, said, "These are Gilmore's lawyers." It was worth losing your pants in Court to see the look on that gal's face.

6

Over the next few days, Earl Dorius did a burn about the disposition of Gilmore's ashes. Under public health statutes, the strewing was illegal, and could have been prevented if he'd known in advance. Then he found out the prison had heard, but did not contact him. He had to tell himself to forget it. That was not the sort of thing you could pursue, and besides he was feeling pretty tired. Bob Hansen told him to take some of the compensated time he'd accumulated after working almost every night since November up till nine or ten.

Earl wanted a quick vacation, no place special, no long time, so he drove his wife and family down to Orem where they had relatives. Just off the freeway, he saw a TraveLodge, and walked in to book a room. As the girl started to write up the registration blank, the phone rang and Earl heard her say, "Don't worry, Mr. Damico." When she hung up, Earl said, "What does Vern Damico have to do with this motel? If he or Mr. Schiller owns it, I'm leaving."

"Well," the girl said, "Mr. Schiller and his staff just checked out yesterday." Earl said to himself, "I can't get away from Gilmore."

Afterward, Earl often thought of that lonely moment in the corridor up in Federal Court in Denver when he looked out the window after hearing Gilmore was dead, and people were coming to work. He had been all alone. Even while giving the argument, he had been a solitary figure, and so it had been appropriate, somehow, to be aware of himself looking out, watching others do press interviews on the plaza. He had to admit he felt a certain disappointment and did his best to laugh and tell himself that he was going in for masochistic martyrdom. If he had wanted to work himself silly just to make sure each little job was done right, then he better develop himself emotionally to a point where he didn't care who got the publicity.

He was sure able to test this demand on himself real soon. In a couple of weeks the Utah Historical Society visited the office and interviewed everybody for one of their volumes on the State's history. They never came, however, to Earl. He was out of the office that day. It turned out pretty much like all of the Gilmore business — he was always away from the main action when media or historians were there. The key thing, he told himself, was to stay glad it got done.

7

SALT LAKE TRIBUNE

Order Probe of Gilmore Photo

By George A. Sorensen
Tribune Suburban Editor
January 28, 1977 — The Utah State Board of Corrections Thursday ordered an investigation how Time and Newsweek magazines carried pictures of Gilmore drinking from a minibottle of whisky shortly before the execution.

SALT LAKE TRIBUNE

Gilmore's Execution Cost State $60,000

By George A. Sorensen
January 30 — It cost the taxpayers of Utah more than $60,000 to bring convicted murderer Gary Mark Gilmore to trial and keep him alive through two suicide attempts.

With the exception of the actual trial costs, estimated by Utah County Attorney Noall T. Wootton at $15,000 to $20,000, all other figures are based upon extra help or overtime.

More than 200 of the prison's total staff of 320 were called back at 3 A.M. on the morning of the execution.

Utah Attorney General Robert B. Hansen estimates it cost $19,000 for the extra work of his deputies and secretaries. Some put in as much as 30 hours straight during the last day and night.

8

One of the hardest things for Toni Gurney was to go up to the University of Utah Hospital for Gary's clothes. They had been sitting in a storage room for a few days and finally turned so rank, they had to freeze them.

Toni was given this icy bundle, and put it in the trunk of her car, but on the way home, it thawed out. By the time she got back, she was close to being late for work, only there was no question. She had to get those clothes in the washing machine, right away. The odor had all the stink of mortal loss.

9

Over the weeks, hate mail began to slow down and Shirley Pedler came back to some kind of daily routine, but it felt peculiar to come into the ACLU office and not have the halls jammed. So much of her emotional energy was still attached to Gary Gilmore that the normal world seemed bizarre and very small.

Not only was Gilmore dead, but she was in some kind of separate reality herself. Once in a while, like a mist passing across the sky, she would feel a strange communion with him, as if a thought had passed back and forth, and she felt happy that the strain was removed from his life and he had been set free. It was paradoxical, but she felt good about that.

CHAPTER 43

To Kiss and Tell

1

In Chicago for the final assembling of the *Playboy* interview, Schiller and Farrell worked around the clock and didn't finish until five o'clock Sunday evening, the 23rd. That was one week to the hour that Schiller left the TraveLodge Motel to drive to the prison for the beginning of the last night.

When they turned it in, they thought they were handing over 19,000 words, still a comfortable length, since *Playboy* had contracted to print 15,000, but a word count came back later that evening. They were up to 25,000. Art Kretchmer, the editor, who Schiller thought looked something like Abe Lincoln — a young good-looking Jewish Abe Lincoln — said, "I'd be scared to cut a word." Barry Golson agreed but was dubious about finding more space. "Nothing else we could run," Kretchmer told Golson, "is as important as going all the way with this," and he pulled a piece of fiction.

Then, Schiller tried to convince Kretchmer to break the standard format and use INTERVIEWER and GILMORE rather than PLAYBOY and GILMORE, but suspected there wasn't anything Hugh Hefner would insist on more than the interviewer being made synonymous with *Playboy*.

Farrell wrote an introduction which Barry Golson had the pleasure of rewriting — he had Schiller on his turf at last! — and then

Schiller wanted to go to sleep, Farrell wanted to go to sleep. Debbie, however, had been brought to Chicago to do the last-minute typing, and now that they were done she wanted to swim in Hugh Hefner's famous indoor pool at the mansion where you could watch the swimmers through a glass wall in the underground bar. She wasn't an ex-Playboy Bunny for nothing. So Kretchmer opened up the mansion. Nobody was in town. Nobody was ever in the mansion anymore now that Hefner was in Los Angeles, but Debbie was able to go swimming while Farrell and Schiller just said, "Oh, no," and lay out in the sauna at three in the morning.

Back in Los Angeles, Schiller heard from Phil Christensen, Kathryne Baker's attorney, who called to say that Nicole was going to be released. Schiller had a flash of the press standing at the front door of the hospital. Here he had never met Nicole and didn't know what she thought of him. Couldn't even be certain she was going to honor the contract.

Naturally, Larry Flynt's new skin mag, *Chic,* called at just this time to offer $50,000 for a series of nudes on Nicole. $50,000! They were being very polite. Using the word "nudes." Maybe they didn't know how to say "spread-shots." He told *Chic* he would like them to come up with a list of photographers. That was a ploy to keep them off for a while. Then, Larry called Kathryne Baker and said, "I think it's important Nicole be taken immediately out of Utah, or the press will hound her. You and your kids need a vacation. Have you ever lived at the beach?" Kathryne said, "Nicole really loved the beach when we were up in Oregon."

"All right," said Schiller. "I'll get a house in Malibu. You and Nicole and your family come as my guests. I won't impose. Just come out and have a month off in a different environment."

Kathryne said that would really be wonderful. Larry scrambled around and made arrangements with Western Airlines for tickets for Nicole and her kids under phony names and prepaid the six trips, and called Jerry Scott to go to Kathryne's house at a given hour of the morning to pick up the baggage and bring it to the airport, then return for Mrs. Baker, and coordinate with Sundberg to have Nicole released at a precise time from the hospital so Jerry could zap her to the airport. They figured it would be exactly a thirty-five-minute drive, and would put a ten-minute variance on it. Pick her up forty-five minutes before the plane was due to leave. All arranged.

Nicole was not only getting ready to leave, but had, in fact, even gone up the hospital corridor one last time to pick up her street clothes, when a girl asked, "How do you feel about Gary?" Nicole said, "If he was alive, I'd do it all over again." They turned her right around and put her back in the hospital.

Schiller was on the phone the next four or five days. He spoke to Dr. Woods and the other doctors. He spoke to Kiger. He kept describing the environment he would put Nicole in. Promised to have a doctor standing by if something happened, swore she'd be secluded from the press. He would *underline* that promise. He sent Kiger a telegram that set it all out, then a longer letter by courier. He suggested that the hospital have the Court recommend her release, thereby lifting the hospital off the hook.

The plan went into effect all over again. Only this time, Schiller decided he would fly to Utah. No way was he going to be caught on the wrong end again, waiting for things to happen. Lucinda was sent to Malibu and found a place for $1,500 a month, and Schiller slapped down the rent and deposit, and took off for Utah where he arranged to meet Nicole in Ken Sundberg's office. While sitting there, a phone call came from Vern who said he had the cartons Gary wanted to give Nicole. What should they do about them?

"Well, Vern," said Schiller, "I got to tell you. My attitude is, don't hold anything back." "Do you want to look at the boxes first?" asked Vern. "No," said Schiller. Vern said, "I got this tape Gary recorded for Nicole on the last night. I've listened to it." His pause encouraged Schiller to say, "How bad?"

"Well," said Vern, "it asks her to kill herself."

"Then," said Schiller, "I think we should not give her the tape." He thought for a moment and said to himself, "Maybe I could be there when the boxes are opened." At that moment, he was ready to hold them back too, but Gary had told her about them in one of his letters.

While still waiting for Nicole in the office, he got a call from Phil Christensen. The old lawyer had a new contract he wanted Nicole to sign. It would establish 20 percent of her income as his fee. Schiller hit the top. "We," said Christensen, "have invested a lot of time," and the lawyer went on to describe the hours put into the effort, and the future work. "No," said Schiller, "let her make her own decision." He had the feeling Christensen's heart wasn't altogether in it.

Half an hour later, Nicole showed up. It was easy. The press had had no idea she was being released that day. On going to Court, the hospital had gotten the Judge to agree to let her out in 24 hours, while announcing that the release was four days off. So the press had thought her coming-out party was 72 hours down the road.

There was Schiller on the second floor of Sundberg's office with Sunny and Peabody, when this girl with a super figure walked in wearing jeans and a shirt and very quiet. She kind of floated by him and picked up the kids and hugged and kissed them. They were really delighted to see her. "Mommy, Mommy," they carried on. Nicole started to cry, and Kathryne Baker started, but the kids didn't. They were holding toys in their hands and were saying to Nicole, "Look what Uncle Larry got us." She turned then, and Schiller was delighted. Much more attractive than he'd expected, and he thought there was character and subtlety in her face considering she was a quietly wild-looking kid. That was splendid. It elevated Gilmore immediately in his mind. Gary and Nicole weren't some sordid romance, but an interesting relationship.

Schiller now knelt to the floor, and said, beaming at her, "I'd like to introduce myself. I'm the big bad wolf, Larry Schiller." She had no affectation. Just said right off the cuff, "Gary told me about you, but you're not what I expected you to look like." She spoke in a soft voice that was full of her own breath, as if she put a lot of thought into each word. What she had to say came out slowly, but had a strong personal quality for a girl so young, and Schiller thought he knew what she meant. Gilmore had kept referring to him as a smart tough guy from Hollywood, so she had been expecting this dapper dude. Here he was bulky and disheveled with his parka on. Of course, he had worn that for effect. No suit and tie for meeting Nicole. A perfect choice. Hell, she had no suitcase, no nothing.

He let her play with the kids for a while, then took her off to a side office, sat her down, and said, "Look, you don't know me from

Adam. I can say to you that Gary, for whatever reasons, trusted me with a lot of things. I've made plans I'll explain to you, and if you think it's something you'd like to do, then we have to leave here in five minutes and catch a plane. If it's something you don't want to do, then no hard feelings." He gave her the reasons why he thought she should come to California, and said, "You know, a lot of people have warned me you could try it again," said it straight out. She nodded like she respected him for remarking on that. Then he added, "I've got this little house on the beach. You can take walks and think about things. I'll be there." He hesitated but decided to bite the bullet, and asked her if she remembered signing any contracts, and was she aware she had a contract with him, and she said she was. "All right," he said, "what do you think? You want to do it?" "Yeah," Nicole said, "I'd like to go to California." Then he added, "Your lawyers also mentioned a contract for you to sign before you leave."

"Do you think I should?" she asked.

They were getting along like hot dogs and mustard. "Well," he said, "I won't tell you what's in it, but it's a pile of crap."

She smiled again. She had a great smile, he thought. It came out of some place in the center of her, and spread slowly across her face like whipped cream. She had full lips and it gave her a great, tough grin. It said, "Come on, you're no better than I am." He was surprised how fresh she was. A remarkably clean young lady. On this promising note, they left the office, went to the airport, and were off to California.

On the plane, however, she began to slump. He could feel her pulling away from everybody. She no longer looked her own soul. More like a waif in a house whose windows were wet with fog. Schiller felt a worm of fear stir right in the pit of his gut.

2

In L.A., waiting at the airport to pick them up, Lucinda was thinking of some of the acts she had heard Gary talk about to Nicole on the tape recorder, the kind of things Lucinda had never heard anybody else say. So she could hardly believe it was Nicole she now saw coming toward her down the runway, but she felt, to her surprise, overwhelmingly sorry for her. Nicole seemed so small and alone, as if plucked from another world, and put in this one without the capacity to grasp it. Yet this was the same Nicole coming toward her now with her mother and children, carrying her little *Newsweek* magazine that had Gary on the cover. The magazine was what made Lucinda feel the worst. It was as if Nicole had no way to grasp anything. Looked numb and out of it. She seemed far off from Larry. Lucinda couldn't tell if Nicole hated him, or hated all of them. There seemed to be nothing coming off her but this refusal to have anything to do with anybody.

After the drive out to Malibu, Larry took Nicole and her to the grocery store and Lucinda watched him spend something like $160 on food for the Baker family. It was probably, Lucinda thought, more food than they'd ever had together in their lives, but Nicole didn't say anything. Just walked up and down the aisles. Larry would say, "Well, think we need some of this?" but she just kept walking through this incredible Malibu supermarket with all these dressed-up moneyed people around her.

Larry kept buying, as if to compensate for the awkwardness of the situation. Two full baskets before long. Nicole would just kind of smile, like food was the last thing she had on her mind. At one point Larry asked her if there was anything else she wanted, and she said, "Yeah, like I think I'd like some instant potatoes."

Later, driving Kathryne Baker around L.A., out on the freeway with this skinny high-strung, very madeup little woman, Lucinda listened to how Gary had come over to Kathryne's house with guns, and she was always terrified of him. It was almost as if so much attention had been given to Nicole, that Kathryne wanted to get in with her story too, and was telling it right in front of the children. It came out in a jumble. But Lucinda was fascinated. When the kids would interrupt, Lucinda wanted them to be quiet.

The first thing Schiller told Nicole after they got back from the supermarket was that she was going to have to take on responsibility for the house. There would be a thousand dollars in cash available as expenses this month, and he would leave whatever part of it she wanted now. The station wagon was also there for her. Now he would say good-bye for a while. The moment he left, however, it came over him that Nicole might open those boxes Gary had left, read something he wrote, and kill herself. She had the kind of calm to do it. That was when he got scared shitless.

He had said good-bye to her with a great big smile, had told her he'd be around the next day, and she should take it easy and feel right, but he could feel how surprised she was that he was leaving her alone this first night away from the hospital, alone, that is, with her mother and kids. He said, "Hey, you're your own person. If I see you tomorrow, fine. If you don't want to see me tomorrow, nothing lost." That was what he said, but he had never been so scared as on that ride home.

In fact, he couldn't hold out till he got back. Two-thirds of the way to Beverly Hills, he stopped and called, pretending he had just gotten in. "Want to let you know I'm home safely," he said in a voice that couldn't sell ice cream, but, of course, had to hear her voice to be sure she hadn't packed it in.

3

Nicole did open the box that night. Gary had left her a Meerschaum pipe which Nicole didn't know was of value. She thought it looked great for blowing soap bubbles. Then there was the watch Gary had broken at the estimated time of execution. She thought it was neat of him to do it. After all, what would it mean if she'd just been handed a watch? Then there was a Bible in the box. Gary wrote he had been sent enough Bibles to open a holy store, but this one arrived on the day he had attempted to take his life the second time.

She read through newspaper stories he had left her on Gary and Nicole, and looked at a picture of Amber Jim, who was a ten-year-old girl prizefighter who had written to Gary. Plus a bunch of letters from Amber Jim. Nicole actually got jealous reading them, even though Amber Jim was just a little girl. It also made her feel like crying. It was the first thing that brought Nicole close to the reality of all those people besides herself who had been thinking of Gary as the time of his execution came near.

Then, she saw a picture of Richard Gibbs. Underneath it, Gary had written, "Undercover agent and a rat. Stool pigeon. He really fooled me." A lot of pictures of Nicole and her family at various ages were in the box, and letters sent to Gary from a lot of people. A St. Michael's medal. A navy blue sweat shirt was the best. It didn't stink, but it did smell of him. Smelled nice. It was just a great sweat shirt, and she didn't want to wash it. She wore it that night and wore it a few times after, and never wanted to wash it, but after a while, it got funky and she had to.

4

Schiller didn't start the first interview for a week. Then it was a problem where to get privacy to do them. The house at Malibu had three bedrooms upstairs, a kitchen, dining room and living room on the main floor, and on the lower level, by the beach, a playroom. Her mother slept in one bedroom, the Baker kids in another, and Nicole was planning to share a big, king-sized bed with Sunny and Jeremy, but she preferred to shack out on her cold, windy porch in the late January and early February winter sunshine of Malibu. It was cold and windy, but she chose it. Virtually moved out there. All her books were on the porch.

They ended up having interviews in all kinds of places. Now that she was out of the hospital, Nicole hated to be confined to a room, so Schiller would start his tape recorder in restaurants, or take her for drives and talk in the car. After some days of that, he came to discover that she was going to give him more than he'd ever hoped for, more in fact than Gary ever did or maybe could.

She seemed to have a commitment to the interviews as deep as the beating of her heart. It was as if she had to tell him the story as once she had told it to Gary, and tell it all, tell it not to satisfy her guilt (and sometimes he thought she felt very guilty), no, tell for some deeper reason. Schiller was profoundly confused why she was so concerned to give it all forth and explain what had happened in the very best way she could ever understand it. Why she was as fair, he decided, to a true description of everything that was not good between Gary and herself as to everything that had been good, until Schiller began to wonder if she had gone through hell and come back with one simple message, "Nothing is worse in all the world than the taste of bullshit in your mouth."

Of course, sometimes the interviews went slowly. She would admit the most amazing matters, told him about Uncle Lee almost as soon as they started, but little admissions would bother her a lot and she would be embarrassed by the oddest things. Sometimes Schiller would have to wrestle with her most astonishing reluctance to provide a detail he considered trivial.

SCHILLER   Now open the crack in the door a little bit. (long pause)

NICOLE   I can't, Larry.

SCHILLER   You can talk about murder, you can talk about Gary choking you, you can talk about Uncle Lee molesting you, and you can't talk about Barrett fucking around with your head?

NICOLE   Yeah, I could probably. But I can't just say specific things that he said.

SCHILLER   Why not? (long pause) Is Barrett holier than thou?

NICOLE   (laughs) Fuck you, Larry. I'm not going to talk about it. I'm not going to say what I don't want to say.

SCHILLER   You're just doing that to prove that you're stronger than me, that's all.

NICOLE   No, I'm not doing that to prove anything.

SCHILLER   Yes, you are.

NICOLE   I'm doing it because it embarrasses me.

SCHILLER   How can you be embarrassed with me? Now come on. Do you want me to turn off the fucking tape recorder? Is that what's embarrassing you? I don't understand how you can be embarrassed with me. I really don't.

NICOLE   Good. You never will. (pause)

SCHILLER   Come on, I've got to understand this. I've got to have an example of it. Because it comes up all the time. Come on, don't play games with me. Come on.

NICOLE   (laughs) Oh, God. (whispers)

SCHILLER "Oh, God," come on.

NICOLE Larry, I'm trying. I can't say it, all right? I'm really trying. I can't. Forget it.

SCHILLER I'm not going to forget it. I'm not going to forget it.

NICOLE Okay. Another time.

SCHILLER I need to know it this time. Not another time. Give me one example. I mean, you're off there in Midway because of what Barrett did with your goddamned head.

NICOLE (laughs) I didn't say Barrett was the cause of anything that happened on Midway.

SCHILLER No, you didn't say he was the cause. You said he made you feel a certain way. By things he said to you.

NICOLE Yes.

SCHILLER Don't give me that smile. (laughs) Don't give me that smile. You're looking out there, you know. And then you turn around and give me that little smile.

NICOLE (laughs) I'm laughing at you.

SCHILLER What?

NICOLE I'm laughing at you.

SCHILLER 'Cause I'm so naive?

NICOLE No.

SCHILLER 'Cause I don't have the experience to fantasize or imagine?

NICOLE No, it has nothing to do with that. It's that you don't give up and you keep sneaking back.

SCHILLER I'm a little sneak, right?

NICOLE Yes, sometimes. (long pause)

SCHILLER You were fucking around. What got you fucking around on Midway?

NICOLE (long sigh; longer pause; another sigh; still more pause — chuckling to herself) Whatever got me fucking around I don't know, but there's one thing I know. I've always known it and I just haven't even thought about it for quite a while. (pause) I got into this cycle or something of picking up guys that either had never had a piece of ass or guys that were . . . you know, that hadn't had a . . .

SCHILLER   Good lay?

NICOLE   Yeah.

SCHILLER   Right.

NICOLE   Just there staying away from good-looking guys, guys that looked like they could get just about any sweet piece of ass they wanted.

SCHILLER   Right. And you went after the guy that looked like he hadn't gotten laid or never had a good piece.

NICOLE   Right.

SCHILLER   And what was the motive?

NICOLE   (long sigh) Goddammit, you're the shrink. No, you're not, right, I know it, I know it.

SCHILLER   What was the motive?

NICOLE   You just ask me so I'll tell you. It's really obvious to you, though, isn't it?

SCHILLER   No, so help me God, it's not.

NICOLE   I can't believe that.

SCHILLER   It's the truth, kid. So help me.

NICOLE   Aw, that innocent voice.

SCHILLER   'Cause if I knew . . . (laughs) Now just listen to me, Nicole. If I knew, I'd say it, and I'd ask you to confirm it. You stop and think the way I work with you. It's the truth.

NICOLE   (little laugh; long pause) Well, okay, it was because Barrett had me convinced I wasn't any good and so the, the only thing I could do was . . . go with somebody that didn't know what good was.

SCHILLER   You're saying that Barrett had you convinced you were a lousy lay?

NICOLE   Yeah.

When it came to interviewing, Schiller knew he had met his match. Maybe there wasn't a disclosure he had gotten in his twenty years of media that hadn't been built on some part of Bullshit Mountain, but with Nicole he got along. He didn't have to use tricks that often and it moved him profoundly. He took a vow that when and if his turn came to be interviewed on Gilmore, he would also tell the truth and not protect himself.

Now Schiller was certainly back with Stephie. He was in love. He was going to marry his princess. He saw it as belonging to the best vein of his luck. But he couldn't believe the other side of his luck. It was that he was friends with a girl for the first time in his life. Something like affection for himself began to come into Schiller when he realized that the monumental gamble he had taken that Nicole would not commit suicide was probably going to win out. One of the reasons he could trust her not to take her life for too little over the weeks and months and years to come, was because of her friendship for him. She wouldn't do it to him for too little. So he went on with the interviews and at times was ready to cry in his sleep that he was a writer without hands.

CHAPTER 44

Seasons

1

April joined the Baker family out on Malibu after a hard time in the hospital. The patients and staff, she announced, had really laid it on her, and banged her head on the wall. Books and newspapers kept coming in. It was horrible. She kept reading all about Gary.

Now, at Malibu, she was still panicky. Out of her sleep she would cry, "Mama, are you all right? Are you sure you're all right?" The night would go on.

In the daytime, April and Nicole would squabble. They had never gotten along. Things might get better, things might get worse, but certain things Kathryne could count on. One of them was that April and Nicole would spit like cats before the day was out.

2

Later that winter, Noall Wootton was having martinis with a couple of attorneys in the Sheriff's Office of Salt Lake County, and one remarked, "These fellows still want me to prosecute Nicole for smuggling pills in to Gilmore." Noall Wootton said, "Bill, for hell's sake, what's that going to accomplish? Forget it."

"Well," said Bill, "I already have. I told them I declined it. I am not interested." Under it all, Wootton would have loved to question Nicole to find out how she did get the pills in.

Sam Smith called Vern one day and wanted to know how they smuggled the liquor into the prison.

"You must be dreaming," Vern told him. "I don't know how."

Sam called again. Tried to get him to open up. For some reason, it remained a mystery to Vern.

3

After the month in Malibu, Nicole decided she liked living in Los Angeles, with her kids, and so she took a house out in the San Fernando Valley that didn't cost too much. Just a shabby little ranch bungalow, five blocks from the very end of town. She could almost have been in Spanish Fork. The desert began down the street, and the mountain rose not a mile away. Nicole tried to keep the kids in day school, hold a job, and go to school herself, but it was a dull stretch. There was no man. There was nothing in her life.

She bought a camper with some of the money Gary had left her, and got a driving license, and went out to Utah and came back. She had not had sex since that night in October with the Sundowner in the middle of Gary's trial, but late in April, returning from Utah, she picked up a hitchhiker. It had been a long, difficult stretch with all kinds of guys trying to make out, and Nicole had been wondering if she could go for the rest of her life without it. Being faithful left her feeling choked up and dull and bored and itchy and intense.

After she made love to the hitchhiker, she no longer felt Gary's presence near. She didn't feel it after that for a long time. Felt as if he had gone away. That left her depressed and close to dead. Still, she kept on having sex. It didn't solve anything, but not having sex also solved nothing. Either way, she was not going to fall in love.

Still, sex left her feeling ugly. She tried to figure it out. She was the one who was living. If she had tension and could get rid of a little by making love to somebody, and then, once they were gone, even the memory of them was gone, and had nothing more to do with her, or her body, or her heart, or her memories, so where then was the treachery to Gary?

Still, sex left her more and more out of touch with him. She was drifting in her heart. It was hard to get started on any program to improve herself. Larry told her she was smart enough to walk right out of the swamp by herself, but the truth was she felt lazy and was tempted to say, "Oh, fuck it, I'm in a swamp. I'll stay here."

The thought Nicole really wanted to lose was that there was no more Gary. It was a possibility she did not like to consider. It was too depressing to believe he might not be on the other side.

4

Several times that year, when friends would get to talking about Gilmore, Barry Farrell, in the course of the evening, might volunteer a tape. People were curious to hear Gilmore's voice. So Barry would play one of the cassettes, but listening to Gary's voice would totally chill him out. The tapes were so interesting to other people that they never wanted him to turn them off.

5

Larry was now doing interviews with various people in Provo who had known Gary, and Lucinda kept typing the transcripts. After a couple of months when that job began to peter out, she went to work for David Frost who was doing a series of television interviews with Richard Nixon.

Lucinda did the work in Los Angeles, transcribing Frost's tapes in an office building in Century City from four o'clock in the afternoon until about eight o'clock in the morning three days a week. There she was, locked in this empty skyscraper with Richard Nixon's voice coming out of a tape recorder, and it was not nearly so interesting as Gary Gilmore. She kept hearing Gilmore's voice, and in her mind, he sounded like a cowboy. Mean, gravelly, twangy, economical, boyish, vulnerable, full of love squeezed into tight little pellets.

6

A year after the execution, Kathryne Baker wrote to Schiller:

You know, Larry, I used to feel sorry for Gary, but what he's done to my girls, what he's still doing to them, well I could kill him a hundred times over — I live with Gary every day, the fear of him in April, is driving us all crazy! when night comes for her, its a nightmare for all of us. She is scared to death of the dark because "he's out there with a gun killing people." She doesn't say Gary . . . only "He" — and she's truely haunted — at 4 AM last week, hysterical, "He's out there killing people, now he's gone to kill more people — hurry, we got to get up there before He kills more!" this is how it is all the time — even in Her sleep — when She sleeps. It makes no difference if we are all here, She must be reassured all night that He can't get in & kill us, no one sleeps the whole night because April wakes us every hour with "Are you allright mama — what are we going to do??!" I tell you Larry I hate Gilmore so bad I wish he was here so I could kill him! April . . . from the things she say's in her sleep & her panic at the sight of blood, I guess Gary's shoes and pant-legs must have been covered with blood & brains, I guess so if the wall's were splattered, I don't know what to do anymore, I can't talk to Sissy about her feelings towards Gary, she hides them, but will relate to music and cry long for Gary, it's in poems — I can't talk to April about Gary, because she don't & won't mention his name hardly ever — night before last in her sleep she said, "there he is with blood on him & that crazy look in his eyes." now who, other than Gary would be tormenting her dreams! I know that crazy look in his eyes — it was there when he came after his gun, when he took April with him — sounds like I need a shrink too huh?? ha ha Well I don't, I'm O.K. just need help in fighting the ghost of Gilmore.

Nicole was sitting in her kitchen one morning in the small apartment she now rented in a small town in Oregon which was where she had wandered after L.A., and she was having coffee with the guy who had been with her the night before. She was reaching out for something on the table when all of a sudden her hand looked strange. She saw the ring of Osiris that Gary had given her, and it was broken. The setting had cracked.

She had built up a lot of control over all these months, but suddenly it just hurt so bad that she bawled right there at the table, two seconds after she saw the broken ring. It was the first real big cry she'd had about Gary in a long time, a month or so.

She was not sure there was any such thing anymore as Gary. She didn't know if that was where her belief rested. He was a lot out of her mind. He might really be dead.

7

In Christmastime of 1977, Vern bought barbells and delivered them to Utah State Prison for the convicts. Gary had asked him to do that after the execution.

It had not been a good year and it did not get better. Vern's leg was so bad he needed another operation, but he had no money. Because he could not stand on his feet for a full day, he had to sell his store, and then there were the lawsuits against Gary's estate. The State of Utah sued him for Snyder and Esplin's legal fees, and the companies who had guaranteed the life insurance on Max Jensen were suing, and there was still a $1,000,000 suit from Debbie Bushnell. Then Ida got a serious stroke, and Vern fed her three meals a day in the hospital for three weeks and tried to teach her to walk and talk again. Since her hospital bill would come to $20,000, he forgot about his own operation.

8

From the day Brenda told her that Gary committed the murders, one of Bessie's legs turned in at the ankle. Then, from the day Gary was killed, that leg would no longer allow her to walk. Up till then, she had been able to make it over to the office for mail. Now, although the office was only three trailers away, she did not try. The leg didn't want to walk.

Sitting in her chair, she would remember the haunted house in Salt Lake where the nice Jewish lady had been her neighbor. Bessie would think that whatever it was that lived in the house, whatever it was the nice Jewish lady had warned her against, must in those years have begun to live in Gary.

Now she heard that Ida had a stroke. Vern turned around one night in the house, and there was Ida with the stroke. Bessie could have told Vern. Whatever had attached itself to Gary long ago in that house in Salt Lake must recently have attached itself to Ida. Bessie would not, however, tell Vern. When all was said, she did not know Vern well enough to inform him that the apparition was now sitting in his house.

She did, however, think of her mother-in-law Fay and the old house in Sacramento where the furniture wouldn't stay in place. Bessie sat in her chair among the coffee cups and the saucers on the table of this trailer, sat in the faded nightgown that looked one hundred and two years old, and said to herself, "I have reached the point of no return from Hell."

Outside the trailer park, automobiles went by on McLaughlin Boulevard. Once in a while, a car would drive under the battered white wooden archway at the entrance, come up to her dark windows and stop. She could feel them looking. She had received letters that threatened her life and she ignored them. Letters could not hurt a woman whose son had taken four bullets through the heart.

She also received letters from people who wrote songs about Gary and wanted her permission to publish. She ignored such letters also.

She would just sit there. If a car came at night, came into the trailer park, drove around and slowed up, if it stopped, she knew somebody out in that car was thinking that she was alone by the window. Then she would say to herself, "If they want to shoot me, I have the same kind of guts Gary has. Let them come."

Deep in my dungeon
  I welcome you here
Deep in my dungeon
  I worship your fear
Deep in my dungeon,
  I dwell.
I do not know
  if I wish you well.

Deep in my dungeon
  I welcome you here
Deep in my dungeon
  I worship your fear
Deep in my dungeon,
  I dwell.
A bloody kiss
  from the wishing well.

— old prison rhyme

FINIS

An Afterword

1

This book does its best to be a factual account of the activities of Gary Gilmore and the men and women associated with him in the period from April 9, 1976, when he was released from the United States Penitentiary at Marion, Illinois, until his execution a little more than nine months later in Utah State Prison. In consequence, *The Executioner's Song* is directly based on interviews, documents, records of court proceedings, and other original material that came from a number of trips to Utah and Oregon. More than one hundred people were interviewed face to face, plus a good number talked to by telephone. The total, before count was lost, came to something like three hundred separate sessions, and they range in length from fifteen minutes to four hours. Perhaps ten subjects are on tape for more than ten hours each. Certainly, in the last two and a half years, Nicole Baker's interviews have added up to thirty hours, and conversations with Bessie Gilmore may come to more than that. It is safe to say that the collected transcript of every last recorded bit of talk would approach fifteen thousand pages.

Out of such revelations was this book built and the story is as accurate as one can make it. This does not mean it has come a great deal closer to the truth than the recollections of the witnesses. While important events were corroborated by other accounts wherever possible, that could not, given the nature of the story, always be done, and, of course, two accounts of the same episode would sometimes diverge. In such conflict of evidence, the author chose the version that seemed most likely. It would be vanity to assume he was always right.

A considerable amount of time was spent trying to establish the sequence of events. My researcher, Jere Herzenberg, discovered that people had characteristic flaws or tics in recollection. Some would always remember separate episodes as taking place a few days apart, when, in fact, if one had a provisional calendar already constructed from other sources, a particular adventure might be two weeks apart from another. Since accurate chronology soon showed itself as crucial to understanding motivation, every effort was made to get it right, and not for the sake of history alone. One understood one's characters better when the chronology was correct. Of course, many an event could simply not be given an exact date (as, for instance, the spring night when Nicole and Gary cavorted on the ground in back of the mental hospital). One could only situate it approximately, and hope no critical error of sequence had been made.

Secondary material, like newspaper quotes, allowed a few liberties. Sometimes words or phrases were removed without inserting marks of ellipsis, and very occasionally a sentence was relocated or a paragraph transposed. It was not done to make the newspaper copy more arresting or absurd; rather the procedure was to avoid repetition or eliminate confusing references.

Gilmore's interviews were trimmed, and very occasionally a sentence was transposed. The aim was not to improve his diction so much as to treat him decently, treat him, let us say, half as well as one would treat one's own remarks if going over them in transcript. Transition from voice to print demands no less.

With Gilmore's letters, however, it seemed fair to show him at a level higher than his average. One wanted to demonstrate the impact of his mind on Nicole, and that might best be achieved by allowing his brain to have its impact on us. Besides, he wrote well at times. His good letters are virtually intact.

Finally, one would confess one's creations. The *old prison rhyme* at the beginning and end of this book is not, alas, an ancient ditty but a new one, and was written by this author ten years ago for his movie *Maidstone*.

Also, the cross-examination that John Woods makes of a psychiatrist who administers Prolixin comes in fact from an actual interview by Lawrence Schiller and myself a couple of years later and has been placed in Dr. Woods's mind with his kind permission.

Moreover, the names and identifying details of certain characters have been changed to protect their privacy. Naturally, any similarity between their fictitious names and those of persons living or dead is purely coincidental.

2

It is always presumptuous to say that a book could not have been written without the contributions of certain people since it assumes the book is worth writing in the first place. Given the length of this work, however, it may be safe to assume that any reader who has come this far must have found something of interest in the preceding pages. Let it be said then that without the cooperation of Nicole Baker, there would not have been a way to do this factual account — this, dare I say it, *true life story*, with its real names and real lives — as if it were a novel. But given the intimacy of the experience Nicole Baker was willing to communicate to Schiller and then to me, I had enough narrative wealth from the start to feel encouraged to try for more.

As has already been indicated in the last pages of the book itself, the work of those interviews with Nicole belongs in the main to Lawrence Schiller. Many of them were completed before it was even certain whether I would take on the job. In the months after Gilmore's execution, Schiller would go each week to Provo or Salt Lake and there conduct two or three long interviews a day. By the time the contracts were signed and I was ready in May 1977 to commence my labor, Schiller had already collected something like sixty interviews and would yet do as many more and make countless trips to Utah and Oregon. That was the first of his invaluable contributions to my task; the other was his willingness to be interviewed himself. Maybe he wanted the best book he could get, but Schiller stood for his portrait, and drew maps to his faults. He exposed his secrets in the confidence, doubtless, that old methods revealed, he would now be spurred on to more cultivated techniques, and so he not only delivered the stuff of his visions but the logic of his base schemes, and in the months that followed, he did not feel regret, or seem to have second thoughts. If he did, he kept them to himself. Without Schiller, it would not have been feasible to attempt the second half of *The Executioner's Song*. A profound appreciation, then, to Nicole Baker and Lawrence Schiller.

There are others I would like to thank with the recognition that they contributed far more than one might expect. Vern Damico, Bessie Gilmore, and Brenda Nicol are three whose names come first to mind, and their contribution was large and they gave unstintingly of their time and were always available for checking discrepancies and verifying details, as well as offering the personal flavor of their own personalities to the work. Indeed, part of the pleasure of writing this book was to make their acquaintance. In almost equal measure, I would like to thank April, Charles, Kathryne, Rikki, and Sterling Baker, as well as Jim Barrett, Dennis Boaz, Earl Dorius, Barry Farrell, Pete Galovan, Richard Gibbs, Toni Gurney, Grace McGinnis, Spencer McGrath, Robert Moody, Ron Stanger, Judith Wolbach, and Dr. John Woods, but indeed to establish such categories is unfair to all the others who were interviewed, since nearly everyone was generous in the effort to portray his or her portion of the story. Let me list their names here: Anthony Amsterdam, Wade Anderson, Gil Athay, Kathy Baker, Ruth Ann Baker, Sue Baker, Mr. and Mrs. T. S. Baker, Jay Barker, Bill Barrett, Marie Barrett, Thomas Barrett, Cliff Bonnors, Alvin J. Bronstein, Brent Bullock, Judge J. Robert Bullock, Chris Caffee, David Caffee, Ken Cahoon, Cline Campbell, Dr. L. Grant Christensen, Rusty Christiansen, Glade Christiansen, Val Conlin, Mont Court, Virginius (Jinks) Dabney, Ida Damico, Michael Deamer, Pam Dudson, Porter Dudson, Roger Eaton, Michael Esplin, Mr. and Mrs. Norman Fulmer, Elizabeth Galovan, Richard Giauque, Frank Gilmore, Jr., Stanley Greenberg, Steven Groh, Dr. Grow, Howard Gurney, Phil Hansen, Robert Hansen, Ken Halterman, Doug Hiblar, Dr. Howells, Alex Hunt, Julie Jacoby, Albert Johnson, Dave Johnston, Judge David T. Lewis, Kathy Maynard, Wayne McDonald, Rev. Thomas Meersman, Bill Moyers, Johnny Nicol, Gerald Nielsen, Captain Nolan, Martin Ontiveros, Glen Overton, Lieutenant Peacock, Shirley Pedler, Margie Quinn, Lu Ann Reynolds, Michael Rodak, Jerry Scott, Craig Smay, Lieutenant Skinner, Lucinda Smith, Tamera Smith, Craig Snyder, David Susskind, Craig Taylor, Frank Taylor, Julie Taylor, Wally (of the Sundowners), Wayne Watson, Dr. Wesley Weissart, Noall Wootton.

In addition, the following: Don Adler, T. Aiken, Paul J. Akins, Mildred Balser, Mary Bernardie, Frank Blalm, Tony Borne, Mark Brown, Vince Capitano, Warden Hoyt Cupp, Dynamite Shave, LeRoy Earp, Richard Frazier, Duane Fulmer, Sally Hiblar, Mildred Hillman, Dr. Jarvis, Detective Jensen, Tom Lydon, Harry Miller, John Mills,

Bill Newall, Andrew Newton, Dr. Allen Roe, Lieutenant Lawrence Salchenberger, Bishop Seeley, Linda Stokes, Captain Wadman, Captain Harold Whitley, Tolly Williams, Dr. Joe Winter, were interviewed. For reasons of structure, they did not appear (except for an occasional reference to their name) in the pages of this book, but their influence on it was not small. Many trips were taken to Oregon State Prison to interview guards and prisoners who had known Gilmore during his many years in that institution, and the author's understanding of prison life was powerfully aided on the official side by Warden Hoyt Cupp who offered many kinds of invaluable cooperation including most specifically his own tough estimate of prison conditions, by Captain Whitley, Lieutenant Salchenberger, and security officers in Segregation and Isolation, and by Paul J. Akins, Vince Capitano, LeRoy Earp, Andrew Newton, and Tolly Williams for their recollections of Gilmore as a fellow convict. A debt of real measure is also due to Duane Fulmer who furnished a clear, well-written, and highly detailed manuscript of life at MacLaren School for Boys. These contributions, while not appearing in the book directly, formed an indispensable subtext, a body of private material, so to speak, out of which one was far better able to comprehend some of Gilmore's motivations in the last nine months of his life. To their assistance must be added the letters of Jack H. Abbott, a convict who has spent much of his life in Western prisons and sent to me a series of exceptional letters, well worthy of being published, that delineate the code, the morals, the anguish, the philosophy, the pitfalls, the pride, and the search for inviolability of hard-line convicts in language whose equal I have not encountered in prison literature in recent years.

Mikal Gilmore was kind enough to make available his piece in *Rolling Stone,* March 10, 1977, about his visits with his brother, and Sam Smith allowed a tour of his prison.

Finally, a most special word of appreciation must be offered to Colleen Jensen and Debbie Bushnell for consenting to give a portrait of their husbands, and thereby obliging themselves to relive the most shattering and excruciating hours of their existence. No interviews were more painful for subject and interviewers both, and none were more valuable to the balance of this book.

For assistance in research and typing, thanks are due to Janet Barkas, Dean Brooks, Sister Bernadette Ann, Clayton Brough, Murray L. Calvert, Molly Malone Cook, Peter Frawley, Kathleen Garrity, Lenny Hat, Jere Herzenberg, Diana Broede Hess, Susan Levin,

Francis Lorsen, Mary Oliver, Donna Pode, Dave Schwendiman, Martha Thomases, and to Mike Mattil who did a gargantuan job of styling with considerable speed and skill.

To those who were asked to read and comment on this manuscript: Norris Church, Bernard Farbar, Carol Goodson, Robert Lucid, Scott Meredith, Stephanie Schiller, and John T. Williams: my continuing indebtedness. I would add here the name of Judith McNally, who not only read and commented on this manuscript, but did ten years of work in one as my secretary, interviewer, research assistant, and critical reader. This work could not have been written in fifteen months without her.

Last, to the memory of that good, fine, and devoted man of literature, Larned G. Bradford of Little, Brown, who passed away on May 12, 1979. He was my editor for ten years, and he would have enjoyed the publication of this work.

Arena

☐ The History Man	Malcolm Bradbury	£2.95
☐ Rates of Exchange	Malcolm Bradbury	£3.50
☐ The Painted Cage	Meira Chand	£3.95
☐ Ten Years in an Open Necked Shirt	John Cooper Clarke	£3.95
☐ Boswell	Stanley Elkin	£4.50
☐ The Family of Max Desir	Robert Ferro	£2.95
☐ Kiss of the Spiderwoman	Manuel Puig	£2.95
☐ The Clock Winder	Anne Tyler	£2.95
☐ Roots	Alex Haley	£5.95
☐ Jeeves and the Feudal Spirit	P. G. Wodehouse	£2.50
☐ Cold Dog Soup	Stephen Dobyns	£3.50
☐ Season of Anomy	Wole Soyinka	£3.99
☐ The Milagro Beanfield War	John Nichols	£3.99
☐ Walter	David Cook	£2.50
☐ The Wayward Bus	John Steinbeck	£3.50

Prices and other details are liable to change

ARROW BOOKS, BOOKSERVICE BY POST, PO BOX 29, DOUGLAS, ISLE
OF MAN, BRITISH ISLES

NAME. . . . .

ADDRESS . . . .

. . . .

. . . .

Please enclose a cheque or postal order made out to Arrow Books Ltd. for the amount
due and allow the following for postage and packing.

U.K. CUSTOMERS: Please allow 22p per book to a maximum of £3.00.

B.F.P.O. & EIRE: Please allow 22p per book to a maximum of £3.00

OVERSEAS CUSTOMERS: Please allow 22p per book.

Whilst every effort is made to keep prices low it is sometimes necessary to increase cover
prices at short notice. Arrow Books reserve the right to show new retail prices on covers
which may differ from those previously advertised in the text or elsewhere.